ONE DAY A YEAR
1960-2000

Christa Wolf

ONE DAY A YEAR
1960-2000

*Translated from the German
by Lowell A. Bangerter*

Europa
editions

Europa Editions
116 East 16th Street
New York, N.Y. 10003
www.europaeditions.com
info@europaeditions.com

Translation by Lowell A. Bangerter
Original title: *Ein Tag im Jahr*
Translation copyright © 2007 by Europa Editions

The publication of this work was supported
by a grant from the Goethe-Institut

Library of Congress Cataloging in Publication Data is available
ISBN-13: 978-1-933372-22-8
ISBN-10: 1-933372-22-2

Wolf, Christa
One Day a Year: 1960-2000

Book design by Emanuele Ragnisco
www.mekkanografici.com

Printed in Italy
Arti Grafiche La Moderna – Rome

CONTENTS

NOTE FROM THE PUBLISHER

Christa Wolf's husband, Gerhard Wolf, furnished this text with many valuable and colorful footnotes that constitute a rich repository of intimate details concerning the Wolf family, their friends and acquaintances, and events and personages prominent in Germany during the years dealt with in this memoir. His footnotes are indicated in parentheses with the abbreviation G.W. Additional footnotes have been provided by both the translator, Lowell A. Bangerter, and the editor, indicated in parentheses with the abbreviations Tr. and Ed.

Note from Gerhard Wolf

These notes are intended to identify persons and relationships that are necessary to the understanding of the diary entries. Names of authors and persons from contemporary history who are not directly related to the entries and events whose familiarity can be assumed were not included.

The Beautiful 27th of September

I did not read any newspaper.
I did not gaze at any woman.
I did not open the mailbox.
I did not wish anyone a good day.
I did not look in the mirror.
I did not talk with anyone about the old days
     nor with anyone about the future.
I did not think about myself.
I did not write a line.
I did not start any stone rolling.

*Thomas Brasch**

---

* Thomas Brasch: "*Der schöne 27. September* (The Beautiful 27th of September)."
Thomas Brasch gave voice to a special kind of reception with his poem "*Der schöne 27. September* (The Beautiful 27th of September)," which also provided the title for his volume of poetry of 1983, Suhrkamp Publishing Company, Frankfurt/M.
For the volume *Ein Text für C.W.* (*A Text for C.W.*) for the sixty-fifth birthday of the author (Janus Press, Berlin, 1994) he wrote for her the poem "*3 Wünsche für C.* (3 Wishes for C.)."

1. The place that between here and there again
will always let you go, but never pass away.
Stay, it calls to you, away at last remain.
I want to be your land. Be my rest today.

2. The word that everyone can spell,
who does not write what's grasped by all, you see.
Never is it I, oft you, and sometimes tell
me when you turned yourself at last to me.

3. The time that lies twixt now and darkened view
and lasts quite suddenly unceasingly,
as though it opened wide your doors for you
and stopped. I'm here again, you see.

My Twenty-Seventh of September[1]

How does *life* come to be? The question concerned me at an early age. Is life identical with time in its unavoidable but mysterious passage? While I write this sentence, time passes; simultaneously a tiny piece of my life comes into being—and passes away. Does life thus consist of innumerable microscopic pieces of time like that? Remarkable, however, that we cannot catch it. It slips away from the observing eye, even the hand that diligently takes notes, and in the end—even at the end of a period of life—it has constituted itself behind our backs according to our secret need: more substantial, more meaningful, more exciting, more significant, more replete with stories. It shows that it is more than the sum of the moments. Also more than the sum of all of the days. At a certain point, unnoticed by us, those routine days are transformed into time that has been lived. Into fate, at best or at worst. In any case, into the course of a life.

The invitation extended to writers of the world in 1960 by the Moscow newspaper *Izvestiya* immediately fascinated me. Describe as exactly as possible one day of that year, specifically the twenty-seventh of September. It was a revival of the undertaking "One Day in the World" that Maksim Gorky had begun in 1935, which had not lacked appeal, but was then not

[1] Christa Wolf's first diary text of September 27, 1960, was first published in the July 1974 issue of the periodical *ndl* (*Neue Deutsche Literatur*) and in 1980 included in the volume *Gesammelte Erzählungen* (*Collected Stories*) of the Luchterhand Publishing Company, Darmstadt/Neuwied (now in Christa Wolf, *Werke in 12 Bänden* [*Works in 12 Volumes*] abbreviated in what follows as *Werke*, (*Works*), 1999, Vol. III, pp. 366ff.).

continued. So I sat down and described my twenty-seventh of September of 1960.

So far, so good. But why did I then also describe the twenty-seventh of September of 1961? And all the twenty-seventh of Septembers that followed, until now—for forty-three years, now already more than half of my adult life? And cannot stop doing it? I am not aware of all of the reasons for it; I can name some of them: first of all my horror in the face of the forgetfulness that, as I have observed, especially carries away with it the routine days that I treasure so much. To where? Into oblivion, of course. Transitoriness and futility as twin sisters of forgetfulness: again and again I was (and am) confronted with that eerie phenomenon. I wanted to write in opposition to that inexorable loss of existence. One day a year, every year, should at least be a reliable buttress for the memory—described purely, authentically, free of artistic designs, which means: left to and at the mercy of chance. I could not and did not want to control what those chance days brought to me; thus apparently insignificant days stand next to "more interesting" ones. I could not avoid the mundane, nor seek or even stage "significant" things. With a certain measure of excitement I began to anticipate what that "one day of the year," as I soon called it, would bring me in the current year. Keeping the records became a sometimes enjoyable, sometimes burdensome duty. It also became an exercise against blindness to reality.

It did prove to be more difficult to capture developments in this manner. All of these individual daily records cannot, of course, claim to stand for the forty years from which they were insularly picked out. But I hoped that the punctual collection of data at regular intervals might in time result in a kind of diagnosis: an expression of my desire to see through relationships, people, but primarily myself. I made note of—often beginning on the same day, usually continuing into subsequent days—what I had experienced, thought, felt on that day, memories, associations—but also the events that captivated me, political occurrences that concerned me, the condition of the country in which I lived, taking interest in it, until 1989, and—that had not been foreseeable—the phenomena of the collapse of the German Democratic Republic and those of the transition into a different society, a different state. And of course my sometimes suddenly, but more often gradually changing attitudes toward all of those complex, complicated processes are reflected: conflicting, offensive expositions. In that sense these notes are more than simply material; they also became—even if not in the least complete—proof of my development. I had to resist the temptation to correct earlier misjudgments, unjust assessments from today's perspective.

These diary pages differ distinctly from the rest of my diary, not only in their structure but also in content and in stronger thematic constraint and limitation. But even they were not intended for publication, as, for example, those other texts were from the beginning, the ones that take the course of a day as the basis for a work of prose: *June Afternoon*, *Accident: A Day's News*, *What Remains*, *Desert Journey*—pieces of evidence for my fascination with the narrative potential to be found in almost any arbitrary day. Whereas an express decision was needed to publish these writings, in which the "I" is not a literary first-person narrator, but presents and surrenders itself unshielded—even to those glances that are not guided by understanding and sympathy.

Why do I do that? My experience is: proceeding from a certain point in time that can no longer be identified after the fact, we begin to view ourselves historically, which means: embedded in, bound to our time. A distance is created, a stronger objectivity with respect to ourselves. The self-critically examining eye learns to compare, thereby becoming not gentler, but perhaps somewhat more just. We see how much generality there is in even the most personal things and consider it to be possible that the need of the reader to judge and pass sentence can be replaced by self-discovery and, in the most favorable case, self-perception.

Subjectivity remains the most important criterion of the diary. That is a scandal in a time when we are supposed to be buried in material objects and become material things ourselves. Even the flood of apparently subjective, shameless revelations with which the media pester us is, of course, a calmly calculated component of this world of goods. I do not know how else we could escape and confront this compulsion toward objectification that is being infiltrated right into our most intimate feelings, other than by the development and the relinquishment of our subjectivity, without regard to the effort that it may cost. The need to be known, even with our problematic traits, with errors and mistakes, underlies all literature and is also a driving motive for this book. It remains to be seen whether or not the time for such a risky venture has already come.

But the decisive reason for publishing these pages is this: I think they are a testimony of the times. I regard it as a kind of professional duty to publish them. It seems to me that our most recent history is in danger even now of being reduced to and defined in easily manageable formulae. Perhaps reports like these can contribute to keeping opinions about what has happened in flux, examining prejudices once more, dissolving bitterness, recognizing personal experiences again and gaining more confidence in them, permitting foreign conditions to come somewhat nearer . . .

I have maintained the authenticity of the texts. Slight abridgments were carried out. In some cases sentences had to be stricken for the purpose of protecting individuals.

April 2003

When I first wake up, the thought: The day will again go differently than planned. I will have to go to the doctor with Tinka because of her sore foot. Outside doors slam. The children are already up and about. Gerd is still sleeping. His forehead is damp, but he no longer has a fever. He seems to have gotten over the flu.

There is life in the children's room. Tinka is reading from a picture book to a little dirty doll: The first one wanted to warm his hands; the second one wanted to warm his gloves; the other one wanted to drink tea. But there was no coal. Stupid!

She will be four years old tomorrow. Annette is worried about whether we will bake enough cake. She calculates for me that Tinka has invited eight children for coffee. I overcome a minor scare and write a note for Annette's teacher: I request that you send my daughter Annette home early at noon tomorrow. She is supposed to celebrate her little sister's birthday with her.

While I am fixing sandwiches, I try to remember how I spent the day before Tinka was born, four years ago. Again and again I am stunned at how quickly and how much I forget if I do not write everything down. On the other hand: it is not possible to record *everything*; a person would have to stop living. Four years ago it was probably warmer and I was alone. In the evening a girlfriend came to spend the night with me. We sat together for a long time. It was the last intimate conversation between us. She told me for the first time about her future husband . . .

During the night I telephoned for an ambulance.

Annette is finally ready. She is a little sloppy and disorderly, as I must have been as a child. Back then I never would have believed that I would reprimand my children the way my parents reprimanded me. Annette has misplaced her purse. I scold her with the same words that my mother would have used: We can't throw money around like that either. Just what are you thinking?

As she leaves, I take her by the head and give her a kiss. Goodbye! We wink at each other. Then down below she slams the house door shut with a loud bang.

Tinka is calling for me. I answer impatiently and try sitting down at the desk. Perhaps I can at least get an hour of work done. Tinka is singing a song to her doll at the top of her lungs, one that the children like very much lately: "In the evenings, when the moon shines, out into the town . . . " The last verse goes like this:

> In the basement once quite late
> They were eating from a plate
> In the night one evening mild
> Came the stork and brought a child . . .

When I am with her, Tinka never fails to appease me. She knows full well that the stork could not carry any babies at all; that would be outright cruelty to animals. But if you *sing* it, then it really does not matter.

She begins screaming for me again, so loudly that I rush to her at a trot. She is lying in bed and has buried her head in her arms.

> Why are you screaming like that?
> Well, you don't come. Then I have to scream.
> I said, I'll be right there.

Then it still takes you a long time to get here here here fear fear fear. She has discovered that words can rhyme. I unwind the bandage from her cut foot. She screams as if on a spit. Then she flicks the tears away with her finger. At the doctor's office it will hurt me, too.

Do you intend to scream like that at the doctor's, too? The entire city will come running—Then *you* have to unwind the bandage for me—Yes, yes—Can I have pudding soup this morning?—Yes, yes—Cook me some!—Yes, yes.

The foot pain seems to ease. While getting dressed she does not scratch under the tabletop with her fingernails and is ready to burst out laughing. She wipes her nose with the hem of her shirt. Hey! I shout, Who's blowing her nose in her shirt there?—She throws her head back and laughs unrestrained: Who's blowing her nose in her shirt there? Snot shirt . . .

Tomorrow is my birthday, so we can already be a little bit happy today, she says. But you've forgotten, of course, that I'm already able to get dressed by myself—Haven't forgotten it. Just thought your foot was hurting too much—She awkwardly threads her toes through her pant legs: I just do it much more carefully than you—There are tears again when the red shoe is too tight. I push one of Annette's old house slippers over the injured foot. She is enthusiastic: Now I have Annette's slipper on!

When I carry her out of the bathroom, her healthy foot strikes against the wooden box next to the door. Boom! She cries. That thumps like a bomb!—How does she know how a bomb thumps? It has been more than sixteen years since I last heard a bomb detonate. How does she know the word?

Gerd is reading in Lenin's letters to Gorky; we arrive at our old topic: art and revolution, politics and art, ideology and literature. About the impossibility of congruent thought structures for—even Marxist—politicians and artists. The "private" world that Lenin grants Gorky (and more than grants: that he presupposes) even with all his intransigence in philosophical questions. His consideration, his tact even with all his rigidity. Two partners with equal rights work together; the one who knows everything is not confronted with the one who must be taught everything. Candid and generous mutual recognition of competencies . . . We come to the role of experience in writing and to the responsibility that we have for the *content* of our experience. Are we free, however, to have arbitrary experiences that are perhaps socially desirable, but for which our origins and personal nature make us unsuited? We can become acquainted with many things, of course. But *experience* them?—There is a dispute about the plan for my new story. Gerd presses for the further transformation of a plan that has remained too superficial until now into one that would be appropriate for me. Or do I intend to write a report? Then go ahead, in that case I could get to work immediately. I become slightly upset, but deny it as always, when in reality I sense that "there is some truth to it."

Have I read this? A little article by Lenin entitled "A Capably Written Little Book."[1] The reference is to a book by a "member of the White Guard who was embittered almost to the point of mental derangement," *A Dozen Daggers in the Back of the Revolution*, which Lenin discusses—half ironically, half seriously—certifying that it reflects "expertise and honesty" where the author describes what he knows, what he has experienced and felt. Lenin simply assumes that the workers and farmers would draw the right conclusions from the clear, expert descriptions of the old bourgeoisie, of which the author himself is not capable, and seems to believe that it is possible to print some of those stories. "We should encourage

[1] *Lenin's Collected Works*, 2nd English Edition, Progress Publishers, Moscow, 1965, Tr. David Skvirsky and George Hanna, Vol. 33, pp. 125-126. (Ed.)

a talent"—which, on the other hand, is irony, but also independence. That brings us to talk about the premises for independent behavior in a country where socialist society must develop under assumptions and conditions like those that we have here. About reasons and bases for provincialism in literature.

We laugh when we realize what we talk about endlessly day and night—as they do in schematic books whose heroes we would criticize as implausible.

I go to the doctor with Tinka. She talks and talks, perhaps to talk away her fear. One minute she demands that I explain a picture on the wall ("Why don't you think it's pretty? I think it's nice and colorful!"), the next minute she wants to be carried because of her sore foot, and a minute later she has forgotten all the pain and is balancing on the stonework surrounding the front gardens.

Our street leads to a new apartment building that has been under construction for months. An elevator lifts carts filled with cement sacks and transports empty carts back down again. Tinka wants to know exactly how it works. She has to content herself with an approximate explanation of the technology. Her new, unshakable belief that everything that exists "is good for something" is good for something *for her*. If I am afraid for the children so often, then above all I fear the unavoidable violation of that belief.

When we go down the steps of the post office, I clamp her under my arm—Not so fast, I'll fall!—You won't fall—When I'm big and you're small, then I'll run down the stairs that fast, too. I'm going to get bigger than you. Then I'll jump very high. By the way, can you jump over the house? No? But I can. Over the house and over a tree. Should I?—Go ahead!—I *could* easily do it, of course, but I don't want to—So, you don't want to?—No—Silence. After a while: But in the sunshine I'm big—The sun is hazy, but it casts shadows. They're long because the sun is still low—Big right up to the clouds, Tinka says. I look upward. Small clouds of mist hang very high in the sky.

In the waiting room, a lot of idle talk. Three older women are sitting together. The one, who speaks the Silesian dialect, bought a blue sweater yesterday for a hundred and thirteen marks. The event is illuminated from all sides. All three of them complain about the price. In a tone of superiority, a younger woman who is sitting across from the three of them finally involves herself in the inexpert discussion. It turns out that she sells textiles and that the sweater is not an "import" at all, as the Silesian woman had been assured when she purchased it. She is indignant. The saleswoman elaborates on the advantages and disadvantages of wool and synthetic wool. Synthetic wool is practical, she says, but if you want something really elegant, you take wool—A good thing will come again, says the second of the three women, and I look imploringly at Tinka, who is preparing to ask a question that would certainly be inappropriate. In the West, a sweater like that costs fifty marks, says the Silesian woman—Oh, well, the second one declares, convert it: one to three. It still amounts to a hundred and fifty marks—That's right.

There is probably no point in getting mixed up in their conversion calculations.

I got the money from my daughter, says the Silesian woman. I could not have bought it from my one-hundred-and-twenty mark pension—All three of them sigh. Then her neighbor says, I have always been for that: simple but fine—I look at her surreptitiously and cannot find anything fine about her—She, undeterred: This coat here. I bought it for myself in 1927. Gabardine. Peacetime goods. Can't be worn out—Horrified, I look at the coat. It is green, slightly iridescent, and outmoded, but there is nothing else remarkable about it. A coat really cannot be eerie. Tinka tugs at my sleeve, whispers: When is nineteen hundred twenty-seven?—Thirty-three years ago, I say—She uses one of her father's expressions: Was I already thought of back then?—By no means, I say. I wasn't even thought of yet—Good heavens, says Tinka—The Silesian woman, still thinking about her blue sweater, comforts herself: At least I won't freeze in the winter.

The third one, a scrawny woman who has not said much previously, now comments quietly triumphant: Thank God, *I* don't have to worry about all that . . . Questioning look from the others. Finally: You have relatives over there?—No. That is, yes. My daughter. But she simply arranges it. There is a gentleman. I don't even know him, but he sends me what I need. He just had another inquiry sent, asking what I still lack for the winter. Pure envy in the eyes of the others. Well then! You can't have it any better than that these days.

I do not say anything. I gave up trying to read long ago. The doctor's assistant calls all three of them out of the room.

Tinka remains very quiet when the doctor presses around on the wound. She is pale. The hand that I hold becomes moist. Did it hurt? the doctor asks. She makes her impenetrable face and shakes her head. She never cries in front of strangers. Outside, when we are waiting for the bandage, she suddenly says, I'm happy that I'm having a birthday tomorrow!

The sky has clouded over. We are already looking forward eagerly to the bricklayer's elevator. Tinka would have stood there for a long time if she hadn't had to quickly find herself a little corner. Then she becomes quiet. She is thinking about the large black dog whose house we must soon pass. As always, at that place she tells me that this dog once bit a woman's finger. It must have been years ago, if it is true at all, but the legend of it has made an indelible impression on Tinka. The impact of storytelling!

The mail that I find waiting at home is disappointing, a meaningless card from a girl who says nothing. On the other hand, motorcycles stop a couple of times in front of the house, express and telegram messengers, substitutes for the telephone. One brings the galley proofs of Gerd's book on Louis Fürnberg.[2]

While the food is cooking I read children's compositions on the topic of "My Most Beautiful Vacation Day," which were left in the library of the railroad car factory. A nine-year-old girl writes: "Things were wonderful in our vacation camp. We had a free day. We could go wherever we wanted to. I went into the woods. I saw a large deer there and a small one. The two of them lay there and did not move. They were so tame that I could touch them. Then I ran back quickly and got the camp leader. After all, it was not far to our camp. I told him everything and he went with me. He led the large deer on a rope, and I was permitted to carry the small deer. We had a small barn, and I put both of them in there and fed them every day. That was my most beautiful day."

I am inclined to give that girl the first prize in the competition for her improbable story.

After the meal I ride to the railroad car factory,[3] to the work brigade's Party meeting. In the streetcar an older couple

[2] Louis Fürnberg (1909-1957), lyric poet and storyteller; after emigration and exile as a Jewish communist antifascist in Palestine, returned to Prague in 1946; escaped the Stalinist Slansky trials of 1952 and was able to emigrate to the German Democratic Republic in 1954, where he lived in Weimar as the deputy director of the National Research and Memorial Sites.
Fürnberg had friendly ties with C. and G. Wolf (see: L. Fürnberg, *Briefe 1932-1957* [*Letters 1932-1957*], Berlin, 1986). G. Wolf wrote "*Der Dichter Louis Fürnberg— Leben und Wirken—Ein Versuch* (*The Poet Louis Fürnberg—Life and Work—An Essay*)", Berlin, 1961, and published his *Gesammelte Werke in 6 Bänden* (*Collected Works in 6 Volumes*), Berlin and Weimar, 1964-1972, with Lotte Fürnberg; with Rosemarie Weimann *Der Briefwechsel L. Fürnberg mit Arnold Zweig* (*The Correspondence of L. Fürnberg with Arnold Zweig*), Berlin, 1978. Fürnberg's poem "*Antonin Dvořák, Sonatine op. 100*" is found in Fürnberg's final volume of poetry, *Das wunderbare Gesetz* (*The Wonderful Law*), Berlin, 1956. (G.W.)
[3] In the nationalized railroad car factory in Halle/S—At Ammendorf, C.W. interned in a socialist workers' brigade—background for her narrative *Divided Heaven*, Halle, 1963, on which she began work in 1960. (G.W.)

searches desperately for the ten-pfennig piece that they need in order to be able to buy the tickets. They spent all of their money while shopping. I offer the woman the ten-pfennig piece. Major embarrassment: Oh no, oh no, they could also walk. Finally the man takes the coin, insisting that it is so embarrassing for him. Such a thing is probably only possible among us Germans, I think.

I have not been in the factory for a few weeks. The hall is filled with half-finished railroad cars. Apparently the production stoppage has been overcome. I rejoice too soon.

Willy does not notice me immediately. I watch how he works with his new device for preparing the press frames. He and J., his brigade leader, developed this simple but practical device and submitted it as an improvement suggestion. With it they cut the time for this process in half. There was whispering behind their backs in the factory and bad blood developed. Today I should find out what is really happening.

Willy looks up. Well, my dear? he says. He is happy. He still has things to do. I sit down in the brigade shed that they themselves call the "open cow shed." Still forty-five minutes until quitting time, but three are already sitting here waiting for the time to pass. Still not enough work? Shaking of heads. The scene in the hall was deceptive—And what are you doing with the rest of the time?—Occupation theory, they say. Iron storehouse, lumber storehouse, plank repairs—And the money?—That's right. We receive the average, of course—They are in a bad mood, resigned, angry—depending on their respective temperaments. And the worst thing is: they no longer hope for the decisive turn for the better. Lothar says: In January we'll be in a mess again, even if we kill ourselves trying to meet the final quarter plan quota. The money's being thrown away on overtime. Is that supposed to be profitable?

His money is right, but he is irritated about the fact that the factory is unprofitable. Can the factory director go to every work brigade and explain what is happening with the factory? No, he can't. But it should be explained, and very clearly, and if at all possible every week based on the latest production updates. Uninformed people are beginning to act irresponsibly.

Meanwhile the conversation turns to the factory party last Saturday. Jürgen tells about the trouble that he had when his wife drank too much and he had to take her home in a factory van after she had publicly slapped an obtrusive colleague. I was so angry that I got drunk again the next day, he says. He is a little afraid that his wife made him look foolish. Then the others begin telling about similar incidents with their wives, matter-of-factly, without any feeling, the way that men talk about women. I think: The obtrusive colleague undoubtedly deserved the slap . . .

Nine comrades come together in the Party leaders' meeting room. They come in their work clothes, unwashed. There is a woman among them, with cheerful, lively eyes. In the brigade I once saw her slam her fist down on the table. Here she says nothing.

Enough chitchat: Let's begin, Willy says. He is the group organizer. I know what he intends to do today, and with anticipation and respect I watch how he ruthlessly moves toward his goal. In front of him lies the report for his brigade's public rendering of accounts. I am familiar with it. But the comrades from the neighboring brigade, the competition partners, are a bit dazed in the face of the twenty-three pages about the others, who, aside from any friendship, are really their rivals. And if a person is familiar with the complicated history of the two brigades, which were actually once *one* brigade . . . The star brigade of the factory under the leadership of P., who sits across from Willy, constantly wiping off the perspiration, and feeling like he has been outwitted.

Willy begins reading rapidly and indistinctly from the

report, a carefully selected section. The hands holding the page tremble a bit. The atmosphere in the overheated room must have a soporific effect on the uninitiated.

Nobody takes quotations as seriously as Willy does. He reads aloud what Lenin said about increasing work productivity. And what is happening here with us? he asks, interrupting himself. A colleague says, Before we wanted to become a Brigade of Socialist Labor, we were always in agreement. Now there is constant grumbling—Willy raises his voice. Now he talks about their improvement suggestion: the very device that I saw in action earlier. There were enormous billows of smoke! he says and lowers the sheet of paper. He looks over the top of his wire-rimmed glasses directly at P.: A fifty-percent savings! That has never happened before—not here! Doubts were raised about the reality of the suggestion. Yes, even you, P.! Don't say anything, it's my turn. But the suggestion is real. There's nothing shaky about it. Obviously we got a bonus. Obviously the two of us will earn a lot in the next three months. It will amount to a thousand marks for me, if you want to know. And what about it? Does material incentive perhaps not count for us comrades? Everything would have been all right if the two of them had distributed their bonus and stopped up the mouths with a few bottles of beer. But that's the end of it! shouts Willy. Egalitarianism doesn't exist anymore. And at the brigade's next evening party we'll buy a round.

That gave rise in the section to the underhanded question: Are you a communist or an egoist?

And that, Willy cries out, now agitated and stammering, that we all knew. Or didn't we? And how did we comrades behave? Not in the least like comrades. How could we?! We didn't even agree amongst ourselves. More concrete! shouts someone from the neighboring brigade.

Willy, louder and louder: Certainly! As concrete as you

want! In the factory administration the two of us are recommended for designation as activists. Who speaks against it? Comrade P.! The Party leadership wants to hang our picture on the "Avenue of the Heroes of Work" on Republic Day. Who advises against it? Comrade P.! Concrete enough?

Perhaps I might be permitted to say something now, too, P. insists. Please, says Willy. Just one more thing: it's about the cause and not about whether I don't like your face or you don't like mine. Everyone here at the table is familiar with P.'s statement from the time when Willy, with his "retrogressive cadre development," was new in his brigade: He or I—that is the question here. There's not room for both of us in one brigade—On May Day P.'s picture still stood on the "Avenue of the Heroes of Work." Both of them must have forgotten and thought many things that they would not admit to themselves, so that discussion can occur at all as it does today. One must not expect the conflict to climax and be "settled" according to the rules of classical dramaturgy. It is already a lot that P. admits: Your suggestion was concrete. It's right that you receive the bonus—After that his supply of self-denial is exhausted. He evades, drags out an old story about which he holds forth verbosely. He cannot simply admit defeat that way. It goes back and forth between the two brigades. The tension sinks. Even Willy has to back down at one point, which is pretty difficult for him.

The brigade's report is still lying in front of him. In a week P.'s people are also supposed to be that far along. Suddenly they become uneasy about the work. Willy allows himself that last small triumph and everyone notices. But that is enough now. They have to come to an agreement. They discuss who should help P. If you're willing to accept an old rabble-rouser like me . . . Willy says—Old idiot! P. responds.

Somebody comes up with the idea that they should invite their wives when the brigade renders an account of itself. That

is in keeping with the times. Nobody can speak against it publicly, but it becomes clear: the suggestion has no ardent supporters. The wives, one of them says, really have enough to do
with the children, especially after quitting time . . . Günter R.
is happy. A man can only bring his wife if he has one.

Well, and you? Willy snaps at him. Don't you have one?—
No, says Günter. Not anymore—And just what's the matter
with your marriage? Don't you start slipping on me because of
that sort of thing! Willy says menacingly—Günter is the
youngest man at the table. He makes a dismissive gesture with
his hand, but has become bright red in the face: It's nothing!
Not worth talking about!

Later P. tells me: Günter had been sent to the sister factory
in G. for a few weeks to give socialist assistance, and when he
returned home unexpectedly one day, he met his wife's foreman coming toward him from his bedroom. Then, of course,
he went to court with it the very next day. But nothing can be
mended there anymore . . .

Gradually the mood has become cheerful. They tell jokes.
When I claim that they all want nothing to do with culture,
there is a protest. The invitations for the presentation of the
report are passed around, white double cards on which the
word *Invitation* is printed in ornate gold lettering. That is just
distinguished enough for them. They want to invite a lot of
guests, want to "be an example," as Willy says. He lets the
meeting grind on loosely now, is hardly tense any longer, and
looks quite satisfied. He winks at me and grins. Very sly, I say
to him later. You have to be, my girl, he says. Otherwise you
don't accomplish anything.

I quickly go home, agitated, with disturbed thoughts. Once
again I hear what they say, and also what they do not say, what
they do not even reveal in their expressions. Whoever succeeded in penetrating that almost enigmatic web of motives
and opposing motives, actions and counteractions . . . Making

the life of people great who appear to be condemned to small strides . . .

At this time of year, as evening approaches it is already cold. I buy the things that I still need to bake a cake and take along a few birthday flowers. In the gardens the dahlias and asters are already wilting. I remember the enormous bouquet of roses that stood on my nightstand in the hospital back then, four years ago. I remember the doctor whom I heard say: A girl. But she already has one. Well, it probably won't matter to her . . . His relief, when I already had a name. The nurse who lectured me about how undesirable girls still are sometimes, and all the things that a person can experience in that case, especially with the fathers. They simply don't come if it's a girl again, whether you believe it or not. That's why we are not allowed to say what it is on the telephone, a boy or a girl.

Everyone wants to help bake the cake. The children get in the way. Finally I put on a fairy tale record for them in their room, "Peter and the Wolf." Afterward they scrape out the batter bowls until they are taken away from them. Annette talks about school: We learned a new song, but I don't especially like it. *Republik* [republic] is rhymed with *Sieg* [victory]—what do you think about that? I think it's boring. We have a new Russian teacher. She was amazed at how many words we already know. But do you think that she told us her name? Not at all. Yet we all had to write our names on a seating chart. I don't think she does it because she wants to be mean—They mill around restlessly and do not want to accept the fact that that they still have to sleep, even during the night before the birthday.

In the oven the cake rises over the lip of the pan. Now that it is quiet, it seems as if I can hear it rising. The pans were too full. The batter expands and expands and drips into the oven and sends a burnt smell through the entire apartment. When I take the cake out, one side is black. I become angry and find that I have nobody to blame but myself. And then Gerd comes and calls the cake "a little black." Then I tell him indignantly that it is because the pans were too full and because of the inadequate stove and the gas pressure that is too high. Oh, well, he says and withdraws.

Later we listen to the violin sonata, Anton Dvořák's *Opus 100*, to which Fürnberg wrote a poem. A lovely, pure piece of music. My anger dissolves. Simultaneously both of us notice that we smell of burnt cake and begin to laugh.

I must still write something, but everything disturbs me: the radio, the television set next door, the thought of the birthday hubbub tomorrow and of this fragmented day in which I accomplished nothing. Morosely I set the birthday table, arrange the wreath of lights. Gerd leafs through some little book, finds it "well written." For some reason even that disturbs me.

I look through the beginnings of manuscripts that lie stacked on my desk. The protracted nature of the process that we call writing embitters me. A few faces have already emerged from the simple brigade story, people whom I know better and have joined together in a story that, as I can clearly see, is still much too simple. A girl from the country who comes to the city for the first time in her life, to study there. First she does a practicum in a factory, in a difficult brigade. Her boyfriend is a chemist; he does not get her in the end. The third is a young foreman who, because he made a mistake, is sent on probation to work in this brigade . . . It is remarkable that these banal occurrences that have been "taken from life" intensify their banality to the point of intolerability on the pages of a manuscript. I know that the real work will not begin until I find the "higher idea" that makes the material presentable and worth telling. But it can only be found—if at all, which I seriously doubt this evening—through this long preliminary work whose futility is clear to me.

I know that neither the pages that already lie there nor the sentences that I write today will remain—not a letter of them. I write, and then cross out: As always Rita was hurled as swiftly as an arrow from her sleep and was awake without any memory of a dream. But a vision had to have been there. She wanted to hang on to it, but it faded away. Robert lay next to her.

Before I fall asleep it occurs to me that life consists of days like this. Points that in the end, if we have been fortunate, connect a line. That they can also fall apart into a meaningless pile of spent time, that only a continuous unswerving effort gives a meaning to the small units of time in which we live . . .

I am still able to observe the initial transition into images before falling asleep. A road appears. It leads to the landscape that I know so well without having ever seen it: the hill with the old tree, the slope that gently falls to a watercourse, meadows, and on the horizon the forest. That you cannot really experience the seconds before falling asleep—otherwise you would not fall asleep—is something that I will always regret.

Yesterday, when it was actually supposed to be that "day of the year"—a tradition that I really would like to begin—I did not think about it all day. Not until this morning, as I awoke, did it occur to me. It was not a joyful idea; I felt reluctant to dutifully remember yesterday by writing about it. Leafing through older diaries I again saw all the things that I forget if I do not write them down: almost everything. Especially the important details. So let's write. And immediately a test as to what I still remember about yesterday, what I can capture, "save" of the things that rapidly grow pale in my memory. And push aside the question: Why save it? Just what is important about an average day in an average life? What causes me to disregard the warning: Do not view yourself as so important, which was impressed upon me early on? Conceit? But isn't conceit, viewing oneself as important, the root of all writing?

(Noted in parentheses, since it is actually embarrassing: during the last week, since I was unfortunately ill again—the old illness: heart pains, insomnia, and weariness—I read a compilation of documents from Goethe's life: *Truth and Fiction Relating to My Life*,[1] letters, journal pages, and I thought again: I *must* write things down, even if only to register every day matter-of-factly. No intention to write "beautifully." Key words, facts, minor outpourings of the soul.)

[1] *The Autobiography of Goethe: Truth and Fiction Relating to My Life* by Johann Wolfgang von Goethe, University Press of the Pacific, 2003. (Ed.)

At best, it is the framework of the day, the framework of most days, which is made of harder material than the filling, which most likely constitutes actual life, which is a little different each day. The alarm clock at six-thirty, the first look out of the window at Amselweg, an overcast sky, clouds drift, but rain does not seem to be in the offing. Early autumn leaf coloring. Some bicyclists who have to go to their factories, among them surely some who are riding to the Ammendorf railroad car factory. The name is a signal that arouses a series of images within me. Certain production paths at the plant have meanwhile become fixed in my mind and I can trace them on my inner map, with a certain degree of satisfaction: I have acquired something that was unknown to me.

Silence in the children's room. In the bathroom the usual procedures and activities. Gerd is already in the kitchen and has begun to fix breakfast, goes into the bathroom. Unfortunately I must now awaken Annette. When I cautiously open the door to the children's room, it turns out that both of them are awake, sitting quiet as mice in their beds, and reading. At least Tinka calls what she is doing with the picture books that she has piled on her bed "reading," about which Annette gives me a sympathetically indulgent glance. She does not have to smear her little sister's deficiencies on bread and feed them to her. She herself is engrossed in a book of fairy tales. Sometimes, before beginning a new fairy tale, she asks whether it ends "well" or "badly." How I understand her! But what is good, what is bad? Annette is quite certain in that regard: if the good is vindicated and wins out, the fairy tale ends well. Once I tried to sow a slight doubt in her certainty: Didn't she feel sorry when the evil stepmother had to dance in glowing hot slippers at the end? Oh, no. The main thing is that Snow White is alive again and married her prince. The fates of the secondary characters are insignificant, and the evil antagonist must certainly be punished. When I was a child of Annette's age, I

scratched out the eyes of the witch in the picture in my book
of fairy tales. During the summer Annette and the children
from the building and the neighborhood put on "Little Red
Riding Hood." As the oldest, she was the director. She took
her task very seriously—just as she does every task. Before the
performance in front of a neighborhood audience, she was as
excited as a real director before his premiere. She has laid in a
stock of favorite fairy tales that end well and that she reads
again and again. What is it this morning?—Cinderella—Come
on, get up—I want to finish reading it first—But you know
how it ends—All the same. From her bed Tinka makes the pre-
cocious comment that you can't stop in the middle of a story.
Otherwise you have to keep thinking about it. Right now she
is full of worldly wisdom.

We reach a compromise. Annette comes to the breakfast table
on time, spoons up her oatmeal, rolls her eyes at the cautious
question of whether or not she has packed her schoolbag, and
then, after she has already gone down the stairs, has to come
back again because she has forgotten to pack her Russian book.
I wisely refrain from making any comment, and Annette refrains
from giving any sign of understanding. That way we are even.

I stand on the little oriel balcony next to Gerd's workroom
and watch her go. She is wearing the dark blue jacket with the
plaid lapels. Her ponytail bobs and the hollows of her knees
flash. Pantyhose are still out of the question, indignantly rejected. As it does every morning, my heart tenses a little bit when
she leaves. As I do every morning I ask myself if we should have
insisted that she go to the other school, which is further away
and to which she would have to ride the streetcar, simply
because it is a Russian school where the best pupils from all of
the schools in Halle are gathered together. I wait for her to turn
around once more. When it is almost too late, she does it. I
wave, she waves back. That exchange comforts me every morning, irrationally.

Tinka has gotten partially dressed, is standing in the bathroom pretending to wash, imitates something like brushing her teeth, and looks up at me from the corner of her eye in the process. I remain serious and pretend not to notice anything.

While she puts on her stockings, with which I help her somewhat because they are new and tight, she casually explains to her shabby teddy bear, which she has generously permitted to continue sleeping in her bed, that there are unfortunately no toothbrushes for teddy bears, otherwise she would buy him one and watch every morning and evening to see that he brushed his teeth thoroughly. The teddy bear uses my deep voice to resist. He is afraid of brushing his teeth. He thinks that the toothpaste tastes horrible and brushing would hurt his teeth. Tinka has a completely different opinion about that, of course. The toothpaste tastes a little bit like raspberries, and her teeth do not notice anything about the brushing. At most they begin to hurt if you don't brush them. But the teddy bear is stubborn and unperceptive. Tinka has to argue with him, first gently, then more and more fiercely. He resists to the end and shouts after us in an impertinent tone as we leave the children's room that he will never ever brush his teeth. Tinka scolds loudly back at him. She is earnestly concerned and indignant. On the one hand, she knows exactly, of course, whose voice the teddy bear used, but on the other hand she is convinced that she was speaking with *him*, and with nobody else. The two contradictory insights and opinions run alongside each other unchallenged in her mind. I wonder if becoming an adult means being able to keep reality and the world of imagination strictly separated—at least in the latitudes where we live. Primitive peoples live in a world where the animals speak and the elements are personages. If you force them to become "adult," they take refuge in alcohol. In what substitute did our ancestors take refuge when a nature that was endowed with nymphs and elves and gods was taken from them in order to dissect it into usable components?

"Bread and honey" is the motto for every breakfast. There would be no point in offering Tinka something else. With her father she discusses the teddy bear's character in endless detail. He makes things too easy for himself with the claim that teddy bears are difficult by nature and then has a hard time backing down from his point of view after Tinka has given him a lot of evidence for her teddy bear's gentleness. Finally she is ready to put on her shoes and her parka, to shoulder her little lunch bag, and to walk to the nursery school with me. In my mind I memorize what I have to buy, but Tinka wants to discuss one more problem. In our neighborhood a young couple got married. Tinka has learned the details of the ceremony. Why does everyone get a ring when getting married? she wants to know—So that the other people see that you are married—Tinka thinks about that. Then: I see. Then a man who doesn't have a wife only looks for one without a ring—That's about it—But what if all the girls have a ring and the man still doesn't have a wife?—Then he remains alone. That happens—Can he then at least have children?—Hardly. You always need a father and a mother for that—Too bad. But then he's sad, isn't he?

I drop her off at the nursery school, which, oddly enough, is called "Free Soil." I am not permitted to give her a farewell kiss or wave to her. She goes in with her back straight.

It must have been eight-thirty, yesterday, on the day that I am describing. It is part of its framework that it is eight-thirty when I walk home from the nursery school and while doing so buy the necessities—milk, butter, apples, mincemeat—and sink into thought. Yesterday, as I have often done in recent days, I may have thought about what the two years in Halle have actually brought us to date. In any case: insight into new circumstances that were previously completely foreign to us. A city that is defined by the industry around it—in the process, of course, also by air pollution. The contact with the railroad car builders in Ammendorf is the greatest gain. But also: more and more frequent symptoms of overstress, heart pains, sleeplessness: once again too fragmented, worn down, driven away from what is actually important. Too much trivia: little articles, meetings, publishing work, diversion, being torn back and forth between different responsibilities, none of which bring me complete fulfillment—except when I can write. The *Moscow Novella*[2] did create a stir as a preprint in *forum* and apparently contributed to the softening of the cultural-political atmosphere. I can actually only see it as a magazine story now. I have success with it at readings, but I intend to be careful now and forever not to take that as a yardstick. What entices me: to rework that material again, for a film, together with Konrad Wolf,[3] who is interested in it and with whom we have already met at Deutsche Film-AG, the German Democratic Republic's film company. The figure of Pavel gives him the opportunity to introduce autobiographical elements. A new level, a reinforcement of the characters and their motives seems conceivable to me. And what penetrates to us from Moscow about the new Soviet films by the young filmmakers must impact the spirit and style of our films: no pathos, no concession to the need for the "heroic," instead of that the quest for the behavior of the figures in everyday life. In that respect I am in total agreement with Konrad Wolf who has

[2] C.W.'s *Moskauer Novelle*, Halle, 1961, was printed in the Berlin student periodical *forum*. (G.W.)

[3] Konrad Wolf (1925-1982), film director; 1965-1982 president of the Academy of Arts of the German Democratic Republic (East Germany); had friendly ties with C. and G. Wolf through joint projects. A jointly written screenplay for *Moskauer Novelle* could not be filmed, primarily because of objections from the Soviet authorities; in 1964, however the film *Der geteilte Himmel* (*Divided Heaven*). A film project *Ein Mann kehrt heim* (*A Man Returns Home*) of 1964/65 was given up. G. Wolf participated as a scene editor in the production of Konrad Wolf's films *Ich war neunzehn* (*I Was Nineteen*), 1969, and *Der nackte Mann auf dem Sportplatz* (The *Naked Man on the Athletic Field*), 1974. K.W.'s film *Sonnensucher* (1958) was withdrawn after the premiere and has been shown only since 1972 on television and in art film theaters. (G.W.)

apparently been looking for a long time for material that suggests the use of those stylistic devices. It seems to suffer greatly under the prohibition of *Sun Seekers*—his film, which we haven't seen—In "our" film the present-day layer will cause the most difficulties: how to present the fact that Pavel and Vera, who meet again, between whom affection grows again, who seem made for each other, part again—but part in a manner that is not final, different from the way they parted back then, after the war ended. At that time the law of necessity, the dictates of the relationships between our two nations, governed things, today it is understanding. Features of real human freedom were achieved together. The life of a person like Vera is no longer dominated by the dully animalistic dependency on prejudices and emotions. How to portray that believably, without pointing a finger?

When was I at my desk yesterday? About ten, later than I wanted again anyway. The top of the desk is covered with piles of pages. The new story that has kept me occupied for more than a year. I have started at least five times. The transformations of the title already indicative: "Discoveries," "Encounter," "At the Time of Parting," perhaps not final yet. Ultimately, under the influence of my experiences in the railroad car factory, it was supposed to become a brigade story like the many that exist now. A girl from the country who intends to study pedagogy in the city does an internship in a brigade of a railroad car factory. The brigade is famous, but inside it something is rotten. A young foreman who did not notice the brigade leader's manipulations is transferred into the brigade, has a very difficult time there at first, Rita falls in love with him, the two of them find their way to each other, the brigade heals . . .

Thus a narrow story, with elements of commentary, tied to a specific purpose, utility literature, and contrived, superficial, provincial—a word that now, with our help, is becoming very modern. In my next conception, to which I clung for (too) long, after her first year of study at the college of education in West Berlin, a girl meets her former boyfriend again, who fled the country almost a year earlier. She spends an afternoon with him, but is already married to another man—the foreman from the first version. So for her the whole thing is now only a farewell, albeit a more wistful one. Thus Manfred is already more of a focal point, somewhat better, because it is more problematic, but again the tiresome triangle relationship. For a long time I thought in circles until Gerd said: You ought to begin when she comes back from Berlin. So a new variation: Rita is not married yet, she comes back from the encounter in West Berlin totally disheartened, has to help out in her old brigade, the factory is in extraordinary difficulties, not least of all because of a stoppage in West German deliveries. She finds herself again through the exertion of work—narrated in flashbacks. She and Ernst, the young factory director, draw closer to each other.

The young factory director with his problems should thus move more into the foreground as a positive figure. It was an intermediate step to the realization that I must write the love story of the girl Rita Seidel. A story with an unhappy ending caused by the disastrous division of Germany that breaks her boyfriend, Manfred. Manfred is driven to the point—primarily by himself—that he leaves the country. Rita stays here, although she almost perishes in the process.

I had begun to realize that conception before the 13th of August. I did not have to change it. The fact that Manfred *could* now no longer leave at all is no argument. Their love is shattered before that, not by the fact that he leaves. However, the parting now has something final about it and cuts even deeper.

One page today, handwritten, corrected on the typewriter in the afternoon and added to the pile of the latest version.

At noon boiled meatballs with caper sauce that Gerd made,

one of the few dishes of Brandenburg cuisine that he learned
from me; otherwise he contributes more to our menu from his
more refined Thuringian cooking. When we eat Königsberg
meatballs, *Mohnpielen* (a dish made with poppy seeds, white
bread, and other ingredients), blood sausage with sauerkraut,
or kale, I always see my grandmother standing at her stove (her
"cooking machine") in her kitchen apron. I climb hand over
hand along a chain of thoughts whose individual links seem
quite logical to me, until I reach the comment that I utter:
What catastrophes had to take place in order that we could
become acquainted with each other—How do you arrive at
that?—Through my grandmother—Gerd tries to follow my
chain of thought: fascism, war, flight, a foreign place of residence as a possibility for meeting each other—Which grandmother? he asks—The one whom you know. Who before she
died knitted a wool sweater for Annette. Who always called
you "Yerhard"—The other grandmother, who starved to death
while fleeing, does not come into the conversation.

To my surprise, what does come into the conversation is the
question of what actually, very concretely, kept (and keeps) us
in the German Democratic Republic, when so many have left.
(That question has now, of course, also become an undertone
in my story.) To answer immediately on the negative side: we
know what they are playing "over there," and that we do not
belong there. On the positive side: that here in our country the
prerequisites for becoming human are increasing. Theoretically quite clear. Practically: are they really increasing? Don't we
often strew sand in our eyes about the "inner relationships"
that "our people" have? For example: their relationship to the
past. One evening when the Ammendorf brigade was at our
house, things only got lively when we exchanged war memories. And it is that way with many people. It is infinitely difficult for them to be critical of themselves.

And the "political consciousness" of the workers, which is

lauded in the newspapers? Many economic successes are obviously caused by material calculations of the workers in favor of their pay envelopes, which, of course, cannot be otherwise. But in Ammendorf I have learned that something like the honor of the factory is not unimportant to the workers, and that the comrades convey something like "consciousness" in laborious daily discussions. After all, in our brigade they are now building ten windows per shift, which still seemed utopian to me a year ago. And they are proud of it, which they would never admit.

But so many whom we would never have thought capable of doing it had disappeared the next morning, toward the West. I had the feeling: the country is bleeding to death. And the functionaries who sit in their armchairs in the offices and exercise bureaucracy contribute their share to it. How long, we ask ourselves, can we continue to take comfort in Brecht's words: "We who wanted to prepare the ground for friendliness could not be friendly ourselves"? If, however, friendliness were to disappear, just what would be the sense of all this tremendous effort in this country?

Midday rest. Read in Aragon's *Holy Week*, which gives me technical stimuli, in order to be able to distance myself from the constraints of prose construction from the nineteenth century, which is regarded as realistic in our country, and take more liberties with respect to the material. Brief nap. Coffee. The one typewritten page that will remain the product of this day and which, of course, altered the handwritten text. A meager result, I tell myself that almost every day while I walk to the nursery school to pick up Tinka. I must be there as punctually as possible at four o'clock. She is already standing at the door ready to leave. I will never forget her expression when I did not make it once and picked her up as the last one—How was it today?—Fine—What did you play?—A be-ba-boogeyman is going around in our circle—I see. What else?—I can count to ten—You could already do that—Now I can really do it well. Tomorrow is my birthday. Do I have to go to nursery school then, too?

She has never more clearly stated that she would rather stay home. There is no point in asking her directly. She does not say anything if she does not want to—Tomorrow I'll pick you up at noon. We'll celebrate your birthday in the afternoon. A transformed, cheerful child hops along beside me, while I feel how my heart grows heavy. The children have often been sickly of late and have needed care. The doctor, who is friendly, to be sure, but whom they hate because he always prescribes sweat cures, thinks that Halle's air is affecting their bronchial tubes. He says that you have to be hardened already to be able to stand the chemical fog here. But I am sure that they also sense my silent despair when the days run away from me. Sometimes I make them suffer for it, which is not right and magnifies my despair. There really is something to the idea that if she has children a woman in "arts and sciences" *cannot* accomplish what it is possible for a man with the same talents to accomplish. An issue that I have often thought about, one that leaves behind a bitter residue and that makes Gerd furious. But the children are growing, and someday concentration will really *have to* come into my life again—if I have not already unlearned it by then.

At home Tinka hands me her lunch bag and immediately slips around the corner of the building into the garden to her friend Olaf who has already been waiting longingly for her. From the kitchen balcony I see them sitting on the rickety bench by the bower, engrossed in a conversation that I would very much like to listen to. It is probably not an exaggeration to assume that Olaf is Tinka's first love. But I must endure another restless half hour before Annette comes home as well—again she did not catch the streetcar on which we expect her to arrive, again I had to imagine all the things that might have happened to her. Perhaps she is tired, doesn't pay attention to the stops, and has too many demands placed upon her by the long school day. I am greatly relieved when she comes up the stairs. Our greeting is passionate, an entire evening and a long night lie ahead of us when we are all safely together and I do not have to worry about anyone. It is not just since the war and my flight; even when I was a child I had this fear of catastrophes, which I try to hide from Gerd, but he always senses it. He gathers the children while I make supper—yes, the children would like Königsberg meatballs—and looks at the "adult picture books" with them, a favorite activity. They most like to engross themselves in the pictures by the naïve painters.

When I enter the room to call them to supper, Tinka is just closing one of the picture volumes: Do you only have pictures of workers?—Why?—I don't want to look at them anymore—Why not?—I don't know. They're boring—But workers are very important—Important, yes, but I don't want to look at them all the time—Then what would you rather see?—Oh, other people. Or how I play with Berit in the children's room . . .

Gerd is delighted. Literary criticism on a high level, he says. The future reader makes her needs known. Take that, Madame Author. No workers if possible—I have to punch him for that. Tinka immediately takes his side and places herself protectively in front of him, while Annette, with her sense of justice, gives her opinion that Father should not have spoiled the pleasure that I take in the workers. She knows what I am writing right now.

The supper is rather turbulent. Tinka uses transparent tricks on us, one after another, trying to get out of us what kind of presents she can expect tomorrow. The three of us are an impenetrable front. Annette likes it when she finds herself among the grownups on such occasions. She is permitted to help set up the birthday table in my room, put the five candles in wet sand on the plate, and decorate it with aster blossoms, while Tinka already lies in bed and plays the lonely, outcast child. In the end they both receive their goodnight song, preferably *"Der Mond ist aufgegangen* (The Moon Has Risen)" because it has so many verses. Each time, after the last verse, Tinka says: But fortunately we don't have a sick neighbor, do we?

We make ourselves comfortable in the room. I get around to the newspapers for which I had no time earlier and that I leaf through in ten minutes. Apparently it is a matter of portraying "Bonn" as isolated following the closing of the border on August 13th: "Washington Angry About Bonn." "Only Brandt Still Favors Adenauer's Policies." "Rebuff of Brandt Course at Social Democratic Party Meeting." "The Packing of Bags in West Berlin: firms such as AEG, Siemens, and Osram have begun to move important production divisions to West Germany." "Bonn After the Election: tax burdens increase, prices rise rapidly." And then entire pages of enthusiastic letters from the public to the office of the state council on the defense law: "We are Protecting Our Republic." And in culture: "A Glorious Beginning: Felsenstein's Enchanting *Midsummer Night's Dream* at the Start of the New Season." And: "On the Trail of Garagin and Titov: a School Observatory on Auguststrasse."

My brother calls on the telephone. He wants to know how we are doing, if the children are healthy. Superficially everything is all right. I notice that he is not in the best mood. Then he blurts out how he envies us that we both work free-lance, and that, of course, is not without justification. (He is right about that. Because the atmosphere and the unreasonable demands in the institutions weighed us down too much. We, first Gerd, withdrew from the respective organizations.) Horst: In the factories and at the university there is "no good air"— But a fresh breeze is blowing in from above now, I say—He does not believe it. Tactics, he says. Too many cowardly people without ideas and initiatives are sitting in the chairs. We greet each other with forced smiles at meetings and do not say what we think of each other . . . How familiar I am with that!

Horst gives a few examples from his area, in which wrong decisions that are made out of stupidity and cowardice immediately cost hundreds of thousands of marks. Bad. I could not fall asleep for a long time because of it.

I wake up in a foreign light that makes orientation difficult in what continue to be unaccustomed surroundings. After twenty days in the new apartment no habits have yet formed. However, here, too, the kitchen is to the left of the entrance, and diagonally across from it the children's room, from which a dialogue resounds that apparently demands much patience from Annette. I stand in the doorway and listen without immediately being noticed. Tinka wants to know why quite a few children in Annette's class still stutter around while reading, as she told us yesterday. They simply don't like reading, says Annette vaguely—Why is that? What do they like, then?—Being lazy and eating chocolate is easy for them— That's easy for me, too, Tinka declares vehemently. Do you think that because of that reading won't be so easy for me?— Reading will be easy for you. You already know most of the letters. But who knows if arithmetic will be easy for you?—She leaves Tinka filled with dismay.

At breakfast Annette is quiet. I try to cheer her up with cocoa and her favorite liverwurst. I know that there would be no point in asking her why she is so reticent. She is a person who has a difficult time getting used to new things, and the

---

[1] The Wolf family moved from Halle/S. to Kleinmachnow, Förster-Funke-Allee, in early autumn, both as a result of attacks in the Halle Party newspaper *Freiheit* in connection with disputes about the Twenty-Second Party Congress of the Communist Party of the Soviet Union and in view of a closer collaboration with the DEFA German film workers group in Potsdam-Babelsberg on film projects. (G.W.)

fact that she has already had to change schools a second time in her four school years is not good for her. She has not made any friends yet. She says that all the girls in her class already have a friend. She cannot bring her qualities to the surface and win over the teachers immediately. It hurts me to see that she is having a hard time. I would like to help her but have to admit that I cannot. She leaves half of her sandwich lying there. When I ask her if she isn't hungry, she shrugs, and Tinka, who appears in her pajamas, declares: She says when it tastes the best you have to stop—Old tattletale, Annette jumps down her throat. I grasp the fact that the half-eaten sandwich belongs to her self-castigation program, like the chewing gum that she threw away and the movie she didn't watch on television. She wants to prove to herself how strong her will is.

My God, how she resembles me, if she only knew it! A series of images from my childhood rolls past my inner eye. I see myself as an awkward child, vulnerable, which I will not admit for anything in the world, craving affection, but incapable of obtaining that affection through kindness or even by currying favor. Why can't a person pass on such experiences, at least as consolation: it will pass?—I hug Annette tightly when saying goodbye, wave to her from the kitchen window. Her child's limbs have become gangling. The transition to teenager is in the offing.

Was it selfish that we moved away from Halle almost precipitously, tearing the children away from their accustomed surroundings? But the old family doctor, who always prescribed sweat packs, said to us: If you want to avoid having your children's bronchitis become chronic, you must move away from here. Away from the chemical zone, away from the fog. Into the good air here in the vicinity of Berlin. Where I—I must admit it—feel just as foreign as the children do.

Anyway, at breakfast we now no longer read *Freiheit*, but the *Berliner Zeitung*, which I open less apprehensively than the Halle newspaper, which accused me in several articles of a "subjective distortion of the Twenty-Second Party Congress" and of deviationist tendencies—because I had unreservedly defended Alexander Tvardovsky's speech at the Twenty-Second Party Congress of the Communist Party of the Soviet Union,[2] which had appeared under the caption "It Is a Matter of the Truth," while it turned out more and more that the Party—i.e. the functionaries—oriented themselves on Sholokhov's speech and demanded from every writer the avowal that he was "first a communist, then a writer." I still become miserable even now when I think of the discussions in the various committees, of the cowardice and the hypocrisy that were even worse than the dogmatism of those who at least believed what they said.

Suddenly we had to be careful what we said to whom; in official committees we had to listen to horrible insults directed at writers. I found out about negative characterizations that circulated about me in the "apparatus" and experienced physically how a person is defenseless against defamation under certain circumstances, and how a person can easily be ground up if he or she ever winds up in this abject, self-sufficient apparatus. And then the blow, that our film *Moscow Novella* was rejected by Soviet agencies; that Konrad Wolf could no longer wait for the situation to improve and turned to new material, that all of our work was thus in vain. Those were dreadful days. I could not work and we began to look around for another place of residence . . .

All of that runs as a pale film behind the articles that I am reading: "Achieving the Q for the World Market—City Coun-

[2] Alexander Tvardovsky (1910-1971), Russian poet of popular verse epics; received honors as editor-in-chief of the journal *Novy Mir* (*New World*) (1958-1970). At the Twenty-Second Party Congress of the Communist Party of the Soviet Union in 1962, he defended the anti-Stalinist reform course; Mikhail Sholokhov (1905-1984), Russian prose writer (Nobel Prize 1965) contradicted him. (G.W.)

cilors Conferred About New Technology"—The East German news service: "One hundred and thirty-five women from the Federal Republic, with a total of 260 children, applied for admission to the German Democratic Republic during the last four weeks"—"Disturbers of the Peace Rebuffed. Bonn Ultras Pursue Front City Politics and Agitate Against the German Democratic Republic at UN Headquarters"—"Every Citizen of the Federal Republic 129 Marks in Debt."

Gerd reads aloud from *Neues Deutschland*: "Foreign bishops at the protective wall. Thanks to the border soldiers for peace watch."

It is reported that Anna Seghers[3] read from *Excursion of the Dead Young Girls* in the crowded cellar theater Katakombe in Frankfurt am Main. Prior to the presentation "anonymous smear sheets against the writer's appearance were distributed." At the opening of the Frankfurt Book Fair, Witsch, the chairman of the publishers' committee in the West German Association of the German Book Trade, called the publication of *The Seventh Cross* in West Germany a "misuse of freedom." The Luchterhand Publishing Company, Neuwied, confirmed, however, that it will publish "the great antifascist novel by Anna Seghers"—I can still see the old teacher's shaky handwriting on the blackboard of the school in Bad Frankenhause, the title *The Seventh Cross*, we had to read that now. It was 1948; we read the Rowohlt rotary press edition. I try to imagine what my situation would be without that book, without the other books of Anna Seghers.

[3] Anna Seghers (pseudonym of Netty Radványi, 1900-1983) was born in Mainz into a Jewish family. In 1925 she married the Hungarian writer and sociologist Lászlo Radványi. In 1928 Seghers joined the Communist Party and the Union Proletarian and Revolutinary Writers, which marked the final break with her bourgeois origins. Novelist, essayist, and short story writer, she is best remembered for her novels about the persecution of Jews and other groups in Nazi Germany. She gained international fame with *The Seventh Cross* (1942) and "Transit" (1944), a story about the fate of a group of German refugees in southern France. Seghers's major themes were social injustice and political upheavals of modern age. (Ed.)

The old question arises between us: Is there *one* German culture? In light of such reports I am almost inclined to agree with those who speak very resolutely of two German cultures and cite Lenin's definition of culture. But we all too quickly forgo our claim on literature that is created in West Germany—for example, Heinrich Böll—and do not hesitate to expand the self-sufficiency that is forced upon us and perhaps necessary in other areas to include culture. This must have disastrous consequences; we will hardly be able to get hold of West German literature anymore, and how is anyone—in the East or in the West—supposed to be able to write at least somewhat reliably about German problems? I ask. Won't we sink into provincialism? Or, over the decades, will West Germany become just another country for us, like Austria? Is a lasting, fundamental division of the nation really taking place? A horrible, enormously painful process.

Unfortunately, the symptoms of isolation with respect to the East are also obvious. I do not know which is worse. The Soviet works that were born and are being born from the intellectual discussion following the Twentieth and Twenty-Second Party Congresses are only hesitantly printed or shown here and without much publicity, and sometimes not at all—for example films like *Clear Skies* or *Peace to Him Who Enters*.[4] Justification: we do not have to participate in their mistakes. But can you turn this process of liberation from lies and ignorance back again? Gerd does not answer. I have the impression that he is somewhat skeptically awaiting the reception of my story, which I finished writing and gave to the publisher in spite of all these other involvements in recent months. He does not express him-

---

[4] Grigori Chukhrai's *Chistoe nebo* (1961): aka *Clear Heaven*; aka *Clear Skies*. Alexander Alov and Vladimir Naumov, *Mir vkhodyashchemu* (1961): aka *Peace to Him Who Enters*. The films, the second of which was only available in the Russian version, stimulated the discussion about our own film creations through their critical, anti-dogmatic attitude toward the Second World War. (G.W.)

self openly, simply says *Divided Heaven* is not really a title that overflows with optimism, is it? Then I shut up again.

Mrs. G. comes. She is a massive person, but agile and tireless in spite of that—one of those women who like to clean, which I do not understand, but I am careful not to let it show. A beautiful autumn, says Mrs. G. Although she has only been with us for a short time, she knows what needs to be done without anyone telling her and needs no guidance. I always wait somewhat fearfully for her tidings during the first few minutes. Since bad news seems to fly at her and she believes in the inevitability of vicissitudes, which we must accept stoically, she always provides us with the latest catastrophe reports. Today it is the suicide of a man whom we, however, do not know. This town is ideal for people who commit suicide, says Mrs. G. Nor is it any wonder. She thinks that the building of the wall that forms a fence through this city really might "weigh heavily on a person's mind." I ask her if she has been directly affected by it—Not directly. The fact that you can no longer go from Düppel to West Berlin on the commuter train actually should not matter to her. She would not have done that anyway. It was too arduous for her. But the fact that it is no longer possible, that does irritate her. And some people are hopping mad, of course. They had been sitting on packed bags and wanted to leave; now the trap has snapped shut—Can the fact that Mrs. G. has two deaf-mute children contribute to her hunger for other people's misfortunes?

I go shopping. How different the mentality of the people here is from that of the people in Halle. Right from the beginning we found it odd that the Western stations come into your house on so many frequencies here; we were not accustomed to being deluged with their news broadcasts. In Halle I had felt a certain amount of relief in the railroad car factory when the borders were closed, because before that we had to be afraid that the plant would be stripped of engineers and technicians. Now that there is no longer any intervention from outside, people will finally speak plainly to each other, they said in the directorate. Now a person will once again be able to criticize openly.

I pack my bags full in the grocery store and carry them home. All the faces are strange. I do not know the code to decipher their expressions. It is eleven o'clock when I return. The editorial office of *forum* calls. Heinz Nahke speaking. They want to pre-publish *Divided Heaven* beginning in November. A thrill of pleasure goes through me. So you like the manuscript? I ask. Nahke, in his usual placating manner, passes on a rather positive opinion—But the publisher still does not have permission to print it! I say. Nahke says that they are not subject to that. And besides, the manuscript fits their program precisely—Which program? I ask—To promote the discussion of socio-political questions among the young intellectuals—And you think you'll get away with that?—Signals from above suggest we need that very thing now—From where "above"?—Not on the telephone, Nahke says. But now we must support the right trend. Perhaps such an opportunity will never come again—I won't stand in the way, I say—Exactly, he says. We have to join forces.

Suddenly the world looks different. The paralysis has disappeared. There are people who are counting on me, who do not rank me among the deviationists, but among the forces that they want to "join" together. It really was good for us to move here, I say to Gerd. He is immune to exuberance. If "trends" are fighting against each other up there, it could become dangerous for those who wind up between the fronts, he says. But that does not change anything now. When a train departs, we have to jump aboard.

Meanwhile Tinka has tried to make friends with children in the neighborhood and returns with the news that they are all "stupid." Nothing more can be gotten out of her. She never says a word if she doesn't want to. In addition to that she makes the face that announced to me even when she was a toddler that she had battened down the hatches. She goes into the children's room to paint another series of princesses. In any case there are no children here that I could invite to her birthday tomorrow. That worries me. While I make Königsberg meatballs once again, Mrs. G. is busy in the kitchen. We soon won't be allowed to call them Königsberg meatballs anymore, she says, voicing her opinion—Why not?—Because Königsberg won't exist much longer. All that is no longer supposed to be true. They will now soon call them "Russian meatballs"— Oh, no, Mrs. G.—It does not seem proper to give Mrs. G. a lesson on causes and effects in historical developments. Besides, my confidence that every person can be cured of his or her false beliefs through evidence has meanwhile significantly diminished. Oh, Mr. Brecht, I often think, people really can see an apple fall to the ground and simultaneously believe it when someone claims: It isn't falling. And there it is still the matter of more obvious natural laws!

But, I say to myself, Mrs. G. is nonetheless open-minded with regard to people with disabilities, because as deaf-mutes her two children are themselves disabled. She becomes furious when speaking about rebuffs her children have experienced.

Annette comes home. The last class was cancelled. That has lifted her spirits, since it was mathematics. We discuss how we should organize Tinka's birthday without children. Go to Potsdam and eat ice cream, that much has already been decided. A bit meager, we both think. And how would it be, Annette says, if we visited a castle? Given she is so obsessed with princesses? Sanssouci! I cry. A good idea! And we won't tell Tinka, but simply announce a surprise.

Lunch is good. Mrs. K., our landlady, is an inexhaustible topic for the children. That she does not like children is obvious. They get their revenge by snapping up and spreading bad reports about her from sources that remain a mystery to me. Annette has learned that she is unbelievably miserly—so miserly that she saves the soap powder that she would use for her wash and instead hangs her things out on the line to air them out. Honestly and truly!

The mail brought invitations to different kinds of meetings. To judge by the topics, they want to start some kind of ideological offensive against the impact of the revelations of the Twenty-Second Party Congress, with which people here, of course, are only partially familiar, unless they read the *Presse der Sowjet-Union*. That is probably the other "trend" that the forum wants to undercut . . .

Weary, as I always am in the middle of the day, I lie down. For lack of other reading material, am again reading Aragon's *Holy Week*. This genre of modern historical novels is just the right kind of thing for me to read now so that I can distance myself a little bit from the present, which really does come at me too hard, and at the same time develop a keen eye.

A few letters, mostly refusals, are the only things created on my typewriter today. At around five we leave for Gross Glienicke, not without first preparing supper for the children, leaving the Schlotterbecks' telephone number with them, and checking with Mrs. P., the nice young engineer who lives below us, to make certain that she will be at home and look in on the children. They're not babies anymore, the two of them claim.

Through Stahnsdorf, Babelsberg, Potsdam, past Sanssouci, everything still new and unfamiliar. I try to see as much as possible and to impress it upon my mind. I try to count: since the end of the war I have moved nine times. Will we remain here long enough to be able to develop something like a feeling of being at home again? Do I actually miss this? It occurs to me that I have never asked myself that question before.

The Schlotterbecks⁵ live in a simple one-family house.

⁵ Friedrich Schlotterbeck (1909-1979), writer; as a communist in Hitler's Germany, because of antifascist resistance he was in concentration camps and prisons for ten years, was able to flee to Switzerland in 1944; all members of his family—mother,

Frieder had invited us in order to initiate us a little bit into "how the rabbit runs here." We met Aenne and him for the first time only a week ago at the first meeting of the Writer's Union in Potsdam, where, not least by Frieder, notes were struck—critical, even sarcastic—to which we were not accustomed in Halle. I had spoken to him about that and asked if it would not be more prudent to be a little more careful. A questioning look in response. The invitation followed.

For a little while we are still able to sit on the open wooden veranda behind the house. The day remains mild into the evening. In addition to Aenne and Frieder, Wilfriede, their daughter, and their little grandson Aram, who can obviously wrap his grandparents around his finger, are present. Tomatoes are lying on the table, which Frieder grew himself, and apples from the garden. At six on the dot he appears with a tray on which five filled champagne glasses stand. They always begin the evening at this time with a glass of champagne. So, Aenne says, to good neighborly relations! We drink. She adds: Every evening

father, sister, brother, fiancée—were executed while they were confined and accused of being jointly liable for his political crimes. Schlotterbeck immigrated to East Germany in 1948 with his wife, Aenne Schlotterbeck (1902-1972). In the German Democratic Republic, during the course of Stalinist trials they were again sentenced to prison.

A key figure for the charges in the Prague Slansky trial against the so-called "subversive conspiracy center" and resulting subsequent trials in the German Democratic Republic was the US citizen Noel Field (1904-1972), who was the director of the American refugee aid program (USC) in Switzerland during the Second World War; in all of the show trials he was named as the central US agent; was sentenced to prison in Hungary and remained in Hungary after his release from prison.

C. and G. Wolf were friends with the Schlotterbecks until their deaths. G.W. published a new edition (Halle, 1969) of Friedrich Schlotterbeck's report about his fate during the Nazi era, *"Je dunkler die Nacht, desto heller die Sterne* (The Darker the Night, the Brighter the Stars)" (first edition, 1945), and was the publisher's reader for his book *Im Rosengarten von Sanssouci* (*In the Rose Garden of Sanssouci*), Halle, 1968. C.W. gave the eulogy at Friedrich Schlotterbeck's funeral and remembered him in her *"Rede auf Schiller* (Address on Schiller)" on the occasion of her receiving the Friedrich Schiller Memorial Prize in Stuttgart in 1983 (C.W.'s *Werke in 12 Banden*, Vol. VIII, pp. 379ff.); for a West German new edition of *"Je dunkler die Nacht . . . ,"* Stuttgart, 1986, she wrote the afterword *"Erinnerung an Friedrich Schlotterbeck* (In Memory of Friedrich Schlotterbeck)," (*Werke*, Vol. VIII, pp. 439ff.) (G.W.)

with the first mouthful of champagne I think about the many
scoundrels who would be mad as hell if they could see that we
live and that we enjoy ourselves. And about those who know
and are mad as hell that they can no longer do anything to us.

And why can't they do anything anymore?—Kruschev, says
Frieder. Times are changing—And Aenne: Don't rejoice too
soon—Aram insists, and sips a little champagne, too.

I help Frieder carry the glasses into the kitchen, which is
beautifully and practically arranged, like apparently everything
in this house, and apparently frequently used. Frieder lifts the
cover from the large pot where something is simmering. Potato soup, he says. I'm the cook here. He tastes it, adds spices
from different small containers until he is satisfied, lifts the pot
from the burner, and puts it on the table in the dining niche in
the large room. I bring dishes and spoons, bread is cut and
placed next to it, the others are called in, and the soup is
served and eaten with something approaching reverence. Such
a delicacy has never been served to us before under the name
potato soup. Frieder puts on his roguish expression. Yeah, it's
a Swabian recipe—I notice his Swabian dialect today more
clearly than before. While he enumerates the ingredients for
the potato soup and Gerd makes an effort to remember all of
them, I imagine Frieder, with his almost bald, oval peasant's
head, as a Swabian fighter in the peasant wars or as an ill-
humored monk or priest, perhaps even as a member of the
Swabian school of poets, a friend of Hölderlin. He fits into
many clothes; he does not fit into fine robes. Where was his
home in Swabia?—Stuttgart-Untertürkheim, he says. A workers' settlement. My whole family worked for Daimler. I was a
carpenter—In the meantime we have learned some things
about the fate of his family: that the Nazis exterminated them.
We do not ask more questions—Yeah, says Frieder, his name
is common in the area around Stuttgart. By the way, since we
were supposed to know literature: we surely knew that one of

the robbers in Karl Moor's band in Schiller's *The Robbers* was named Schlotterbeck?—We did not know it, to Frieder's satisfaction.

Wilfriede says goodbye. Aram must go to bed; she lives in Berlin and still has an hour's ride ahead of her. After she has gone, Aenne says: To call a child *Wilfriede* in Germany in 1944—that also took courage for her mother—So is Aenne not Wilfriede's mother? Frieder not her father?—We do not ask. Frieder says: Wilfriede is the daughter of my sister Gertrud, whom they killed. And, almost without a transition: Oh, by the way, you're sitting in the chairs of Dresden's Nazi district leader Mutschmann! They are ostentatious brown leather armchairs into which you sink. They were given to them in 1947 when they moved from the West to East Germany, to Dresden, and of course had nothing, and certainly no furniture. They were administrative staff members of the Red Cross and brought a Red Cross supplies train with them, and that had also been quite a prank—Frieder seems to still be gloating about that, even now.

Of course we want to know more, everything possible about them, without questioning them all too obtrusively. And they notice that and give us the bits of information that present themselves, always casually, without emphasis. Primarily they actually want to talk with us about "the situation," about the power relationships in the district. The fact that in the Writers' Union the "reasonable people" are in the majority—we had already noticed that. We could imagine how this does not necessarily please the functionaries "in the district." Varnishing the truth is not dead, says Aenne. They are being put under a lot of pressure by Berlin to finally bring us to our senses—But then you talk so intimately and openly with them? I ask— Frieder says: I've already noticed that it disturbs you. But first of all: they are also human beings and receptive to human conversation. Second: don't think that the Twenty-Second Party

Congress didn't shake them to the core, too. And third: with respect to us they have a guilty conscience, and I simply exploit that shamelessly.

Aenne reins him in and tells him that he had better not dare to give us one of his political lectures. Nor did the conscience of the comrades really seem to be all that guilty. Otherwise they would long since have given them back their old Party books with the correct date of entry—That's another story— How so? says Aenne—Now we do want to know what they are talking about—Oh, when they were let out of the socialist prison, after a time they were rehabilitated, to be sure—they had been locked up "because of false accusations"—but in their new Party books they had entered a new, incorrect entry date, and since then Frieder had been fighting to have his correct entry date in his Party book, specifically the one from the 1920s. He has been in the Party much longer than all of the wiseacres and armchair farts, says Aenne. And he wants that documented. There he's as stubborn as an old jackass— Frieder grins at that.

But what did the false accusations consist of? we now want to know. Oh, that's a broad subject. Just a few intimations. Does the name Noel Field mean anything to us?—Didn't he play a role in the Slansky trial in Prague?[6]—Right, as an "enemy agent." And their trial had been a weak offshoot of the trials in the socialist sister nations. But while in exile in Switzerland, as a staff member of the Red Cross, Aenne had met Field, who also arranged help for victims of the Nazis, and that had led to their downfall. To be sure, after Stalin's death they had silently dropped the charge of "enemy agent activity" and replaced it with other absurd accusations. In any case, the

[6] Slansky trial: 1951 (see also footnote 5); Stalinist trials with anti-Semitic tendencies against leading members of the Communist Party in the CSSR under General Secretary Rudolf Slansky, with numerous death sentences or long prison terms; the condemned people were not "rehabilitated" until 1963. (G.W.)

two of them had sat—she two, he three years—in Bützow—
Bützow?—In Mecklenburg. A prison for men and women. We
can go there some time if you want. Frieder almost died there,
rupture of a stomach ulcer—To be locked up by your own
people, Frieder says almost apologetically. That takes an awful
lot out of you, of course.

We say nothing, but they can guess our thoughts. Well, of
course you sometimes get fed up with the nonsense, says Frieder,
and you want to give up. But then everything that you did before
would have been in vain; then all of that Nazi shit would have
won after all. The price was too high. We just have to pull ourselves from the swamp with our own hands. And go on.

And if the swamp is stronger?

You mustn't even think that, says Frieder.

When we say goodbye outside, standing before the front
door, he puts his arm around my shoulder: You always have to
rattle the bars of the corral, girl, he says. Otherwise the walls
will close in on you and smash you in the end.

On the way home we have no desire to speak. It is dark, a
bizarre moon accompanies us. At home we look into the children's room, the children are asleep. As agreed, Annette has
put a large dish of fine sand on the table and laid a note next
to it: Don't forget to set up the candles. I press six birthday
candles and a larger "life light" into the damp sand and decorate the table as always with aster blossoms. It is not yet midnight and we are in bed. Gerd hands the open Hermlin[7] book
over to me. Read, he says. It's fitting. When he wrote that, he
was as old as we are now. I read:

[7] Stephan Hermlin (1915-1997): G. Wolf edited *Gedichte Stephan Hermlins* (*Stephan
Hermlin's Poems*) for Reclam in Leipzig in 1963 and wrote the essay on Hermlin in *Literatur der DDR in Einzeldarstellungen* (*Literature of the GDR in Individual Treatments*); C.W. remembers Hermlin's poem in her obituary on the poet "*Der Worte
Wunden bluten heute nur nach innen* (Today the Wounds of the Words Only Bleed
Inwardly)" (*Werke*, Vol. XII, pp. 674ff.). On the friendship with Hermlin of many
years standing see also the contribution "*Nicht beendetes Gespräch* (Unfinished Conversation)," Berlin, *Freibeuter*, 63/1995. (G.W.)

The time of wonders has gone by. Beyond the blocks
The arc lamp suns have now gone down and out of sight.
And when they strike, we're startled by the faulty clocks,
And now the cats are gray again in fading light.
For merchants and for heroes evening falls across the
skies.
The heartbeat falters like this line, something chokes the
cry.
The wall inscriptions and the flocks of birds advise:
Our youth is gone. The time of wonders has gone by.

. . . and it ends:

The wounds of words are now still bleeding inwardly.
The time of wonders perished. The wasted years are gone.

I begin. It is the "middle of the day" when I sit down at my desk—finally! It is already 10:50—and I begin with a statement by Anna Seghers that I just read in an essay written last year on the occasion of Nazim Hikmet's birthday . . . She quotes Hikmet:

"Unlike most writers he often needs more time for a poem than for a stage play. That clarifies his life for us, which is in part driven, in part paralyzed. And divided into individual harsh acts.

> Thus have I freed myself
> From all big words,
> From all question marks.
> Sedately I entered the ranks
> Of the great struggle.

In this way, we gather around him, close, sedate, freed from big words."[1]

In that one sentence a person can unfurl the entire debate in which we have been involved since the end of last year—and I

---

[1] Nazim Hikmet (1902-1963), Turkish communist poet, often forced into exile, he also occasionally resided in the German Democratic Republic; friends with Anna Seghers; in the German Democratic Republic numerous volumes of his poetry appeared in German; Anna Seghers quotes from Hikmet's poem *"Die Welt, Freund und Feind, Du und die Erde* (The World, Friend and Enemy, You and the Earth)" (N. Hikmet, *Gedichte* [*Poems*], Berlin, 1959, pp. 68ff.). (G.W.)

especially in recent weeks. It becomes more and more clear to me that it is not a matter of a chance collision, of misunderstandings (at first I myself still wanted to take it that way for fear of the consequences); it is a basic difference of opinion *not* on questions of literature, but on political, "general human" questions. Last night on the telephone Konrad Wolf said: "You are probably aware that we live in a time of the class struggle, especially the ideological class struggle . . ."—I: "But surely not of class struggle within the Party!" He: "Why not? If that stops, we don't need the Party anymore!" I: "But will you permit me to forgo shouting hallelujah about that?" He: "Nobody asks that of you."

Of course, calling it class struggle is not correct. It is even more complicated. It is actually a matter of replacing an old generation of communists with a new one, which will always bring conflicts, of course, but is now enormously critical because of the simultaneous necessity to deal with the cult of personality (which has very little to do with individuals anymore). To step down, to see your own limitations, must be enormously difficult. In addition to that: specifically in the area of ideology and pedagogy, during the last decade and a half the most unpleasant characters have systematically pushed their way to the top and now hold important positions (also people, by the way, who do not understand much about the field, which gives their struggle for their seat a tragi-comic element). In the Czech Soviet Socialist Republic they have now reorganized the entire government—an act that certainly would not be advisable here. But the slow process of "reorganization" brings problems, of course . . . For example, Walter Ulbricht[2] has difficulties getting a youth

---

[2] Walter Ulbricht (1893-1973) was a German communist politician. As First Secretary of the Socialist Unity Party from 1950 to 1971, he held arguably the most central role in the early development and establishment of the German Democratic Republic. (Ed.)

communiqué[3] with the sharpness that he would like accepted in the politburo. It is being attacked (or watered down) by the same people who are attacking *Divided Heaven* in Halle and elsewhere. The attack is not so dangerous because they usually hide the true reasons for their opinions and build a structure out of suppositions, distortions, and suspicions, which cannot stand up, of course. ("Decadent lifestyle" is the least of their accusations against me.)

To be sure, we have different opinions about life, about what is true and false, genuine and counterfeit, positive and negative. But I think that it is too early to conduct that discussion openly. So it proceeds on the level of appearances: I am forced to reject human baseness and am able to involve myself relatively little in the matter. In recent weeks I have swallowed quite a bit. At times, I was really down (I saw what lies ahead of us!), and I was especially hurt by the disappointing behavior of some people. On the other hand: they are not succeeding. The book is mentioned (in spite of violent opposition) in the youth communiqué. A lot of people, even leading comrades, maintain their opinion.

Just now a card from Kurella[4] in which the man as a whole is visible:

"Dear Christa! I just read your 'Terra incognita' (an article in *forum*) with great pleasure![5] What you wrote about the elec-

---

[3] Youth Communiqué: Resolution of the Central Committee of the Socialist Unity Party, initiated by Walter Ulbricht: "*Der Jugend Verantwortung und Vertrauen* (To the Youth, Responsibility and Trust)" for the modernization of the youth, cultural, and scientific policies of the Socialist Unity Party; directed against Erich Honecker, who condemned this policy as a "false orientation" and "revisionism" (see also: Second Plenary Session of the Central Committee of the Socialist Unity Party, 1966). (G.W.)

[4] Alfred Kurella (1895-1975), writer, cultural functionary; as a communist, emigrated to the USSR; 1957-1963 in the politburo of the Socialist Unity Party and after 1963 a member of the ideology committee of the politburo; significantly involved in the cultural politics of the Socialist Unity Party. (G.W.)

[5] C.W.'s essay, "*Wo liegt unsere 'terra incognita'?* (Where Does Our 'Terra Incognita' Lie?)," which contains a quote from the diary of Max Frisch from January of 1948 (Frisch, *Gesammelte Werke* (*Collected Works*), Vol. II, p. 554), appeared in *Forum*, 18/1963. (G.W.)

tion and about literature is—a commentary on the youth communiqué! And an excellent one! Isn't that a good, satisfying realization for you yourself? You mustn't take the peculiar series of articles (so as not to call them something else) appearing in *Freiheit* too much to heart. This is no way to eat!—Getting a 'taste of it' is sometimes part of the deal! Heartfelt greetings, A. K."

The same A. K. who came up to me at Ulbricht's birthday reception with Dr. Thiessen,[6] introduced me to him, and said: "Unfortunately also married. But probably not above the norm?" . . . The fact that I *do* take the people in Halle to heart is *also* a part of the "deal," but of my own personal deal, which, one way or another, has to be brought into harmony with things in general . . .

Another letter: from DILIA, the literary agency in Prague. They write to me that a Czech women's magazine wants to pre-print *Divided Heaven* as a serial. I am very happy about that!

The most unpleasant thing about these sudden unfounded attacks against a book or against a person is that the process of self-criticism is slowed down. You stiffen against it. You hunger more for praise than you did before. You take it more seriously.

That must not happen to me under any circumstances!

This morning—now I am writing retrospectively—I rolled around lazily in bed with Tinka for a long time. School didn't start today until late. She exploits her position as the littlest girl, stretches herself, and encircles me with her charm. She still smells good. I cuddled with her and was reminded of how she lay next to me as a baby, as a warm little clump. Enthusiastically she grasped the association and demanded "baby sto-

---

[6] Prof. Peter Adolf Thiessen (1899-1990), professor of physical chemistry; 1935-1945 director of the Kaiser Wilhelm Institute for Physical Chemistry in Berlin; 1945-1956 a specialist for atomic research in the USSR; in the German Democratic Republic 1957-1965 chairman of the Research Council of the German Democratic Republic and member of the State Council. (G.W.)

ries." Father warned her: Mom is just thinking aloud. After all, she's a writer!—I protested: Invention is not my strength!

It was stormy today. Sunshine alternated with dense clouds. The loose window next to me rattled. Actually we should already be turning on the heat. I am now often weary during the few days between our "tours" through the Republic. Today I have "aches" in my left shoulder for the first time. Hopefully they will go away!

Later Baldauf came from the Deutschland station and brought the newest product by Günter Grass: *Dog Years*, for me to review. In the process we became conscious of how little we actually know about intellectual developments over there. There is almost no discussion anymore. We no longer see the background before which such a book appears at all. Recently, during a discussion with students someone said: For me West Germany is a country like any other—like France or Italy—only German is spoken there.

No isolated opinion among twenty-year-olds. So the two parts of Germany are inexorably moving apart?

Tinka says: "Now I'm going to close my eyes. Then I'll see myself as a baby. And you?" I saw her, too, and saw myself as well: young, cheerful (which surely is not true at all), unburdened by so much. I often yearn to be young, but not to be naïve. Can we long to know less about everything than we know? The process of disillusionment, a background theme of my story, continues unceasingly. Sometimes we become alarmed (as I am doing right now). But Seghers said it very well: "Sedate, liberated from big words."

Of course: this also entails a new freedom . . .

In the afternoon: Tinka has just come in, thoughtlessly opening the door. I am startled and get upset with her. She says: "Are you jumpy?" Yes, I am. Sometimes at night I wake up with a start and scream. That never happened to me in the past.

Gerd says he found a piece of paper in one of Fürnberg's

diaries, with a real prayer on it, a plea for protection for himself and his family, addressed to God. From the time of the Slansky trials . . . I ask myself: What must be happening inside a person who is a communist to his last breath to make him cling to the mystical as a final way out?

Tinka is just now straightening up her school case—she has a hard time with careful treatment of the books and notebooks. She still does not take school very seriously. So far she has not had any problems to solve.

An afternoon program "for the older generation" is being broadcast on Free Berlin Radio. In a nutshell: cheese for the soul. "They sure know all about it!" says Gerd.

The pain in my shoulder becomes annoying. Am I going to have to have my tonsils removed after all?

Today at noon, while I was shoving the shish kebab onto the skewers, I said to Gerd: In Prague they want to publish *Divided Heaven* in a women's magazine. See, he said. The Czechs really are the best!—Mrs. G. laughed and said: But they are not very clean!—I gave my opinion on that point. She: All that may be true, but the refugees who came from there in '45 were rather dirty. I: We also came as displaced persons, dirty. If you don't have anything, it is easy to get dirty. Mrs. G. remains unconvinced. A few days ago, when we were eating garlic, she said: Now we'll stink like the Jews!

Last week in Weimar I had the experience of seeing a seven-year-old boy call after a Negro on the street: "Look at how dirty he is! He never washes!" When put on the spot, he evades and then backs away with a shyly cunning look on his face. He knew exactly what I wanted from him. ". . . continuously engendering evil must give birth . . ."

The day is almost over. I am already bringing it to a close because I know how it will proceed: supper, putting the children to bed, two hours with newspapers and a book, while getting more and more tired, and then to bed.

This time the "one day a year" fell on a Sunday. But even then I did not have time to write. I will probably have to make a "week of the year" out of it. For my daily routine hardly says anything about me anymore. It is forced upon me. I am afflicted by gloomy reflections about the extent to which the writer (and of course other people especially) may be manipulated in our society. When, after a book, the number of invitations to readings rises to seven hundred, they become one of the seven Egyptian plagues. When many of them are clearly a matter of routine, a matter of striving, with the help of the author, to check off an item on the cultural agenda, you feel miserable enough. Then, even a national prize is not worth rejoicing about anymore. On the contrary: it burdens me. It is extremely difficult to draw a line under all of these public demands. They are electing me to PEN. I can do nothing about it. They shove me onto the advisory board of the presidium; I am not asked and I am not even there. Every newspaper wants an interview with me, or a picture. Every West German or foreign journalist is supposed to visit the monument to the fallen soldier at Treptow, and me. Of course, this is also an opportunity to remove someone from the field of battle. I am again quite nervous. I can hardly take an afternoon nap anymore. Whether I want to or not, I am in danger of seeing everything from the point of view of my own ego. There are signs of that with me, which Gerd signals. Now and then there is a small, insignificant collision that would be unthinkable under "normal" circumstances. Perhaps I am beginning to become too self-important. Gerd says: You don't enjoy life at all anymore. There is something to that. I am becoming wry, a bit tense, and pigheaded. I begin to think that it is improper for me to have all that money. I urgently want to produce something new. But aside from the fact that I am not able to work without interruption, I am also not to that point. I have not worked exactingly and hard enough. That is the worst thing.

The new plan came into existence in the following way: on the telephone, after he had attended an international film symposium in Moscow, Dieter indicated that our film had virtually failed. Two days earlier, following an Academy discussion, an article had appeared in *Neues Deutschland*, under the title: "Motion Picture Art's Lucky Hour." Quick as a flash and very clearly I grasped the weakness of the film: its artificiality. In the same moment I thought: I must write about that. What I mean is: about the process of finding the truth in two respects: First, as a "simple" process of the ever better (or just beginning) recognition of the dialectic nature of reality and its artistic representation, and second the achieving of distance from that truth, which actually again proves to be one-sided, limited. The pains experienced in doing so, and the satisfaction. The influence of the environment on it—very often negative. How we are hindered in seeing or saying the truth. How they want to push art aside as a decorative embellishment and not view it as one of society's vital organs.

Is that an artistic topic at all? It should be clothed in a report about the day of a film producer. A day when he receives a prize and simultaneously recognizes how inadequate his work has been. The conflicts to which artists in particular have been subjected in recent years should intersect in that man.

I was horribly in doubt. Not only that my own national prize makes the treatment of such material excessively difficult for me—(first I thought: Now I cannot write that anymore at all)—even in itself. Is that a topic?

On a recent evening I discussed it with Konni,[1] who is busy preparing his Goya. He says that the most important thing for him about this material, next to the problem of the artist, is the topic of intellectual inquisition. I asked, Do you think that a person can only deal with this topic right now within the context of historical material? He: Yes! Otherwise you never get to the principal level.

That is how it is. I now see before me already how I will constantly have to cut off the threads at the top, so that the whole thing does not go too far. It is very difficult, perhaps impossible, to write in a way that in the process you do not think of an audience. That you only write "for yourself." That would be the right way to write.

Sometimes I think that for our generation the intrusion of reality comes almost too late, in any case at the very last moment, and processing it demands extreme effort.

Konni said: *The* topic, one that has not yet been touched at all, is, "Germany today." That had become clear to him again during a birthday party for Christel's grandma ("Grandma's birthday"), where West and East met together and everything was represented, from soldier anecdotes to socialist agitation.

That means, I said, a great, multi-level novel of the society, like the kind Tolstoy wrote? Yes, he said. Or: small stories in which the entire spectrum of problems of recent years is reflected indirectly. That is more or less how he saw my material, but it seems to me that it is more direct and has essayistic elements. (Is that really appropriate material?)

Konni told about his recent encounters with Michail Romm,[2] who was in Berlin to collect material for his film

---

[1] Konrad "Konni" Wolf. (Ed.)

[2] Michail Romm (1901-1971), Soviet film director; master of the classical revolution film *Lenin im Oktober* (*Lenin in October*) (1937); *Neun Tage eines Jahres* (*Nine Days of One Year*) (1961); *Klarer Himmel* (1961); an initial dispute with Stalinism, *Gewöhnlicher Faschismus* (*Ordinary Fascism*) (1965). (G.W.)

about fascism, *Triumph Over Violence*.[3] (At home he has a finished scenario for it, but one that he cannot film. It treats the conflict between the generations, which, of course, officially does not exist.) While there, he also found new documents about the 1939 pact between Hitler and Stalin. For example: two days after the attack on the USSR, oil and iron ore were still being delivered to Hitler's Germany! Romm thinks it is possible to conclude that between dictators, no matter of what social order, there is or there arises a certain affinity.

Angel Wagenstein[4] compared the situation after the Twenty-Second Party Congress to a champagne cork that has popped out of the bottle and can no longer be stuffed back into it for anything in the world. Romm counters it with his image of the two flies sitting on the wheel of a one-horse cart that at times ploughs through mud, and at other times moves over dry terrain. The flies cheer when they're high and dry and "on top," and curse when they are drawn through the mud. So they become angry about the independent movement of the wheel. But they forget to ask where the whole cart is actually going. And that in particular, Romm thinks, would be the most important thing today . . .

He also told Konni about the prohibition of the second part of the Eisenstein film *Ivan the Terrible*, whose separate phases he experienced. One day they were all invited to the Central Committee. Eisenstein was also there. The film was shown.

[3] *Obyknovennyy fashizm* (1965), aka *A Night of Thoughts*; aka *Echo of the Jackboot* (UK); aka *Ordinary Fascism*; aka *Triumph Over Violence* (USA); aka *Trumps Over Violence* (USA). (Ed.)

[4] Angel Wagenstein (b. 1922), Jewish Bulgarian film scenario writer who wrote screenplays for numerous films of the DEFA German film workers' group; friends with Konrad Wolf since their studies together at the Moscow All Union Institute for Cinematography. Wrote the screenplays for Wolf's films *Sterne* (*Stars*) (1959) and *Goya* (1971); *Pentateuch oder Die fünf Bücher Isaaks* (*Pentateuch or the Five Books of Isaac*), Berlin, 1999. (G.W.)

They all had a distinct feeling: a film against Stalin. Nobody could say that aloud. They beat around the bush. Romm said that he should finish the third part first. Perhaps then they would be able to see things more clearly. Pudovkin[5] wanted to know what he had actually intended to say with the film. Eisenstein responded: "What I intended to say, I said."—In any case, nobody came out and said it. Meanwhile Eisenstein had a heart attack, lay in the hospital, and the film was shown at high levels. Adamant rejection. Romm is assigned to convey that to Eisenstein. He makes it cool and brief. Eisenstein remains calm. He asks: "What is the reason for the rejection?" Romm answers with the sentence that was officially communicated to him: "In the film there are distortions of historical events." Eisenstein responds: "Well, if you have nothing else . . ."

While ever we do not write about such things, we remain superficial. One serious question is: does this problem actually interest "the nation," the masses of people? Isn't it a typical intellectual problem formulation (yesterday during a film discussion in the National People's Army we noticed that many people are not willing to pursue such questions)? It has to be dealt with in spite of that. After all, it is a determining factor in life everywhere! Recently in the executive committee of the Writers' Union (that also lies temporally within this week of the year!) the secretariat itself, apparently under pressure from below, brought up for discussion the problem that many writers (I believe, all of them) think that they themselves and their union are powerless. Certain phrases were used, like: "The powerlessness of the author vis-à-vis the institutions," which is now generally accepted as fact. A result of that is the lack of contribution by the union members to the life of the union. Many feel that they are a "democratic façade," "dues payers," and see the union as a "debating club." All of that is correct.

[5] Vsevolod Pudovkin (1893-1953), Soviet film director, best known for Russian silent films and his influential theories of montage. (Ed.)

Walter Kaufmann,[6] who traveled for several weeks between the German Democratic Republic, Finland, and Sweden on a small coastal motor ship with a small crew (fifteen men), told us how bitter most of those very capable and politically "clean" young people are toward the political instructors and toward the administration of the shipping office. How they make comparisons between the accomplishments of our ships and analogous West German ships—not in order to run away to the West, but in order to improve our methods. They, and the young captain, are punished severely if they try to act rationally. He refused to bring an old ship from Egypt back to the German Democratic Republic with a lading that was too heavy for it. He was relieved of his command, demoted for refusing to follow orders, and sentenced to land duty. With a new captain, quick to volunteer, the ship broke in two not far from Rostock. That captain was punished. The first captain now commands a small ship, but has no intention of climbing any higher. (Similar reaction, although for different reasons, on the part of the Ammendorf plant director, who also does not want to climb up the ladder.)

A typical story here in our country: the man who was punished for common sense and now quietly contents himself with a position that insufficiently challenges him.

I must look for other stories like that. The Meternagel story of the man who always had to do things that went beyond his abilities is also such a story, but seemingly a contrasting one.

The day before yesterday, in the Potsdam Cecilienhof PEN Club: discussion. Historical room of the Potsdam Accord. An abomination! Ernst Schumacher said as he entered: "No won-

[6] Walter Kaufmann (b. 1924), writer of Jewish origin; General Secretary of PEN (German Democratic Republic) 1985-1993; took up residency in the German Democratic Republic in 1956 following exile in Australia; reportages and novels, a. o. *Wohin der Mensch gehört* (*Where the Human Being Belongs*), Berlin, 1957, *Die Zeit berühren—Mosaik eines Lebens* (*Touching Time—Mosaic of a Life*), Berlin, 1992 (see also: C.W., *Akteneinsicht*, Hamburg, 1993, pp. 152ff.). (G.W.)

der—here they were incapable of thinking up anything better!" Gloomy wooden paneling halfway up the wall and a penetrating moth stench. High windows. The flags of the four powers in small format and a picture in which the four main signers are visible. For the first time the sacred round table was desecrated by profane activity, even though school classes were steadily led past and stared at everything. I asked myself: What do they think of the illustrious circle that is gathered here?

A discussion about German literature after the two world wars was planned. Günther Cwojdrak[7] opened the session, cautiously. One of his ideas proved fruitful: Why isn't there this comprehensive portrayal, *the* great novel, after the Second World War, as there was after the First? At the beginning Arnold Zweig[8] told a few anecdotes, reported about the genesis of his *The Case of Sergeant Grischa*, which developed from a piece that supposedly nobody wanted to print because of the expressionist trend. No publisher would even accept the book—at least not Ullstein. They did not want any more war books. Zweig called that the "suppression of the war." Afterward Ludwig Renn[9] told of similar experiences. Zweig's novel and Renn's book were then first published in *Die Frankfurter Allgemeine*.

Anna Seghers spoke on the problem of distance. Back then, after all, the writers had written from direct experience, without distancing themselves (Barbusse). Why isn't that possible for the young generation? Seghers said: Because they used their time to become "opponents of themselves." Franz

---

[7] Günther Cwojdrak (1923-1991), literary critic, publicist; with Willi Bredel and F.C. Weiskopf a joint founder of the journal *Neue Deutsche Literatur*, 1952-1957 its editor. (G.W.)

[8] Arnold Zweig (1887-1968), German writer and an active pacifist. (Ed.)

[9] Ludwig Renn (1889-1979), pseudonym of Arnold Friedrich Vieth von Golssenau. German novelist, best known for *Krieg* (*War*, 1928), a novel based on his First World War battle experiences, the narrator and principal character of which was named Ludwig Renn. The stark simplicity of the novel emphasizes the uncompromising brutality of combat. (Ed.)

Fühmann[10] joined in and confirmed that. During the entire
time, I had the feeling that the topic has not even been touched
yet, at least not in its current variation. Then Ernst Schumacher was the first one to talk about the consequences of the Cold
War. Hermlin interjected that Soviet literature is actually just
now really beginning to grasp the Second World War artistically. That the strong signs of degeneration recent books so
quickly exhibit have to do with the cult of personality and the
Cold War, with their impact on the thoughts and feelings of the
people, including the writers—That is where we should have
started talking. The fact that the Third World War would be a
nuclear war, and that this weapon must also influence and
change the way to fight against its use was not at all a matter
for debate.

Yesterday, after a film presentation, an evening of discussion
with the National People's Army in Potsdam-Eiche. Afterward, a brief get-together with the officers. They talked—thoroughly congenially—about their difficulties in training the
troops. There is no positive attitude toward compulsory military service. Most of them come unwillingly—and the best
ones in particular!—due to the unproductive period that they
have to spend in the National People's Army. Some say: Then
I'd rather work for eighty marks in an agricultural commune
for eighteen months; then at least you know what you have
done. In the army they do only what is necessary, always getting by, just short of punishment, just not wanting to stand out,
etc. The officers spoke about political discussions, which must
apparently be quite open, at least in part. For example, that we
let the retired people go to the West because we want to be rid
of them. Nor is there, said the officer gloomily, any convincing
political argumentation about it yet. Or: there are debates

---

[10] Franz Fühmann (1922-1984), story writer, autobiographer, essayist, children's writer,
poet. (Ed.)

about theory and practice in socialist economic management (all come from factories, of course!). There the officers suffer from their relatively long isolation in military barracks. Then, on maneuvers, they say, the soldiers stand their ground, even when they get nothing to eat for thirty hours under order. (By the way, it is said that there are isolated cases of conscientious objectors who are sentenced and locked up.) The officers longed very much for "pre-military training."

That is only a fraction of this week's problems.

In a review of the *Coriolan*[11] performance by the Berlin Ensemble, Brecht is cited: "That the individual is apparently irreplaceable will continue to be an enormous topic for a long time." The actual topics are of *this* kind.

So, historical themes are the only ones to be dealt with?

Several evenings back, Walter Kaufmann conducted a test with me. Which milieu, which city, which streets do I know so well that stories occur to me when the name is mentioned? For him Melbourne was still the source of material, and lately the USA. For me, Landsberg. My flight. The village of Gammelin. The tuberculosis sanatorium. Frankenhausen. The university (in a limited sense). Later it becomes more difficult. Or is the production of literature a "topic"? From a certain time on I no longer see milieus, but individual people or a general atmosphere in front of me.

My plan up to 1970:

Fräulein Schmetterling (*Miss Butterfly*) (1964), screenplay
Das Preisgericht (*The Jury*) (1965), novel
Seghers piece (1965), essay
My book about 1945 (1966)
The novel (up through and including 1970)[12]

---

[11] 1952-1955 adaptation of Shakespeare's play by Bertolt Brecht. (Ed.)

[12] *Fräulein Schmetterling* (*Miss Butterfly*), film by C. and G. Wolf, 1965, prohibited (see: "*Kahlschlag—Das II. Plenum des ZK der SED 1965. Studien und Dokumente* [Clear-Cut—The Second Plenary Session of the Central Committee of the Socialist

I still forgot to write that on that evening we discussed the problem of cynicism with Konni, which is closely related to the so often visible phenomenon of the "second face" under the mask. *The Jury* will specifically portray how a man who is unconsciously on the edge of cynicism is saved from crossing that boundary by a powerful self-critical shock. Günter Görlich[13] interjected the question of whether or not that is also the problem of so-called "simple" people. Konni gave examples from the brigade: how the "second face" becomes visible very quickly under the influence of alcohol.

Finally, I want to write down my curriculum for the last week and a half:

23 Sept.: in the afternoon: state ceremony, memorial service for Grotewohl
  in the evening: at Konrad Wolf's
24 Sept.: executive committee meeting Berlin
25+26 Sept.: scrubbing after the painters at home
  in the evening at Kaufmanns'
27 Sept.: Mrs. Krause here in the afternoon
28 Sept.: Tinka's birthday with nine guests
29 Sept.: in the afternoon: PEN
  in the evening: PEN reception
30 Sept.: in the evening with the National People's Army in Potsdam-Eiche
1 Oct.: in the evening "social gathering," with the German Writers' Union, Potsdam

Unity Party 1965. Studies and Documents]", Berlin, 2000).
Preisgericht (Jury): Unfinished manuscript (C.W. Archive Foundation, Academy of Arts, Berlin).
Seghers piece: never developed beyond preliminary notes.
My book about 1945: plan in regard to *Patterns of Childhood*, Berlin, 1976.
The novel: plan not carried out. (G.W.)

[13] Günter Görlich (b. 1928), writer of novels and books for young people in the German Democratic Republic. (Ed.)

2 Oct.:　　　nothing

3 Oct.　　　discussion of the factory collective contract in the IHT[14]

So now I have not written anything at all about my impressions at the state ceremony in connection with Grotewohl's funeral, which in my opinion was hollow, depressing in the old style. The Soviet delegate used the same unbelievable phrases that he would have used on a similar occasion ten years ago.

Nor have I yet written about Michail Romm's evaluation of Soviet cultural policy today: not yes and not no. They had recognized that "after it" (after the Twentieth Party Congress) they had still gone "too far," and even Ilyitschov does not know how to proceed from here.[15] The initial impact of explosive excitement after the Twentieth Party Congress has stopped, the trend is moving backward. They are all sitting there waiting to see what will happen.

I have not yet described how Konrad Wolf, on the night when he wanted to drive me to my obscure hotel, came to his new Fiat and found that the back window had been smashed in with a rock that lay on the back seat, and how he then noticed that his nylon raincoat, which had lain there, was missing. A new hooliganism is developing around Alexanderplatz.

Or yesterday evening: young Potsdam poets read poems aloud. A stupid brew of autumn and love poetry from the twenties. And what have I written this week? An open letter for *Pravda*.[16] These diary notes. Coming up today: a miniature

[14] IHT Stahnsdorf: Institute for Semiconductor Technology of the Academy of Sciences of the German Democratic Republic in Stahnsdorf. (G.W.)

[15] Ilyitschov (b. 1905): Secretary for Cultural Politics in the Central Committee of the Communist Party of the Soviet Union. (Ed.)

[16] C.W.'s letter for *Pravda*, not locatable. (G.W.)

speech on the fifteenth anniversary of the German Democratic Republic in Potsdam.[17] An article for the magazine *Sowjetfrau*.[18] All that is impossible. I must now employ the tactic of having them say that I am not home, or else really go away . . . A small apartment on Alexanderplatz in Berlin would be nice.

[17] Miniature speech: see "*Eine Rede* (A speech)," C.W., *Werke*, Vol. IV, pp. 54ff. (G.W.)

[18] Article for *Sowjetfrau*: under the title "*Fünfundzwanzig Jahre* (Twenty-five Years)" in C.W., *Lesen und Schreiben* (*The Reader and the Writer*), Berlin, 1971. (G.W.)

The twenty-seventh of September passed without my reporting on it. I had migraines, felt lethargic, sick, and unable to work, sat and lay around, let things slide, neglected my diary. Noted down a few quotes from Pavese's diaries,[1] which I was reading. On 19 June, 1946 he wrote: "I begin to write poems when the game has been lost. We have never seen that a poem changed things."

Apparently I did not have the desire or the strength to put down in writing as well my growing feeling that the game has been lost. Without concentrating I worked on a novel, *The Jury*, which I had actually already abandoned, prepared a contribution for a discussion that I wanted to have with writers during a meeting in the State Council, but which I put aside because Werner Bräunig[42] was sharply and unexpectedly attacked by Walter Ulbricht in *Neue Deutsche Literatur* because of his Wismut Company novel and had to be defended. That was less than three weeks before the 11th general assembly of the Central Committee on the fifteenth of December, which I attended with feelings of anxiety. After that my

---

[1] Cesare Pavese (1908-1950), Italian poet, novelist, literary critic and translator. (Ed.)

[2] Werner Bräunig (1934-1976), writer; well acquainted with C. and G. Wolf (G.W. was the publisher's reader for his first works, *Waffenbrüder* [*Comrades in Arms*], Halle, 1959; poems in the anthology *Bekanntschaft mit uns selbst* [*Acquaintance with Ourselves*], Halle, 1961); a preprint from his planned novel about the uranium mining of the Wismut Company, *Rummelplatz* (*Amusement Park*), unleashed substantial criticism (*Kahlschlag—Das II. Plenum des ZK der SED 1965. Studien und Dokumente*, Berlin, 2000). (G.W.)

diary begins again on the twentieth of December and will be cited here as a typical illustration for the year 1965.

Perhaps in the near future the diary will be—Gerd and I argue about whether it will be in the next year, or in coming years, or at all—the only art form in which a person can still remain honest, in which one can avoid the compromises that are otherwise necessary or becoming unavoidable everywhere. The general assembly has decided: reality will be eliminated. Anna Seghers says: "There have been worse things. Under Stalin the people were put against the wall—not any longer. Is that perhaps not progress? Besides that, it will pass. Or it will remain the same. Then we will have to adapt to it."

That was on the second day of the plenum,[3] after I had spoken there, had tried to save what could be saved, and had left without applause, halfway overwhelmed; after Paul Verner,[4] while purposely misinterpreting me, had polemicized against me (he claimed that I had demanded absolute freedom for art, while I had spoken about our laboriously acquired free relationship to the material; he protested against my plea not to let the dialogue with West German writers be broken off, using examples in which the dialogue had led to an "ideological hodgepodge," etc.). Anna Seghers was sitting outside in the foyer reading a newspaper. She had me called out so that I heard only part of the polemic. I was still glad that I had spoken, although I saw what the result would be and especially how useless it would be. Anna Seghers encouraged me: It is

[3] The Second Plenum of the Central Committee of the Socialist Unity Party in December of 1965 entered the history of the German Democratic Republic as a clear-cutting plenum because at that meeting a line was presented that was hostile to art; i.e., the prohibition of twelve DEFA films; C.W., a candidate of the Central Committee from 1963 to 1967, was the only one to speak against that policy (see "*Kahlschlag—Das II. Plenum des ZK der SED 1965. Studien und Dokumente,*" Berlin, 2000). (G.W.)

[4] Paul Verner (1911-1986), member of the politburo of the Central Committee of the Socialist Unity Party, 1959-1971. First Secretary of the Berlin district executive committee of the Socialist Unity Party. (G.W.)

good that you spoke—She was in the process of reading the report of activities that Honecker[5] had presented the previous day and was quite perplexed. She found such passages "captivating," where, on the occasion of Brezhnev's visit, a "successful hunt" is mentioned. "That will especially interest the people," she said.

Then she insisted upon going to the Near Eastern Museum with me during the lunch break. "Five minutes!" she said when I declined. She had already been there once that day with "the other" grandmother. I must go with her to see something "really beautiful."

Because of the heavy traffic, we waited a long time to cross the street. "You simply have to jump in, the way you do in any large city," she said. "I don't for your sake," I said. "Oh—the worst that can happen is you get run over, and I've already been run over once." "Then you should have had enough of that." "Oh—after that I was able to write such beautiful things." "*Excursion of the Dead Young Girls.*"

On the way she kept asking people how to get to Kupfergraben, although I assured her that I knew the way, and switched back and forth between talking about her love for the Near Eastern Museum and her concern for the plenary session. "It is bad that they praise my book (referring to Paul Fröhlich[6]); they will destroy it. I had some other problematic stories, but they were not finished yet. They will be added to the second edition."

At the entrance to the museum she is not keen on having to pay again, since she had already been there once on the same day. Finally she is given free passes. "Now simply follow along

---

[5] Erich Honecker (1912-1994), German Communist politician who led the German Democratic Republic from 1971 until 1989. (Ed.)

[6] Paul Fröhlich (1913-1970), member of the politburo of the Central Committee of the Socialist Unity Party; beginning in 1952 First Secretary of the Leipzig district executive committee. (G.W.)

behind me and look at the things that I show you. You can look around longer another time." She raced through the first room ("The lions have marvelous fangs, don't they?") into the corridor that leads to the magnificent turquoise-colored Ishtar door. "Isn't that beautiful? They had their difficulties, too, you know. Back then it was a matter of whether or not you could portray God in human form. The Islamic people created these beautiful animal figures for that. And now come on. We're going to the Pergamum altar that the people of Berlin are so proud of, and then I'm going to show you just what decadence is, for here we are only one century before Christ, while the heyday of the Greeks was six hundred years earlier . . . Strangely enough, this morning there were nuns everywhere. I wouldn't know why they come here and look at all the naked asses. And now I'm going to show you the first statues of the gods, those youthful figures, you feel a little gay just at the sight of them." In the air she traced the back part of one of the truly very beautiful hermaphroditic statues of the gods with her hand—"That is the most beautiful thing about them . . . "—"You see, they had more trouble than we do, and something that beautiful came out of it. By comparison, all the gonorrhea in Bräunig's Wismut book is really unimportant . . . "

On the way back, she offered to make a bet with me. If it is "as bad as ever" in March, after the Party Congress of the Communist Party of the Soviet Union, she will buy Gerd and me lunch at the *Operncafé*, followed by a comprehensive tour of the Near Eastern Museum; if, on the other hand, things "improve," lunch is on us. I told her that I didn't expect that we would have to pay.

"The word *life* is only another expression for *conflict*," I have just read in the Chaplin book that lies open next to me. And in my presentation at the plenum I said that we cannot write if we find ourselves in a deep conflict . . . But in the sense that I meant it, I was perhaps right after all.

I was very afraid before I decided to speak at the plenum. Konrad Wolf and the Sterns[7] had implored me the night before, insisting that somebody absolutely had to say something. If nobody tried to speak against this attack on art, then it would grow very dark. For me it was primarily a matter of warding off the suspicion that the Writers' Union had become a Petöfi Club,[8] that is, a counterrevolutionary center, and voicing my opinion on the denunciation of Bräunig's book (the article from the Wismut people against him is in all the newspapers, even in the district press, while the number of copies of *Neue Deutsche Literatur* in which his Wismut novel chapters were pre-published is ridiculously low), and of suggesting something about the only conditions under which art can arise. In between, I made half-hearted efforts, confessions—I knew in advance what my problem was: to seek to prevent the worst from happening without knowing exactly whether or not the moderately bad was worse.

Perhaps there was also an unconscious wish to draw the fire to myself. I accomplished that.

As I spoke—after all, I had only a few key points; after I had asked to speak, they called on me ahead of many others, the third or fourth speaker—I was quite calm. The image of a steamroller moving toward me was before my eyes. Afterward I was pleased that I had spoken and snapped at Helmut Sakowski,[9] who, as we were leaving, said: We should all speak

---

[7] Sterns: Jeanne Stern (1908-2000) and Kurt Stern (1907-1989), writers of film scenarios and reportages; members of the communist youth movement, emigrated to France, participated in the struggle against Franco in Spain; were exiled in Mexico, emigrated in 1946 to Berlin/German Democratic Republic; friends of C. and G. Wolf. (G.W.)

[8] Petöfi Club: Club of Hungarian writers and intellectuals (Georg Lucàcs, Tibor Déry and others), which participated in preparing for the Hungarian revolt of 1956; after that was regarded in the language of the Socialist Unity Party as a "counterrevolutionary group." (G.W.)

[9] Helmut Sakowski (b. 1924), writer of novels and television plays, 1963-1973 candidate of the Central Committee of the Socialist Unity Party; beginning in 1973, a member. (G.W.)

as you did! I said: Well, do so. Throughout the day I maintained my composure and observed with interest how the others behaved toward me—every shade of behavior was represented, from furious rejection to abashed disregard and furtive approval—but, I did not feel well physically, went to the doctor, who measured my blood pressure—160, she said, too high for such a young woman! But of course she did not ask about the reason for the high blood pressure, which she well knew. Young? I thought. Thirty-six. Is that young? I felt old.

I then went to see the Strittmatters.[10] Erwin lay in bed and had everything behind him for once. "I have begun to realize myself," he said, "and I don't want to let myself be hindered in doing that." I, too, should have let up. Nothing could be done. Laxness created Iceland, Hamsun, if you will, Norway, Tolstoy and Pushkin Russia. Shouldn't there be some people here who could undertake to create this country? Nothing would stand objectively in the way of it. But naturally we are not even permitted to say that at all. Who would understand it?—Our garden, he added, has now been preserved forever—in my story "June Afternoon."

The motif of loneliness that always appears when we insist, even if only in our thoughts, on "that which really is."

The next morning, after sleeping only half the night in the Sterns' guest room, suddenly my strength was completely exhausted. I physically shook at the thought of having to go "there" again. I returned to the doctor at once, had to wait. She discovered that in spite of the medication my blood pressure had risen even more. It can't go on, she said, to my relief. We must stop. She certified that I was ill. I hardly took what she said seriously: that it cannot go on this way. That I must draw certain strong conclusions from my susceptibility. That

[10] The Strittmatters: Erwin Strittmatter, author of *Wundertäter II* (*The Miracle Worker II*) and his wife. (Ed.)

these attacks were damaging my blood vessels and in twenty years it would be all over for me. That simply not everyone can stand "that." Moreover, too much is required of our people. We should do something about that. Four weeks of vacation twice a year. Travel.

If my blood pressure were not so unstable, I would have had to endure the torture. I was almost grateful for the disorder. Through miserable slush I rode home with a friendly taxi driver. The man was balsam to my soul. I had the feeling of leaving much more than a convention behind me.

And that is probably how it was.

The pressure on the root of my nose and my ears remained during the next few days. Sleeping pills seem like a benevolent, gentle salvation to me. I was only able to skim the newspaper, in which my speech had been printed. Naturally, they had omitted the sentences regarding my protest against the dressing down of the Writers' Union as a Petöfi Club; had also, however, stricken that attack in Fröhlich's speech. The reason for my appearance and the thing that was most important to me about it had thus never existed. They adulterate reality, I said. Gerd said: What do you expect?! I threw away the newspaper like something that had been poisoned and have not touched it since then.

Konni Wolf told me in a long telephone conversation that he was especially furious with the people who had gotten us into this mess (Biermann, Havemann[11]), and who offered "them" the means to take care of the others; to proclaim the program: protests are not welcomed. He would now most like to create

[11] Wolf Biermann (b. 1936 in Hamburg) is a German songwriter, poet and former East German dissident. In 1976 the Politburo decided to strip Biermann of his citizenship while he was on tour in West Germany. Biermann's exile provoked protests by leading East German intellectuals, including C.W. Robert Havemann (1910-1982) was a chemist, communist and an East German dissident. He was put under house arrest in 1976, which continued until his death in 1982. In 1989 he was rehabilitated by the Communist Party. (Ed.)

a "nice film about the present." "The worst thing we could do would be to do nothing."

He still does not see this total limitation to any honest experiment the way I see it. Anna Seghers says one must try to say certain things differently so that "the most important thing" in a book is preserved. Instead of: "They slept with each other," "They lay down together in bed," etc.—If it were a matter of that! Even she does not see what intrudes upon my mind.

Nonetheless, we must see to it that "what exists here" survives. It does begin to resemble the "over there" in certain ways, but it really is so much better in many things—beginning with its foundation—and the only protection against it. To leave—no, I have not yet reached that point, even in my thoughts.

But what can I still do honestly? The book about '45? Hardly. The film with the women's episodes? Out of the question! Television will express its thanks for our planned studies from reality. Perhaps narratives: *The Quest for Christa T.* A children's book: *Being Good for a Whole Day*?

But a curtain has fallen behind me. A way back into the country lying before that curtain, a harmless country, no longer exists.

Jessenin poems.[12] The man in black. From that entire period nothing remains of all those super-revolutionary poets except for the three who committed suicide: Blok, Jessenin, Mayakovsky.

Did I suspect that this time it was a matter of being pushed into reality? From the beginning this painful, tense feeling. The poison that I almost consciously ingested. Now I can no longer tolerate a drop of it. Every pose has fallen away from me. To think that there are always new realities behind this one.

---

[12] Sergei Aleksandrovich Yesenin (also Esenin, Jessenin) (1895-1925), Russian lyric poet. (Ed.)

By the way: Anna Seghers can stand extremely astonished in front of the State Council building, scrutinize it, and ask: For God's sake, what is this thing here?

The walls around us move closer together. But in the depths, it appears, there is too much room.

TUESDAY, SEPTEMBER 27, 1966
Kleinmachnow, Förster-Funke-Allee

Ten minutes to nine, work begins. Woke up shortly before six. During the half hour I remained in bed, thought about today's impending appointment with M., what I will say, what I won't, how much of it is true, how much half true, what he himself will understand, what I may learn about it. In the meantime, it occurs to me that it is that "one day a year," but fortunately I forget it again and again and it does not damage my candidness. Gerd asks how I slept. Quite well, I say, and that is at least something. Does he still love me, I ask him, or has some nightmare crept into his heart overnight that works against me. I kiss the old place on his cheek. Even that, both of us know it, has already become a bit routine, and I ask myself to what extent the difficulties of this year are not simply my very personal difficulties, of a talent that is too small, of an ambition that is too great, of a life that is too sickly, too half-hearted, from which simply nothing more can be elicited. "People live peculiarly," Gerd suddenly says. "What do you mean by 'peculiarly': close together?" "Not only that. Just peculiarly. That would be the only thing that literature should attempt: to describe the peculiar life of people as peculiar . . ." Warm shower, cold shower, some hummed melody. The mirror. At noon today I will put on makeup, a mask, because I do not have a different one, but perhaps that is also a self-deception. I examine myself, but the double life that I have occasionally lived in recent weeks—that I reacted mechanically to the external events, to words, news reports, but that inside of me a totally different, deeply despondent life unrolled, always ran in a circle, and apparently could not be stopped—that is probably past. I am perhaps still preoccupied, but no longer obsessed. I should not view it as that important, I think. Just who says that I of all people make this immoderate demand of myself and also have to fulfill it? Be more modest. Do more modest things well . . .

Annette criticizes my hairdo; I should not brush all the hair toward the back. Tinka stands on a chair without any pants and taps her forehead at her. "Look," she says, "my new dog and my teddy bear have already made friends." They lie tightly embracing each other on her pillow. Annette is amused that I simply say "hm" in response to Tinka's surrealistic comments. "Today my hair is all turning outward," she says in despair. I garnish the children's breakfast with red peppers (Tinka: "A nice breakfast!") and prepare the sandwiches for school. While they eat, Gerd gets up and I fix our breakfast. While I was in the bathroom, two articles fell into my hands. A former Catholic clergyman, Harold Mitchell Koch, justifies his decision to leave the USA and to ask for asylum in the USSR: "I took this step because I do not agree at all with the politics of the Johnson government, as a protest against the unjust war that the USA is conducting against the people of Vietnam." In the USSR he could openly voice his opinion about it. "I finally grasped the fact that the Soviet Union comes closer to the ideal than any other state. Their leaders are upright men who strive to have their people become rich, but not themselves. They fight for justice and equality and have clearly outlined plans of how that can be attained . . . After that I took a look at America and saw that the Saigon of today, with its corruption, its black market, and other dubious transactions is a miniature version of today's America: getting ahead at any price, using all permissible and impermissible means; man is man's enemy and not his equally entitled brother." Writes about resurfacing McCarthyism in America: "Fascistic reprisals and loss of freedom."

The other article, nothing significant, an interview with Korneichuk[1] under the title: "Applause Is the Author's Reward." Calls the human soul the "cosmos" of literature, calls for a revision of the aesthetic definitions in the realm of form: "I am angry when I hear the talk about how at the time of the cult of personality our literature was intimidated and remained silent or did not reflect the truth. Talentless works distort life in any era, but talent always tells the truth." As an example he then names his play "The Front." "The truth" has become an abstract, almost meaningless concept. At this moment I consider whether or not we should bring that American who left the USA here to interview him in the context of a scenic report before the television camera . . . For a long time I have been searching intensively for such a documentary opportunity, in which I can become completely engaged, without reservation, in order to gain a bit of distance to the other "real" matters, and also to have the feeling that I am doing something useful.

At breakfast we talk about the Negro riots in San Francisco, which they were talking about yesterday on Western television, and which broke out because a policeman shot a young Negro boy, who had probably stolen a car, "while trying to escape." "There is also a border there," I say. "Shooting goes on every day there, without a wall." We remember yesterday's Western television film *Justification for a Judgment*, which focused on one of our young border soldiers who had shot a border crosser and then run across the border himself, and who was put on trial over there. A film that attempted to be both a warning and a revelation, that was naturally supposed to have an under-

---

[1] Alexander Korneichuk (1905-1972), Ukrainian Soviet dramatist and state functionary. (G.W.)

mining impact, and did. "By the way," I say, "I would only shoot if I knew with certainty that I had a criminal before me." That has been very clear to me since a deer was shot down before my eyes recently. That cynicism of the hunter and the last leap of the deer into the air unexpectedly wounded me very deeply—That is perhaps the problem in general: that the longing for gentleness, to finally see humaneness and goodness in the people, has become so overpowering, and that we still and again and again have to be hard, that we change ourselves in the process, that our goals change with the methods that we must use to achieve them or to survive at all. It is bitter that we are supposed to leave precisely this to the coming generations.

The newspapers. Federal Minister of the Interior Lücke made a pitiful attempt yesterday to wash Lübke's past clean.[2] It was beneath the dignity of a head of state to concern himself with that kind of charges. Not a word about the facts—Additionally, official reports about Ulbricht's trip through Yugoslavia. Nothing about culture in *Neues Deutschland*, I am happy about that. In the *Berliner Zeitung* it says that books by me were supposedly sold at the Frankfurt Book Fair. One of the usual general articles by a scholar of German literature about the successes of our literature, but also once more mentioning a few of the figures under attack: the Kirschs,[3] Mickel, Braun. Geisler expressed himself very positively on the German Democratic Republic over there and attacked the anticommunism of his society. "He will soon be better than we are," I say. "Perhaps we really are behind?" "Sometimes I would like to know what is going on in your head," says Gerd.

I clean up, wash off, Mrs. Sch. is ill. Then I write these three

[2] Heinrich Lübke (1892 –1972), President of West Germany from 1959 to 1969. (Ed.)

[3] Sarah Kirsch (b. 1935), poet, and her husband; at the time friends with the Wolfs and in active correspondence with them; G.W. published early poems in the anthology *Sonnenpferde und Astronauten* (*Sun Horses and Astronauts*), Halle/S., 1964; S. Kirsch emigrated to West Berlin in 1977, settled later in Schleswig-Holstein. (G.W.)

pages, hastily, inexpressively, dutifully. Now it is a quarter to ten, and I begin the real work. I am on page 109 of my story. I see the end, but every day starting again is difficult.

Addendum: Earlier I had to fill out eleven of those donation certificates for the project "A Thousand Bicycles for Vietnam."

In two hours, one page, sluggishly, without concentration. Every word temporary, approximate formulations. I read in Bachmann: "I heard that in the world there is more time than understanding, but that we are given eyes to see"—and I am discouraged.

October 1st

Because this day does require completeness: potatoes were peeled, boiled, and mashed, with them fried eggs and cauliflower. I dressed meticulously, got ready, spent more time than usual on my hairdo, makeup, even my eyes a little bit, the gray checked suit—I wanted to look chic, in order to get into the right mood, almost accomplished it. Drove the car to Schönefeld. It was a slightly hazy but beautiful fall day. I like driving that stretch of road. You do not have to be cautious; you can think while sitting at the steering wheel. I drove rather fast, then parked the car with the others in the small parking lot in Schönefeld and boarded the commuter train, which was still quite empty. At the later stations other people got on, many workers; I remember one of them, he wore a white protective helmet, a bear of a man, very self-confident, but not rough in dealing with his colleagues. It occurred to me that the "better people" really ride in cars and not on the commuter train. I had my sunglasses on, felt protected, and could observe. The feeling of not belonging, of walking among stage props, was no longer as strong on that day as it had sometimes been in the past. I again shopped with more determination—in the clothing store on Alexanderplatz, two white blouses, one of them for Irina, a poodle for her daughter, a pair of stockings for me—and began again to take some things with humor. It was clear to me that this was the product of anticipating the appointment with Prof. M., and that there was naturally also something like danger in it—but *danger* is already too strong a word. I rode the commuter train to Friedrichstrasse and waited a quarter of an hour for the number 9 bus, because one had just left in front of me. The people who walked by. A few narcissistic, astonishingly dandified young men caught my eye, *jeunesse dorée*; I do not believe that they were foreigners. A young woman, early twenties, got off a bus, came toward me. She was wearing a black, bat-winged coat, black modern shoes with wide heels, asked directions to Hannoversche Strasse. Even her eyes were beautifully lined in black, but she had brown hair, straight, nicely coiffed. She spoke with a North German accent, from Hamburg or Bremen, then even had a sketch from the travel agency on which Hannoversche Strasse could be found. I followed her with my eyes as she walked away. She was one of those young women into which I would like to transform myself. With regret I then try to look haughty.

By the way, Berlin seemed a bit shabby yesterday, especially in the area around Friedrichstrasse. Paint is falling from the façades, some luster was missing. I was probably seeing it with the eyes of the lady in the black, bat-winged coat.

In front of the government hospital as always a crowd of cars; as is so often the case when I go on foot, I feel a bit displaced, but at the same time enjoy that feeling, am a bit startled when I think I see acquaintances, and am happy when I am mistaken.

I just have time to freshen up and to read in the *Eulenspiegel* lying there, something about the spectacular character that *Spiel mit* (Play Along) will have on television on October 7— and then I am already being called in. As always the polite tone of the nurse, who knows my name. The nurses are paid better here than in other hospitals.

M. still has to close the window and make a few remarks about the autumn that has finally arrived. I am somewhat nervous because I remember my wretched appearance last time. The obligatory question: How have you been doing?—Better. It varies, but better—You look better—It's all artificial—Really?—Yes, I think so—How do you sleep?—Not especially well, but it will get better—I could still give you a different medication—or do you have the feeling that you are calmer. Because this is the prerequisite for everything else. We already talked about that—you have to deal with the questions of substance yourself—I know. It is clear to me that this is not a matter for the physician . . .—I would not say that in such absolute terms. Things are connected. And according to our materialistic philosophy, emotional complications *have to* be connected to physical ones. Besides that, there is nobody in the Party who would certify you as being ill for six months. So you need the physician, and our method also seems to stand the test—For some time now I have felt better. Before, I was occasionally only free for a few hours in the evening. Besides that, it is all really part of my profession. I would be very happy if I could do something else now, for example, what you do . . .—Of course, some have it easier. Actors, for example. I recently talked with M.K. He is boiling inside, of course, but during the day he can let off steam in a new role and calm down, and you can't do that—To a certain degree, I can—But only in a purely reflective sense. Or in a more vital sphere of life—as you recently spoke of the fact that perhaps something would already have happened, if you did not have the children—But for weeks they were not there for me. I was there for them, but not they for me. I talked to them, reacted, but in reality something else was going on inside of me. So, even that is not a sure protection—Certainly not. And it is also not such a simple matter for others, who are not in your profession. It's like this: through the rapid and drastic ideological changes of recent years, the moral frame of reference has been lost for people who think. What older communists talk about when they say that the people died cheering for Stalin when it was he who had them killed—that really doesn't exist anymore. I am now reading *The Vicar of Wakefield*. It is delightful how steadfastly he can fall back on his Christian religion in all of life's situations. Our people have lost that. Nothing new offers itself yet. Now most people are not educated enough to mentally process that conflict. The neuroses augment—Lack of education? I really don't know . . .—But of course—

In my mind something else can be added. It is clear to me that one can only cope with the current situation literarily with great maturity and a strong talent. I do not have that. Up until now I have been oriented toward a different kind of literature. The awareness of the necessity of this adjustment causes additional difficulties for me. These are the recent problems—With respect to maturity, you are right. As far as talent is concerned—thinking about that is unproductive and it leads to narcissism. But it is already there in literature: Proust did it better than we could do it, or Thomas Mann . . . We like to climb to those heights sometimes, but they are fixed end points. You have to come down again. You can't go on from there; it is not a basis. You have to ask, in a completely new way, the questions about individuality for the new class that has come to power—I know. I must look for that, for what I can do—That does makes me happy. I see that you will make it—

I no longer know how we got around to the next segment of conversation. He suddenly said that neither the patients of the government hospital nor his colleagues, who only worked there, had any idea what things are really like in our health system. That in hospitals entire stations have to be shut down for lack of personnel. In his area people sometimes lie for three weeks with a brain tumor and cannot be operated on. Naturally, some also die because of it. But for that there was the splendid slogan: Every profession helps itself with its own strengths! But in agriculture they have not been able to get by using their own strengths for fifteen years. Every year the students dragged themselves around on potato fields for four weeks instead of at least going into the hospitals as ward attendants. Then the profession would help itself with its own strengths. But that slogan does not appear to apply to agriculture. But if you say anything, the faculty Party leaders respond: Comrades, there shall be no discussion. You have to understand that!—I: Last year I lay here in the hospital for a week. It became clear to me what it means never to come in contact with reality—Obviously. Those people only drive their cars. They no longer know what happens on the commuter train, much less what normal people may think. They think they are being ridiculed when they see a poster hanging in the vegetable store: Bottle things—Prepare for the winter! And in all of Berlin there is not a single canning jar for sale. At least the Stasi,[4] who are always wandering the streets, should report something like that . . .

We talk about the "fundamentals of Marxism," which in his opinion need no reexamination, only a cleansing, restoration, observance. But our leading functionaries lapse, of course—pardon the blasphemy—into biologistic thinking . . . Kruschev only demonstrated greatness in coming to an agreement with Kennedy: We will not make war. Cuba was the proof of that. The murder of Kennedy was thus a turning point . . .—They could no longer afford him as president—That's the way it is. All the forces of democracy that he wanted to mobilize, the

---

[4] The Ministerium für Staatssicherheit (MfS / Ministry for State Security), commonly known as the Stasi (from Staatssicherheit), was the main security (secret police) and intelligence organization of the German Democratic Republic. (Ed.)

Peace Corps, etc.—couldn't work anymore. After that it was only a question of time, of how long Kruschev could last. I made a bet with my wife that he would only remain until the next Party Congress. She said: You're crazy. But then even he had to step down a year earlier. His greatest mistake was the total overemphasis of material interest. That has now led to our economic theory, to the absence of ideas and ideals. There are no real intellectual problems anymore. The young people find no basis for argumentation. They are sliding down into foreign realms, the church, into our field to biologism. Recently in Vienna, at a convention of anthropologists, without any opposition from us, the main lecture was about the biological bases of culture. Well, now it cannot get any worse.

Fine, but what should we do with respect to literature in this situation? Write about utopias? Given that the relationship of the individual to the society really is the province of art after all—not its province exclusively, of course, but not everyone is inclined to read philosophy in its pure form. One could now say, of course: Just simply write, without regard to whether or not it "succeeds." Only: we do not write only for ourselves. Being isolated as we are, it is hard to write.

M.: And nevertheless you have to cope with these problems thoughtfully. He reminds me about the conversation between the devil and the Grand Inquisitor in Dostoyevsky, and how interesting it is that Dostoyevsky gets no further than the observation that every bureaucracy corrupts the once pure idea. Thus the politburo as a collective Grand Inquisitor that would kill Marx immediately if he returned to the earth, just as the Pope would have to kill Christ . . . So the prototype has already been written. Why then should I read it in Christa Wolf's writing—pardon me for becoming personal—if Dostoyevsky already has it? We must break that circle intellectually—So, the utopia after all?—What it means literarily, I don't know. It can be solved on a purely intellectual level—That is not of much use to me. I need *vehicles* for those thoughts. Just which *section* of our society should break this cycle into which we have apparently fallen? Just who?—I don't know that either. I don't belong to the inner circle either. But it is so terribly interesting to watch developments over there. Erhard, the pure economist, cannot hold his own in politics, Strauss is at the door. We, of course, constitute the antithetical equivalent to that development. The pure economists here cannot hold their own for longer than two or three years either . . . We have to think these things through rationally and have a little patience—What do you recommend as a remedy?—A puritanical ideology. Puritanical in content, not, of course, in the ideal of abstinence. A moral ideology that offers ideals. Thus, renewal of the fundamental principles.

I do not see where that is supposed to come from and that it would still be possible.

By the way, earlier in the conversation we talked about the behavior of the American soldiers in the Korean War and in the Vietnam War. Back then, in Korea, they were still dropping like flies. They convened entire conventions of psychologists to deal with that fact. In the meantime they must have done something with the people, what, I do not know. But in Vietnam they do not collapse.

Returns to his favorite topic: biologistic thinking, which presents itself historically as cyclical thinking, and Marx's brilliant idea of *development*—which, by the way, for a long time had its idealistic equivalent in the Catholic idea of sinful birth, the life of man in sin, and his final salvation. Then we come to the nothing-but-façade people who show no inner movement for decades, and to the question of how they do that. He is just as amazed as I am. He can only see them as monsters; he is not exactly familiar with the inner mechanism. The realm of things that have value for them is probably extremely limited, simple as that, and for them absolutely no dangers would arise from

others . . . In general, of course, a functionary, if he is to function, must not be familiar with any feelings of guilt, remorse,
etc. We surgically remove that from him, of course. At first I
misunderstand him to mean that the psychologists participate
in those operations, but he says: No, just read our newspapers.
There may be mistakes, but no individual guilt—That, of
course, is the very question upon which literature was halfway
unconsciously focusing, and why it was stopped with such brutal force. And we really do have to think about that. But I
believe that something is being bottled up there, which, if it
does not find a release, will once more break forth in a totally
unexpected place . . .—Exactly. So the writers will then continue to paste flesh and muscles properly around those wire
façade figures, so that they will still stand erect for a little while
longer . . .

I accuse him of meanness. The tone has become more spir-
ited, sardonic, almost a skirmish. He has confidence in me
again, gives me something to swallow, is no longer gentle with
me, and expresses his satisfaction with my condition. I had
decided to contain myself, I say, and I almost want to apologize for the last visit. He: Please don't. No, objectively your
condition has improved—I say that in those last few weeks I
sometimes needed self-confirmation, which you simply take
wherever you can get it. Ask jokingly if, in his large selection
of pills, there isn't also a tablet for emotional hardening—Just
say apathy pill.—No, they do not have to go hand in hand—
But it does. The negative side of sensitivity just happens to be
the risk of depression. There is a pattern of illness in psychiatry where the patient can feel neither pain nor joy, but is simply apathetic, complains about it in moving words, but actually does not *feel* the loss anymore, but complains about it
only based on memory. That is worse than depression. Those
people usually hang themselves—Can they be helped?—Of
course. We give them medicine . . .—You do everything now

with pills—We can also do it in other ways, but it is simply faster with pills.

I elucidate my observation that there are people, an increasing number of people it seems to me, who resemble those sick people in the realm of normality: who keep their feelings and passions well tempered, never reach the verge of a real conflict, are able to swallow everything, if not process it, never know devotion or even moral steadfastness in love, nor see any reason for it . . .

Yes, he says, that is technology. It produces this human commodity, and we cultivate it—But to have to live among such people is a horrible vision of the future . . .—How so? You can still live among mentally ill people who still have all of that. Besides, since no hereditary biological mutations occur among these people, everything can be reclaimed in coming generations. If technology is not apathetically imitated, the way the pupil copies the teacher's A, but if we *play* with it . . .

M. promises me a copy of a preface that he is in the process of writing, with documentation that can be helpful to me. I promise to give him my next piece of work to read and to let him know how I am doing after the trip. After all, he has a medical interest in that . . .

When I leave, I have been with him for an hour and ten minutes and am, as always, very relieved. The relief lasts for the entire day. It is like coming to myself on a higher level; many things are clear that I only felt and could not formulate. In many things I am stimulated to contradict, am thus led away from resignation in any case, and toward activity, and that is what he wants to achieve: remain active, continuing the renewed effort to grapple with the problems . . .

He proceeds, of course, from a high view of literature, from the literature of the models; he proceeds from the idea that a model that has been thoroughly treated does not have to be repeated, and in the process basically leaves little hope and little room for the mediocre talent. For therapeutic reasons, of course, he must express himself more gently when such a person sits before him as a patient.

Addendum concerning the apathetic, "those who move along a well-tempered middle line": "I am actually happy when such a person begins to drink," says M. "Then I really see that everything is not lost."

I do not fool myself and know that my relationship with him is burdened with a certain affectation, a kind of transference, as Freud observed it, but even that was all right with me, even important. It broke through the fear of approaching inner desolation that I sometimes almost wanted to view as an unavoidable attribute of growing older.

I left Robert-Koch-Platz on the bus. At the Academy of Arts an event was just ending. I saw people come out and go to their cars, again with an almost maliciously joyful feeling of not belonging. Suddenly some acquaintances came slowly down the sidewalk. Reflexively I turned away in order not to be recognized. A Japanese proverb says: A man toward whom you harbor feelings of hostility is like a sack of stones on your back. How many stones . . . ? At the stops along the way to Alexanderplatz, only a small number of those waiting were able to get on the bus, it was the rush hour. Those who remained behind were angry, but by now resigned. At Alexanderplatz, in typical fashion I first waited for a few minutes at the wrong taxi stop, one that had probably been out of service for weeks because of construction, without anyone taking down the sign. A man took several snapshots of his girlfriend in a casual pose by the outdoor advertising pillar. When I finally found myself standing at the right stop, I had to wait quite a while, but the taxis moved in rapid sequence. In the end, Ursula Püschel[5] appeared, whom

---

[5] Ursula Püschel: Germanic literature scholar, theater producer, writer; did work on Bettina von Arnim. (G.W.)

I really hardly know, whom I have usually always greeted only superficially. She was suddenly friendly and open, and I had believed that a mutual prejudice existed between us. "Were you at that conference today?" she asked. "At which conference?" I had completely forgotten the invitation, but then remembered that some sort of discussion on realism involving writers and German literary scholars was supposed to take place. "I couldn't have gone anyway. I'm on the sick list." "You probably didn't miss much anyway. I'd like to know just what is going to happen at the annual conference . . ." "Oh well, all they do is demand declarations of loyalty from everybody. There really are some things that could be discussed . . ." And in that vein back and forth for a few minutes. (The next day I heard that an executive committee amply supplied with prominent figures and a total of four writers had appeared at that aforementioned conference.)

Then my taxi came. I rode to the Central Committee's guest-house to pick up the Ehrlichs.[6] Addendum to M. (Today is already the third of October, so I am still preoccupied with that). Yesterday I once again read with growing excitement the passage from *The Brothers Karamazov* that M. had recommended, Ivan's poem about the Grand Inquisitor. After that, what Anna Seghers writes about it in her Dostoyevsky article. It became clear to me that this is the level on which literature has to move and that it remains unattainable for me. I got a headache, became irritated, and was upset about the fact that I have continually reacted too subjectively of late. I thought that in a large novel or a similar creation one should try to portray the difference between our generation and the older one, where both would have to have worthy representatives—the way that the Grand Inquisitor is also a worthy representative

---

[6] Ehrlichs: Wolfgang Ehrlich (b. 1909), member of the politburo of the Communist Party of Israel, and his wife. (G.W.)

of the Jesuits. Alyosha even calls into question whether this Jesuit who acts out of *love of mankind* exists at all, while Ivan says: And if there is only *one* such Jesuit, his solitary tragedy, his secret being that he is without God, is worth portraying—I now understand M. better. The tragedy of those who began as communists and during the course of their lives forgot or had to forget to believe in that idea, that is, in mankind, is probably also worth portraying (and not just a variation on the church theme, as he probably thought). How we gradually become addicted to thinking about expediency. Freedom as a gift that is too heavy for the human masses and is therefore carried by the few who silently make the sacrifice of being in power, deciding, acting, giving people faith, taking their torments of conscience upon themselves, giving them peace . . .

Anna Seghers sees in that only a product of Dostoyevsky's recantation, a recantation forced upon him following his death sentence, lifted at the very last moment, and his banishment, in order to be able to continue writing: for living and writing were one and the same for him. She sees no immediately relevant sharpness in that conflict—or she suspects it but emphatically repudiates it. In that she belongs completely to her generation, one that believes in progress and thinks that what they have fought and suffered for must take place exactly as they have foreseen it. But she has a strikingly sharp feel for the tragedy of Dostoyevsky, who *could* not have finished writing his novel at all without getting into a deep, unsolvable conflict with his own convictions of loyalty to the czar and his religious censors. How the compulsion to artistic truthfulness can drive great writers into that conflict . . . Tremendous material.

Here I dryly pass on in a single layer the abundance of thoughts that then disturbed me all day long. In any case, I begin to suspect how fundamental the difference between the generation of Anna Seghers and our generation is and must be: there the classical clarity, but also rigidity, here the agitated, unresolved unrest. Everything is in flux, we flow with it, seek to hold on here, then there, and the roots tear off again and again. First we blame ourselves, then others, notice that neither one is correct, and do arrive, if we are honest and moderately sensitive, near the verge of despair. I became aware that Anna would have to reject my *Quest for Christa T.* story flatly.

At the first suggestion of the possibility of such a novel, Gerd immediately got worked up. This morning in bed we meditated about it: no conventional form, process specific material from the time as well, not force everything in around a single protagonist, take the sixties, Berlin, the old new things and the new old things; that the people hardly understand what is actually happening to them, show the forces that actually drive it—but what kind of forces are they? The economic ones?—Yesterday evening, when I was again confused and despondent, he advised me just to do something else for a while, to go into a factory, not to write, to come to myself. I would very much like to do that. But how should I do that? He justifiably reproaches me with my narcissism, my one-sided thinking. Transition stage, but how difficult it is.

Back to the "day," on which I have now, at a quarter after five, finally arrived at the Ehrlichs' place. They are expecting me, get in, and ride along to Schönefeld. You wouldn't think they suit one another, he a somewhat softer, even now and then sugary type, she sterner, "more forceful," as Gerd says, hardworking. The taxi driver, who comes from the Treptow area and talks about his childhood: about catching fish in the Stralau, about the tunnel leading from Zenner under the Spree. A young man, a dyed-in-the-wool Berliner, lighthearted, natural. And on that evening I, too, am lighthearted and answer him in kind.

The last part of the trip in my own car. I explain the border situation. The conversation about Israel begins, which then does not cease all night. Either they really like to talk that much, or somebody has planted the idea in them that they should not embarrass me with uncomfortable questions under no circumstances—there is no talk about us. Sometimes I hear them talking as if through a fog. I become weary, and my thoughts revolve around the conversation with M. But what they say about Israel interests me. I do not know anything: from how many nations the two and a half million there have come together, how there is a stratification in social esteem among them, that all Jews definitely are not equal (the Yemenites as the "Jews among the Jews"), the Arab problem, the tiny Communist Party that has even split—the one wing has become nationalistic—the influences of foreign capital, etc. Everything viewed rather soberly and materialistically, while we, because we are not in opposition, actually still see our little country in a rather idealistically distorted manner, determined in part by wishful thinking, in part by disappointment.

When they have gone, the washing of the dishes. Annette comes home late from a youth forum on *The Laughing Man*,[7] eats everything that is left, goes to bed. She already has her own life. On television there is the last part of a boring and poorly made crime film, then a farewell to Ludwig Erhard after his America trip. In bed a few more pages of Druon: *Rendezvous in Hell*,[8] too superficial and disgusting. I fall asleep without sleeping pills.

[7] "*Der lachende Mann* (The Laughing Man)," television documentary by Walter Heinowski (b. 1927) and Gerhard Scheumann (1930-1989) about a legionnaire in the Vietnam War. (G.W.)

[8] Maurice Druon (b. 1918), French novelist and member of Académie Française. *Rendez-vous aux enfers* (*Rendezvous in Hell*) London, Rupert Hart-Davis, 1959. (Ed.)

WEDNESDAY, SEPTEMBER 27, 1967
Kleinmachnow, Förster-Funke-Allee

A t around midnight we were still out and about: visiting Claudius,[1] who—after my reading in the Potsdam clubhouse last night—took us home with the Schlotterbecks and Lilo Sch., to his beautiful, large work house, which he has decorated with Vietnamese souvenirs. We sat there for a few minutes more, after we had railed, as always when writers are together, at "the situation." The Claudius couple had made fun of Bernhard Seeger's[2] nouveau riche mannerisms, and I had passed on the anecdotes that were told to us on a recent afternoon by the Romanians: about the ship full of Romanian writers that is sailing across the Black Sea and on which a joker suddenly announces over the ship's radio the supposed state prizes (the paroxysm that then breaks out); about Dunayevsky,[3] who takes bitter revenge on a colleague who had his door barred during his absence, and for doing so puts him on a plane for Siberia, drunk and without any papers.

We rode home with Lilo Sch., who seems a bit stiff and as if she were constantly doing her duty. I was feeling better after

---

[1] Eduard Claudius (1911-1976), writer, occasional diplomat; author of the Spanish Civil War novel *Grüne Oliven und nackte Berge* (*Green Olives and Naked Mountains*) (1945); *Menschen an unserer Seite* (*People at Our Side*) (1951); the autobiography *Ruhelose Jahre* (*Restless Years*) (1968); a friend of C. and G. Wolf. (G.W.)

[2] Bernhard Seeger (1927-1999), writer, member of the Central Committee of the Socialist Unity Party beginning in 1967. (G.W.)

[3] Isaak Osipovich Dunayevsky, aka Dunaevsky or Dunaevski (1900-1955), Soviet composer and conductor who specialized in "light music" for operetta and film comedies, frequently working with the film director Grigory Aleksandrov. (Ed.)

having been afflicted all afternoon with some kind of stomach cramp—which I did not want Kunert[4] to notice. Instead of writing new scenes for him, I would much rather have continued to read in my schizophrenia books, although it is clear to me that I must not become too deeply engrossed in that. The time of my susceptibility is coming back, and with it the question of whether or not I am equal to "all that" in the long run. During a discussion like the one last night they do not notice any of that in me, and I myself feel that being together with people is the best protection.

This morning I had a very remarkable dream. I returned to a city that was supposed to be Landsberg, but with which I was not at all familiar. Unfortunately I now remember only fragments of the dream, whose atmosphere was strange: very clear and at the same time fantastic; I wondered how I came to be there and how everything proceeded so naturally. An important role was played by a girl in a turquoise-green dress, who appeared continuously in our room, and by water, which was supposed to be the Warta River. At the end I was in a large hall, with long, straight rows of chairs in front of me, all filled with people. I sat at a simple rectangular wooden table and was supposed to read (somehow the audience had something to do with a semi-military organization, but had a friendly attitude toward me). I had a little booklet in front of me, on good, thick paper, printed in a beautiful large font, in the Polish language. I was supposed to read from it. I had written it. I was a bit amazed, but the whole thing did not seem absurd to me. I knew that I would live in that city and among those people.

Gerd let me sleep this morning (I had awakened during the night, as I often do after readings. M. immediately stood like a shadowy figure before me. Everything that had been said yes-

---

[4] Joachim Kunert (b. 1929), director of the film *Die Toten bleiben jung* (*The Dead Remain Young*), based on the novel by Anna Seghers, for which C.W. wrote the scenario. (G.W.)

terday in the discussion was recapitulated again. I noticed that the doubt about my profession can always be pushed aside only for a few hours). He fixed breakfast for the children and for us, even oatmeal for me. During breakfast we talked once more about *The Quest for Christa T.*: that on the whole Konrad Wolf likes it very much, that he finds fault with some linguistic affectations. Whether I should now give it to *forum*, the way the editor wanted yesterday, or rather to *Sinn und Form*.

Then I wash up, even polish the shiny copper plates with Sidol, take care of the flowers—everything just so that I will not have to sit down at my desk immediately. After having given up on the *Unter den Linden* story for the time being— after four weeks in which I really tried to sink my teeth into it somehow—I will now, after our trip to Bulgaria in October, have to begin the '45 book. I want to try to tell it using an alienated first-person narrator, to an imaginary group of questioners who have a right to an explanation. Before that—in other words, now—I still have to do a chapter in *The Quest for Christa T.*, about which I am not yet quite sure: a "grabber," as Gerd calls it, toward the end. I have been putting that off now for several days, up until this moment, when every pretext disappears.

Leafed through the papers of Christa Tabbert[5] once more, looking for connecting links. Quotes like these: She "seeks to find out what the people unconsciously reveal to her." She "never wanted to let them take from her the right to live according to her own law." She knows "that her strength was her ability to be new again and again, to see in a new way." "What a great temptation to open up these diversiform human lives and their relationships."

"The encounter. The 'genial place' that has been prepared

[5] Christa Tabbert, married name Gebauer (1927-1963), friend of C.W., protagonist in C.W.'s *Nachdenken über Christa T.*, Halle/S., 1968. (G.W.)

for it inside of you, where you have collected everything, your own center, from where—after going through the learning stages that have made you into a 'normal product'—you also recognize your profession as a calling, an original one at the actual beginning, after all the coincidences of private life fall away and necessity is equal to inclination."

All that often as a "she," in the third person, denying her self. The thought comes to me to write about that very phenomenon in the chapter that is still open: the transfer of one's own problems to a third person—and thus even more clearly to create a fiction within the fiction, for the Christa T. figure is already in large measure a medium for transferal.

Sarah sends poems. An answer to the letter that I wrote her last week.

After all, she is in the same condition as you are, says Gerd—As I was a year ago, I say.

He reads her poems:

Puzzle

Two white women cooks
four red palms
pluck black birds
where, Beloved, are you?
uoy ees morf ym wodniw
(You see from my window)

Gerd says: Like your schizophrenic poems (from the Navratil[6] book that I got from M.). I say, I would really like to write a Hölderlin story, if I could grasp that subject matter—his poetry—but I can't do that—Take a different person,

---

[6] Leo Navratil, *Schizophrenie und Sprache—Zur Psychologie der Dichtung* (Schizophrenia and Language—on the Psychology of Literature), Munich, 1966. (G.W.)

where it is somewhat easier, he says—Gunderode, I say—He: Yes. Do that.

Our conversations always go that way.

Another poem by Sarah:

What a perfect, white-faced clown I am
In the beginning my nature was carefree and happy
but what I saw drew my mouth toward my feet.

First I believed the one thing then in the other
now I no longer cut my hair and listen to
how your nails and mine grow how the little chicks
lose their down they gain fat
it cries and cries

I say what I have seen strangely enough
the people misjudge it is a matter of serious things
how funny they say if I tell of a misfortune
when they should laugh they are frightened

Only sailors and chauffeurs notice what I say
those in the blue jackets can prove everything with examples
have the coordinates in their heads
what you drank before and after and then they remain quiet

She can express her condition completely, says G. Perhaps that condition is not large and general enough, but others should decide about that.

The children come from school, early. First Annette, wearing a black pullover that she currently loves most among all her clothes. She immediately leaves again, to buy edging for the black miniskirt that Mrs. P. is sewing for her and which dominated her thinking for a while, because it was supposed to be finished for the school party, which she was looking forward to immensely, before the school party was prohibited because the Party secretary of the factory did not want to tolerate the band, the "twens," in his rooms. Tinka comes home quite tired, stretches out by me on the corner sofa, and reports on the impending Young Pioneer election that she is supposed to direct and that is enough to make her "throw up." She repeats that several times. She will not let herself be elected to a function again. She pushed others forward. She talks about a swelling of her gums, initially asks cautiously and in general if such a thing is "dangerous," if a person has to go to the dentist in such a case. I feel the place on her gum and explain that it is simply a new tooth coming in. She is very relieved, had already thought it was "something bad." Just why do you imagine such things? I say. She: I just have a lively imagination—Annette comes back, whines about the fact that she is still not getting any wisdom teeth. General fooling around breaks out. Tinka imitates her new biology teacher, who lisps. She wrote her name on the board: Glaede, and Stefan said to her: Mrs. Gla-e-de—the Pioneers of the fifth grade . . . We laugh to the point that we almost choke on the rice.

We talk about Father's ambivalent relationship to foreign words (when he talks about the student who spoke "*en cörpore*"). He tells how he recently very much wanted to use the beautiful word *tectonics* for the description of a picture in Bobrowski, but unfortunately tectonics has something to do with the surface of the earth, so the ignoramuses would not have understood what he meant.

While I am washing up, in a flash of inspiration Annette is trying to transform a common proverb: When you want to think, get yourself comfortable . . . but she does not succeed. Father suggests: When you want to think, don't get behind the wheel; cars are not for deep thinkers.

Tinka has been chewing and speaking very carefully because her gums hurt. She confesses that Lutz reconnoitered our future street, on which our future house lies, and paced off for her the distance to the bus stop: more than a kilometer!

Before going to sleep, I read in Binswanger's *Schizophrenia* about poor Ellen West[7] who wore herself down in the conflict between excessive gluttony and the overpowering compulsion to be slender. In the quotes from her diaries I find that she was probably a gifted girl who was in search of the absolute, who found no footing in her environment, and that she didn't have to go insane.

On the telephone they tell me that something has gone wrong with the car for the trip to the Soviets tomorrow. Palaver back and forth.

When I sit down at my desk again, I think that this is how everyday happiness looks and nothing more can be expected anymore. That would not matter, if only I did not fear injuries.

I drive to Potsdam. A magnificent warm day. Autumn sunshine, deep blue sky. For some time driving has been a kind of relaxation and diversion, even if I have to force myself again and again to focus on the traffic. I have become accustomed to daydreaming while driving, because I usually sit next to the driver. In Potsdam, while going across Lange Brücke, I wind up in a horrible traffic jam. They are moving at a snail's pace, and I am wedged in between motorcyclists, tractors, and military vehicles. Finally I reach the reason for the delay. The traffic is being diverted into one lane around an accident. A grayhaired woman is lying on the street, unnaturally bent, the way we always see corpses in crime films. Next to her crouches a younger woman—her daughter, I assume—holding the stricken woman's wrist. She has her other hand in front of her eyes

---

[7] Ludwig Binswanger (1881-1966), considered the founder of existential psychology. "Ellen West"—a pseudonym—is considered one of the classical cases in psychiatry. She suffered from an eating disorder and depression and at the age of thirty-three committed suicide. See: L. Binswanger, "The Case of Ellen West (An Anthropological-Clinical Study)," Existence, May, R., Angel, E., and Ellenberger, H. F. (eds.). New York, Simon & Schuster, 1958. (Ed.)

and is weeping. As we drive on, we encounter the police ambulance with its blue light and emergency signal.

I am happy that I do not have to drive much further to reach the dressmaker's. The image, although I was able to see it for only a few seconds, has become fixed in my mind.

Fitting. Palaver about the assistant's illness. She is expecting a child as well and is fortunately beyond the sixth month, in which things had gone badly during an earlier pregnancy. Now she has tendovaginitis. So Miss B. is swamped with work. She remembers last year with horror, when she had to pay sick benefits for two employees for several months. But those are simply the risks in a women's business—She is happy that my figure has not changed, complains that she hardly gets around to sewing for herself—or only when she travels to a convention and does not want to appear again in the same suit.

I run my errands: buy a frock for Tinka in the children's store; turn in my list of orders for the coming year at the book store (the manager of the bookstore tells me how much she enjoyed "June Afternoon" in the *Neue Texte* series; at the fair they were officially informed that my new manuscript is not yet finished). I have the books wrapped and buy prizes for the birthday party at the toy store. Then there is still the matter of birthday candles and a small lamp. I pick that up at shortly before six and am completely loaded down when I return to the car. (The lamp sellers are both very unfriendly and inclined to advise against buying their lamps.) On Klement-Gottwald-Strasse I now encounter many young people, among them two with harsh yellow patterned shirts that all the people turn around to look at. The light falls from the gate into the street on the Platz der Nationen, evening sunshine. When I drive off, I already have to turn on the parking lights.

The lake near Werder is unreal in this light, a mirror over which an orange-colored light spreads, in it black fish trap poles, the outlines of boats, fishermen. One night we saw a gigantic, four-deck, brightly lighted steamer sailing here, until it became clear to us that a normal excursion steamer had doubled in size through its reflection in the water.

I leave the car on the street in order to avoid a repetition of the scene that took place once with the renters on the lower floors of my parents' apartment house in Werder, when we had parked in the driveway of the building late at night. For a few days my father has been out of bed intermittently, but very frail. As always after such illnesses old age seems to come in spurts. My visits are the only happy diversion for both of them. I receive fried liver and an egg. They ask about our affairs, about the possible move. My father has again found newspaper clippings about *Divided Heaven*. In reality, my parents are totally occupied with their own affairs. The bathroom is not going to be fixed up now after all, because they are out of money, and my mother had an hour-long argument on the stairway with the renter below, gave him "a piece of her mind," because he constantly complains that they are still walking around over his head at night. A distinct pensioner complex reveals itself again and again: "We retired people in the German Democratic Republic seem to have no rights at all anymore, we should simply hang ourselves," etc. With pride I am shown an envelope that Horst had printed for himself: "Dr. of Engineering." My father is inclined toward fretfulness, while my mother seems to thrive on such tasks as cooking according to a strict diet and keeping each of his impulses under control. In the neighboring apartment lies an uncontrollably fat woman who suffers from a "rose" (erysipelas), and she has to do the shopping for her. She is unsatisfied. She comes to the car with me. I do not like to drive in the dark. The oncoming lights irritate me. At the very end, when I am already in Kleinmachnow, I react violently and inappropriately to a car that is apparently crossing the road but in reality traveling along a parallel street.

Unloading of the purchases, setting up the birthday table (it is completed with jewelry selected from my own pieces, which Tinka always wants as accessories). On television there is an unspeakable series film from "over there" about an oh-so-human director's family. The director runs away from an official celebration to drive his truck and trailer to the branch establishments in person. Mrs. P. finally brings Annette's black skirt, which has become too short and is still longer on one side than the other. It is now no longer what she once wished for. Now she herself doubts that she can actually wear it, tries to sit in it, then returns again wearing a light-colored jacket over it. We say it is pretty and that she should go ahead and wear it. (Tinka is already asleep. She had deliberately left the window open in order to hear me coming and to be able to look at the prizes. But she has been consoled by thoughts of tomorrow. Apparently, she went around all afternoon saying to herself: It's my birthday tomorrow!) Annette does not understand Sarah's poems, probably also does not want to understand them. This makes Gerd furious, they squabble. Father cannot stand a different opinion, says Annette. I read her two or three poems aloud and then it's all right.

Gerd tells me that Sachs[8] called. He wants to come on Friday, set up a contract for *The Quest for Christa T.* after all. We discuss tactics. When Annette is in bed, we talk some more about Sarah and about me in the process. Gerd says that he really doesn't understand these fits that she has. The reason for them is too small. Well—if, for example, you live in isolation as an antifascist under fascism—then you could despair. But here?—But it is a matter, I object, of despairing of yourself— Then you would really have to be very ambitious, he says, have made up your mind to do a great deal, to despair in that fashion. For him it is more a matter of doing his thing. He already

[8] Heinz Sachs, chief publisher's reader for the Mitteldeutscher Publishing Company. (G.W.)

knows that no world literature will come out of it. Where would world literature be created at all these days, and who would decide it? But that doesn't mean that everything else is nonsense. And it is only because a person is known, is to some degree a topic of conversation, that an over-dramatization of that person's conflicts occurs within him or her. Just as Kant would not have left his wife if he had not had *The Auditorium* in reserve.[9] And for women this inadequacy complex is apparently especially difficult to overcome. With talent, sensitivity also increases. That's the way it is. He admits that he doesn't even dare try to tackle the "abnormality" that fascinates me so much right now, out of fear of sinking into it.

Now you're angry, he says. No, I say. I am annoyed with the fact that I started it. I don't want to talk about it anymore— You always think that nobody else can understand it, he says, and you flee into isolation.

I do not respond to that. There is some truth to it. But I have now been understood in that stratum of my being that I myself hardly knew before. The preoccupation with psychiatric literature is really a thirst for knowledge, of course. I really want to find out just what this accursed soul actually is, just how the brain functions, etc. Besides that, I do not hide from myself the fact that through this material I remain in a certain sublime contact with M. And third, my experiences of recent years, which were far-reaching, give rise to the wish to clarify those experiences for myself, to integrate them.

I rapidly fall asleep.

[9] Hermann Kant (b. 1926), German writer resident in East Germany until German reunification. *The Auditorium* (*Die Aula*) (1965) was his first novel. (Ed.)

OCTOBER 30, 1968
Kleinmachnow, Fontanestrasse[1]

H ave been home for five days. Before that, five weeks in Mahlow,[2] at the hospital in the forest. A repeated experience: in the hospital you are unable to keep a diary, though you ought to have abundant time for it. But even your inner life is put into overdrive. This time I even forgot the "one day a year." Want to write something about the entire time instead of that, five weeks with their hodgepodge of people. Seems as if this kind of writing things down is the only thing I can do. I shall write nothing about the death of my mother, which occurred during that time. There is a barrier there that I do not want to break through.

Am alone today. It is Wednesday. Went back to bed when the children had gone. Read Colette and slept until a quarter to eleven. The dangerous feeling of paralysis announces itself again, but shall not arise. Some see the Third World War coming. We suggest successes and declare that anyone who does not think as we do is wrong and hostile. I can't read it anymore. It is an effort to pull the newspaper out every day.

Annette says: Even when your whole face is happy and you don't hide your feelings, your eyes are sad . . .

I know that she is right.

I will probably have to write "the book." Am simply not yet

[1] In January of 1968 the Wolfs moved from Förster-Funke-Allee to Fontanestrasse in Kleinmachnow. (G.W.)

[2] Mahlow: Town in the suburbs of Berlin with a hospital, specializing in the healing methods of Prof. Vogel ("Water Vogel"), a therapy of holistic medicine with application of special diet and water treatment. (G.W.)

clear about the prototype, there are several possibilities among my colleagues, depending on whether the type who develops himself toward autonomy or the characterless adapter is the focus. Probably a mixture of both.

Klaus Höpke[3] wrote as a beginning to his article—on which literature helps life and which does not—beautiful sentence: "Having success is a duty"—That is perhaps how I should begin the book. Take an inventory, like Musil. In a similar tone, but of course not so stuck-up, essayistic.

Upon my mother's death, Anna Seghers wrote me: I should not forget how many people like me and "warmly surround" me. But when I asked her not to read my galleys of *The Quest for Christa T.,* which I had sent her, of all times, one day after the Höpke attack in the State Council, because I did not want her to become involved in the matter (which will surely become very complicated)—she then wrote a bit peeved that I really would have to permit her to read it now. And she could never ever understand why something that they said about my writings struck me to the core. After all, it was intended only for the mind.

But does it strike me "to the core"? Does the old insecurity arise again and again? Until now I thought: No. Today I think: Perhaps it does.

Now, while writing, I begin to feel better. Just the process of writing already helps. So it will probably remain the only thing for me after all. But "life"—that is: political, national life— runs along the old tracks. Sometimes it seems to me that it races toward a bad end. And we stand next to it and give woe-begone commentaries. But once you have jumped the tracks with such force, you do not get back on them again . . .

[3] Klaus Höpke (b. 1933), 1964-1973 editor for art and literature of the newspaper *Neues Deutschland*; 1973-1989 Deputy Minister of Culture and director of the Central Administration for Publishing and the Book Trade of the German Democratic Republic, which had to authorize the publication of all books. (G.W.)

Longing for Gerd. Nothing more could touch us, not even a passion that happened to me. And should happen, but won't.

Today it is very mild, like September. Only the leaves blow forcefully from the trees and rustle dryly in front of the door.

Is it worth it to remain firm?

What did I actually read in the hospital?

Döblin: *Vertreibung der Gespenster* (*Driving Away the Ghosts*)

Fontane: *Der Stechlin* (*Stechlin*)

Schach von Wuthenow (*Man of Honor*)

Balladen (*Ballads*)

Briefe (*Letters*)

Vor dem Sturm (*Before the Storm*)

Carl Zuckmayer: *Als wär's ein Stück von mir* (*A Part of Myself*)

Regis Debrais: *Revolution in der Revolution* (Revolution in the Revolution)

Musil: *Mann ohne Eigenschaften* (*The Man without Qualities*) (little)

Max Frisch: *Bin oder die Reise nach Peking* (*Bin or the Journey to Peking*)

We are contemplating an *Eulenspiegel* film.

I am now reading the Stubbe[4] material.

Five weeks in which I have written nothing. In retrospect, they represent a closed complex that I can remember.

A Friday noon, when I arrive. The forest house, my narrow room at the very top, number 95. I rearrange it, move the

---

[4] Hans Stubbe (1902-1989), professor, geneticist; 1945-1967 director of the Institute for Domestic Plant Research in Gatersleben (Saxony-Anhalt), which organized numerous meetings of scientist with artists (see also C.W., "*Ein Besuch* (A Visit)," *Werke*, Vol. IV, pp. 283ff.); H. Stubbe wrote the afterword for C.W., *The Reader and the Writer*, Berlin, 1971. (G.W.)

round table to the window, reflect, there I will sometimes sit and write, also brought the genetics materials along. Nothing came of it.

Dr. L., who seems somewhat bent and shabby, without my being able to say why. He is very polite, even extremely friendly, perhaps the first shy doctor that I have met. Distinguishes himself in the volleyball games through enthusiasm and good serves. Takes turns with Dr. B., a woman who is likewise friendly, but reticent, somewhat harsh. Both have probably been in practice for only two years.

On Sunday my first conversation with Dr. K., the head physician, who summons me to his room although it is already nine o'clock in the evening, and when I leave it is almost eleven. A thorough and extensive anamnesis; never experienced anything like it before. Symptoms traced back to the basic functions: heat balance, circulation, blood pressure, food, bowel movement, breathing, etc. Sleep, of course, and that is my biggest problem. Blood pressure, the second number of which has not gone under 100 for years, is also objected to. Nevertheless, I go from 145:100 at the beginning to 140:90 at the end. The intensive Kneipp cure produces its successes. In the sauna it sinks even more.

I have no desire to become acquainted with anyone, to talk much. I want to go for a walk, discover the familiar paths again. I notice that in five years I have forgotten everything. On the second morning somebody addresses me by name, using the familiar *du* form. It is the wife of Bobby Reimer, who has already been there for almost five weeks and has lost twenty pounds. Her skirts and pants flap around her, but she distinguishes herself at the wall bars, doing knee bends, which are so difficult for me. She was in the Fichte Youth and tells everybody that she is sixty, but is only fifty-six. She runs like a corporal and talks unceasingly with an unbelievable Berlin brogue. She knows where there are overgrown patches of ground on which pears and apples are lying around, where nuts can be found, and where they sell fruit cheap. She carries away as much of it as she can; she is accustomed to doing that from way back, to not letting anything go to waste. Sometimes she is obstinate: for example, if someone disturbs her when she is sleeping. In the beginning she ran weeping through the forest because she did not sleep at night at all and they did not give her anything for it. Enthusiastically she tells about her stay in Yugoslavia last year. She went alone and enjoyed everything, especially swimming in the lukewarm water. She brings bedridden people flowers from her walks. Later I hear that some thought she was a spy. I find that very unjust. Naturally she believes every word that is in the newspaper.

Mrs. N. comes a few days after me, because of continuing headaches. They have her fast for a few days, so that her bowel movements become normal. Then she is put on the famous "K3 mild" diet, which I, too, follow for three weeks: large amounts of raw vegetables and fruit, in addition, rye crisp and butter mornings and evenings, at noon potatoes boiled in their skins and butter. Mrs. N. is the wife of a veterinarian who teaches at the university, her "little man," Siegfried, who is her everything. She can talk about him for hours: that he is "overweight" and should also go to Mahlow or eat less, that he should not drink so much with Dimitroff, a Bulgarian friend, while she is away, that he once allowed himself to have an affair, years ago with a girl, which absorbed him completely, so that he got behind in his habilitation, with which she, his wife, now helps him: "Just what should I do, Mrs. Wolf?! So, you know, back then I almost cracked up because of that affair—that's how it is, when, as a woman, you concentrate so completely on your husband and have no other work. So if we had separated—I would not have known what I should do!" Now she has been working in a Berlin outpatient clinic for five years. There she is something like a senior clerk and feels deeply rooted in her enterprise. She tells about the different doctors, especially a professor, a gynecologist, whom she mothered a bit (he is a bachelor) and who repaid her by taking "everything" out of her. Following early ovarian infections she had no children. Now she tells about the consequences of the operation: hot flashes at the most inappropriate moments, hormone injections, which in turn made her voice deep, etc. "So, if it is not an absolute necessity, I would not advise anyone to do it!" At the same time she offers me the address of her professor, in case it did "have to be" at some point—In just as much detail she tells how the hairdresser improperly colored her hair and that her husband ridiculed her instead of pitying her; or how she had a breast operation years ago in which they never determined whether it was cancer or not. (She had a copy made of the results of her last operation and always carries it with her.) Or how during his last visit her husband explained his tardiness to her by saying that he could see from their window that his tire had a "flat" and that he would first have to change the tire. "But you know, Mrs. Wolf, it then occurred to me during the night that we live on the eighth floor. So it is impossible for him to see from up there whether or not the tire is flat! He probably got drunk with Dimitroff. I then wrote that to him the very next day. After that he called me on the telephone: So, my little Euschi, it has been a long time since I laughed the way I did about your letter . . . Oh well, he claims to have seen it when he came down. I can believe it or not . . . "

She is quite funny and easy to like, and she is not without self-irony, just not without the naïve conviction that she is something "better." Nevertheless, she is very devoted to her work, has headaches because she becomes angry when her husband suggests to her boss that she perhaps will not return, remembers everything that she did not finish before she came here, is, of course, somewhat proud of the fact that her substitute cannot quite deal with it, shows her amazement when she determines who I am on our first walk. "I would have envisioned you to be quite different!" And she cautiously complains about her room-mates. The first one, Mrs. H., comes from "meager circumstances" in the country. She herself is small and like a little mouse, does not talk much, but hears everything and knows all of the conditions in the hospital and all the gossip. Every day she discovers new pains in herself, Mrs. N. thinks, because she does not want to leave. "And I can understand that. She has never had a vacation in her entire life. But on the other hand, her husband is really doing just as badly. He can hardly move because of rheumatism, and as long as she is here, he, of course, cannot leave the cattle and go to the hospital . . ." Then comes Mrs. B., who has to fast. Of course she is quite broad, especially down below. Now she, on the other hand, has a peculiar body odor that spoils Mrs. N.'s appetite. Mrs. N. also grew up in the country; her father must have had a farm in the vicinity of Magdeburg. She proudly says that she rode a horse and her husband first met her as a young girl in riding boots and a riding habit. She immediately made an indelible impression on him.

The three of us take our walks during the first two or three weeks. Anna Reimer leads us to the lake Märchensee, which is somewhat larger than I remember it. The only mushroom season of this year begins, but it is luxuriant. Sometimes we even find edible boletus mushrooms in passing. Mrs. N. has a good eye for mushrooms. The weather continues to hold. There is little sunshine, sometimes we take our umbrellas along, but we do not let ourselves be deterred from walking three or four hours every day. Supper is at five o'clock already, and after that I walk with Wolfgang Heise[5] for another hour: our philosophical-political evening walks.

[5] Wolfgang Heise (1925-1987), philosopher (*Aufbruch in die Illusion* [*Departure into Illusion*], Berlin 1964); beginning in 1972 professor of the history of aesthetics at Humboldt University in Berlin; interlocutor and advisor for authors (Volker Braun, Heiner Müller, and others); friends with C. and G. Wolf, wrote the afterword for her narrative for the film *Till Eulenspiegel*, Berlin/Weimar, 1972. (G.W.)

The newspapers search for justifications for the invasion of Czechoslovakia primarily from the comments in the Western press (according to which, the Dubček people where planning a "change of system"), we comment on it in the evenings and exchange information, and especially seek for the "productive point of departure" from which we can still work. We have in common our endeavor not to let ourselves be pushed completely aside—H. knows some who now sit and pout in the corner with their clear consciences. He fears that like the plague, but did not sign the faculty resolution that welcomed the invasion, anticipates unpleasant discussions, seeks contact with the theater (Besson), talks with me about a possible idea for an *Eulenspiegel* film. While thus engaged, we trudge through the almost totally unlighted Mahlow. Some evenings, when we are still standing in front of the door to the forest house, Dr. K. comes out. He provides us with new information that is often wrong: Biermann has been arrested. On one occasion he runs off to get me the issue of *Neues Deutschland* in which Anneliese Grosse[6] argues polemically against Eda Goldstücker.[7] From Heise: the Prague issue of *Konkret* with commentaries by Peter Weiss, Heinrich Böll, Erich Fried.

One afternoon H. and I walk as far as Blankenfelde, then another time to Dahlewitz, where we drink coffee and eat a frankfurter with Mr. D. in the Waldeck Café and then ride the steam train to Blankenfelde, and from there take the "Blue Buck" back to Mahlow.

[6] Anneliese Grosse: Germanic studies scholar, literary critic. (G.W.)

[7] Eduard Goldstücker (1913-2000), born in Slovakia, of Jewish origin, in the communist movement from his youth on; emigrated to Great Britain in 1939, before the German invasion; after his return home in 1945 in the diplomatic service of the CSSR. In 1953, in connection with the Slansky trials, condemned to life imprisonment, released in 1956; Professor of Germanic Studies at Karl University in Prague, in 1968, during the "Prague Spring," president of the Czechoslovakian Writers' Union; after the invasion of the Warsaw Pact troops emigrated again to England; in the nineties returned to Prague. An acquaintance of many years standing, friends with G. and C.W. since the late fifties (see also: E. Goldstücker, *Prozesse—Erfahrungen eines Mitteleuropäers* (*Trials—Experiences of a Central European*), Munich and Hamburg, 1989. (G.W.)

I inherit Michael D., the student, from Heise, who has known him for a long time. He is twenty years old. One evening, when I enter his room to take him something, he is alone and begins to tell me a story. A few weeks earlier he had attempted to commit suicide. "It was because of a girl, the daughter of acquaintances. We have been close friends for a long time, but she never let me get too close. She showed me her poems, and I showed her mine. Hers are better, I find. I could talk with her about everything, only I did not know if she wanted to go further. And at that time, on that evening, I wanted to kiss her and was stupid enough to ask her first. Then she simply went 'Phff' and turned away. I left then, and I really felt like I could have spit on myself in the mirror. You must not think that I did it because of her; it was because of me. I could no longer stand myself. It was a Saturday. I told my parents that they should let me sleep late the next day. I thought, of course, then I would lie there very quiet, as if I were sleeping, and they would not notice for a long time. Fortunately—or unfortunately, depending on how you look at it—the sleeping pills lay on my father's nightstand. Dr. K., of course, wanted to know exactly what you think before doing it, whether or not, after taking the pills, you want to undo it, and so forth. But once you have gone that far . . . Naturally you think about it once more before you swallow the stuff. But once you have taken it, you would be ashamed to run quickly to your parents and to say: I did this and this, so pump out my stomach . . . Nor would you do it if you knew what comes then. Somehow the body seems to resist. In any case, in the morning I was not lying in bed but under the table. Thus they quickly noticed what was wrong and took me to Oskar Ziethen Hospital. Then I am supposed to have struck out around me, attacked the doctors, yelled, and cursed them. Anyway, they brought me back. Then I was taken to Wuhlgarten, to the security ward. Everybody who makes such an attempt has to go there. Then you lie

there with many others, even truly insane people, also with
notorious drunks who are brought in at night and create an
uproar and get everything dirty. The food is also bad. K. visited me and got me out of there. He said that I should tell you
my story sometime; perhaps it interests you . . ."

Obviously the girl only gave him the last push. He showed
me poems by her: pleasant, clear, a real gift not yet discernable.
Besides that a prose piece and a poem by him. The prose, a
simulated monologue, exposes his state of mind during his
school days: he expects the death blow at any moment. He
must have had great difficulties getting along with his class,
must have always played the scapegoat for the rougher students. He was in the "Gray Cloister." He is tall, awkward, not
at all inclined toward sports, quite hostile toward mathematics,
altogether too sensitive. After leaving school he worked for a
year in the state library and got along amazingly well with his
colleagues. That was his first taste of success. Now he is studying Slavic languages and literature, which he never wanted to
study, but which now interests him very much, and even during his first year he turned in some successful essays and also
got along well with his fellow students. This disappointment
with the girl must have followed more deep-seated failures. He
does not trust himself. Has also never had a girl.

His parents: father about sixty, was a Social Democrat, during the Nazi era resistance activity, eight years in prison. After
the '45 law, became a vice-president at Humboldt University.
Now retired for some time. Remains aloof, not everything has
gone as he had wished. The mother a little over forty. In
Michael's opinion, she married his father after the war in order
to be taken care of. By doing so she did not create a personal life
for herself (she was a nurse), was never gainfully employed. Is
beginning now to find her own friends; the marriage is not
going well. Supposedly the father does not get a divorce because
he is afraid that the mother would not be able to manage alone.

Michael is completely occupied with himself; other people interest him less. Once he introduced me to a friend who comes to visit him: the son of E., who lives with his mother away from his father, whom he hates because of his corruptness. The boy is studying theology, but cannot become a pastor for "reasons of conscience." On the side he is an extra with the Berlin Ensemble. He behaves in an old-fashioned polite manner and addresses me as "Madam."

A few times we go—Michael and Mr. Sch., his roommate—to the linden garden by the railway station and drink a vodka. Mr. Sch. is a not quite definable man, a mathematics teacher at an agricultural college. His father is a television director, as a result of which Sch. comes in contact with problems that are actually not his own and that are hard for him to get over. But he would like to join in the conversation, join in our grumbling a little bit; on the other hand, I can imagine that demands a totally different attitude from him. He talks in detail about the dream house that Felsenstein[8] is having built in Glienicke, and which is supposed to have cost four and a half million. That is really hard to believe.

I hear motor noises from the street. Can see from the window how Gerd maneuvers the car into the garage, that tin hut. The children have already gotten out and they stomp up the outside stairs and ring so impatiently that I run down the stairs as fast as possible. I open the door for them, say: Well! Behave yourselves!—Hunger! Tinka screams. Gerd comes up the stairs with sacks. Everything for a good supper in them, he says.

[8] Walter Felsenstein (1901-1975) was a theater and opera director, manager of the Comic Opera in Berlin after 1947. (Ed.)

Wake up after six, hear Annette getting ready.
Headache, from the back of my neck, as has often been the case recently. Can't go back to sleep. Think about yesterday's Wogatzki[1] television play (*Under the Sign of the Original Ones*), find that next to the concept of "sing out" in music, they should also introduce the term "play out" in dramatic art. A shameless, poorly made, artificially reproachful apologia for existing conditions, which can only be created, of course, through distortion: but if that's what they want. There are young people who become intoxicated with it. (In *Neues Deutschland* there is also an apologia for the apologia: Here the signs of the original ones are established for art.) I remember the telephone call last night from Dr. M., who announced that Annette is being invited for an admissions interview to begin her studies and gave a few hints about what they expect of her. Her problem, whether or not she should accept the female role in a Camus play that the Youth Group intends to stage here. She was very tempted and also wanted to discuss it with the people; the reasons for not accepting the role were purely pragmatic ones that she reluctantly gave in to—Tinka, on the other hand, is supposed to go to Berlin to the meeting of the Young Socialists . . .

Gerd takes Tinka away; I fall asleep again, until a quarter

[1] Benito Wogatzki (b. 1932), writer, wrote television plays in the style of pragmatic socialist realism; *Im Zeichen der Ersten* (*Under the Sign of the Original Ones*), 1969. (G.W.)

after eight. When I look out the window, Maxel, the tomcat, is looking for a way in. I let him in. During breakfast, on Free Berlin Radio the report: Dubček[2] spoke at the meeting of the Central Committee in Prague and refused to declare his behavior of last year to be politically wrong. Husák[3] pleaded to remain president of the legislature. Clever, says Gerd, who is just now reading Isaak Deutscher's[4] Trotsky books and is excited about them. Everything repeats itself. Back then nobody simply wanted to believe that Stalin was such a monster, and Trotsky refused to fight against his opponents personally. Besides that he saw that the mood of the people had already changed and that nobody really knew the history of the Revolution anymore. Krupskaya had been blackmailed by Stalin, probably with the threat of exposures from Lenin's private life, into speaking out against the opposition. ("I will put another of Lenin's widows in your place.") A line: By supporting the ideals of the Revolution, Trotsky prepared his own suicide.

I take a pill for my nerves, consider soon after going to bed whether or not I should go to M. again and ask him: Do you have something for fear?—I see that the next few years will be bad,[5] that I can only retain my integrity to some degree if I do not subject myself to the ugly public events, but that this must again lead to a certain degree of isolation and remoteness from

[2] Alexander Dubček (1921-1992) was a Slovak politician and briefly leader of Czechoslovakia (1968-1969), famous for his attempt to reform the Communist regime (Prague Spring). (Ed.)

[3] Gustáv Husák (1913-1991) was a Slovak communist politician, president of Czechoslovakia. (Ed.)

[4] Isaac Deutscher (1907-1967), British journalist, historian and political activist of Polish-Jewish birth, became well known as the biographer of Leon Trotsky and Joseph Stalin and as a commentator on Soviet affairs. (G.W.)

[5] "That the next few years will be bad...": How justified C.'s fears proved to be emerges from the dossiers of the state security police, who monitored and watched the building on Fontanestrasse (see also: Jörg Magenau, C.W., Eine Biographie (C.W., a Biography), pp. 205ff.). (G.W.)

everyday reality . . . I feel it now in every contact with the public. The private world that we have constructed for ourselves cannot endure forever. I follow the sound of every car that drives past our home during the night.

We go shopping, the final things for Tinka's birthday. The cooperative, the bakery, stand in line everywhere. The day is not cold, but gloomy, windy, and rainy. Max, the tomcat, almost kills himself trying to get the rabbit that Gerd cuts up to put in buttermilk until morning.

As always, I now let Gerd leaf through the newspapers. All they contain now, intensified by the approaching twentieth anniversary, is self-adulation. The group of those who are now successful has sharply separated itself from those who are now unsuccessful. The presumptiveness with which history is distorted and the masses are prevented from learning from it is depressing.

I receive a letter from a woman in Gardelegen who had already written to me once, a German teacher or lecturer, I believe. She has not been successful in obtaining my new book. She writes about writers who change, who transcend themselves, and about others who do not do that, about a conversation about literature with a West Berlin student on a train from Hungary, about morality and immorality among the people, etc. Never before have I had so much personal contact with so many people, especially young ones. All of them are also a product of this society in which they live, but in which they often feel helpless. Recently, at the boring Potsdam literary ball, a young woman journalist from the Liberal Democratic Party said to me: We really don't want to have everything poured into our skulls. We do want to think for ourselves . . .

The veal shank sizzles in the oven. Gerd moves around in the house. I feel good here. But for how much longer?

I work on the material for the *Eulenspiegel* film, read a book about "the thousand-year Reich," *Revolutionary Messianism and Its Survival in the Modern Totalitarian Movements*—Gradually begin to see our time "from above" (even if not from a distance like the "neighboring" Milky Way system that the astrophysicists gave me as a photograph at the discussion last week). In the process I become a bit more detached, but not more confident.

Maxel climbed up the tree and onto the terrace, asked to be let in by scratching at my door, and is now looking for a place to sleep. He just crept into my large brown satchel. Then he will jump into my left desk drawer and will stay there for hours.

I am reading about the "free spirit movement" in the Middle Ages, people who in each case gather around one of their own and worship him as a god—after which they are no longer capable of committing any sin. Among the prerequisites for their existence is the practical rejection of monogamy. The rest of humanity is viewed as their servants and slaves, as subhuman material.

I am reading about Hans, the piper of Niklashausen.

At noon I put the peaches on the cake, finish the topping. A Western station reports that the government of Czechoslovakia has stepped down and that Svoboda has assigned Cernick[6] to form a new government. Commentary: The "reformers" are supposed to be excluded.

The children come at a quarter to one. We eat our veal shank and drink wine with it. Annette tells about a flag ceremony that they had today: at the beginning of the Hans Baimler competition for pre-military education. While the flag was being raised, a flag poem was recited. We say: That is how it was during our entire youth. Why should you have it better than we did . . . ? I am miserable at the thought—Then, after

[6] Oldřiich Cerník (1921-1994), Czechoslovakian Communist political figure, Prime Minister of Czechoslovakia from 1968 to 1970 and supporter of the Prague Spring reforms of 1968. (Ed.)

the director, an officer spoke. He made it seem as if the secondary school were nothing more than an institution for the production of military personalities. The ninth-grade classes had to recite a pledge in which the term "steeled youth" occurred several times, and an Ulbricht quote was cited on how the socialist youth are supposed to be.

A boy in her class, whom they call "pussycat" and about whom Annette has already told me a lot: that he rakes in money and since last year has been planning the exact time when he intends to become a candidate of the Party—this boy has now invited the class members to become members of the Society for German-Soviet Friendship. They would look great, etc. *He* wants to look great. Half of the class wants to join, the other half does not. "Pussycat" went to the class teacher to complain. She, who sees right through him, has to praise him for the good initiative . . . The children wash up, we lie down, I sleep for an hour and a half as I usually do now in the middle of the day and have no desire to wake up. In the end, for the first time in a long time, I dream about Christa T. again, but I do not see her, am simply in her apartment, a spacious suite of rooms beneath the roof, which Gustav shows me, all beautiful, remarkable old furniture, a lot of atmosphere; there is also a bedroom with proper marriage beds, which amazes me very much in the dream. I throw myself across one of the beds, am very tired. There is also a peculiar child's chair with expensive inlaid work that is enthroned up high on a tapering pyramid of elaborate panels and makes a deep impression on me in its absolute uselessness. I know that we talk about Christa, but I do not remember what we say.

I wake up with pain in the back of my neck from the rhythmic shoveling noises made by the after-hours brigade that is working next door. Gerd lies there and reads and reads. You are racing through your Trotsky, I say—He: But it's like a crime novel. He bursts out laughing scornfully and says: Until 1927 the opposition in the Soviet Union could still express itself in publications, but then Stalin got too far into a corner and had the material confiscated. The opposition—whose members were scattered on vacation at the time and hastily came traveling back—was reproached for having its things printed in the print shop of a former White officer of the Wrangel army. The members of the opposition responded that they did not have their material printed at all, but hectographed it themselves, and that the former White officer did not belong to their group, but had been sent in as an agent provocateur by the secret police—The answer of the secret police: So? What was wrong with the Revolution making use of a White officer to expose the counterrevolutionaries?—The accusation was exposed as untenable, but clung to the Trotsky people. On the tenth anniversary of the Revolution an absolutely disciplined mass of people is already demonstrating under the ordered slogans and no longer looks around for Trotsky—In the long run this reading material really is somewhat depressing, says Gerd.

I make coffee, whip cream, we eat and drink while on television the Beat Club lets off steam, film clips that show long-haired girls and young men in ecstasy. At the end the woman moderator says: And something else to take with you: go out and vote tomorrow, perhaps it will be the last time—What does she mean by that? I ask—It's obvious, says Annette. If the German National Democratic Party wins—perhaps there won't be any elections anymore at all.

Tinka calls out: I'm having a birthday tomorrow! Then I'll be a year older—One day! I say—Tinka becomes furious. Nevertheless: thirteen already!—Annette: Oh, I have that far behind me . . .—Come on! Tinka snaps at her. You are always four years older than I am. Because of that you will also die four years sooner!—She shuts up in dismay, wants to take back the thought: It would be best—oh, that won't work, of course! It would be best if we all died together much, much later!—

She must apparently be imagining our earlier death, which is unavoidable, and gets tears in her eyes. Then she measures her height against Father, she does not want to be taller than Annette, not shorter and not taller.

Now I am sitting downstairs at my desk in the vestibule. Tinka is practicing her Telemann piece on the piano and petting the tomcat. Father is working on Hölderlin in his room,[7] Annette on mathematics in hers.

Tinka is teaching the bewildered tomcat to play the piano.

I call the Böhmes in Gatersleben. How's it going? Moderately well—Gerd shows me a lead article by Anna Seghers that she had in *Neues Deutschland* on the twenty-first of September, and which he just now found while cleaning up newspapers: books and transformations. Agreeably simple in tone, she makes no mistakes, talks about a child's wish for books in which magical transformations occur. She ends with: Much later, with an undertone of amazement, people will report quietly and beautifully, penetratingly and simply about the transformations of our days. She believes that, fortunately for her. I do not anymore.

We eat fried rice for supper, leave then very quickly, for the movies, want to see *Time to Live*. We have to run in order to get there on time. There is *Avengers of the Mountains*, a Soviet color film. Yes—the other film will come later. We walk back, this time slowly. We talk about how we can get a room for Annette if she is really admitted to the university, and if at all possible two, because she wants to live with Gunther. In the lamp store we look for a lamp for the vestibule. In the fur store there is a black fur suit for almost 900 marks. Should I give you that? Gerd asks. I'll pay that amount just like that!—At the picture painter's place—she offers a portrait for fifty marks and promises to paint any motif you want—hangs a seascape.

---

[7] G.W.'s text: *Der arme Hölderlin* (*Poor Hölderlin*), Berlin, 1972. (G.W.)

I feel sorry for the woman, says Tinka. In front of the gas station we find that the sky looks like the ocean. Then we come to Förster-Funke-Allee. There is still a light on at our place, Gerd says. The entire floor is lit up. Our successors have visitors. A child is being carried around in someone's arms. The apartment has changed a great deal.

On television Kai Uwe von Hassel implores his countrymen to go to the polls: Every missing vote helps the "extremist groups." On the Second German Television Channel a hair-raising spy film is playing, in which as always the Soviet agents are portrayed as killers and cold-blooded idiots. On that channel Reich-Ranicki with a scathing critique of the new Grass book, *Local Anesthetic* and a detailed review of the memoirs of Mr. Speer, who is still fascinated by Hitler but admits his complicity. He also shares the blame for Auschwitz—Then he must be executed, I say. Annette says: You always want to execute immediately. He has been in prison for twenty years. Not everything can be solved by capital punishment—On the other channel, Karl-Eduard von Schnitzler[8] declares that in our country the people freely and openly decide their own politics, while over there lies, hypocrisy, and exploitation rule. Gerd says: We really don't know which of the two worlds is better.

We set up Tinka's birthday table. I tussle a little more with the tomcat. We go to bed.

I read until eleven-thirty in *The Road to Obliadooh* by Fritz Rudolf Fries, which Thomas Reschke[9] gave me because he found his generation and his vital consciousness expressed in it. I read about the burial of an angel painter in the fifties and about a Christmas and New Year's celebration. A totally disil-

[8] Karl-Eduard von Schnitzler (1918 - 2001) was an East German journalist, propagandist and host of the television show "Der schwarze Kanal (The Black Channel)" from 1960 to 1989. (Ed.)

[9] Thomas Reschke (b. 1932), translator of the most important works of Russian or Soviet literature, among others the works of Michail Bulgakov, Boris Pasternak, etc. (G.W.)

lusioned vital consciousness actually is assumed here, even disillusioned puts it flatteringly. There has never been anything
there to become disillusioned about. I have to accept that
there is such a thing, apparently, but it is foreign to me. But I
read my way into it.

Gerd says, as usual: Aren't you going to turn off the light
pretty soon?—I do it. I cannot sleep, spend a little time thinking. We are clamped in between the two halves of a murderous
and suicidal insanity. As punishment for the fact that we are
also unable to succeed in getting the others to accept reason,
we will depart together with the irrational people. Or be
locked up by them. Just where are we heading with our fruitless negation? The affirmation for it is still missing—or the fertile soil in which it could take root and grow.

In Obliadooh everything has already happened. The word
humanism is no longer spoken, nor do they mourn about it any
longer. Are they now "further" than we? Aren't you asleep?
Gerd asks at around twelve-thirty. His old worry: Is something
wrong?—Nothing, nothing at all, I reply quickly—he does not
know that during the last week I have frequently been taking
meprobamate again. I am simply not tired—Sleep, poor child.
I do.

SEPTEMBER 27, 1970
Kleinmachnow, Förster-Funke-Allee

OCTOBER 3 – OCTOBER 18, 1970
Warna, Schipka Hotel

K leinmachnow, Saturday, the third of October. Day of
departure for Bulgaria. The previous Sunday was the
"day of the year"; I made as many mental notes as possible that day, but during the week I had no time to write any
of it down. Intend to catch up on the way.

Sudden panic about the winter, weariness. During the day I
write the last pages of the tomcat story.[1] It is imperative that it
be finished so that I will not have to get it out again after vacation. As always, packing the suitcases takes longer than one
wants. By the way, it is clear to me that my weariness originates
with the indecision about what I will do with the tomcat story.
Should I send it off to the publisher or not? Is it good enough
for me to provoke a row because of it? Do I want the row at
all? Günter Caspar[2] advises me not to: A gentler wave is just
now rolling in, and we should not put any rocks in its way . . .
What is the reason then for a "gentle wave" at all? I note that
I would most prefer to have peace, conceive a cycle of seven
satires, none of which would be publishable, and I would also
then leave "Revised Philosophy of a Tomcat" alone. I am no
longer able to deal with all of my mail. Gerd seals a few doors
with adhesive strips. Annette receives a list of behavior rules.

---

[1] C.W.'s narrative "Revised Philosophy of a Tomcat" in *Unter den Linden—Drei unwahrscheinliche Geschichten* (*Under the Linden—Three Improbable Stories*), Berlin, 1974 (see also: *Werke*, Vol. III, pp. 435ff.). (G.W.)

[2] Günter Caspar (1924-1999), chief publisher's reader for the Aufbau Publishing Company from 1956 to 1963, after that director of the readers' department for "contemporary German literature." (G.W.)

At eight-thirty in the evening the taxi is waiting. The driver has heard a report of beautiful weather in the South. Where we live it is decidedly cool and rainy. In the airport waiting room stands Mrs. Philipp, our tour guide, with a sign around which we gather. The group consists of 47 people. In the press at the baggage counter I notice that I become too aggressive. When somebody pushes their way forward, I push back. A little more time in the transit lounge, a cognac, then again in the dreadfully jostling crowd through the barrier, into the bus, and onto the plane, an IL 18. We wind up sitting in the middle, by the wings, where it roars very loudly. Departure at ten o'clock. They introduce Flight Captain Wuttke to us over the loudspeaker, and the three flight attendants (in the gangway one of them kept saying: Ladies and Gentlemen, if you push like that, we'll be going back, and there will be no flight!). Flight plan: Prague, Budapest, Bucharest, we see nothing of it. Tinka, who was very hungry at first, then, did not eat anything. Shortly before the landing she admitted that she had been afraid: because of the storms. Even I could only eat a little, a piece of bread, a cup of tea . . . Meanwhile it was midnight Central European Time.

On this fourth of October, a Sunday, I am going to let a second "day of the year" begin, into which I intend to filter the real one, the twenty-seventh of September. I have made up my mind to record this vacation as precisely as possible.

We land on schedule at 12:50 at the airport in Warna (where it is an hour later, of course), experience again how the southern air lays itself on us like a warm, damp sheet, and climb onto one of the three waiting buses. Gerd looks for stars; they would signal a clear sky and that tomorrow the sun might possibly shine, for which we have an uncontrollable longing. We ride through nocturnal Warna. Only the main streets are wet, so it will have been a sprinkler truck and not rain that wetted them down. Half an hour of country road, then we stop in front of a large beehive, our hotel, the Schipka. Nothing but round balconies like honeycombs that—which we cannot yet know—will be illuminated until ten o'clock at night with green neon lights, but which are now dark at after three in the morning.

In the hotel foyer the assignment of rooms, not without conflicts, because there are not enough beds; for us and Tinka there are two adjacent double rooms, 803 and 805. I sign up a young blond girl as a roommate for Tinka, Lilo, who continues to negotiate for a long time at the reception desk for a single room that had been promised her in Leipzig. Then the two of them quickly make friends. Lilo is a thin, neurasthenic type, 28, suffers from sleep disturbances because of the uninterrupted overwork caused by the Leipzig Fair, has a steady job with Jugendmode, the state-owned youth fashions company, and has gathered together a very nice wardrobe for herself there—We liked our room immediately, wood paneling and beautiful simple furniture made of the same wood. We unpack quickly and are in bed at four o'clock. A married couple next door (as I now know, gastronomes from Lübbenwerder, small man, large woman) apparently wrapped each shoe in crumpled paper. The closets of two adjacent rooms form a piece of wall, so that you hear every word from next door when one or even both closets are open. (Now, for example it is the following afternoon—dialogue from next door. She: Just why do you want to wash now? He: Just leave me alone! She: We're not going out now. He: No. She: We're going to rest a little bit now. He: We can do that. She: Then you don't need to wet down your hair and comb it!—And so on . . .) In any case, during our first night, they spent more than a quarter of an hour smoothing out the crumpled paper in the closet.

The next morning at nine, we meet in the hotel foyer, exhausted from lack of sleep. Our little Bulgarian interpreter, Tanya, announces all kinds of excursions and events to us. It was raining horribly, and it stays that way all day long, bleak! It could not have been worse, I said, if only we had stayed home. Unfortunately I also thought: All that money! Tinka, who now sees us very critically, complained today about my moods. In addition to that, my bronchial tubes and my vocal chords immediately made themselves noticeable, damned mist! I thought. I just got that behind me at home and wanted to cure it completely in the warm air of the South. We eat breakfast in the Sotschi Restaurant. I walked through the rows of tables with my coat flying and knocked a butter plate down, but did not pay any further attention to it, as if I had a perfect right to knock over butter plates if it has to rain outside. (At some point that day, I was saved by the idea that I ought to pay close attention to all external conditions, to remember them and note them down, as if I might want to write about them. The only interesting thing in life is writing, I said. Gerd does not like to hear that.) All right, the breakfast is somewhat meager: round soft rolls, butter, a slice of cheese or canned sausage, lukewarm Lipton tea or Nescafe. Tinka gathers up the leftover pieces of sugar for her horses at home. While the girls go to the hotel and sleep, we walk around in the rain yet for a little while, see that beautiful construction is being done here, imaginative, that trees are left standing wherever possible; the sidewalks are laid out with natural stone—it is unfortunately being cut directly in front of our hotel, causing considerable noise.

Then we, too, lie down. I read in my *Feathered Serpent* by Edgar Wallace. Gerd brought along the classical legends of antiquity again, which he always reads in the South, where, in his opinion, they belong. He wonders about the Prometheus legend. The man did provoke Zeus earlier, he says, so that it was his fault that mankind did not receive fire—did you know that? And then chained to that rock for 30,000 years—very nice. And when he is freed earlier than anticipated, Zeus contrives this ring for him in which a splinter of the rock is set, so that he can save face . . . They were always clever—He reads a sentence aloud to me: Those who have just come into power must be especially hard-hearted.

Behind the soberly written pages of my *Feathered Serpent* a perspective leading far into the future suddenly opens before me. In thirty thousand years, how will the people who live here look back at us? Why do we always have to believe that they will be smarter than we are? Have we become "smarter" in thirty thousand years?

After the mediocre dinner in the Moskwa Restaurant, where the only decent thing was the salad, I try to reach the Schlotterbecks, who, at the very same time as we, are vacationing in the vicinity of Warna in a journalists' clubhouse. We are informed: They are sleeping now, call back later. So, I can sit down on the balcony and begin to report on the twenty-seventh of September from memory and on the basis of a few notes.

A Sunday with nice weather, but cool. We get up earlier than we usually do on Sundays. Tinka tries on dresses. The red corduroy skirt has a broken zipper; the dress from last year that Tinka had counted on is actually too small. I say, it is still good enough, but barely, Gerd says, it looks somewhat tiny. At breakfast Tinka is in a bad mood. She is not comforted by Annette assuring her that she knows how she feels. Frieder Schlotterbeck comes, the speaker of the day, who is supposed to open the series of events in preparation for the youth initiation ceremony. We go to the school. I introduce Frieder to the principal and to Tinka's teacher. The children clearly look like they are in a transitional state, no longer children, not yet adults. The parents look like socialist philistines. Finally it begins. Two young people fiddle piteously on their violins and then a sparse choir sings. A girl recites something. Then Frieder, twenty-five minutes, somewhat unfocused. He talks about the difficulty of becoming an adult, puts in a good word for the young people with parents and teachers. Political phrases do not occur, but he speaks penetratingly about the concept "human being" and warns the youth against ever being condescending toward others, like: the farmer is also a human being, and so on. Professor Z., who is sitting in front of us, grimaces, whispers to his wife. Frieder receives his chrysanthemums; the choir, the violins, and the girl speaker come again; grim boredom descends upon the meeting.

On the way home, two boys from Tinka's class, Tille and Matze, ride around on their motorcycles, although it is prohibited. Frieder tells how he helped a boy from his neighborhood. Because he had not gone through the "youth initiation," he was not going to be permitted to enroll in the secondary school, even though he had the required grade-point average. Frieder helped him receive just treatment after all. At home, I give him the tomcat story to read, and Frieder says: That is a broadside against them, there will be a row. You must think about that. Gerd thinks I should very innocently submit the text as a manuscript and that it is not at all that sharp.

Frieder leaves, I bake apple dumplings for Tinka's birthday and fill the cake with vanilla cream, so that in the afternoon, before she leaves, Annette gets some of it. With what is left of the whipped egg white I dry meringues in the oven. Then we eat our Szeged cutlets. I am continually reminded of Max the cat, who died of the epizootic cat disease while I was writing the tomcat story, for which he did provide me many details. I can still see him, the way he scratched at the glass door with his front paws, see his light-colored belly (today, a week later, all that is already past—that's how fast it goes!).

After our naps we clean out Tinka's closet and discover to our dismay that almost nothing fits her anymore. She is now one meter seventy-two. We divide the sorted things into four piles for four families that have children who could use the clothing.

I interrupt the writings, call the journalists' club again, and this time Frieder is there. We do not have any leva for the bus yet. Frieder describes the route for us; the promised fifteen minutes become half an hour, all of it in the rain. On the way we see all kinds of strange plants, many of them in the gardens on the slope, which are still in private hands, with small bowers and summerhouses: fig trees (Tinka: Aha, that's how the famous fig leaves look in nature!), a kind of almond, remarkable yellow apples, and grape vines, of course, with large blue grapes, all of it glittering and dripping from the rain. In the journalists' club we initially go the wrong way and then come from behind, through the restaurant, into the old building. At the reception desk they are at a loss. Fortunately we run into Aram, who guides us. Children of different nationalities romp through the building, play hide-and-seek, sit around on the broad, carpeted stairs, which Aram creeps up and down on all fours. The Schlotters are in room 303 and have just had coffee. They are still quite filled with the odyssey of the first night. They arrived one day later than their tour group because at the airport in Berlin they suddenly discovered that Aram also needed papers. Then they stood in front of the clubhouse in the dark, on the street, with no way in, until Frieder found an open window through which they climbed in and then spent the night in armchairs in the foyer. I tell about my prohibition against leaving the country, which almost prevented this trip. On that occasion I learned that I am on a list of people that they do not want to let leave the country.

In an adjacent building there is a very cool bar-like establishment, where we can drink a cognac and a Nescafe. Beneath a shawl Aenne hides the bandage that she still wears on her neck since her thyroid operation, during which, as she probably expected, cancer was discovered. Through a ruse, from a nurse she surreptitiously obtained the diagnosis that they had intended to keep secret from her. She wanted to know the truth. There is no talk about the illness, instead we talk about dreams. Frieder does not dream at all and that must also mean something. Instead he has intensive daydreams. He governs.

He puts their youthful ideals of a just world into action. He knows that it goes exactly the same way for other old communists. In reality, he says, in a few years nobody will give a hoot about us anymore. We will be swallowed up by progress. I protest, not very convincingly. I remember the youth initiation aphorism that Frieder once received: The best must leap into the fissure of the times. And if that fissure is an abyss?

But Frieder also knows stories about old communists who begin to dote at the end. For example, a man from Stuttgart, a legendary figure who was the military leader of the revolt of '23 in Stuttgart, had to live illegally during the entire Weimar Republic period, "legalized" himself with false papers during the Nazi era, always worked illegally, and was never caught. Now he walks around Berlin without any teeth and checks to see that people do not park in front of garbage cans, because the garbage collectors will then not pick up the cans.

Aenne dreams on the highest level. For example: she works her way forward with Walter Ulbricht across the icy, totally empty Glienicker Bridge near Potsdam. They cling to each other, alternately fall down and help each other up again. He also foolishly carries a rectangular block of ice under his arm, which slides back and forth and is an additional hindrance.

Now listen, we say, the Glienicker Bridge is only used to exchange spies!

Franz Dahlem[3] wrote a long letter to Aenne and asked her for information on a series of points. He is now writing his memoirs, the time is favorable; he explains to her about the injustice that was done him in 1953, about Noel Field and the Slansky trials. As if that were totally foreign to us! laughs Aenne bitterly.

---

[3] Franz Dahlem (1892-1981), functionary of the Communist Party of Germany, member of the politburo of the Central Committee of the Socialist Unity Party and cadre chief of the Socialist Unity Party; in connection with the investigations of connections to Noel Field, expelled from those functions; 1956 "rehabilitated". (G.W.)

I remember what I dreamed last night: I am being taken, halfway resisting, across the border into the West; there is shooting, a woman aims at me with a tube, I run, but do not make any headway, jump onto an empty departing train, and am thus over there. A large empty room, an unfriendly, distrustful landlady, I am very alone, as I had always imagined it, and am now supposed to write a great book. Annette is supposed to be the next one to come. I advise against it.

Yeah, says Frieder, German dreams.

We go back into the dark, still under the rain, and talk about my plans. The childhood book must be the next one. Not in the first-person form, or alternating between first and third person. No chronology. Perhaps this way: the trek in the first half of 1945, blending my childhood into it, which actually does not come to the surface until this flight. Technical problem that arises again and again when I write prose: how do I bring the stacked layers of which "reality" consists safely over into my linear writing style? (Obviously by no means only a "technical" problem.)

Suddenly, to our right something cries in the bushes, shrilly, at brief intervals. A small white kitten creeps out, which would almost still have to be nursed and has lost its mother. I pick it up; it clings with its claws, seeks for warmth, cries and cries. We spend a quarter of an hour trying to decide what we should do with the little thing. Take it along? But to where? And how will we feed it? Abandon it? Then it cries louder and creeps further up on me. I take it in my arms and we walk the few hundred meters to the government building. In response to our shouts, the militia sentry actually does come out of his sentry box. He opens the door in the fence, and we explain the situation to him through gestures, with scraps of Russian, and the kitten cries and cries. He finally takes it in his arms and pets it. He has kind, sympathetic eyes, probably a boy from the country, he keeps it.

The cure doctor here has prescribed massages, herbal baths, and inhalations for me. The next day, on Tuesday, I receive the first treatments. At noon we eat only a few sausages. I sit with Gerd on a bench, where he apparently loses his wallet, with thirty food coupons and seven leva.

Oh well. Then in the bathroom I let my watch fall on the tiles. It breaks. We feel that with that we should have appeased the jealousy of the gods. Our mood is excellent. With our little immersion heater, we boil coffee water in the glasses provided for brushing our teeth. So now I am sitting on the balcony, and I will continue with my recapitulation of the twenty-seventh of September.

In the afternoon Hörath came with Lydia, a student from Novgorod, who is studying German language and literature in Leipzig and is working on Ernst Moritz Arndt's ties to Russia.[6] She complains that the foreign students here have so little contact with the German students and families, criticizes the insufficient education in world literature here and the inadequate interest of German students in their studies. She asks why my book (The Quest for Christa T.) *is officially viewed so much more negatively in the German Democratic Republic than in the Soviet embassy—I did not know that. In Leipzig she met an eye doctor from Odessa, whom she wants to marry, and then she will work at the university in Odessa as a lecturer. Leipzig as a meeting place for Russians—I like that.*

When they have gone, I measure out cloth that has already been lying around unused for a long time, for pillowcases, and while doing so listen to a report on the sociologists' convention in Warna. Annette listens to it, too. I ask her if the psychologists, among whom she belongs, could not complement the sociologists in their problems and methods: the one group concentrates on the individual, the other on social processes. She sees rather the

---

[6] Ernst Moritz Arndt (1769-1860), German patriotic author and poet. (Ed.)

differences and a certain danger that the sociological problems that are more evident and would seem more relevant to the contemporary technically oriented societies could contribute to leveling out the methods by which the subject is approached. I sit by her while she eats supper early because, as always on Sundays, she has to catch the bus at seven-thirty. Yes, yes, she says, she has already become accustomed to her Berlin room to some degree. I know that certain aspects of her studies and certain lecturers create difficulties for her. She does not talk about that today. The pain of parting is no longer quite as sharp as it was in the initial weeks, when I always had to sit down in her room for a while after she had gone, to console myself.

The three of us eat supper. There is something trivial on television. Gerd sticks the fourteen candles onto the large French cheese plate that we got from the Sterns. The gifts are spread out. I leaf through the newspapers again . . .

. . . which I brought along with me. I do not have time to quote from them now because we have to go eat; the sun is just disappearing behind the mountains, and it rapidly becomes cool. It is five in the afternoon. A mallow-colored twilight descends, and then all at once it gets dark. I straighten up the room a little more, and then we go to the Koscharata, a restaurant that is set up to look like a sheep shed. We wait for our lamb. Within an hour an uncanny German coziness develops. First a Bulgarian band plays folk music; then they begin with corny German waltzes. Up front on the right there is a table with about ten women, most of them somewhat older, most somewhat plump, an entire throng of unlived life. One of them is asked to dance and then more couples go out on the dance floor. Suddenly a girl dressed in pink (from that table) jumps forward, begins to writhe, to weave her way through the tables, and then, prodded by applause, performs a solo number. At the end the splits, applause. Cheering at the women's table.

Near us an entire company of men. We learn: trade organi-

zation gastronomes from the German Democratic Republic.
Tinka's mocking laughter prevents her full development. Gerd
recognizes one: his former youth platoon leader from Jecha. He
also pronounces it nicely, "yaycha." Imagine him younger and
with short pants, says Gerd. He tells wonderful jokes: A lieutenant asks a fellow what he would do if he were driving a car
on a country road and a Stuka started to dive at him. Oh, he
says. I would deceive that guy. I'd signal for a right turn and
turn left! At the table they laugh so hard that one of the women
has to run hurriedly to the toilet amid the roaring laughter of
the crowd. At the next table a fat agronomist: Who is the very
best *Kellner* (waiter) in the world? The *Kellner Dom* . . . [7]

Separated from us by a palisade wall, a Western and an Eastern couple draw closer together. The Westerners are from
Hamburg, the Easterners are trade organization innkeepers
from Lübbenwerda. The woman is considering whether or not
she could transform an empty barn in her vicinity into a restaurant, and the woman from Hamburg encourages her vehemently. In general gastronomy is actually better in the German
Democratic Republic than in Bulgaria, even if they do more
here on the surface. Back and forth about restaurants in
Warna, about menus, etc. Then the man from Hamburg (who
apparently originally comes from somewhere in the East)
declares that he does not insist on his right to a homeland, and
he is for the recognition of the German Democratic Republic.

Meanwhile, between the women's and the men's tables a
kind of singing competition has developed: *Trink mal noch ein
Tröpfchen* (Just drink another drop) . . . , *Heute blau und morgen blau* (Drunk today and drunk tomorrow) . . . , *Warum ist
es am Rhein so schön?* (Why is it so beautiful on the Rhine?)—
that brings them all together. Gerd's former youth platoon
leader tries a solo: *In der Heimat, in der Heimat, da gibt's ein*

---

[7] A word play on *Kölner Dom* (Cologne Cathedral). (Tr.)

Wiedersehn (In the homeland, in the homeland, there's a reunion there) . . . The waitresses, for the most part pretty girls, perhaps students, walk back and forth with rigid faces, serving. It does not occur to the singers at all that someone could see no value in their offerings.

On the way back, to Gerd's irritation I say that it is boring at health resorts.

The "great" book, once again we talk nonsense about it. It would have to be open toward all sides. The year '68, the year of the final disillusionment, perhaps as a framework. It could be called directly that: *The Year.* A motto: Alone with our era. Another: Keep the wound open. Employ: diary pages, letters. Previews and flashbacks, tell entire stories, episodes. No "exposé," no resentment. Simply a document of the times: how people live in this time. I go to bed again with my *Feathered Serpent.* Suddenly it occurs to me that the two of us, Gerd and I, should write a utopian crime novel together under a pseudonym, probably a new genre. Gerd is skeptical. What should be in it? he says, and: Under a pseudonym we should write something entirely different!—In spite of that I like the idea.

The next morning. A radiantly beautiful day. Around ten to Druschba, the buses are cheap. Made a stop at the journalists' club, where we met the Schlotterbecks in the room of the famous Soviet painter Shukov, who had just depicted Aram. They proudly show us the drawings. For his part, Aram had drawn Shukov, with an enormous "sex apparatus," as Frieder expressed it, and to which Aram gave the commentary: It is for two men at once. From another Russian, who was also there in the room and with whom Frieder is supposed to have come to a quick agreement about the relationship between the artist and power (by pantomime, through imitation of upright and devotedly bowed carriage)—from him Aram swiftly stole his lighter, threatened us later with it (it has the form of a pistol):

Hands up, no false moves! By means of trickery the pistol was taken from him by Gerd and Frieder, so that he had to think that he had lost it. Then he said: I'm sure that the pistol probably thought to itself, I want to run away, and so it ran away.

So we rode to Druschba, sought and found the warm mineral bath, a basin under the open sky into which a warm spring with a temperature of at least 45° C flows from the side. Although it smells slightly of sulfur, the water is tasteless. The bath was just being drained, but still had enough water in it that we were able to roll around in it for more than half an hour. Even Aenne, with her neck bandage, otherwise quite immobile, enjoyed it a lot. Frieder even tried a pike dive; he is still young and flexible. Afterward we lay in the sand behind the dressing tent in the sun. After twelve a cool wind arose, which remained through the afternoon, but was still plenty of sunshine. At noon, by a circuitous route we sought out the cloister cellar restaurant. A waiter, a badge on his suit: "*Chef de sale*," hardly left our side, good soup, a bratwurst with white beans, a nice red wine: Mönchsgeflüster. The waiter told of his trips to the German Democratic Republic, spoke very good German; a black and white cat was there (the same costume as the waiter) that had a miserable shattered and improperly healed leg and limped horribly, then two kittens, five to six weeks old; we brought them out from under the table, they meowed, and we put them in our laps.

On the way back we stop to buy a pot to boil water in. In the hotel Gerd lies down immediately. I make coffee, sit down for a while on the balcony, and note down a few headlines from the newspapers of the twenty-seventh of September:

The entire collective struggles to save time for new production—National anger in Italy about Nixon visit—Thorough analyses of moon rocks begin—Arabian heads of state admonish King Hussein of Jordan to cease hostilities—Industrial production in the COMECON countries increased during the first half of

1970 by 8.7%—Your children, our children: who is educating them? Every teacher is simultaneously a political leader—Günter Schabowski [8] *: Service—no longer modern? With the defeat of the oppressors the socialist revolution also objectively did away with the contrast between serving and ruling—A monument to the land reform, two plowshares stretch fourteen meters into the air, visible from a distance upon them the writing: Squire's lands in farmers' hands. Münzer's grandchildren fought it out better— Washington mobilizes its "fifth column" in Chile. Goal: to prevent at all costs the inauguration of Dr. Salvador Allende of the victorious* Unidad Popular, *who was elected during the presidential election, and to avert the danger of a popular front government.*

Gerd wakes up, looks out at the beautifully colored sky, and declares that we ought to have a cottage on the Mediterranean. I say he should not talk nonsense. He continues to fantasize: Or live on the island of Hiddensee all summer. His blood is flowing freely and he is more thoroughly warm than he has been for a long time.

Well, and then it is the evening of the sixth of October, the wine-tasting in the Ambassador. Shortly before we left, the lights went out in the entire town. I do not know who all may have been stuck in the elevator, but in any case we walked down the eight floors in the dark. Tinka had already gone ahead with Lilo. I became indignant. Gerd called me prudish. I did not let him get away with that. After all, she is not an adult yet, as one might say. The mood was not especially good. Then the two of them had decently reserved seats for us, at a table with our tour guide, Mrs. Philipp, the tour guide of another group, and a few younger people.

It began rather stiffly, we said: An atmosphere like the one in the sheep shed will not develop here. On the tables there

---

[8] Günther Schabowski (b. 1929), Socialist Unity Party functionary, member of the politburo of the Central Committee of the Socialist Unity Party, journalist; beginning in 1968 on the chief editorial board of *Neues Deutschland*. (G.W.)

was a bottle of white wine (muscatel) and a bottle of red wine (cabernet or mavrodaphne), so mediocre. At the beginning, our interpreter, Tanya, proposes a toast with cognac to the Day of the Republic, the twenty-first. The tour guide joins in, and with that they have that behind them. We eat our small plate of hors d'oeuvres with hard sausage, sheep cheese, a few mushrooms, stuffed tomatoes, etc. We pour our first glass of white wine. The older gentleman across from us (as we learn later, a Mr. Peters from Waldheim) describes the merits of the hot spring in Druschba. Then he tells his first joke: A German man, who is staying on the Bulgarian Black Sea coast as we are, falls in love with a Bulgarian girl and asks her: Wouldn't you like to go into the woods with me for a picnic?—I'd like that, she says, but shouldn't we eat something first? The laughter begins—so things do get better! The jokes are always told with one hand in front of the mouth, away from Tinka. After all, there are young girls at the table! She notices that she is spoiling things, becomes irritated, now really does not want to be too young and becomes naughty. Reproaches us for remaining in this company, wants to know why we laugh and sometimes sway along with the others, instead of causing a row or leaving.

And across from us the young married couple that I had already noticed at the airport (she had pushed her way forward). She has short hair, the way the fashion was years ago, a rather deep voice, and is an athletic type, perhaps thirty-two. He, late thirties, has melancholy eyes, seems a bit droopy and listless, significantly less active than she is. Gerd sees that he has a facial tic that probably should make him interesting. Later we learn that they are from Cottbus (Peters immediately wants to have them recite the *"Cottbuser Postkutschkasten* [Cottbus mail coach box]") and that the woman is a teacher. We do not yet know his profession; perhaps it has something to do with history, because she asks him about some Bulgarian kings in order to be able to interpret the wall paintings. Lilo whispers that she cannot stand the woman; she immediately addressed her with the informal *du*; and that she feels it is disgusting how she leaves her husband in the lurch and flirts with the other young man (it was a very modest flirt, but she really conversed mostly with the two young men on her right, of whom the one suddenly asked the question: What is actually normal? Apparently a brooding loner.) Lilo says she does not understand the woman, her husband does represent something. In the bathing suit we can clearly see that he does not work with his muscles (he actually does have a flabby, seemingly dead upper torso); he is probably an academic, while Mr. Peters, who is getting more and more into the swing of things and now begins to sing (*"Im tiefen Keller sitz ich hier* [I Sit Here Deep in the Cellar]"—Yes, Ladies, I was once a member of a men's singing club!), in Lilo's opinion, has some small farm with state support in Waldheim—nothing major, his intelligence is not at all sufficient for that.

The main course consists of pieces of some kind of meat (boiled, as it usually is here), French fries, and the good *schopska* salad. Meanwhile they are singing loudly at our table and swaying with the music: *"Trink, trink, Brüderlein trink!* (Drink, Drink, Little Brother, Drink!)"* Diagonally across from Peters sits Mrs. Sauer from Leipzig, a diabetic, eats a lot nevertheless; she is short and fat, but very agile and has a bubbling Rhineland temperament. Mrs. Peters addresses her as "Mrs. Sweet"—because of the sugar! She surprises us with a number of Rhineland songs in a remarkable soprano. It is time for *"Heute blau und morgen blau"* again, the unavoidable *"Warum ist es am Rhein so schön?"* and *"Mein Hut, der hat vier Ecken* (My Hat, it Has Four Corners)."* The neighboring tables probably envy us; a professor from Ilmenau rises, toasts Mr. Peters: "To our Schaljapin!" At the end of our table sit several fat ladies, among whom a blond in a white blouse stands out especially, who supposedly (according to Tinka's story) fished away a piece of cake from the man who was sitting behind her on the airplane. She has her big moment when she auctions off the three carnations that she bought from a woman selling flowers.

Mrs. Peters pesters her husband to dance with her, and then the blonde also begins dancing with the fat, dark-haired woman next to her, and Mrs. Sauer with the similarly fat short woman next to her, who has glasses and a pug face and always says: Mrs. Sauer does not like this, Mrs. Sauer prefers that, so that one would think she were Mrs. Sauer's mistress or employee, but then they only have a concert subscription and drink champagne together, once a month, Mrs. Sauer does not like any other alcohol. Mr. Peters and his wife are heartily invited to a champagne breakfast in Leipzig. Champagne does not run out at their place. Mrs. Sauer is probably a business-woman.

Nothing but single women, many pent-up desires. The young people (thus we) are made fun of. Why can't we be so lightheartedly cheerful? Not sing along for a change? Sway along? Or begin to sing a song ourselves?—The young pseudo-Casanova who watched last night at roulette says: They are right, of course. Often the so-called parties of the young peo-ple are also very unimaginative, nothing but beat and necking and then home. I defend the young people; Tinka says, better a beat party than a hundred of those Rhine songs. Mr. Peters tells more and more daring jokes, in response to which Tinka, who has also drunk her two glasses of wine, no longer knows where to turn her eyes, but she laughs without embarrassment, shows clearly that she understands the jokes and despises the entire group. At around ten-thirty Gerd takes her and Lilo home; she has additionally admitted to me that she is a twin, that her sister looks just like her but is very different from her in character. She is a teacher.

Some samples of the jokes: Ladies, if you only knew how

much we like to have you among us and that it is our greatest enjoyment to be in your midst![9]

Or: A man dies in an accident. The pastor goes to his widow to comfort her and also brings her a Bible. The man's pants are still hanging in the closet. The widow points to them and says: Pastor, what was in those pants is not in any Bible!

In between Mr. Peters says a few things to the interpreter that he considers to be gallant (after all, the girl needs encouragement; she is doing this for the first time and is making an effort!). The fancy cake has also come and gone and been eaten by all of the fat women. After that the obligatory grumbler comes from next door to complain to the tour guide about all kinds of things. He is drunk and ends every sentence with "Bang! Finished!" He is not going to spoil our mood. Then he tells a little Erna joke. (Peters had already offered "The landlady had a son.")

We feel that it is time and we leave. Outside it is rather mild; a different air seems to be blowing in, stars. Gerd's wallet mysteriously lies quite innocently and untouched on the table. Too bad, he says. I would have gladly made a small sacrifice. During the night we are awakened several times by loudly returning people.

A radiant morning. Gerd continues to fantasize in bed about where he would like to live: a Greek or an Italian island. Has the South caught you? I ask. I know it is not the South; it is the reluctance to return home. (When did the change actually occur, that we were no longer happy to return?) We walk on the beach; the clouds move inland; it is windy, but there is nothing but sun. We have gotten ourselves a green windbreaker. We enter the water, which is hardly more than 17° C, but bubbles like champagne. We send the girls to the hotel, walk for the twenty minutes to the Schlotters', and find them still in the

[9] The German original is a word play on *Mitte* (midst or middle). (Tr.)

dining room in conversation with a Pole who was in a Siberian camp for twenty years and his wife, the widow of the famous General Walter of Spain,[10] who was killed after 1945. Solzhenitsyn will receive the Nobel Prize, we hear. They still do not know if he will accept it.

Aram, overtired, is supposed to go to bed, but first he has to tell a joke: Dad, do grapes have legs?—No, of course not!—Then I just ate a dung beetle—We sit in the foyer on their floor until well into the evening and drink tickling apple wine and sweet maraschino. I say to Aenne: Strange. I can drink as much as I want and I don't get drunk!—She claims that it is a sign that I am in spiritual equilibrium. Only unstable types quickly become drunk. The two of us laugh heartily. The Schlotters tell stories from their time in Dresden when they, freshly imported from Switzerland in 1948 as attendants for a Red Cross convoy, had "quite naïvely" remained in the East and worked, he in the city administration, she as a journalist with the *Tägliche Rundschau*[11] (Aenne: "Because I did believe completely in the justice of the cause that we represented!"). Wild stories about uncompromising clashes in a vacation house with philistine union members who envied them for the special food they still had with them from Switzerland. That's right, Aenne shouted at them, she liked to eat well, and she had absolutely no guilty conscience about it, because she was not one of those who had bellowed "*Heil Hitler!*" for twelve years. Then it was quiet in the place, she says. And then afterward some people came creeping up and expressed their joy at our victory. They themselves had always secretly eaten the extra rations that they had brought from home in the lavatory.

---

[10] General Walter Karol Swierczewski (1897-1947), officer in the International Brigades against Franco in Spain, after 1945 Deputy Minister for National Defense in Poland, murdered by fascist bands. (G.W.)

[11] *Tägliche Rundschau*, daily newspaper published in 1955 by the Soviet occupation forces. (G.W.)

Or our orgy on the Weisser Hirsch! says Frieder. Alternating with each other they describe an evening after a theater performance (*"Stella!"* says Aenne. The men were enchanted!) in an international tourist hotel on the Weisser Hirsch in Dresden, where people had to pay with foreign currency ("We still had some!"), where they rapidly got drunk, where Frieder threw the champagne glasses at the chandelier and the other old comrade who was with them began to walk on his hands through the hall to prove that he was still in good condition as a worker-athlete. The manager came in black breeches to throw them out ("Such an SS face, I really enjoyed him!"). The whole thing ended with an automobile accident and a case of trade organization beer in the room where they lived at the time.

Once Frieder leaves, Aenne says quietly to me: By the way, I inquired about it—F. died of the same thing that I have. I dispute that rigorously. In F.'s case it was leukemia and nothing can be done about that yet. In her case it is something completely different.

Slowly, wheezing, Comrade Horvath from Bratislava comes up the stairs. The Schlotters know that he was condemned to fourteen years in prison during the Slansky trial, but had to serve "only" two and a half years. He sits down at our table and talks about what all of these old comrades constantly turn over in their minds: the causes of the deep crisis in which the international workers' movement finds itself: misuse of power by a small clique. Marx and Engels analyzed the homo oeconomicus, but Marxism did not concern itself with the feeling human being and neglected to draw out the rational kernel from the different schools of psychology. H. is 58, looks much older, recently retired. Last served as a specialist for regional planning. The national responsibility of factories, which has theoretically been established in your country, is something one is not even permitted to speak about here. He still believes that Dimitrov's popular front approach of 1937 was right.[12] The youth here, he says, still live in the spirit of 1968 and play tapes with the speeches of the Prague Spring, but the number of people who still cling to those ideals continues to crumble. The foreign troops are now in the country for an unforeseeable length of time. While in '68 we could have defeated the counterrevolutionaries, from whom they supposedly had to save us, with our Party books. Our great mistake, he says, was the complete abolition of censorship—It turns out that in the twenties H. was in the same Party cell with Louis Fürnberg; he participated in the Slovakian revolt that had Husak as its military leader. His first wife was shot by Slovakian and German fascists. His third wife, who has joined us, who is not a member of the Party, must always simply shake her head in wonder at these utopians. She is far more skeptical and probably more realistic than he is.

We leave late. Frieder takes us to the bus. Sometimes Aenne doesn't believe the diagnosis, he says, and thinks that the operation will resolve everything. Sometimes she is insufferable and I can only imagine what is going on inside of her. And sometimes I no longer know what to do.

In the hotel Tinka has halfway overcome her boredom with the *Feathered Serpent*. Lilo was out with an older gentleman, a gas station owner from the Eifel, whom she rudely calls "Grandpa." He told her about his midlevel entrepreneur's worry of getting eaten up by the big guys. The Americans especially, to whom everything will soon belong, are merciless partners. The telephone is always next to his bed. At night, when the large tank trucks make their deliveries, he or his wife must go out and check to make sure that they do not get cheated. Once he made a major coup. A friend from the city adminis-

---

[12] Dimitrov Popular Front Line: Georgi Dimitrov (1882-1949), Bulgarian communist labor leader; 1935-1943 General Secretary of the Comintern that worked for a popular front against fascism. (G.W.)

tration gave him a tip, and he built a gas station on a street that now, as predicted, is being torn down and turned into a construction site along with the entire surrounding field, so that they have already offered him triple the price for his piece of land and the state is building him a fully automated gas station on the new highway.

Well, says Gerd, we'll never be able to grasp that kind of thinking either. We drink another glass of red wine on the balcony and talk about the book. So, tackle the childhood book right now. Subtitle something like: *A Childhood in Germany*. Or perhaps: *An Obituary for the Living*. Describe the flight, even the difficult incidents, truthfully. An expulsion from the paradise that was, however, no paradise, as it turns out. Work out parallels to today through precise description of the education mechanism. I need school books from back then: reader, history, biology. Then I can prepare myself to work for a few years, I say. Gerd says: Be happy. I would also like to be able to write something very bad again. I say: How about finally doing Hölderlin?

I go to bed with Bulgakov's *Molière*. Tomorrow we will go to Warna and then finally walk along the golden beach for once, clear to the end of it.

A t ten after one in the morning the telephone rings for a long time, but the ringing breaks off just before Gerd is able to run down and pick up the receiver. I still have a bit of a stomachache from the Chinese duck we had yesterday. I consider who may have called us, and imagine Annette in some kind of emergency. But it was surely a wrong number. (Gerd does not sleep the rest of the night.)

At 7 the alarm clock, get up, wake up Tinka, who is already awake and as always takes a long time to get ready. Meanwhile, on the news I hear about the argument over the expulsion of 105 Soviet diplomats from England, about the delay that it will cause in the preparations for the European security conference. Nothing new from China, where for the last week vacations for the army have been cancelled and preparations for the big parade on October 1st have been broken off, etc. Abroad they are wondering about Mao having a serious illness and internal political power struggles.

The cat Napoleon, who has just given birth, is fed oatmeal porridge, which she first rejects but then, when I take it to her bed, licks up with relish. Little Karl, her newborn son, is beginning to crawl; his little front legs are already very firm. I straighten things up a bit in the large room. Ask Tinka again if she really does not want to invite anyone to her birthday celebration. She says no. This year she has no desire at all to celebrate. I cannot get anything more out of her. She is now very quiet, also leaves most of her soup in the bowl.

I shower, oil myself thoroughly, in the process am already thinking about getting to work. For a short time I am consoled about my reluctance to write my telephone conversation yesterday with Brigitte Reimann,[1] who is having the same problem. She has not been working for weeks, cannot concentrate at all, not even write letters, nor read either, is unhappy, but hears from all sides that no work is being done, which strengthens even more the feeling of unreality, the feeling of living amid props and of not being herself at all. Can she still fall victim to schizophrenia at this age? Nor does she go out on the street at all anymore, etc.

I know: if I just let myself go a little, I could very quickly produce all of those symptoms. But what for? To escape from work? Perhaps—to give myself credit, I want to assume it is so—the difficulty is that it is impossible to write with the necessary sharpness and the necessary ties to the present and to think of publication at the same time (I know, of course, that the analysis of my own character structure is already difficult enough in itself), but I still want to publish this book if at all possible. Thus certain censorship boards function quite dependably in my own head, but I set out every morning to fight consciously against them. (When I had to read galley proofs for a new edition of *Divided Heaven*, I sometimes shed tears about the unbroken world view that it still radiates.)

I started over again, more objectively, without introducing an "I," using old material. Now on page 6.

I eat my soup, try in vain to reach a number in Brandenburg to reclaim our defective record player, initiate the anxious and fussy Miss St. once again into the mysteries of our washing machine, then clean out the refrigerator, water the flowers, and

---

[1] Brigitte Reimann (1933-1973), writer, friends with the Wolfs since 1964 (see B. Reimann–C. Wolf, *Eine Freundschaft in Briefen—Sei gegrüsst und lebe* [*A Friendship in Letters—Be Greeted and Live*], Berlin, 1993). (G.W.)

now sit here, at 10 minutes after 9, have a period of two hours ahead of me and get to work.

Weariness and paralysis, but I do not intend to surrender to that. It is the process of growing old, yes. And that I already know too much and no longer expect anything new. Holding out with things that are not new requires practice.

A glorious day, warm, clear, and sunny. At 11 o'clock I go for a massage. Miss Hahn and her colleagues are conversing—the children in the first grade are supposed to bring felt pens that cost 6 marks—with what utensils they were sent to school in 1945 and the first few years after that: slate or cardboard tablet, slate pencil, cardboard school case . . . The conversation shifts to when teachers still struck pupils, with a cane or with the cover of the wooden pencil box on the cheek. (I can't listen to such stories.) The massage is painful, but does me good and makes me tired.

On the way back I still buy sweets and flowers for Tinka, roses. In the flower shop I have to wait because a funeral parlor is picking up its wreaths and bouquets, 150 marks' worth. The people are rather busy and not at all sad.

At home a surprise: Annette is there. I am very happy. Everything looks different when the whole family is together. She hid behind the stove. For lunch she gets the Chinese duck soup and the Chinese duck from the previous day. It is as if she brings life with her. (We have decided, in four years, when Tinka graduates from school, to move away from here, to Berlin, and meanwhile to expand Meesiger. Then to divide the year between winter in the city and summer in the country. We cannot grow old here in Kleinmachnow; it makes a person melancholy. We must change once more.) Tinka also comes to lunch on time. It is cheerful and lively. The children understand each other well, tease each other . . . I see what I now always lack otherwise. Tinka so alone between us—that is not good either.

I sleep for half an hour, take down the laundry, sew my pants, make coffee, whip cream, open strawberries. At last, everybody around the coffee table once again. (In between, Tinka brings a tape down to two tall boys from her class for their class party on Friday evening. Annette runs to the kitchen window to look at her little sister's potential admirers.) Annette tells about her first lesson in autogenic training, the fact that she does not succeed in making her arm heavy. We talk about hypnosis. She now likes her studies somewhat better; she has more time and a few classes that touch on her actual interest. She has also become accustomed to Berlin. She has a prospect of getting a room with a kitchen, in a building on Invalidenstrasse. (They, she and Rainer, have been offered a three-room apartment, for a 750 mark bribe, but they are not going to do that.)

She talks about the child that she wants to have next year as if it were already here. She then intends to interrupt her studies for a year and has already painted an exact picture for herself of how it will be. She is communicative in general, talks about Rainer, about the difficult situation in which he finds himself: nobody understands exactly what his actual artistic intentions are and earnestly discusses them with him. He often has doubts about himself, is being driven into isolation, which he is resisting. Annette also tells about his first marriage, how deeply it hurt him that the woman wanted to use the child to blackmail him to go to Bulgaria with her; the distrust that has remained inside him since then—Annette is very mature in her judgment, objective, at the same time involved. By the way, she does not want to and should not take any more money from us; Rainer wants to support his family himself. Any kind of participation in social organizations has become impossible for her; she feels that everything is "pseudo"—in contrast to her friend Gunter, who is very active and fights against the theory of small strides. It occurs to me that I, too, no longer adhere to that theory and am basically no longer able to believe in any possibility of far-reaching change, that I am, of course, crippled by that and do not really do anything. It is enough to drive a person to despair. Gerd, on the other hand, thinks about the large amount of work that he has before him, about the prospect that his Hölderlin piece will be published, and is actually in good condition, although his spine gives him a lot of trouble.

Then I bake an apple pie, following Lotte Janka's recipe.[2] Meanwhile, Annette and Gerd eat a little bit of supper. Tinka has gone out with her new friend Marina to the song club.

We take Annette to the bus stop in the car, and we ourselves drive to the parents' meeting. Almost all of the parents have come; the classroom is crowded. Mrs. B., in a green pants suit, follows the teacher's plan—which is divided into three parts: political-ideological education, learning results and learning motivations, connection to social organizations—in reporting about her intentions. Everything is well thought out, precisely arranged and organized. The class is already being praised as active and interested. They are striving for maximum performance, each student has to bring forth the ultimate effort, even the slightest political unclearness is to be eliminated, and supervision has to be precise but unobtrusive. A "positive nucleus" has already formed, she gives the names of students who were recommended for functions by everyone, Tinka is not among them, like a fool, I am somewhat offended by that. (Later we hear from Tinka that the suggestions for those names originated with Mrs. B.)

In me the same feelings arise that now come in all meetings:

[2] Lotte Janka, wife of Walter Janka (1914-1944), director of Aufbau Publishing Company from 1952 to 1956; in 1957 sentenced to five years in prison for "forming a counterrevolutionary group"; 1962-1972 director with the DEFA-German film agency; advised C. and G. Wolf in connection with film materials, director of *Till Eulenspiegel*; the Jankas, friends of the Wolfs, also had their residence in Kleinmachnow (see also: C.W., *"Wider den Schlaf der Vernunft* (Against the Sleep of Reason)," *Werke*, Vol. XII, pp. 158ff.). (G.W.)

uncanny foreignness, coldness, depression almost to the point of fear (have I then really become such an outsider?), migraine headache (that is still not gone this morning). The members of the parents' activist group introduce themselves; Mr. Th., a lawyer, makes his inaugural speech, not very congenial. I constantly ask myself how Tinka sees this, how she lives in this dilemma. But all that seems to go off much more simply and naturally for her. She is still awake when we come home, wants to hear what happened. I am happy at how little she aspires, how little need she has to push herself to the front. "Let Annette M. do the Free German Youth," she says. "She is a short, fat girl. She runs around everywhere and can organize well, and she is also terribly enthusiastic."

After that we watch an English film about a millionaire who has to flee to Mexico because of fraudulent business dealings, and while on the train to Mexico seizes the passport of a fellow traveler, whom he drugs and throws off the train without knowing that the man himself is being sought in Mexico as the murderer of the governor. When the millionaire finds out about it, a game of confusion begins, in which the real murderer of the governor dies. In spite of that, the Englishman is not out of the woods; in the end he is run over and killed on the Mexican border by a pursuing car. Then you feel sorry for the brutal, selfish man—a film that awakens sentimentality in the wrong direction.

On the late news it is announced that in 24 hours Radio Canton will make an important special announcement, from which we hope to be enlightened about the internal situation in China.

In bed I still have to say that it is terrible to imagine what people do to each other every minute, everywhere in the world. Gerd defends himself against my tendency to dramatize. He is lying on his heating pad to ease his spine. I have a headache, have taken a pill, immediately turn off the light, and soon fall asleep.

I get up at 6:30. Remember fragments of my morning dream, Honecker has been removed from office, I am with his successor, who tells me intimate details that I have forgotten. Only the atmosphere of complicity and comradeship between us remains in my memory. Then Margot H. was also suddenly removed from office. I saw her from a distance; we were all in a larger room in a summerhouse. Some women who had worked with her until now and had kissed her ass were now running her down. Above all they ridiculed her false modesty when she said again and again that she still had something to *learn*. (The word was repeated by the women with the presentation of several examples.)—Suddenly I have to let myself be photographed with a married couple whom I am supposed to be acquainted with—the man is an officer. The people then live in the same summerhouse with the Honeckers; we walk along a narrow path that slopes down on the right toward an embankment, at the bottom of which are flourishing garden plots, summerhouse colonies. The married couple (who obviously must have been checked very thoroughly in order to be able to live in the same house with the Honeckers) wants to move out of there—I feel sorry for the politicians.

Under the shower in the basement (the bath has not been functioning again for a week) I think about my Minka plan, which had occurred to me the night before: a naïve, originally sensitive girl in our time and our world. Only after some effort do I remember what I wanted to begin with.

I put on lotion, get dressed, wake up Tinka, then the cat, who slept in the back in Annette's room on the blue pad. I tickle her, look unsuccessfully for fleas in her fur.

While putting on lotion, I am reminded of the pain behind my left ear, of the little cartilaginous knot that I have felt for months, that has been worrying me again recently, although the ear doctor and the dentist do not find anything, also probably smile a little bit about it, and Gerd reacts to my hints with irritation. If I had only three or four years to live, I probably would not change anything, still try to write the book and finish it in time.

I fix breakfast for Tinka and me, fry bread, boil eggs, and pour orange juice. The cat comes to her corner to eat; I let her out. The news that I listen to while doing those things (Free Berlin Radio): Norway rejected entrance into the European Economic Community by a 53% majority—Japan favors good relations with China over the economic birdcalls from Moscow because it no longer wants to be an object but a subject in the power triangle Washington-Moscow-Peking—The German Democratic Republic exchanged with the Federal Republic of Germany more than 100 political prisoners for two spy leaders—The Soviet ambassador Vinogradov arrives in Cairo again after an absence of more than two months—The Arab states reserve for themselves the right to resolve their conflict with Israel by any means, even military ones.

Tinka at breakfast, quiet. Radio music, which she insists upon in the mornings. I ask her if she really goes to school reluctantly every morning. "Not *yet*," she says. No, she has only been afraid of a teacher or a subject once, specifically in the first grade, when she was afraid of Mr. Schröder, who then became her favorite teacher . . . At the time, it became quite dark in the class when he came in . . . She does not want to finish the orange juice and we divide it among the other glasses. We talk about attending the theater on the evening of her birthday; we talk about the fact that we parents will not be there this evening, and that this evening at Secondary School IV she has a performance with her singing club. Her German teacher, with whom she had an argument about the interpretation of the song "*An die Freude* (Ode to Joy)," gave her an "A" for her elaboration and criticism in her file folder and identified the numbers of the stanzas in which a militant and revolutionary spirit are supposedly expressed, which Tinka so clearly misses.

Now she always wears pants, a pullover, and a colorful sleeveless jersey, puts her parka on over them, leaves.

I water all of the flowers and then put Annette's laundry in to soak. At eight o'clock I am sitting at my desk, which is an ideal that I so seldom realize. I write the first three Minka stories, about her dreams, her ideas, and her sympathy for the politicians. I imagine that I could give Gerd a series, illustrated by Tinka, for his birthday (immediately seems utopian to me again).

I am cold; I make myself a glass of Nescafe and speak a few words with Miss St. about her sister, who, to please her brother, helps out in his household in Stahnsdorf and with feeding the cattle in the agricultural commune. She did not want to join the agricultural commune; her brother pays her. She has always hoped to get away from here, but she can't and has to endure it. Nor will she be able to accept a different position. She says that she is finished—all of that presented dispassionately and without a breath of any claim to life: from a different time.

Across from my window, on the other side of the street, I can watch the day-to-day progress of the maple leaves in turning yellow. Next door, at the neighbors' place, the parquet stripper produces a horrible hissing sound as it works.

The sheet of paper for the first page of *Patterns of Childhood* is still in the typewriter from yesterday, but I do have to start over again. I write a good page and a half that I intend to let stand for now without knowing whether that will help me at all. For I cannot work for weeks on every page of the manuscript as I have done with this beginning. I am temporarily in a better mood because I seem to succeed in putting together a few sentences that were, for the most part, completed previously, but with regard to the whole I am and remain disconsolate and hopeless. I talk briefly with Annette, who is here because of Rainer's trip to the West, about the Ritters' book on liberal family education. She is still lying in bed. Allergic sniffles. Less than two months more until the birth of her child.

The mail comes. A remarkable, friendly letter from Lieselotte Welskopf-Henrich,[1] the invitation to the genetics colloquium in Kühlungsborn, a card from Siegfried S., that he finds *Self-Experiment* "heavenly."[2]

10:30: I get ready, makeup, etc. Am wearing the rust-colored suit.

11 o'clock: We leave in the car, first take the water heater from the kitchen to the public services shop, and then buy twelve roses for Kurt Stern on Lenin-Allee.

On the way I tell Gerd that I now have a beginning. He is of the opinion that I can write only out of negation, out of inhibition, and that I therefore subconsciously bring about that condition for myself.

Berlin. At one o'clock in the afternoon, Gerd is in the Academy. I drive to the copyright office, where I go to Mr. G. and pick up intershop checks from my West German honorarium for *The Quest for Christa T.* in the amount of 500 DM; then, by a roundabout way to the People's Theater to get tickets for *The Robbers*, then to the children's department store to buy baby things for Annette. I meet Gerd in the Friedrichstrasse inter-

---

[1] Lieselotte Welskopf-Henrich (1901-1979), historian, writer of works about Greco-Roman antiquity and books for young people about the life of the Indians. (G.W.)

[2] Siegfried Streller (b. 1921), professor of Germanic studies, Leipzig, guest professor in Prague 1972-1976. (G.W.)

shop. We spend all of the first check. Then, in the used book store on Unter den Linden, I found a book with French-German idioms for the Sterns, in the art store the Oelschlegel[3] record for Tinka, in the U-Wu-Bu store[4] sausages and cartons of orange juice. At noon—cold cuts (Hungarian salami) in the Lindeneck. Next to us a table with Arabs and two fat Berlin floozies, very young girls, the one blond and obviously ordinary, the other with black hair, a child's face that she has covered with makeup and a lascivious mask, porcelain cheeks, eyes with heavy makeup, bright red fingernails, cheap rings. Otherwise older, uninteresting customers. The waitress with a sharp bosom, silver, enormous wig. Afterward we immediately meet a few more women with wigs. Gerd says: Do they think that is beautiful?

We drive to the Aufbau Publishing Company (2:30 P.M.), to see Sigrid Töpelmann,[5] who was just at the hairdresser's and is wearing a brown corduroy dress that looks good on her. It concerns the *Eulenspiegel* manuscript that we have brought with us, and my three "improbable stories" (that is what Gerd called them), which they want to look at. (Caspar: "If we want to push them through at all, we will have to treat them as grotesque tales and illustrate them ludicrously.") There is also the matter of an invitation to a meeting with young writers of the Aufbau Publishing Company.

We stop at the *Sonntag*[6] office to deliver pictures of Gerd (they want to introduce his Hölderlin story), then to the store

[3] Vera Oelschlegel (b. 1938), actress; beginning in 1975 manager, director at the TIP (Theater in the Palace of the Republic in Berlin). (G.W.)

[4] U-Wu-Bu stores: colloquial "*Ulbrichts Wucher-Buden* (Ulbricht's Usury Booths)," select stores for luxury articles at exorbitant prices. (G.W.)

[5] Sigrid Töpelmann (b. 1935), Germanic studies scholar, publisher's reader of C.W.'s works in the Aufbau Publishing Company, Berlin. (G.W.)

[6] *Sonntag*: weekly newspaper of the Cultural Society for the Democratic Renewal of Germany; from 1955 to 1957 Heinz Zöger (1915-2000) was editor-in-chief and Gustav Just (b. 1921) was deputy editor-in-chief there, until they were sentenced to prison in connection with the Harich trial; after them Bernt v. Kügelgen was editor-in-chief until 1977. (G.W.)

on Lenin-Allee to shop, especially to buy the yogurt that Tinka likes so much. Outside we get into a heavy downpour and get quite soaked while traversing the hundred meters to the car.

At 4:30 P.M. at the Sterns' place, until 10:30. Drink coffee, have supper (roast beef). Kurt had his sixty-fifth birthday a week earlier. They tell us about France, about Jeanne's family home in Burgundy, where she has now become a foreign visitor through the pedantry of her brother-in-law, who is a joint owner, about the friction of the first six weeks, which they described as a test of nerves, the sometimes comical reactions of their granddaughters in the German Democratic Republic, who are very sheltered from foreign influences here, then about their never-failing enthusiasm for Paris and their shocked depression when they returned: everything stagnated. With amusement Kurt quotes the last sentence of a welcoming address by PEN President Kamnitzer[7] on the occasion of his birthday, who assures him that his example demonstrates how, as a communist, one can be without illusions and yet enthusiastic. (He is certainly not without illusions, but neither is he enthusiastic anymore.)

Jeanne tells about her search for material about the Berlin Huguenots, during which she initially encountered a Mongol, then a Hungarian with a Spanish name. We laugh until tears come. Kurt tells about the crossing to Mexico, about the family of the wealthy gynecologist who traveled with them, with whom the Sterns unintentionally became involved in all kinds of injustice. Jeanne says that as emigrants they lived with their backs turned to the country of Mexico and were not fair to the country; she had much to do with the sons of the upper middle class whom she had to teach French. She talked about a house that was exotically magnificent on the one hand but squalid on the other, where they lived for a while in imitation

[7] Heinz Kamnitzer (1917-2001), professor of history, writer, president of the PEN Center of the German Democratic Republic 1979-1989. (G.W.)

of Bodo Uhse[8] in order to cure their daughter Nadine of tuberculosis.

In between, repeated questions and speculations dealing with the old topic, "whether or not anything will change." As if that were a decision from above over which we could have no influence. Rumors are floating around that censorship will be eliminated; the same people who say that, however, signal danger for the "processes that have begun to function so well." I ask myself: Would we know what to do with a liberal breeze if it were to come? The atmosphere is relaxed and intimate. We like to visit the Sterns. Jeanne has a more pleasantly assured instinct regarding moral questions. We then talk about the difference in eating habits between France and Germany, etc. Drink vermouth, red wine, even champagne. At ten-thirty we drive home, taciturn and weary. Annette is still awake. Plumbers from the service center had come and had offered to repair our defective pipe system "privately." We carry our purchases up from the car, unpack, and put everything away. I read one or two pages yet in the *Radetzky March*,[9] then go to sleep.

[8] Bodo Uhse (1904-1963), writer, like the Sterns emigrated as an antifascist to Mexico by way of France and Spain (participation in the struggle if the International Brigades); in 1948 returned to what later became the German Democratic Republic; 1949-1958 editor-in-chief of the periodical *Aufbau*; 1954-1962 member of the executive committee of PEN in the German Democratic Republic. (G.W.)

[9] Joseph Roth, 1932. (Ed.)

I am describing that day two days later, i.e. on Saturday, the twenty-ninth of September. Tinka turned seventeen yesterday (a date that she seemed to fear and endeavored to ignore). In the morning I dreamed about her. We were visiting a doctor (unfortunately I have totally forgotten the image of his practice that was strongly visible to my inner eye after I awoke, as well as the cause and all of the other very involved circumstances) who told me that Tinka was healthy (about which I was relieved), but that in the course of the next eight years she would change from a pretty to an ugly girl (I even *saw* that new, ugly face; it had the features of a severely mentally impaired child). I was startled and figured out that she would be twenty-five. The doctor told me that the process could not be stopped. But Tinka did not know anything about it, and I immediately told myself that she must never learn of it. I awakened disturbed. Did not tell anyone about the dream. (A few days before that I had read Eichhorn's story of the illness of his mentally retarded grandson Peter: "Is That a Senseless Life?" Besides that, I worry about Tinka's increasingly severe back pains, which result from her spinal scoliosis.)

On the twenty-seventh—for the first time in years!—I did not think about the fact that it was the "day of the year," until the afternoon, during the drive to Berlin, specifically at the major crossroads just this side of Adlershof. This realization touched me in a remarkable way. What was occupying me to that extent?

I got up early, as always, fixed breakfast, ate scrambled eggs with Tinka in the kitchen. Tinka is always grouchy now in the mornings, barely responsive. The prospect of the hardly satisfying (on the contrary: frustrating) school puts her in a bad mood. She "sags." Besides that, she informs me that she is definitely a "late riser" and for that reason has not yet "gotten started" in the morning. It occurs to me that the next day is her birthday and that I must still buy a pie crust, birthday candles, and flowers. As always, we listen to the news and to commentaries. Chile is the focus of our interest. (I am astounded that we hear hardly anything anymore about the successful night landing of the three American astronauts from Skylab, Alan Bean, Jack Lousma, and Owen Garriot.)

My satisfaction when Tinka gets enough vitamins in the morning and drinks milk. She leaves. I shower in the cellar (because the water heater in our bathroom is permanently out of order), then wash up. Gerd quickly goes shopping. I do the bedroom. He returns with Drechsler, the upholsterer, who measures our chairs and tells us how much upholstery cloth we need: 4.25 meters. He offers to upholster the chairs "privately," because he has an opening right now. Why is your name Drechsler (Turner) if you are an upholsterer? I ask. He says he enjoys his trade.

I make telephone calls, first to Günter de Bruyn [1] regarding the appointment with Jurij Trifonov [2] this evening, in which

[1] Günter de Bruyn (b. 1926), writer, friend of the Wolfs, exchanged views with them; (see: C.W., *"Preisrede—Laudatio zur Verleihung des Lion Feuchtwanger-Prises an de Bruyn 1981* [Prize speech—Laudation on the Occasion of the Conferral of the Lion Feuchtwanger Prize on de Bruyn in 1981]," *Werke*, pp. 210ff.; de Bruyn about C.W., *"Fragment eines Frauenportraits* [Fragment of a Woman's Portrait]" in *Liebes und andere Erklärungen* [*Declarations of Love and Other Declarations*], Berlin, 1972; B. Pinkerneil, *"Gespräche über C.W.* [Conversations about C.W.]," *Text und Kritik*, 46/1994; G.W., occasioned by G. de Bruyn's *"Mein Brandenburg* [My Brandenburg]" in *Die Poesie hat immer recht* [*Poesy is always right*], Berlin, 1998). (G.W.)

[2] Jurij Trifonov (1925-1981), Russian writer; his father was executed as a Party functionary in 1917 (see: *Im Widerschein des Feuers* [*In the Reflection of the Fire*]); wrote

they had initially wanted to participate. But now it turns out that they already saw Tr. the previous evening and walked with him along Friedrichstrasse. As a result, Günter wants to return to Blabber immediately. At the moment he is so nicely involved in work, is right in the middle of it, and it is so much fun for him that he feels that any interruption is annoying. Mischka[3] calls and we make an appointment for Saturday afternoon. Annette asks me to bring the cough syrup for the baby girl, who still has a cough.

At a quarter to ten, I sit down and begin working with the notes for the eighth chapter: "War." The usual four sheets of paper are laid out, on which I note the usual "four levels": travel level, level of the past, manuscript level, level of the present. I now dubiously approach the focal point of the self-analysis (entry into the young girls' club and what followed that). These notations are always fun for me. Later they will no longer stand separately next to each other, but merge with each other. Sometimes I consciously experience that moment of melting together (in an artistic idea); on that morning I only reached the point that it became clear to me that I should begin this chapter with a description of my preparations for work. (Today, a day later, probably under the influence of a piece by Kütemeyer: "Illness in Its Humanity," I already take note of the fact that I must present this entire complex of ideas, "war," as a pathological knot in the lives of these people.)

socially critical novels (a. o. *Das Haus an der Moskwa* [The House on the Moskva], 1977); in friendly contact and exchange of views with the Wolfs. (G.W.)

[3] Mischka (b. 1905): Wilhelmina Slawitzkaja, from a Jewish-German family; born in Riga; worked as a communist beginning in 1928 in the Comintern in Dimitrov's office; married the communist functionary Kurt Müller, who entered a German concentration camp in 1936, was declared dead to his wife, but, freed from Sachsenhausen in 1945, was a delegate for the Communist Party of Germany in the federal parliament. In 1953 he was arrested by the Russian KGB as an "English spy," returned to Germany in 1955, where he saw his wife Mischka (meanwhile married to Naum Sawitzki, whom she had met in a concentration camp and with whom she had been exiled from 1936 to 1955) again through the mediation of Lev Kopelev and Heinrich Böll. Came together with the Wolfs several times. (G.W.)

Could only work until twelve o'clock. With the mail came a letter from Helga Pf.,[4] from which the fact suddenly emerged that her husband is seventy years old. Now many things became clear to me. She found a father substitute in him, a man who surely no longer gets too close to her very often. Proudly she reports about her success in feeding his birthday guests and describes their trip to Italy together ("Of all the cities in Italy, Florence is my favorite").

Fix lunch. We eat grit sausage, fried potatoes, cauliflower, tomato and pepper salad. Tinka is now usually able to eat with us because she has only five classes. As always, she complains about "the K. woman" (history and civics), with whom she spoiled her last chance when the woman overheard Tinka and her art teacher in a conversation about her spinsterhood. ("I feel sorry for her, of course, but what should I do . . . ?") Her second problem is Mrs. M. in German. Just listen to what she has thought up this time: Tinka sits down on the coconut mat in the vestibule and reads aloud from her file folder the four points that they will "apply" as criteria for any book or other work by any author. (Of the kind: how does the author reflect reality in his work? etc.) Simply aids for an insecure teacher who has no real connection to literature. We try to encourage Tinka. But she is already asking for the first work to which she must "apply" those points: Büchner's *Woyzeck*.[5] I give her the Reclam edition, say that she was not supposed to get it until tomorrow for her birthday: "Terrific!" By the way, she says that most of the people in her class have no real feeling for *Woyzeck*. The language is foreign to them, the contractions.

Gerd: Have you seen how red the sumac trees are? Some-

---

[4] Helga Pfeiffer: school friend of C.W.'s. (G.W.)
[5] Karl Georg Büchner (1813-1837) was a German dramatist and writer of prose. His unfinished and most famous play, *Woyzeck*, was the first literary work in German whose main characters were members of the working class. (Ed.)

what early, but pretty—Tinka: What sumac trees? (She is not familiar with anything in the garden.)

The most important midday news: In Chile the junta has posted rewards of 4000 pesos (? . . . or whatever Chilean currency is called) each for the capture of seventeen leading members of the *Unidad Popular*. All political parties are prohibited. They are supposed to have destroyed a secret partisan training camp. (In the *Märkische Volksstimme*[6] our text with the signatures of the Potsdam writers was printed: . . . "incapable of having a clear view of the brief period of time that remains for their dictatorship . . . " By request we changed it to "limited" period of time. But even that is probably too optimistic. A nightmare, and our predominantly pleasant daily life continues unchanged . . .)—The American senate rejected the most-favored-nation clause for trade with the Soviet Union, as long as Nixon cannot prove that the USSR is permitting the emigration of its citizens who desire to emigrate and does not require more than a nominal fee for it—Initial commentaries call this decision a very serious obstacle to the Nixon-Brezhnev politics of détente—In addition, they report about Herbert Wehner's special tours. While in Moscow with a delegation of West German legislators, he immediately declared at the airport that in the Federal Republic they had "overdrawn" lately with respect to Berlin, and then engaged in secret talks with unnamed Soviet partners, which the Christian Democratic Union calls a "scandal." Wehner let it be seen that of late he is no longer in full conformity with the Eastern politics of the federal government—

Tinka and I wash up together; Gerd is still looking for secondary literature on Büchner for her. It is almost two o'clock and we lie down. Tinka declares that she also wants to read *Buridan's Ass*.[7] Before going to sleep I read a little bit of *Mira-*

---

[6] *Märkische Volksstimme*: daily newspaper in Potsdam. (G.W)
[7] *Buridans Esel* (*Buridan's Ass*): novel by Günter de Bruyn. (G.W.)

cle Worker II[8] that does not move me much, so that I do not move ahead. While we are getting up and getting dressed, Gerd casts prophylactic reproaches at me, saying that I will undoubtedly let Henniger[9] talk me into taking on a function again. During the discussion the subject comes up that I always talk for a long time on the telephone (which has not been the case for a long time, and I say that, too, without success), that I always need people (which is true); undoubtedly I would sit for who knows how long with Henniger; what did I have to talk with him about anyway? He, Gerd, would be outside again in ten minutes. That I can never say "No"!—I become irritated because I do not see any reason for these rebukes and because Gerd seems to experience the difference of my nature on that point in a purely negative way, but I tell myself that there would be no point in getting upset, surrender of course, and then I am upset.

Tinka lies in the vestibule for a long time and sleeps. I wake her up and put a piece of the previous day's plunder in front of her. Agreement about taking a key along and coming home. Sunglasses are quickly fetched; it has gotten light outside. I have put on my new dark blue pants, with it the colorful red blouse, black leather coat, and the supposedly "colorful" shoes that Gerd just resignedly called a "wrong purchase," because I wear them too seldom. Piles of bags are taken along, as always. Departure always like for an expedition.

We stop in Teltow. I obtain no birthday candles, nor a pie crust. To say nothing of flowers. Then we silently drive the stretch that I was able to drive precisely in my thoughts that morning. Gerd curses several times when he "gets stuck" behind tractors and trucks at town exits; he complains about the roads, especially as we come into Berlin in Schöneweide,

---

[8] *Wundertäter II* (*The Miracle Worker II*): novel by Erwin Strittmatter. (G.W.)

[9] Gerhard Henniger (1928-1997), First Secretary of the Writers' Union of the German Democratic Republic. (G.W.)

and watches as a Wartburg, which he had shaken off several times, moves past us in Adlershof after all. (Soon after the point where it occurred to us that it is the "day of the year.") We do not talk much; I am not thinking about anything special. On the square in front of the State Council building, where the Palace of the Republic is being built, the pile driver is still active. Gerd lets me off at the Writers' Union. I still have some time, buy a set of underwear for Tinka in the clothing store, black woolen gloves for myself, then look in the baby shop for Jana articles, but do not find anything that could tempt me.

Henniger has to be summoned. He offers me coffee and begins a rather noncommittal chat about the convention preparations. (The cat just ran out, and I got myself a cognac, Martell, and put on a new record: the Bach family.) I am informed about the convention: what will take place when, who will speak, how the foreign delegates will be dealt with, how long everything is supposed to last, etc. The coffee comes. We both know it is a matter of preliminary fencing. I ask myself (influenced by Gerd's warnings) if I am perhaps too obliging. (At the end Gerd had said to me—programmed me: Be firm without being obstinate.) I praise the Union's initiatives for social questions, for the establishment of a periodical—decisions that are supposed to be "pushed through" even before the convention. H. is as hasty and overzealous as ever. I remember having heard that after the ninth plenum he did have the courage to oppose the series of articles that was coming out in *Neues Deutschland* (which was intended to contain nine pieces), so that it was stopped—I would not have believed him capable of that.

Then he comes out with the expected "request" (why do my hands now begin to sweat?). I am supposed to become a member of the executive committee. Of course I decline decisively, albeit obligingly. He explains that the executive committee has

become an authentic administrative organ, should be strengthened, that the suggestion came from Anna, she pleads with me
to agree—I repeat my refusal (actually: my difficulty in being
able to say no. Others do not get into this situation in the first
place). I cite my work load, my impending trip to America,
that I am on the PEN executive committee, and that I have
enough with those things—H. insists, describes work possibilities. Back and forth for more than half an hour, during which
I reveal my true reasons a piece at a time or at least hint at
them, a balancing act, not to relinquish too much of that—
especially not the fundamental things. Thus I say that I have
doubts about the Union's work possibilities, do not want to be
invested with any responsible leadership function in it. The last
convention and other similar and worse cultural-political periods had made such a lasting impression on me that I could not
brush off the suspicion that exactly the same things could happen again. (I could work against that very thing in the executive committee, H. countered, and it was difficult for me not to
laugh out loud.) A good statement occurred to me: Such a
function would "burden" me much too much. I repeated that
several times. Naturally I would assist otherwise, wherever
possible. As I am also doing now. Right at the end—he should
not take that as the central motif—I become cocky and see
myself induced to say that it would also be better for them if I
were not there. I would never sign such resolutions as the one
on the occasion of the awarding of the Nobel Prize to Solzhenitsyn. (Voilà. In addition I say—oh, we cautious people!—that
does not mean, of course, that I "identify completely" with S.)

All right. He is very sorry, but must simply take note of
everything. We agree that he will dwell on the reasons as little
as possible. Then I leave, buy paper napkins across the street,
and meet Gerd on the corner of Unter den Linden. It is five-
thirty and is starting to get dark. I like Friedrichstrasse in the
evening light. Then we drive to the Hellerau store and buy the

blue-green upholstery material after all. We were originally eager to get the green cloth with the red in it, but it is no longer available. Then you simply convince yourself, this one here, of course, is "also pretty."

The hotel Unter den Linden, we call up to Jurij Trifonov's room, and he comes. I go to the toilet; the toilet attendant sits on her stool in the corner and asks everyone to leave the door open. Gerd is standing in the hall with Jurij; I would have recognized him. Gotten broader, says Gerd. (Today he says, he had "lost it," he remembered him as being more slender and lively.) Jurij has a cold. We go to the pharmacy across the street, obtain throat lozenges, cold drops, and aminophenazon. Drive off. In the car we already ask him how the colloquium was (Topic: Conflicts in Life—Conflicts in Literature). He simply laughs. I say that I have just heard that it was the best one ever—Well, then he could imagine how the others were.

On the way the topic of conversation immediately turns to the recent policy of no longer jamming certain Western radio stations in Moscow.

We drove to the Ermeler Haus restaurant, refined quiet, coolness, draft; until nearly closing time we are the only guests in our little nook. All of the waiters in tails. We are served by a young one with a child's face and a child's curls. We order veal steak *au four*, Gerd an exotic duck dish. (During the hour and a half we begin to freeze.) At the end little pancakes filled with pineapple, which are baked and filled at the table. All of it (a cognac, a vodka, and juice in addition) for ninety marks in the end.

Table conversation: exchange of information about Solzhenitsyn and Sakharov[10] (we agree that Sakharov, through his appeal to the Chilean junta with respect to Neruda, hurt himself and proved to be politically naïve. On the other hand Tri-

[10] Andrei Dmitrievich Sakharov (1921-1989), eminent Soviet nuclear physicist, dissident, and human rights activist. Winner of the Nobel Peace Prize, 1975. (Ed.)

fonov says: It is great, what the two of them, Sakharov and his wife, did, what they set in motion). What Trifonov has written in recent years: three stories and a historical novel about the Russian terrorists of the previous century, which are supposed to appear here. How his escaped cousin—Dyomin—who published a book in the West and works for Radio Liberty, makes any trip to the West impossible for him. Which people sign the appeals against Solzhenitsyn with regard to the Nobel Prize: first and foremost the literary union secretaries, and among them unfortunately Aitmatov[11] and Bykov[12] as well. But why did the old, almost dead Katayev[13] find it necessary? we ask ourselves. Trifonov cites an open letter from a woman (was it Chukovskaya?[14]) against those signers, whom she declares to be "dead" at the moment of their signing . . . We also talk, later, about Mandelstam's second book *Century of the Wolves*, which Trifonov, despite some injustices to some people, also considers to be a "great book." (Just as he does Maksimov's *The Sixth Day of the Creation*[15].) He does not hold Kaverin's *Double Portrait*[16] in such high esteem; he thinks it is too "literary." Nor does he feel that it was right that Kaverin wrote a

---

[11] Chingiz Aitmatov (b. 1928), Russian writer from Kyrgyzstan; father a victim of Stalinist terror in 1937; became famous through his narrative *Jamila* (1962) and *The White Steamship* (1972); multiple meetings with C.W.; in 1989 he appointed her a member of the editorial board of the periodical for world literature *Inostranaya Literatura* (*Foreign Literature*) in Moscow. (G.W.)

[12] Vasil Bykov (b. 1924), writer from Belarus; became known through his critical novel about the Second World War (*Die Schlinge* [*The Noose*], 1972). (G.W.)

[13] Valentin Katayev (1897-1986), Russian writer. (Ed.)

[14] Lidiya Korneyevna Chukovskaya (1907-1996), writer, human rights activist; friend of Anna Akhmatova; wrote *Ein leeres Haus* (*An Empty House*), Zurich, 1967; *Untertauchen* (*Submerging*), Zurich, 1975; *Aufzeichnungen über Anna Achmatowa. Tagebuch* (*Notes about Anna Akhmatova. Diary*), Tübingen, 1987. (G.W.)

[15] Vladimir Maksimov (1930-1985), Russian writer of socially critical novels like the one mentioned here, *Die sieben Tage der Schöpfung* (1972); emigrated to Paris in 1974, there editor-in-chief of the periodical *Kontinent*. (G.W.)

[16] Venjamin Kaverin (1902-1989), Russian writer of socially critical novels like *Das doppelte Portrait* (1973), here the topic of the conversation. (G.W.)

rudely negative letter to the old, ill Nadeshda Mandelstam about her second book. (Impression that Trifonov is one of those people who are "out of danger" and developed patterns of behavior that permit them to live without the possibility that their hearts will be touched and destroyed.) Later, when we are with Annette and Rainer, he tells about the conflict concerning whether or not, after Tvardovski's dismissal,[17] he should continue to publish in *Novy Mir*. After a year he did it. Tvardovski understood him, but others criticized him for it.

At the table he also talks about his new wife ("a good woman"); she is also a belletrist, they live in two apartments, and his daughter (21) does not accept this woman. It is very complicated. It would be better if she married, but that does not happen either.

The food is good, the atmosphere in the restaurant too exclusive and lifeless. It would have been better if we had gone to a simpler restaurant. Tr. tells about a committee that has now been established and determines translation policy. Bunin[18] is on that committee. He is not a "limpid" man. Tr. voices funny judgments. About a participant in the colloquium he says: He is a nothing, zero point zero. (I correct: Zero point zero one.) About the trial of Yakir and Krassin[19]: The result is equal to zero (I: –100), because no Western correspondents were there.

We drive to the children's place, are frozen stiff, and have to warm up in the car. Annette is in her rust-red sweater, looks good and "cozy." We confer at first for a few minutes about Jana: that she now still has a cough (however, she does not

[17] Aleksandr T. Tvardovski (Russian 1910-1971), formerly editor-in-chief of *Novy Mir*. (Ed.)

[18] Nikolai Bunin: Russian translator from German. (G.W.)

[19] In 1973, after being tried and found guilty, Victor Krassin and Pyotr Yakir officially admitted their "guilt" for having passed "anti-Soviet" material to the West. The trial was condemned as a mere "show trial" and the confessions were said to have been forced out of the two men. (Ed.)

cough in our presence). I ask myself if a resistance of the little body to the crib is not being expressed there. At ten o'clock, when she has to take her penicillin, we take her into the large room. It is difficult for her to wake up, but she does not cry at all, as always. Simply looks at us sternly.

On the wall is a new picture by Hermann: "*Selbstportrait mit Pappnase* (Self-portrait with False Nose)." Good, but somewhat too direct for me. From the photographs that he inherited from his grandmother Rainer has created two montages and hung them on the wall in old frames. An old, very beautiful chair now stands in the corner. We quickly make tea. We have also brought rum along. Because of his cold, Jurij is quite worn down. The conversation initially focuses on films. Annette tells us that she has just seen pictures of Neruda's funeral on television, the thousands who walked behind the coffin and the many along the street. Many wept. They shouted: Long live Allende, long live the *Unidad popular*. They sang the *Internationale*. She was very impressed.

Later a few old issues of *Der Spiegel* go around. I read a few sentences about Gabriele Wohmann, who has been married for twenty years to a teacher who is six years older than she is, who calmly says: With the husbands in her books, she did not always mean me . . . In addition there is material, published by lawyers for the Baader-Meinhof Group, about the "torture" in prisons of the Federal Republic. (Solitary confinement, not enough to drink during a hunger strike.) The whole thing composed in a pronouncedly rude tone: "Head Federal Pig Martin" etc. Unfortunately causes shrugs because we are reminded of those who are really tortured. Trifonov is interested in Western television. (In Moscow he watches only sports. The question is discussed as to whether the Moscow team can and will really go to Chile to the world championship return match.) Just then there is a report about new measures to revive Polish villages and Polish agriculture. In vain we wait for the reading of Pavel Kohout's *Manifesto*,[20] which he gave to Austrian Radio. Then Trifonov is tired. At ten-thirty we leave and drop him off at the hotel. He says, with reference to Annette and Rainer: Nice young people. I: It is good when you can keep your children as friends.

On the drive back we hear the report of a Western correspondent, who realistically and even prejudicially describes the conditions in the stadium in Santiago, where at least 4,000 people are being held captive and waiting for their hearings. The weeping women outside, all of them poor people. How a new batch of prisoners is brought in on a bus: "Supporters of a Marxist regime that did not have a single political prisoner. Images that I would never have wished to see in Chile . . ."

A nightmare, day and night.

The guard at the Berlin border flashes a green signal from his hut. Does he at least have a little stove inside? Gerd asks. A horrible job. The most useless people!

There is still a light on in Tinka's room. It is twenty minutes to twelve. Next to the telephone lies a note: "Roehrichts were here. Brought beautiful dahlias and Karl-Hermann's *Joys*."[21]

Tinka attended a reading of Plenzdorf's[22] from his new play based on *Buridan's Ass*. She tells how full it was, describes the changes in the figure of Miss Broder. Then she had listened to a "fabulous" Armstrong program on television: One should undoubtedly take more interest in jazz.

We carry our Berlin purchases upstairs. The cat Napoleon shows up and wants to eat yet. I get Tinka's birthday presents out of Gerd's closet and set them up in the vestibule: without

[20] Pavel Kohout (b. 1928), Czech writer; after the collapse of the "Prague Spring" of 1968, under publication prohibition; has lived in Vienna since 1978. (G.W.)

[21] Karl-Hermann Roehricht (b. 1928), painter, writer; lived at the time in Freienbrink near Berlin; friends with C. and G.W. (see also: *Unsere Freunde, die Maler* [*Our Friends, The Painters*], Berlin, 1995). (G.W.)

[22] Ulrich Plenzdorf (b. 1934), writer, screenplay author; wrote a play and later the screenplay based on Günter de Bruyn's novel *Buridans Esel*. (G.W.)

flowers, without candles! Blouse, skirt, underwear, socks, many books. Egg liqueur. Chocolate. We count off the minutes until midnight; Tinka sits on the stairs. Then she is permitted to enter the vestibule. She is hugged, a casual congratulation, she looks at the gifts, we drink a toast with egg liqueur. From Annette a card with a Modigliani woman on the front, and the wish that she may become as slender again as this woman . . . She just couldn't resist that, says Tinka.

The day is over. Great weariness. In bed I read a few more paragraphs in W. Kütemeyer. Encounter the "case" of those who suffer from rheumatoid arthritis: inflammation as a sign of deeper existential problems. Think about my recently arthritic knee joints. See half anxiously, half curiously (yes: hungrily) all that still lies in store for me, even literarily, so that perhaps the mechanical process can be interrupted after all. Twelve-thirty. Sleep.

(On that day there was also a politburo resolution on the improvement of the health system in the newspaper—understandable following the flight of doctors in recent months.)

I have given myself a vacation from the manuscript today; it is a liberation. I woke up early at five and read in the third diary of Anaïs Nin, of all passages the one in which she describes her collapse and her gradual healing by a psychotherapist. Her case is completely different from mine. She suffered under the obligation of having to go all out—both psychologically and physically—for other people. I probably suffer from a dependency on the good will and the sympathy of others, a result of my childhood and the dependency on authority figures. After every meeting or session—as they now pile up again—I am a mental wreck, especially when I have also spoken myself and must always tell myself afterward that I let myself get carried away again and revealed too much. A feeling of shame always remains. I ask myself then if I really spoke for the sake of the cause. That happened to me after the conversation with Hoffmann[1] in the PEN executive committee, and yesterday again, after the debate in the Academy about the letter from Dieter Noll[2] on the situation in the schools. I asked if they actually knew that tens of thousands of students unwillingly, disgustedly, go to school, that thousands of parents do not know what they should advise their children

---

[1] Hans-Joachim Hoffmann (1929-1994), director of the culture section of the Central Committee of the Socialist Unity Party, beginning in 1973 Minister of Culture of the German Democratic Republic. (G.W.)

[2] Dieter Noll (b. 1927), writer. Novels: *Die Abenteuer des Werner Holt* (*The Adventures of Werner Holt*), Berlin, 1960/63; *Kippenberg*, Berlin, 1973. (G.W.)

with respect to their behavior in school, and that thousands of teachers are tired of school and sick. I shared my observation: On the one hand this large group of indifferent, inexperienced, undifferentiated young people, who are basically bored and seek intoxication. On the other side, those who have completely internalized the social standards and are one day faced with a fiasco like this Jurk, whose path I briefly—and perhaps superfluously—sketched out. Then Neutsch[3] broke in: But there are also totally different examples, and what is the point of this pessimism again?

Yesterday on the way back—with Eduard Claudius, who said that basically all of that no longer affects him—and in the evening I was still irritated, resolved again just not to speak anymore in the future, not to push my way to the front. Notice at the same time that deep inside I really cannot stop tying continuing hopes to phases in which a greater freedom of movement is granted to us and to me as well: just as if it were possible to renew this social coexistence once more from the ground up after all, which now threatens to peter out and ossify in clichés, follies, and unproductiveness. Each of them had to know that the schools are only a symptom of that, and nobody said it. It is these very half measures, this dishonesty that gives rise to my shame afterward. I reproach myself for my cowardice and at the same time know that boldness would not be of any use. I feel that I am walking out onto a field again on which I can only lose—in the worst case, myself.

This specific fear is the deepest layer of my irritation.

I came home soaked with sweat, battered, and tired. Talked briefly with Tinka, who soon left for gymnastics. Bathed. A call came from Herta Wegner, saying that my father was lying in the hospital, in the liver ward. Taken aback, I asked if the doc-

[3] Erik Neutsch (b. 1930), writer. Novels: *Die Spur der Steine* (*The Trail of the Stones*), Halle/S., 1964; *Der Friede im Osten* (*Peace in the East*), Halle/S., 1974-1989. (G.W.)

tor considered his condition to be serious. No, no. An inflammation that could be treated better there than at home. For the first time I addressed her hesitantly and with conscious effort using the informal "*du*": acknowledgment of the rights that she—now also as his nurse as well—has acquired with respect to my father. This morning—I had resolved to make it "easy" for myself today—I ordered a taxi to go to the hospital at lunchtime.

Last night I talked with Tinka about what had been discussed during the afternoon at the Academy on the topic of school. She was tired, had a headache—as she unfortunately often does now—but was very loose and open. She was full of her afternoon with Stephan: A really clever and nice boy! Who had then suddenly said: Studying philosophy—is actually impossible. When he placed his signature on the application, he had had misgivings similar to those that he had with his signature on the three-year commitment to the army.

Tinka wants to do only things that can be done from within. Has she actually never felt the need for functions, for "social" activity? Never! she says so convincingly that we have to laugh. She really has never needed it. Her opinion is that in contact with the leaders—on whatever level—you can only become bent and corrupt. Does she then, I ask, also have misgivings now, when she applies for the stage direction class? No, she says decisively. Not that, not at all. But neither would I break down in tears if it did not work out. She does not want to make herself dependent on external decisions about her life: If I am not accepted—well, then I will still go on living—She sees the only real value of life in honest relationships with other people, in a web of friendships—Aren't you dependent at all on the opinion that teachers and other authorities have of you?—No! she says with conviction. Not at all!—She thinks that perhaps we silently reproach her for not necessarily finding her happiness in work, as we do. Annette is different in that respect, although both of them were raised by us . . . But in different phases, I say—She wants to know if her phase is better or worse—Perhaps better, I say—Because I can perhaps become happier? she asks—As evidence for her lack of concern, she tells how she quickly withdrew from a student newspaper when she noticed that it was going to indulge in empty talk. "I'm simply not available for that, and that's all there is to it."

Later, she still protested against the term "generation conflict": I think that is simply stupid. You are not a different generation from me. Of course you're older, fortunately, and have different problems than I do. It's good that I appreciate this, and that we show each other where we are different, and also where we don't understand each other. Obviously each of us sometimes reproaches the other with something, but I don't think it's with anything fundamental. I like it that way.

I was happy. She definitely did me good, and I told her that. Then we looked for two poems that she could recite in her sponsor's brigade on the anniversary, and she made comical, sarcastic comments about the possible reception of this or that text that I suggested to her.

Now it is a quarter to twelve in the middle of the day. A magnificent roaring rain just began.

For the third time somebody calls who wants to talk to the CI, Central Institute, which now has a number similar to ours.

In the evening I read more in the diary of Anaïs Nin, slept from eleven on, but woke up at five because of my inner disquiet. Continued to read. Also found comments about the fact that a woman who is creative is plagued more severely by feelings of guilt than a man: because she takes something away from the man, to which, according to her innermost belief, he is entitled (and from the children: how well I know that feeling!). And because she feels more guilt with respect to the people that she describes in this or that form. Apparently it is more difficult for women to "invent" their figures than it is for men—Now that very thing, of course, is my—one of my—problems at the moment. When I gave myself a vacation from work on the book today, I felt very, very relieved, recognized under how much tension I constantly find myself through this work pressure. That I apparently exert and force myself more intensely than I think. (Now—in spite of this "vacation"—but what do I mean here by "in spite of"?—I have a migraine today, which I can perhaps keep under a certain degree of control with Titretta.)

At six I happen to look outside. The cat is standing down below, looking up at the bedroom window. I let her in. She does not want to eat, lies down at my feet on the bed. Tinka, who gets up at six and has to go to work, shows me her passport pictures before she goes. The one is stupid, she thinks, the other fat. Before that we perform a whistling concert through the doors.

She leaves. I lie down to sleep. I think: Now I should have a dream that illuminates my difficulties for me. I dream the following:

I am having a birthday. We are living in a house that is foreign to me, but in the dream it is familiar and comfortable. Large, bright rooms that merge with one another. Only my family is there. I go to a table where I probably expect to find flowers. But there are none there (nobody sent flowers), and that disappoints me somewhat. Then the doorbell rings. I go out through a kind of terrace door and see that several cars are parked along the street (among them, by the way, a light blue VW). Behind a post to which the bell is attached (the way it is here at our place), the visitors throng: six men dressed in gray gabardine overcoats, with gray hats on their heads, emphatically discreet, but by their numbers promising nothing good. Smiling and greeting me, they come up the stairs toward me (this stairway again resembles our flight of stairs in Bad Frankenhausen). All of them are faceless except for one who has a Menjou goatee and is their spokesman. With a smile he says that he congratulates me on my birthday and that he has a suggestion that I will undoubtedly welcome very much. I want to know what it is about before I let them in. On their behalf, for a nice fee, I am supposed to write a text in which I represent the views of the public in my own way. This text would be sent to all households, and everyone would be forced to read it. Well? A person could not wish for greater effectiveness—Horrified, but hiding my horror, I ask them to wait outside and go back into the house through a different entrance. Gerd wants to know what they want. I tell him while I hastily use an electric pot to make coffee, for which I am very thirsty. Gerd says hardly anything, just looks at me intently. I know it myself, of course. I drink only a swallow of the coffee, feel strengthened, and go to the people at the door. On the right side there is a row of rabbit hutches. The six men are standing there, smiling—as I now see, there is also a woman among them—and ecstatically petting the rabbits: demonstrating their German disposition. The woman turns around and laughs at me hideously; she has teeth like a horse—But now they want to come in—They could do that, I say. But the matter has already been decided: I would not accept the assignment— The man with the Menjou goatee says soothingly: Now, now, a person really could not decide that on the doorstep! As a many-footed mass they push their way into the veranda—Or, says the man with the goatee, smiling maliciously—or should we bring you the telephone book?—Why that? I say—So that you will grasp how many readers you will lose by your refusal—

I woke up when the telephone rang, was determined not to go answer it, and instead recounted the dream to myself, which I immediately liked very much and which brought me a great deal of relief. When it had rung eleven times, I ran downstairs after all. An irritable, impersonal woman's voice (as if it belonged to the dream): Well, who is there? I, irritated: Whom do you want?!—She: The CI—I, impolitely: Wrong number!

The next morning, September 19, a Thursday at 9:20. I am sitting on the terrace in bright autumn sunlight—yesterday, of course, the weather was hazy, melancholy, gray—today, clear colors, little air movement, a veil of thin clouds across the sky, with patches of deep blue. Youthful voices coming from the stadium. The construction machines at the swimming pool are silent today. Birds can be heard. I sense that I must continue writing in the diary, that I should take another day off from the manuscript. I cannot "work"—as if this here were not work!—when too many unfinished fragments have built up inside me. The basic motif of my writing, coming to terms with myself, prevails rigorously; I can and must not ignore it, as often as it seems to me to be my basic weakness: "subjectivism."

Quickly now, before I get busy on yesterday again, my morning dream of today: At a table in a room that is not large several people sit putting stamps on addressed envelopes. Among them Anna Seghers, Steffi Spira,[4] Günter Kunert (who, however, looks different than he does "in reality"), and a man whom I think I recognize as Ulrich Plenzdorf. I am standing in the next room, looking through the half-open door. Anna Seghers says that Kunert has never really seemed to her like a person from another generation. She says that to Steffi Spira while they all unwearyingly continue to lick the back sides of stamps and then stick the stamps on the envelopes—as if doing piecework. A.S. looks to the side and sees me standing in the doorway, and undoubtedly thinks that I am now envious of Kunert—and I am, but not very—and says to me: Nor are the two of us really strangers!—I see through her motive, but in spite of that I am quite happy about that admission, finally sit down—which I had wanted to do for a long time—next to

[4] Steffi Spira (1908-1995), actress, friend of Anna Seghers. (G.W.)

Kunert at the table, also lick stamps that all have different, brightly colored motifs, are for the most part quite large, and hardly fit on the envelopes; they often overlap the edges a great deal. Kunert stands up, walks around the table, intimates to me that in reality A.S. really does not know much about him. For example, she doesn't know that his father always whipped him on the legs when he was a child. He makes the motion of whipping . . .

Explanations for that: yesterday I received a letter from Kurt Batt,[5] saying that I should write my contribution for the volume being prepared for Anna Seghers's seventy-fifth birthday. In the evening I was still thinking about it, and that it should deal with "gratitude." The dream probably expresses my resistance to that. Plenzdorf is among the three editors of an anthology, of whom one, Klaus Schlesinger, called me yesterday and also requested a contribution from me. I had thought of Kunert often in recent days because I want to ask him if he is going to remain on the editorial board for the Chile volume, even though Biermann's poem is not being accepted, with unacceptable justification. I will withdraw from it—I cannot explain the stamps. "Sticking stamps on," an expression from home during the war; but in that case the reference was to food stamps.

So back to yesterday. I baked pancakes for my breakfast after I had taken two Togal (the beginning of a headache) and had enjoyed a cold shower. Drank coffee. On the radio they expressed themselves in derogatory terms about the displeasure that President Ford caused with the announcement of the amnesty for Nixon—and in certain circles with the simultaneous announcement of the very limited amnesty for Vietnam conscientious objectors. The plane with the three Japanese ter-

[5] Kurt Batt (1931-1975), literary scholar, in 1961 chief publisher's reader in the Hinstorff Publishing Company. (G.W.)

rorists who had the French ambassador and several members of the embassy in The Hague in their power for a hundred hours took off in the direction of the Near East. 750,000 DM ransom. Ford let the admission slip out that the CIA spent a significant amount of money in Chile to undermine Allende. After all, all major powers did the same in their respective spheres of influence. The CIA did not arrange for Allende's fall . . . Among other things this report continues to saw the legs off of Kissinger's chair, who was, after all, Nixon's security advisor.

Listening to the news in the morning is a kind of addiction.

I clean up downstairs and make the beds. Then Tinka comes home early. They had let them leave at work because yesterday was an ÖKULEI (Economic-Cultural Direction System) event; everyone had gotten drunk and could not appear because of hangovers, not even her immediate supervisor. Tinka brings Brummel along. Detlef appears later. They listen to loud records in her room and smoke a lot, which disturbs me. Drink tea. (I just moved my mosaic stand and the chair from the left to the furthest right corner of the balcony, where the sun will soon emerge again from behind the poplar tree. In the shade it is very cool. The cat Napoleon comes up the pine tree and prowls around my legs.)

I talk with Brummel. Yeees—if school were fun! he says. That would be perfect. But nothing will come of it. That would only lead to psychosis.

So I am writing in my diary, and I do not mean this report. The mail. Nothing special. Newspapers. As always, I leaf through them in ten minutes. In *Die Junge Welt* it says that I recited the Neruda poem "Insomnia" at the Neruda tribute in the Congress Hall ("In the middle of the night I ask myself: What will happen to Chile? What will happen to my poor, poor, dark country?") with personal perplexity. I am perplexed!

Rainer comes, brings books. We talk for half an hour. I about the pedagogy discussion yesterday, he about the discussion with the Hungarian film directors on the weekend.[6] How a totally different language prevails there, a self-awareness that is not attainable for us. "The Party secretary stands *behind* the camera!" is one of their maxims. From our side stupid appeasement by the DEFA film agency directorate. Rainer blurts out criticism of them: "The others always come and show us their films, and we always stand there and give reasons why we can't do anything." As it always is with Rainer, a slight self-consciousness on both our parts in personal conversation. I encourage him to take a look at *Franziska Linkerhand*.[7] He says that Ralf Kirsten's film *A Pyramid for Me*[8] turned out to be very interesting, that it destroys the legend about the generation of the fifties. As a precaution it will not even be announced for delivery at all before the twenty-fifth anniversary of the German Democratic Republic.

I then continue to write, send Tinka shopping, dry her hair with the blow dryer, eat a few spoonfuls of bean soup, change clothes quick as a flash—brown suit—because the taxi driver has come half an hour early. He is pressed for time. We talk about the weather ("Somebody must have been naughty again"), the construction of the swimming pool, the construction of Stahnsdorfer Strasse, which is supposed to be opened for traffic on October 3rd.

Potsdam. I have him drop me off at the parking lot on Platz der Einheit, pay eighteen marks instead of 16.60, and he wishes me a good day. Stores closed. Sit down in the milk bar, always mindful of the motto of the day: Indulge yourself!—

---

[6] Discussion with Hungarian directors: discussion in the DEFA film agency. Albert Wilkening (1909-1990), 1952-1976 with interruptions chief director of the DEFA film agency. (G.W.)

[7] *Franziska Linkerhand*: novel from the literary estate of Brigitte Reimann; see above. (G.W.)

[8] *Eine Pyramide für mich* (*A Pyramid for Me*): novel by Karl-Heinz Jacobs (b. 1929), writer, as a film by Lothar Warneke (b. 1936) not realized. (G.W.)

and drink coffee with ice cream. The waitress stands at the bar with her back to us and eats soup, constantly interrupted by her work. She will get ulcers that way, I think. Does she have children? She is no longer young, not especially attractive, rather skinny, one of the nice kind.

Ten minutes to the hospital. Station I, room 5. This is where my mother also lay before she died. My father is lying in a six-bed ward on the left by the window. Herta Wegner is already there. Until noon my father had a medicine drip bag, in order to fight the inflammation quickly. Now the pain is gone. In spite of that, through his behavior he appeals strongly to our sympathy. Mrs. Wegner exhibits concern and solicitude down to the last detail. All the details of his condition yesterday, the doctor's visit, and the admission to the hospital are presented to me. Otherwise the conversation trickles along laboriously. The usual admonitions on my part. At a quarter to three I leave.

Buy some things for Tinka's birthday in the youth fashion shop, where the young girls crowd around polo blouses. These shopping situations always seem foreign to me—On Bassin-Platz at this time of day a bus going directly to Kleinmachnow leaves every twenty minutes. It has seats with fold-down boards and reading lamps. In the next seat two older women are conversing—to my amazement the one says that she is over 80—about the other woman's poodle. That she always has trouble because he pushes off his muzzle. The old woman says she will not get another dog; it is no longer worth it. Then they talk about Kleinmachnow physicians, whom they seem to know more or less well, calling them by name and characterizing them precisely. When she gets off at Lenin-Allee, the dog woman actually is warned by the driver that her dog is not wearing a muzzle.

My headache gets worse again. I get out at Meierfeld and shop yet in the market hall. It is drizzling. When I get home, a severe headache, am exhausted, tired. Tinka is sitting in front of the television set with her best friend Schnulli. They are watching *Love and Intrigue*. Both of them are smoking like crazy. It is very warm. Tinka has set the heat at 70. You must be crazy, I say, and jerk the window open. She rebukes me for that in the evening.

I lie down on the bed, read in Anaïs Nin's diary, sleep a little bit. The headache has eased when I get up at around seven in the evening. We eat supper: Tinka pancakes, I sausage sandwiches and tomatoes. Gerd calls. He is in Weimar; his stomach is bothering him. I warn him about the stomach flu that is supposedly going around. He then says there is a meningitis epidemic among children there; even Lotte Fürnberg's granddaughter is affected.—I immediately call Rainer to warn him about it because of Jana. I learn: Jana does not want to go to sleep. She is sitting at the table quite wide awake. I can hear her talking loudly in the background.

We turn off the television set and sit down at the round table. Tinka fills out the questionnaire for her college application. Then we work together on the autobiographical statement. Of course she is now crowding everything together exactly as I had predicted she would. She has not even been to the doctor yet. In a bad mood, I reproach her for that. She becomes obstinate and does not want to hear that. My headache becomes worse. Then we have to laugh again and produce absurd formulations and connections ("Because both of my parents are in the Socialist Unity Party, I have had piano lessons since I was nine years old." Or even the other way around). It is so terribly difficult. We cannot write candidly, are blocked.

At shortly before ten, both of us go to bed, quite frustrated and tired. Tinka does not look good, also often has headaches. We say "Good night" to each other a couple of times.

I listen to something else about Jean Améry's book *Lefeu, or*

The Demolition, read in Anaïs Nin's diary, turn pages, have a somewhat difficult time going to sleep. My head. An annoying obstacle. Woke up this morning at six-thirty without a headache.

B ad night. Gerd is unfortunately afflicted with allergies in this house. It can no longer be cat hair, but naturally (that is the right word for it!) we are surrounded here by green, which we all like so much, but which blooms at varying times, and by farmers, who spray all kinds of stuff. But through the open window shutter came clear air and the first cold nights are announcing their arrival. I did not go to sleep until about one-thirty, read again in Max Frisch's second diary[2]; there is a self-indictment there in a fictitious dialogue and hidden within quotation marks, the important sentences of which read:

"For example, you lived in a society that you call abominable. You demanded changes etc. That follows from your numerous words, not from your actions. Or do you feel that you acted according to your express creed? . . . According to the dossier you did not live very differently from other profiteers who feel that this society is in order."

. . . "So you contented yourself with being comparatively innocent?" "You remain silent."

So do I—my head is burning with thoughts about apparently insignificant things: Annette's move. What she still needs for the new apartment. The beginning of Tinka's studies at the directors' college (as expected, she is throwing herself completely into her studies, is learning in speech training to walk with her behind clenched together and to say "a lot of rub-

---

[1] Neu Meteln; beginning in 1974 and until 1983 second residence of the Wolfs in an old farmhouse in Mecklenburg. (G.W.)

[2] Max Frisch (1911-1991), friends with C. and G.W. (see also: Max Frisch, *Tagebuch 1966-1971* [*Diary 1966-1971*], *Werke*, Vol. VI, pp. 143ff.; C.W., *Werke*, Vol. VIII, pp. 21ff., Vol. XII, pp. 280ff.). (G.W.)

202 · CHRISTA WOLF

bish" with her lower jaw stuck out in order to obtain a sharper S. "I do not see myself as a film director," she says, "not that
you think that. But I simply will not let myself be driven to
despair.") I think about our own efforts with regard to changing apartments and moving from Kleinmachnow to Berlin. For
a whole afternoon we drove through hot Berlin, looking at
apartments that would be a possibility for a multilateral apartment exchange. Everywhere: the noise. Gradually you do
become horrified about how people live.

And again and again: Jana. How we should protect her so
that she does not suffer too much because of her parents'
divorce. How to relieve Annette, who is now too heavily burdened: living alone with a child and her profession. How to
help her find joy in her life again. Now that we have spent a
night there, her apartment, which was so difficult to obtain,
seems unreasonable to me. At night you begin to sweat, you
cannot open the windows because of the street and construction noise. Jana screamed every hour or two. These tracts of
new buildings are anti-human, not built for people with their
different needs, but for well-functioning worker bees. And
they are beehives—I ask myself if I am perhaps developing into
a mother who exaggerates things in her worry about her children and children's children . . .

Then I went to sleep after all. Toward morning I dreamed a
long series of experiences that I have unfortunately forgotten;
near the end I sat at a table with a woman who, I believe, was
my mother. She pushed an account statement toward me; from
it I gathered that I had 255,000 marks in the account. A quarter of a million! I thought, startled and relieved.

Gerd's comments at breakfast in the kitchen: The more
money you have, the more you worry about it. From his first
prize money, 2,000 marks, we bought a rug in 1955. After that
we had nothing left. Then, a few years later, with all of the
money that we had, we bought a car, the yellow Trabant, with

which I first backed over a freshly planted little tree before the eyes of the mayor in Werder. After that the account was empty, and we did not count up the money again. Today we have a few tens of thousands, and if it gets below that, we start counting again—The need for security, with which we were previously—when was "previously"?—not acquainted. Is probably also tied to the fact that the new book is progressing so sluggishly and that I always secretly expect not to be able to write anymore. And that I continue to feel responsible for the children, who are no longer children, even financially. For example, I always shop for them, too, think about them unceasingly, and think for them as well. Find relief for myself by remembering the difficult times in my life and the fact that I did "make" it. Constantly the guilty conscience that a man does not experience.

My thoughts continue to flow during the quiet breakfast and reading the newspaper. "Magnificent Beginning for the Nineteeth Berlin Festival" "Five Franco Opponents are to be Executed Today" "Gathering of the Berlin Combat Group Commanders" "Antifascist Resistance Against the Franco Regime Increases" "Immediate Freedom for Luis Corvalan" "Meetings with the Builders of the Western Section of the Baikal-Amur Railway."

Today everything is an effort for me, so I note down only a few headlines, but then I do copy down a few sentences from an essay by Werner Neubert[3] about Walter Benjamin. Under the title "Constantly in Search of Constructive Answers," with ideological conformity he writes: "Much confusion in middle-class evaluation standards had to be overcome, however, before individuating the direction in which only the passionate search for new solutions could promise answers: the scientific

[3] Werner Neubert (b. 1929), editor-in-chief of *Neue Deutsche Literatur* 1966-1974. (G.W.)

world view that is inseparably tied to the revolutionary work-ers movement." Yeah, yeah, I think. Except that for Benjamin certainly no vulgar infusion of the "scientific world view" would have been a possibility.

I am reading "A Magna Charta of Equal Rights." Twenty-five years ago the law for the protection of mothers and chil-dren was put into force, which had the goal of "pointing in the direction of a socialist future in which women and girls would participate in the production process with equal rights." With satisfaction I observe how "women and girls" make use of the chance for these—relative—economic equal rights (which, of course, bring a lot of overload with them), but in the process do, to a large extent, avoid the danger of letting themselves be integrated and used "like men," and instead of that develop needs that the economy can no longer cover: register their claim to a complete life. In that sense they have already sur-passed men in their emancipation, and I really do not know if I should at all wish for them the opportunity to occupy super-vising offices in the "Party and state apparatus" as well—the way that apparatus is constituted.

While I am considering all that, I have started to straighten up the kitchen, in which dishes and food scraps are still lying around from last night. We had a party for our after-hours brigade, the workmen who faithfully helped us to make the house inhabitable, bricklayers, cabinetmakers, and carpenters who spent many an evening and many weekends with us and not only expanded our bathroom and the barn but also told us their stories. I learned what kind of food to cook and what kind of sandwiches to prepare for them. Yesterday they were here with their wives, thirteen people. Gerd cooked them a proper and substantial *soljanka* soup. I had baked two pans of tomato cake, and at the end there were two large pieces of cheese on the table. Beer in quantity, the good *Lübstorfer*. It was loud and jovial. The men, of course, no longer had any inhibitions in front of us, and the women also overcame their shyness. Many of them come from East Prussia, West Prussia, and Silesia. Mecklenburg, of course, was a haven for refugees—for our family as well in 1945. It was almost midnight when they left.

Now I finally have eyes for the weather, for nature. First I step outside the kitchen door and inspect the sky: blue, as it has almost always been this summer; it will get warm. The flock of swallows flies up from the two oak trees. The pond toward the Schomakers' place has long since dried up. Even the stork from the main village has meanwhile grasped the fact that it will not catch any more frogs here. In front of the house, where we all sat at a long table last night, a few full ashtrays are still lying around. Beer bottles lie in the grass. Far away I hear the sound of a motor; they are probably plowing the fields on the other side of the hill.

There is no way around it; I have to sit down to do my work. It is already after ten. Actually I do not want to work. It seems pompous to me. Gerd can only shake his head at this, and I don't mention it to him anymore. But the feeling is real. My typewriter stands in the little room where my old peasant's bed also stands, and a writing cabinet, everything "noodle style," the old furnishings give the room a good, homey atmosphere. I must finish the fourteenth chapter today.[4] "I must" is probably the unspoken phrase that always accompanies me. So I must describe how the life of Bruno Jordan, who is supposed to be shot by Soviet soldiers because he accompanied French prisoners during their march, is saved by a Frenchman. I try to write it exactly the way that my father told it to us. While doing so, many other images go through my mind. I conclude with a statement by Lenka, which I invent, of course: What madness this whole thing. Or don't you think so?

[4] "Fourteenth chapter": C.W. is working on the manuscript for *Patterns of Childhood*, Berlin, 1976. (G.W.)

One single page. That is today's entire yield. I neither want nor am able to begin a new chapter today. Instead of that, I listlessly turn to the pile of mail that I brought along from Berlin and that has decreased far too little, and we already have to drive back to Kleinmachnow tomorrow! I am able to write one or two more letters declining invitations. Unfortunately I am incapable of simply preparing form letters for it into which I would then only have to insert the name of the inviter and my own signature. I am afraid of offending the people who send them, who often take great pains with their letters.

Gerd is calling me. The food is ready. A favorite standard meal: potatoes boiled in their skins, linseed oil, and cottage cheese. I am too tired to talk, lie down immediately, and fall asleep. When I wake up more than an hour later, I notice that I have a fever; the thermometer confirms it. So it has already been inside me all day. Half angry, half relieved, I remain lying down. I read—interrupted again and again when I doze off— in de Mendelssohn's Thomas Mann biography *The Magician*, fascinated as always by this eminently German figure. Amazement at the accomplishments of this life is mixed with something like sympathy, because he, I believe, is among those male artists who have that "splinter of ice in their hearts," of which one of them once said that it made it impossible for them to love—a horrible inability, which in the case of Thomas Mann may have been intensified by the lifelong suppression of his homosexuality. I ask myself if my inhibition in the writing of this specific book does not also come through my striving not to injure anyone if possible—through a cold, loveless perspective.

Gerd comes with the report that we have neither electricity nor water. The central village pump is out of order again. The joys of life in the country, he says, hardly disturbed. There was still enough water for tea in the kettle, and at such moments we enjoy the advantages of our propane tanks.

Now I must get up after all and gather a few things together that we want to take home (Aha! Unconsciously Kleinmachnow has become "home") with us tomorrow. Among them all my writing materials in divers bags, more and more books—which are driven back and forth—and all the unanswered mail. Little clothing. I do not really feel sick, just a certain amount of weakness. Nevertheless, we still go out for a short walk, to say goodbye for this time, as far as the "Neanderthal," the geodetic vantage point on the hill behind the tail of the "tomcat," as our village is called by the natives. The view is beautiful, but just what does that mean? The landscape is graduated, the horizon autumnally close, heavy, plastic clouds, toward the darkness a veiled, waning moon, all constellations clear. We both have the feeling: this is it! without saying it aloud.

From the tap in the cellar some water still flows, with which we will be able to wash ourselves scantily in the morning. There are enough candles in the house, romantic atmosphere. For supper we drink juice and eat what is left of the large cheese from yesterday, and salad with it. I do not have much appetite. We do not watch television for lack of electricity. So, early to bed, not reluctantly. Before that a call from Annette that relieves me a great deal. She does not feel all that uncomfortable in her new apartment, and Jana is adjusting amazingly well to her daycare. The woman who runs the daycare seems to like children. She *sings* her instructions, which removes the odor of orders from them. Both of them are doing well, I hear. I notice how a weight falls away from me.

I cannot read by candlelight. So I turn onto my side and try to fall asleep quickly.

I n the last little while my dreams have seldom been preserved by my long-term memory. Today, one day later, I must already think about how I woke up yesterday, exactly when I got up. It did not occur to me until last night that it was the "day of the year"—not until I was arranging the table with Tinka's books for her birthday. So I did not experience the day consciously, and today I can tell the difference. Now I remember that after waking up, my reading material from the previous evening came to mind: Hans Mayer, "Goethe, Essay on Success." The formulation of the question had fascinated me: the claim that from his Weimar period on and then especially after the French Revolution, Goethe, as a lone individual, had lived and written *against* the rudimentary German middle class, sought historical compromise, produced either fragments or weak pieces of literature, isolated himself more and more, and documented his view that he stood against the times through the decision not to publish *Faust II* during his lifetime . . .

Around seven I get up, shower, and fix breakfast with Gerd. Here comes the newspaper already, early. I glance at it starting with the back page: "*Berliner Bühnen* (Berlin Stages)," television schedule; I do not pay attention to the sports news. A photograph: The space traveler Valeri Bykovsky looks up at

---

[1] In April of 1976 the Wolf family moved from Kleinmachnow to Berlin, Friedrichstrasse. (G.W.)

the tree that he planted in 1963 after his first flight into space, next to him, smiling, his colleague Vladimir Aksyonov. The picture moves me in a different way than the bombastic reports about "Soyuz 22" during recent weeks. So they plant a tree after their flights—perhaps mechanically, perhaps routinely. But perhaps it is also an act of respect paid to the earth whose beauty is now close to them again—Otherwise many headlines that become intoxicated with greatness: "Energy giant," "Hundreds of thousands." While I scan the international page of *Neues Deutschland* again, I think, an investigation ought to be conducted sometime about the primitive form of partiality that is expressed in our press in the placing of adjectives. The experienced—and not only the experienced—reader immediately knows whether he is dealing with a friend or an enemy, depending on whether or not in a headline a death notice is called "moving," contacts are called "intensive," or suggestions are called "concrete." I find no examples for the opposite side in this issue (check to see if that is coincidence!), there the rejection is mostly expressed in verbs: "condemned," "drives," or in nouns: "maneuver," "delaying tactics." For the hundredth time I resolve to read the newspapers more carefully again, from other points of view.

On the culture page a brief review of the film by Nicolaou[2]/Gass, which undoubtedly only a few people saw, because at the same time on the second channel of West German television *Scenes from a Marriage* by Bergman was playing, about which the entire German Democratic Republic is now talking,

[2] Thomas Nicolaou (b. 1937), Greek writer and translator who lived in the German Democratic Republic; author of the film *Hellas ohne Götter* (*Hellas Without Gods*), 1957, for the documentary director Karl Gass; grew up in the German Democratic Republic as a child of Greek emigrants, translated Greek poets (for example Janis Ritsos) into German, C.W.'s *Cassandra* into Greek; lived with his wife Carola in Drispeth near Neu Meteln, friends with the Wolfs; later his work for the state security police was revealed; lives in Greece. (G.W.)

in the tenor: Yes, that's exactly how it is. Somebody is finally saying it for once. Which did amaze me a little bit. (I should also examine that amazement more precisely. Why had I actually not thought that marriage weariness is just as severe here as it is elsewhere?)

Mrs. B. has arrived, at a run as always. She claims that it is cold outside, at least colder than advertised. I am able to contradict that claim, and now I finally remember what I had forgotten for so long: that right at seven-thirty I had run out to turn the wrong Wartburg key back at the shop on Marienstrasse, which I had mistakenly taken with me on Friday when I picked up our car from the repair shop. It pleases me that I already know the people in the shop, the shop secretary's dog whose name is Bovi, it is her third one of the same large terrier breed, and you are always warned when he is eating his meat in the corner of the office; the white-haired supervisor, all of them friendly. The key, of course, had already been given up for lost; they had not been able to repair the car to which it belonged; there had been trouble, but: "The main thing, it's here now."

Then I walk around the block, looking for our gas fitter, who still has to inspect the gas line and have a gas meter attached. He is not in his office; I walk around the corner, and bump into him, Mr. W., in front of the gateway that leads to his shop; he is just on his way to work. He says the boss wanted to come to our place himself. We continue to talk a little bit back and forth, about his vacation in the CSSR, etc., and then the boss comes. He talks his way out of it again by saying that Mr. W. had not been "free." So fine: Thursday.

In the mornings I like to walk among people who are going to work. The makeup of the women who come toward me is still fresh. Many wear the modern calf-length skirts, combinations. Noticeably many Western textiles—I get milk from the store and take it along.

Only then breakfast, reading the newspapers. By the way, the headlines on yesterday's front page read: Elect the Candidates of the National Front on October 17. (Their pictures on the outdoor advertisement pillars, I do not take the time to look at them.) In addition, a beautifully arranged photograph that features a twenty-three-year-old mill shift supervisor who is a candidate for the People's Chamber, among his colleagues—all of them smiling—in the background the fireworks of a mill. During the election campaign the amount that they are ahead of schedule increases—The electoral assistants began their work on the weekend—Appeal from Helsinki: Strengthen the fight for disarmament!—Worldwide solidarity with the patriots of Chile—Workers' strikes in the capitalistic countries—And smaller: Leftist forces of Lebanon striving for conflict resolution—Kissinger plan rejected.

We actually quit reading that long ago, more than likely bored. What did we talk about at breakfast? When Tinka will come, who is at Ralli's place,[3] celebrated her birthday with him. I don't know of anything else.

At around nine I sit down at the typewriter. I write two pages of *Summer Piece*,[4] half of page 54, page 55, half of page 56. I know that I must stop at eleven. In addition to the doctor's appointment in the afternoon, at Gerd's urging I had them give me an appointment with the gynecologist in the Rössle Clinic. Since Maxie[5] has been lying in the hospital on Tucholskystrasse with her breast operation, I am supposed to be more careful, strictly keep the quarterly check-up appointments.

[3] Ralli: Ralf Thunberger, friend of Tinka Wolf. (G.W.)

[4] *Sommerstück*: C.W.'s narrative, Berlin, 1989. (G.W.)

[5] Maxie Wander (1933-1977), Austrian author who lived in the German Democratic Republic; friends with C. and G.W.; C.W. wrote the foreword for Wander's book *Guten Morgen, du Schöne. Protokolle nach Tonband* (*Good Morning, You Beautiful Woman. Reports Based on Audio Tapes*), Berlin, 1977 and "*Zum Tode Maxi Wander* (*On the death of Maxi Wander*)" (see: *Werke*, Vol. VIII, pp. 111ff.). (G.W.)

Even if it is only two pages—the fact that I am working at all will save the day for me. There is hardly any possibility that I will release *Summer Piece* for publication, if only because what I have written is too close to what I have lived, too many people would recognize themselves and be offended, and gossip could develop. But while writing I do not have the feeling that I do anyone an injustice, because an unfeigned sympathy ties me to all of the figures who appear there. Actually I cannot understand why I procrastinated for almost the entire summer, only to finally write quite genuinely, even in the first-person form: the very thing that I had initially not wanted to do at all. I am aware that in this story I probably play the same role again that I do in life: seeing through things, lightly floating above the situation, passing judgment, without being judged if at all possible. (My other side, the passionately involved woman, will not be present as strongly here—I am giving her a leave of absence for this text.) In "Maria" I describe my counterpart, which strongly fascinates me—Once again I anticipate that only material that cannot be published for different reasons drifts toward me anymore, and yet the diction in *Summer Piece* peculiarly seems as if I intended to publish the story: not like a diary, not like these writings here that already oscillate between the compulsion toward the privately discreet and the compulsion toward the publicly indiscreet.

I describe how "Lorenz" changes in the village under Maria's influence, how hard it is for "Irene" to tolerate that, how "Bella" and "Benjamin" arrive and are loved by "Maria." While doing that, I constantly think about how our relationships to each other have changed in the course of a year, how friendships have become looser, Maxie now lies there and feels abandoned, "Bella" has not worked since February and lies on her nice lounge chair and waits for mail, which, when it comes, does not help either, because what she longs for cannot be in it: that he wants to come to her and perhaps even take her with him. ("I have been made for the purpose of loving somebody—why can nobody be found? And it is very possible that I will perish because of it, and I cannot do anything at all about it . . .") I ask myself if this current knowledge should resonate in the text, which describes the previous summer. If depth can only be attained through the second time perspective, if that perspective should not lie indirectly in the sentences at the distance that is being expressed. If I am writing this, it is only because nothing else inside me is as urgent and because I neither can nor want to write. In addition to that—as contrast or confirmation—all this turmoil that I procure for myself and which Gerd constantly rebukes: You don't find any peace at all.

At around eleven Tinka comes. She missed the bus because of construction work, and she had need of a bit of "movement." I say: Comb your hair. She, indignant: I don't tell you that you should comb your hair. I leave, go the parking lot, drive to Buch, the stretch that I already know so well, along which I am always reminded of Brigitte Reimann, silently warn myself several times to concentrate on the traffic. As always I wonder how many villages there still are until Buch. It is a warm day. I leave my leather jacket in the car and go into the waiting room for the office hours of Professor E., wait in front of the glass door; a few women are in the cubicles. Again and again this atmosphere of haste, silence; the women do not say a word, wait for the examination as though hypnotized; sometimes one of them says: It is always terrible here.

E. says to me when he comes out, yes, yes, he would take me in right away. I gradually notice while I am sitting in the waiting room that his office hours have not yet begun. It is almost one; some have been sitting since eight. After the first group of patients has been summoned through the loudspeaker, the office assistant comes in and calls me. I am led into the consultation room—privileged—can say my little piece, which is not long, of course, and am immediately examined. Two swabs are taken, hastily; hastily I get dressed again, and the examination assistant is emphatically friendly. E. has found nothing remarkable.

Relieved, after a short time I am already back outside in the sunshine, in the heat. A woman is standing next to the street with her daughter. They beckon urgently and I stop. They want to know if I can take them to the railway station, then they would still catch their train. I have the impression that something depends on it for them. The woman is plaintively upset. I take them with me, then park by the store and as always buy two large bags full that I can hardly carry away. It is very clear to me that there is often some sort of shopping mania behind it, to which I can give in because I am not financially restrained. I also want to provide for Tinka when we are away, cans, bottles of fruit etc. I have to stand in line for a long time at the cash register. The store is crowded, but only two cash registers are open. Peculiarly, in such instances I often think that the wives of our leaders do not have to shop, and if they do, then in shopping places where there is enough personnel and no waiting.

In front of the store, after I have already carried the bags to the car, I meet Mrs. R. I hesitate a moment, but then do make myself noticeable. She is happy, and together we go into the Parkschloss Restaurant to eat lunch, smoked pork spareribs that are too fat, with potatoes that are half raw. She will turn 55, I learn during our conversation. She would really like to invite me, but that would already be a bond that is too close for me. Recently I have been using part of my tactical ability to avoid letting too many people get too close to me.

(Wednesday, 9/30/76) It is also characteristic of "the day" that I describe it in small pieces. That is how fragmented my life is now. Tomorrow we are going to Tübingen, so the day before yesterday I was at the hairdresser's, then at the dressmaker's trying on my cape. Then in the evening I cooked Chinese food. Ralli and Käthe[6] were here, a big night for Käthe who told us how she became an actress without any training. We drank several bottles of wine, even champagne, and it went on until two. In the morning I had a headache—that was yesterday—and then I had to go to the Writers' Union to pick up our papers, in the afternoon to the publisher, picked up a proof copy, learned that the book (*Patterns of Childhood*) with more than 500 pages is only going to cost 9.90 marks, which I feel is too cheap; that there are difficulties with the printer, that they still do not know if it will be out in time for Christmas business, etc. Then we drove to Potsdam to the dentist, went in to see my father—the day was over. "After the seventh of November"—that is now my magical date—concentration will have to become a strict act of will.

So on with the text—it is not yet six o'clock in the morning. Naturally, the day is especially busy, and I at least want to finish this description: the conversation with Mrs. R. It was about the sentence in her last letter, she had never liked doing the housework, also did not like to cook, but because they had the four children, of course, and her husband was such a very busy scientist, she did not have any other choice at all. And that for twenty-five years. I ask about the scraps of bitterness that must be bottled up in her as a result—I understand that much. She married late—at the age of thirty—had her children late, and it all seemed to be a great happiness that she wanted to enjoy. The topic of conversation turns to Bergman. She did not see *Scenes from a Marriage*, but she tells me how astonished she was when her daughter said on one occasion: Yes—your only aim in life is to have a happy marriage! To this day she has not wanted to understand that statement completely, because it fits her too precisely.

She also talks about her attempts to write about her brother

[6] Käthe Reichel (b. 1926), actress, friends with Brecht; engaged at the Berlin Ensemble, then at the Deutsches Theater in Berlin; friend of C. and G.W. (G.W.)

who was killed in the war, which I strongly encouraged her to do. I again tell the story of how we almost burned down in Meteln, and also talk about Maxie because Mrs. R. had the same operation but did not receive radiation treatments because the "seat of the illness" must have been minimal.—For a second it occurs to me very vividly how many times I have thought about cancer here, in the environment of the Rössle Clinic, or at home (because of my mother, because of Brigitte, Aenne, Maxie). A fear of cancer has not developed within me.

I drive—it is still warm—to the Baumann Clinic at a little before three, along the road on the clinic grounds, which I now also know so well. Probably still in connection with the thoughts about cancer—why no fear? Do I believe that I am immune—do I think what I have already thought so often: that the very worst thing has not happened to me yet? Of course I experience some things, even bad things, but I emerge whole and healthy from such life crises, even illnesses. The tuberculosis could have been worse; we could have lost a family member during the war or during our flight; I could have become involved in completely different conflicts; my tachycardia could have run its course less good-naturedly—just to name the things that immediately occur to me. Instead of that, however, what I write is also not very good, I believe.

In the Baumann Clinic my turn comes very quickly. Dr. F. has the young woman doctor represent him, to whom I can only say that I am doing well, except for the few migraine attacks. Her examination seems to confirm that. My blood pressure while lying down is 130/80, a fabulous reading for me. After a quarter of an hour I am outside again; I was only able to read a few pages in the book that I took with me: Hans Erich Nossack *Emergency Service*. It describes a suicide epidemic happening five years earlier in which the first-person narrator, a chemist, "participated" as a member of an emergency crew, and by which he was especially severely affected.

His wife had committed suicide and taken his two children with her. I do not read that until the evening, in bed, but from all kinds of hints you have to suspect something of that sort from the very beginning. The book is probably supposed to expose the cover-up tactics, but it belongs to the genre of synoptic literature.

I drive back quite cheerfully (as I always do when I do not have to remain in Buch; for me that town has become a synonym for illness) until I reach the second town from it. There I stop behind a store, and somebody looks at me so strangely in driving past. It turns out that I have been driving for the entire time without having released the brake. There is a stink of burnt rubber, all the tires are smoking, and the hubcaps are hot. Just what is that a sign for this time?! I will not say anything about it, I decide. So for the time being I go into the store and let the wheels cool off. Inside I have to wait for a long time for a basket. Then I get a few things, a breadbox at last, for example, and drag myself back to the car again heavily burdened. The car is no longer smoking, but the hubcaps are still hot. On Prenzlauer Allee I look around for flower shops, stop a short distance past the commuter railway station, wander through a few more textile shops without buying anything, and then actually do obtain two small bouquets of yellow roses, but just not three as I would have wished. There, you see, that is all that I am blessed with.

By the way I drive I note that I am getting tired; people honk at me several times and point at their heads with their fingers. Since nothing happens, I remain quite calm, arrive safely at the Reinhardstrasse parking lot, and then quickly buy a book of Shakespeare's for Tinka in the bookstore. Gerd and I then unload the car. We carry the bags upstairs, a very familiar process in all the apartments that we have had. (I quickly count them up: if I include Jena, this is our eighth—simultaneously with Meteln, which would be the ninth: too much expense that we have to deal with on our own; I often feel how that drives me outward.)

It is after five. Tinka is not home yet. We drink a quick coffee. Tinka comes and sits down at the kitchen table. We warm up the green peppers that Gerd had cooked, and talk a little bit about what went on with her today. She is dead tired, of course, because she spent two nights with Ralli celebrating her birthday and hardly slept, but she goes to the theater with us. At around six, Hinte and Schönebeck, our furniture movers, come. They will finally set up the last cabinet in the bedroom. I fix supper for them yet, put out the "joker," and give each of them twenty-five marks—I calculate that setting up the cabinet costs us over sixty marks. It is absolutely insane, but in money matters we act without thinking, as long as there is some. I only have time to change my blouse and then we have to leave. Gerd says each time, how nice it is that we can get there so quickly (to the Deutsches Theater, I mean), and when we come out: How nice that we will soon be home.

They present Shukshin[7]: *The Standpoint* and *Capable People*. It is the premiere, and Wolfgang Heinz[8] is the producer. As expected, we know many people in the audience. First we immediately encounter Helga Paris,[9] who wants to show us the Meteln summer pictures sometime (she called me yesterday: Ms. Soubeyrand[10] and Ms. Karusseit[11] want to do something together with me. I would not be disinclined, but theater?). We also saw Kurt and Jeanne Stern immediately, but then it

[7] Vladimir Shukshin (1929-1974), Russian actor, film director, and prose writer; aroused attention in East and West with the film *Kalina Krasnaya* (Red Guelder-Rose). (G.W.)

[8] Wolfgang Heinz (1900-1984), actor, director, 1963-1969 manager of the Deutsches Theater in Berlin. (Ed.)

[9] Helga Paris (b. 1938), photographer, friend of C. and G.W. (G.W.)

[10] Brigitte Soubeyrand: director, at times in intensive work discussion and correspondence with C.W. (G.W.)

[11] Ursula Karusseit (b. 1939), actress and director. (G.W.)

was already starting. Heinz sat motionless up in the central box. It became evident that Shukshin is not a dramatist. Nice ideas are flogged excessively (Three hours for that, Tinka said, it really does not have to take that long!).

I forgot—and since I do not want to forget anything, I will go back to it—that before going to the theater I made a quick telephone call to Isot Kilian to excuse Tinka for yesterday because she had to take care of Jana while we were in Potsdam and Annette was at the hairdresser's. Talk back and forth, explanations of her principles for controlling the students. I: But they are all adults! After that she calls again because she could not get the sentence out of her mind. Compliments for the *Sinn und Form* discussion.[12] In return for her courtesy she asks for a copy of *Patterns of Childhood*.

During the intermission we stand at first with Jeanne and Kurt in the very warm and humid air in front of the theater, talk a little bit about the play, about their trip to Rostock, and then we go upstairs to have a drink. We constantly see aged acquaintances. The three theater critics stand together like augurs: Keisch,[13] Cwojdrak, and Kerndl.[14] By the way, next to Tinka a man is sitting who could have come from Gogol's *The Government Inspector*—he has muttonchops and very fat cheeks—he sleeps through almost the entire play. Tinka laughs herself sick.

The "capable people" then turn out to be a band of racketeers who are supposed to be turned in by the wife of one— Fred Düren, Lissy Tempelhof. Very nice, we also had to laugh, but the effects were based purely on the costumes. Gerd

[12] *Sinn und Form* discussion: discussion of C.W.'s *Patterns of Childhood* in the periodical (29/30/31/1974) between the literary critic Annemarie Auer (1913-2002), Stephan Hermlin, and Kurt Stern. (G.W.)

[13] Henryk Keisch (1913-1986), writer, 1974-1985 General Secretary of the PEN Center of the German Democratic Republic. (G.W.)

[14] Reiner Kerndl (b. 1928), dramatist and theater critic. (G.W.)

laughed to himself for a long time, specifically about that style of clothing. A harsh retort: In a certain situation Düren cries out that he just now thought that his wife was with the police—Böwe says: But you have been living with her for fourteen years!—Düren: So what? All that is supposed to have been around before.

The applause was moderate, but nevertheless one could take the evening as an indicator for "all the things there are." While leaving I also run into Erika Hinkel.[15] She has developed a harder face. We exchange a few words about Mrs. Blomberg,[16] who needs a place in a home for the aged in Berlin, which E. H. can perhaps procure for her. Gerd makes himself scarce, of course. ("Isn't it wonderful that we'll be home right away?")

Tinka, dead tired, lies down on her belly on my bed; I lie down beside her. We eat an apple, and after that her stomach hurts. Of course we try to persuade her, especially Gerd, that she must live a more regular life, otherwise she will get stomach ulcers. She, of course, does not want to listen to any of that. Yes, yes, she says, and then gets up in a huff and leaves. I am already familiar with that and no longer think that I could change anything about it. I read a few more pages in Nossack. Next door, Tinka is running bath water. She comes in again and says: By the way, I was supposed to say hello to you from Tenschert a long time ago. Then she disappears. After a while Gerd says: Turn off the light soon, will you? So I turn off the light and quickly fall asleep.

---

[15] Erika Hinkel: assistant in the secretary's office of Kurt Hager (1912-1998), who was a member of the politburo in the Central Committee of the Socialist Unity Party, responsible for culture. (G.W.)

[16] Elena Liessner-Blomberg (1897-1987), painter of Russian origin, lived in Germany beginning in 1922, like C. and G.W. lived in Kleinmachnow, friends with them; G.W. edited the book *Elena Liessner-Blomberg oder Die Geschichte vom Blauen Vogel* (*Elena Liessner-Blomberg or The Story of the Blue Bird*), Berlin, 1989 (see also: *Unsere Freunde, die Maler,* cited above). (G.W.)

TUESDAY, SEPTEMBER 27, 1977
Meteln—Berlin, Friedrichstrasse

Early, perhaps around three, I had to get out of bed. The two glasses of tea with rum from last night made themselves noticeable. Outside it was almost as light as day because of the enormous moon that has been in the cloudless sky here for several nights. Cold besides. The regenerative night furnace is just barely able to heat the cottage. At temperatures below freezing, it does not succeed. I soon fell asleep again, woke up for good at six. Although in the evening—in accordance with a suggestion in a television program about dreams—I had given myself the order to wake up when I had an important dream, and to retain it, the morning dream fled inexorably away. In my still half-fuzzy consciousness a searching and feeling after firm objects began, to which my thoughts could cling. I tried to make note of those objects, since after a time it occurred to me that today is the "day of the year." It is already difficult for me to reproduce them in my memory.

Whenever I spontaneously "let myself think," it is still a matter of coping with the shock of this year—Biermann's expatriation and the consequences. I am still entangled in an inner monologue on that topic, searching for justification and self-justification. I mentally tried out a dialogue with translators in Buckow, whom I will travel to meet tomorrow, and for several minutes I lapsed into a wishful dream that Sarah[1] had

[1] Sarah Kirsch had moved to West Berlin in 1977. (G.W.)

returned and we were setting up an apartment for her. For days I have also observed in myself a firming up of my determination to be here, whatever that may mean now for the future. Considered an atmosphere, a mood for the middle portion of my Kleist-Günderrode story,[2] which still seems too ponderous to me, still lacking inspiration. It is a lengthy, tedious process for me to work out inspirations of this kind, the smaller, more skillful ones. Other, "greater" ideas come more often, apparently without effort. (Just when Gerd says that in his Fürnberg afterword the publisher eliminated the name Ernst Fischer,[3] I am thinking that I should someday write something entitled "Nobody." So, during this summer a wealth of plans: the night before last a dialogue occurred to me on the topic of "disassembly," which I wrote down yesterday morning, which Gerd would immediately recognize as too flat and not even finish reading.) I am happy about the idea that made "fiction" into a multi-layered set of materials, about which I also had new ideas this morning, after six, and which I must now "only" work out. As is so often the case, I reflect on the boundaries against which our taboo-schooled thinking constantly strikes. Because it is getting lighter and lighter, from the bed I see the rose by the typewriter, find it beautiful, and am happy. Gerd asks how late it is—Six-thirty. (He never has a watch within reach.) Not at all warm in here, he says. I admit, my throat is somewhat tight. The first raw autumn air always affects my throat. He immediately wants to do something about that, just does not know what, grieves after the

[2] Kleist-Günderrode story: *Kein Ort. Nirgends*, Berlin, 1979. (G.W.) Karoline von Günderrode (1780-1806), German author. On 26 July 1806, she committed suicide by stabbing herself on the banks of the Rhine River. Günderrode's work first received the critical attention that it deserves in the 1970s and 1980s with renewed interest in Romanticism and through C.W.'s critical writings. (Ed.)

[3] Ernst Fischer (1899-1972), Austrian scholar of aesthetics; was expelled from the Communist Party of Austria in 1969 because of his non-dogmatic Marxist essays (see also: *Das Ende einer Illusion* [*The End of an Illusion*], Vienna, 1973). (G.W.)

good tablets that we had last year in Tübingen when I had to fight down an angina. Or was it two years ago in Switzerland? It seems unbelievable to me that Tübingen was only a year ago. Excitement and mourning and despair seem to stretch time out.

At around a quarter to seven I get up, run bath water, and listen to the news on Radio Germany: Norway is ready to participate in an economic embargo against South Africa. Israel will tolerate representatives of the Palestinians in the Geneva negotiation delegation. The president of the World Bank, McNamara, warns against exaggerated nervousness in evaluating the economic situation. The developing countries must be helped more so that they can become equal partners with the industrialized nations. The press review discusses the expediency of the Christian Democratic Union's request to prohibit the three smaller "C" parties in the Federal Republic. By so doing they would unnecessarily revalue the Moscow-dependent German Communist Party upward. Besides that, they would push the members of the communist groups into the well-prepared underground, where it would be harder to keep an eye on them than it is now. No new news in the Schleyer kidnapping case. The large crisis staff has met. Bonn will not confirm nor deny that it suspects that the kidnapped man is on a ship in Dutch waters.

Pedicure. Personal grooming. When I am doing well, I take less offense at my physical imperfections—Meanwhile, Gerd heats up the kitchen stove. I fix breakfast, toast bread, make tea for him, coffee for myself, and still have to laugh about the excited discussions that have taken place in recent weeks regarding the price of coffee, regarding the distasteful invention "coffee mix" for six marks, about the jokes that are going around about it: What is the difference between coffee mix and the neutron bomb? None. Both should be banned. Or: Coffee mix even destroys organic life, but it also eats away the utensils. Or: Ho-mo-six.[4]—Our station is broadcasting long excerpts from the speech that Erich Honecker made yesterday in Dresden during the opening of the Party apprenticeship year. Over there they offer particular commentary about his comments about the international shops and inquire as to whether or not the apparatus wanted to forcibly make him appear to be unreliable, since it wrote into his speech the claim that the international shops had been "reduced" to the justifiable number, which simply was not true. I unconsciously control my distance to those complaints. Yes, it works. A lot of time lost with false "commitments." Not to take oneself so seriously, to evaluate realistically one's own role is perhaps also a kind of acquiescence. I could not write *Patterns of Childhood* again; I would lack the boldness to do so. They drove it out of me, I think—Really?

At breakfast we talk about the fact that the elderberry jam that we made yesterday tastes very good but unfortunately did not thicken, find out for me about the trains to and from Berlin, and talk about K., who is supposed to find out today if there is anything cancerous in her abdomen. Gerd gets upset about the fact that she did not go to the doctor at the first signs and does not understand the fear that a person has of it. I give him the counter example of Inge K., who immediately went to the doctor but was not treated correctly, so that it may now also be too late. He becomes irritated about the "fuss" that K. makes about everything. I call attention to the fact that her manner of being distraught and clinging to others has intensified during the last two years, she has aged considerably; it is as though vitality inexorably leaves her, and then the characteristics that disturb him so much become much more visible.

For weeks Gerd has been doing only trivial publishing crap, and has not found himself a topic that he could tackle. This

[4] The German original, "*Ho-mo-sechs*," is a word play on "homo-sex." (Tr.)

year, for the first time, neither one of us gave a single thought to our wedding anniversary. I ask myself—asked myself yesterday before going to sleep, when I had again read *The Touch* by Bergmann—if I, too, secretly long to be overwhelmed by a passion, instead of longing for this harmonious, unquestionable, and dependable warmth, this proximity, this solicitude. In the past perhaps, yes. I have become aware that that chapter in my life is finished (the woman in the Bergman film said: I am already thirty-four . . . ! And I am forty-eight, that means, upper limit of the middle generation). Only that chapter? At my age isn't it self-deception to still expect the most important work from the future?

I clean up a little bit and sit down at the typewriter to write this. I am aware that this is my favorite way to work, when the work mixes itself into the days and eats them up, when one cannot be separated from the other. Gerd says that hundreds of starlings are at our apples again. An enormous apple harvest this year. Since my childhood I have not looked as calmly and as closely at how an apple sits on the branch, nor observed the deep September sky as intensively as I have this year. Why is it that here I have the feeling of "being alive" far more strongly than I do in the shallow bustle of Berlin? And why have I poked my nose into that shallow hubbub for so long? Lost so much time by doing it? That would probably be a reason for mourning, more than anything else, and for regret as well. But my store of mourning and regret seems to be used up for the time being; there actually is something like an economy of the soul, which, when overburdened, will one day say, actually unexpectedly, "Enough."

When I fix my morning drink in the kitchen, and then bring it upstairs, through the windows I see Otto Schomaker's brown horse grazing on our meadow. A beautiful horse with a glistening coat, the only joy of Otto's life, which he, however, denies, saying that he actually keeps the horse only for Hartmut, his son.

It is now 9:45. I want to spend another hour on the Kleist piece, have given thought to how many associations there are that have arisen from technology, which he and his contemporaries could not have, but which are natural to us. I write only a few sentences. Gerd washes his pullover. The mail comes, no letters for me. In the *Weltbühne* under the title "In the Fastest Way" a short article by Annemarie Auer in which she announces that she has been told that Landsberg/Warthe did not lie in the former Warthe district, in what was later Hitler's Warthegau, as she had claimed in her anti-*Patterns of Childhood* article in *Sinn und Form*, but in the territory of the German Reich, nevertheless near the border. This "mistake" could distort some of her arguments into "something harmful" and, if not corrected, become a lie. But she did not have anything to retract from her "thoughts while reading." A book that many people like could also endure controversy, which belongs just as much to the search for historical truth as the book itself . . . My heart immediately races and I feel heart pains at the new infamy. As if this small "error" would not have thoroughly changed the historical basis and all the moral premises of the book: whether one lives together with oppressed Poles as their oppressor, as A.A. claimed, and spends her childhood that way, or does not . . .

Gerd says angrily: Why are you getting so upset?!—Yes, why? Because of the intentional malice that strikes out at me there.

Now the little mouse in our false ceilings moves around in the daytime, too. Just now the two large pear trees on the other side of the street were occupied by hundreds of starlings that made an unbelievable racket. I clapped my hands—a dense, dark cloud of starlings against the sky.

Friday, 9/30/77, in Meteln again. Meanwhile the weather has turned. Yesterday it was raining when I arrived in Schwerin again, richer for the knowledge that I am not as stable as I still thought three days ago, that announcements about certain meetings can still depress me. But I must reconstruct the Tuesday without being able to fall back on notes. So I continue on after the cloud of starlings and gather up my things for the trip.[5] Gerd brings two beautiful old glasses for Tinka for her birthday and a sack of apples from our own harvest. He has already cut and washed spinach; I peel potatoes, cook them and the spinach, fix fried eggs, and wash up the breakfast dishes . . . What I thought while I was doing it I no longer remember, so a superficial image of that day will now have to be created here. It turns out—which can also be verified in the narration—that the external events and acts remain sharper in the memory than what transpires inside—often synchronous with it. Similarly, people also say to me about *Patterns of Childhood* again and again that the almost conventionally narrated parts and the figures that are developed there mold the memory image of the book for many readers, much more strongly, in any case, than the reflections. The question of a young Polish woman yesterday at the translation seminar: We live so much with the Jordan family, we identify so much with it—couldn't we forget the six million dead in Poland as a result of that? Focused on that phenomenon, on the power of what is narrated, on its power to control things as compared with what is only thought. Must be considered for future writings.

I washed the lunch dishes yet—now I remember: I had become indignant, took the eternal dishwashing as a pretext for the aversion, which in reality revolved around a suppressed fear; this self-assertion program that I have firmly made up my mind to carry out shows its flip side. I am less eager to admit to myself the recurrences, the fear that is generated by a ridiculous little article, the fantasies—self-tormenting ones—that

[5] Trip: Switzerland October 14-November 1, 1975; Tübingen October 1-21, 1976. (G.W.)

immediately attach themselves to it and make me disheartened and immediately permit the wish for self-destruction to emerge, which I seriously and systematically want to overcome. It is clear to me that I will have to live with that—but that means *live*; it must not limit me. Perhaps I owe many of my tests of courage to the unconscious resolve that I do not intend to let myself be restricted by my fear. With it, enormous and imperative after this year (which was actually "too much," but Gerd was right, of course: I must view it differently. This time is the way it is, and I am the way I am in it, and I do not have to "endure" that, but take note of it and live through it . . .) a longing for peace and quiet that pushes away everything else. For a corner in which they would simply let me live, without suspicion, without revilement, without the compulsion to have to protect myself constantly from others and from myself because I am the way I am or am becoming something else. To write this down requires a conscious effort because of the bottomless naïveté and impossibility of fulfilling such a wish. That corner does not *exist*. There is only this field of tension (here or there) in which people like me always stand between the fronts, always have to be attacked from both sides, then have to figure that under that burden they will change: become too sensitive, even unjust, thus offer raw surfaces, which then increases the liveliness of the campaign. It is almost a question of material. How must nerves be constituted, those that endure in the end? Sometimes I wish for a collapse that could possibly procure me a break for a few weeks. But I am meanwhile so hardened that I can live on the edge of my strength for a very long time. No more than a slight increase in blood pressure sometimes, a bit of heart and stomach pain, more frequent migraines. It was worse in the past, for lesser reasons.

Recently somebody wrote me that the number of my potential readers in this country must decrease more and more, that this is a regular occurrence. I believe it, too.

The wounds are still painful, and I am also afraid of that pain, which exceeded in its cruelty anything I had known before. So, with those feelings, I sit in silence next to Gerd in the car; he sometimes strokes my knee, but does not press me as he often does otherwise, when he immediately wants to know the nature and origin of a mood in order to argue against it.

The air is cool and clear. When we turn off into Lübstorf, Gerd says: Here a person really can feel at home, don't you think so?—I think how precious a feeling of attachment to a home town is and how difficult it would be to give it up. All of my thoughts have had that duality for a few months. I think that I would never again be able to feel at home anywhere, if I were to leave here. And I ask myself how high a price I would be willing to pay under certain circumstances for that feeling of attachment. I ask myself what price I unconsciously pay every day, a price in the coin of looking away, not listening, or at least remaining silent. I often wonder if the bill is yet to be presented during our lifetime. If not, I must present it to myself. I do not know if I can muster the strength again for the ruthlessness that would be necessary there. That is, perhaps, the central question for the continuation of my work, which I would sometimes simply like to give up.

The apples on the trees. The foliage is beginning to change colors. The hills on the left. The different shades of brown on the plowed fields.

Gerd drops me off at the railway station in Schwerin; I immediately buy a round-trip ticket, observe in myself, as I do each time I travel by train, the familiar reflexes: indignation toward the people who fumble around for so long at the counter, then on the platform a certain enmity toward the crowd of potential fellow travelers, which seems very large to me, too large for a train, but which then does distribute itself; everyone has enough room and I am already looking at the people more kindly. This time, I pay almost no attention to fellow travelers, have no desire to observe them, take note of only the likeable family in the compartment on the other side of the corridor, who seem to deal kindly with each other. I am tired, sleep a little bit, and then read more than half of the new book by Otto F. Walter: *The Degeneration*.[6] A montage novel, describing the rise and fall of an attempt by some young Swiss (and a somewhat older journalist, Blumer, the identification figure of O.F.W., who interests me the most, by far) to live together in a group that is similar to a commune. A young couple, Leni and Rob, who start it, are simply killed at the end by lower middle-class people who have gone wild—The book in its radicalism quite certainly courageous right now, where over there an air of pogrom is arising against "terrorists" and so-called "desk culprits," where this book—even if it does not say anything new—uncompromisingly rejects the idea that one can live in a capitalistic society without perishing on the constraints; it is probably what Walter himself has learned in recent years, which he describes now, barely transferred into the literary domain. Here, too, I skip the plain newspaper notices from Switzerland, press my way with difficulty and somewhat reluctantly into the historical excursions into the story of the marriage, also do not find too much sense in the quotation of passages from Gottfried Keller's *A Village Romeo and Juliet*,[7] although the language—set against the other language forms in the book—has an almost legendary quality, as if drawn from a different source from our language: heavier, weightier, nobler, made of a more permanent material; but also not so inviting for use—Again the experience: where the book, shyly and reluctantly, divulges something about the author's

---

[6] Otto F. Walter (1928-1994), Swiss writer, amicably acquainted with C.W. through his work as chief publisher's reader of the Luchterhand Publishing Company (1967-1973). (G.W.)

[7] Gottfried Keller (1819-1890) was a Swiss writer whose best known work is *Green Henry*. (G.W.)

self, there it touches me, there I want more of it. Not the purely technical problems of writing, but the problems of a man in his early forties, who has failed in his profession (journalist), who has let his life slip away and wants to begin over again with young people. Since I know O.F.W., I look at the cracks in this presentation, in the places where he wanted to and had to hide things, with sympathetic forbearance. I see his great vulnerability.

(Just looked through a Suhrkamp catalogue in which new poems by Peter Huchel are advertised. In the text it says: Nothing heals, the vulnerabilities prophesy a fatal end. I make a note of "Nothing heals" as a possible title for a piece of writing. In an unfamiliar way the catalogue gives me courage, the faces of the authors who look at me, among them Thomas Brasch. It has to work out, after all; I have to go on. A sudden, bewildering, and pleasant contact with myself, with the part of myself that is exposed while writing and that I was forced to hide while caught beneath the wave of meanness that crashed upon me during this past year: as much courage as is necessary to present it again, after all. Will I ever find that again, aside from moments of happiness like this one?)

(A title that points in the same direction would also be, by Elke Erb[8]: *The Manna of the Injuries That Taste Good.*)

Berlin-Lichtenberg. The crowded railway platform, under perennial construction. In the crowd I suddenly see two people coming toward me, who I really must know; it takes a few seconds before it becomes clear to me who they are and that they are there for me: Käthe and Kreisel. They pick me up with his car (much talk about broken seals; he has not been able to obtain replacements for three months, so now he has turned to self-help and made some for himself). I say to Käthe: Well, you

---

[8] Elke Erb (b. 1938), poet, well acquainted with C. and G.W.; see also C.W.'s conversation with E.E. as the afterword to her volume *Der Faden der Geduld* (*The Thread of Patience*), Berlin/Weimar, 1978 (in: C.W., *Werke*, Vol. VIII, pp. 87ff.). (G.W.)

seem to be doing fine!—Yes. It was only an inflammation and everything is fine—That takes a load off my mind. We talk while we walk along the platform, about her relief, about the fear that she had before. Peculiarly I had "known" it, of course—but that was perhaps just one of my maneuvers to postpone the truth. (Gerd told me yesterday how often he thinks of the sentence: The laughing man has not yet received the terrible news. That is the kind of lifesaving help that he needs.)

In the tunnel I say that I still need flowers for Tinka. So, on the way we look for flower shops and finally stop. I take five aster plants, Käthe a bunch of daisies that she will put in a copper jug, which she will give to Tinka. She says how kind Tinka always is to her when she is not doing well. Kreisel says he feels that we concerned ourselves with the Biermann affair[9] for too long. We should have let go of it a lot sooner. He is sorry that last winter we did not get around to doing our Hegel series: a weekly philosophy hour. If you concern yourself with events for so long, you do miss out on arriving at concepts and pieces of knowledge. I say that I really did gain new knowledge during the past year, that I had encountered concepts: it was very important for me—He cites reasons why he does not say anything political in closed rooms.

They both come to my place to drink tea. The door to Tinka's room is open; she is sleeping, snuggled under her green blanket. We slip past. I fix tea while Kreisel looks for the place with the "black holes" in *Patterns of Childhood*, in order to show me a sentence that is physically wrong, to be sure, if you think your way into it the way I do, but is nevertheless correct. It is the sentence that talks about the "collapsed event horizon"—a concept that the physicists supposedly understand in a different sense from the way I apply it there. I have forgotten in which sense. Just as I have forgotten what K. then said about his new work, about a not insignificant discovery that he succeeded in making by using a neutron field as a measuring background. His fantasy of the double world is fun for me: what is wave in our world is corpuscle there and vice-versa, and the two worlds exist next to each other and within each other. That would be an amusing idea for a science fiction story. By the way, K. is quite certain that there are rational life forms all over in the universe. They probably even shield themselves from us late developers, he thinks.

I go to Tinka's room; she wakes up and says: Just where did you come from?! I was just dreaming about you—She sits down with us and drinks tea. Is very tired because she spent the night with Ralli, who was celebrating a birthday. But does not look bad. Soft, when I kiss her.

When Kreisel has gone, then Tinka, too, who is watching a film about the rehearsal work on *Peasants* by Heiner Müller,[10] Käthe tells me how she sat and desperately read during the morning (*Muschg, Albisser's Ground*), did not call the hospital until one-thirty ("very quiet"), heard the good news, hung up the phone, and then screamed three times like an animal, as if she were screaming stones out of herself.

When she has gone, I clean up a little, change clothes, make the apartment warmer, eat another open-faced sandwich, and then go to Walter Kaufmann's place to look at Tinka's possible future apartment. The Berlin apartment has not yet lost its eeriness for me since it was monitored, since they forced their way into it. The cold, desolate, and dirty foyer. The street, where I have to give myself a shove to go out onto it because the feeling is still there that I am being watched. The dark

[10] Heiner Müller (1929-1995) controversial East German dramatist and writer. (Ed.)

Oranienburg streetcar. At the very end, to Alexanderplatz, the number seven. Three flights of stairs. Kaufmann has visitors, a Polish Jew whom K. met in Israel, his girlfriend whom he brought with him from Poland, and Kaufmann's girlfriend Lissy, a redhead. The Polish woman does not understand a word of our conversation and is bored. I drink cognac, Kaufmann whisky. We are talking about his Israel report, just published in *Neue Deutsche Literatur*, without certain passages, however, in which, for example, Zionists were described—it now appears as if there are only communists in Israel. A tragicomic story about his uncle, who invites him to a restaurant and in the end does not want to pay for his friend, whom he has identified as a communist. My relatives! says K., and I tell a little about my aunts in West Germany. Then we talk about the apartment that would be ideal for Tinka. K.'s friend Lissy knows how to get it. She would only have to reregister with the police, nothing more—At around nine-thirty I leave again, measure the time, the shortest route to our place takes fifteen minutes. The streets are already empty.

Tinka is not home yet. I call Gerd on the telephone. Nothing on television interests me. With painful admiration I read a series of texts in the quarto booklets by Biermann, which are lying here right now. Sadness as well.

Tinka comes. We talk about her theater, about the *Galileo* rehearsals. We go into the kitchen and eat something, talk while we are doing it, go to bed, she lies down on Gerd's bed, and we continue to talk. How the actors have been spoiled by the choreographic production style of recent years, perform imprecisely, sound, on the other hand, overly precise, hardly capable of being spontaneous. Her nightmare, that she would sometime have to do the rehearsal plans that the other assistant is now doing, while she runs the prompt book. She says she is one of the few people whom she knows who is totally fulfilled by a job that is fun for her. She would not like to know how many in our country would end up taking drugs if they came here. She tells about a long night of conversation with her mentor and a fellow student. She says she can no longer listen to the malicious joy of the Western stations regarding our difficulties. Her desire to become productive. My joy about that. We talk until midnight, then I turn on the light once more to congratulate her. She is twenty-one. Just exactly when was I born? She asks. At around eleven in the morning, I say, and again I see before my eyes the large lamp that was fastened over the table on which I lay in the labor room. The whiteness, brightness. The white coats of the doctors. My happiness, a fragment of which has remained and is being revived. I then fall asleep quite quickly, while Tinka softly slips away because she is afraid that she will disturb me with her cough, which persists following the serious bronchitis and pneumonia that befell her during the period of the arguments about our Biermann intervention and the monitoring by the state security agents.

WEDNESDAY, SEPTEMBER 27, 1978
Meteln

The day begins at night, at "zero o'clock"—an expression that always seems mysterious and a bit eerie to me. We are sitting downstairs in the "hall," which was once a pigsty; the fire in the fireplace has burned out and we have searched in vain in the Bachmann books for the quote "with my burnt hand I write about the nature of fire,"[1] which my Polish translator, Mr. Blaut,[2] wants documented. I have leafed through the reports that were published by Reclam, which document Dostoyevsky's trial in the year 1849. Drank cognac, later vodka—every evening some, in spite of the warning that the female liver has a much harder time breaking down alcohol than the male one. Several times we tried in vain to call Carola[3]; all we hear is a busy signal. It is undoubtedly out of order again, but a slight uneasiness remains because she actually intended to come in the evening, and because Thomas is in Hoyerswerda on a reading trip. In the country you worry about people, especially if one of them lives alone and out of the way. Tinka called again. The furniture for her apartment, which Ralli and a friend picked up this afternoon with a large truck, arrived; a telegram from Halle cancelled an appointment with the publisher for Gerd, thank God. It is still "zero o'clock," and now the end of an American movie from the year

[1] "With my burnt hand...," Ingeborg Bachmann; quote from the novel *Malina*, Frankfurt/M/, 1971. (G.W.)

[2] Vladimir Blaut, translator of *Patterns of Childhood* into Polish. (G.W.)

[3] Carola Nicolaou, wife of Thomas Nicolaou; see above p. 209. (G.W.)

1976 (a date that always awakens unpleasant associations for me) is playing: *The Killing of a Chinese Bookie.* A remarkably unconventional film, which nevertheless, toward the end, slips off more and more into the usual pursuer-pursued cliché, but only at the very end, when the nightclub owner Cosmo Vinelli, who had been forced to commit the murder by the gang to which he owes a lot of money, is sitting among his girls again as they put on their cosmetics, as he was at the beginning—during which, by the way, he (which we suspect but hardly have shown to us) slowly bleeds to death—then it gets better again. His last appearance on the stage of his shabby club, when he introduces his troupe; how he stands next to the street and the blood seeps through his jacket; how right at the end, over the credits, the girls sing a little song that ends: We did not believe that we loved him, but we really do—That was all right.

I note in my diary a sentence that does not come from me: Today begins the first day of the rest of my life. To live as if it were the last day. What would I do? Do *differently* than usual? What and how would I write?

Gerd goes to bed. The last news at ten after midnight, second German television channel: The espionage suspicion against the Social Democratic Party representative Holtz and the personal advisor to Egon Bahr[4] has been eliminated; the bishops' synod of the Protestant Church in East Berlin ends with the unanimous resolution that rejects the introduction of military science into the schools of the German Democratic Republic and more than ever calls for an education of the youth in the spirit of peace and international understanding. US President Carter has lifted the weapons embargo against

[4] Egon Karlheinz Bahr (b. 1922), journalist and director of the Berlin Press and Informations Service; former member of the Social Democratic Party of Germany, Secretary to the Prime Minister's Office from 1969 to 1972. M.P. in the Bundestag from 1972 to 1990 and federal minister from 1972 to 1976. (Ed.)

Turkey—The weather: cloudy with patches of blue sky, show-
ers, fifteen degrees Celsius.

The electrical furnace unit in the vestibule hums extremely
loudly, stops—because of the changeover switch—when I turn
on the hot water and wash, but then starts up again all the
louder. "Caloderma Cream." Almost every time I have to
remember how, as a child, I used the wrong intonation with
the names of the creams that my mother used. That is how long
a brand endures, in reality and in memory . . .

Twenty after midnight. Go to bed, in the brown bed beneath
the wooden roof, one of the great pleasures. The long sleep of
recent days, following the great weariness that had accumulat-
ed through the work on the Günderrode essay, through the
stays in Berlin and Leipzig. Reading material: Oscar Wilde: *The
Portrait of Mr. W.H.* Given Wilde's great fondness for significant portraits, I believe, one might expect that he was in possession of a self-portrait that meant a great deal to him; the
homosexual components that he laboriously restrains or ardu-
ously permits to emerge in his works—depending on which
drive was stronger within him: the character type of the idler
who is disgusted with the world—probably first in Büchner's
works, in *Leonce and Lena*—I read it yesterday again for the
first time in a long time—in Büchner's case wrested from a pain,
in Wilde's case from a sentiment that can hardly be hidden
behind the banal, moralizing plot of *The Picture of Dorian Gray.*
While in Büchner's work the banality of the ending, the "happy
end," is consciously put forth as an ironic alternative: nobody is
punished, the moral laws are really put out of force, he is serious about it; he is also beyond disappointment, beyond indict-
ment, and thus also beyond hope. Wilde, strangely enough, is
not. He is tied to the morality of his era, as a negative print.

(It is now ten-fifteen. I interrupted this text, which I am writing while sitting on my rostrum in the upper room, went down,
got the two newspapers from the mailbox—the mail goes to

Berlin—scanned the headlines, discovered that the film *The Summer People* is playing at the studio cinema in Schwerin, informed Gerd, and we decided to drive there. I got a few apples ready, homegrown, and turned over the record with the Schubert sonatinas for violin and piano . . .)

With Büchner and Wilde: the difference between being moral as an author and moralizing. That must be pursued.

I slept in stages, probably dreamed, did not remember anything, when suddenly, as I awoke, the name "Cyril" occurred to me. That is, of course, the name of Wilde's hero who provides evidence that the object of the Shakespeare sonnet is a very young actor from Shakespeare's troupe. The night seemed long to me.

When I awoke, I saw a rectangular patch of sunshine on the rostrum on which I am working. So the sky, which had been clear and star-studded during the night, had "held," pleasant after the persistent rainy gloom of this autumn. I fell asleep again, heard Gerd get up, wanted to sleep and slept (under the motto: this is my vacation, which I need), and got up at seven-thirty. I looked out all the windows to see if Otto Schomaker's horse was still in our meadow (the horse Jochen, to which the veterinarian was brought the day before yesterday, because it was lame; it has a hematoma on its right rear leg, and yesterday the entire family made a pilgrimage across our meadow to see how the horse was doing), but it was gone. I thought repeatedly about the fact—in contrast to earlier years—that today is the "day of the year," and that this knowledge will cause me to live this day more consciously, but also perhaps distort it. In any case, I do not say anything to Gerd, so that he retains his candor.

He is sitting downstairs at the typewriter over his Kunert article,[5] has already been coughing for a while, which woke me

---

[5] Kunert article: G.W., "*Der lebende Vers* (The Living Verse)" in *Kunert lesen* (*Reading Kunert*), Munich/Vienna, 1979. (G.W.)

up. I walk past him in my bathrobe; he grabs me and gives me a hug—Warm sleeping bag—Under the bathrobe I am warm. You don't feel that through the material.

The colors. Above the yellow sunflowers in the green petroleum bottle, the light through the eastern skylight. All the windows should be washed, one of the most hated jobs. Below, the one pale red geranium in the window, the orange-yellow flowers in the green marmalade jar, the bouquet with the last lupines and the two dark red roses, all picked yesterday, when it had finally ceased raining and I could wash. For that reason there is little housework today.

In the bathroom, the new bubble bath, poisonous colors, anti-plaque toothpaste; I do not follow the direction to brush my teeth for two minutes after every meal using soft, circular motions. While I let water run into the tub, I catch myself humming the melody of the song: "*Hörst du mein heimliches Rufen?* (Do You Hear My Secret Call?)"—which I have probably not heard for years, to say nothing of sung: Let me kiss you just one more time, show me your dear face . . . Now where does that come from? I bathe, take a cold shower. Rubdown with the new towel: also one of life's pleasures. I think of Kunert, who recently said in Leipzig: If the hope for a perspective has really ceased, then you develop a new enjoyment of the moment—I am already humming another tune again from "before"; it comes from the same sentimental supply as the first one: Rosemarie, Rosemarie, for seven years my heart called for you . . . So what is going on this morning? Where is my subconscious heading, or what does it let drive it? In a chain of associations, I arrive at the others, at "our" songs, which accompanied me for many years—for the entire childhood of our children—and which I hardly sing anymore, if not subconsciously. Some connecting links that I forgot, hardly perceived—and I am already in the autumn of '76 again, in January of '77, in that meeting, in my attempted defense. I must forcibly break off the series of images. It no longer hurts, that is true. It is only still "there." How experience becomes memory and present becomes past. Some day, that, too, will be cut off from me, I will feel like I am a different woman, my behavior will have become foreign to me. The motif of becoming foreign to oneself occupies my mind; perhaps it can become the primary motif for the fantastic story called *Fiction* that is working within me but is not yet finished.

My face very close in the mirror. Aging, no longer an abstract word, daily experience. It occurs to me how my hip hurt again during the night and I had a difficult time finding a comfortable position. Skin with large pores around my nose. More and more new pimples that result from my disturbed hormone balance, in which the female hormone gradually begins to decline. Recently I read in one of the soothing articles that the body does have years to adjust to that. Newly burst small blood vessels on my cheek, the cover makeup has to cover up more and more. It does not bother me, although I sometimes ask if my body, like my spirit, has also had its full, rich life, "I" do not still owe it something as a result of my onesidedness. Now, in the country, it receives its due, of course, more than it does in the city. The senses open up here, and they wither away quickly and painfully in two or three days in the city. That is one of the strains of Berlin.

What does it mean that I—although I have never been "beautiful," although I have always been aware of the flaws in my figure, although I have seldom been desired by other men—as a woman do not have an inferiority complex? As a young girl I was actually oriented that way. Living together with Gerd and the intensity and perhaps my success in writing were probably sufficient to satisfy my hunger for a full life.

Get dressed, the old, thick jeans, the brown turtleneck sweater, casual. Fix breakfast, listen to the news while doing so (eight o'clock). Still the hysterical espionage affair, then the

Near East agreements from Camp David and other reports that I wanted to note down but have forgotten. I fix scrambled eggs with onions, tomato, and garlic. Coffee. Gerd comes, brings the utensils into the room—Smells good, he says. I think that politics, its goals and forms, together with the men who carry out the policies, is hopelessly outdated and old-fashioned, not at all in a position to grasp the problems of the present, let alone bring them closer to a solution. Oriented toward power and influence and support of economic goals, each of its "successes" leads us into new dead-end streets, and what the politicians celebrate, the people, if they only understood their own interests, should unceasingly deplore, even combat. But the majority of the people do not understand their interests; they trot along on the well-worn, misleading path with their heads hanging, and the few that break out of the institutions and try new forms with new goals are hopelessly alone and at a disadvantage. Nevertheless, they are the only hope.

Breakfast, also one of life's great pleasures. Along with it the Dresden Cross Choir with madrigals and folksongs. It tastes good. We talk about the question of how long Tinka has been "well" again—oh, no, I ask Gerd if he actually sometimes thinks about the process of aging. He: Why not? You probably think that I don't reflect about anything—I: I don't think that, but I want to prod you to let me participate in your reflection process—He: Why always immediately participate? . . . I: And why are we married? He: Surely not in order to share every reflection with each other—I: Yes, for that very reason. By the way, growing old does not frighten me. Just being old, being old and fragile for a long time. He: Yes. Being ill is dumb— Then we talk about our negligence in fighting illness: that he still has not been to the doctor to have his inguinal hernia examined. About the possibilities of getting near a good doctor. Then we talk about Tinka's time in the hospital, about her protracted pneumonia. Gerd denies—typical for him—that it was only last year. She was already well by then! We count up, present the evidence. Where Tinka is concerned, Gerd likes to make mistakes. I express my worry that she could start smoking again—Then about our country problems: what to do with the apple harvest, how to slip our way into the overworked cider mill, where to get somebody who will prune the trees during the winter, where to get fruit bushes, where to get a hedge, where to get paint to coat the fence—The record has just ended, the tone arm jumps up when I go out with the tray, clean up in the kitchen, and wash up, which I do not like to do, three times every day, but Gerd is right: better to do it myself than to be free of any housework . . .

Telephone, a call from Ingeborg A.[6] I want to tell you something, she says. A few days ago, she had gone to the legal information office with five other women and girls from her library, because they suspected that their director was not strictly abiding by the labor-law regulations, and they were told that they were right! Now they have filed a complaint. People in the workplace are very angry with them—even the labor union leaders, who actually should represent their interests, believe that their action was "underhanded"—Oh, I say, they will be angry there for a long time. They won't forgive you for something like that very quickly—I know, she says, once before, two years ago, a colleague asked for information from the district leadership of the Free German Trade Union Federation; she then left because she was no longer able to stand it—The syndicate of the employers vis-à-vis the employees in socialism as it really exists, I think. Ask her about her writing. She says: Coming along slowly. She must now laboriously distance herself from the character that she has laboriously approached for four years, otherwise it would turn out that only she is always right and all the others are only hypocrites and windbags and

[6] Ingeborg Arlt, librarian, writer; in correspondence with C.W. (G.W.)

so forth, and that is not true either—Yes, I say, that should actually not be the focus either. Since human beings have behaved egoistically for as long as the world has existed, we actually should investigate why they do it and not get stuck on condemning them, i.e. in moralizing—She says, then she would probably have to be as smart as I am in order to manage it (that is the same old tune, I like and dislike hearing it, in equal measure). I say, the bad thing is only the fact that deeper insight into these problems leads us in a crazy circle, but I would not want to burden my young colleague with that. We'll get that later.

(Gerd has now come after all—was not able to let it go, because he was amazed that I wrote six pages—to have a look at the page headings. Aha, he says. I call him names because he is also no longer candid now. He says, you can write that down along with everything else, that I am no longer candid either: a typical occurrence.)

Ingeborg A. does not want to accept the title of "colleague." I ask her how old she is. Twenty-nine? Back then I had not published anything yet either. But at forty-nine, she says, she will definitely not be like me. No, I say, but also *somebody*, just different. She says, yes, a hedgehog. She has taken the expression from one of Luxemburg's letters: Go after the philistines like a raging hedgehog. By the way, during a recent evening she had heard me read on the radio, from the Kleist-Günderrode story, and she had been unsatisfied because she thought that it was the entire text; not until later did she realize that it was only a small part. But I must also have some hedgehog in me; otherwise I could not understand Kleist and Günderrode so well—Sure, I say boastfully, they were very afraid of me! We have to laugh about that. I suggest to her that she should call her attack on the library director the "Hedgehog Campaign." She goes on to talk about the former midwife who now works in the library because her earnings in the clinic "with that responsibility" were too small. I admonish tolerance: Midwives really are paid too little. Yes, she says, but then she should simply say that she left because of the money and leave the responsibility out of it—She should, I say, keep me informed about the results and the successes of the Hedgehog Campaign.

I think, while I am still drying the dishes: They are still doing something. I gave it up as useless and am cutting myself off here. At breakfast Gerd said that I would probably have enough material, even if I did not leave. He is right there. You always want to "change" something, he says. Otherwise you do not feel well. It is true.

It is twenty to twelve. We go over the hill to Carola's. The sky has clouded over, no more sunshine. As we walked over the hill past the "Neanderthal" to Carola's place, it occurred to me that this morning, as he came out of the kitchen with the breakfast tray, Gerd said: Christa and Gerhard in the farmhouse . . . Life is sometimes very strange, don't you think?—And that I completely shared that feeling of strangeness and alienation: that we live here, and so forth—only a few years ago it would have been an absurd idea to us. Now it is the thing that makes life possible at all. The second addendum (my inclination toward precision is eating me up!): Ingeborg A. asked me what I am working on now. I said, since I had the "Günderrode shit" behind me now, I would write something "for me" and then something *else* only for me—in order to find out if I could still be honest. When you write for publication, you are not dishonest, of course, but something always gets shoved between your head and your hand, and it is very good to find out now and then if you can still get rid of that intermediate layer (it is, of course, only *one* of the reasons for "writing for myself," but *nonetheless* one).

We hardly talked on the way. Gerd complained once that a field was sloppily cultivated. Together we became indignant at the fact that work on the paved road to Meteln had been broken off right in the middle because the machines were with-drawn to Schwerin to the Great Fallow Field, where some sort of project is supposed to be finished by October 7; that the road is so narrow and is already crumbling on the edges, so that winter potholes can already be anticipated. Just why, we asked, can nothing be done properly in our country any-more?—I thought, as I walked through the tall grass, across the pastures that also remained unused this year, how I used to fret about all of these mistakes and identified with every bit of negligence, every failure, and when all that began to stop: a long, painful process before that identification turned into joy-less malicious glee, into that nagging laughter with which I par-ody myself and that is foreign to me. I know that a remnant of that identification mania lies in the need to seek "guilty par-ties" who are responsible for this creeping alienation. But they do not exist, and if they do, they are subject to circumstances. Others are not there because they were not needed and there-fore not tolerated. You can explain the failure of Marxist experiments from the Marxian point of view.

The autumn colors. Brown, brownish, and brownish-green predominate, dark green on the edge of the trees, beginning change of color to yellowish, still hardly perceptible. (Today I read in the newspaper that yesterday in the territory of the German Democratic Republic the day was "too cold for the season"—the most frequent weather report of this year—the storks were already flying south at the end of August, the swal-lows were flocking together now, and flocks of wild geese would meet on Dambeck Lake before their departure.) After two or three days of rain the roads are impassable, and every autumn that creates a feeling of hopelessness, even rage: that the tractor drivers avoid the small effort to lift their plows when they cross the roads and thus ruin them; that everything of that kind has become immaterial to them.

The sky was cloudy, not gloomy; there were strips of brightness. At Carola's: the elderberry bushes with their heavy, black, juicy berries. The door was open, the living-room windows as well. She was ironing. Was wearing no makeup, therefore more girlish than usual. A cat was running around, marked almost like our Max. She immediately jumped into my lap and stayed there, purred, and let herself be petted the entire time, even offered me her belly to pet. Gerd tries to make a telephone call, but her telephone is, as so often now, out of order. She brought apples, fresh nuts, and quickly carried the basket of ironing away, so that Gerd did not see it. As always, when she is alone, the house quickly seems uninhabited, cool. We talk about making cider and make an appointment with her for the afternoon. When we leave, the sheep slips into the kitchen behind her and then walks out in front of the door again, like the real lord of the manor. We feel its black, greasy wool, the beginnings of horns on its head. Carola calls it Tulichka. For her every animal becomes a child.

She talks about the abominable state of affairs with the cosmonauts—Jähn and Bykovsky—how in Schwerin a newspaper woman in a kiosk was completely surrounded by their portraits and said furiously: For weeks we have been living on nothing but that!—Thomas is on a reading trip to earn money. He cannot stand any insecurity, she says. She tried to persuade him that it would be better to finish writing his stories first, but he needed a money cushion—now, however, they have nothing at all.

We go back. By mistake I put on Carola's rubber boots, which are torn in back. With them Gerd's old leather jacket. You look like you are from the country, he says. Proper.

At home we eat leftovers: the pea soup, to which I mistakenly add thyme instead of marjoram, a green pepper. Dishwashing again. In bed a few pages of Oscar Wilde—the story changes more and more into an essay about the Shakespeare sonnets. Shakespeare never viewed those sonnets as important works; they made the rounds in a few copies among a few friends. Oh, our presumptuousness and our impatience!

It is pouring again at noon. As always I sleep in two stages: I do not *want* to be awake yet, *want* to lose consciousness once more . . . Upon awakening I retain from a dream that I forget— only this much: somebody was beaten—the following absurd sentences: "Atom, why are you talking about that? Atom is really nothing more than an onion. Albrecht's Watch and onion, those are the true signs now." But who said that? And how do I arrive at Albrecht's Watch? I am now often fascinated by the remarkable images that I see before falling asleep, or immediately afterward, the sentences that I hear (not think).

Carola comes. Departure. In the village we obtain rubber boots for her, Gerd picks up the laundry, I loan C. fifty marks, she has spent her money for the boots. On the way, I tell her about the girl (why?) who was locked up at Hoheneck [7] because of a signature against the Biermann expatriation, and I achieve the desired effect ("To me it is as if she had also spent time in jail for me"). Schwerin is full, hardly a parking place to be found. The three of us walk through the streets, Gerd always off to the side or ahead of us, I look for material for a skirt, do not find it, buy fresh bread, by which we set great store, go into the antique shops; yesterday Biedermeier items were being sold, everything is gone; marked with a red dot. It just cannot be expensive enough, the people buy it; after all, they do not know what else they earn their money for. We seek L.'s cottage in a back yard. L., who attaches himself tenaciously to us and is either an informer or a person who does not notice when people want to shake him off, who suddenly appears at our home and brings books to be signed . . . Gerd hangs the bag with the books on his door handle with a note containing the false message that we have to return to

[7] Hoheneck: women's prison of the German Democratic Republic. (G.W.)

Berlin . . . I say to Carola that it is actually immaterial to me if they watch us here, too, but then correct myself. No, I do feel better when I feel somewhat freer. I notice that as soon as things are peaceful for a few days, I push aside the awareness that they are serious about it.

In Schwerin we buy a heavy pair of stockings for me on Carola's advice (in those you will be quite warm, you'll see!), then records: Paganini, Telemann, Handel, Bach, and Giehse doing her Brecht interpretation. I now buy records constantly, as if I had to lay in a supply for times when I will not leave the house.

Then a few Reclam books in the bookstore, which is arranged so soberly and unclearly. Georg Heym, Tibor Déry, Franzos . . . While taking our money, the book dealer says that she does not like this kind of paperback book very much. I say, that is a prejudice of the Germans, the French actually have only hardback books. I noted that the revolving shelf with the East German books did not tempt me at all; I did not pull out a single one of them.

Meanwhile, Gerd had obtained tickets for *The Summer People*, and then we looked for a café and failed to find one as usual. Shortly before six we quickly bought some cake at a bakery, sat in the car and ate it, cream puffs and lemon cake . . . we drove to Leninplatz and parked. It was a little after six and beginning to get dark. A few strides up and down the street, which immediately becomes desolate after the stores close. Carola told us how she always used to walk through Leipzig on Sunday mornings, how unspeakably desolate it had been, with everything as if it were riveted and nailed shut.

In the movie theater we then obtained the coffee that we had wanted. I had some vodka, cooled with ice. Sentimental music was playing. Only about twenty people were there. *The Eye Witness* [8] feature showed all kinds of remarkable incidents

[8] *Augenzeuge*: DEFA film agency weekly news program. (G.W.)

with animals, among them pictures of a fur-bearing animal farm, showing how carefully the animals are tended and cared for in preparation for death. I had to resist viewing that banal process as something symbolic, but in his perverse care and his cruel egoism the man seemed like a monster to me, like the only monster on earth. And he is.

Then, in glowing colors, the cottage where the summer guests live. The fragments of sentences that draw nearer, their argument about the nature of literature in the narrow vestibule of the cottage. How each of them, one after another, is drawn into the plot and characterized. The peeling window frames. The whitish ball lamps on their tall poles. The dresses and blouses of the women who played their roles perfectly. The furniture—everything was correct. I wanted to inhale the sentences that they spoke, hold on to and not forget them. The perplexity of the first time came again, this time not with the undertone of despair, but almost of satisfaction. (In the background, always the thought of the girl. I resolved to maintain contact with her, to send her books. Feet are wiping themselves off on her while I write, am published, and stand around at receptions.) I thought that my notes of recent days about "anguish of the soul" were disgraceful; today I already no longer think that.

At the end of the film I was happy rather than shattered—not the same as last time. Even the knowledge that every new turn of the wheel brings nothing new to light, "until the end of the world," could not affect me at the moment. Today it can, however. Even while I still sat in my comfortable movie seat and resolved not to avoid clear, courageous actions but to seek them, I also knew that I will not carry out that intention, that I am not free to do what I want, not even to want what I want. That is actually what "growing old" is; to know that and yet continue to live and to seek and find joy and pleasure.

On the drive back—we still had to stop at the gas station—

we frightened Carola with the term "military dictatorship," which she could no longer get away from and which I then regretted. Why do we have to make her afraid? She could not eat; she has often been sick recently, not in her stomach but in her soul.

Remarkable how they succeed in *The Summer People* in having all the characters receive their due, each from his or her point of view. The writer—to what extent does Gorky identify with him? He, "written out," as they say, who admits that he writes because he must live, and who, if he were honest, would throw away his pen, go out into the country, and raise potatoes: he in his painful search for the "new reader," he, who remains an observer and has the final word: Everything is immaterial. Who once, when Varvara, who loves him, talks about her former admiration for him, bursts out: Just what do you all want from me? Am I supposed to be a hero simply because I write stories? I am a totally ordinary person, and you do not want to grant me that . . . I know the feeling.

What primarily concerns us about the film, of course, is this eternal, constantly repeating separation of the people and the intellectuals, and the fact that they cannot come together, cannot relate to each other, do not concern each other: the one group eternally teaching, lecturing, the others led by and dependant upon totally different interests.

Today again this fear of physical destruction. It must be the autumn, what else? And the ghosts that we ourselves conjure up, who make us afraid. Should it then be true and our only salvation that we must at least halfway sell ourselves to the lesser evil in order not to be swallowed up, mocked, and destroyed by the greater one? Oh.

In the evening the three of us drank a large bottle of Badenser wine, ate cheese, liverwurst, and garlic sandwiches, and talked. Gerd went to bed; I sat at the farmer's table in the corner with Carola until twelve-thirty. We talked about where the hatred of many colleagues toward us comes from. All right: the mediocre must use their opportunity—but why desire to stomp on the others? Both probably belong together—they are two sides of one coin. And yet every time that I am confronted with a concrete case it causes me great uneasiness. They are insolent and shameless and cruel, we must not be deceived about what they will be capable of doing if the last reins are removed from them. And once, if "one" sees herself driven into a corner, one could use them. (It was a reference to the Writers' Union in Frankfurt, names are unnecessary.)

My left arm hurts from writing. A while ago I was listening to the first part of Schubert's *Winter Journey* once again, which I now crave. For a long time last night I made an effort to strengthen Carola's self-confidence, for example vis-à-vis her Greek grandmother who takes the reins in the house and does what she wants with Carola. Never, never will she be able to put up any resistance against her, she says, and I chewed her out: Just whom did she think she was helping by making herself so small and causing herself to disappear? . . . But I really don't have any right, she just repeats again and again and makes me furious. Let's talk about something else, she says. Everywhere in the world I see only the same thing: that the people are destroying themselves—Her final, amazingly naïve illusions: But I do believe very firmly that the Soviet Union wants peace and would always, always champion it—The mechanism of power is still unknown to her.

Shortly after midnight I consider whether or not I should call Tinka, but then let it go, perhaps she is already asleep, I think. We go to bed, Carola in the front room, where we fired up the beautiful new green tiled stove. Together we make the bed with bedding we just bought for Jana. I think about Annette and Honza,[9] who are in Warsaw, and ask myself if I

---

[9] Jan (Honza) Faktor, Annette Wolf's second husband. (Ed.)

would have the courage, if I were younger, to bring a child into the world now.

I read a few more pages of Oscar Wilde, Gerd is already asleep. I fall asleep at shortly before one. Toward morning I dream about a man who is being pursued; I no longer remember the details, only that he is running through streets and I am always next to him, like a movie camera. And then again I am suddenly in an apartment on the top floor of a new apartment house. The wife of that man lives there; she rolls a gray overcoat together into a bundle and throws it through a window down to the street where her husband is still running. I, however, am suddenly expecting a child. I see myself in the dream, which is strange, and you cannot tell by looking at me. But there is an electric apparatus in the apartment; when I touch it, the indicator moves and shows how far along the labor is already—which I do not feel—and that I have to go to the clinic. I pack my suitcase and notice with horror that I have not prepared anything for the child. All of Jana's rompers are hanging around the place, but I really cannot take them. Perhaps they are not very clean at all. I let the air out of inflated rubber animals and stuff the casings in my bag so that I will at least already have a toy for the baby. Gerd is also amazed about the child that is supposed to be coming . . . When I wake up, it is seven-thirty, and Gerd is getting up. The sun is shining, but I am still tired and do not want to get up. I sleep until eight-thirty and then get up.

The first thing in the morning, a reddish light from the round window above my desk. Gerd jumps up and looks out the round window across from it. The sunrise is clouded over; we see only its reflection in the opposite part of the sky. Gerd says that unfortunately he has already been awake for a while. One of us often says that in the morning, he thinks. I wake up in the night. It occurs to me that I screamed twice in my dream. Gerd says, yes, once it was a kind of cry of resistance, the second time a kind of scream for help. From the second time I remember only a glowing red color in which this dream was bathed, my deep anguish, and that I could not cry out aloud, that I heard my own thin little voice and in spite of every effort did not bring out a single full tone. It occurs to me, and it does amaze me a bit, how promptly the fulfillment of the "wish" followed, that in the evening before falling asleep I thought that I would most like to scream now as if in my sleep, in order to make Gerd aware of me and my needy condition. I did not do it, just as in general the hidden appeals that I formerly permitted myself have become much more seldom since I no longer make anyone else responsible for my condition, since I no longer feel sorry for myself, since I have been forbidding myself to worry Gerd unnecessarily.

It is after six and actually we are still weary. What is causing me not to make any headway with my work, he asks from the other bed. I do not want to make a mountain out of a molehill and seek to allay his disquiet. It will come. Perhaps I am simply still too deep in the material. I do not say what I felt yesterday: fatal barrenness, discouragement, and depression—I have, he says, not really been able to sink myself into a piece of work at all this year. The Frankfurt lectures have been left unfinished—I think fleetingly that I should not have agreed to do them at all, that I should not do anything theoretical now at all, in order to prove to myself that I can still write. I wanted to finish the story, I say, that I wrote in June, July, and August ("What Remains"). He: But you could have seen in advance that it would offer insurmountable difficulties. We should talk about things earlier. I: I can't do that—It is true. I cannot talk about material in advance because it then loses its glow and its charm.

You are familiar, he says, with conditions of relief and non-relief—I say: Yes. The day before yesterday, when I heard about the amnesty,[1] that enormous relief. Only then did I feel the lead weight that otherwise rests on my shoulders—But you really can't, he says, commiserate with everyone who is in prison. You didn't do that before either—No. Nor do I understand any longer how I could live with that before. Today this entire country presses down on my shoulders, and only occasionally do I become free of it so that I can straighten up more easily. But that would be the same somewhere else, of course—Not quite, he says. Somewhere else it would not concern you—So, a self-deception—Yes. But where does this indissoluble identification with this country come from? Why do you never get rid of it?—I say, if they had been able to get rid of it, Sarah Kirsch and Günter Kunert would not have left. It is actually that from which they had to flee. And I will always remember the moment—it was after the Biermann expatriation, it was in

[1] Amnesty: On October 11, 1979, about 20,000 people in the German Democratic Republic who had been sentenced to prison for mostly "political crimes" received amnesty, among them Rudolf Bahro (sentenced to eight years in prison in 1978 because of his book *Die Alternative* [*The Alternative*], 1977). (G.W.)

Hungary, on the bus from Hevis to the airport, when I promised myself that if I am able to free myself and continue to write, totally independently, I can remain here; if not, I must leave.

We know all that, have discussed it a hundred times. While we are talking about it, it seems to me as if the cramp is relaxing, as if, by bringing personal things up for discussion, I will also manage to complete that Bettina afterword after all, not simply as a cold piece of diligent work. (Now, while I am sitting at the typewriter, which I always see as the first object in the morning, against the gray window curtain on the little technical stand, now that dry weariness behind my eyes is already there again, and it is fortunate that I have this here to write today. It is already a quarter after ten.) G. says that he, too, knows such paralyzing conditions, he simply takes care not to become aware of them as depression. If he does become aware of them, then for weeks he can do virtually nothing but fritter away the days—That would be what I would like to do now, too, I say. But I am even more afraid of that than of the laborious work that I force myself to do for hours at a time.

It is a gray day, milder than those that have preceded it; now the wind comes up. All summer long I saw the apple tree standing very close to the window where I work, from the time of the succulent blossoms until now, where a fullness of large, greenish-red apples hangs from it. I have never experienced such a thing before, nature in its yearly cycle. It is a real treasure, something new. A piece of happiness. I think that this simple act of lying together and talking with each other is happiness, an intimate hour that I want to take into myself and preserve. What more do I want? I often count up the things that contribute to the fact that I am doing extraordinarily well. I tell Gerd that and think, I have to manage to feel as well as I am doing. (Again something that I want to "manage" to do . . .)

Gerd says how it amazes him that the people here, whose

lives are a single bad wearing-down process, nevertheless get up every morning at five and go to work. Otto Sch.'s compensation for it: being sick on occasion (and then he really is) or to get drunk in Drispeth and make speeches about the salvation of the world, so that people think he belongs to the Jehovah's Witnesses.

I come to the images that I involuntarily see when I lie there with my eyes closed, or during autogenic training, or shortly before falling asleep. Gerd says that he does not see such images, that he sees only circles or dots. I do not want to believe it. He simply has not concentrated on it yet, I say. Describe the loose condition of expectation that I have to bring on, so that the images "come," arise, are not projected into the eternal field of view. I could imagine, I say, that painters find motifs in that way. One sees quite wonderful colors and very strange motifs. I tell him what I "am seeing" at the moment and what I have already forgotten, as in a dream. He has doubts about the spontaneity of the process.

It occurs to me that this entire observed day falls under the Heisenberg uncertainty principle. It is deformed by my constant viewing of it. It does not pass as it would otherwise pass. It wins and loses through consciousness.

We go back to sleep for a short time. As I wake up, I say: I just saw very clearly an enameled funnel from which a coarsely woven net was hanging. You do see surrealistic images, Gerd says. Yes, I say, I see them often. And landscapes. In my thoughts I also ride into a tunnel on an express train, just to see what kind of landscape opens up on the other side. I really do not know it in advance—Gerd cannot really imagine that, and I am amazed that I have never spoken about it before. I myself have probably also only been consciously aware of the phenomenon since the autogenic training with K.

We jump up. I grab my things, place them on the dresser in the vestibule, and enter the kitchen in my bathrobe, while

Gerd takes a shower. Wash up the dishes from last night's supper—very seldom do I leave it undone, because I like to come into a clean kitchen in the morning, but last night any chore was too much for me. I then shower thoroughly, very hot for a long time, then cold for a long time. At the same time I listen to the news on Radio Germany (the spoon radio continues to hold out for that): Senator Dahrendorf[2] stepped down because of his involvement in the poison scandal in Hamburg; Genscher[3] spoke with Gromyko[4] in passing at the UN meeting: Further "confidence-building measures" should be agreed upon between East and West. The new government of Cambodia permitted some international aid organizations to open offices in the capital city in order to help the starving people quickly and "impartially." Images from a nightmare appear before my inner eye. I know that I will quickly forget them again.

In the kitchen it smells like coffee and fried eggs. This is the best odor, Gerd says. Homemade blackberry jam is on the table. For the hundredth time Gerd praises the stove that heats the kitchen so quickly. He has already put the plums that lay in sugar overnight on the stove, where they now have to "dehydrate" for two hours over a low flame. We eat the black "goat bread," as it is called here because it is so cheap that the farmers feed it to their cattle. I take my pills: a Digitoxin, half an Obsidan. (All that serves to firm up the memory of these days that are slipping away, which are my lifetime: I will not have another.) Lard that we rendered ourselves. Dishwashing after

[2] Ralf Gustav Dahrendorf, Baron Dahrendorf (b. 1929), KBE, German-British sociologist, philosopher, political scientist and politician, member of Free Democratic Party, and from 1970 to 1974 commissioner in the EU. (Ed.)

[3] Hans-Dietrich Genscher (b. 1927), German politician and chairman of the Free Democratic Party. Foreign Minister of the Federal Republic of Germany from 1974-1992, making him Germany's longest serving Foreign Minister. (Ed.)

[4] Andrei Andreyevich Gromyko (1909-1989), Soviet politician and diplomat, Minister for Foreign Affairs for the Soviet Union from 1957 to 1985, Chairman of the Presidium of the Supreme Soviet from 1985 to 1988. (Ed.)

breakfast, even the jars for the plum jam. Gerd talks about Arendt's new poems[5]: They "run on." He wants to suggest abridgements to him. I express doubts about the principle and its validity.

I try to call Annette. Briefly hear Franci's voice, but the connection is very bad, and when I try again I do not get a connection. Our telephone—a chapter in itself. Sometimes I think: Perhaps they are not listening in on us here. The letters mailed in the German Democratic Republic arrive quickly and appear not to have been opened. I almost do not want to believe it.

With a few flicks of the wrist I clean up downstairs, make the beds upstairs, and sit down at the typewriter to write this text. By then it is already almost nine-thirty. My eternal wish, to sit at my desk by eight o'clock, remains unfulfilled; the resistance to writing is too strong, has made an accomplice of my need to have order around me.

Later Annette calls—What I am doing—Keeping house, keeping house—How are the children doing—Well. They are also very lively. Jana has adjusted very well to the school. She notices no change at all in her behavior. She, Annette, will become a member of the parents' advisory committee and wants to find an assignment for herself in which she can use her professional experience as a psychologist. Jana has desisted again in her desire to go to daycare. Benjamin is as sweet as ever, now screams very little, and sleeps through the night until quarter after six: Children just go through phases—I respond evasively to the question of how I am doing. We ask ourselves

[5] Erich Arendt (1903-1984), lyric poet and essayist, translator of Latin American and Spanish literature (Pablo Neruda, V. Aleixandre, M. Hernandez, Gongora, and others); close friends with G. and C.W.; G.W. edited various anthologies of his poetry and wrote about his works (see: G.W., *Wortlaut Wortbruch Wortlust* [*Wording Word Breaking Word Lust*], Leipzig, 1988; *Vagant der bin ich* [*Traveling Scholar I Am*], Berlin, 1993); editor of Erich Arendt's lyric poetry for the Rimbaud Publishing Company, Aachen. (G.W.)

if the amnesty is valid for everyone, Annette thinks it is. The Thirtieth Anniversary was thus worthwhile . . . As always she asks if we are not thinking of coming back. In the winter she wants to have parents again for a change—What do you need them for? I ask—To talk all she wants, she says. As far as they can see, Franci is doing quite well—I think, but do not say, that Annette has six years behind her that were not very easy, and that she is really holding her own. I say that we do not want to go to Berlin now because I have to write my Bettina afterword, which is as hard for me as cutting down trees, and that I cannot interrupt it again now—It is accepted.

Meanwhile Mrs. Sch. has brought the mail in, in it also a small book package from Luchterhand. A letter from Günter de Bruyn with an invitation to go to the university in Bamberg, which he tries to make palatable to me, and above all the following paragraph: "Mr. Gysi will represent our dyer and dressmaker as her attorney. The last thing that I heard from her was that she succeeded in moving an official to deliver a knitted dress that she had promised the 'sibyl' to the editorial office on time." The dressmaker is Jutta Braband.[6] I do not know why this news consoles me a little bit: as if a human hand were reaching out from the frightening anonymous apparatus. And also: if she is thinking about her delivery dates "in there," perhaps she is not doing too badly. I think of the text that I entitled "Green Nuts" and that was supposed to be dedicated to her. (She uses the green nuts to dye her cloth.) Will I write it?

A poem from an admirer, addressed to Gerd, dedicated to me: "Why I Cannot See Christa Wolf"—It would be embarrassing to me to write it down here. Gerd says that somebody should say to the sender sometime: Girl, stay on the carpet—

---

[6] Jutta Braband (b. 1949), fashion designer at the time, was arrested in 1979 for oppositional activity; C.W. appealed for her release to the politburo of the Socialist Unity Party; after 1989 representative of the United Left; 1990-1992 delegate in the German federal parliament for the Party of Democratic Socialism. (G.W.)

But it would not do any good. A kind of true passion is in gear there, and I cannot reject her because I sense the talent and do not want to damage it; it has been damaged enough by others.

Among the books is one with critical essays on the feminist movement, which appears to be interesting—A card from Dieter from Italy—A letter from one of my Italian translators, who is in Berlin at a time when I am not there. Am happy about that, happy about any visit that does not take place. Do not want to talk with anyone, although I often have a strong longing for people here, a longing to work with people. Yesterday, at the overly long *Faust* rehearsal in the Schwerin theater, I sensed again how this act of working alone taxes me in the long run. Gerd reads a sentence aloud to me from the critique of *No Place on Earth* in *Sonntag*, by the Schlenstedts[7]: that I denounce practice. It is a misunderstanding. If I cannot accept, cannot adhere to today's wrongheaded practices, it does not mean that I would reject action in general. And in spite of that, the question always remains, as a barb: did I give up too soon? Should I have made further compromises in order to remain "inside," in order to be able to do something?—But what?—There is no answer to that.

At around eleven we fill jars with the plum jam and then I write for another hour on this text—live in order to describe it!—now it is after twelve. I will go into the kitchen, cut the cutlets into little pieces, fry them with onions and paprika, and fix rice to go along with it, cauliflower.

Now it is three twenty-five. I had lain down at one-thirty and resolved to be sitting at the typewriter again at three o'clock, but I slept this long. Always very tired in the middle of the day. Before falling asleep I saw a girl with a white dress on a swing, perhaps tied to a few sentences from Bettina's *Goethe's Correspondence with a Child*, which I had just noted

[7] Dieter and Silvia Schlenstedt, literary scholars in the GDR. (Tr.)

yesterday: "Those magical charms, this ability to do magic, are my white dress; but Sir, this suspicion cannot be contested, that the white dress will also be taken off of me and that I will walk around in the usual ones of common, everyday life, and that this world, in which my senses are alive, will founder."— It is possible that Bettina did not write those lines until she was a fifty-year-old woman, in fulfillment of prophecy, while still remembering what troubled her as a twenty-year-old. This disenchantment of the feminine—she experienced and endured it in her own life; we do not know what it may have cost her to create a counter-world for herself—Before falling asleep I had read in Bettina's Günderrode book, the pages where she seeks to describe why she cannot write creatively: "My conscience hinders me in writing" . . . "I probably have a dark idea of why I do not write, simply because the deep things that powerfully seize me, so that there would be electrical power in the language, are something that does not legitimize itself in the world of feeling, or in order to express myself more quickly and without circumlocution, because it is *nonsense* that surges in my soul, because it is nonsense that my thoughts tell me over and over again, because it is nonsense that forebodingly takes hold of me as the highest essence of wisdom"—I think that in my essay this nonsense-thinking that suspects that it is wisdom, this feminine re-evaluation of the given facts and relationships from which Bettina draws the power to act ingenuously, even "foolishly," should play a larger, a primary role. My getting stuck certainly announced to me, as is always the case, only that I have not yet grasped the thing by the right handle. If I can trust the lightness that I now feel, it will now go better.

While I wrote this, Gerd was still lying in bed, reading in the new Luchterhand book *Overcoming Speechlessness*. He quoted from an essay in which it is explained that the Mycenaean culture was the last one that still had matriarchal elements, that afterwards, a large gap of three hundred years came, and then something entirely new began in which the old culture was lost and symbols that were once considered positive mutated; the sphinx, for example. Immediately appeals to me as a motif, belongs to my Cassandra sphere, for which I must collect things from this winter on, and specifically as much as possible even over there. I see myself riding around and feel somewhat enlightened.

I gave Gerd the new contract from Luchterhand (for the volume of stories that is supposed to appear in the spring) and asked him to compare it with the old one—Your secretary, huh? He says. It will come to that yet—Sure, I say, it would be nice—Then from downstairs he shouts questions and information at me; at the end he says: *Exchanging Glances* was a very good title—I was just thinking the same thing, I say. I have already finished my very strong coffee; his is standing in the kitchen and getting cold.

I must add that while fixing lunch I listened to the news and "Current Events of the Day," attempted to attain Bettina's inner view, and came again and again to the formula: everything is wrong. All these men who see themselves and each other as important, who deal with "politics," which means the same as: distributing power. How each of them makes a great effort not to lose face. Now the 2000-3000 men of the Soviet military brigades are in Cuba, now the two great powers have become engrossed in that small troop, and neither of them can back down, and there will be a war sometime about something like that, one that nobody wants, but also that nobody can prevent, because the mental attitude to which they are all subject leads directly there. I often ask myself how I must think differently, behave differently—we have to begin somewhere, so with ourselves. Not slip into that one-track thinking with them, not be just as stubborn, just as bestially serious as they are. Rather difficult when your neck is on the line. Right now, for example, in

Leipzig they are expelling Erich Loest[8] from the Writers' Union, and he will then probably also leave. Among the news reports was also the one that the Palestinians are gaining ground in the UN and the Israelis are losing ground because of their uncompromising attitude; besides that the other powers want to get at the Arabians' oil. And everything is that way. Feeding the world will become even more difficult this year, but it is a matter of power and influence. I do not see how these lines, with catastrophe lying at the point where they cross, could be forced in another direction. Someone also talked about the ridiculous contributions, when compared with the armament expenditures, which world hunger relief has at its disposal . . .

Here in our country now, before the Thirtieth Anniversary, there is only noise and the beating of drums anyway. Gigantic lists of honors in the newspaper, which I hardly leaf through. Gerd reads the reviews, says that a new generation of writers is forcing its way to the forefront and will have to fight its way through, even if their first books and plays are still very proper. Now, however, even forty-year-olds here are still viewed as "the rising generation."

It is four-fifteen. I still have to "take care of the mail," the eternal nightmare. The mail folder that is always full.

9/28/79: I wrote six letters: to the copyright office, so that it would approve the Luchterhand contract for the stories, among which is also "A Little Outing to H." that cannot be published here, which I did not directly point out; to Altenhein about the stay in Darmstadt; to the Darmstadt Academy with regard to a hotel room in October; to the Frankfurt City Theaters, Peter Palitzsch,[9] about a possible meeting in October; to a female student in West Berlin to

[8] Erich Loest (b. 1926), German writer born in Mittweida (Germany). Also writes under the pseudonyms Hans Walldorf, Bernd Diksen and Waldemar Naß. (Ed.)

[9] Peter Palitzsch (1918-2004), German theater director who advocated politically involved theater. (Tr.)

accept an invitation to a discussion about the possible effects of antifascist literature, and to the de Bruyns. That is now almost the normal relationship between my "Western" and my "Eastern" mail, I notice it myself with some amazement, even a bit concerned. The "official" contacts are becoming increasingly limited here, the opportunities to move around in the institutions are gradually disappearing completely, but the institutions will not change anymore in my lifetime . . . Actually I have never strived toward a role on the sidelines.

With haste and in a great hurry I got ready for the reading, put on the brown dress, stuffed a lard sandwich into my mouth in passing, gathered up all my books, and put on my cosmetics while Gerd was already driving the car out of the garage, then quickly wrote a birthday card for Tinka, on the front of which the Schwerin theater and the cathedral were portrayed in color, and at a little before six we drove away. It was only then that we noticed the sky.

The skies here are unbelievable, and yesterday was one of the most beautiful. A red sunset, its colors reflected through a field of clouds consisting of strokes, a geometrically almost faultless, rare formation, and between the individual glowing red fields the open sky, pale blue and apple green: I showed Gerd what I always call "apple green," and as always he wanted to insist that it was blue. A different kind of blue. On the way I turned pages in the books to make sure of what I would read, without carefully preparing the text as I always do otherwise. Near Lübstorf we had to pass three heavy trucks with double trailers, no idea where they came from. It rapidly got dark, and on the road to Schwerin we hardly saw the red sky on the right at all, because of the trees, but on the left its reflection and the other end of the firmament—another phenomenon that I first really become familiar with here.

We drove to Tinka's place, Robert-Blum-Strasse. I got out. As always Mr. M. was working in front of the building; as always the dog Felix was yapping furiously on his chain behind the sign: CAUTION, VICIOUS DOG! Mr. M. kindly let me through; their veranda, where they always sit and watch television, is now the way they wanted it: with a sofa and chairs. I put a rose in the bottle with a handle on Tinka's little round table; the old pepper can filled with prunes, and an envelope with our card and some money. "Happy birthday tu yu," Gerd had written on the envelope. I became irritated that I had forgotten her towels. As I went back down, I asked Mrs. M. if Tinka always came home late. She did not know, she said in her lax way. The dog already knows her now and no longer barks at night, so she does not hear when Tinka comes home. At the theater it probably always gets late, of course. Outside the raging Felix again. We drive on, mail letters, and go along Obotritenring in the direction of Crivitz. Once I startle Gerd with my hasty reaction, as I shout "Careful!" just when he, as he so often does, is looking somewhere else and not at the road and I believe that he has failed to see a motorcycle rider. My reactions would startle him much more than the real moment of danger, he says. I admit it, but find that he looks around too much while he is driving. He sees everything that happens all around us, while I can only watch the road—Otherwise we do not talk very much, search a little bit through a few ultrashortwave stations, but then give up.

In Crivitz we are too early, first look for the place in the wrong direction, and then it is seven-twenty when we arrive. A new school where it still smells like whitewash and paint, Polytechnic High School II. Mrs. B. is already waiting; the room in which the reading is supposed to be, normally the teachers' room, fills up. Tables with glistening Formica tops set up in a horseshoe formation, poison-green placemats that have no function spread out on top of them, on the wall a radiant, youthful Honecker in front of a sky-blue background, undoubtedly arranged that way by an advertising specialist.

Mr. St. gives the introduction. He is the subject instructor for German and organizes the cultural life in Crivitz. He wears a Party insignia, is approximately as old as we are, and has a scar on his face. He does not speak extravagantly, mentions the approaching Thirtieth Anniversary several times. I read from *No Place on Earth*, the beginning, slightly abbreviated. Am not very focused, orient myself on a few faces that I have noticed, am not very convinced of the quality of what I am reading. After thirty-five minutes I stop.

There is no break, unlike what is often otherwise the case, and a woman who is sitting across from me, who does not have a beautiful, but a good and interesting face and is about my age (she walks with a cane, I notice later, and I learn that she is an eye, nose, and ear doctor) immediately says that she read the book like an extended poem; the language had a suggestive impact on her, and then she read it again for "content." She wants to know if the language in this book was influenced by the language forms of the time about which I wrote—A second woman, with her back to the first. She must admit that the reading was difficult for her. She is not used to this kind of literature. For example, I use no quotation marks at all, and then the reader does not know exactly whether a person has spoken or only thought a sentence, and sometimes the reader also does not know who. She then immediately read the book a second time and in the process also understood the title. And now, during the third time, when I read it aloud, she understood everything—A female colleague who is sitting behind her says that she is right—To the left an approximately forty-year-old man—the men are in the minority—by the way, the women also dominate mentally—The reproach has been raised against each of my books, of course, that it is difficult; for him they had always pushed open a door that enabled him to occupy himself with something, they had stimulated him to think . . .

That gives me the opportunity to say something about the

misjudgment of many years standing in this country, according to which reportage with contemporary themes has been declared to be part of what is actually worthwhile literature.

The discussion is astonishing. A librarian from the scientific general library of Schwerin says that literature only begins for her with books like this one. But she was startled when she recently worked in a normal lending library, at how the people there walked around as they did twenty years ago, and that they also, as they did twenty years ago, exchanged stacks of crime novels—We once believed, I said, without being contradicted, that in the future everyone would need art, but like many other beliefs this too proved to be an illusion; as long as the operating method does not change and the producers of material goods come home dead tired after eight and a half hours of work, they would not be able to feel any need for art; but even if the workday were drastically shortened, as it may indeed be, I do not believe that all people would need art. People are too different. For me it already means a great deal to encounter a circle of people now and then, in which I see the beginnings for such a new coexistence with art.

Another librarian, perhaps forty years old, a very attractive woman, brown hair, slender, a striking face, tastefully dressed, said something deeply touching. While reading such books as mine, she feels that they, the readers, actually lack words when dealing with their deepest concerns, and that what they could not say is expressed there.

I try to explain some of the problems of the role into which an author, who has to speak as the representative of other, silent people, can very easily be forced. We come to the desired concept of "dialogue." The knowledge remains that in our country literature must often serve as a replacement for other opportunities for self-realization that are withheld.

For a long time the discussion revolves around the concepts of conversation, communication, and dealing with one another. It is quite clear that this touches upon a central problem of their lives: that they are limited to functioning in a one-sided profession; that they have forgotten how to talk with each other; that people do not open themselves to each other; that each one wants and is able to talk only about him/herself, but not to listen to someone else; that they have never learned to express their innermost needs and feelings. Everyone's interest in these topics is great; there is often general loud talking amid which I can hardly understand who is speaking: a great deal of pent-up dissatisfaction with their way of life. Among the older people and the men, uncertainty as to whether they can demand what they lack. Among the younger people more dissatisfaction and self-awareness. A young man in a red pullover asks if there is not a "natural threshold," for drawing others into confidence, and if it is not very good that such is the case—I talk about the culturally injected shame threshold—But it really is quite natural to be ashamed; we do say to the children: Shame on you!—Oh, no, I cry. I hope that I have never said that to my children—But how did they get along well in school then?—Oh, they already knew how they were supposed to behave. Next to me Mr. St. becomes active. He is the one who most closely represents the norm, but avoids the appearance of wanting to regiment and lead people by the nose. Basically, he says, it is first of all good if a person wants to deal with a problem on his own. Especially, as a responsible person you cannot run to somebody else with every triviality, you simply have to get hold of yourself sometimes and restrain yourself—Yes, I say, but we were not talking about trivialities. And I had also seen many a responsible person who lost himself in the end because of too much self-restraint, too much getting hold of himself, leaving only the shell of his function— just because he believed that it did not permit him to speak openly about his problems with others, even a "subordinate"—That way, however, someone says, you can never achieve self-knowledge, which he had found to be the main thing in my books. It was discussed quite openly that our society does not recognize self-knowledge as a value and does not promote it in any way.

Continuing to refer to the text and the problems of the figures, whom she saw as contemporaries, as a point of departure, the first librarian directed the discussion toward what was for her the very significant question of adaptation. The practice, i.e. the existence of the human being, is still the most important thing, and thus we see ourselves confronted daily with a wealth of demands to which we actually do not want to submit ourselves. How should one behave under those circumstances?—I made it clear that I found that question to be very justified but difficult to answer, since it cannot be resolved; and that I, in a non-alienated work, simply have much more freedom for self-realization than others do—She said: At the hairdresser's—we could probably tell that she had been there—she had just read a statement by Simone de Beauvoir, who intended finally to begin doing only the things that were fun for her. When, asked the librarian, will I finally be able to begin doing what is fun for me?!—Laughter filled with heartfelt understanding. Mr. St. puts his oar in. To do what is fun for a person is actually seldom possible in normal everyday life. We simply have to do what is necessary, and then we will become aware that it often gradually becomes fun: when something comes of it. It depends, of course, on success.

A pretty blond girl who sat on my left in the second row along the wall and had already involved herself often in the discussion contradicted him: That was not the intent of the question. What was meant was: how should we behave when we constantly have to do something that is against our convictions? Fortunately, she is not a teacher, but as a student she had already felt how wrong the entire educational system was—for example, precisely in this one point: giving grades—Mr. St.

concedes that the teachers also often wind up in conflict about that, but that the students expect an evaluation of their accomplishments and the teachers had to force themselves to give it—The blond girl insists that the teachers should let the students feel their conflict. But she had often had the impression that it was really fun for the teachers to use grades to make the students afraid.

In the room there was a clear tension between the tendency to cling to conservative norms and an urge toward something new; I could tell by looking at some faces that they were hearing many a thought for the first time; flabbergasted, they burst out laughing. Not one of them protested against anything; the atmosphere was not conducive to that. It was clear that they did not give voice to those questions anywhere else, but that they also knew how far they were permitted to go and where they could not become concrete. The discussion lasted for an hour and a quarter, always with the same level of liveliness and intensity, amid great interest and tension. Mr. St. honestly meant it at the end when he said that he was happy that everything had transpired so freely, that no recipes were distributed . . .

Then I had to sign books; a young woman, thirty-five, as I found out later, began once more with the problem of adaptation, with the education of children, etc. Whether a person could still feel capable of doing something at the age of thirty-five. She now wanted to move to Güstrow, no longer to work as a teacher as she had until now, but as a physicist—Shortly after that, she came to us and asked us to drop in on her former teacher with her, who lived right around the corner and invited us to come. We went with her.

A small two-room apartment in a new building, somewhat cramped, full of books. The teacher, Miss R., our age, lives alone. I had already noticed her at the reading but she had not said anything. Somewhat short, plump, a brown turtleneck sweater. An electrical heater is turned on, wine and juice are brought. Gerd sits somewhat cramped with the young married couple on the sofa. The two young people want to unburden themselves. Tell about their conscious decision against a beautiful house in the country—which undoubtedly would have led to isolation—and in favor of a small apartment in Güstrow, where they expect to find professional opportunities and a circle of people with whom they can "talk." He is a chemist in the district sanitation department. She has great problems with educating children. She herself had been held back to a great degree, and she did not want to do that to her children.

Miss R. talked about the curricula for German. For twenty-one years she has had to treat Gorky's *Mother,* even twice, and *Faust,* and she is already bored with her teaching, and *The Vassal* is not understood at all by the ninth-grade students. There are fewer and fewer students that like German: "What good will that do us later? We don't need it!"—fewer and fewer who read serious literature in the eleventh and twelfth grades. Gerd was particularly perplexed about that—but was it actually any different in the past?

At the beginning the young married couple said that they had just heard again that I had also left, that I was no longer in the German Democratic Republic at all. But they really were not able, says the very nice, somewhat naïve young woman, to believe that—it would really make everything that I have previously written untrustworthy; it would really contradict all my commitment . . . I hesitantly say to her that I understand all those who have left in recent years. At the same time I once more grasp precisely why these people do *not* understand them. And why there is actually something like betrayal of these readers in it, even if the one who has to leave bears no responsibility for it. Do we not, I later ask Gerd in the car, for the sake of these people, in order to stay here, in order to retain this incomparable audience, simply have to be ready to compromise? Perhaps, he says doubtfully—The evening was extraordinary.

We leave at around a quarter after eleven. Downstairs the young woman says that the two of them feel a certain attachment to this teacher because she helped to arrange their marriage; once, when she saw them dance at a reunion, she said to them: The two of you actually fit quite well together. That strengthened them in their affection—Good people. If this were the "people." Or had been . . .

In the car I tell Gerd that at the end of the reading that first librarian—the one that had been at the hairdresser's—came to me to tell me that she would totally subscribe to the first half of the congratulation on my fiftieth birthday by Anna Seghers, which was printed in *Sinn und Form*—What do you mean? I asked—That you are beautiful, said the woman—One woman to the other—that is also something new.

On the way back, the streets are almost empty. Once, a remarkable animal with green-glowing eyes scurries across the road in front of us. Fortunately a kitten remained sitting at the edge of the road. Gerd says that he has only once run over an animal, a rabbit. It occurs to us that we have seen hardly any deer and rabbits this year, in contrast to other years. Last winter was too severe. When we turn into our lane, the dog Lux comes up wagging his tail and follows us into the yard. We had driven directly toward the Big Dipper and wondered how it could be called the Great Bear. For another few minutes I look into the sparkling sky that buzzes with silence. Dozens of constellations. The Milky Way.

Very tired now. Take off my makeup, go to bed. A few pages in the Günderrode book. Half past twelve. Light off. Fall asleep.

SATURDAY, SEPTEMBER 27, 1980
Meteln

I do not wake up very early. I slept through the night because I had taken a sleeping pill. Outside sunshine, everything seems less oppressive than it did last night. The thought of my thyroid problem, of that "knot," of the operation that is becoming necessary, of the still uncertain nature of this illness, is there immediately. It permeates the days like a gas and changes what I usually call reality. I know that I still do not really believe that it could be cancer; do not know how I would behave then, if I have to believe it. If I could work as intensively as I now imagine. If a paralysis did not come over me. Think that all of these fantasies will become embarrassing and ridiculous if the suspicion should dissolve.

Gerd comes. His hair smells like the hay in his pillow wedge, a smell that I like. We talk about Uwe Johnson.[1] Gerd leafed through his Frankfurt political lectures; during the evening I read the last pages aloud to him, where Johnson says that this suspicion of his wife has been proven that she was foisted upon him by the Czech secret service to prevent his *Anniversaries* from ending as planned: with the Soviet entry into Prague in August of '68. I consider that construction to be a sign of paranoia, perhaps unconsciously forced into his mind in order to escape the still unbearable truth: that his wife simply had a love affair with another man, thus preferred that man to him, Uwe,

[1]Uwe Johnson (1934-1984), German writer, editor, and scholar. He left the GDR when he could not get his work published there. His fame subsequently spread in the Federal Republic. (Ed.)

for a while. We talk about the participation of neuroses in writing. I repeat my thesis, that I am much too normal. Gerd calms me as always: I am not at all that "normal," many people do consider me to be exalted—a somewhat ridiculous and fruitless dialogue. My remorse about all the lost time, this decadeslong effort to detach myself "here," my inability to see an alternative "over there"—perhaps that very thing is my neurosis: difficulty in dissolving ties. Blocked by the knowledge of the other side that truly does not entice me to cross over and remain—all of which Johnson did, and for which his three important books now stand. But also the destruction of his person.

It goes round and round in my head that four years ago I grasped that our situation is hopeless; that since then I have tried to process this knowledge less in narrative prose than in essays; that perhaps my body very quietly sought for its own way to express that hopelessness, that feeling of being strangled; that this suspicion, however, might just as easily be an inadmissible mysticism; that illness, *this* illness in particular, should and must not be taken as a metaphor (although the question of the psychosomatic factors of each and every illness remains).

We go to sleep once more, get up late, and do not eat breakfast until about ten o'clock outside. My two oaks are beginning to turn yellow. After everything has been cleaned up and washed, we ride our bicycles along Rote Flöte to visit Thomas and Carola. On the paths, puddles from the last thunderstorm during the night, impassable places. The day is—well, which word is suitable?—magnificent, glowing. One of those inimitable autumn days. The gold behind the blue.

At Tommy's house we encounter only him at first. He is coming out of the grandmother's room, in which he now intends to work, is serious. I embrace him. He is reading *Neues Deutschland*, he says. We go to Regina's house, where Carola and Regina are picking plums. Activities like this one are suitable for soothing Carola and connecting her to life again after the death of her grandmother. The men walk through the tall, wet grass to the woods to look for mushrooms. We three women sit in front of Regina's house and drink coffee. Talk about the grandmother. At the end she was quite tender and did not resist her help, says Carola. She felt that was nice of her. Two days before her death she said that in two days she would go away. Both of them had then believed that. The entire house had been filled with her loud, wheezing breath, and when it suddenly ceased late in the evening, she went into the room and did not really know: was she dead or not? Even before that, her pulse could hardly be felt. But, I say, the flesh does change then. Yes, says Carola, that is true—Before her death she had also said that she and Thomas, they were both good people, they should get along with each other, stay together, and go to Greece. She would have liked to have lived for one more year, she said, in order to be buried there. But she did not resist death at all.

The men's mushroom harvest is meager. A few remarkable specimens are identified using Regina's mushroom book and then rejected. All five of us sit in the sun in front of the little cottage, talk about this and that, and feel very good. From time to time Carola quickly gathers information about my illness, shyly, as if behind her own back. We talk about the economic situation, about the state of affairs in Poland—by the end of the year the economic situation there is supposed to get worse, they say—about the "Weapons Brotherhood" maneuvers that just ended, and about the number of police in Berlin during the convention of the inter-parliamentary union.

When we are about to leave, it is decided that we will eat over at Nicolaous's; we all feel the urge to remain together for a while. A garden table is placed in front of the house, cold meat, onion soup, coleslaw, homemade white bread, and wine.

It tastes good, the sun is warm, and everything is completely calm. The edge of the forest is no longer green, but eggplant-colored. I see everything very clearly, as if forever and as if for the last time. Must we yet experience such moments over and over again? I talk about that with Carola behind the kitchen, with the four cats dancing around us.

Why do we actually wish for a longer life? I kid myself in saying that I would still like to do the *Cassandra* material; nobody else could do that. That is true, but if it does not get done, nothing will change either. The material is seething in me, repeatedly sentences emerge, but I do not write them down, and I lose them again. I am unfocused.

Back beneath the gigantic blue sky. We lie down and fall asleep. I sleep for a long time, for almost two hours. When I wake up, Gerd has already left. I find him on the meadow harvesting apples. I get myself a basket and gather up the apples that have fallen on the ground, put the bruised and rotten ones on piles that we will then take to the compost heap, pour the good ones, the ones "to be given away," into our large basket. The miller's bearded friend comes and asks if he should order tiles for us, but the tiles from Dahlewitz are not durable enough for our gable; and besides that, the lime and the cement have not come either. We have already given up the idea of building this year once the roof has been patched provisionally. The topic of conversation is Karl Lars, the only thatch roofer in the vicinity, who fell from a roof because of a faulty hook—on the very day when he had *not* been drinking, everyone says. Who is now still in the intensive care unit, has hardly regained consciousness, and is being fed intravenously. A double fracture at the base of the skull and a broken lumbar vertebrae. He will never get on a roof again, everyone says. Karl Lars, who was part of the landscape.

My feeling of a loss of reality: as if somebody has bored a hole in the plastic bag that has been slipped over us, and now the air is rushing out. The sky is well-suited for that feeling, because in its intensity it is already unreal again. I see the figures of the three of us on the meadow from afar.

We go in, close the windows in the front part of the house, which is still supposed to swallow as much sunlight as possible. I sit outside on the bench in the sun and pit plums. Ask myself how many years I will yet sit this way on the bench in the fall. How many years I still want to do it at all. Suddenly an age jolt.

I prepare yeast dough and put it in the back part of the house on the edge of the stove to rise. Meanwhile, R. comes and helps Gerd carry the individual pieces of the heavy oak cabinet—Gerd "thawed" it with paint remover and then removed the paint remnants from it over the last few days—through the kitchen and upstairs into our bedroom, where it will be set up between the beds. It is large and beautiful. Gerd decides to rub oil into it *after all*, so that it will become darker and so that the grain of the oak will "show up better." Meanwhile, I put the dough on the metal sheet, cover it with plums, put the sweet pastry crumbs on it, and put the whole thing on the stove again. As I shove the cake into the oven, the Tetzners [2] arrive from their trip through the three cities: Schönebeck, Rehna and Gadebusch. They are enthusiastic, brown, and refreshed. While Gerti and I get busy making salad out of peppers, cucumbers and tomatoes, Gerd and Rainer put the top of the writing cabinet in the bedroom on the bottom part. We all go to admire the work. How nice the cabinet looks. How beautiful the room has become. How well the Greek blankets go with the red Mecklenburg wood tones . . . Everything somewhat feigned with me, because of a layer of indifference. Today it does not matter to me how this or any other room looks.

[2] Tetzners: Gerti Tetzner (b. 1936), writer (see also: *Ein Briefwechsel* [*A Correspondence*] in: C.W., *Werke*, Vol. IV, pp. 213ff.) and Rainer Tetzner (b. 1936), writer; friends of the Wolfs. (G.W.)

When the cake comes out, Gerd shoves the large, foil-wrapped fish in the oven and adds a few potatoes that are also wrapped in foil. That takes three quarters of an hour. Meanwhile, we set the table—it grows hot in the kitchen—Gerd makes a shrimp cocktail and gets good, cold white wine from the cellar. Slowly we begin to eat. It tastes good. We are cheerful and tell jokes. Finally the fish and potatoes are done: an often repeated process, the way Gerd takes both out of the oven, unwraps the fish, probes it, examines: Can we eat it yet?—For me the day is full of repetitive processes, the good daily routine. And I ask myself—why right now, why today of all days is all too clear—if it is "necessary" to experience a hundred or a thousand more repetitions of these same processes. The impulse to want to continue living (that is already a treacherous phrase: to want to live) must come from the new thing that I am aiming at; otherwise I might resign myself to a judgment behind my back. I think about the two books that I read about experiences of people with cancer that significantly enough bear the title *Judgment*: one by Hildegard Knef and one by Soloukhin,[3] who also reflects that remarkable arrogance that lies in taking oneself to be too important, while millions of people to whom nobody ascribes a value simply perish unnoticed every day. I think that this "judgment," if it were to be passed, could possibly free me from a series of secondary judgments. Immediately ask myself: Should it only be possible at that price? Are those secondary judgments still so binding? And how do they read? It is clear to me that in my next book I must call them what they are; that it is also probably for that reason that I push it along in front of me: I always have my reasons for "laziness," since I do not feel at ease in it, of course. This book would be the new thing for which I would like to live, no: *want* to live—and the children whom I would like to

[3] Vladimir Soloukhin (1924-1994), Russian writer, representative of the Soviet "village prose." (Ed.)

spare the mourning, although, on the other hand, without me they would have to become independent more rapidly—Stupid thoughts that I do not like to write down.

After the meal we go into the room with the fireplace; a new bottle of wine is opened, bright red Badenser, which we enjoy very much. The conversation turns to the world situation: the war between Iraq and Iran, which, like most things these days, has traces of insanity. The fact that since the beginning of this year every somewhat sensitive person has sensed that a dark, impenetrable curtain hangs before the future. I often think of the Goethe lines: "The future curtains / pains and good fortune / step by step from our gaze / and yet not frightened / we still press forward . . ." With the ending: "We tell you to hope." Steel was still unknown to Goethe as a material: curtain, in order to remain in the poem: "covering" of steel. Observing how people carry out their daily routine, I ask myself: What do they hope for? Do they hope at all? For what do they hope for their children? Is that impetus, by which for generations people hoped for "something better" for their children than what they had personally experienced, used up? Isn't that state of being tired of committing oneself actually a state of being tired of hoping?

Rainer knows figures from the last UN inquiry about the state of armaments in the world. According to the UN there are now probably three tons of TNT for each person, the Great Powers can destroy each other thirty or forty times, and so forth. Feelings are numb with respect to those numbers; we laugh a little embarrassed and snobbishly, indignation, protest would be totally inadequate. Gerti gives the opinion that it is impossible to write these days without reflecting that threat. Thus one can no longer write a "closed story"—which is an aesthetic short circuit. Gerd, tired and somewhat irritated, argues against the idea that perhaps now in every story the nuclear threat appears. But that was not what Gerti meant. Rainer arrived at the motif of the magic broom that he uses in his work, simply in order not to have to deal with the topic directly. I talked about how inadequate that image appears today, as Goethe himself intensified it in the final image of *Faust*: to the blind Faust who, in absurd self-delusion, incorporates the shovels of the lemurs that dig his grave into his vision of the future: "To stand on free ground with a free people . . ."

We then talked for a long time about the question that I brought up, of whether the literature of the German Democratic Republic had actually produced enduring accomplishments. We arrived at names like Bobrowski, Müller, Braun, Mickel, Sarah, and perhaps Kunert [4]; we spoke of poets and dramatists—but in prose narrative? Did this reality not offer enough for writers of prose? Has it forced them into provinciality? Does the disastrous tie to ideological restriction make itself visible in prose in an especially disastrous way? We sought for names that were comparable to Böll, Grass, Arno Schmidt, even Lenz und Koeppen, Johnson, Andersch— found none except Seghers—the earlier Seghers—and then Bobrowski again. Fries, all right. Strittmatter in his respectable third *Wundertäter*: provincial nevertheless. He simply does not "create" this country as he had once undertaken to do. The others, people who work journalistically, bring problems to light, but they, too, do not create a new literary landscape. But there's the problem. We have been overburdened with problems and conflicts all these years and have not had our minds and our hands free.

That would gradually come for me now, I believe. I also believe, however, that *The Quest for Christa T.* is an attempt, and that a book like *Obliadooh* by Fries, which is still not being published, similarly works toward that. Fühmann, too, when he has processed his past.

[4] Johannes Bobrowski, Heiner Müller, Volker Braun, Karl Mickel, Sarah Kirsch, Günter Kunert—all well-known GDR writers. (Tr.)

Now it would probably be a matter of rehabilitating those years that lie behind us, after the fact, by treating the life material, which they did provide in ample measure, in literature. And now, I add bitterly to myself, my inner calculation, which was based upon the assumption that I still have twenty years, might possibly be thwarted.

I told the Cassandra story the way it now presents itself to me: Cassandra, the oldest daughter of King Priam of Troy, does not simply want to take care of the house like her mother and her sisters. She wants to learn something. The only possible profession for a woman is that of seeress, soothsayer (which ages and ages ago only women practiced at all, when the supreme deity was still a woman: Gaia; which, however, during the course of struggles that apparently lasted for thousands of years, gods contested the seeresses' right to practice, for which the Oracle at Delphi is a striking example, in which prophecy is given in two superimposed layers: above, the god and the priest, below that, the woman). Apollo declares that he is willing to teach Cassandra. As payment he demands that she submit herself to him. When she, disappointed, horrified, denies herself to him, he pronounces the curse upon her. She will see and speak the truth, but nobody will believe her— During the siege of Troy by the Greeks she sees and foretells the fall of Troy. She loved the city more than any other. She foresees her own fall along with it and does not close her eyes to it either. She warns them against falling for the trick with the Trojan horse, but the king, intoxicated with the prospect that the Greeks were leaving, lets it in anyway. Cassandra has been declared insane anyway and is later installed as a servant in the temple. When Ajax rapes her beneath the image of Athena in the holy sanctuary, Athena turns her eyes away—she can do nothing more for her servant. Ajax is punished, and the spoils, Cassandra, pass to the victor Agamemnon. She is supposed to give birth to twins—but probably on the long voyage home to

Mycenae as a prisoner from Troy. Now she remains outside, in the wagon, while Agamemnon goes into the castle to be murdered—as she very well knows. Clytemnestra asks her several times to come in; they know, of course, that she is the daughter of a king, even if now a prisoner, and they will treat her honorably. The chorus—in Aeschylus's version—unsuspectingly encourages the hesitant woman. Then she gets up, goes in alone, and is slaughtered.

Gerti is concerned with the question: Why does she go? As a sacrifice? Or because she has no other choice?—For me it is quite clear. Even if a person has no other choice, there are two ways to walk the unavoidable path: a free one and one that is not free. Cassandra chooses the free one.

In bed I read some pages of *Edith's Diary* by Patricia Highsmith and am unable to find the fascination that many have for this author. Before I turn off the light, I open the one wing of the bull's-eye window. The night is cold with a bright moon. I think, as I have done so often in recent days, and am permeated with the knowledge that everything is phony. My writing, my failure to write. My wish to live, when I assumed that I would perhaps not live much longer, was not phony. My feelings for the children, my joys and worries are not phony. My moments with Gerd, especially the ordinary ones, are not phony. At noon, irritated, as he always is when dealing with such matters, he asked me: The thing—he meant the thyroid—does worry you after all!—Why shouldn't it?! I should have said. But I said: Nonsense. Of course I sometimes think about it . . . He: I can see how you are talking yourself into believing something there!

That is a basic pattern for dialogues between us. I must belittle and hide a worry or a fear that he, just because he, too, worries about it, does not want to see in me. The real dialogue, in which one knows how the other is doing, and still *wants* to know, transpires below the surface—although after twenty-eight years a weakening of interest would probably be understandable.

In the evening we had—I forgot to report about it in its place—also talked about the question of what literature, damn it all, actually is. How it is different from the multitude of texts that are sent to me in large numbers—just now again the diary-like writings of a young woman from West Germany who very precisely describes the separation from her husband, a certain G., and her depression afterward. Who apparently appropriately describes her childhood in the shadow of a mother who endlessly mourns a husband who died prematurely. Why should that now, I asked, *not* be literature? Sociologically it is not. Much great literature is also self-revelation. *Must* then this fiction element, the displacement into the non-I, the so-called generalization, be there in order to make a piece of writing into literature? Did I not just discover for myself in the Bettina essay the meaning of insignificance, of rejection of form—which, of course is also a rejection of misrepresentation? And can no conclusions be drawn from that? Or is this very flood of unliterary, autobiographical writing a sign of the fact that I seek to divest myself of the falsifying forms?—At the same time it can simply be inability.

It became a night in which for the first time in a long time, even without a sleeping pill, I slept again without waking up after five hours.

Addendum, three days later: Interestingly enough, I "forgot" to mention an entire train of thought that occupied me on that day, which lies almost a week in the past. Surprising even to me, during the evening conversation among the four of us, I said that I actually did not believe that I could still call myself a Marxist. Not that I would not continue to consider Marxist economic thought—above all with respect to its criticism of capitalism—to be correct and important. But that thought represents only a small segment of human life—just like politics, which has held us in its clutches for far too long. And, perhaps the most important thing: I doubt that the role the economy plays in the motivation of human deeds and misdeeds is as determining as Marx claims. They, the Marxists, concern themselves very little with human nature, which—even that has developed historically—works *against* them with enormous irrationalities that transcend their own economic interests. The sober economic calculation: if it would at least prevail! No, it probably lies within Marxism itself, as it has presented itself until now, that it could come down to this purely pragmatic economic doctrine and to this utilitarianism, from which not another spark can be struck and which yields nothing for art. I insist upon mysteries that cannot be unveiled by applying an economic law, and upon human autonomy that the individual cannot surrender to a higher organization with its claim of omnipotence, without destroying his or her personality.

Wake up. Remnants of dreams that fade, distance themselves faster and faster from "me," and finally dissolve, as they usually do now. A thought, still fleeting, that becomes a motif of the day: that what we call "forgetfulness" increases, is contingent upon age, undoubtedly; but is it not possibly also contingent upon time? Are there perhaps reasons for the agency that is responsible within us for "retention," for memory, to deny us that retention? Not only the often-mentioned flood of enticements but also the nature of the enticements may be repulsive to the instruments of memory, which are not at all neutral, of course, but emotionally charged. But why then does forgetfulness, misplacement, strike my little Moscow watch, of all things? Which has been lost for three days and which I miss every morning when I read the time from the ancient, enormous wristwatch with the almost crumbling armband. Seven o'clock. So six, since sometime last night daylight-saving time fell back to Central European Time and we did not notice anything.

I feel that it is even earlier, since I went to bed late last night; the last phase of yesterday (it occurs it me), the one that came after midnight, already belongs in this entry. While I pick up my things, slip downstairs—in order not to disturb Gerd, who is still asleep—and shower, I memorize, pre-formulate what I am noting down now about last night: the auction of art prints and "curiosities" in the dining hall of the children's vacation camp in Gallentin,[1] which occurred *before* midnight; but *after* midnight we then sat at the oilcloth-covered table in the mess hall, which, like the entire vacation camp, is empty in the autumn, thus a place where artists were able to organize a weeklong open-air painting event and now, following the auction, were counting their money—more than they had expected—beneath neon lights in the front part of the room, while in the back part of the usually inhospitably bare room, which the artists had completely transformed with green bushes and colorful decorations, people were dancing in the dim light. While we were still talking, we began to write and to draw on the inside of a large double sheet of paper that was lying in front of us on the table, each with the writing instrument that he or she happened to have at hand: Ranft[2] placed a stick figure in the middle; I wrote on it in Sütterlin script: In the center stands the human being. At the same time Helga drew a heart and wrote in it: Gerhard loves Christa. I continued: hopefully . . . somebody else added: . . . for a long time yet . . . ; Hannes then, last line, in Sütterlin script: . . . Alliance-insured. And so on. Butzmann[3] drew a rectangle, wrote on the edge of it: Reserved for Butzmann ("For realism!" he shouted), drew a landscape in it with a few strokes, Werner Wittig his even sparser landscape in a second rectangle, Ranft his figures in a third. In between I had explained

[1] Gallentin: Village in Mecklenburg in which an open-air exhibition initiated by the gallery director Klaus Werner and the painters' group of Clara Mosch (Karl-Marx-Stadt) took place; participating East and West German artists included among others Manfred Butzmann, Michael Morgner, Torsten Kozik, Dagmar and Thomas Ranft, Anneliese Schöfbeck, Klaus and Rolf Staeck, Werner Wittig and Max Uhlig; C.W. read from the manuscript of *Cassandra*. The event was sharply watched by the state security police. (G.W.)

[2] Thomas Ranft (b. 1945), designer and graphic artist; well acquainted with the Wolfs. (G.W.)

[3] Manfred Butzmann (b. 1942), painter and graphic designer; friends with the Wolfs (see also: C. and G. Wolf, *Unsere Freunde, die Maler* [*Our Friends, The Painters*], Berlin, 1995). (G.W.)

that this would be a birthday present for my daughter who would be twenty-five on Monday, upon which the sheet of paper was declared to be a "synthesis of the arts" and wildly worked on, finally even with impressions by Klaus Staeck's brother, which he inconsiderately and to Butzmann's dismay placed in the latter's sky, and which proclaimed, in the center is always the human being . . . and the animal, somebody continued. Art slogans were printed on it; they fought over the space that was still empty; in an indecipherable hand a congratulation was placed on the back in addition. Staeck made a gondola ride-ticket from Venice, valid for the year 2016— Tinka's sixtieth birthday.

I packed up the precious sheet of paper. A woman, whom I meanwhile knew to be the director of the "property," asked me for a certain book and I agreed to send it to her, spoke with her about the difficulties that she had and would yet have with the office of permits and registration because she had not registered this open-air painting event—which was privately organized—on time or according to regulation at all. Her answer surprised me, almost made me ashamed. This week had given her so much that she would gladly proffer her back to the lashes just to have it. This is a so-called "simple woman." I do not know what could be more encouraging.

In pitch darkness we ride home with the Helms[4] through a dark Bad Kleinen, talk—as always during this summer—about thatch roofers, roofing, and construction problems; a kind of fever has broken out, which for me, perhaps in exaggerated measure, has taken on a different accent than I would have given it before: not to build yourself in but to make the earth habitable, to put on a roof, to fix up a house, even if you remember every day that it could be destroyed in a few years.

[4] Helms: Helga Schubert (b. 1940), psychotherapist, writer; and her husband Johannes Helm, professor of psychology, 1975-1983, lived in the neighborhood of C. and G. Wolf in Neu Meteln (1974). (G.W.)

Sow seeds for flowers right now, I thought this spring, and sowed many more than usual; hang pictures on the wall right now, we said to ourselves, and bought pictures, and I often asked myself, as I did this morning, if beauty—a word that for me, used that way, stands within invisible quotation marks—has not taken on a new meaning under the real, immediate threat of the destruction of *all* evidence of our culture, both the ugly and the "beautiful"—what meaning?

It occurred to me, I think while I am taking my shower and at the same time letting the previous evening run past my inner eye, how many words I am gradually (and the speed is increasing) placing in quotation marks; a process that indicates that these words are being drained of meaning; often, of course, they are words from the class of the beautiful-good-true, thus from the realm in which ethics and aesthetics have melted together. An essay that could be written about the quotation marks, could be organized as a commentary or even historically: use of the quotation marks in earlier times—and in the process would soon arrive at the inflation that this punctuation has experienced in reaching the present ("experienced" would probably also have to be in quotation marks?), evidence not only for the loose treatment of symbols but also for the stronger awareness of the corrosion deep within the body of language, which has as a consequence—also as a prerequisite?—that word and meaning no longer coincide, and that thus a series of facts, processes, characteristics, conditions, and contradictions will remain unlabeled.

Not everything that has pressed us so hard is covered in the end by the expression "end of the world," which was borrowed from early myths—to name just one example, I thought, and ridiculed myself: this one of all things!—but had become aware that some of my thoughts have already been moving in another direction since the word *awareness*, and that this direction was more clearly marked by the term "body of language": *Aware-*

ness Through Movement is, of course, the title of the book by Moshé Feldenkrais[5] that has kept me occupied for days, and which gives me a feeling of freedom and happiness as I read—the two words are, of course, synonyms—in a way that I had not known before. Specifically in a way that has the body as its point of departure: the linguistically clear, simple, and precise description of functional relationships (for example the relationship of thinking habits and schemata to falsely established moving processes) or of delicate exercises that make the movement apparatus more functional, in that through introspection directed at bodily processes the individual learns to correct his self-image—this inner consideration of myself was already dissolving tensions and producing more freedom as I read. So that I, standing on the bath mat and closing my eyes, used ideas to go beneath my skin and produce a warm flow that went along with a feeling of being friends with and approving of myself: not produced by reflection, logical conclusions, or by emotions, which usually follow the thoughts or are tied to them, but by a physical sensation. Here something takes place that I have suspected for a long time and have subconsciously sought: the relationship—I look for a more suitable word: the coincidence, the state of unity of spiritual-intellectual condition and bodily feeling on a physiological basis. But simply *not* interpreted in a vulgar materialistic fashion—as dependence of mental processes upon their physical "bearer"—but dialectically: like thinking and acting, in the process of moving oneself, determine one another. (I had already been similarly fascinated by the description of the "Doris case" by Feldenkrais: how in the tiniest steps of months-long cooperation, a woman whose functions had been disturbed or destroyed by a failure of certain brain centers learns anew

[5] Moshé Pinhas Feldenkrais (1904-1984), engineer and judo expert, founder of the Feldenkrais method, which was designed to improve human functioning by increasing self-awareness in movement. (Ed.)

through habituation: forms new paths for nerve impulses that were being lost.)

What especially captivates me about Feldenkrais's way of looking at people is his approach. It is not ratio or strength of will, not force in any sense, no matter how broadly taken, nor even "self-control" that he considers to be the key for the healing of the fundamental injuries from which modern man suffers, but a change in orientation to what has been falsely learned, habituated, and conditioned, a change that begins with physical postures and movements and (does not yet) end with purely one-sided rational thought. *Patience* is one of his key words. He is far from presenting himself as an apostle of civilization, but one cannot avoid expanding and generalizing his thoughts and exercises—for there are also some of those in the book. Will a human being who is friends with him/herself be able to or have to be teeth-gnashingly hostile toward others? Will people, occupied with the finer processes in nature, feel within themselves and in coexistence with others a great desire to use violence, even when others disturb them greatly, when they consider them to be injurious? Will a nation that is certain of its identity have a compulsive need to maintain that identity through the destruction of other identities?

But what nation—above all: what *great* nation is certain of its identity? Is sovereign enough to include even the mistaken developments, even the crimes in its immediate past as warnings, as lessons for its present day? For example (to say nothing of the German atrocities during the Hitler era): the Soviet Union the crimes of the Stalin era, the USA those of the McCarthy era and the Vietnam War? In compensation, I am certain, the longing for violence shoots into those unfinished psychic zones; from them, from them *as well* emerge wars in modern times. So that logically, according to linear logic, what is not mastered, not thought, unspoken, not regretted, and not understood continues to beget evil. That we should thus, in literature as well, reflect on other, nonlinear, "deeper" lying sources of deliverance, life—not "survival"! (The letter from the Federal Republic with its questions that point in that direction, which I have not yet answered, not only because of general lack of desire because of letter censorship, which is impervious, but also because of a special perplexity in the face of the demands of that letter.)

Get dressed. News reports: *Solidarnósz* congress in Gdansk continues deliberations. Vigorous and prolonged debates of the delegates about the arbitrary decision of the executive committee to agree to a compromise with the government concerning the question of the appointment of plant managers— Hijacking of a Yugoslavian commercial plane with 100 people aboard by German-speaking hijackers, landing on Cyprus.

Last night at around one o'clock, before going to sleep, I also read in the Rowohlt paperback book that Klaus Staeck had given us: *Too Much Pacifism?*—edited by Freimut Duve, Heinrich Böll, and Klaus Staeck. I leafed through the contributions of some authors, and some sentences fixed themselves in my mind: Böll: "And yet I am certain that the Germans are not only peace-loving, but also capable of peace; they are simply without peace in a manner that still needs to be analyzed. They have not experienced what could be called a *deep* peace for a long time, and those who once experienced it—at around the year 1910—were tired of it."

Why do we hear no voice from intellectuals from the USA? No Bellow? No Malamud, no Vonnegut . . . More Böll: "These Germans are not against the condition of peace, but are allergic to the word; it simply has a communist ring for them and it could turn out in an analysis that even the Versailles Treaty contributed to the denunciation of the beautiful word and peace is equated with 'shameful peace.'" . . . "In light of the armament capacities, of course, the word *balance* is as deceiving as the word *harmony*. No, superiority is the motto . . .

Naked insanity, absurdities all around. And then there are those who are still amazed that people are not only going insane, but also acting insanely." . . . In a future nuclear war, defense is impossible—So the existing power systems of the superpowers have to be strengthened, because their very disconcertion can be a motive for "preventive strikes"? So do the revolutionary processes in Poland paradoxically increase the danger of war? Or do they diminish it—in the sense that nations that govern themselves are not warlike? But does this process come too late to still have influence on the neighbors?

Unkind question: Must we respond to the slogan: Better red than dead! with the counter-slogan: Better white than dead!?

Jürgen Fuchs [6]: "When we hear what is happening, for example, in South American states, in the Ukraine, and in Cuba, we regard East German cultural politics, in spite of the sharpening of criminal law and carping, biting censorship, with somewhat different eyes." . . . "Will we have war?" Brecht asks in a letter from the year 1951. His answer: "If we arm for war, we will have war." For days I have been thinking: Hitler has caught up with us! The victors of the Second World War have adopted his insane concept of destroying Europe into their strategic plans.

Carl Amery [7]: "Today it is no longer a matter of the survival of the state, but of the survival of people and—probably—of the survival of humanity . . . No longer the end of the world, but the end of Europe; that is simply and movingly the meaning of the new strategy . . . If we want to defend ourselves (and I am in favor of that), then the few thousand nuclear warheads that are lying around here must unfortunately leave the country. Our defense has only one chance, if it offers no rewarding targets for nuclear missiles . . . Below that of the nuclear mis-

---

[6] Jürgen Fuchs (1950-1999), German writer and civil rights activist. (Ed.)
[7] Carl Amery (1922-2005), novelist, environmentalist, and one of the spiritual fathers of the German Greens. (Ed.)

siles, however, there is only one single kind of warfare that must be taken seriously: guerilla warfare. Guerilla warfare and social defense, those are the two possibilities that we have . . . We must become a society that can be defended in any case. It will, as matters lie, no longer be able to be capitalistic, at least not given our situation and our population density."

Is there for the rest of the world a plausible argument why Europe—the Europe of the colonial rulers and exploiters of natural resources and consumers of the wealth and food of the world—why the ways of thinking and the culture of the white European ought to survive?

For months my mind has been producing, whenever I do not control it, thus also at night, questions. How could the dissolution of the perverse coupling of productivity to destruction still be conceivable? Then, after those illuminated letters, a hasty text begins: It would be conceivable only after the surrender of the respective favorite myths of both sides—"socialism!"—"freedom!"—from which the ruling classes live just as much as they do from their material privileges. So we perish because of our or our rulers' flight from reality. I have known that for a long time; sometimes I know it with indelible clarity. An end to the arms race is only conceivable through the advance concession of unilateral disarmament on the part of the USSR—So not at all. And this paper, all papers will burn along with it (always my horror, even before Brecht's precautions for his immortal works in case of a catastrophe!), all the pictures, all the statues, and all the churches of this culture. All the children.

Fix breakfast, always accompanied by radio music, radio news reports. The different shades of blue in the kitchen, I only have to do a few last things, Gerd has set up everything: melon with bologna, egg, homemade jams, cheese, light and dark bread. The height of luxury. We are not permitted to send any food to Poland. A sad slogan is making the rounds among workers: The Poles will live tomorrow the way we work today!

A gray day, calm, not cold; it is as if all nature stands still. I tell Gerd how it becomes *even* clearer through the works of Feldenkrais, how injurious any training is, especially that of children, because we do not lead a reflex by way of the nerve paths from the mind, from the willingness and maturity to carry out an activity or a function, to action, to motor activity, but force the opposite, the unnatural way: the cleanliness training in all daycare facilities and many families—and it doesn't start there, but much earlier: demand accomplishments, according to some table, according to the calendar, rape the unique living human being, who is then able to defend himself only with counter-violence, who resists, refuses, striking out, shooting.

I read a Hölderlin quote to Gerd: "We are in the evening of our days. We often erred, we hoped much and did little . . . I have often said to myself, you are prey to corruption, and nonetheless I finished my day's work." The ever-returning feeling of the end. I talk about my change in the motivation for the Cassandra material, not only in content but also in the structure of that material. At first it was not much more than the association that everyone has when he or she hears the exciting word *Cassandra*—also to the obvious time relationships that lie within it—and the search for the apparently natural self-contained narrative form. So the work, the deeper penetration into *her* time, into *her* social and geographic situation, yielded *her* possible consciousness and the simultaneously incomprehensible progression in the growth of the danger in which we, too, find ourselves, *and* my shift toward new patterns of literature (or at least away from old ones), which, on the other hand, is due to a different world view; all this together awakened the disquiet in me, the insight that a story, no matter how it is set up, would not do justice to the plan, would not realize it completely, would not totally utilize it.

He has, said Gerd, as we went from the kitchen into the large back room that was once a pigsty and which now seems to us to be the one room that is most suited to us—he has always seen the lectures as a lattice and the Cassandra story not as their highlight and culmination (this is old dramaturgy) but as embedded in the lattice, describing the process leading to it but also that of the critical self-reflection leading away from it. That is difficult to do, I point out to him, for the nature of literature conflicts with the production of a lattice, as Lessing already discovered, since writing can only be done in temporal sequence, i.e. linearly. For that reason it is hardly possible to produce a purely literary "synthesis of the arts" that the observer can grasp at one glance. It has been, of course—for a long time—my tendency to deliver as well the other things that happen during the days, weeks, and months in which a manuscript is created. That is the kind of authenticity toward which I strive. Not simply to deliver "works," that would seem dishonest to me; there is, of course, a dishonesty that is not lying, nor even concealment, but rather: expressing oneself unsuitably.

So my aversion to the literary discussion of those phenomena that we falsely and inadequately combine under the collective title "Stalin era," and which still lies ahead of me, of course, can partially be explained by the fact that I fear that I have not yet attained the degree of sovereignty that would also make such a production artistically productive. The inadequacy that I find in the (necessary) exposé literature, defects of twisted socialist realism; only a basically new way of thinking and feeling can get around this old one, thus new literary forms as well. Not hate and defense, Gerd says that even to him that always seems too small and petty. But naturally, I say, my fear of approaching my own errors once more, as I did in *Patterns of Childhood*, and getting to the bottom of them, is also a motive for my hesitating so long.

The question arises as to whether our relationship with each other has actually always remained the same over the three decades, or how and to what extent it has changed. Just as we ourselves have changed, Gerd says, so our relationship with each other has changed. But how have we changed? In the last five years, I say, by detaching myself from internal entanglements with the power structure I have acquired for myself more freedom from fear, more sovereignty. Gerd says: And also more habituation. In the beginning, every departure of a colleague hit us very hard. But now? Well fine—how many close friends still remain who could leave? . . . Only when I come to those points that are touchy, that were recently painful, do I have the feeling while writing that I am legitimized. He, Gerd says, does not need that feeling. It is sufficient for him to creep into some material, to be able to cover himself up with it. We are different there.

While I walk upstairs to the desk on the platform by the round window and very joyfully take in the view of the landscape that I never grow weary of, I give free play to the thought of what role this domicile here, everything that I combine together in the concept "Mecklenburg," had played in my transformation; if I say with justification: If we had not had this, we could not have endured it in the German Democratic Republic (but even then: what would have been the alternative?!). Everything that we call "life in the country": becoming reacquainted with the seasons. The transformation of a landscape, its shades of color, which I cannot see enough of; individual plants precisely observed in the change of seasons (my two oak trees, which I take quite personally, or the apple tree in front of the window at which I sit with my typewriter). The weather and the storms that affect us directly, the winds that we feel on our skin, the different kinds of air. Materials to which we gradually develop a relationship: reeds, stone, wood, sand, earth. The incomparable joy in the growth of a tree or a bush that I have planted myself. The interest in having the landscape maintained and not destroyed. The proximity to the production of food. The question of whether heavy technology will not gradually ruin the ground, of whether much will not be wasted and destroyed through neglect.

All in all, here I feel life's fullness much differently than I do in Berlin. Strangely enough, the old house is part of that, without my feeling that I am its "owner," and above all this web of people is part of it, the web that weaves itself tighter year by year, and into which we are drawn, more than we originally wanted to be. People from social strata that we would never have touched so intimately in Berlin. So what was originally viewed as a retreat, where we would be protected, even hidden from the destructive demands OF THE CITY and would find peace, has actually become a move toward a different lifestyle, something new that, above all, opens me, my senses, and my sensitivity again. An astonishing experience.

Idyll? No, not at all. Sometimes, however, I do have the feeling that it is too beautiful. A person cannot actually live this way today. We also live this way, however, only because we have given up all hope of change in this country and believe that we have a right to set up for ourselves the place where we can work . . . I remain aware of the conflicting nature of this lifestyle.

Among the new discoveries that life in the country brings with it is the rediscovery of physical labor, which I, actually since my childhood, have sought to avoid as a waste of time. Now it becomes a task to maintain a country property—as a center not only for the family but also for friends, for people who need a place to visit. As a prerequisite for communality. Then garden work, trimming hedges, making cider, and making jam suddenly become meaningful again.

Morning: report on thoughts about the discussion of the first twenty pages of the *Cassandra* text with the creative artists in Gallentin.

Noon news: The USA declares that they want negotiations with the USSR with the goal of a "zero option," which means: dismantling the mid-range missiles of the USSR in Europe and renunciation of the "additional armament" of NATO. During the last ten years the USSR has pushed its rearmament to an unimaginable degree, while NATO has taken preliminary steps toward disarmament (this, in my opinion, a false report)—Between the Federal Republic and the USSR a commission for energy questions is supposed to be established. Representatives of the USSR have revealed to the West German trade delegation that is now in Moscow their interest in not having to intervene in Poland, so that the exchange of goods with the West could continue undisturbed.

At lunch—stuffed green peppers prepared by Gerd—we talk about the poplar trees that we want to plant; where to put them so that they will protect the west gable from the wind. For a long time already it has been more of a crime *not* to talk about trees. We consider all of the things that we have already built and planted here, how expensive the house, with everything connected with it, already is—about seven times the purchase price—and we repeat: If we had not had this . . . and know how the sentence ends.

Noon nap, after washing the dishes. Before that I read the first few pages of Urs Jaeggi's new book, *Outlines*.

If it is true that all frustrations and empty spaces promote war, is it then not also true that censorship promotes war?

In the afternoon, to Mrs. W.'s place, notify her that we would not be there the next morning when she came. She is sitting in front of the house with her husband, protected from the wind. He is worse again. He points to the area over his chest and stomach, which "hurts." He can no longer walk, eat, take care of himself. I suggest calling the doctor so that he will come tomorrow.

At home, when the coffee is not yet ready, Dani and

Joochen. We drink coffee together in the fireplace room. It is about their house. Are they going to take it now, although the daughter of the B.s wants to knock off another piece of land for herself? Is it at all worth it to take that house on which there is so much to do? Yes, of course, since it is not expensive and would be easy to sell again . . . Then about the last meeting of the Berlin Writers' Union: detailed information about the economic situation. Kant's cynical behavior. Statement: Not all members of the United Polish Workers Party are renegades and traitors. The Polish military forces are no longer completely dependable in instances of internal conflicts; there the slogan is going around: Poles do not shoot at Poles. Nevertheless, we do not understand why *we* should do the dirty work— Different topic: the danger of war. The neutron bomb is of concern to us, of course, but does not have any great strategic significance. More important are the cruise missiles and the Pershing rockets that threaten Moscow and Leningrad . . .

Called the doctor, made an appointment for him to come to W.s' tomorrow. So there is dry rot in his house, too, lately the bogeyman of the vicinity.

I try to answer a letter that has been lying here for days. It comes from Freiburg in Briesgau. A few excerpts: ". . . But what is it that causes me to address you? Very briefly, it is worry. But that is too little, too flat. Rather, it is my struggle for hope, for optimism—in a time that makes that so difficult . . . Can I still hope? I have been carrying four phrases with me for a long time now. They came to me from book titles; they burst the framework long ago and have become content: 'Ways out of danger'—or: 'Ways out of danger?' Has the entire sentence lost its justification? So soon? For you? (And when I ask you that, the fact that we find ourselves in two different countries with two different systems in two different power blocks has no relevance. What my question touches upon lies much deeper.)

"What power have you experienced that others can also experience? . . . But I ask you most urgently for an answer! I—we—need a perspective so urgently . . . Respectfully—and with the kindest greetings, yours, Walter D.

"Please, let us risk everything so that peace may prevail between our countries. Everything. Really everything! And even more."

My helplessness. My uneasiness about the role that is given to me here, and at the same time understanding for it and the impression that I cannot avoid it, and impotence, and, as is now often the case, a pestering fury that would like to vent itself in slamming doors and smashing dishes.

My attempt to answer, thoughts that are already noted down here.

Early darkness. Autumnal feeling. The apparent idyll permeated with disquiet, also with longing for the children. Again one of those unbelievable skies, red, streaked, night-blue all around us, apple-green strata.

News: The hijacking of the Yugoslavian commercial airliner by three Croats came to a bloody end on Cyprus with the capitulation of the hijackers.

A very good supper that Gerd makes, with swallow's nest soup, red caviar, and wine.

Television evening. A film about cuckoos, which interests us because of the flocks of cuckoos that are found here in the spring. Unbelievable photographs, remarkable adaptations of the birds—for example, with regard to the color and design of their eggs—to those of the host birds—followed by the broadcast series: *I Bear a Great Name* with the granddaughter of Käthe Kollwitz[8] and the grandson of Otto Hahn. Then a film forum: "We Saw the Truth," in which Andrzej Wajda[9] is inter-

[8] Käthe Schmidt Kollwitz (1867-1945), German artist. She was a committed socialist and pacifist, well known for her themes taken from proletarian urban life. (Ed.)

[9] Andrzej Wajda (b. 1926), Polish theater director. (Tr.)

viewed and segments of his film *The Man of Iron* are shown. Thus the Polish film people are at last allies of the workers for once. That will never happen here. *Never* is a heavy word. Wajda says that he makes folksy and popular movies. "We experience something so fascinating that we must express it."

Gerd says: Well, boys, just watch out . . .

At eleven o'clock a short telephone conversation with Tinka, who is in Berlin; in an hour she will be twenty-five. Painful, painful, she says. Mistress of the understatement. If it were midnight now, I say, I would congratulate you on your twenty-fifth birthday. She says: Thankee, thankee. Family language.

To bed. Tired. Read in Urs Jaeggi again. "Here in your neighborhood, in this Western suburb, there is no insanity because everything is insanity."

Eleven-thirty. Lights out. Sleep.

It is nine-fifteen and it already seems impossible to me to catch up with two wide-awake hours of the day. During the night I had lain awake until long after midnight, probably still excited from the evening because of the results of the Hessian parliamentary election, which had not, as firmly expected, produced the absolute majority for the Christian Democratic Union and the minister-presidency of Alfred Dregger—a quick response by the voters to the plans of the Christian Democrats and the Free Democratic Party in Bonn to oust Chancellor Schmidt, who now, at least in Hessen, have conjured the Free Democrats out of the parliament completely. Great satisfaction here, finally a joyful emotion again with respect to a political development. It had been a long time; by the way, these "politics" do not interest me anymore either; they have become a fixed game everywhere. We clearly saw the inability of even the Social Democratic Party politicians (perhaps with the exception of Brandt) to grasp the phenomenon of the Greens at all.

When I woke up, I immediately saw by the nature of the light that the sun was shining outside. Again a magnificent clear day after the rain during the night. I awoke with the hazy memory of a string of dreams. Is it really only seven? I asked G. Yes. Seven. I got up as quietly and carefully as possible in order not to tear apart the memory of the dreams completely. I am now always happy when I have dreamed and can occupy myself with the dream in order to learn something from it about myself or my condition. Thus today, toward morning, Günter Kunert was in my dream, but a transformed Kunert, transformed into a feminine being. He wore a wig with a permanent wave; his facial features were prettier, smaller, he on the whole more dainty, also more affected. We were in a large group that he entertained with sentences that I have not retained. A certain self-right-eousness, but also brilliance of expression and formulation. We were also probably walking through gardens. They dropped—or was that already in the next dream—the name of Rainer Kunze[1]; I also saw him, specifically the way he appeared recent-ly on television, when he justified his withdrawal from the West German Writers' Union—namely with the secret arrangement of the chairman, Engelmann, with Hermann Kant. Then I was in an enormous stretched-out building that I simultaneously saw from outside: a desolate, unarticulated concrete façade, hardy any windows. There I had to deal with S., of whom I have developed the very recent impression that she lets herself be drawn too much into the non-literary practices of the Aufbau Publishing Company and that I want to talk to her about that sometime. That horrible building must have gotten into my dream as a symbol for the publishing house. Later sequences process ambivalent feelings with regard to colleagues—but then I had to deal with two women whom I do not know, or whose identities I have forgotten. The one lay down in bed in a large room; apparently she was ill. I had to take care of her. The other one, who exhibited peculiar behavior from the very beginning, busied herself in the bathroom. Suddenly I came in and saw how she calmly unfolded the bedding—blue checked pattern—that I had just washed and folded and put it in the water in the bathtub. I was beside myself and told the sick woman what was happening. Yes, she said imperturbably, she does things like that. Somewhat later, when I myself then unfold the same bed-

---

[1] Rainer Kunze (b. 1933), writer in the GDR, author of children's books and socially critical poetry. (Tr.)

ding, which had been folded up again, I notice that it hardly got wet. That relieves me somewhat.

All of these dreams together, if I were to analyze them one at a time, would bring to light a lot of the problems that have occupied my mind in recent weeks. But I would not get to the very bottom of them, because I have forgotten too many connecting links.

While showering I hear the voices of politicians from different parties, who all perceive the Hessen election as an encouragement to pursue the very things that they intended to pursue anyway; and I hear the first press opinions, which are devastating for the Free Democratic Party. I fix breakfast, boil eggs, and make tea and coffee. Change the towels. The concept "addicted to radio" occurs to me. For the sake of fairness I listen to a few sentences from the East German radio station, where in prosaic formulations with a homey voice, an editor gives her prosaic opinion about the film *Sonya's Report*.[2] To be sure, she found parts in the film that touched her, but, she does have to say that the book touched her more profoundly. Notice again that I will not be able to stand the intonation much longer, any more than I can that of the German Democratic Republic's newscasters.

At breakfast Gerd talks animatedly about the book that he is now reading, written by Freeman Dyson, an American of English origins, *Disturbing the Universe*, subtitle: Remembering the Future.[3] The author is an uncommonly gifted scientist, mathematician, physicist, and probably one of the top minds of this century. Gerd finds him likeable, at the same time he concerns himself with the technical mode of thinking that is foreign to us, with the errors of this man, who, before becoming a consistent supporter of a disarmament policy, participated on the American side in all kinds of weapons technology projects. Convincing

[2] *Sonjas Rapport*, a film based on the book of the same name by Ruth Werner (1907-2000) about her work for the Soviet secret service during the Nazi era. (G.W.)

[3] The original version, in English, does not have a subtitle. (Tr.)

are his portraits of Oppenheimer and Teller, whom he—in contrast to the opinion that people commonly have of him—depicts as very likeable. At the same time, the brilliant thinking of this man reflects a certain naïveté in political and social matters. But what a mind! What a breadth of interests! Our minds are occupied by the thought that similar minds cannot develop at all "in our country." That in "socialism" no opportunity exists for persons of genius. That here the colorless bureaucracy immerses everything remarkable in its own colorlessness.

Clean off the table. Every day I am amazed at the many little things that have to be cleaned up. We go out into the yard. Breathe in air that is incomparable. The hand towels are still hanging outside from yesterday, have soaked themselves in the moisture. I straighten things up. Hang up the clothes from yesterday. We possess far too many. At the same time I think about today's work, to what extent I can succeed in overcoming the obstacle that has confronted me for days in the continued work on the Cassandra story. That I must not jump over that obstacle, move it out of the way. I would have to penetrate it and in the process dissolve it, so to speak . . . But how? Narratively: how? The concept of the "wild woman" comes to mind again, which stuck with me last night from my reading of the book *Dreamtime* by the ethnologist Hans-Peter Dürr[4]: Cassandra must have this experience of a wild woman who stands outside of the culture. She must—this expression came to me in the night—"derail." But can I use that expression for a behavior in a culture that was still not acquainted at all with the technology of constructing rails? I thought of the rails in Peter Stein's theater room,[5] on which the cart ran, in which Agamemnon and Cassandra came to Mycenae . . .

[4] Hans-Peter Dürr (b. 1929), German physicist. Director of the Werner-Heisenberg Institute at the Max Planck Institute for Physics and Astrophysics in Munich. (Ed.)

[5] Peter Stein's theater room: Allusion to the director's antiquity project for the West Berlin stage. (G.W.)

At the moment everything in me moves in the direction of transcending culture, perhaps under the subconscious influence of the refrain: Is that all supposed to have existed? It seems to me that I thirst for an adventure, which, however, could only be transcendence of culture, and for which there are no prerequisites because I envision neither the use of drugs nor living in another culture. Except for: writing.

Gerd shows me a dying mouse that lies on its back, wiggling now and then, in front of our glass door. It could have been the one whose patter I heard last night in the false ceiling. A large species, Gerd says. As always in such cases, I do not look at it all too precisely. It could have eaten poison, Gerd thinks. But where? In the little room where the apples are? There he had dumped all of the available poisoned wheat into a hole . . . the image of the cat appears again, which had caught her paw in the marten trap that had been set on one of our trees. That I ran away and got help, but was not able to go there myself. What right do we have to lay hands on the animals? Yes, yes. I, too, do not want the marten to destroy our new thatched roof again. That the mice in the pantry gnaw through the jam jar covers . . .

While I sort as quickly as possible the unanswered mail that is lying around, a heap that is piling up and of which I no longer have control, Mrs. B. calls from our apartment in Berlin. This time she really thought that it was over with for her; she had lain at home alone with her heart racing, too weak to walk, to get anything, etc. I try to order her to go home immediately. To go to the doctor. To follow the advice of the doctor on duty and go to the hospital. She will not do any of that. It is clear to me that she is severely neurotic. I do not know what I could do besides my constant admonitions and pleas. She wants to force them to give her ambulant medicines and leave her alone. Why does she have that kind of horror of the hospital?

Mrs. W. is here, as always since the death of her husband, in a black blouse, a black skirt, and a black apron with white dots. I tell her what she is supposed to do today, then go upstairs to the workroom, and start on these notes. In the meantime, I listen to the review of a book—Dieter Spazier: *The Death of the Psychiatrist*, in which the author apparently attacks the institution of psychiatry once again from within, inasmuch as it is (also) a way for practitioners to protect themselves from those parts of their own nature that they have pushed aside while acquiring a rational, *purely* rational, personality, and which now echo back to them through the mouths of their irrational patients. "It is preferable to tear the tongue out of insanity," it says there. I have to think of Annette, who, of course, has no opportunity at all to let such points of view approach her in her daily routine as a psychologist. Hardly anywhere else is the boundary between reason and insanity drawn and guarded as strictly as it is here in this country. It is no wonder that those who could not stand it ran away and that many over-adjusted people remained here (from which a state, but not a living society, can be made), and that the uneasy ones flee beneath the wings of the Church, which also does not really know what is happening to it.

What seems compelling to me of late is that story about a psychologist who must twist himself into an evil philistine in order to remain functional. Writes letters to himself every evening in order to be able to go to work in the morning. Who cultivates petty malicious pleasures. Who drives his less easily pacified, more creative wife insane.

It is now five after eleven. I get myself one of our wonderful Gravenstein apples, which are saturated with sunshine this year, cut it into thin slices, and eat it with relish, while I attempt to find my way back into my handwritten *Cassandra* manuscript, which has drained away into disorganized notes in recent days.

That intention was frustrated. Mrs. Schomaker threw the mail on the table downstairs. As is always the case on Mondays, almost no letters at all—they come "in bunches"; only a request from the American publishing house Farrar, Straus & Giroux that I fill out a card for the publisher's computerized accounting system. The newspapers—*Neues Deutschland* and *Norddeutsche*—I leave lying there; as always I will not leaf through them until the evening at the earliest: idiosyncrasy is unconquerable. By the way, there was a time—'65, '66—when I could not look at a *Neues Deutschland*, let alone touch one, without breaking out in a sweat. Then I cautiously learned to deal with newspapers again. Thus today I feel absolute indifference, whatever those newspapers may write. Why is that? It is probable that the constantly repeated experience that we ourselves cannot intervene, that everything is already established, that there can be no change because we are residents of a colony—that experience simply creates a colonial mentality in the end: malicious joy of the minor child directed toward the parents when his hands freeze: Why didn't my father buy me any gloves?!

In the kitchen, where I peel my apple, Mrs. W. is at work. I ask her how that story of the boy turned out; the boy who three weeks earlier, in a tavern in Drispeth, had made unruly comments against a local officer of the national police—he, too, a young local fellow who had even gone to school with the former, but who now, because of personal mutual antipathy, blew the incident up, turning it into an insult against the state and on the next day gathered witnesses against the insulter and obtained statements from them, which, in the opinion of other witnesses, were exaggerated. One of those unwilling witnesses was Mrs. W.'s son. I can clearly see how she wants to play down the matter, which in reality disturbs her very much. She says she doesn't know anything. The hearing had taken place and had been adjourned. (Yes, because others had voluntarily appeared as witnesses and shaken the testimony of the police officer.) Her Henry had not been summoned again. (At the time, she had told me how much he regretted having said anything at all.) Now this Uwe has a loose mouth; that fact is well known. On the other hand, he had always run the disco in the Dambeck culture center in . . . This case, of course, is common gossip in the surrounding villages. The workmen who come to our place on the weekends pass the various opinions along, which, however, all come down to one opinion: that you simply have to keep your mouth shut. Yeah, says Mrs. W., it's easy to say . . . It's simply all shit. (In this context, though the two cases cannot be compared, I always end up thinking of *The Seventh Cross*.) She talks about her plans to sell her house. That there are new possibilities there. That her Henry has to leave here because there is nobody for him to associate with. Then comes her favorite topic: gossip about the neighbors. How they cut Horst Sch.'s lip open every which way in the hospital. Yeah, once they get started snipping! That couldn't turn out well either, the split lip and then the cigar always hanging from it—the nicotine on it! It's only just being sent in for analysis. Yes, now we will just have to wait and see. If nothing else, everything that is above the lip will be bad afterward anyway. But you don't know, of course. It may just have gone well. But Mieken—no. (Horst Sch.'s wife) I took a look at her. She goes to the hospital on Sundays to visit her husband wearing the same things that she wears when she goes to the school to clean. And she wouldn't even have the parka at all, if they hadn't given it to her. And have I already told you about the scandal that occurred recently? When the parents from Böken wanted to take their daughter—who is now supposed to become Mieken's daughter-in-law, you know—away from there at all costs? And she didn't go with them? Although her uncle, who is here from somewhere in the West, arrived in a big Western car and stopped in front of the door? But he didn't even get out. But Mrs. E. knocked on my front window—it was already dark by then: Man, just listen to what is going on at Mieken's place again. No, they aren't going to get out of the kneading trough. But who can do it the way Horst does: in the morning a couple of hours in the barn, then in the afternoon another hour, and the rest of the time he sits at the fence and smokes? Were our husbands able to do that? And Mieken even goes along to help him in the barn? When they are all waiting anyway for the two hundred marks that she earns at the school? I simply have to see what she buys at the store, and I already know just what is what. No, no. It's all shit. But still defends her husband. You, when the insurance people come there to collect, then everything is locked up tight at Sch.'s place, and nobody is at home. At the same time, he really is a strong man. He really could work. But no. And if they have no liquor and no cigars there, he is cranky anyway. All shit.

Since the death of her husband a few weeks ago, Mrs. W.'s face has become wrinkled and she has dark shadows under her eyes. If I ask her how she's doing, she says: you keep going, you keep going. She often dreams very vividly at night that her husband is lying next to her. Once in the evening, in the dim light in front of the television set, she had nodded off a little and she gave a start and had the definite feeling that her husband was sitting next to her, and she reached out to his chair. Oh, how I deceived myself! she says. Yes, everything is not that simple. Proudly she shows me the steam horn from the water kettle, which had fallen behind the stove ages ago, and which she found when she finally moved the little kitchen cabinet out. An old, rusty fire starter also became visible. That can probably be thrown away now. She wanted to know if we had already dug our carrots. They should actually be out of the ground by the fifteenth, otherwise the sugar will go into the ground. They say. There may be something to it. Only this year everything is going differently. Still no rain. She still has only a little bit of celery and a little bit of leek in the garden. Everything else is gone. No, now she has her peace at last.

In Mrs. W.'s life there is not a single action, not one opinion in which she was wrong. Never, never has she done anything wrong. It is she who watches the comings and goings for the entire village from her post at the window. Wasn't Mieken at your place recently? She really can't have been at the P.s' place, and she wasn't at Aunt Martha's either, I asked her myself. I know what lies behind the question—that "Mieken" might have offered herself as temporary help in case Mrs. W., as she intends to do, moves to Schwerin. But I act as if I do not know anything. No, Mieken was not at my place. So, you now always have to be at the grocery store by noon if possible, if you really want to get something—they receive goods on Wednesdays, and immediately after there is again nothing. No—things will not be the way they were again very soon, certainly not. But I still got mine.

And how are things going now with your daughter? she asks. So, one more week. But she was already very big when she was here, wasn't she? Yeah—but you often cannot tell by that. It is not always the case that a woman who gets so big also has a large baby—I tell her that during the last ultrasound examination the doctor already calculated the approximate birth weight of Tinka's baby: 3200 grams. That's good, she says. The baby shouldn't be too heavy. So if you take into account that she had everything out front, then it should be a girl. You can't always tell by that. But with me it was that way. With my boys I always grew large in my hips. But I had easy births otherwise. Two or three strong contractions and it was out. Yeah. But back then we also had a good midwife. She lived in Rugensee. She really cheered a person up. And when my first one had slipped out, she said: Well, you were not the last one either with your mother. And that was right. Five more after that. Yeah—it's becoming fashionable again to let the husbands watch. Not bad at all, I must say. Otherwise they don't know at all what a woman sometimes goes through. Oh, a birth! they say. But they should be there. My husband, too, of course. Come on over here, the midwife said to him when he wanted to slip away. The first three were born at home, of course. So, then he stayed. But at the end, when it was a fight to the finish, he slipped out after all. My God, he was still such a very young guy. Well. What has to be, has to be.

Now I do sit down at the desk beneath the bull's-eye window. I prowl around the thought of Tinka's giving birth, as I have tended to do in recent weeks, without imagining all too vivid images. My hairdresser in Schwerin, whose daughter will give birth at the same time, recently said to me: I don't tell her about birth all that precisely. I don't either, I said. We smile at each other in the mirror. It isn't necessary, is it? she said.

Instead of writing as I had intended, I continue reading in the book that lies there open next to the writing paper, and in which I have been reading over the last few days: *The Scientist and the Irrational*, contributions to ethnology and anthropology, edited by Hans Peter Dürr. There are, of course, such "coincidences," where you get your hands on the right book at just the right point in your work, and that is how it was for me with this. In a series of articles this book presents a large number of details about shaman and oracle technique, mostly with reference to Africa. But rituals of that kind cannot have differed so greatly in early Greece either.

I read an essay by Werner Zurfluh: "Flying Outside the Body Through the Holes in the Net," in which the author reports on his out-of-body experiences: about his ability to leave his body while sleeping, with complete consciousness, to move around in a second body, and also to fly and have other transcendental experiences. He describes precisely such an experience of returning again to his body, which "he" sees lying in bed. He reports about techniques of "condition control" that help him to ascertain in which body he currently resides. ("With the second body solid objects could be penetrated . . .") He describes the difficulties that he had in accepting the out-of-body state as reality, because symbolic understanding failed. He does not seek evidence—"The fact of experience and the certainty of experience are sufficient" for him. And then comes a key sentence, for the sake of which I read these and other essays with a certain inner excitement: "If, instead, we initially attempt to prove and explain the phenomenon, then we will only have a paradigm available to us that does not 'allow' experiences of that kind."

It is that very thing that has concerned me for a long time—and last but not least my involvement with mythology led me there, but I know that the question has already been on my mind for a long time. What is reality? How many realities are there? Is there a possibility for having transcendental experiences even without drugs?

Zurfluh explains that the "objectives of human society" lead to the distortion of dreams; he experienced this personally during periods of great strain at the university. Whether or not one decides in favor of "coherent dreaming" depends on what value is given to individual needs and experiences vis-à-vis the demands of society. He himself works part-time as a biology teacher, and his wife also works so that he can devote many hours a day to writing down his dream experiences: a need that I understand all too well. He has also developed a technique that makes it possible for him to remember his dreams—I would like to become acquainted with that! But obviously he is not steering toward a dream life: "He who does not want to cut himself off from the outside world and similarly exclude the nocturnal domain has to concern himself intensively with both, the daily routine and the world of dreams." "If dreams are observed while taking social concerns into consideration, one arrives at neither the dominance of the subject, the ego trip, nor at the determination of personal development by society alone." I myself feel a strong need not to continue to bow to the power of the coordinates where I find myself, but to find other coordinates and also learn to relate to them. I do not know if it is too late. But does what we long for have to exist?

The report of Zurfluh's experience also has an aspect, of course, that concerns language. In order to narrate an experienced reality, one translates it into a linguistic form. In the semantic fields, the "material," the "spiritual," and the "intellectual" components are blended together to form a whole. This continuum is shifted in the direction of an exclusively material understanding by present-day social needs. With that, material reality is automatically given priority, and it must come to a confrontation with the other domains.

The style of the narrative will show how strongly my language is shaped by the terminologies that are at my disposal. For me difficulties arise that are similar to those of a physicist who must describe a quantum mechanics experiment with the language of classical physics—And yet only through narrating what we have personally experienced is it possible to reveal the problems in all their ramifications.

This is an everyday experience in writing. At the moment, for example—that is, for the last three or four days—I have the feeling that behind the text that I have written up until now the outlines of a new continent are appearing; that additional aspects of the figure are opening into the depths that I cannot yet formulate: its transcendental side, a substratum that cannot be defined only socially. So I read around, make notes—am agitated, "lazy," and wait for the saving illumination. Know that I cannot go on this way. In the process simultaneously seek below the surface for the inspiration toward which Gerd presses: to break down the level of identification between me and C. I have a feeling about a possible solution for it (at night; that is why I lie awake for a long time); it would mean plowing the entire text under. Throwing out all of the delivery dates and the publisher's production dates; for this is not something one can accomplish with a tour de force . . .

My most intensive interest is directed toward those comments in the texts of the book that Dürr edited, which concern themselves with the visual and their influence on the perception of reality, thus also toward sentences from the Zurfluh essay like these—He quotes Einstein about the relationship between theory and observation: "From the standpoint of principle it is quite wrong to want to base a theory only upon observable values. For in reality it is exactly the opposite. It is the theory that determines what one can observe . . . Although we are getting ready to formulate new natural laws that do not agree with the existing ones, we do suspect that the existing natural laws function so precisely, beginning with methods of observation all the way to the relevance to our consciousness, that we may depend on them and may therefore speak of observations." But "the possible, that which can be expected, is an important component of our reality that cannot simply be forgotten in lieu of what is verifiable." This is a sentence that made the day worth it.

Since I have begun to quote, it is difficult for me to stop doing it (it has already been the next day for a long time, and it is almost seven o'clock in the evening already and thus questionable whether I can at least finish these notes today); specifically, I want to note down a few more sentences about the meaning of openness to the idea of transcendence—to which, I believe, openness to the idea of utopia would also belong: "The rarity of an observation is provoked directly by the theory, and it is the theory that declares an observation to be irrelevant. If the openness to transcendence no longer stands in the middle of a paradigm, observation may only take place in conformity with theory. Facts that contradict theory are eradicat-

ed and replaced by ideology." And finally, a Dürr quote in Zurfluh: "Thus it appears that our person amounts to very much
more than what everyday culture voluntarily puts before our
eyes. And besides that, it appears that it was the more archaic
cultures in particular that trained man, or at least some people,
to 'empty' themselves of their quotidian natures, as the Indian
says, . . . or to renounce its limitations."

Zurfluh closes: "The human temperament is capable in
principle of out-of-body experiences. But for that it must transcend that social norm which prescribes what 'natural' means.
In a paradigm that does not permit openness to transcendence,
the human temperament becomes subject to a standard that is
inhuman. If, through the application of structural force, transcendence is darkened and ecstasy is labeled flight from reality, then the end of any evolutionary development has been
reached and only the progress of 'more of the same' remains."

It is clear to me that Cassandra must have experienced a ritual rebirth and authentic conditions of ecstasy through which
she brought herself into opposition to her social environment.
But—when I think about my ongoing plans: I finally have new
points of departure for my figure of the magician! A fortunate
find.

At noon we eat "leftovers." Gerd has already put the potatoes on. Then Mr. R., the electrician, comes to mark out the
path for the electrical lines and the placement of the outlets, the
water heater, and the electrical hot plate in the former cattle
barn that is now being renovated into a domicile for Tinka and
her family. We walk across the bare concrete. We want to leave
the corner free, perhaps a sitting nook. Naturally we need
couches. Where they want to sleep, of course, is up to them.
The corner here, says Gerd, I've been thinking, is perhaps a
convenient place for the child. He explains to R. where the windows should be enlarged and where new ones should be cut out
in the walls. It will become nice and bright, says R. A nice room

in general. The men discuss toward which side it will be most convenient to have the door open. It will probably have to be moved again. As R. leaves, Gerd tells him that his nephews were seen breaking into a house whose owners were not there. Highly likely, for them, says R. It's a shame, isn't it?

A nice man! says Gerd, when he has gone. I just made a quick call and didn't even reach him, then he comes on his own. A really nice man.

We sit outside to eat. The radiant, dry autumn weather is holding. A summer that comes only once in a hundred years, they say. We won't experience a year like this again, we say. Behind that is my secret calculation of my lease on life, which will, however, undoubtedly last for a few more years. Even in two or three years, assuming that I do not get seriously ill, I will figure on a period of twenty years. Will think that I can probably reach seventy-four or seventy-five. Secretly observe the seventy-four and seventy-five-year-olds that I know, catch myself thinking that I would not be that frail then, surely less forgetful, hopefully still able to work—for that is what it is really about. The many sentences for an autobiographical book, which have been going through my mind for weeks, should be written down sometime—an autobiography from points of view other than those of external history and chronology—So we eat dill sauce on the potatoes; we have the radio with us and listen to the latest domestic and foreign press commentaries on the election in Hessen; they take Hans-Dietrich Genscher sharply to task. So coalition parties and the Free Democratic Party want to cling to their schedule and to the constructive vote of no confidence against Chancellor Schmidt in Bonn. The fact that following the election in Hessen they have no mandate for it, as Willy Brandt remonstrates, does not matter to them at all. It is about the number of votes that Kohl would get in the legislature. The Free Democratic Party, however, would have to guarantee a solid majority there.

Dishwashing. We lie down, I with my Dürr book again, Gerd with his Dyson. He claims that the year '61 was the last moment when disarmament could have been successful. The Americans had superiority, the Soviets, who had always behaved like they were trying to impress others, had known that, and would have been ready for authentic armament limitations. The opportunity was wasted. Now disarmament has become an almost insolvable problem. Sixty-one? I think. Then "we" built the Wall . . .

I cannot hold on to the fragments of dreams from my nap. I get up, fix coffee, and look longingly at the magnificent sunny weather outside. Sit down at the desk upstairs for two hours, with the *Cassandra* manuscript this time. Recognize, as I skim the last pages and notes, that I must go back a few steps and begin again at an earlier point. That I wanted to bring in the "stealing of the statue of Pallas Athena" too soon, the interpretation of which was so difficult for me. So I draft an earlier scene in the temple—specifically the one in which Hecuba and Polyxena come to sacrifice (why? I do not know yet) and Achilles sees Polyxena for the first time and is immediately inflamed with "love," which in his case means: with lust, and Cassandra feels that "melting pain" which accompanies her visions at that time; she knows: Polyxena will perish because of this animal, but she does not say it. Nor is she supposed to say it. She is a state priestess, not a "seeress." The contradiction within her comes to a head.

I write rather rapidly, unclearly, in an unsatisfying manner, still drafting, not really hitting the mark. I am circling around the real form of the text and I know it. The fact that I know it is disquieting and at the same time lets me hope: I will probably not be content with it too soon, even if I now do not yet see in what manner the difficulty in which I now find myself could be resolved. In passing, I listen to the news. In Israel almost half a million demonstrators demonstrated in favor of the establishment of a state investigating committee to determine who was guilty of the massacres in two Palestinian camps, and against Defense Minister Sharon. That is a great relief to me. How was that state supposed to go on living otherwise? Although not one of the dead will return to life as a result. Nor do I try to imagine all too precisely how those mass killings played out. The bulldozers that pushed the corpses—and was it only corpses?—together, covered them up. Those images now stick in my mind next to the images from German concentration camps, of the burial of bodies following the destruction of Dresden, of the legacies of the Pol Pot regime in Cambodia—it is a sentence on which I cannot comment further.

I need movement, have to go outside. It is shortly after five. Gerd puts the red bicycle out for me—I can do it myself!—Let me do it, the bar of the barn door is so difficult to move—he has gotten his quota of fresh air and movement by cutting the hedges and gathering sorrel on the meadow; besides that, his feet hurt severely and he walks around in my red health sandals in order to straighten them out again. When I ride off, the air is still mild. With every little rise I notice that the summer exercise from the time when we often went to Rugen Lake swimming has unfortunately had no lasting effect. I get out of breath, my heart starts to pound, and I have to get off. From the sand hill I look at our village, the "tomcat," as it lies there with the outlines of every house etched sharply in the glow of the setting sun—how can you tell by looking at this light that it is autumn light? What causes it to appear "golden"?—the front part, the "head" of the tomcat, to which our house also belongs, deeply embedded in the islands of the tall trees, around it the rolling countryside, in sharp relief every line, every outline, and in this evening light. I cannot remember ever having stood up here without having been permeated by the feeling of deeply moving beauty—in any weather, in any season, in any light. It is a secret of this landscape that in all its simplicity it has so many faces, that you never get tired of it. The path to Sch.'s house is as bad as always; he says it cannot be paved with asphalt for reasons of military strategy. Sch. is standing in his shirt in front of the house with an older married couple; we are introduced to each other. They come from Wismar. The man is a member of the hunting club and knows the hunting area here thoroughly. What famous people live here, he says. That there are no longer any deer—or only a few—is clear. They used to find feed here, now—just what is there for them to eat? Besides that, the hard winter of '78 to '79 decimated them. He asks if we have a black sheep dog. He has often encountered one in the hunting area, ownerless; until now he has spared it, but once a dog like that has smelled blood and its wolfish nature breaks forth again—then it is a real pest and has to be shot.

The two of them turn their car around and drive off. Sch. says that he has sent his dog to Wismar, to his wife's apartment, and that it is much too uncomfortable for the dog out here. We stand there for half an hour, until it grows cool and the sun sinks behind the edge of the woods, and exchange gossip and information. He says that he has now gone as far as the cultural ministry to sue for his trip to the West, which he needs in order to do research for a literary project. He was treated quite gently; that is the motto now, but they could not do anything. (When two writers from the German Democratic Republic are standing together, I think uncomfortably, they first talk about trips to the West.) Yes, if he were not a member of the union! Absurd, he says excitedly. Then he will just leave the union. In his opinion—also in mine—"they" want nothing but quiet in the cultural domain right now, just no quarrels there, too. For that reason, the copyright office also approves without much difficulty manuscripts for Western publishers, which are not permitted to appear here. If only a few marks of hard currency come in as a result. At the last authors' conference of the Mitteldeutscher Publishing Company they no longer made any effort to gloss over the situation: that the publishers are left sitting on their books; that only "light works on a simple level" are still being bought. The chief publisher's reader had observed that my books form almost the only exception. That they are also unable to fulfill their export quota. And that those "interesting" manuscripts that could perhaps be sold as books are unfortunately not printable. Absurd, says Sch., he will not go there anymore. Also absurd that of all things his first book is now selling, of which he would prefer not to be reminded any longer. But what else should he live on? His better books are not selling as well, and the manuscript on which he is now working will be unpleasant. So these problems have now also reached the provinces. The conversation unavoidably turns to the supply situation. That in Wismar people have occasionally already had to stand in line for three hours to get meat; but that in Meteln there was still butter for 2.40 marks, which he now buys simply on principle. He almost warns against boxed butter, because it is poured into the plastic hot and as a result harmful materials from the plastic, melted, can penetrate the butter. In the West, for example, vinegar is not sold in plastic bottles—only here! I contribute a few guiding principles from a training session for functionaries that took place recently in Frankfurt/Oder: The eighties are not the seventies—nobody should imagine that. Or: export comes before domestic needs, Berlin comes before export. And if the entire Republic should starve—Berlin will not starve!—We laugh unhappily. Not a trace of a conception anymore, we say. Not even the pretense of one. Only: get through the insolvency! A country could hardly founder any more severely . . . Yes it can. It's much worse in Poland. Sch. says he is amazed that he still tries to be mentally active, to grapple with it, although he then actually thinks it is senseless, on the other hand, and catches himself in mental laziness . . . This very thing, the leadenly gray resignation, the comfortable letting oneself go, has taken hold of most people who would otherwise be creative. Those who are hindered in being so for an entire generation finally give up. Or go away. Mold grows on everyone and everything.

It grows cool. I ride on. On the left, F.'s house that never gets finished. On the right the white roof of the mill, the poplar lane that leads to it straight as an arrow. Some of the poplars that we planted as cuttings from those have died on us during this bone-dry summer. In ten years others should look like these here. The bumpy path to Jammersdorf. All of the colors, which remain clear and glowing and sharply distinct from one another, are now bathed in transparent dark-blue ink. The landscape could be transferred directly over into a naïve picture. Small tractors are still in the fields, digging potatoes. A few people, in pairs, bent, gathering potatoes. In Jammersdorf a man holds his somewhat threatening white dog at heel as I pass by. Good evening. Good evening. Across the field, because the path in the ravine is worse, to Prophet's farm, then past the Laabses' property,[6] on which Mieke Sch. and her daughter gather apples. I ask about the husband. Yes, today the stitches are supposed to come out; on Wednesday he will probably get out of the hospital. The cuts in his lower lip are described for me once more. The dog at Str.'s rages as always when I ride by. It is almost six-thirty. Since daylight-saving time is over, darkness will now come quickly.

I call up the Laabses to inform them that some boys are said to have broken into their house. They intend to come tomorrow.

I still have to write a letter, actually two. A week ago I received a letter from a man in Dresden who is seeking sup-

[6] Laabs: Daniela Dahn (b. 1949), writer, married to Joochen Laabs (b. 1937), writer; friends with the Wolfs. (G.W. was the publisher's reader for the lyric poetry volumes of J. Laabs for the Mitteldeutscher Publishing Company.) (G.W.)

port for a family, for a former fellow worker with whom he is friends. Actually I should forward the entire proceedings, with the request to intervene for this man, to Anna Seghers. Anna Seghers lies in bed, ill, not always clearly aware, in her home in Friedrichshagen, and can no longer be bothered with such problems. I have considered whether or not I should simply send the material back to the man in Dresden with that notification and write to him that I, in order not to lessen the effects of my interventions, have always intervened for authors up until now, and that I do not expect much success if I now take on the case that the man from Dresden presented to me there. A man has been sitting in prison for over two years because he submitted an application for a permit to leave the country for himself and his family, and when that was rejected, he turned to relatives in the Federal Republic and to Federal Chancellor Schmidt. Proceedings were then raised against him for repeated agitation against the state and collaboration with organizations hostile to the German Democratic Republic. Sentence: three years and six months in prison. Apparently the family was supposed to be deported in the summer. The man was moved from Brandenburg to the Karl-Marx-Stadt prison, and then it turned out that the former husband of the woman, who is also the father of the son, refuses to give permission for the son, who does not recognize him as his father at all, to relocate. The man was taken back to Brandenburg. The family's problems seem to have become insoluble. Then in July, in a letter to Honecker, which remained unanswered, the woman asked to have her husband released early at least and to cancel the rest of his sentence because she has fears about his health. And so that is what I had to support in my letter to H. I had gotten it straight in my mind that it would be impossible for me to cross the border unhindered, while a man, E.S., has been sitting in prison for more than three years because he also wants to do that very thing, and not at least try to help him.[7] My reservations—where do they come from? First from the fear that an intervention will only make everything worse than it already is. So I would not give the name of the man who sent me the letter that was actually intended for A.S. Not use the additional information that is in that letter. Had to consider whether or not it could harm the woman if I were to pass the copy of the letter to E.H. on to him again now. Could he see in that a breach of trust on the part of the woman and perhaps react obstinately? So my tone must be polite, almost cooperative.

That already leads to the second reason why such letters are so difficult for me: I do not want to have anything more to do with them, not even as an interventionist for others. On the other hand, the opportunity for such successful interventions is one of the reasons why I remain here and am able to say to myself: I am needed. I can, even if it is in such limited measure, do something. If I were to cut the thread that leads to the top completely, those few opportunities would be cut off at the same time. But I would be freer. I could and should publicly voice my loathing toward practices of locking up unknown people for the same offenses for which they are lenient toward us more well-known figures. If I were to express that opinion—and others—publicly, i.e. on West German television, for example, I would be out, too. Would then only have to think about myself, about my writing, and only have to worry about that. In the long run would probably also be forced geographically across the border.

When I have finished my letter to H., I recognize that I have addressed him incorrectly, with his former title ("First Secretary" instead of "Secretary General")! Thus I must write him again, and condense on the basis of good advice from Gerd.

It is dark. Supper. G. has made sorrel soup. I eat too much.

[7] C.W.'s letter to E. Honecker was successful. (G.W.)

We watch the news while drinking red wine. The same faces again, the politician's dance, suspicions, and commentaries. Kohl: We are on schedule. The leftists of the Free Democratic Party are beside themselves. The Greens will be happy if the entire Federal Republic becomes ungovernable. They wear no ties like all the others. So I actually sit down and watch a group of journalists consisting of two Germans and some Swedes, among them a woman, who converse about Sweden. About the spreading bureaucracy. About the possible dependency of the press on the government that gives it subsidies. I am more interested in their open faces and the manner in which they talk with each other than in what they say.

Gerd goes to bed. When the Panagulis film begins, in which scenes of torture and confinement can be expected, I turn off the television set; I cannot watch that. My dissatisfaction almost every evening. The day ought to bring more. It should not yet be over. Then I wish for people. Conversations. The television: a feeble substitute.

Dutiful cosmetics. Sometimes I think that in earlier pictures I look older than I do now in the mirror. Self-deception. In bed I continue to read in the Dürr book. Gerd recites a sentence from his Freeman Dyson, says that it is interesting, I should also read it sometime. How the man changed from being a collaborator on the neutron bomb to a supporter of peace politics . . . One of the two great powers has to begin to stop, we say. But is there any kind of a chance for that? The refrain of all my thoughts. Shortly after I have fallen asleep, the train of thought continues. Then I think intensively about Tinka. Hopeful thoughts, suggestive. About her magnificent belly which was the most beautiful thing this summer. Did I really perceive it— the belly, the summer? In all of its beauty? Really enjoy it? As unrepeatable? As the best thing in life?

I lie awake for a long time yet.

U ntil after midnight, when, to be specific, this day begins, I read in Chekhov's *Uncle Vanya*, encouraged by Brigitte Soubeyrand and our discussion about her impending production of *The Seagull* in Tübingen. I am quite surprised by the prophetic figure of the doctor, of Astrov, probably the first environmentalist in Russian (and European?) literature, who wants to preserve the forests and already sees them threatened back then. I do not quite finish the first act, am tired, fall asleep. Shortly after I wake up, I can still remember that I dreamed something and perhaps approximately what. I would like to hold on to the dream and call it back—nearly simultaneously it occurs to me that today is the "day of the year"—but I do not succeed. It fades inexorably, as almost all dreams have since the house burned down.[1] Is that a phenomenon of age? Does the protective mechanism that does not let the pain come too close to me also affect sleep, dreams? Do I "want" to repress it? Do I have to, so that an unworthy heartache does not gnaw too severely at me?

I look at the alarm clock that is standing on the floor beneath the green chest, because its almost silent ticking disturbs me when I am trying to go to sleep: six o'clock. Gerd is already awake; he reaches his hand over to me and it is warm. I pick up the Chekhov book again, with which I had fallen

---

[1] On July 11, 1983, the house in Neu Meteln was totally destroyed by a fire; only a few pieces of furniture and manuscripts, C.W.'s diaries among others, were saved; no people were injured. (G.W.)

asleep during the night, and read aloud to Gerd the passage that had amazed me: "One has to be a barbarian without sense and understanding to burn this beauty in one's stove, to destroy what we cannot create again. Man is gifted with reason and creativity in order to multiply what has been given to him, but up until now he has created nothing, but has only destroyed. There are fewer and fewer forests, the rivers are drying up, the wild animals are dying out, the climate has been ruined, and with every day the earth becomes poorer and more faceless . . ." Later this Astrov spreads out a map on which he has noted down the disappearance of species in his district; and what is a genial anticipation at the turn of the century: the question of why man has become destructive. No belief in progress. Deeply momentous thinking, specifically because of its skepticism. A still relevant piece that probably could only have its genesis in a dilapidated Russia where no pseudo-progress, no technology, no economic boom clouded the minds of the liberals. Gerd, who was simultaneously reading in the catalogue of the West Berlin Academy about the Russian futurists, says: Yes, much was concentrated in that Russia back then; even today, the West still does not see that. Beyond that, he is amazed at what a ruckus could be caused through the decades by comments in literary works that are in themselves so limited, as, for example, those of a short text by Blok [2]; amazing, again and again, what literature unleashes—In a very small circle, I say—He: Nevertheless.

He goes to take a shower; I begin to fix breakfast in my pajamas. Turn on the coffee machine, boil eggs, and set the table in the kitchen. I often see now before the background of the present the same scene, when we will be old. What will I still be able to do then, what not? Then I always resolve to do my

[2] Alexander Blok (1880-1921), Russian poet; this allusion is to his epic poem "*Die Zwölf* (The Twelve)" (1918), in which he sees Christ at the head of twelve soldiers of the Red Army. (G.W.)

morning exercises more regularly, to go to the sauna every week . . . And at the same time always the question: Should we really stay here? Newly evoked by Annette's comment yesterday on the telephone. There in the hospital there was a nasty denunciation that also affected her and probably originated with the head physician: in their hospital there is a "conspiring union." That is being investigated now. Foolishness, of course, she said with emphasis on the telephone. He simply gave the names of all of those whom he does not like. And now I think—less disquieted than I would have been a few years ago: Should our children and children's children endure that all their lives? Nailed down to remaining quiet as a mouse, simply in order not to come under any kind of suspicion? And how long will I live yet to protect them? And what then?—When I talk with Gerd about it over breakfast, he says—this conversation that has repeated itself a hundred times!: And what do you intend to do?—I think, I say vaguely, we should leave after all—And how do you intend to do that? With the whole family? Over there, the children would cling to you and you would also be financially responsible for them . . . Here, I said, I also have to regulate anything out of the ordinary for them—Yes, but they stand on their own feet financially—And there they would receive unemployment support for at least a year, could travel . . .—And the political situation? The Kohl regime?— Yes, but since Sunday the Social Democratic Party is in an upward trend again—But that does not change the economic crisis—We have been talking like this for years, sometimes not for a long while, then every day again. Dialogues like this one are floating around in my head for the play that Brigitte has pushed me to write: "What you are doing there as a prose narrative, *Summer Piece*, I would very much like to have from you as a play." While I am thinking about that—already wrote a dialogue yesterday as a sample (Ellen–Steffi), it occurs to me that in a play I would view the characters more harshly. The prose embellishes a little bit, perhaps through the landscape that comes into play much more strongly.

While eating breakfast, in the background we hear comments on Radio Germany about the good performance of the Social Democrats in the parliamentary elections in Hessen and Bremen. Federal Manager Glotz: We are simply modest people . . . That the federal government pays the price so quickly for its anti-populace politics . . . We make it difficult for ourselves in the missile question, and the voters honored that . . . I visualize "the voters" and ask myself when all of these politicians will begin to put sober analysis in the place of the phrase. There is a press review from the East German press; apparently there is a grandly presented peace declaration by Honecker and Mies[3] together. After Krupp, the speaker says scornfully, and means with that Beitz, who received an honorary doctorate last week in Greifswald and whom Honecker congratulates today on his seventieth birthday—after Krupp, Krause now comes to the German Democratic Republic and gives his blessing to the flirtation of the leaders with Krupp. Meanwhile, we eat mixed cereal, eggs, bread, and rye crisp with honey. I drink my good, strong morning coffee, Gerd his tea. From the radio comes the hit of recent months, with the closing line: Visit Europe as long as it still exists—Now we are already laughing about that. Talk about the men of E., our colleagues.

When Petra rings the bell, at shortly before eight, I go into the bathroom. The evening with E.[4] is going through my mind. Her manuscript, which she had given me to read, about a pubescent love toward a teacher, and from which we came to her life. Her father who had a violent temper and destroyed for her the things that she was attached to (for example, a cactus

[3] Herbert Mies (b. 1929), Chairman of the German Communist Party in the 1980s and '90s, winner of the Lenin Peace Prize in 1985-86. (Ed.)

[4] Gabriele Eckart (b. 1954), writer, at the time actively involved in dialogue with C.W. (G.W.)

collection), who sold her to the state security service, where she signed a collaboration agreement at the age of eighteen, which also contained the threat of prison if she ever talked about that agreement. How she then in Berlin, while studying philosophy, when "her entire world view rapidly changed," tried to get away from it, not to say anything, not to begin any conversation; how they came again and again, how they had her in their hands again after they had dragged her out of the bunker where she was hiding after she had strayed too far toward the West on the Bohemian border; then really wanted to have her until somebody advised her: You must tell that everywhere, otherwise you will never get away from them; how she had done that and they really had left her alone, but that she still sees them at more prominent events of the Writers' Union, for example at the May 8 bazaar, and then she becomes afraid again and cannot sleep. Our conversation had begun in the first place, of course, with her fear because of her diaries, in which she has compulsively written down each of her feelings, everything that she experiences and observes, since she was fourteen years old, and which she keeps hidden and only takes home sometimes when she wants to read something in them, material, for she forgets everything that she has not written down, especially everything that has excited her. Then she has an insane fear, has hallucinations, constantly hears the doorbell ring, really hears it, creeps to the door, and goes to pieces. If they put me in prison, that would not be too bad; after all, I could write about it afterward, prison report, just imagine that. But if they take away my diaries, I will not survive that. I always see Bierwisch before my eyes, in Leipzig. I was with him after they had searched the house and carried away twelve wash baskets full. He spent two years in remand custody; they could not prove that he had done anything; then he got out and he got nothing back of all his things—The detailed story of her successful attempt to get her books published via the Central Committee, after she had complained in a letter about the attempts by the state security people to recruit her again; about the disruption of her telephone; and after she, not at all stupid, had suggested that she no longer saw any way out and that she would leave. Which she would also have done. Now the publishing house Verlag Der Morgen wants to publish everything by her. She always finds fatherly protectors. But all that cannot change her nature—shouting for joy to the heavens, saddened to death.

It is eight-thirty. I greet Petra. She says that she hurried to bring us fresh rolls and now we have already eaten. She has me try on the skirt that she sewed for me. She sits down at the typewriter in the large room. In the *Berliner Zeitung* I look through the real estate and apartment exchange advertisements. Gerd has discovered a five-room apartment in the vicinity of Frankfurter Allee, I object that we would not like the location. I also look for bungalows that are for sale. The burning of the house in Meteln has again thrown our situation into turmoil; we no longer want to stay here on Friedrichstrasse. I always see the clouds of exhaust rising in front of my window, and inside I think: I do not want to remain here at all.

I put dinner—the soup that was precooked yesterday—back on the stove for another hour, intermittently fish out the meat, the vegetables, and the bones. Make some notes on the plan for the play. Have now been writing these notes since nine o'clock. Am still thinking about E., who is untouchable, can get upset to be sure, even sick, but after that comes out of an experience almost exactly the same as she went into it. She does not regret that she was together with R., who burned one of her diaries, drinks unbelievably, cheered when his former wife committed suicide ("Now I will finally get my beautiful picture books back and the other things that were awarded to her in the divorce!"), that she exposed herself to him. After all, it was an experience. It might be that someday I will have to describe such a man. Experience is everything!—But she actually does not experience anything, but simply participates in it. Observes the people in her diary like objects. So that I told her: It serves you right that he burned your diary. She had compared him and her real lover with each other in two adjacent columns like insects. I am dumbfounded at her cheerful aversion to ties, which she shares with her brother. In the end it comes out that he loves her and is making plans for how they will live together. And that is what will probably happen, she says. But not until later, right now he still disturbs me, of course. For example, if I have a lover and he is living in the apartment with me . . . I am also quite perplexed about S., whom she repeatedly visits to be idolized by her. To tell memories to her. To listen to music with her. Yes—she is another, contemporary Mignon, a being outside of societal ties, something impish, completely subject to her moods, which rapidly change, eerie—undoubtedly also, if it has to be, destructive.

I call up a certain F. family in Pankow, Parkstrasse, that wants to exchange their five-room apartment for two somewhat smaller apartments. I ask the daughter, who answers the phone, about their wishes, and see that it will become somewhat difficult. I ask if there is gas heat in the apartment. No, stoves. Not good either. But the location is very nice. I ask if we could see the apartment. Yes.

Then I call Helga Paris to find out if there is a camera here that I could give to Tinka. She advises me to get a Minox.

Somebody calls me from Karlsruhe, a woman with a Swiss accent who claims that she has already invited me (she speaks for some organization or association), who has learned that I actually am coming to the Federal Republic, who even knows that I will be free on November 13th and now wants to seduce me into reading in Karlsruhe on that day. I can well understand that, she says again and again, when I decline because it would become too much for me. But I had to call you so that I can tell my friends here that I tried.

While I talk with her, I think about the telephone listener who is free to know that people are asking for me.

A sentence that E. spoke in relation to her "experiences" is still going through my mind today. She said that if she was not open to them, she would have the feeling that she saw herself as too good for certain experiences, for example, those with certain men. It occurred to me, and I talked with Gerd about it, that I have always seen myself as too good for that. That marriage and the family are natural protective fortresses, while a girl like her exposes herself to life unprotected and in the process experiences the other, dark, eerie sides of men, and also of the society. But since she cannot be destroyed, she finds older protectors again and again—she is not at all interested in others—and comes through.

Across the street, by the new Friedrichstadt palace, a yellow grader is busy, surrounded by men with yellow helmets. The ground is being smoothed out. Through the open window holes, which are secured by crossbeams, we sometimes see workers involved in interior work. A remarkable building. "Turkish bath," as someone recently called it, does not fit too badly. I see the sun and the blue sky; I already feel "hollow-eyed" again and want to go out. Want Gerd to come along; he does not look good, works too much, does not get any air anymore. Yeah, yeah, he says. Later. When I am finished with the thing. He means the Bettina afterword.[5] Just let me finish this one page yet, he says, and when I look in again, he becomes impatient, although I only wanted to suggest that I would also drive alone. I'm coming!—Petra receives directions about how to finish the soup. We go downstairs; it is really hot. People

[5] Bettina afterword: G.W. and Günter de Bruyn edited the series *Märkischer Dichtergarten*; which includes a volume on Bettina von Arnim, née Brentano: *Die Sehnsucht hat allemal Recht* (*Longing Is Always Right*), Berlin, 1984. (G.W.)

surge toward us, without jackets, as in the summer. Meteln! To be in Meteln now . . . In the parking lot, while we are pulling out of the parking space—I am reading in the letters that Gerd took out of the mailbox—there is a crunching noise. A Trabant that was too close behind us has lost its taillight cap. Damn it! says Gerd and climbs out. By chance, the Trabant owner just happens to be there. A good thing, he says, that I am here! and assumes that we would otherwise have furtively slipped away. The damage, of course, is minimal. But it is hard to find those caps, he says, gradually becoming friendlier. Where can you get them? Gerd asks. The man gives two addresses of auto parts stores. Gerd offers to drive to the one, while the Trabant owner wants to go to the other one. They exchange addresses. That's what I thought, says the man. We already met once at Wieland Förster's place.[6] When we have laboriously worked our way out of the parking place, Gerd says: His face seemed familiar to me, but I do not know who he is.

We drive down Lenin-Allee; at the end of it is the store. We wanted to go to Friedrichshain anyway. Gerd says that he was too distracted and did not watch properly. He was thinking about the laundry stamps, which he apparently lost. He is constantly looking for or losing something, failing to hear things, is somewhere else with his thoughts, thinking about his text. At the park in Friedrichshain he lets me out and now has to spend the time when he should be walking sitting in a car filled with exhaust fumes. I walk as quickly as possible through the park and am astonished at how extensive it is and at the diversity of trees and shrubs that it offers. Not many people, often lone individuals. Married couples, too, of our age. People with dogs, loners. Breeds of dogs: boxers, terriers, dachshunds, and

---

[6] Wieland Förster (b. 1930), sculptor, writer; friends with the Wolfs (G.W. gave the laudation for the presentation of Förster's book *Begegnungen—Tagebuch. Gouachen und Zeichnungen einer Reise in Tunesien* [*Encounters—Diary. Gouaches and Sketches of a Journey in Tunisia*], Berlin, 1974, *Neue Deutsche Literatur*, 3/1975). (G.W.)

poodles, nicely trimmed. The trees still quite green, on the ground already wilted leaves, isolated branches are beginning to change color. A summer restaurant that resembles a booth, in front of it round white plastic tables, the yellow plastic chairs already stacked in fours. The nice up and down that is created by the two bunker hills. You walk on the rubble of many buildings. On top of the one hill a student is helping her sports teacher measure out some stretch of ground. He thanks her several times before sending her to play volleyball with the others. A small group of boys in athletic clothing comes running up. Two women are jogging; the one is wearing the pants of a yellow suit, the other the jacket that belongs to it. A young woman with a baby stroller. How can I tell that she is a single mother? She is wearing a bright red blouse that does not go well with her pale face and her corn-blond hair. I like it here. I will come here often. I discover another restaurant, Spreeklause, or something like that, built round like a pavilion. Outside people are sitting under wooden canopies drinking beer. Gerd comes at around one and we walk for barely fifteen minutes. Of course he did not get a taillight cap. Irritating for the man, he says. He will not have gotten one either. We talk about Bettina. To what extent she is a Mignon. He talks about the episode that she, in contrast to her normal openness, wrote down very secretly and which was only found in her literary remains: how Goethe passionately kissed her, the twenty-five-year-old, on the breast in Teplitz and then withdrew when he sensed that she was still not aroused.

We drive back. In the parking lot Gerd looks at the Trabants and says what I have just been thinking: If you simply cannot get such a small part, then you are tempted to unscrew one from another car—We laugh.

Petra is waiting with the soup. It tastes good. On the radio a singer is singing a melody from *Cabaret*. Is it Liza Minnelli? I ask. No. She does not sing in German. Someone is imitating her there. Then comes the song, the last line of which in English is: I'll never fall in love again, and which we know in German with the line: Love is over for me. Now a female singer is singing here: I won't get involved in love anymore. How awful! The sour milk that I have saved, as always, has become too old, as always. This time we decide not to pour it out, but to make cottage cheese out of it. I get the sieve, Gerd the handkerchief, and we pour the thick milk into it. After that I hurry to the flower shop and get, besides fall asters, twenty-seven carnations for Tinka's birthday tomorrow. At home Petra and I put the flowers in a vase. I tell her that she can go ahead and leave early, so that she will still have part of the beautiful day, and then I lie down.

Read a few pages in Immanuel Velikovsky's *From the Exodus to King Akhenaton*, especially the introduction, in which there are statements like this one: "The present work will be as disturbing to the historians as *Worlds in Collision* was to the astronomers." Because he introduces a completely new chronology into the history of the ancient world. "Many of those who look to acknowledged authorities for guidance will express their disbelief that a truth could have remained undiscovered so long, from which they will deduce that it cannot be the truth."

I admire such sentences and smile over them. I sleep for half an hour, dreamlessly, and wake up at around three o'clock. Against the white bedroom ceiling I see especially clearly three black flies, which, small and transparent, have been buzzing back and forth in the direction of my gaze just beyond the retina of my left eye for several weeks. Remember how they upset me during the first few days; the fact that I have already almost become used to them amazes me. Read in a pocketbook containing letters and diary excerpts of Rahel Varnhagen, which present how fortunate she considered herself to be as a woman, as a Jewess, and that she considered herself to be ugly.

In her case, too, a severe father must have stifled the possibility of enjoying life at an early age.

Now some good coffee, I say. Gerd says, Yes. And makes it. We each go to our respective rooms to write. I continue to make notes for the piece that I call *A Stay in the Country* in my thoughts, or, like the subtitle of Chekhov's *Uncle Vanya*: *Scenes from Life in the Country*. Would not be bad to declare myself a follower of Chekhov by using that title. By the way, when I listen to what is going on inside of me, I observe that I do not believe I will write a play. So this whole thing is perhaps a waste of time. Or not quite. The work with the characters of the play enables me to see the characters in the prose more clearly.

Gerd comes in: Tell me, how can I say: Achim von Arnim [7] undoubtedly possessed manuscripts by Hölderlin. "Autographical writings." Arnim possessed autographical writings of Hölderlin's?—Autographical writings by Hölderlin, I say. Otherwise people could think that Hölderlin himself sent them to him—Gerd leaves again and I am reminded of the hundreds of times that this scene has repeated itself. I put on a phonograph record: Bach, six sonatas for violin and cello. Look through the letters from today once more: a hard currency certificate from a publisher. An invitation from women of the Lutheran Church to a discussion, which comes from a woman who says she is from Landsberg and refers to *Patterns of Childhood*. In addition, the letter of an Englishman who is spending an academic year in Berlin and would like to meet me. Besides that he would like to "carry on a correspondence with me"—which is the last thing that I want to do . . . Besides that, a small package of books from Luchterhand, which we picked up. Added to that is the certification from the mayor of Meteln attesting

[7] Ludwig Achim von Arnim (1781-1831), German poet and novelist born in Berlin, married to Bettina Brentano, who won wide recognition as a writer in her own right. (Ed.)

to the fact that we cleaned up the property where our fire was, as prescribed by law.

In the newspaper I again find questions from *Pravda* to the Americans concerning the incident with the South Korean passenger plane that the Soviets shot down—evidently when they confused it with a spy plane that was simultaneously in their air space. Quite clear to me that this was a trap of the CIA—but they unfortunately fell into it.

The news that Gustav Just[8] received the Translator's Prize calls up a chain of images from my time in the Writers' Union, where he was First Secretary and was then replaced because of questionnaire falsification. Later, as a staff member of *Sonntag*, he was in prison like Walter Janka . . .

Jaruzelski[9] spoke on cultural politics in Poland. Nobody is being condemned to silence. If books were not published it was because they damaged "the social balance or the interests of the socialistic state." One can ruminate for a long time over those metaphors.

It is approaching five-thirty; I put on a record, the Bach Sonata for Violin and Cello, No. 1 in B minor. I call Annette. How are you doing? Very well. And you?—Is there anything new?—Yes, today my shop steward at work was questioned about me. And they asked him if he thought it was possible that I would work poorly here because of my disapproval of politics—Man, what a mistake—Right. Even if I were full of displeasure about politics here, I certainly would not vent that on my patients—And what did the man say?—Well, only positive things. I was not supposed to know about the whole thing at all. It is so absurd that I cannot really get upset about it. The

---

[8] Gustav Just (b. 1921), deputy editor-in-chief of *Sonntag*, until he was sentenced to prison in connection with the Harich trial. (G.W.)

[9] Wojciech Witold Jaruzelski (b. 1923), a communist Polish political and military leader, Prime Minister from 1981 to 1985, head of the Polish Council of State from 1985 to 1989 and President from 1989 to 1990. (Ed.)

others are much more upset. Apparently that Schlumich wants to become head physician as fast as possible, and I only hope that he cuts his own finger there. I have also been summoned to the cadre administration office for next week . . .—How is the family doing?—Honza is still at work. Jana is wandering around somewhere. She is also doing gymnastics now as part of a team. Benni is here playing—Still doing puzzles?—No, that phase is over. Now he is building apartments. But chestnuts are his main passion. He has carried pocketfuls of them upstairs—But I can understand that—I can too. But I am constantly slipping on a chestnut—I could contribute a few acorns yet, which I recently gathered—No! Please don't. He can play with those in your apartment, not here—Do you have a lot of patients?—Enough—Also interesting ones among them?— Oh, yes—In the near future I need to discuss with you some psychological phenomena that affect mutual acquaintances of ours—Which ones, for example?—For example: frigidity—I don't know all that much about that either—Do they feel their frigidity and want to be rid of it?—Not at all. A person who is really frigid does not feel that either. Only in certain decisive moments of their lives do they sense that something is missing in them—And that someone drinks because of that?—I don't know. I would have to know the details—We'll talk about it on Saturday. (We then discuss who will stay there in the evening on Saturday, when we all get together at Tinka's for Helene's birthday, because they want to go to the opening of an exhibition of Zabka [10] and Benni is supposed to go to sleep there. I offer to stay there.)

When I hang up, the next call is there, from Mrs. Hollnagel in Seehof. She has looked around in the surrounding area, she says, and found out that there is an empty house in Gross Trebow. I know Gross Trebow, the property on the shore across

[10] Rainer Zabka (b. 1950), painter, graphic designer and action artist. (G.W.)

the lake where the people from the twentieth of July met. We had always liked the place. The house that she means is supposed to be situated very nicely, close to the lake. But according to her description it could be one of the estate workers' houses from back then, probably in bad condition. But we will go and look at it. She will make tentative inquiries of the state land office as to whether they would part with it. We are supposed to come to her place for coffee. We would like it so much, she says, if you would move back to this area . . .

I have hardly hung up, and the next call. Sigrid Töpelmann.[11] She asks if they can use excerpts from my Seghers afterword for Luchterhand in the "Read Again" column of the next issue of their publisher's newspaper *Der Bienenkorb* (*The Beehive*), which is due to appear again. We palaver about it back and forth. That would not be especially felicitous, but on the other hand Seghers should be represented in the first issue. Finally I agree to look at the afterword. The editor is supposed to call the day after tomorrow. We talk for a while longer about Sigrid's illnesses, about her Bachmann afterword, to which I promise to contribute the latest Bachmann publication, and her radio interviews.

Meanwhile Gerd has left ("So, I am leaving!") to have the car washed and to buy cheese on Leipziger Strasse. I begin to set the supper table, prepare a cheese platter, open the caviar tin, and put on my makeup. News. Almost three months after the granting of the billion-mark credit through the Bavarian State Bank, the German Democratic Republic has announced its first quid pro quo: the minimum exchange quota for children is abolished. Besides that an ordinance appeared today, in which the bringing together of a family has been given a legal foundation for the first time, the possibility of marriage between citizens of the German Democratic Republic and for-

[11] Editor at Luchterhand Publishing Company. (Tr.)

eigners is granted for the first time, as well as a right of appeal in the case of negative decisions by Republic authorities in this matter. There are already commentaries ranging from "A step in the right direction" to "disappointing."

At a quarter to seven Christoph Geiser[12] arrives, whom we have not seen since we met in Bern eight years ago. He has a stipend from the German Academic Exchange Service to live in West Berlin for a year and has now been trying for three months to become accustomed to the atmosphere of the city. At first, during the summer, in the heat, when there were hardly any culture people there, he simply spent a lot of time at the lake, at Wannsee. Then, since he did not like to ride the subway because it disturbed him so much to have lost his sense of direction when he got off—he had walked through the city a lot. Now he has made some friends, or, as they say there, "contacts." First over the champagne breakfast on Saturday morning in the authors' bookstore; there he immediately became acquainted with Klaus Schlesinger and other East German authors, with whom, he had to admit, he found more ready contact that he did with most West Berliners. The latter were focused so much on the thing that he noticed about West Berlin in general—on consumption. Even on the consumption of culture. They consume theater, film, and concerts; and even communication focuses mostly on consumption: in bars, for example, while they drink a substantial amount. There such an evening passes very quickly and even amusingly. They hardly ever go to bed before two o'clock in the morning, but if you ask yourself afterward what actually happened, you cannot

---

[12] Christoph Geiser (b. 1949), Swiss writer. The conversation also deals with the "passages" in the lectures on *Cassandra* that were questioned by the censors in the German Democratic Republic. In the East German edition, which appeared in the Federal Republic after its publication, sixty-three lines were cut from those lectures by the censors; the author insisted on the marking of the cuts, a process that had not existed in the German Democratic Republic up until that time (see also: C.W., *Werke*, Vol. VII, pp. 439ff.). (G.W.)

think of anything. He now has to see to it that he finds a real working rhythm again. Very often he is also in one of the five bars that he sees from the two windows in his almost empty apartment with three desks and three beds. When he comes over here via Checkpoint Charlie, he actually likes it better. Not as hectic, the people quieter. More like home. Today, for example, he looked at the Schinkel figures that have newly been set up on one side of the Jungfernbrücke, still very white, but he liked the entire ensemble. He sees more architectural poise here than he does over there.

I tell him that it is often that way for Westerners, that without having to experience the disadvantages they participate with pleasure in the advantages of closer human ties and a less well developed technology.

He talked, hesitantly, about his last book, which he had had to revise again because he treated such sticky questions there, questions that then also touched on the personal rights of others. Actually it was about the end of a friendship, but he could not really talk about it yet. He would still be dealing with it until he had read the galley proofs, but his next set of material was already on his mind, and he was moving more and more away from the autobiographical. He asked about the date when *Cassandra* would appear here. I expressed the suspicion that there would be quite an uproar; I would now see how insulted by this book many men would feel. He said, but the feminist theme was really not the main thing; it was actually about an all-embracing topic, the logic of power. He wanted to know which passages were eliminated. I told him. He could have guessed.

I asked him about acquaintances. He had run into Bichsel in New York, in the Village on a street corner. Erica Pedretti [13] was having problems with her children, was also probably ill,

[13] Erica Pedretti (b. 1930), Swiss author and artist of Czech origins. (Ed.)

cancer, as far as he knew. Otto F. Walter[14] seemed to be doing quite well; a new book of his would appear in the fall. Muschg was living in Zurich. The coherence of the Olten authors' group, which, of course, had oriented itself against something, specifically against the calcified social conditions and against the calcified literary business, had now become weaker. Each one had withdrawn more into him/herself but had to see how he or she would get through it financially. His books appeared in editions of 3,000-5,000 copies, so then he had to give readings. There were also support programs from the canton, and he had to accept those stipends. By himself he gets along; with a family it would not work.

I had already quietly wondered what actually might be behind his playing the lone wolf. He looks striking, rather short, not strongly built, very fine hands, a small head, a large, curved moustache on his face, his skin covered with scars resembling smallpox, black curly hair, like an Italian, I wanted to say to him, but I decided I had better leave it unsaid.

Meanwhile Gerd had come home. We ate the caviar rolls, the borscht, and good cheese. Drank white wine. The key word "Oberlin"[15] was mentioned. So he had also been there, 1980. We exchanged memories. Horrible, he said, actually fatal that dark Midwest, that college town. There he was also hardly able to work, but then he got a car and used the rest of the money to travel through the USA. Two of the chapters in his next book would take place in the USA. I remember my old, ancient plan for the book, the background of which was supposed to be my USA experience.

For a long time we talk about our new talents, names like Gert Neumann, Wolfgang Hilbig, and Christoph Hein are mentioned; Gerd brings in his lyric poetry materials by the "young

[14] Otto F. Walter (1928-1994), Swiss writer and publisher. (Ed.)
[15] Oberlin College: C. and G. Wolf were in Oberlin, Ohio, in 1974 as writers in residence. (G.W.)

savages"; we talk extensively, with distributed roles, about Dieter Schulze,[16] who then, again, crossed his, Christoph's path—as a name, as a legend—in West Berlin. The bizarre story of Schulze's departure—which we, a group of authors, had achieved "right at the top," because there was fear that he would become liable to prosecution here; how Fühmann took him across the border . . . Man, says Christoph, you do experience things!

We talked about crossing the border, how it strains us; that each time a decision is necessary to go over and back. He, he said, felt strain at every border, but at this one here especially.

Gerd brought the Seghers stories that I edited for Luchterhand. I wrote something for him in the book; he said that he was not familiar with most of the texts. The few that he knew by her, however, had given him much to think about. We talk about *Transit Visa*; how she, when I told her how much I admire that book, responded: Many of my comrades do not like it . . . About her relationship to the Party, for which he exhibited understanding.

At shortly before eleven, he began to talk about saying goodbye; then he left at eleven-thirty. We, Gerd and I, talked a little bit, saw fragments on different television channels and the last news on the third West German channel. The Club of Rome, which, to my surprise, is meeting in Budapest this time, declared that the number of starving people on our planet will quintuple by the end of the millennium if a radical change in world politics does not occur. The topic for the meeting of the club is: "Food for Six Billion People"—According to the most recent representative survey results, 66% of the citizens of the Federal Republic are against the stationing of US missiles in the Federal Republic, even if the Geneva Convention should

[16] Dieter Schulze: one of the East German authors from Prenzlauer Berg whose works were self-published or appeared in unofficial periodicals; went to West Berlin in 1983. (G.W.)

bring no result—Only sixty-six percent? says Gerd. I say: But that really is a lot.

We go to bed, Gerd, as always, quite rapidly, I after absolving a few rituals and after I have made a few more notes on the pad for the play. Then I read a little bit in the stories of Walter Vogt.[17] It is a quarter after twelve when I turn off the light. I fall asleep quickly. The last thought that I can remember was devoted, a little uneasily, to the Schiller Prize speech,[18] which I now, I said to myself, finally had to start. Would the first words, I asked myself, really be: "The hostile brothers in the works of Friedrich Schiller . . . "?

[17] Walter Vogt (1927-1988), Swiss writer. (G.W.)
[18] Schiller Prize speech: Friedrich Schiller Memorial Prize for C.W. on November 11, 1983; speech of thanks, *Werke*, Vol. VIII, pp. 379ff. (G.W.)

THURSDAY SEPTEMBER 27, 1984
Berlin, Friedrichstrasse

At exactly twelve o'clock midnight this morning I washed out Helene's diaper, which still lay in the bathroom from the day. Got ready for the night. Lay in bed at seven after twelve. Knew that this was the day of the year. Read, as I have done for the last two weeks, since I prepared the lecture for the psychosomatic gynecologists,[1] in Georg Groddeck's *The Book of the It.*

"Please, love, do not forget that our brain, and with it our understanding, are creations of the id; certainly one that in turn works creatively, but does not become active until late and whose creative field is limited . . . Basically, everything that transpires in the human being is done by the id. And that is good. And it is also good to stand still at least once in your life and as much as possible to dwell on the thought of how things transpire entirely separate from our knowledge and power. For us doctors that is especially important . . . It sounds absurd, but it is true, that every treatment of the sick patient is the correct one, that he is constantly and under all circumstances treated correctly, whether he is treated in the scientific manner or in the manner of the medically trained shepherd. The success is not determined by what we prescribe according to our knowledge, but by what the id of our sick patient does with our prescriptions."

[1] Lecture for the gynecologists: C.'s lecture *"Krankheit und Liebesentzug* (Illness and Love Deprivation)" for a meeting of the work group "Psychosomatic Gynecology" on November 1st and 2nd of 1984 in Magdeburg (see: *Werke*, Vol.VIII, pp. 410ff.) (G.W.)

And I, while I read that and remembered the other curiously fascinating claims of Doctor Groddeck, had to ask myself why my id has been giving me this really terrible pain in the right side of my pelvis at night since the summer, as soon as I have lain on my back for a while, so that I do not know how I will be able to turn onto my side and draw up my knees so that it will then be all right. "The ligaments," says Mrs. Gomolka. But why are they suddenly so "worn out"? And my left hip for years? And then this summer these excessive headaches that come from my neck, especially when I am under psychic strain? Yes, yes, I said to myself and thought about the scientists' urge to measure, count, and dissect, and about their resistance to the imponderable human element, which arises from deep frustration, thought, as I have done so often, that there is probably no cure for it, and fell asleep.

This morning I awoke, with fragments of dreams still in my mind, which I immediately forgot. It was a quarter after seven. I got up, ran to the phone in the vestibule in my pajamas, absolved my morning conversation with the Schwerin plumbers who had promised to go to Woserin,[2] where Gerd is anxiously awaiting them, and now simply do not show up anymore. This time the secretary gives me a different number where I could reach the responsible person. Of course, nobody answers there.

The few exercises that I have imposed upon myself. The shower ritual. At the same time, radio: Today Gromyko is speaking before the General Assembly of the United Nations. They are expecting information about whether or not the USSR will accept President Reagan's offer to resume the talks between the superpowers. A discussion between Gromyko and Foreign Minister Schultz was termed "useful." We listen

---

[2] Woserin: In 1984 the Wolfs acquired an old parish house in this town in Mecklenburg, which they renovated and occupy with their family as a second residence, especially during the summer months. (G.W.)

to those things, I think, and they are really all deceptive maneuvers. Reagan is probably readier to talk now because he has driven his rearmament to the point that he intended. Because he needs a smoke screen so that behind it he can continue putting armaments into space. In reality I see no hope for an authentic understanding, which, of course, could not proceed from the premise that the respective other side is the empire of evil. My thinking always follows the same lines. In the People's Republic of China free enterprise is supposed to be permitted again. And financial incentives for workers and farmers are supposed to be introduced—Well, fine. A long way around, with millions of dead, to arrive at that goal again after all. It apparently does not work otherwise. Is egoistic self-enrichment the only motive for doing any work at all? And how will the countries where socialism actually exists exist at all without the surplus production of the capitalist countries?—The French speaker in the UN General Assembly declared that he could imagine a worldwide New Deal.

Then a commentary on the accelerated death of forests in the Federal Republic. The speaker directs sarcastic remarks toward the federal government, which shrinks back from industry, for example, with respect to the introduction of automobiles with greater pollution control. It really must get around, even in industrial circles, that consumption can only take place if the common ecological basis is not destroyed. Two thirds of all trees in North Rhine–Westphalia are sick. (And here in our country, since all industry is owned by the state, the "environment" has no lobby at all . . .)

Get dressed. It is eight o'clock. I sit down and write the first sentences. Have not written anything for weeks, have occupied myself with the lecture for the gynecologists, struggled with the obstacles that arise from fear. Actually even literally "burned my mouth"—on hot gravy. Taken care of little Helene, since Tinka is in the hospital with the new baby

Moritz. Cooked for Martin and Olaf,[3] so that Martin can finish his mural in the nursery in Hohenschönhausen. Silently worked on the plan for the novel—always in the hope that something will come together in such times.

Petra comes and fixes breakfast. It is raining outside. Gerd calls on the telephone. Above all, he wants to know how Tinka is doing and is relieved that I found her doing so well yesterday. I tell him that the great loss of blood apparently did not have a very negative effect; that her hemoglobin numbers are quite good. But today I still do not tell him that during the birth she had a tachycardia. And the baby? he asks—I have not seen him yet. Tinka thinks he is very quiet and very clever— Gerd laughs. I ask: Do you know that Erich Arendt died?— No—Ragna called me.[4] She said that he passed away peacefully, the way we would wish for him—Yes. So that revival was only a last flickering of life—I should tell him when the funeral will be; he will come then—Otherwise we talk only about workmen and construction matters, as we have done all summer. That he obtained stones, so on the weekend the roofers can begin to build the chimney crowns. That they must gather stones for the interior wall in the house. That he is constantly out and around and dead tired at night. That I should send money with Olaf. That he was already able to buy the regenerative furnaces yesterday, very expensive, but now the entire lower part of the house is "taken care of."

We deal carelessly with money.

At breakfast Petra and I talk about routine things, which I now, at a quarter to six in the evening, have already forgotten.

The telephone. Jeanne Stern. She asks me on behalf of her granddaughter Katrin, who works for the Volk und Welt Publishing Company and is supposed to send a letter of condo-

[3] Olaf Gitzbrecht (b. 1964), a friend of the Wolf family. (G.W.)
[4] Ragna Pitoll, a friend of the poet Erich Arendt. (G.W.)

lence to the nearest relative of Erich Arendt, who that nearest relative actually is. I talk about Ragna, who took care of him, who had been his last love, and who was with him when he died. As young as she is—she was probably his next of kin at the end. Kurt, Jeanne says, is still in the hospital. He has a fever, but above all, that great, great weariness and weakness. For such a long time already. Last night, however, his voice had sounded somewhat more animated—I have a bad feeling, and I do not know to what extent Jeanne, who would never express it, feels the same way. (While I am talking with her, I see the face of Erich Arendt before me, the way it was when we visited him for the last time and when we felt that he was already dying, perhaps recognized us for a few seconds, then fell asleep again, and already had his death face. And I also ask myself, more and more often, without fear however, how my death will be. Lonely? Wished for by relatives who are no longer able to deal with caring for a helpless person?)

While I am still talking on the telephone, the family doorbell rings. I hear Helene's voice; Martin is standing outside with her and Olaf. Coordination of the day's schedule. So in spite of bad weather, Martin and Olaf want to try to finish the wall mural as much as possible; it is their race with time until Tinka gets out of the hospital. This evening Olaf is going to Mecklenburg, Martin is going to visit Tinka, and I have to go to the Neruda function.[5] Petra offers to take care of Helene until Martin comes to pick her up. A pot of cabbage stew, cooked yesterday, is given to Olaf to take along for the Woserin workmen. When everything has been clarified, the men depart and leave little Helene here, who begins to play with Petra. I sit down at the typewriter for a short time, write the initial pages of this text, and then I have to "go out" with her. Down onto

[5] Neruda function: Evening event of the Academy of Arts in honor of Pablo Neruda. (G.W.)

the boisterous, roaring, and stinking Friedrichstrasse, where aside from her there are, for good reason, almost no other children. Children cannot live here; the exhaust fumes from the cars poison them. Today, since I am pushing Helene along in front of me, I sense that they are doubly poisonous. Entire clouds come at us and we have to inhale them. Along the Spree we have to stop: "Water!" Then I buy stockings for her and Tinka; enthusiastically she enters all the stores with me, and of course becomes independent at once. "But don't go near that pane of glass there, little girl, you might cut yourself!"—I am always happy when I am outside with her again. In the post office she experiences one of the small dramas to which she is so open. A mother and a perhaps five-year-old son, both in the yellow hard-currency-shop rain capes, are arguing with each other. The woman, frustrated, as she is anyway, does not know what to do other than sit the boy down on the bench "as a punishment" while she goes to a counter. There he sits now, howling. Helene must immediately be picked up in my arms: "Boy is crying." Yes, I say, he is sad. Helene repeats probably twenty times: "Is crying. Is sad."

Fortunately the mother finally relented, sat down next to the boy, and patted him a little bit, even though she also admonished him that in the future he should be "good," etc. In any case, he calms down, stops crying, and both of them leave. Helene also comments in detail and persistently about this course of events. Since I have to wait for a long time at the counter, she has time to try out various games, to run back and forth, to study and "read" the posters, during which she traces the writing with her finger as far as it is within her reach. A signal often flashes within me, that my children behaved similarly, especially: that I behaved the same way with my children as I do now with Helene. Similar worry when she stays outside while I go into the vegetable store on Clara-Zetkin-Strasse and have to wait in line there again, but there are blue grapes and cauliflower that has not yet gone bad. At first Helene remains sitting very quietly in her stroller, because the boy from the post office is also standing outside (she does not recognize him; he has taken his yellow cape off), and she has to look at him quietly now up close. Children are extremely fascinating for her. Then she climbs out of the stroller and hangs onto an iron ring for dog leashes that is set in the wall. Once she comes to me because she has bumped her head and wants me to recognize the pain. I begin to sweat and to hate the people who are in line ahead of me and request "four kilograms of grapes." Then another woman pushes her way to the front, and I can hardly bridle my despair.

We walk along Unter den Linden, I show Helene the fading leaves that are already falling. From one of her picture books, she knows the term "rain of leaves." With all kinds of tricks—because I am really in a hurry—I get her to stay in the stroller and not to push it as she asks to do several times. We go into the fashion store Exquisit, primarily because I want to buy something for Tinka for her birthday, but also to look for a new coat for myself.

Inside it is warm, heated, and in the end sweat streams down my face and body. It is boring for Helene, of course. She wants to run around and touch everything, but that is not permissible in this expensive store. "It is really inconvenient to be in here with such a little child!" I hear a woman say, and I think: Old goose!—I have two dresses written up without trying them on; the saleswoman raises her eyebrows. Then I try on black jackets. They seem too wide to me. I know that I am inclined to buy without thinking, but I do it again and again. The results of such shopping hang in my closet for years unworn, rejected and criticized by Gerd as "phenomena," and usually stubbornly defended by me. I find a blouse for Tinka and necklaces for all three of us—Tinka, Annette, and me. The saleswoman must think that I intend to deal in them, but in this price range even the saleswomen in our country do not show much surprise. Nevertheless, I reap reprimands when I arrive at the cash register with the sales slips that Helene has crumpled and torn. How is a person supposed to insert these slips into the slit in the cash register?—A rebuke that I understand because the work is made more difficult for the cashier; but then from this heavily made-up, blond young girl comes the comment that the sales slip is a document, after all, and that it is everybody's duty to be careful with it. That is German again, I think, and have to grin. I have lost the impulse on my part to protest against it.

We go home almost at a run. At the Friedrichstrasse station we buy flowers from a boy and from an old woman who assures me that they will keep for a long time. They are bog stars, and some of them have already wilted at home and will not recover again. For four marks fifty! I say indignantly. Helene has places where she likes to stop: the fountain waterfall in front of the Hotel Metropol, the water of the Spree, and this time she discovers on the masts of the Weidendamm Bridge the golden "suns" that have been painted on it. "A sun," she cries, and I have to search for a long time before I find it, and see it for the first time through Helene. Remarkable: she shows me these suns; in Drispeth I showed her the first moon of her life, and she has still not forgotten that to this day: "Grandma showed hoon," she still says even now when she sees a moon, whether in nature or a picture book. She forms the past-tense forms by hanging -*et* on the verb stem: "*zeiget* (showed)," "*kommet* (came)." I am amazed that she feels the need at all to express different verb tenses. We still go quickly into the hard-currency cosmetic shop to buy soft handkerchiefs for Tinka. On the street I always look into the faces, unconsciously searching for one that I can feel my way into. In recent days I have had the feeling that they are becoming more and more foreign to me, especially the young people who are groomed in punk style or in the fifties look, about whom we probably no longer know anything.

The foyer of our building is dirty as always, besides being a storage place for stones; the view into the yard still shows the chaotic construction situation, which, of course, according to the plan, was supposed to be finished at the end of May, then at the end of August. Now all of the building's inhabitants have probably given up hope and their protests as well and are happy that there is no pounding and sawing directly in or above their apartments. Each time I climb the stairs I become irritated that the painters applied the dark brown paint so low—the light color above it will be completely stained again in a few weeks, if only by the eaters from the sausage stand next door who come into the foyer and smear the mustard on the walls. But a bell sign has been put up downstairs now, so that you can still be disturbed from the street even in the evening by someone ringing the bell. The workmen, I think, who must put our yard in order, probably set it up as an "object" that must be representative on the thirty-fifth Anniversary. Nobody sees our yard, of course.

At home Petra has lunch ready: cauliflower, potatoes, and the little slices of meatloaf that I had already made the day before and most of which I had fed to Martin and Olaf, the mural painters.

(Meanwhile four days have passed, during which I could only work on this text a few lines at a time, was completely occupied with Helene, with visits to Tinka, and then yesterday, on Sunday, when we hoped that Tinka would be released from the clinic, with her telephone call. The catastrophe had occurred: she would not be released because the pediatrician had heard anomalies from Mortitz's heart and would have to check it again on Tuesday. Whatever happens as a result—another day again that I will not forget, and the other day, about which I must now write, sinks away very rapidly. I have no notes about it and am completing the report during the breaks that caring for Helene leaves me.)

The ritual after lunch: Helene lies down in Grandpa's bed and fiddles around for a while longer. I lie on my bed, read, and then sleep. This time I read Strindberg, specifically the play "The Creditor," the psychology of which seems superficial and unbelievable to me, but it is probably also only pasted together to create character vehicles that could articulate the author's fear of the "woman." And I had believed I would learn something about the handicaps of a creative woman, for after all, this character Tekla writes. But of course she writes badly and has made her husband uncreative, and now here comes Tekla's former husband, unrecognized by the second one, and defames her; and the whole thing ends with the death of her current husband and is interlarded with witty remarks directed against the woman who swallows up everything. It strikes me as being infantile, but the fear seems to be genuine, and I ask myself where this fear of women, which suddenly emerges around the turn of the century, actually comes from, following a decidedly masculine half century in which women had no chance at all to develop themselves mentally. The masculine feeling of inferiority seems to be inveterate. How does it arise? What role do mothers play in the process? And to what extent is—and now I am back with my gynecologists, whom I definitely must not shock, of course, with all too radical problem formulations—the choice of the profession "gynecologist" also dictated for a number of them by needs for revenge with respect to women—Unconsciously, everything unconsciously.

I sleep, dream of Martin and Tinka. Martin is walking along a street, Helene is also with him somehow; he seems sad to me, and I know why, too. He is jealous because of Tinka. Tinka appears in very colorful clothes. I ask Martin just whom he is jealous of. He says: Of Mr. Everyman. I wonder about the strange name and do not grasp the meaning of that answer until I wake up.

Helene is still asleep, as she always sleeps for a long time in the middle of the day. I get up and put on my bottle-green morning robe, because I must change clothes again later anyway. At noon I had not gotten around to reading the mail. It is lying in the middle room on the oval table, a whole pile of it. West mail day. First I glance through the newspapers. "Brotherly Meeting Before the Thirty-Fifth Anniversary": Friendship with the USSR is a matter of the heart for us. Erich Honecker visited the House of Soviet Science and Culture. A photograph: Erich Honecker, smiling radiantly. Two smiling young women in traditional costume and pointed bonnets bring him bread and salt on a tray; next to them stands a smiling older gentleman, the Soviet ambassador—Second front-page story: "President of the People's Chamber Received by the King of Spain." Horst Sindermann brought Juan Carlos I greetings from Erich Honecker. Photograph: a radiantly smiling Horst Sindermann shaking hands with the Spanish king—smiling—between them the interpreter—Further: Great labor accomplishments by collectives for the thirty-fifth Anniversary of the German Democratic Republic acknowledged! Andrei Gromyko had additional meetings at the UN headquarters. Recognition of meritorious workers and collectives with the Patriotic Service Medal in Gold—On the culture page an article on the ninetieth birthday of Otto Nagel and a briefer tribute to Erich Arendt occasioned by his death. Problems: none. We live in the most successful year in the history of the German Democratic Republic.

The letter of a woman from Leipzig, which I find in my mail, corresponds to that. She writes: ". . . For me the fulfillment of a life means the preservation of individuality. Without that prerequisite there is no chance to become a personality at all. But how is that possible in a country where the language is remi-

niscent of a large nursery and one is incapacitated, intimidated, and soon no longer able to react as an 'I'?

"Even the birth of a child, where one is at the mercy of the
medical establishment. The baby is isolated from you, and
every timid suggestion, that the separation, particularly during
the initial hours, does have severe consequences, is ignored
and rejected with flippant, careless responses. When daycare
begins, then the mothers surrender their children every morning again. The trust, the refuge has been destroyed forever. For
in the daycare facility the very thing occurs that destroys a
human being during the formative years. Beginning with the
so-called potty training." She talks about a generation that has
been "played to death," gives examples, and ends:

"For you, a person who has learned to see, the pain must
have dimensions that can hardly be grasped any longer. But
for the very reason that you can see and think, I beg you to
show me if and how there is still hope here, especially for my
children.

"My small longing is only to obtain books without such
great difficulties, and to see originals in galleries, which we do
not have here . . ."

A letter could hardly confront me more clearly with the duty
to remain in this country and the dilemma that is inherent in
that decision. As in this case, more and more frequently
unsolvable problems are trustingly presented to me (and all of
these letters have been opened before they reach me). More
and more frequently I have the feeling that somebody is standing before me whom I cannot help, who probably cannot be
helped. My defense against the demand that such people make
of me also seems to be growing stronger and stronger. Should
I tell her that we have to be happy if the leaders at least have
enough understanding that they themselves want to remain
alive and in that instance also let us live? The report of the
"outcome" of the UN discussion between Reagan and

Gromyko only confirms my sarcasm. Those two men can dare to simply chat with each other without any result, and "the nations" accept that readily in the face of the threat of destruction under which their own leaders have placed them. But who are the nations? The "German nation" that has now just been invoked repeatedly again by representatives of the Federal Republic seems to me to be a phantom, similarly the "nation of the German Democratic Republic." There is one consistency in it: National Socialism ruined the "German nation"—I still do not know if I will respond to the woman from Leipzig, because I do not know what to say. I like to remain silent, have the feeling that I have already said too much—especially when repercussions from the *Cassandra* wave reach me.

The second letter that I open is one from that wave. It comes from the USA, from my New York publisher, who notifies me of his recovery from a long illness and encloses a counter-review of *Cassandra*, which Eva Kollisch—whom I met, of course, during our last stay in New York—wrote in response to a rather derogatory review by Mary Lefkowitz in the *New York Times Book Review*. I was familiar with the Lefkowitz review, of course, had only spelled it out superficially, and silently put it with the reviews that Petra was supposed to file. Now I read with a certain satisfaction in Eva Kollisch's review: "Reading Mary Lefkowitz's attack on Christa Wolf's *Cassandra*, one comes away with the impression that the Trojan prophetess might have had quite a nice life if she had only consented to play ball with Apollo, and that Christa Wolf, East Germany's foremost writer, is an addle-brained feminist and soft-headed communist for thinking otherwise"—and so on. So there.

Thomas Nicolaou writes from Greece that he is supposed to translate the book for a publisher, and some producer would very much like to film the Cassandra story. After a radio play, stage play, theatrical monologue, and opera—now also a film to boot! It embarrasses me to have hit the nerve of the times like that. But would I want to take it back?

In the mail there is also news from Stuttgart that texts of mine—I believe, in this case it was texts from *No Place on Earth*—are to be used in a "representation" performance in a church.

An invitation to a gallery discussion with Carl Friedrich Claus in Karl-Marx-Stadt, which took a week to get here. The appointed date is today.

A letter from the Aufbau Publishing Company. The Suhrkamp Publishing Company wants to print a passage of text from *Patterns of Childhood* in an anthology.

In addition, an accidental coincidence—three letters from women with whom I became friends during the course of the last year: Charlotte Wolff[6] and the two Austrian women, Barbara Streitfeld and Elisabeth Reichart.[7] Charlotte writes from London in her large, scrawled, old-age handwriting, in her sloppy German, about my Doctor Lechner experiences, which I wrote to her about—one of the miracles of this year.[8] (The second is my grandson Moritz, whom I saw yesterday for the first time—it is, after all, already Wednesday, the 3rd of October, today, and Tinka is still in the hospital because she had bleeding again after it had been settled that Moritz is healthy . . .) She writes that she remained especially conscious of Doctor Leitner from *Patterns of Childhood*. I understand

[6] Charlotte Wolff (1897-1986), physician, psychiatrist, sexual researcher (*The Human Hand*, London, 1942; *Bisexualität [Bisexuality]*, Frankfurt/M., 1981; *Augenblicke verändern uns mehr als die Zeit [Moments Change Us More Than Time Does]*, Weinheim, 1982; *Magnus Hirschfeld*, London, 1986; and others). The author emigrated to Paris in 1933, beginning in 1936 lived in London; had an intensive pen friendship with C.W. beginning in 1983 (see also: *Werke*, Vol. XII, pp. 577ff.). (G.W.)

[7] Elisabeth Reichart (b. 1953), Austrian writer; well acquainted with C.W. (see also: *Werke*, Vol. VIII, pp. 407ff.). (G.W.)

[8] Dr. Alfred Lechner (1899-1992), physician who, as a Jew, had to leave Germany in 1938, lived in the USA. C.W. had him appear in *Patterns of Childhood* as the character Dr. Leitner. Thereupon he made himself known, met with C.W. in West Berlin, and remained in correspondence with her after that. (G.W.)

that. She herself is Jewish and she perceived especially clearly how I see and describe Jews, also the orthodox Jews, "who carry the golden chalice from the burned-out synagogue across the street and into a private apartment, wearing long caftans with black caps on their heads. It dogs me in a remarkably personal way. How 'ghostly' those figures are, and—a wonderful world, as tragic as it is. The tragic element does not count in such an event, where the breath of the cultivated world stops.

"How I 'see' you with that Dr. Lechner. The revenant! We are perhaps, if we only knew it, involved in boomerang games. But so near, to enter the 'family' again and anew that way—is a shock—but it has something (for me!) frightening—beautiful—but??

"I can congratulate you. To have your house being finished on a beautiful flat (I love that too) lakebed—the two of you have a home—and you loved the house that burned down—How good it is to be able to live in and with your own world and in a place of residence with such feeling.

"I am only at home at 'my place' (I hope!). All apartments here in England, not in Paris, are like railway stations to me—I sit there ready—to run out. To a train that takes me to a dear woman (?)—No! I do not find her—and in a way I prefer it like that. The eternal student and outsider—I!"

After that she writes about my presentation on psychosomatic gynecology, about the possibility of influencing menstruation problems, false pregnancy, frigidity, vaginal cramps positively through psychotherapy—"But—the big but about psychotherapy—who can be a really good therapist?!—In my opinion only the person who does not belong to any special school—and (this first of all!) who gives himself to the other person (I hate the word *patient*) in his empathy . . ."

Charlotte ended with the question of when we will meet. "I cannot help remembering the words of an English acquaintance who often whispered in my ear: It is later than you think! What do you think of that? I am at an age—hm!!—that the future is short, although I am physically absolutely healthy—"

I will have to hurry and travel to London.

Elisabeth Reichardt intends to come here at the beginning of December. She writes about an inaccessible work about Austrian women's specialists that I had asked her for, about a stage play that she has written, then about her "work day," which, she thinks, I see as "too strict, too rosy." Her work as a publisher's reader seldom leaves her time to sit at her desk for the entire day, and besides that she succeeds "really always with somnambulistic certainty, in putting myself into that agonizing state in which I have an idea, a topic, and am at the same time certain that I cannot frame it, I am incapable—and then I hate myself for my inability and meanwhile also for not being able to deal with this preliminary writing, preliminary work stage, for I am familiar with it now, it is always the same . . . " She writes about K.—the two of them are, I believe, the first couple that became acquainted through me . . .

I think about the fact that in my case it is specifically the preliminary writing phases that are the most beautiful times, when I make notes, invent or seek names, write down outlines, and each time imagine again that the book will be as beautiful and perfect as I bear it within me, see it, during this phase. How it moves. Apparently, when I was a child they did not infect me with the sentence: You are not capable of that. Favored by fate, by my parents, especially my mother, who, to be sure, imposed the strictest standards on me, but who was apparently thoroughly convinced that I could meet them . . .

A photograph falls into my hands from the letter from Barbara Streitfeld in Graz: I, sitting, talking to her, with her standing in front of me with only her back visible in the picture, her straight, rounded hairstyle. The picture of me does not especially appeal to me, just as all of my recent pictures do not especially appeal to me—Barbara S. writes to me about an interpretation of the Bachmann[9] poem "Explain to Me, Love" that is different from mine, not inappropriate, but it does not convince me.

The letter from Charlotte Wolff continues to work within me, her indication that she no longer has much time. I know in various countries some Jewish emigrants from Nazi Germany who are also her age: Alfred Lechner in Canada, Maria Scherer[10] in Australia, Walter Grossmann[11] in the USA, my Charlotte Wolff, the woman in Paris who gave me the red pad of paper, Keilson[12] in Amsterdam, Anita's mother in Rome,[13] perhaps even Franci, perhaps Kurt Stern here—my Jewish friends. Is there not an assignment there—before they die?

Still lying in front of me, something that also arrived with today's mail, is a periodical: *END, Journal of European Nuclear Disarmament*. I already saw it lying there for me a short time ago at Ingrid Krüger's place in West Berlin,[14] but did not dare bring it back across the border with me, because the checks for printed material at the border crossing have become meticulous again, and because the article for the sake of which they sent me the periodical is entitled "Sisters Across the Curtain," and its author is that very same Englishwoman who visited the German Democratic Republic barely a year ago[15] and

[9] Ingeborg Bachmann (1926-1973), Austrian poet and author. (Ed.)
[10] Maria Scherer, a Jew who had emigrated from Germany, who entered into correspondence with C.W. after reading *Patterns of Childhood* and also met her. (G.W.)
[11] Walter Grossmann, Jewish-German emigrant, writer and scientist living in the USA, in correspondence with C.W. (G.W.)
[12] Hans Keilson (b. 1909), psychoanalyst, writer, 1986-1988 president of the PEN Center of German-Language Authors Abroad; emigrated to Holland in 1936; well acquainted with C. and G.W. (G.W.)
[13] Anita Raja (b. 1953), library director in Rome; her mother emigrated to Italy; translator of the books of C.W. into Italian; close friends with the Wolfs. (G.W.)
[14] Ingrid Krüger: publisher's reader for the Luchterhand Publishing Company in Neuwied; established ties above all with East German authors. (G.W.)
[15] Barbara Einhorn, English Germanic studies scholar. (G.W.)

apparently contributed through imprudent behavior to the fact that Bärbel Bohley and Ulrike Poppe were arrested. At that time it was said that she then left the German Democratic Republic in panic; now she writes: "The ever-present terror of nuclear war and the way it erodes all certainties and values is in a curious way a great equalizer, which transcends national and bloc boundaries." She then writes, comparing the conditions within the peace movement in the Federal Republic and the Democratic Republic, while using the different social status of women in the two countries as a point of departure, that the women in West Germany are part of a basic peace movement, that the ones here, on the other hand, operate under the protection of the Protestant Church, and their slogan is: We women want to break the erroneous cycle of violence. She quotes some sentences of mine from the *Cassandra* lectures.

I believe her impressions of the "peace movement" here are no longer up to date. As far as I know, so many have left, and so many others have become discouraged (even Ulrike Poppe had to leave) that the number and intensity of those who struggle for peace has sunk. Besides that, during the last year Honecker's commitment to "damage control" through setting up nuclear missiles has given rise to a certain hope that genuine efforts toward peace could also proceed from the state. That means we must wish that the status quo will be maintained. Changes within the society are not possible; the iron conditions are carved in stone—that is the price for no war. This often seems to me to be the unconscious reason why so many people leave. If there really is no hope for social change, they can also live there, where it is more comfortable and consumer freedom is thrown at the individual.

A letter had fallen to the floor. Alfred Moos from Ulm expresses his thanks for the answer to his inquiry regarding the Schlotterbeck family. He needed the information for documentation about prisoners who were interned in a prison near Ulm (Oberer Kuhberg). Perhaps Frieder will return to his home region after all, after his death.

Helene wakes up, calls for me at the top of her lungs, is sitting red and sweaty in "Grandpa's bed," has to be picked up and rocked a bit. Smells so good, like all children after they have slept. Then she gets moving, goes to the toilet, a new accomplishment, not at all firmed up, each success is still looked upon with wonder and cheered. Puts on her slippers ("by myself!"), then I fix coffee. Petra has brought pancakes with her. I practice with her the two Neruda poems that I intend to read this evening during the Academy celebration of Neruda's eightieth birthday. The first is from the *Extravagaria* anthology and is called:

Keeping Quiet [16]

And now we will count to twelve
and we will all keep still.

For once on the face of the earth
let's not speak in any language,
let's stop for one second,
and not move our arms so much.

It would be an exotic moment
without rush, without engines,
we would all be together
in a sudden strangeness.

The Fisherman in the cold sea
would not harm whales

[16] From *Extravagaria: A Bilingual Edition* by Pablo Neruda, Alastair Reid (Translator). Noonday Press; Bilingual edition January 2001. (Ed.)

and the man gathering salt
would not look at his hurt hands.

Those who prepare green wars,
wars with gas, wars with fire,
victory with no survivors,
would put on clean clothes
and walk about with their brothers
in the shade, doing nothing.

What I want should not be confused
with total inactivity.
Life is what it is about,
I want no truck with death.

If we were not so single-minded
about keeping our lives moving,
and for once could do nothing,
perhaps a huge silence
might interrupt this sadness
of never understanding ourselves
and of threatening ourselves with death.

Perhaps the earth can teach us
as when everything seems dead
and later proves to be alive.

Now I'll count up to twelve,
and you keep quiet and I will go.

I read the very good preface by Erich Arendt to the Luchterhand edition of Neruda's late poems *We Are Many*, constantly
interrupted by the demands that Helene makes of me. I must
look at a certain picture book with her especially often, by

Elizabeth Shaw,[17] in which a girl winds up in a house belonging to bears, three little pigs have all kinds of adventures (unfortunately there is no phonetic notation that could describe how Helene pronounces the little pigs' names, Cilly, Billy, and Willy!), and an actress named Bella goes around with three parrots ("Rappot!"). Day in, day out, this book again and again, the same pictures, the same words accompanying them, and apparently also again and again the same strong emotions that do not use themselves up at all.

Petra calls me to the telephone. An Academy secretary asks me with gushing courtesy in the name of my (?) Party secretary to remember my Party dues. I thank her just as courteously. I go into Gerd's room and try out the locked safe system for the first time, which actually does, after some slipups, give me access to the strongbox in which my Party document lies as well. I have to look up how much I pay, because I forget it from one time to the next. Gerd's room seems empty, uninhabited, and I feel like an intruder with my keys. While I fill out the check at my desk, for the hundredth time it goes through my mind that I am probably the only Party member in the German Democratic Republic who, for exactly the last eight years, has not attended a single member meeting, who announced that in person to the General Secretary, and who asks to be expelled, and I wonder, likewise for the hundredth time, but only fleetingly, how this will resolve itself someday. For me it has resolved itself, is no longer a problem. I still would not have believed that six or seven years ago.

Petra comes from the post office, laden down with little packages and a large graphics cylinder. In the packages are books that were sent to us: to my joy the book by Natalia Ginzburg[18] with her shorter prose works and essays, which was

---

[17] Elizabeth Shaw (1920-1992), graphic artist. (G.W.)
[18] Natalia Ginzburg née Levi (1916-1991), Italian author whose work explored family relationships, politics and philosophy among other themes. (Ed.)

published by the Volk und Welt Publishing Company, and the book by Keilson, Amsterdam: *The Investigation of the Lasting Effects of Concentration Camp Injuries Among the Children of Former Concentration Camp Prisoners*. An edition of letters by Oskar Maria Graf. Several Luchterhand books.

In the cylinder, the *Cassandra* graphics by Angela Hampel from Dresden, seven sheets. We spread them out on the floor. I still like them very much, in spite of a slight fashionable aura that I notice more strongly that I did the first time. The Cassandra motif entirely contemporary. I am happy.

Monique, Petra's daughter, comes, actually wants to pick up her mother, but now stays here to play with Helena, since I, of course, must leave later on, and Martin, who can stay with Tinka until seven, will not come to pick Helene up until eight. For days now, Petra has already been sitting in her room on the floor all day, sorting the manuscript for the exile anthology for Gerd. Helene accepts the playmate enthusiastically; anybody who is a child meets her approval. Thus the two of them romp around in the middle room, while I sit down at the typewriter once more and write a part of this text. Monique has the idea of getting ice cream and Helene is beside herself with joy. She stands behind the door and waits, but Monique returns with an empty bowl. The ice cream store closes at five o'clock already! Such rubbish! Rubbish! Helene says, and: Shit! But fortunately we then find some strawberry ice cream in the freezer compartment and they are all comforted.

Now I have to change clothes. I take the new reddish-brown dress that I bought this morning, dress carefully from head to toe, brush my hair, and put on my makeup. The question is: Aren't the red stockings perhaps really too red? Yes, Petra and Monique decide, the anthracite-colored ones are better. All of us are standing in the vestibule as I get ready to leave. Why are you looking at me that way? I ask Monique. She says, Well, you look good. Black shoes, the ones from Vienna, black purse. A kiss for Helene, who waves enthusiastically and shouts "Bye!" Off to it.

Outside on the street right now there is the big rush before the beginning of the performance in the New Friedrichstadt Palace, which some call "Khomeini's Revenge," but which I call a Roman-Turkish bath. Finely dressed people stream toward the entrance from the commuter train and from the cars, expectant and quite content. Bread and games. And I pilgrimage, with fewer people, to other games that are specifically arranged for the few, so that they also have something to drain off their energy, and so that we can also embellish ourselves with that and it can get into the papers the next day, with a list of names.

We collaborators gather as usual in the "club room" of the Robert-Koch-Platz Academy. Everyone had noticed with satisfaction that once again young people were standing down below in front of the ticket booth. I shook hands with everyone, even those whom I did not know or did not recognize. The number of people whom I do not recognize but should know is increasing. I am especially friendly to those people and do know that they are primarily the reserved ticket holders from the political organs and that I cannot trust their friendship. Three round tables are standing there with the obligatory coffee cups and the obligatory morsels. At the left corner table I greet Scheumann, Teitelboim,[19] his interpreter, and Neutsch; sit down at the middle table with Volker Braun[20]; Deicke[21] is also sitting there then. I ask Volker how he is doing. He is depressed; he cannot stop brooding about his situation in this country, in this part whose leadership has prohibited most of his books and plays in the last

[19] Volodia Teitelboim (b. 1916), Chilean writer, author of a Neruda biography; at times chairman of the Communist Party of Chile. (G.W.)

[20] Volker Braun (1939-2006), writer; close friend of the Wolfs. (G.W.)

[21] Günther Deicke (b. 1922), lyric poet, member of the Academy of Arts of the German Democratic Republic. (G.W.)

few years. I know from experience that those musings indicate
the degree of dependency on this system in which we still find
ourselves. I keep after him in that vein—As I describe my current mood, the word *cheerful* also falls. Immediately afterward I
tell myself how foolish it is for me to claim that "I am at the
same time quite cheerful"—Deicke tells about the roundabout
route his daughter had to take before she could now really
become a book dealer and about the unspeakable obsequious-
ness that she encountered in the process in "his" party, the German National Democratic Party. Someone had told her that
instructions from above are not to be criticized, but to be carried out unconditionally—Teitelboim comes to me, sits down
with his interpreter, and begins to praise my work. He has read
my books, to the extent that he has been able to obtain them in
Spanish or French, and finds them so and so and so. The German Democratic Republic can be proud that I live here. I have
to laugh loudly, but he insists. That is his opinion. He also talks
at length about Neruda, with whom he has been good friends
since '32, is interrupted by Wekwerth, who converses with him
for a long time and praises the two Chilean directors that work
at the Berlin Ensemble.

We then went into the hall. There were still many empty
seats there. Downstairs the tickets that were set aside but had
not been picked up were being sold, and the hall almost filled
up. We contributors sat in front in a semi-circle, Scheumann
opened with a letter that he recently received from a friend in
Santiago de Chile, and which describes the conditions there
more openly than one would ever dare to do in a letter about
the (certainly very different) conditions here. I asked myself if
Chile then perhaps had no postal censorship. Naturally, each
of the participants selected from Neruda's inexhaustible works
something that fit him or her. Neutsch read a declaration of
loyalty to the Party, Sakowski the description of a reading
among workers, and so forth. A Chilean man who is studying

music here sang Chilean songs, but I could not get rid of the feeling that the event was not getting off the ground. I do not know if I was the only one who felt that way, that here a dutiful exercise was being conducted, or if I perhaps projected my own half-guilty conscience onto the others. The second poem that I read is from *Critical Sonata*:

Maybe We Have Time

Maybe we still have time
to be and to be just.
Yesterday, truth died
a most untimely death,
and although everyone knows it,
they all go on pretending.
No one has sent it flowers.
It is dead now and no one weeps.

Maybe between grief and forgetting,
a little before the burial,
we will have the chance
of our death and our life
to go from street to street,
from sea to sea, from port to port,
from mountain to mountain,
and above all, from man to man,
to find out if we killed it
or if other people did,
if it was our enemies
or our love that committed the crime,
because now truth is dead
and now we can be just.
Before, we had to battle
with weapons of doubtful caliber

and, wounding ourselves, we forgot
what we were fighting about.

We never knew whose it was,
the blood that shrouded us,
we made endless accusations,
Endlessly we were accused.
They suffered, we suffered,
And when at last they won
and we also won,
truth was already dead
of violence and old age.
Now there is nothing to do.
We all lost the battle.

And so I think that maybe
at last we could be just
or at last we could simply be.
We have this final moment,
and then forever
for not being, for not coming back.

Now again as well, while copying, I notice that I do not
entirely understand the "message" of the poem, and yet I
understand completely the tragic vital consciousness that it
expresses. A ray seems to radiate from it, which people understand. The people clapped—Volker read a piece about police
and literature from *Residence on Earth*—a formulation of the
vision that Neruda had of the end of the struggles in which he
was involved, and which is also Volker's vision. It is just that
there will be no end to those struggles or, worse, that the struggles ended long ago and what is still to take place are fatal
shadow skirmishes among equals and equally matched oppo-

nents, which people like us can only watch—they cannot be stopped.

There was a young Chilean writer there, who did not leave Chile until '83, was arrested and tortured there twice, and sentenced to death twice. He had beautiful blue-black hair; he read poems that were undoubtedly good, and we could not tell anything by looking at him.

Scheumann read off one of those totally useless, inflationary protest letters against the terror in Chile. People clapped. I thought of the collaborators who probably wrung the text out of themselves in work that lasted for days, a text that accomplishes nothing, nothing, nothing.

After the presentation some people from the audience came. A man shook my hand—a remarkably limp hand-shake—because I "had read best." A young woman gave me a purple aster from one of the tables of the Café Praha, as a thank-you for my tribute to Fühmann, which she had just read in *Sinn und Form*. An older, nice-looking Chilean woman who lives in the German Democratic Republic came with Volodia Teitelboim to tell me that the two of them, while climbing a mountain in Addis Ababa during the summer, had talked about me. And now—there are still mysteries!—we were all standing here together. A woman came to give her express approval to the choice of poems that I had read (and which had been selected by Gerd). She had found there again thoughts that were similar to those in my *Cassandra*—Some do notice it.

Then most of us sat together for a while longer, as usual, at the long table in one of the rooms, cognac, juice, coffee, sandwiches again. I sat down with Renate Richter. Deicke, next to me on my left, told me some more about his brother-in-law in Thuringia, who had always been two hundred percent loyal, but now that they have forbidden him, an associate in the district attorney's office, to pursue certain crimes of highly placed individuals in the district, even he is beginning to have doubts.

I said goodbye to Teitelboim, who gave me his Moscow address on a little card. It consisted of only numbers. Talked then briefly with the Chilean poet, whom I found likeable, with whom, I felt, I would quickly get on the same wavelength. He now lives in Paris. We agreed to meet again some other time.

On the street I caught myself humming to myself. Those are the old melodies . . .

At home I found a despondent Martin waiting, who had either left his key hanging in the shed of the children's facility for which he is painting the mural, or had left it lying in the car in which Olaf was on his way to Woserin. I tried to reassure him. At present it is just a bit much for all of us. We sat together for another moment, saw and heard on television that Gromyko's speech before the UN General Assembly had not struck any conciliatory notes. Then I went to my picture postcards to look for one for Tinka, on which I wrote a happy birthday message. In the process, the cards with the children's drawings from Auschwitz fell into my hands again. This time I forced myself to look at them. Hopelessness. Again I thought—and I think it more strongly with every year that separates us from those events—if that had been done to my children and if I had unfortunately had to survive: I would not forgive. I would hate and hate, intransigent to the end of my days.

Martin got ready for the night in Gerd's room. Little Helene lay sleeping in "Grandpa's bed." I read some more in the stories of Natalia Ginzburg. She moved me. The pain at the death of her husband, which she articulates, made me sad, so many years later, in such a different place. How many pains that I fear. I saw the salamander go through every fire . . . And nothing hurts him—I will never be a salamander.

In the middle of the night I was startled out of my sleep and sat up straight in bed. Somebody called my name loudly and distinctly. I could not, even after the fact, identify the voice. It was a man's voice. I thought: I have been called.

Wake up for the first time early, at around five o'clock, in a strange room where I cannot orient myself. A sentence fragment from a dream is still in my ear, Annemarie Böll says to me, with reference to an old automobile in which I am sitting: But that is Death who is riding along with you. I cannot put the other pieces of the dream together, but gradually remember where I am: in Cologne, Hotel Königshof, in room 416. Also immediately sense again my feeling of being physically ill, am sweaty, the cold has firmly entrenched itself. I see my foreboding of yesterday confirmed, that it will not stop at a cold, and go into the bathroom, take Toxiloges drops and a Neo-Angin, and also two Togal tablets, lie down again, and am happy that I do not have to get up yet. Think, as always these days, of Annette.

At six the powerful ringing of the bells in the cathedral begins, which is quite close by. After that, I fall asleep again and do not wake up until about eight. Gerd has already been in the bathroom, asks how I am feeling, and tries, as he always does, to suggest that I am feeling well, while I quietly curse the fact that we came here. Shower. Get dressed. Enjoyment of the perfect bathroom, of all the hotel comfort. On the nightstand, the copy of *Der Spiegel* that we bought yesterday, which Gerd has already read. I quickly scan the article about the anthology *Contact Is Only a Side Issue,*[1] the second version of which was

---

[1] Anthology *Berührung ist nur eine Randerscheinung—Neue Literatur aus der DDR,* Cologne, 1985, edited by Sascha Anderson and Elke Erb; introduced thirty authors of

published by Kiepenheuer und Witsch after it had to be
pulped because of flaws in the printing. The author of the
review, who had already made a film about three young East
German poets and is now in the West, unfortunately does not
write a literary review, mentions no names, examples, avoids
any literary evaluation, but occupies himself only with the
political background, presents a few pieces of intimate information, but is nevertheless correct in his observation that for
decades thinking and doing were subject to a "duality" in our
country: socialist or not socialist, for us or against us, either–or.
A polarity that also had an impact on the content and language
of art. He sees in the group of young writers that is articulated
in this anthology "life as an attempt to overcome social collection, duality, that conflict not only in the mind, but also in
everyday life and in writing."

While I am reading that, the images in my mind: the over-
crowded readings in apartments in Prenzlauer Berg two or
three years ago (also already a thing of the past), the people
who come to us when they need money, our conversation in
the copyright office, where we declared our solidarity with
those young writers, but also our own conflicting relationship
to them, more accurately: to some of them: the unconditional
narcissism of the young men, the so-called "connections" that
founder beneath their inconsiderate egoism, the gradual disintegration of the "scene," their conceit. All children of the parents of our generation, youth that have been left alone.

We breakfast rather quietly. A Cologne newspaper reports
what is planned for the afternoon in the Gürzenich festival
hall: "Böll celebration in all rooms with loudspeakers": 1107
guests would attend the commemoration ceremony in the large
hall, in side rooms an additional 700 seats have been set up in
front of monitors, 700 complimentary tickets have been given

the German Democratic Republic with initial texts that did not appear in the German
Democratic Republic. (G.W.)

out, etc. Some names of prominent figures who have said they are coming are given; I ask myself again what I am doing here. My cold is working its way toward a climax; I notice how the inflammation is spreading to my bronchial tubes. In the room, it is nine o'clock; once more the loud ringing of the cathedral bells. I take all kinds of medications, four or five different kinds. Telephone: first Viktor Böll. He states his fear of possible chaos in the afternoon. Gives us Lev's number, I call him, Raja is on the phone, is happy. Calls Lev. I give him Viktor Böll's message: if he were to forget his manuscript this afternoon, he would strangle him with his own hands. Just what does he think?! Lev shouts. He doesn't know me very well! For the flu he recommends thirty grams of vodka, pepper, eat some bread afterward, then go to bed, sweat, and everything will be fine. I say that I lack the training for that, and that I would give preference to Togal—Western softness! he curses. Announces that they will bring us various books to take along. "We're as productive as rabbits, after all!"

We start out, mild, warm air, sunshine. The cathedral. Gerd thinks that its towers "seem somewhat too squat," "break off somewhat abruptly," I do not think that and look up and down at the seemingly naturally generated stalactites. We turn into the pedestrian zone, carefully select pants, pullovers, and shirts for our daughters. I leave, as always when we shop together, the final selection to Gerd, and am happy that he does not slow down. The real enthusiasm that I once had on such occasions is missing. I look at the people that surge toward us on the street, all of them buyers, especially women buyers, well dressed in strikingly loud colors (the young ones), in the windows as well the new screaming green, the new screaming red. It occurs to me how I once wanted to explain the expression "screaming color" to Jana when she was little and found no colors around us that I could show her as an example. It occurs to me how Annette told me two days ago how her eyes were

opened to other people as she walked across Alexanderplatz
with her worries; how she suddenly became so close to them.
It occurs to me, it occurs to me . . . I can, I think, no longer see
anything without drawing from it a cue for an earlier experience. For example, even in *Der Spiegel* the article about "the
great plagues," prompted by the new plague of AIDS—then I
see us on the airplane from New York to Columbus, Ohio,
reading the American newspapers in which the first articles
about AIDS appeared. Now, I think, while the many young
people surge past me, it is said that thousands of them will contract AIDS by 1990, and thousands will die of it by the end of
the century. And *Der Spiegel* appreciatively makes itself a story
out of that, and even that does not concern me anymore, just
as so much no longer concerns me.

On the corner a new Laura Ashley store has opened; we go
in. A figure, to the left of the entrance, obviously a mannequin
dressed in the Laura Ashley fashion, bends its upper torso forward in the course of its programmed mechanical movements
just as I pass it. Involuntarily I jerk back and stare into its
motionless porcelain face. Oh! says a woman behind me in the
Cologne dialect. That can really startle you. I turn around
again. Is that really a mannequin? Yes, a mannequin. Why does
Veronika F. come to my mind at that moment? The woman
about whom they reported this morning after the news, saying
that she has been missing since yesterday afternoon, eighty-
four years old, suffers from spells of disorientation, and is possibly wandering around the city in a blue housecoat. While I
look at the beautiful new dresses and blouses of Laura Ashley,
I think of the old women whom I have seen "disoriented"—my
mother, Anna Seghers—but they could no longer walk then,
nor wander around in any city. I also think, this Veronika F.
could have been a figure for/by Böll. A. S.—mother figure,
Böll—father figure, I think, surprising myself. Both dead now.
By the way, I will read in the newspaper this afternoon that

Laura Ashley has also died, yesterday, before her new Cologne branch opened, "due to the effects of a fall on the stairs." She began as a simple seamstress and then later created her own style, "unwelcome bulges hidden beneath pleasant ruffles and tucks"—and here they open the new branch in her name, for the heirs. Upstairs you get a glass of champagne—you let them hand it to you, Gerd instructs me, you do not take it from the tray yourself—petits fours, cheese pastry. Here somebody who is unemployed could feed him/herself gratis, we think, but he/she would have to be well dressed to come in here. I would not meet Veronika F. here; disoriented, she roams through other regions of the city, perhaps sparse, abandoned parks. I feel the jackets and coats, feel poorly dressed, as I always do in such stores, coarse. Gerd urges me to buy a pullover; I take the bottle-green one because I am thinking about Böll ("dark-haired women should wear bottle-green"), at the cash register Gerd receives two tiny bottles of perfume as an extra, packed in colorful boxes that Helene would like.

See, see, see . . . On the street only the eye is required. Quickly past the cathedral once more. (Every time I am here and walk through the streets, the hidden question walks along with me: Could I write here? Would the writer's block of recent months dissolve here? Since it undoubtedly again has something to do with a hesitation to get too close to myself—would it disappear here of all places, where everyone has to appear in the proper light in order to be noticed at all?) On a side square a young artist producing a picture with chalk on the slabs of the sidewalk, using a model that he is holding next to him. Few people see him—a too familiar process. I should buy myself some shoes yet, I resist; we will see tomorrow just how far the money will stretch. Now we quickly find our way to our hotel and wait in front of the door. Mr. von Hanstein comes; he is as shy as I remember him from Leipzig. NANCY REAGAN MEETS MRS. GORBACHEV, I read in passing, in

November, in Geneva they want to have tea together. God bless them. Could I, too, be "disoriented"? Oh, yes. That can all happen to me, too. Wander disoriented through the streets of a city that I thought I knew but that is now quite foreign. I experienced such a thing, by the way, when we visited Landsberg again.

(It is already the fifth of October when I write this, in Woserin, which at first I still call "Meteln" in my thoughts.)

Fifty-six million marks' worth of annual sales has no meaning for me. The Lempertz sales gallery does that much business, which does not mean at all, however, that young Hanstein is a millionaire. Perhaps he is, but he has worked hard since taking over the enterprise at a very early age from his father, who died in an accident. Their earnings are only a portion of the profits of the auctions, we learn. I enter a pharmacy and buy even more medicines, vitamin C, cough syrup, and a cold remedy that warns people with heart rhythm disorders against itself, so I will leave that alone. Only when we are standing in front of the building does it become clear to me that the Cassandra figure that H. wants to show to us is set into the façade up above and in large measure covered right now by scaffolding. So we see fragments of the figure from below. However, because it was done by Gerhard Marcks as a continuation of the Barlach figure frieze for the St. Catherine Church in Lübeck, it is conceived as one that is to be viewed from below. If we want to see more of it, we must climb up on the scaffold; that can only be done from inside, through a foyer window, to which we have to climb on a small ladder, and from which we must cross a meter-wide chasm to reach the scaffold. I am amazed at myself, that I attempt it without contradiction and actually accomplish it. Then we are standing right next to the figure. Gerd says that she is similar to Rosa Luxemburg, in profile, viewed from a very specific facial angle. Later we learn that for many years Marcks had a Jewish lover who served as his model. Perhaps a similarity in type existed there. I like the figure very much, her expression, her attitude, her strength. The left hand, wrapped in the robe, drawn up to her breast, the right falling downward, pointing. In antiquity, H. says, this had been the pose with the meaning: let the earth be my witness. He believes that Marcks was familiar with that meaning and intended it. I accept it joyfully, as I do the total, unaffected, but at the same time lamenting the nature of the figure in general. Its authenticity. A document about the Lübeck figure frieze calls her "resigned," later: "renouncing." I like that better. Mourning, renouncing. Not fearful, giving ground, not exalted. The figure here is, so to speak, a duplicate of the Lübeck one, in terra cotta, the people in Lübeck knew nothing about it, nor did they need to know, and the people of Cologne simply did not notice what was hanging there when they walked past down below. Marcks saw her here, felt it was good—Just for us, they unwrapped the figure from the covering that is supposed to protect it during the construction work. I am happy that I saw it. We follow the same awkward and not really safe route back into the building. One simply has to conquer the figure for oneself, I think, and that is fine.

In the office of Mr. H., books are passed around, among them very expensive ones that H. produced with woodcuts by Marcks. Then the edition of the fairy tale "The Fisherman and His Wife" costs five hundred marks, and since we, too, have brought books with us, Mr. H., who apparently cannot bear to receive gifts ("but I do not deserve that at all!") almost wants to give us such a book as a gift; but then I cannot stand that—in contrast to Gerd, who looks greedily at it, and I resist. Then we receive very beautiful stationery, decorated with a Marcks woodcut, and also building blocks from the Bauhaus period, for little Helene. We walk through the three stories of the building that are used by the Lempertz sales gallery, where pictures that were left over from the auction hang on the walls. A

wonderful print by Nolde sticks in my mind, and a portrait by
Liebermann. In the showcases art objects, also vases, etc.
There is a department for old furniture, among the things a
very tricky table that one can pull out on different levels, a
Tibetan department, etc.; thirty employees, many of them aca-
demics. How much he would like to be lazy for once, says Mr.
H., but the competition from New York and London is right
on their heels, so they have to take everything that is offered
them, seven large auctions a year, each time a complete catalogue (he shows us one, gives us a brochure to take along, in
which magnificent pictures by Nolde, Kandinsky, and Picasso
were each being sold for half a million marks. During the
whole time my mind is occupied with the revelation that Barlach was unable to finish the Lübeck figure molding, not only
because he died before he could do so; even before that "nothing more occurred" to him. That is, of course, what I have
recently been afraid of, that I could be empty; if the desolation
is not being created by my hesitation to penetrate into the next
lower level, to let myself be totally permeated by the mental
freedom that I believe I have acquired, to let it flow relentless-
ly into my writing).

And now Mr. H., whose kindness knows no bounds, and
whom I like more and more because of his shyness, his modesty, his passion for art, and his expertise—now, after everything else, he wants to drive us into the Severin quarter,
because I asked where the Severin Church is located, which
plays a role in *Billiards at Half-Past Nine*.[2] It is my, our old passion to seek out places from literature in cities that we visit; it
is the most intensive way for me to assimilate cities. Thus we
now do get into a real Mercedes after all; we will not, I think,
encounter the confused Veronika F. here either. Only in front
of the Santa Maria Church in the capital, where H. stops first,

[2] Heinrich Böll (1917-1985), 1959. (Ed.)

where a fat man in a horizontally striped pullover is sitting on a bench, apparently drunk—a confused woman could also sit there, I think. Only absolute sexual fidelity protects from AIDS. Next to the church, the *Mourning Woman* by Marcks, similar to *Cassandra*, she, too, impresses me, and Gerd discovers in her as well the Rosa Luxemburg profile. We enter the church and see in the entryway the photographs of its almost total destruction, hard to believe how it has been rebuilt. When the first bombs fell on Cologne, says H., they precisely measured and photographed all the churches and other architectural monuments down to the last millimeter. Thus, after the war they were able to fall back on that documentation. He shows us the outlines of the "parallel churches" in Rome and Jerusalem, which are inlaid in the floor. The enormous world impact of Catholicism jumps out at us. The beautiful old door. The tour around the church, an entire architectural landscape, H. says, and I experience it that way, too. Unfortunately on one side a home for the aged built in front of it. Just how were they able in your country, says H., to demolish the old University Church in Leipzig only a few years ago? Were there really no artists who could join together to prevent that? I feel ashamed of our "artists," who in that, as in many other instances, thought and think only of themselves.

He tells about the sad incident connected to plans to give a square in the city of Cologne Böll's name. Somebody who was not familiar with history recommended, of all places, the Appellhofplatz for that—an old square where the Appeals Court stands, which played an important role in the rejection of Prussian claims to the Rhineland. For example, back then they succeeded in maintaining governance of the Rhineland under the Napoleonic Code, and not under Prussian law. And of all names, they now wanted to remove that name from the city, which would have been a misuse of Böll. He had suggested that the square in front of the city library, in which Böll's literary estate is also housed and which had no name, be named after him. (I remember a press report from this morning: the city of Cologne had taken over the archives from Böll. Viktor Böll supervises them; the city has no publication rights, but pays the family over 100,000 marks annually. The writer had declared that his expenses exceeded his income, and for that reason he needed the money. I remember what Böll told us years ago about his enormous tax liability.)

Severin quarter, so old Cologne. The church, streets. Old houses. The streets themselves more colorful from advertising than is good for them. Is there a Café Krone here? A Hotel Prinz Heinrich? Böll probably invented the names. I see a café that could have served as a model. Böll was born here in the vicinity, we learn. H.'s father was acquainted with Böll; he, Böll, really knew his way around the old churches and always preferred the Romanesque to the Gothic Cologne. Since this morning I have understood that completely. H. was later afraid to continue his acquaintance with Böll, although he once asked him to do so when he happened to meet him with his crutches at the main railway station and drove him home. But he did know how that man was literally besieged and exploited.

On the drive back into the city center, H. gets around to talking about his most recent horrible experience. Two weeks ago he was sitting in an airplane when a heron flew into one of the motors as they were taking off from Rio, Brazil, whereupon the motor stopped one minute after the takeoff. The plane had to fly back to the airport while draining the fuel for twenty minutes—otherwise the plane would have exploded upon landing anyway. They all sat there wearing life preservers and none of them believed that they would come down safely—especially he; he has a pilot's license, had once been a glider pilot, and was able to imagine vividly what would happen if only one of the little metal parts, some of which were constantly freeing themselves from the motor, were to end up in the motor. Or if the entire wing, and not just pieces, had sud-denly broken off. More than two hundred and fifty people aboard. And no panic, no screaming—a remarkable calm. He was only angry with the people who there, 150 meters below them, would continue to live while he was dead. Even when they then landed on that thick foam-rubber mat, the cheers were still limited. Now, however, he suffers from insomnia and lack of concentration and uses every opportunity for diversion, such as that of driving around the city with us. It was remark-able what he had to think about during the twenty minutes that he thought were his last—even about people whom he did not know were so important for him—I find the man more and more likeable; he apparently has to talk about his experience.

After we have said goodbye, we quickly have something to eat in the vicinity of the hotel. While we are waiting, I leaf through *Die Zeit*, scan headlines: AUSCHWITZ LABORA-TORY—SCHILLER'S PRECIOUS REMAINS—A case that remains a mystery. What happened to the poet's skull?—PAR-ENTS UNDER THE INFLUENCE. I feel quite miserable, cough, sniffle; something bad seems to be in my limbs. In the hotel I immediately begin to change clothes, while Gerd lies down—then it turns out that he did not take note of my repeated answers to his question as to when the event was to begin and stuck with his original assumption that it began at four o'clock and that we would thus have to be there at three. It was shortly before two o'clock and we were supposed to be there at two. Gerd could not control himself, I was irritated anyway, he repeated that if I had only told him that earlier we would have come back to the hotel sooner, so that I could have taken a nap . . . A course of events that I know very well. In spite of that I still had to prepare the brief preliminary materi-al that I would have to present before the actual reading. Gerd rejected the first version as too commentating and gave point-ers for the second one . . . If I had felt better, even that could not help but have amused me because it has constantly repeated itself for decades.

I put on the gray jacket because several people have already told me that it is "elegant," "smart," "looks good on me," the black skirt—Gerd also asks again each time if it is new—and it is four years old. Very good, he says then.

The hotel doorman explains the route to us; it turns out that this explanation is of little use to us, and people answer us on the way: What? You want to go to the Gürzenich?—Finally we do arrive. Viktor Böll, who bears no familial resemblance to the other Böll branch, receives us and takes us into the room where the other participants are already waiting. I find the atmosphere impersonal and inhospitable; only Lev gives us a hug, of course. Of the others hardly anyone speaks a word to us, including Grass and Lenz. At midday I had heard on the radio that Veronika F. still had not been found; she will not stray into this room either. Lev rolls up papers, talks about his work, implores me to visit them. I want to see you, he says. He has the feeling that time is growing short for him. He has a tumor in his bladder, which he does not have examined more closely. At his age such a thing does not grow as rapidly any longer . . .

Behind his aged face his earlier one appears to me again— not so very different, by the way (he has not changed very much)—which I knew in Moscow. His large form in the Moscow apartment that was too small for him, how he kicked the telephone around like a little dog because he suspected that there were listening devices in it. Our walk through Moscow on the day when there were anti-Semitic invectives in the periodical *Ogonyok* again—against Lilya Brik [3] and her husband. His anger, his rage, his far-reaching walking stick.

---

[3] Lilya Brik (1891-1978), known as the muse of Vladimir Mayakovsky; Neruda called her the "muse of the Russian avant-garde." (Tr.)

Before that: the introduction at A.S.'s home, who wanted to make him see reason, but too late. Böll was something like an absolute point of reference for him; twice I experienced how he tried to explain the West's rotten messes and "swine" to the Russian. The walk in the park next to his Cologne apartment, where he explained to me why he turned away from Solzhenitsyn. The afternoon in his (new) Cologne apartment after Böll's funeral. And now today. Only in intimate conversation between the two of us signs of weariness. Afterward he will be the first one after the high mayor of Cologne (who makes a "decent" speech) to step to the speaker's desk, and he will not give up the microphone for almost half an hour, read letters from Moscow on Böll's death, and after, for a long time, an essay by Böll on the Sakharov incident. While I sit in the second row, at quite a distance from him, I will notice an impatience in myself, but no longer the petty fear that overcame me for a few seconds when I saw his name yesterday as the first one on the program and had to think: Man, how they will chalk that up against me at home!—Now, in my second row, I felt satisfaction instead, defiance: Let them!

Isn't this an extraordinary duplication of events, Lev says: This morning they buried Axel Springer,[4] the very person whom Hein actually meant in his book about Böhnisch[5]—the federal president went to the funeral. Here he declined—I find that quite all right, also for the sake of clarity—I scrutinize the other participants around the large rectangular table, see— which was already obvious from the program—that I will be the only woman (once again), once again also those mixed feelings of bitterness and triumph, my own sex remains behind, but to where should it advance? And what drives me onto this rostrum?

[4] Axel Springer (1912-1985), publisher of the German news magazine *Der Spiegel*. (Tr.)
[5] Böhnisch (b. 1944), title character in a book by Christoph Hein. (Tr.)

Gerd found it appropriate that one "of ours" should also be here. I did, too, in theory, but had no desire to be here, none at all. And now this disgusting cold besides, which is getting worse. So now, while we are finally sitting in this large hall, in front, on the right side, and the prominent people—among them Bastian, Petra Kelly, radio and television people—have filed past us; after, the shameless radio people in front of the door quickly pushed one more (green?!) microphone in front of my face: Mrs. Wolf, a brief interview!—I: Leave me alone. I have the flu!—An answer that I immediately felt was foolish—while I am thus sitting there, listening to the mayor, who at least would like to bring the great son home to his city piece by piece (in which he is right and is doing the right thing, since he does not do violence to him and also remembers the time when they virtually ostracized him, '77, when Cologne remained loyal to him), then Kopelev,[6] who takes full advantage of his freedom, I believe—I feel how an insuppressible urge to cough rises again and again from my bronchial tubes. So I cough, with the corresponding dreadful head pain, and press my hand against my bronchial tubes to warm them. Then follows the unavoidable, predictable dialogue with Gerd: What's the matter? I: I have to cough—Gerd: Rubbish. You don't have a cough at all. You are simply excited. You are getting tense—I: Of course I have a cough. I am not at all excited—Gerd: Suck on something—I: I have been constantly sucking on something!—(That is true. I constantly have Neo-Angin or Ems salt lozenges in my mouth.) I can see that we will not come to an agreement, prefer to be silent, cough, try to suppress the urge. I really am not excited;

[6] Lev Kopelev (1912-1997), Russian Germanic studies scholar and writer; after political imprisonment in 1957, for the time being rehabilitated, expelled from the Communist Party of the Soviet Union in 1968 and discriminated against; 1980 emigrated to Cologne and was expatriated from the USSR. For the Wolfs especially important because of his three-volume autobiography; in active, friendly exchange of ideas beginning in 1965, frequent encounters (see also: G.W., *Die Poesie hat immer Recht*, Berlin, 1998, pp. 66ff. and pp. 100ff.; C.W., *Werke*, Vol. XII, pp. 607ff.). (G.W.)

I am never excited before such appearances. And here I am not even reading my own text, but the Schrella Nettheim chapter from *Billiards at Half-Past Nine*, before me Grass with a (somewhat too long) excerpt from Böll's *Letter to a Young Catholic*, after me the leader—or how do you say it?—of the Gypsies in the Federal Republic, Lolotz Birkenfelder,[7] with whom I would have liked to have spoken earlier, but I was too shy to speak to him. While Grass is reading, he asks me with gestures if I want something to drink. I say yes, relieved, and he opens a water bottle, pours for himself and me, and I feel that this small gesture is friendly and courteous. He reads from Böll's essay on Eichmann,[8] "Order and Responsibility."

Exciting, courageous, provocative, and liberating: Wallraff's speech,[9] "No Farewell to Böll," no eye remains dry there, and the official Federal Republic cannot hide that behind a mirror. Once I am startled myself when he reveals that Böll once brought a "victim of persecution" "across the border" "in the trunk of his car"—what kind of victim of persecution? Which border? And should one divulge that, give the detractors grist for their mills?

Beautiful, fresh, and sassy, the Cologne songs of the group BAP, moving the Chinese woman who has actually traveled here to read the beautiful chapter from *Group Portrait with Lady* about the writer's torn jacket—here, I think, the confused Veronika F. would have fit into the book, there she would have found people who would have taken care of her—but this way: where might she now be wandering around? Then it occurs to me how Annette recently told me that she encountered a con-

---

[7] Lolotz Birkenfelder, Gypsy poet and leader. (Tr.)

[8] Otto Adolf Eichmann (1906-1962), high-ranking Nazi and SS official. He was charged with facilitating and managing the logistics of mass deportation to ghettos and extermination camps in Nazi-occupied Eastern Europe. Captured by Israeli Mossad agents in Argentina, indicted by Israeli court on fifteen criminal counts, including charges of crimes against humanity and war crimes, he was convicted and executed. (Ed.)

[9] Günter Wallraff (b. 1942), German writer and journalist. (Ed.)

fused woman in the middle of Alexanderplatz, who was talking to herself aloud, also cursing, moaning, and weeping, and
whom everyone avoided. With her professional experience
Annette recognized what the problem was there and spoke to
the woman: You are not doing well right now. You need help.
She called her clinic, put the woman on a bus, and the woman
said to her: You are the only person who understands me . . .
Yes. I once met a woman like that on a Moscow bus. She was
sitting directly across from me; I tried to calm her using pantomime and glances, but in vain. I could not speak to her, of
course. My Russian would not have been good enough.

While we were leaving, a few of the visitors asked me for an
autograph. The side rooms appeared to have been empty. The
next day in the *Kölnische Rundschau* it said in large letters: Böll
drew only a few—while at least 1500 people had come. And in
the feature supplement the headline read: "Larger Than Life:
Heinrich Böll." Oh, how I understood Böll in his fury against
the yellow press.

Across to the city hall cellar restaurant, Grass is annoyed
with Kopelev, he really should have known that Böll never shot
that one-sidedly, against the "Soviet ruling powers," for example . . . Asks if I was not delegated by the German Democratic Republic to attend a cultural convention of the Conference
on Security and Cooperation in Europe in Budapest. I laugh
and say: You misjudge the situation. And he answers: You say
that to me every time—I do not remember having said it
"every time," but resolve definitely not to say it again.

In the restaurant a relatively small room is occupied by more
than a hundred people in no time at all, the closeness oppressive, the heat bad, and the air terrible. Wine, juice, and morsels
of food are passed around. I do not get any of that because I
constantly have to talk with somebody who appears in front of
me. First I want to tell Annemarie Böll myself something about
the impact of Böll's death in the German Democratic Republic.

She says, yes, she received an incredible number of letters, even from Turkey, and she had to say that it did comfort her somewhat—I ask how she is doing—Oh, quite well. She has the children, of course, and they are very kind. Sometimes better, sometimes worse. Nevertheless, a lot of work is coming at her, and trouble as well. Through disputes with the publisher. René, of course, wanted to print some things by his father . . . Well, she would not rush anything, but give herself some time. She also tells me that shortly before Böll went into the hospital, for an entire week there was a very severe tax audit going on in their house—And? I ask—She: Well, a large additional tax payment. But we'll make that all right. I am just so sorry that Hein was not spared all that.—Raja arrives, gives me her book [10] *A Past That Does Not Pass Away* and one by Lev. In Raja's book I find a card: Dear Christa, Back then I read your book, *The Quest for Christa T.* and was in the middle of this manuscript. Hopefully you will understand why that and others (*Cassandra*!) were so important. Yours, Raja. I want to have the books, but must simultaneously consider what will happen if they unexpectedly check my apartment on Friedrichstrasse, perhaps because of anger at my participation in this event, always the old fears, I think, the books will just be lying downstairs in the bag . . . Raja understands that I do not want to visit them in the evening, that I feel too ill. I, on the other hand, understand that it would mean a great deal to them to talk with us. Their homesickness is unappeased, and they can only respond to Westerners who ask them how they are doing: Fine, fine. They can tell us how they are really doing—we know it anyway.

Uwe Timm [11] comes. I did not know him and am amazed that he praises *Cassandra*. I had thought he would be too far

[10] Raja Kopelev: Raissa Davydovna Orlova-Kopelev (1918-1989), American studies scholar, writer; second wife of Lev Kopelev; expatriated with him from the Soviet Union in 1981. (G.W.)

[11] Uwe Timm (b. 1940) one of the most successful contemporary authors in Germany. (Ed.)

left for that, but he has already been out of the German Communist Party for a long time, which is now really a branch of the East German Socialist Unity Party, and he just did not want to do it as spectacularly as Kroetz. We talk about the film that Egon Günther[12] made based on his book, then others come, publisher's readers from Kiepenheuer und Witsch, readers, Fritz J. Raddatz, whom I meet in person here for the first time, Klaus Staeck, who sits down outside with me in the bar, where it is not as hot and the air is more bearable, and asks me to sign books. We arrange that, he takes a few pictures of me with his Polaroid camera, I confiscate at least the picture with my tongue stuck out, ask about his brother who had to go over there from Bitterfeld against his will at the beginning of the year. He had been deeply rooted in our country, is now constantly ill, but was never ill before.

One or two hours have passed. We now leave as well, covered with sweat. I say goodbye to Viktor Böll, wonder if Böll would have liked this celebration. The usual daily thought of death, sometimes now even comforting. See again and again that what happens (to me) after that does not concern me.

The people here spray apart; there is none who would take an interest in another person. Well, fine, we will go eat alone, but perhaps somewhere else for a change. Down the lanes to the Rhine, to have been in Cologne and not on the Rhine! So it was flowing there, past the pleasure boat that was moored firmly along the shore there. A dark stream, on the other side up high the illuminated letters: FORD, 4711. Oh well, clear conditions and the romantic mood is not in vain either. Many people out and about, the shoreline promenade has changed—in the direction of American taste—since we were here the first time. One restaurant after another, all promising local foods (just what we do not want), and Cologne beer. Around a street per-

[12] Egon Günther (b. 1927), German writer and director. (Tr.)

former a large audience. He has erected something like a pocket guillotine. Susanne, a girl from the crowd, still quite young, fresh, natural, has volunteered for an experiment. First, however, in an obscene manner, a carrot is beheaded. After that, Susanne has to stick her hand through—"Are you afraid?"—"Yes."—"Well, I am too!" They talk and talk, the audience laughs, and below Susanne's hand there is still a smaller opening for the carrot. At the last moment, when the guillotine comes down very threateningly, Susanne's hand is jerked up, remains whole, while the carrot falls into pieces. Joyful shouts from the audience, laughter, applause. We are in the Rhineland.

We land then in the Nudelbrett restaurant after all, do not believe our eyes when, after we have already ordered, we discover Brigitte Soubeyrand at one of the other tables with another woman, an actress, as it turns out. All four of us move together at one table, eat different kinds of noodles, and drink red wine. Now, of course, our conversation is about the theater, more precisely: about the theater in Cologne, about "Maria Stuart," which Brigitte wants to produce here (now after all), and about a certain actor that she cannot get for a certain role. Oh, you know, she says, things are difficult here, I can tell you. She "threw" a discussion, offered a compromise. The actor was to be asked if he would not like to play both roles—that of the fool for the other, preferred director, and that of the father confessor for her, a role that she sees in a completely new light and wants to fill with this specific young man in order to emphasize the erotic element in the faith of Maria Stuart—but when the meeting then convened again in the afternoon, to her disappointment "the management" decided against her. The theater manager then takes her along into his room and then also wants to tell her that even he does not have it so easy in this new position, in the big city . . .

I am tired! Oh, I am tired! We learn that the other woman,

the actress, will play the nurse in Brigitte's production. A nice role, all four of us say. She explains the unemployed actors' technique of using small temporary jobs to enable them to start over in receiving unemployment compensation again and again, for otherwise after a year, of course, they "have no further claim on benefits." "That is really difficult for many here, you!" After a week of Cologne, even Brigitte is "very wiped out," and dreams of how she can create a group within her team, in which trust and security rule, better: prevail, or how do you say it? Can develop. (This language of power!)

I cannot eat any more, cannot drink any more wine, can hardly speak any longer, am just tired, tired. We leave. The pavement artist has finished his picture, crouches next to it with his cap turned upward next to him. I have to go over, throw something into it. Gerd already knows that, no longer tries to stop me. The young man does not look up. Only when I then walk a few steps to the foot of the picture, compare it to the original (van Dyck: "The Family"), and look at it more closely, does he lift his head slightly and smile a little bit. I should not, I think to myself, have given him the money until after I had looked at the picture, his work. I should have had more respect for his dignity, his pride.

Veronika F.? I did not meet her. There is no more talk about her. In the hotel I take a hot shower, soothe my bronchial tubes, swallow all the liquids, drops, and pills, and am relieved. It went all right again, it did go well once more. In the last news of the day we see the widow of the great democrat Axel Springer, very well-groomed and composed, "in a simple black dress, decorated only with a diamond brooch" walking behind the casket, all of the prominent people with her, resembling those who sat in the first row today in the Gürzenich and were unable to clap at all for Wallraff, and also the Springer grandson Sven, who was recently kidnapped and still, I read, suffers from feelings of anxiety. Undoubtedly, and I feel sorry for him, the boy, only: this, too, is not my world, after all. But where else is it? "In search of a habitable language in a habitable world" read the statement by Böll that they placed over the event this afternoon, with his picture "larger than life," yes, there you are, showed him in the attitude of lively conversation. And that is perhaps what living is: being on that search, speaking, facing other people.

Television off. Light off. No more talk. Gerd's hand. Fall asleep.

SATURDAY, SEPTEMBER 27, 1986
Zurich

Z urich. I am thinking about what I experienced during the final hour after midnight before we drove to the hotel. The last discussions and conversations after the "Cassandra" performance in the Theater an der Winkelwiese. I am sitting in a leather armchair, next to the wall, by Mr. Zweifel, the patron of the little theater, of whom it is said to me several times that he accepts the responsibility for it, even for the loss that the theater might incur. I was not able to find out to what extent he is also a financial backer. During the morning the director had said to me that he fought long battles to obtain continuing support for the theater from the city treasury. If there were 120 people at the performance, then at least forty to fifty of them had joined Zweifel afterward. A few young women had attacked the director because of the text selection; I had defended him, not quite convinced, because even I found that selection to be one-sided. The entire complex of women in the caves was missing; Cassandra was portrayed as a solitary fateful figure. A small circle then sat around me, some of them on the floor, next to me on my left the woman with the reddish curly hair who had introduced herself as the former wife of Paul Nizon, now works in a library, and told me why she had not been able to read the afterword to the "Frankfurt Lecture" by Nizon: "Always the same, always the same. He cannot stop focusing on the same poets each time." A young man was there, Hannes, the boyfriend of the actress Barbara Magdalena Arendt. He works in television and had wanted me to consent to a television interview. I talk about my experiences with the press and television, coloring my speech with anecdotes, and why I now refuse all interviews if I do not know the people who ask me for them. He understands that, but finds it exciting that I came here, knew nobody, was not familiar with the production, met the director, then saw the production, talked with the actress, etc. He talks about how he felt while reading *Cassandra*, what affected him there as a man, and also what had made him furious. It is an unusually open confession for a man. He wept during the entire performance, he says. From several directions all at once, I am being encouraged to accept the offer from the university for next fall to give lectures and seminars there. Suggestions are made as to what I could do, etc. When we then leave with the director and his wife Viumje, I am inclined to accept those suggestions and return. We go to the car; the woman drives; she is an art historian and tells us a little about what she does. On the way they talk about their home outside of Zurich, you can now only live outside the city anymore; the city is empty on Sundays, of course. They invite me to come on Sunday, and we talk again about the work on the text, etc. The ride is short; most places in Zurich are not far from each other. After one o'clock, I am in the Leoneck Hotel on Leonhardtstrasse. I have to ring the bell. Get ready for the night then in my room, open the small refrigerator once more in the slight hope that they perhaps put something to drink in it. But again I find the old ham, the old yogurt, and the spoiled cheese that were left by some very distant predecessors and quickly close the stinking refrigerator. In bed I then read some articles in the most recent issue of *Die Zeit*, for example the one by Marlies Menge about Carl Friedrich Weizsäcker's appearance in the embassy of the Federal Republic. I think about whether or not I could have described and evaluated it that precisely and note that I am actually gradually losing that journalistic ability to grasp,

describe, and evaluate an occurrence rapidly. Another interesting article that I begin to read there is about the mental, philosophical, and political effects of the reactor accident in Cher-
nobyl. The author, Beck or Becker, discusses the question of
whether or not this accident simply annuls certain other standards of order and value that were valid within Europe for an
entire historical period, specifically, for example, the class conflicts, for example the evaluation of a society on the basis of the
equality of its members, which forms the basis of the socialistic approach to things, of course. He talks about the fact that
through the radioactive contamination, the equality, even of
those who helped to cause that contamination, is automatically established. And that in this manner other laws, which, to be
sure, continue to function—as, for example, that of the class
struggle—are subordinated to the primary aspect. In any case,
that is a way of looking at things which fascinates me and
which, I believe—or in any case I think about it before I fall
asleep—will presumably increase in importance during the
coming years, in that it will occupy the attention of more people, and in that more people will assimilate that approach into
their thinking.

I wake up rather early, before seven, long before I actually
have to get up, read some more in the article that continued to
work within me during the night, as well as other things in *Die
Zeit*, leaf through the program for Zurich, listen to the news,
hear that an accident had occurred in a nuclear reactor near
Basel, an admittedly lesser accident, but one that was also not
reported to the responsible authorities, that they are angry
about that, etc. I hear that in Washington additional talks are
underway between the US Secretary of State Schultz and the
USSR Foreign Minister Shevardnaze about the case of the US
journalist Danilov, who is suspected of espionage, and the
Soviet spy Sakharov, and again think about the absurdity of
world political affairs that use such insignificant cases to tor-

pedo important meetings like the summit between Gorbachev and Reagan. By the way, I notice that Swiss Radio broadcasts all spoken programs in Swiss German and only the news in High German. Later I hear that there is also criticism of that, that the French-speaking Swiss, for example, criticize this more recent practice because they can then no longer listen to that station; they do not understand the Swiss German either, and the standard language has lost more and more ground in recent years. Even in the schools they speak Swiss German in most of the classes, as I learn at midday from the son of my hosts. I eat breakfast—it is, by the way, a lean breakfast with little variety—in this not especially good hotel. Then I walk through several streets to the railway station and cross the pedestrian zone. In the underground shopping corridor I begin to look for certain things, for example, for a pullover that Jana wants, but which I do not find in the end, at least not with the neckline that she would like. I then walk for a short distance along Bahnhofstrasse, buy myself a blouse and a sweater, and observe the people who are on Bahnhofstrasse in bright crowds on this Saturday morning, strolling up and down, sitting in front of the stores, and shopping. I see the show windows of the very expensive stores in which there are only very few customers, but which must also exist, and I again have the impression that Switzerland is a country in which somebody without money must feel especially uneasy and especially excluded. At twelve-thirty I am back at the hotel, and I am picked up by Professor Böhler, who had called me and offered me that job for next year at the University of Zurich. In the car he is already talking about how he hates Zurich; he and many other intellectuals feel that it is a city that isolates, separates people from each other, and simply a city of capital, of big money. He tells how much he enjoyed, on the other hand, having much more contact with people at the university in Columbus, Ohio. There, in half a year he had received more than twenty invitations from colleagues, and when he came back to Zurich, during the same period of time they had received exactly one invitation. Even in the same department at the university they would hardly cultivate private contact with each other. Actually he cannot explain either why it is that way, but everybody that I talked to complained about it.

He lives on the other side, in a quarter that was inhabited more densely by Orthodox Jewish families than it is today. We see some families in black, the father with a black hat and a black tie, going to the synagogue. In his building, too, for example, lives a family named Rothschild, and the Böhlers tell me that on the Sabbath—it just happens to be a Sabbath on which we are out and about—they have sometimes forgotten to do some task or other in advance, which they are not permitted to do on the Sabbath, for example, turning a stove on or off, and that then the Böhlers do it for them. I very much admire the apartment into which I am led, very bright, white, and full of green plants. We were fortunate, they say. By the way, I often hear that. All the people in the West who live very well say that they were fortunate and that actually there are no apartments, at least not ones that are that nice. I am shown a grand piano that was just painted by a lady artist. Each member of the family plays music; sometimes there are house concerts. The woman, whom I like very much because she is so natural, is a photographer. She does portrait photography. Apparently the salaries of Germanic studies professors are rather high, for such an apartment in this quarter must be very expensive. They show me avocado trees that were raised from pits, and I decide to try it once more after all. In one room we sit on modern seats at a large, oval glass table. There is also a thirteen-year-old son, Stefan. A very good Swiss meal, beginning with melons, with a good soup, with chopped vegetables and crisp bread, and with cheese, coffee, and wine as well; the whole thing goes on until four o'clock, and during that time we talk about Zurich, about the literature of the German Democratic Republic, which these German literary scholars feel has more vitality than the literature of the Federal Republic, about conditions in our country, in theirs, about the schools, about apartment rents, house prices, about what we eat, who cooks, what we cook, and of course about political conditions, in any case a spectrum of that which interests Central Europeans these days. At around four, Böhler brought me—no, not Böhler: his wife brought me to my hotel at around four o'clock, and now it seemed to me that I should accept the offer to come to the university in Zurich, although there had been much talk about how encrusted the conditions are there, politically not very pleasant, and how much I would have to figure on being overrun by a lot of students, especially female students. When we drove in at the hotel, I had the feeling that I should take it on. Of course I was very tired, of course the time was much too short for me to really rest, but nevertheless I did lie down for half an hour, then quickly got dressed, thought about whether or not I should call Max Frisch and tell him that I would be coming a little bit later, but I did not reach him. Fortunately I drove off in a taxi on time, into the old city where he lives, fortunately, I say, for he was standing outside on the street waiting for me.

(For better or worse, this first part was recorded on tape—a practice that I have never engaged in before, and which, as far as my time is concerned, signifies an emergency situation. During the last two weeks since my stay in Zurich, my primary work has been the revision and then the correction of the summer piece for this year, which I have labeled a "text," and which up to this point bears the title "Accident, Description of a Day." I have never before completed the description of that other day, which I have imposed upon myself for twenty-six years now, as late as I have done this time. Because of that, details that would have been especially important to me have probably been blotted out or obscured; nor do I have any notes. Thus, without any aids I will attempt to write down my recollection of the meeting with Max Frisch, which, on the evening of that day, did last for five hours, from six o'clock until after eleven; and since we actually talked without any break, a very large bundle of sheets would result if I could—or wanted to—write down that verbal exchange word for word.)

When my taxi stopped, Frisch was standing on the other side of the street. I was startled and reproached him for waiting for me outside. Otherwise finding him would have been a bit complicated, he said, as he led me through the stone and pillar landscape of the new building in which he lives. An elevator to the fourth floor. Tour of the apartment, which, like the entire building, had been built by "one of our younger architects—who are still good." His apartment is situated on three levels, an impressive, somewhat cool, undoubtedly expensive place. From each of the floors there is access to a balcony, to two balconies, and then on top to a beautiful roof garden, which he could actually make use of, if it were not for the fact that for the last year (or even longer?) directly behind his building the construction site—an offshoot of the citywide construction site—of the new Zurich subway has been operating, which, of course means: significant shaking of the ground, significant noise, pile drivers, and enormous, heavy crane arms hanging overhead. For God's sake, I say, how long is that supposed to go on?—For two more years, he says. And I am seventy-five—Can't you move?—To where? Even back then I didn't find anything else.

He gives me the impression of being a man who actually does not know where he should live. The day before he had just returned from Ticino, where he goes (just how? Possibly driving his own car? I did not ask that) when he can no longer take the air in Zurich. He has emphysema and flees from the gas-laden city air, but on the other hand, in Ticino he is then completely alone, which he is also not able to stand for very long. I believe that it is not simply an imagined need, but that this famous and wealthy man essentially does not know how and where he should live. To be sure, he is unmistakably Swiss, but his homelessness is evident. During the first few minutes he already emphasizes that he does not live alone, but the woman with whom he now has a relationship, "Katrin," does not live with him. She has a profession, is a therapist for severely behaviorally disturbed children. During the course of the conversation Frisch tells me that a boy recently said to her that she was an especially stupid cow and that he would someday cut her up into very small pieces with a knife—Frisch talks about her several times, how they spend their weekends, what she says about the fact that he wants to keep an expensive car and is now having it refurbished again, which will cost just as much as a new car . . .

He has considered and prepared everything precisely. The champagne glasses stand on the low glass table directly next to the window front of the living and dining room on the middle floor; a little plate of shrimp is ready, champagne is opened. We talk first—I bring it into the conversation—about the topic of "resignation." I note that this is an irritating topic for him. Following his speech in Solothurn, with which he said goodbye to his colleagues and professional life, he was often addressed concerning it, and also probably, from the left, accused of resignation. He repeats that his insight into the true conditions does not necessarily mean "resignation," but on the other hand he does not want to hide the shattering nature of that insight. His motto is: resistance. Resistance wherever possible, pouring sand into the machinery, so that the large operations move more slowly, delay whatever possible in the hope that meanwhile alternatives will develop.

We talk about the theater. I tell him about the premiere of

Cassandra in the Theater an der Winkelwiese, ask him if he actually always went to the performances of his plays. He says no. Only in Zurich, where he had previously already seen portions of the rehearsals and could, to a certain extent, have an influence on the production—then he also went to the premiere. Elsewhere hardly at all, he couldn't stand it. He talks about the variability of the productions; an especially unsuccessful one had given him the greatest doubts concerning his play, and he had made changes, which then, in a different, "proper" production had proven to be superfluous, etc.

Several times we come back to the USA, to his stay there in a "loft" with Lynn from *Montauk*. Then he had not been able to stand it there anymore, not only because the relationship with that woman was over. The USA seemed to him like Germany in 1937. To be sure, all comparisons and parallels were warped, but that nationalism, which reached far into the ranks of the intellectuals, really did seem eerie to him. There he was simply unable to discern any resistance at all anymore.

Later we talk about Uwe Johnson. I remind him of our only evening with the Johnsons in West Berlin, when Uwe and his wife both intensively reproached us for living in the German Democratic Republic, where a writer simply could not speak the truth. Frisch begins to remember the evening. I indicate that I am very well aware of that truth problem, was aware of it even back then. Frisch says, as an interjection: That, of course, had been the crux of the matter with *Patterns of Childhood*, that I evaded certain critical points about the present because I knew that I would have had difficulties at home because of them. I do not say much in response to that. When I wrote *Patterns of Childhood* it would not have occurred to me to draw any parallels between German fascism and Soviet Stalinism. I saw those two phenomena, in spite of a series of manifest similarities, as fundamentally different. That very thing was the problem, one could say. I still have no satisfying answer to it that I feel is "right," because it covers my very different, in many things contradictory, experiences in those two systems.

Frisch talked about how unconditionally Johnson and his wife always had to be right. He again recounts the episode with Jurek Becker,[1] whom he took to see Johnson and who was viewed by him as a means of humiliating him: the Jewish former concentration camp boy confronting the former National Political Educational Institute student. As so often, aggressiveness as an expression of feelings of inferiority. When they lived in the neighborhood in West Berlin, they sometimes drank a lot in the evenings. Once they went out on the street, determined to drive off into the night in the car. Marianne tried to prevent them from doing it and asked Elisabeth Johnson to help her, and she simply said: They are grown men; they must know what they are doing—I felt cold in the company of those upright people who did not tolerate any weaknesses in themselves and did not pardon any in others.

Frisch seems to be still grappling internally with the fact that the last conversation he had with Johnson ended badly, gruffly. A man who cannot accept anything, Frisch said. Unseld had financed a one-year stay for him in the USA, and he, Frisch, had offered him that loft, which he had already moved out of, but in which Lynn still lived (as big as it was—since it was basically a matter of a single enormous room—he would not have been able to work there if Lynn were there), and he offered to pay Uwe's rent for him. Uwe had said he could come up with $400 a month for it, but he had to know that that was ridiculous for such a dwelling. It cost $1200 plus $600 in additional costs. Uwe was supposed to assume those expenses, and he hesitated and hesitated, did not agree to or reject the offer, until he, Frisch, during the last telephone conversation, said:

[1] Jurek Becker (1937-1997), novelist who became famous in the GDR, then moved to the West. Best known for his novel *Jakob der Lügner*, which was filmed in the USA as *Jacob the Liar*, starring Robin Williams. (Tr.)

So Uwe, do you want the apartment now or not?! He then probably hung up. Two weeks later Johnson was dead.

How difficult it is these days to maintain a friendship.

Frisch talked a lot about a plan that he had given up on, to write an autobiography of money. He regretted that in *Montauk* he had already hinted at so much that he could now no longer do that at all. After all, he certainly had not risen from a dishwasher to a millionaire, but in his childhood they had also gathered fallen fruit in order to have a meal in the evening, and they were really poor. And now . . . It becomes clear to me that this advancement, financially as well as otherwise, means a lot to him, that a truly desired element of self-conformation lies in it; being only a good, even famous writer would perhaps not have been enough for him. He tells me how the truly wealthy people suddenly began to talk with him about money, about prices, even about the kind of prices that amount to millions. The other standards of value—money!—are also simply internalized here by those who fight against them. He talks for a long time about an obtrusive man who tried to fleece him in Rome, how he sometimes helped him, sometimes turned him away, and he comes back to other episodes in his dealings with money, which in part are already in his diaries. Several times he also mentions a prize that he is supposed to receive two weeks later, in California, I think, so and so many dollars, a good prize, but he cannot travel there for health reasons. Apparently that is still important to him.

It occurs to me that a slight speech impediment, an occasional hesitation in speaking, is becoming clearly apparent. That is how, I think, it may also have gone for Kleist. Frisch has grown old, his features have blurred, are no longer clear. He himself is not fatter, rather broader. Almost white, sparse hair. Once he calls old age "humiliating." To my question: Yes, he is also bored. He has given up writing in order not to repeat himself. The elements of his autobiography are used up—well, the

Jewish woman to whom he was engaged as a young man, and so forth . . . We are familiar with that, of course. He reads. Right now, strangely enough, Gottfried Benn, and after not having done so for a long time Nietzsche once again.

I try to imagine a writer who has finished his work while he is still alive. From an interview that he gave to a leftist weekly newspaper and in the meantime had sent to me, emerges among other things that he finds these comrades' exclusive interest in his political opinions annoying. He enumerates for them the titles of his books as evidence for his permanent commitment. He must have the impression that he is being forgotten as a writer more and more. To me, however, he says that the two of us cannot complain. After all, our books continue to be read by young people.

He tells me in detail—we are still sitting with our introductory champagne—about a visit to the Federal President of Switzerland. How he had invited "him and his friends"; how he insisted upon going there alone, because otherwise the others would again wait until he said something; how he then took a taxi to the address that had been given him, got out, went up the stairs, rang the bell, and the Federal President himself opened the door for him—no protection, no security measures. But otherwise: a man who did not know what was going on in the country. Who had no contact with the everyday life of the people, etc.

Frisch also has everything prepared at the dinner table. He fries two steaks in a rectangular pan, with them broccoli and spinach from frozen food packages. It is ready quickly, tastes good, with it a dry white wine and fruit. Everything very thoughtful and well planned. No break in the conversation.

I talk to him about the long interview that was broadcast on West German television, but which I did not see. Of which I am familiar with only one sentence with respect to Bachmann. He feels, when he—often—thinks of her, dreams of her, no guilt, but regret—What is the difference between guilt and regret? I ask him. He says: The cameraman immediately asked me that, too. Regret, not about guilty behavior, but about things that were missed, things that did not happen, things that were not done . . . He does not want to go into detail, which I understand. What causes me to ask about that? He talks a little more about that long television interview. At the end of the fourteen hours he had also asked himself if anything had come out of it that he had not already said in his books or in other interviews . . .

Rather late I say: Now we will again not get around to talking about what you didn't like about *Cassandra* (he had written me that he had had objections with regard to the lectures, and I thought I understood them to be with regard to the Bachmann parts). I had seen the lectures lying on a little side table. He said, but we could talk about that right now. By now, of course, much time had passed. He should have written to me immediately, at the first impulse. Now it would undoubtedly be given too much weight, etc. On the advice of his lady friend he had taken the lectures with him on vacation, had begun to read in them and had sometimes become so angry that he had thrown the book against the wall. Just what is it that irritates you so much? his lady friend had asked, and he had said—and he would now say that to me, too: I did not mention my husband at all, with whom I was traveling; he only appeared briefly a few times with G. If it was about feminism, then go ahead, do it right; I behaved toward my husband the way male writers usually behaved toward their wives. And second: he felt that the description of my trip to Greece was irritating. There I had apparently had the feeling that if I was so privileged that as a citizen of the German Democratic Republic I could travel to Greece, then I should faithfully and uprightly describe the journey—that was how it struck to him; now he was really familiar with Greece, and perhaps could not be described differently, but then he just did not want to read it that way.

I immediately had the feeling that those two points undoubtedly had disturbed him, but that they were nevertheless only
pretexts, for a person does not throw a book against the wall for
such reasons. He did not tell me the real reasons. Instead,
apparently because he himself was offended, he tried to offend
me, and he succeeded. I said, with regard to Gerd and our relationship with each other, I was so shy that I did not want to portray him in a book, and thus his reproach was not valid for me.
As to the other point, I could not say much—except, that a person can simply also go to Greece too late and then describe
something with which everyone else is already familiar.

The evening continued, but it had a crack. I had probably
not expected envy, aggressiveness from this direction, too. I
became aware again that I am an annoyance to a number of
colleagues; Frisch is not among them, his irritation is partial. I
will never forget how in the dark winter of 1976, after the Biermann expatriation, he and Marianne came through Checkpoint Charlie to our apartment on Friedrichstrasse to document their solidarity with us, and what a great help that really
was for me—He then encouraged me to come back to Zurich
next year, to the university, but beneath the surface he advised
me against it by describing to me how reactionary this university is, that they would misuse me for their own image, that the
women would overrun me as a cult figure, and so on. At the
same time, he offered to bring me together with the "right"
people—When I left, I was determined not to accept the invitation to the university.

Very kindly, he brought me back downstairs, wanted to have
a farewell drink with me in a bar, but it was too full. He even
accompanied me in the taxi to the hotel and considerately took
me—after all, he was responsible for me—to the hotel door. I
would call him again the next day, I said. Do that, he said. I did
not do it, and I now regret it.

The previous day runs into this day. At a quarter after twelve midnight, I say: It is a quarter after twelve. We are still sitting at the kitchen table with the Hoffmanns,[1] the book dealers from Eutin. Following the Schwerin performance of Shakespeare's "Winter's Tale," we ate rutabaga soup, drank tea, and are now talking about the swampy politics in Schleswig-Holstein, about the work routine of married book dealers from Eutin, about the different modes of behavior of people "here" and "over there" ("Now you also say "over there," Mrs. Hoffmann says). When in the theater—they performed in the royal stables in Schwerin with unnumbered seats—people were asked to move together again, everyone did so happily and without grumbling—"over there" that would be impossible. First of all, everyone would insist upon his or her right to the seat that was paid for, upon the right of money. And that the tickets were so cheap and then even "almost a supper" came with it (at the appropriate point during the performance there were lard sandwiches and a glass of wine) . . .

In bed I then read in the program interpretations of "The Winter's Tale," and thought about to what extent one could have depicted what seemed on the stage to be a rather simple structure in a somewhat roughened, more contemporary manner. Whether or not, on the other hand, one can simply relate

[1] Hoffmanns, owners of Buch & Grafik Hoffmann (Hoffmann Book & Graphics Co.), Eutin, where C. and G.W. went for readings and lectures. (G.W.)

a tyrant of the Shakespeare period directly to "Stalin, Mao, Pol Pot," as was done in the notes to the work by Christoph Schroth, etc.[2] did not immediately sleep. The tea made itself felt. Awoke while it was still dark, pursued the dream fragments that are now all lost; that repeated itself twice. Then it was a quarter to eight on my clock. I did an abbreviated version of my morning exercises, went across into Tinka's bathroom, because we are letting the Hoffmans use ours, and learned there from the radio that during the night standard time had begun again. So it was seven o'clock, and I could have slept longer. I immediately thought that I could use the hour that I had gained for these writings. The news reports said that there were substantial differences of opinion between Kohl and Strauss. The West German Mrs. Brinkmann, who had been released from captivity in Chile, called for an intensification of the fight against the military dictatorship. She will go back there as soon as possible. A signal that constantly repeats itself: admiration for such people who knowingly expose themselves to physical violence. I could not do that. The fleeting thought that I will buy myself free of that—in the near future again with the money from the prizes, which unfortunately lie ahead of me, which I will distribute.

Religious music. Shower. I ask myself how authentic my shock at receiving the new prizes really is, if there could be some ambiguity in it (as there is with other similar emotions): that I want it and do not want it. This time I am certain: I do not want it. I fear the envy of the gods and of my colleagues. I fear the increased burden of responsibility and the ever increasing attitude of expectation that already makes writing

[2] Christoph Schroth (b. 1937), theater director; 1974-89 stage play director at the Mecklenburg State Theater in Schwerin; had work discussions with C.W. in connection with various productions; occasioned by his *Antikeprojekt* (*Antiquity Project*), C.W. read from *Cassandra* in the theater (see also: *"Wo ich bin ist keine Provinz"* Der Regisseur Christoph Schroth [*"Where I Am Is Not a Province": the Director Christoph Schroth*], Berlin, 2003). (G.W.)

difficult for me now. At the same time I know that I draw this kind of attention to myself and am also able, if I want to (wanted to), to find out how. Through a tricky behavioral pattern I offer myself as an identification figure. All of these problems, I now realize again, played a role in my dreams last night.

After breakfast I sit in my room at the typewriter. It is ten o'clock. Gerd drove to Sternberg with the Hoffmanns to register, and then on to Güstrow. I drank a glass of homemade elderberry juice and am now watching the giant starlings that circle against today's strong wind above our back meadow and go into the elders. Beautiful, very large birds with elegant wing surfaces and a light gray dress shirt, over it an almost black swallowtail coat, peck at the elderberries and then defecate reddish blue. A beautiful, cool, clear, windy autumn day, large deep-blue patches of sky, white, whitish gray cloud masses. At night it is already cold, with temperatures down to five below zero centigrade. We have already forgotten that the summer was so bad.

For breakfast we had country eggs, cottage cheese with herbs, grapefruit, and ham. My but you live healthy, said Mrs. Hoffmann, and then you laugh about us! (You see, they have gone over completely to naturopathy, measure the water lines in their house, move the bed and the television if they stand in an unfavorable location, and have been drinking only water for three months, no alcohol. But they almost work themselves to death for their bookstore . . .) Mr. Hoffmann describes his walks through the weekly market in Eutin, recommends its eco-cottage cheese to us ("with fried potatoes! A delicacy!"). We learn what "mud pan" is where they live; he tastes our ham and is told about what is on offer at the delicatessens. In the background news commentators hold forth on the possible variations for the new Schleswig-Holstein parliament of: who must or can go together with whom in order to put together a mathematical majority.

Mr. Hoffmann would like to know if it is actually true that the Poles became afraid of a reunification of the Germans when Honecker visited the Federal Republic. I say: Like the French. Hoffmann thinks that Kohl should walk around among the people here wearing a cap of invisibility sometime and hear what they have to say about his stupid talk about "Germany"— but I again am not so sure about that. And so on. Hoffmanns built in the sixties, and now their house is not sufficiently practical, for example, no dining room-kitchen combination. Actually no plan for a workroom. But they do not throw things away. When you see what people put on the streets beside the Dumpsters on garbage days! Entire sets of furniture. Sofas and chairs. They have had their washing machine for thirty years. Had always bought used cars up until this last one, a Saab. We clean off the table together; I put the dishes in the machine. Before that I sat with Gerd on the edge of his bed and tried to figure out how to set our new alarm clock back. The sun was shining in through the window. I saw Gerd in his typical attitude, somewhat impatient, then triumphant. ("She showed me how to do it. We must still have a description. Just where has it gone now?!") A good everyday moment. Much too seldom am I prepared for those signals, which I, if I only want to, can receive daily, hourly—lucky person.

Without success I still try to call Carola to find out if I perhaps left my raincoat, which is missing, at her place during my last visit.

Now it is ten-thirty. I will begin to write the eulogy for Thomas Brasch as the recipient of the Kleist Prize, which I will have to give on the twenty-fifth of October. That is why I stayed here, of course. In Berlin I will not have much time for that.

I have hardly begun to write, to work out the very first page—which I had already outlined—more precisely, when Frank appears in the kitchen. With his family. We could not stand it in Berlin anymore. We had had it up to here. So at breakfast we said to ourselves: Let's go to the Baltic! But that really is a little bit far, and then we thought to ourselves: Woserin is also quite beautiful—slight despair. I do not let myself be interrupted for more than twenty minutes, put out something for them to drink, and sit down with my text again. But now it is no longer the same. I constantly look at the clock. At twelve-thirty dinner has to be prepared, my peace is gone. Unfortunately I am not the type to work on in spite of such a disturbance. So I go into the kitchen. Biene and I fix fried potatoes and fried eggs; I get herbs and pickles . . . I learn that in his distance learning program Frank failed two intermediate examinations. Why? He didn't enjoy those subjects. And the worst thing is that he also does not know for sure what he wants to do; he cannot imagine doing what he is now studying for forty years. He has even gone to the Chamber of Technology already to inquire about opportunities to learn a trade, but they did not give him any prospects at all. Biene, too, is completely overtaxed with her eighth-grade-graduate apprentices. On the days when she teaches them, she is all worn out in the evening.

I understand that here a young man is afraid of being ground up in the mill of production and that he sees no alternative at all for himself. That he is rattling around aimlessly in the box. Unfortunately he does not have by chance any talent for one of the possible "free" professions. And he has the greatest fear that someday he will no longer notice at all what is happening to him.

A while ago I read a few lines from the diaries of Virginia Woolf and was peculiarly touched by many a similarity in our feelings. But she never lost her focus. I? Appear to be in the process.

Now, while I am writing this—at two in the afternoon—a black wall of clouds had appeared, "squalls," it begins to rain and hail. Bad weather. Over in ten or fifteen minutes. A low from the direction of Ireland, the radio announcer says.

At eleven-thirty on the twenty-eighth of September I continue writing. If it were not my duty to describe the twenty-seventh of September each year, I would not write a line about the rest of yesterday. After I had lain down, had read a few pages in Per Wahlöö's *Operation Steel Jump*, and had slept a bit until Gerd returned and lay down, I got up, played a little ball with Bastel and Frank and Biene on the meadow, drank coffee, ate homemade plum pastry, and talked with them about their daily routine. Then the call came from Dieter.[3]

Helmut had just died while the doctor was working with him.

All of my disquiet and nocturnal fear had been confirmed.

It would be a small comfort, I immediately thought, if we were certain that his death was unavoidable after the accident. But we simply do not have that assurance after our experiences with that hospital. And after the nurse had no idea at all that a man was dying there. Which Dieter, who wanted to make his Sunday visit to him, saw immediately.

I was completely beside myself. I cannot and do not want to write about it. Something was there that concerned only me, far beyond the pain caused by that premature death. A horror and a sadness that I think I will now never get over, that I will be saturated with for the rest of my life. Something that concerns human life and destiny in general and which we do not learn as long as we are young. Which defies discussion. Now I see what depresses the older people so much.

At some point a line went through my head: I do not seek my salvation in growing stiff. / The shudder of horror is the best part of being human—*Shudder*, that is the word. I shudder. In the night I wake up several times, shuddering. That we

[3] Dieter Wolf, "the call came…"; Helmut Wolf (1942-1987), half brother of G.W.; died in a Potsdam hospital following a serious automobile accident.

must all die? Not only that, I believe. That we have lived and do live incorrectly? Yes. That perhaps even more.

I was completely filled with a great love for Gerd. In the evening, in bed, as I was still reading in a book by Gert Heidenreich, *The Woman Who Collected Stones*, he was already turning off the light in the next room, and I heard him breathing loudly. I listened to his breathing and wished to be able to hear it for a long time yet—for as long as I live.

We had to spend a few more hours with Hoffmanns, of course, talk with them about the different ways to build houses, about the prices of land and materials, about the different ways that workmen behave. Had to make the pan of mixed vegetables that I had planned, watch the news, and eat.

I then called Annette and Tinka, also told them how things had gone in the hospital and that Dieter intends to make a "report" about it—Helmut cannot be brought back to life again. I constantly saw him in front of me, as he was a week earlier, when we even took him a radio and thought that he was over the hump. He believed that, too—Tinka then told me about their visit to Martin's brother in Rostock—how depressingly miserably some people have to live here. That she had jumped into the ocean when the water temperature was only twelve degrees centigrade, Helene and Anton, too.

I would have liked to gather them all around me and to hold them each individually.

When the day begins, at midnight, I am still sitting in the large room in front of the television; I am watching the last fifteen minutes of the play "The Blessed Ones," produced by Bergman. It is a television play about the increasing insanity of a married couple, which begins with the wife and eventually leads them to suicide. I see in myself again the resistance to the "insane" behavior of the woman that injures herself and her husband, a resistance that goes to the point of aggression, since that behavior seems extremely egoistic. I am aware that my aversion to those "insane people" is triggered by the trouble and the attacks that I have experienced from them. Besides that, I say to myself, if I were to let myself go completely, I could also very easily drive everyone around me up the wall, but I just pull myself together as long as it is at all possible (as I do again today), so that, for example, Gerd is not also burdened with my depression. The fact that these are all defense and protective mechanisms is only too clear to me; in spite of that, I did not let myself go to the point that I watched a married couple committing suicide with an overdose of pills with satisfaction. After all, I say to myself, the great dictators of this century are also insane, paranoid—why must the healthy always suffer under sick people of that sort?

The keyword "insanity" remains operative, seems to stand like a signal over this day. The news last night brought the report that the black Canadian 100-meter Olympic winner Ben

Johnson will perhaps be disqualified because his urine sample after the victory (in a new, fantastic world-record time!) revealed traces of anabolic steroids. They showed a brief interview given by Johnson during the training period. He said, grinning: Today my muscles are so hard. That comes from those vitamins, you know, those muscle-building vitamins that I take. Those are good pills—Reporter: Yes, yes, the vitamins . . .

The final report: Riots in West Berlin in the vicinity of the opera house, where the participants in the World Bank conference that begins today had a gala evening. The demonstrators shouted "Murderers!" and cursed and spit on the participants. They also destroyed automobiles and shop windows in the city. Seventy people were "provisionally arrested" by the police, who used clubs. I turn off the television set, turn off the light, take the glasses, and walk across the vestibule into the kitchen. Gerd is already asleep, and I am also tired. The usual washings and rituals in the bathroom. Open the window in my room, a pale glow lies on the landscape; the full moon comes from the left from behind the large linden tree; there are also a few bright stars in the sky. ("When pale snow beautifies the fields . . . " Not really appropriate.)

I get into bed, read for another half an hour in the book of an American: John Traute: I—Arturo Bandini. A very young man obsessed with the idea of becoming a writer and getting rich in the process takes out his inferiority complex on a young Mexican waitress. Preface by Charles Bukowski, who discovers an affinity of temperament.

I see a connection between Ben Johnson, the black runner, and Arturo Bandini, who rises from the poorest social class: the envy and ambition of the individual who falls short. The megalomania that develops from ambition and striving for success. I believe that a large percentage of our problems that are getting out of control can be traced back to this kind of masculine megalomania, and I read the book with a certain degree of uneasiness. Put it down around one, fall asleep after a while, wake up at around three, have to go to the toilet, am horrified by my mirror image: grown old; back in bed I see that the moon is apparently shining directly through the window, the window cross casts a shadow on the curtain.

When I wake up at seven o'clock in the morning, it is light (standard time!). I try to hold on to the fragments of dreams, but do not succeed. I go back to sleep until a quarter to eight, then get up, because after eight o'clock the electricity is supposed to be turned off, so that I can still take a shower. Again the weight of depression that has come again and again in recent days, since in the otherwise so enthusiastic letters from Rosemarie and Günter about *Summer Piece* the possibility was indicated that critics would feel themselves called upon "to offend me," and above all, since the question was presented in Günter's letter: "When does one betray a person to art?" To be sure, I have firmly resolved not to surrender to my depression; I want to put up resistance, mentally work against it; I intend to enumerate the arguments that speak in my favor and not simply surrender to the arguments that speak against me. I also do that today, at first without success. Like every day since the operations, I comb out a handful of hair.

While I am in the bathroom, the radio is on. A description of the "riots" last night in Berlin. Then the news: Ben Johnson has actually been disqualified; the gold medal has been taken away from him. He has been expelled from the current Olympic games. Later we hear: The Canadian sports ministry has banned him for life. A fate that unexpectedly depresses me. We saw that powerful muscular colossus strutting around, then triumph; we saw his mother in the stadium, who could not watch the race at all, who held her head bowed and prayed. It was the only possibility for this man to catapult himself upward socially and to become wealthy. He is a weak personality. Not only his life but also that of his family has been destroyed. Question: Can one still compete at all in this highly demanding sport without anabolic steroids? Claims: 70% of the athletes are probably using drugs. Mr. Neckermann reveals his shock: What industrialist will now still put money into a sport that is saturated with doping?

I fix breakfast and call Gerd, who is already sitting at his typewriter, wanting to take advantage of the time when there is still electricity. We talk about the latest news, turn it this way and that. G. is occupied with his intensive work on the essay about Sarah Kirsch,[1] which he must "manage to do" by the end of the week.

(Now I can continue to write with the typewriter. The electricity is on again. It is twenty minutes to four.)

At eight o'clock we hear a short radio broadcast in honor of Bucharin's one-hundredth birthday.[2] His youth, his studies that were encouraged by Lenin, how he found himself in the leftist opposition to Lenin for a time, then, under Stalin, thoroughly criticized his industrialization and collectivization policies . . . The "dozens of millions of dead" during the collectivization. How they isolated Bucharin until he was arrested in 1937. That he was tortured, signed absurd accusations. How he, "whose arms they had dislocated," probably felt that the death sentence in 1938 was a release. How he now, beginning this year, has been rehabilitated in the Soviet Union, posthumously readmitted into the Party, and is constantly mentioned in the press . . .

We increasingly listen to such reports in silence, exchange looks at most. There is nothing more to be said about it. We talk only briefly, worried about a report from yesterday. In a speech, in which he had also warned about the recently bloody

---

[1] G.W.'s essay on Sarah Kirsch, "*Ausschweifungen und Verwünschungen* (Excesses and Imprecations)" in *Text und Kritik*, 101/January 1989. (G.W.)

[2] Nikolai Bucharin (1888-1938), Soviet politician and economic theorist, initially a disciple of Stalin, but later rejected him. (Tr.)

clashes between Armenians and Azerbaijani, Gorbachev had said: Time is running out on us. We are losing the game—Spoken, to be sure, with respect to economic reform, but one can naturally interpret those sentences much more fundamentally. And what will happen, I ask, if he falls? Will the military then come into power? Gerd does not believe that. He only wonders why Gorbachev does not come up with any fundamental ideas for solving the problem of supplying provisions in the Soviet Union. He certainly cannot believe that after a few appeals the people will spit in their hands and begin to work; he should know them better than that. Or perhaps not? It should really be possible to visibly improve the supply situation in a few centers. A kind of Marshall Plan should be introduced—I say, perhaps they do not want to put themselves that far in debt and make themselves dependent.

The electricity goes off, as expected. I rinse off the breakfast dishes with the last water that comes out of the tap and then go to the post office. At last! says Mrs. B., the first customer! She is sitting there reading the newspaper. It is cold in the small room. She says: I must do something, the stove is broken—On the small table to her left, an overflowing ashtray. I pay for yesterday's telegram, to Rome, good wishes for Sandra's baby. Seventeen marks eighty, sixty-five pfennig per word, says Mrs. B. She describes her colleague's reaction when taking down the telegram: To Italy! For Heaven's sake! And in English besides? Then you will have to spell it out!—In addition, I register our radio and our television set here, fill out forms to cancel the newspapers from the 1st of November on, and then exchange a few more words with Mrs. B. That she delivered her geese on the weekend, which she had fed all summer, and that she got far more than 4000 marks for them—almost 3500 marks pure profit, when the expenses are deducted. That is quite a lot, she says, where we can use every mark.

Outside, a penetrating drizzle has begun, not a soul on the

village street, yellow leaves are falling from the linden trees. My head is spinning with the arguments that I wrote to Günter de Bruyn in response to his letter about *Summer Piece*, in which, among other things, he discussed the problem of a method that employs other, close associates as "material." I ask myself if my counterarguments—that one can also create a literary monument for somebody; that I live in a very unliterary manner with the people whom I love, pay the full price of happiness and pain for the peaks and valleys of that coexistence, and am only able to see us all as characters much later; that I attempt to deal with myself as ruthlessly as possible—if all of those arguments are only defensive assertions, rationalizations for an inability: for apparently, of course, if I remain in the present, I can not only invent, but I come back to experienced material, i.e. also back to "real" persons again and again. When I think of future plans, that circumstance appears to become a handicap for me. At this point I always call to mind the names of other authors who remained close to their own life's material—Thomas Wolfe, Salinger—and then I read a few pages in Joseph Conrad's *Nostromo*—which thematically does not interest me very much at all—and envy him the objectivity of his nonetheless subjectively colored presentation.

So the thought carousel is in motion; and uneasily I register the fact that that I am already once again unable to stop it. And I had actually been able to think, in the hospital, when I was ill, that after that the depressions, the act of circling around such problems would no longer afflict me. I "knew," of course, that I had secured a respite for my soul at the cost of my frazzled body. Now I see that the problems have not been resolved, and whether I can deal with them in a more sovereign manner than before is doubtful.

I am now approached on the village street by a young, intelligent-looking man whom I do not know and cheerfully greet in return. The storm has knocked hundreds of chestnuts from the trees. I step on them, but I no longer bend down to pick them up; I have gathered enough of them. The institution director's wife is in the cooperative store; in order to say something at all, I ask her if she is responsible for this weather. She says: No, not her, and then says goodbye and leaves. Just as Mrs. M. is about to pack my eggs, which I am buying as instructed for Tinka and Martin's party, the mail car comes. Mrs. M. has to go outside and leaves me standing there. Simultaneously meat is delivered at the back door; two boxes of sausage are missing. I hear her talking back and forth with the driver, yes, the boxes were incorrectly labeled and delivered to a different sales outlet, she should call them up; what, she doesn't have a telephone? Well, then she will have to weigh out the goods and write a report about what is missing, and he will confirm it. And so on. I become impatient. Finally she waits on me again; I do not buy much, of course, in addition to the milk and eggs, just two bottles of Grauer Mönch, also for the party. Mr. B. comes in and asks the sales clerk if she can use fish. She says: No, she will be closing by noon today, and she would therefore not get rid of the fish. I ask him what kind of fish he has, he says: Pike and perch. I say we would gladly take a pike. He says that he will bring one and that I should come to his place at twelve.

Back through the drizzle. Again the young man comes toward me; he is carrying a machine part. Then the old neighbor woman comes, and finally even Mr. W., who touches his cap. Good day. Good day. One of the new young women with a child greets me without smiling—I notice that in general with all these young women. They do not condescend to friendliness.

I have forgotten the key to the mailbox, put the bags down on the veranda, and have to go back. Only one letter is there besides the newspapers, from Günter de Bruyn again, this time to Gerd; he asks him if they have to put up with the new regulations in the contracts for the Poets' Association of the Brandenburg March, according to which they will no longer receive any West shares of the honorarium for books sold in the West. We also believe that they do not have to put up with that. Gerd wants to call the legal counsel of the Writers' Union, but does not reach him.

I sit down in my wicker chair and scan the newspapers. Honecker is traveling to Moscow for a working visit. The satellite "Cosmos 1900," which has gone out of control and has a nuclear reactor aboard, burns up in the atmosphere at the beginning of October—In Teltow a new kind of rabbit plague has appeared. One third of the citizens of Schwerin are too heavy. Consumption of alcohol and abuse of medicines are continually increasing. At least thirty to forty percent of the patients who seek out their family physician indicate emotional causes for their illness. (Why does such a report comfort me?)

I sit down at the desk and begin these writings, by hand, because the typewriter needs an electrical connection, of course. The little battery-powered radio is on. In the "Office Hour" they talk about cancer illnesses; a pleasant doctor's voice talks about the fact that they must not lie to cancer patients. Cancer patients call up and describe their sufferings, their operations, and ask questions in order to have their hopes confirmed. There are short reports: In the German Democratic Republic alcohol consumption is two and a half times as great as in the Federal Republic (no wonder, I think, with the spreading monotony and boredom). According to recent investigations, children in cities with lead-processing industries become bearers of real intellectual deficits.—At the beginning of October the working group for mucoviscidosis—a word for a metabolic illness that leads to death in young people, which I hear for the first time—will sponsor an information day.

At twelve I go over to B.'s, knock, since the bell does not work, and wait a few minutes until B. comes with his bicycle.

He forgot the pike. I am supposed to pick it up later this afternoon. So we do fall back on the beets; I go to the garden and
harvest the greens as the rain increases, while Gerd is already
putting the potatoes on. Should I do that? he had asked me as
I was going out. I said, No, I quite enjoy doing something like
that. Otherwise I feel too lonely—Lonely? he then asked when
I came back—I said something about being "depressed." He
asked: "Why?" I indicated the reason: my anxiety with regard
to the appearance of the book and its consequences next year,
my brooding about the letter from the de Bruyns. Gerd says,
but I really should have that behind me now, after this year (he
does not say: "on the brink of death," but I know that he thinks
that). Those really aren't capital matters now—The words help
me. I can clearly visualize my condition in the hospital again
and my firm conviction that after that capital threat[3] the other
problems would no longer press me so much.

I fix myself a fried egg. Gerd refuses to eat one because of
his cholesterol level. We eat, but I cannot wash up because
there is no water. I stack up the dishes and lie down somewhat
relieved. Gerd comments on the report that Rakowski[4] is the
new Polish minister president: Now he probably thinks that he
can save Poland. They always think that, otherwise they would
not do it.

Before falling asleep I read in the *Wochenpost*. Gerd had
pointed out the article to me in which the faulty performance
of the computer during the most recent Soviet space landing is
described in detail: how two attempts to land failed in that
manner, but then the man "calmly" observed: We will make it
the third time—If not, no additional attempt would have followed. Air and food supplies in the small landing capsule

[3] Capital threat: Following an appendectomy C.W. developed a life-threatening case of
peritonitis, background for the later narrative *Leibhaftig* (*In the Flesh*), Munich, 2002.
(G.W.)

[4] Mieczslav Rakowski, Polish politician, journalist, minister president. (Tr.)

would have quickly run out; they would not have reached the space shuttle, nor could a backup space ship from the earth have helped them anymore—

My mind is occupied at least to an equal extent by a court report: Three youths, apprentices, oppressed, tortured, humiliated, beat, and vented their anger on a fellow student, Daniel, for years. The entire class watched coldly, teachers and educators left it at occasional warnings, until that boy no longer wanted to attend the trade school. How those three fellows, who have now been labeled "rowdies," came before the court, I do not know. They received two years of probation with a threatened prison sentence of eight months—they are supposed to work "diligently" in their collectives. As always the authorities do not get to the bottom of the motives for their behavior. It is said that they themselves were once picked on in their class—but that really was not a justification for their behavior—Perhaps it is. Above all, however: why does that behavior continue from generation to generation? Why is there this struggle for preeminence among the youth, which can often only be decided through the oppression of weaker individuals for one's own benefit? "Three Against One" is the title of the article. As if that were the essential thing about this case.

I also read Tinka's article about the Godot production in the People's Theater again, am happy about her fluid style, her certain judgment, but am also irritated about the two sentences that were added to her article without her permission—an appeal not to let it rest with waiting!—tomorrow she will be thirty-two, I think, still young, young.

I sleep. At a quarter to three I get up, still no electricity. We decide "to go out for a little while" for a change and to drink tea after that. It begins to rain. We arrive at B.'s, and Mrs. Buchholz, who complained about how long she had had to wait in the doctor's office in Sternberg, calls through the doorway: Did you turn off all of your water taps? The electricity just came on!—Then Gerd trots back home; he wants to sit at his little machine, and it is also raining too hard. So I make tea, take him his glass, quickly wash up the midday dishes, and while doing so hear from the radio (this is a media day!) a report about the Kranichstein Literature Days, which I had never heard of before. It begins with the reporter asking himself why writers actually go to that sort of event at all, since they really should know that it is a matter of platforms for the self-stylization of the critics at the expense of the authors—in this case it was a matter of prizes and stipends from a literature fund; the critics ran down the authors to the point that one of the prize-winners later furiously rejected his stipend. I was in complete agreement with the reporter; I have often asked myself why anyone goes to that Bachmann Prize critics' spectacle and throws him/herself to the gathered augurs as fodder—I would never do it. Do the authors have a thicker skin? Do they have illusions, or what? So, now to the typewriter, to describe the day. Thus writing eats up life; that always becomes most clear on this day. That is one reason why I cling to this report (other reasons: a possibly productive set of material is piling up, and: I am placing points of memory in the ocean of forgetfulness).

So I write until five-thirty, then I break off to write little Helene her birthday letter. I invent a story about the very small dwarf Erwin who does not find himself a suitable wife until late, Malvida, who is now expecting a child and is becoming moody. Writing the letter cheers me up a bit. Additionally a card to my father, to whom I announce my visit at the beginning of next week. I see before me, as so often, the images of his old-age misery; I do not hide from myself the wish that he might die before his prostate cancer becomes noticeable. With horror I see the danger of having to experience something similar, for one of us in advance, but must ask myself at the same time, why I then did not simply take advantage of the opportunity to depart decently, which offered itself this year. If it will not always be that way, if I, too, will not, as my father does, postpone the date of my own death further and further, even if it is, as it now is in his case, only for one or two years. I also know precisely—and especially since this summer—that the involuntary death wish, which always arises in circumstances of depression, is not "authentic," i.e. not permanent and that it does not hold out against the normal frame of mind, yes, becomes foreign and incomprehensible to it. I still ask myself how it was possible that I did not fully and clearly recognize the danger in which I found myself during the initial weeks in the hospital. So apparently there really are those defense mechanisms of which the doctors speak, and for the person who is endangered they are impenetrable—if a thoughtless word does not break through that protective shell.

Just when I want to go mail the letters, Gerd calls me to the telephone. My English translator of *Accident: A Day's News* is calling from Berlin, where she is participating in a translators' seminar. I answer a few more questions for her with regard to quotes in the text. She says that she and her husband have lived with that book for months and had even argued about the translation, but that it was a productive argument, and asks if I would not like to come to England in the spring when the book appears. I say no. Then we talk about the title, *accident* is not a perfect translation for the German word *Störfall*. At first they had wanted to call it *Mere Accident*, but the publishers had been against that, and I, too, do not feel that it is a good title. By the way, there was also the same difficulty with the translation of that title into other languages. We almost always have to make cuts there.

So to the mailbox; it is not yet seven and almost dark—standard time!—I ring B.'s doorbell for a long time before she opens the door: A pike? My husband undoubtedly forgot it!—

That is how it is. Crestfallen, Mr. Buchholz wants to ride to the fishing cooperative once more to get the pike; I prevent him from doing that. He will definitely bring it tomorrow after breakfast. (While I am writing this—it is the next morning—a gigantic pike is lying on our kitchen table.)

Television. The seven-o'clock news. Pictures of the enormous hall in which the World Bank meeting is taking place: all of them money and currency experts, well-to-do people. Several hundred of them pay hard currency to stay in the noble hotels of East Berlin, are picked up and returned in luxury limousines, are immediately let through at the border; state security watches out for their welfare, and those young people who, under the wing of the Church in the German Democratic Republic, also protest against exploitation of the Third World by capitalist financiers, are urgently admonished to maintain peace and order and are constantly checked. That is how things have changed; the state, which still calls itself socialist, protects and defends capitalist financiers, while young Christians represent socialist ideals and use their tracts to attack the functionaries and the "clerics," of which the latter, however, just demanded a "society with a human face" in their synod . . . Whereupon the first representative of this state, at a martial event commemorating the anniversary of the armed industrial militia groups, turned against "people who really should know better" and documented the humaneness of our society in the fact that during the last year thirty thousand apartments were turned over to their occupants . . .

Telephone again. Irina Karintzeva, the Russian translator of *Accident: A Day's News*—she, too, is at this translators' seminar. Regrets immensely that we cannot see each other. When asked about the "situation" in her homeland, she becomes sad and melancholy. Oh, everything has gotten worse. They could already see that at the Party conference, the way the elections went, for example, and now they are experiencing the consequences. The opposing forces, you understand, are strong and getting stronger. The economy—well, we did not think that it could improve rapidly; but it really should not constantly grow worse! She feels hurt by many things that are now happening. Yes, of course, if "he" (Gorbachev) did not come through—that would be inconceivable. An unimaginable catastrophe!—She will call again; I am supposed to identify a contribution from my essays for her new periodical *Horizont*.

Gerd gives me the fifteen pages of his essay about Sarah Kirsch; he calls it "Excesses and Imprecations." I read it; he sharpens a pencil expressly for me, so that I can correct commas and draw a few squiggles in the margin where a sentence does not seem harmonious to me. As always I read the poems about which he writes, now differently from before, understand them better, and see the relationships into which he places them. I am especially touched by the section in which he differentiates between Sarah's own tone and the tones of her masculine lyrical collaborator. Is that actually true, he asks, when I write here: They speak pornographically and mean eroticism? I had also wondered about that sentence, believe that it is more correct to say that they speak pornographically in order to avoid eroticism—He accepts it that way—I have probably mortally insulted some people here, he says. I try to soothe him because I do not like to think that he might be exposed to the aggressiveness of those authors who are, of course, easily insulted.

I fix supper, farina soup for Gerd, who has stomach or intestinal problems and is therefore on a diet; for myself I warm up the goulash from the day before yesterday. I get myself a large bottle of beer from the cellar to go with it. I then eat too much, although the time is past when I had to make up for the pounds that I lost in the hospital. Gerd cleans up; I actually watch—which happens very seldom—the "Dallas" series, infinitely desolate, but there "isn't anything" on any of the other stations, and we do not want to watch the Olympics again right now. On our station there is a comedy that Gerd feels is even worse than "Dallas," and unfortunately watching television in the evening has become too much of a pattern for us to simply do without it. Rewarding then, "Contrasts." First a contribution from an East German environmental group about Bitterfeld, pictures of a destroyed, wretched landscape, statistics about the health burden of the people who live there, corroded buildings, desolate cityscape. Commentated by a young man who assisted in one of those environmental groups until July and is now in West Berlin. After that an extensive report about the extermination of all life in the Werra River by potash factories in the German Democratic Republic, which shamelessly pour all of their waste water into the river without purifying it and are now demanding that the West provide, without compensation, a newly developed desalinization system, which they, however, do not want to deliver because some by-products are produced with it, for which the West itself has laboriously developed a market in which it does not need any competitors. Infuriating, sad pictures of the dead, foaming river.

It is ten-thirty. I usually stay up much longer; today I am tired, undoubtedly also because of the beer. In bed I read the manuscript *Bottom Attitude*, which Cornelia Wyhl[5] sent me from Zurich. I pushed it around in front of me for two weeks. Now I am fascinated after all, although I cannot hide from myself the fact that the text is not pleasant and probably does not have much chance with publishers. While reading, I clearly see her before me; I also believe that she really expresses herself in this text and that she is gifted. In spite of that I must ask myself if I did not give her too much hope in Zurich last year—a question that I have already often had to ask myself and which

[5] Cornelia Wyhl: In the winter semester of 1987 C. and G.W. assumed responsibility for Adolf Muschg's writing seminar at the Technical University in Zurich; there they also met Cornelia Wyhl. (G.W.)

I would most prefer to resolve by not repeatedly championing talents that find it so difficult to gain acceptance. Only, when you have them in front of you that just cannot be done . . .

It is eleven-thirty when I go to sleep. Once I wake up at around three, have dreamt that a theater group, to which Tinka also belongs, wants to stage something by me. Again we sit in large rooms that are unfamiliar to me. There is talk. What I remember most clearly is that Käthe R. is with us and participates objectively, if not courteously, in the conversation, and that this circumstance comforts me as I wake up.

When I wake up for good at seven, I still feel the pressure of depression and fear in my stomach region, and the thought carousel starts up again. Then Gerd comes over from his room. So, are you still brooding?—Yes, I say—You have too much free time here and are alone too much. And these days I am also not the right conversational partner for you, he says—I say again: Yes. He says, with Günter de Bruyn, his somewhat apodictic attitude is also interlarded with a shot of professional jealousy. I should keep that in mind; it is not intended to be malicious, but it is quite unavoidable. As for the rest, he feels that it would be good for us to enter once more into a more vital working relationship with the two of them in this way; and I say (and also mean it) that I feel that way, too. We should, he says, start talking about my next book sometime. Actually I am in a very good position right now—free, without responsibilities; in my place he would drag out that excuse with my illness for at least the entire next year and not let myself get involved in too many events again—Yes, I say, I do not want that either, but here I have lost contact with the new generation, and I want to look around a bit there—Yes, he says, do that, but purposefully, in a way that is already related to your work. And then during the winter we should simply talk about it a bit. Perhaps the whole thing could simply be called *The House*—Yes, I say, that would be possible, but I already have a better title: *The Labyrinth*. He says: Yes, that works; all that is missing is a grotesque idea, like with *The Master and Margarita*—Oh, God, I say, you're telling me!—Oh, well, he says, it will be all right. Don't get discouraged, don't be despondent. You don't have any reason to be.

At that moment I suddenly feel that way, too. Only then is the previous day over for me. In a different mood I can later gather up the many, many nuts with him outside, which are now either falling "naked" from their hulls that have burst open on the tree, or are lying in the grass in their green or brown mushy skins, and which you have to pick out with gloves, because otherwise your hands will turn brown and remain that way for weeks. I like that housing of the nuts very much; I examine precisely the white slime that still envelops many of them, and the little brown clump of hair by which they cling to the hull.

Then I sit down at the typewriter to finish these writings.

FRIDAY, SEPTEMBER 29, 1989
Woserin

The weather seems to be holding today as well. When I draw back my curtains this morning at around seven-thirty, I can hope for a similarly deep-blue sky that is interwoven with enormous white cloud formations, like yesterday, when we presented that sky to the Aichers,[1] while they were still at the small rural railroad station in Blankenburg and had hardly gotten off the train with their suitcases, in lieu of other sights: Well, aren't these northern skies something special? They generously admitted it. The only one who did not appear to be deeply astonished that this meeting, which had been arranged for this day a year and a half earlier at their place in Rotis, was Otl. For him it was quite natural to keep such long-range promises. Only that which is precise becomes concrete! is one of his maxims, which are all drawn from experience, never from theory alone. Had they crossed the border at Herrnburg easily? They had. Without difficulties? Without. The East German border guards probably have reason to be polite to Western travelers.

[1] Aichers: Otl Aicher (1922-1991) and his wife Inge Aicher-Scholl (1917-2000), with whom the Wolfs had become acquainted in 1987 on the occasion of the awarding of the Geschwister Scholl literary prize to C.W., were in lively, friendly contact with the Wolfs afterward. The Wolfs visited the Aichers in Rotis/Allgäu in May of 1988 and the latter reciprocated by visiting the Wolfs in Mecklenburg in September of 1989. Otl Aicher described that encounter in his text "*Mecklenburg Herbst 89* (Mecklenburg Autumn 89)" (see: Otl Aicher, *Schreiben und Widersprechen* [*Writing and Contradicting*], Berlin, 1993). For the books of his Gerhard Wolf Janus Press Publishing Company, established in 1990, G.W. selected Otl Aicher's typography *rotis*; Aicher advised Martin Hoffmann in the production of the first titles and gave G.W. the first manuscript of his political essays, which was then published by Janus Press. (G.W.)

We drove the two short stretches via Brüel and Sternberg to Woserin, which we know in detail, but which I saw with other eyes in their presence. All of the street damage, all of the run-down houses along that stretch, to which I am accustomed, caught my eye. Like a backdrop, the image in my memory traveled along from the neat villages and small towns of Allgäu, in which Otl Aicher's "Autonomous Republic of Rotis" lies. No material, we would later say, no foreign currency. No material! we also said as we showed them our house, which, after all, we had been rescuing from its decay, putting in decent condition for five years; it was habitable, certainly, and more than that: a work and vacation house, also for the children, grandchildren, and friends. It had already added patina, already produced stories, even myths, but could you tell that by looking at it? Or did you see above all its flaws? So that they did not have to say it, we said: There is still much to do, and Inge, affectionately—sensitively—perceived its virtues, finally the incomparable view from the windows of the guestroom, while Otl, the expert, had Gerd describe for him the condition in which we had found the house, the individual steps of the reconstruction, and the immediate plans. Amid this knowledgeable discussion my fainthearted fear that "we" would come off too badly in comparison with "them" disappeared, although, of course, all of our unceasing, almost uninterrupted talk since their arrival, if you really think about it, was one single act of comparison. And when we then, after a simple "all-German" vegetable soup and Mecklenburg red jelly, and after a short nap, went to the lake and "to the hills," I knew once again that this is my landscape. We stood silently on the lakeshore and took the silence into ourselves, and I asked myself if the Vorall-gäu region from which the Aichers came could ever look as melancholy as our early autumn lake, which lay there dark and mirror smooth. To the left, the racks for trout breeding, on the right shore the gentle beginning of the autumn coloring of the

beech forest. All of these, I was aware, were contrast images to
the landscapes to which Inge and Otl had been accustomed
since their childhood.

They were amazed at the large cooperative barns. We
explained the organization and the production approach of the
farm cooperative and then saw, from the hills, the large herd of
cattle lying on the meadow chewing their cuds. When the milk
truck came, the cows trotted amiably and placidly to the milk-
ing barn and patiently took their places—an image that Otl
had never seen before. Is that productive? he wanted to know.
Economical? He asked about the milk production and retail
prices. There we had to pass.

In pairs—two men, two women—we went a little way further through the beech woods; Inge and I talked about children and grandchildren. I complained that my large supply of
songs was running out and that no new ones occurred to me
during the singing periods with my grandchildren. Inge was
familiar with the problem, and she taught me: "*Ich armes
welsches Teufli, ich kann nicht mehr marschieren* . . . (I, poor
foreign devil, I can no longer march . . .)"

At home we immediately pushed the radio button in the
kitchen and listened to the news reports, which—since the
Hungarians took down the border fences between them and
Austria, and Austria opened its doors to East German citizens—deal primarily with this one topic: the stream of refugees
from the German Democratic Republic. Hundreds have again
arrived in Austria from Hungary, in their own cars, on buses,
and by train, and in the Prague embassy there are meanwhile
close to five thousand people, among them many children;
they live in extremely tight quarters in tents in the embassy garden, where the grounds have been transformed into a morass
by the autumn rains; they talk of the first cases of diarrhea
among the children, and the word "dysentery" has already
appeared. Apparently nobody knows how this debacle might

be ended. In Warsaw, too, several hundred citizens of the German Democratic Republic have taken refuge in the West German embassy. The new government under a minister president from "*Solidarnósz*" is more cooperative toward them than the authorities in Prague and has assured the refugees that they will not be deported to the German Democratic Republic against their will.

Otl took note of the many news sources in our house; that had not occurred to us before. It is natural for us to listen to news on Radio Germany every half hour. All of our senses are focused on Berlin. We could not hide our dejection and perplexity. After supper we sat around the kitchen table, talked about the reasons for this exodus of East German citizens, and Otl suggested that each of us should try to see his or her country from outside and to convey to the others what he or she saw there. A kind of game that quickly became serious. We should have recorded it on tape. Today already, one day later, I can no longer remember all of the details of our conversation, which, accompanied by a few bottles of red wine, lasted into the night. While I take a shower in Tinka's bathroom—we have turned our bathroom over to the Aichers—get dressed, and prepare breakfast with Gerd in the kitchen, I try to remember again the most important points of our "system comparison"—that is what we ironically called it late at night.

The initial situation after the war, said Otl, was actually similar in the two states: the lower classes of the populace had lost their aristocracy, which had been too deeply involved in the Nazi crimes; economically everyone had sunk to the lowest level, and everyone "was" what he or she acquired through personal effort. When reconstruction began, in the Federal Republic there were enormous opportunities for creative individuals, which were not directed and limited by the state; the market economy had been able to develop its virtues in many small and mid-sized businesses. They had, Otl said, lived for a long time without internal social conflict, in what many believed to be the most democratic democracy. While in your country, Otl said, under the other occupying power, from the very beginning people were led by the nose and dispossessed . . .

. . . and above all things were dismantled, we said. What was still standing with respect to factories, machines, and even railroad tracks was dismantled and taken eastward . . .

. . . Yes. We had paid the reparations for all of Germany, said Otl, while in the West they had gotten a good start thanks to the Marshall Plan. And many had seen themselves as being justified after the fact. They were validated by the fact that they were supposed to legitimize their democratic attitude through anti-communism, and otherwise, after a brief phase of de-Nazification, remained undisturbed . . .

. . . while here, we said, the administrations, the schools, the justice system, and the army were rigorously cleansed of Nazis, and the word "antifascist" appeared in the state designation: antifascist democratic fundamental order, which never made the claim that it was a bourgeois democracy, which, of course, had been so susceptible to the National Socialist ideology. Back then, after the shock of learning the truth about the misdeeds of the Nazi regime, that very thing won us young people over for this new state: the fact that it grabbed the evil by the roots and tore it out . . .

. . . But, said Otl, replaced that evil with the thoroughly organized state . . .

. . . Which we had supposedly wanted to vanquish, but which unfortunately, during times of intensified class struggle, was not possible . . .

. . . As in our country, during the period of the Cold War, the strict observance of human rights was unfortunately not possible.

Thus our respective new upper classes each used the other German state as the enemy image. But, we said, our state—

much more than theirs—had remained a state of the common people; villa districts like those that we had seen during occasional visits to Frankfurt am Main and Munich and Hamburg do not exist here. There are not those social differences; the children of workers were given preference for entrance into the educational institutions—and not, as was the case in their country, subjected to discrimination. And there was—which we considered to be the most important thing—no private property with respect to the means of production, no private firms with their devastating consequences; we had always focused our eyes on that when despair with respect to this state was about to overpower us in recent decades. On that basis it should be possible to reform, to improve, and to democratize it. After the suppression of the Prague Spring, however, that hope evaporated for us, but without the Federal Republic, for example, appearing to be a desirable alternative for us. We had consciously practiced living without an alternative.

Perhaps, says Otl Aicher pensively, this place here, an enclave in the middle of Mecklenburg, and this point in time, when your state is being put into question by masses of people, will suddenly permit other insights and views regarding our two countries. I thought: And the improbable meeting of these two couples here and now. How would our marriage have actually turned out if we were living in the Federal Republic? Would it have "turned out" at all? Would it have endured as it has done here, where the external pressure causes the wish for *one* certainty, for *one* durable element to become so strong; the wish for a person upon whom you can depend unconditionally and absolutely and under all circumstances. And I became painfully aware that resistant people like Otl and Inge could not have lived in the German Democratic Republic. And we probably not in the Federal Republic. By the way, Inge said, most people here surely do not know at all that we still have to pay a fine because we participated in the protests against nuclear armament; that in our country people are still sitting in jail for doing that—Even we had not known that.

As a state, the Federal Republic, Otl said, is perhaps a democratic democracy, but—contrary to what they had hoped for in 1945 and to what the founding fathers of the Basic Law would certainly have wanted—not a democracy of human rights but a democracy that protects property and consumption. Over-consumption in the meantime—it is needed to keep the wheels of the economy running. For that, false needs must be massively supported or awakened: freedom to drive for free citizens! In practical terms an advertising slogan for Mercedes as a motto for freedom in general.

Yes, but—didn't the thousands of East German citizens that were now pouring into the Federal Republic want that very thing? Consumer goods? we asked. Otl and Inge saw that as understandable after a period of lack. One ought to be able to buy a well functioning automobile in Central Europe these days at an affordable price in a reasonable amount of time, Otl felt. And not wait for twenty years for a weak product. And our thoroughly planned state with its totally controlled economy was just not able to do that—to satisfy justified needs. And all of the state machinery is centrally managed and controlled from above in exactly the same way, perhaps originally oriented around Hegel's ideas at one time, but, although the opposite is always claimed, quite mechanistic with its "wheels of progress" that will unavoidably move history toward a happy final condition.

We could also see that as a goal, we said. We called it communism. We noticed that the lauded dialectic and with it the contradictions and the opposition were more and more rapidly, more and more strongly eliminated, and we criticized that, but initially considered it to be a correctible error. Or a necessity of the class struggle. Until we recognized it as intended and legitimate under the prevailing circumstances—under the authority conditions here.

They had also had to swallow many a toad, said Otl. Last but not least, under the banner and under the pretext of anti-communism, they, radical democrats that they were, had experienced a hollowing out of democracy, in the direction of a representative democracy in which governing does not occur from the bottom up; in the direction of a party, actually a two-party state in which the ruling and the opposition party are united to form a power cartel and the parliament is employed as a mechanism for agreement. The Federal Republic was put out of operation.

I do not know—was it the same melancholy with which we looked at each other and, toasting each other, drank the last swallow of red wine? We stepped outside once more and looked up into the star-studded sky. Like in Rotis, said Inge. And Otl, after we had said good night to each other, while still on the stairs leading to their garret, with a kind of grim humor: Most of history up until now has been in vain. A statement that followed me into my sleep.

A glorious day. We want to show the Aichers Mecklenburg. At breakfast we decide to drive to Güstrow today, and specifically "by the back way," where we will pass through forsaken villages, with neglected manor houses, with the rows of tiny, adjacent servants' and field workers' houses, built of red bricks, and those half-timbered houses of the somewhat more well-to-do small farmers, where the farmers who belong to the cooperative now live, whose wives still take care of the front gardens and now, in the autumn, draw the most beautiful colors from them with dahlias, asters, grass-of-Parnassus, and mallows. Those farmers' gardens are different from the ones where we come from, the Aichers say, and Otl: It's obvious, of course. Different social structures produce different construction methods. The enormous fields without border markers simply fit together with the enormous barns on the outskirts of the villages. Is that the future of agriculture? But the Eastern

Elbe estate whose ruins he now sees here for the first time
probably wasn't it either . . .

We drive first to Barlach's studio house on Inselsee. Here,
and later in the Gertrude Chapel, I see the often seen Barlach
figures with new eyes. They agitate and comfort at the same
time; I would like to find out how. For a long time I stop in
front of the "Doubter" who wrings his hands in pain, but
whose face has already found peace, as if he were now even
permitting himself to doubt and to fall away from the faith: I
cannot do otherwise. As if he could, since he seriously believed
and now seriously doubts, forgive himself at last—Then I
stand for a long time in front of the wooden sculpture of the
Wanderer in the Wind which Barlach created in 1934 when it
was clear to him what kind of era had dawned. He pulls himself together. He holds his helmet-like head covering tightly; he
draws his coat more closely around him; he makes sure of his
strength. The opposing wind is strong, but he will endure—
And today for the first time I actually "see" the group "The
Reunion," which touches me deeply, I do not know why. The
two men are Jesus and doubting Thomas, I read. Thomas, who
did not want to believe that the resurrected Jesus appeared
before him until he had touched Him. Now he almost falls to
his knees, clings to Him, and looks at Him earnestly pleading.
He, however, does embrace the pleading man, holds him, too,
but rigidly looks past him. Not punishing, not perhaps vindic-
tive. So fine, the unbeliever is transformed into a believer. But
He himself, who is believed in: what does He believe in? The
pain has distorted His face into a mask. Oh, if you knew! the
sightless eyes seem to say. He is lonely and must be so.

That is how it is, says each of these figures. No concession.
There is lamentation. But no self-pity. That is just how it is, that
bad. And to know that, therein lies the comfort.

Until now, Otl and Inge have not sought experience with art
this far into the East. It becomes clear to me that a powerful

east wind must blow toward them from Barlach's Russian figures, distance, and the smell of the steppes—toward them,
whose life and works faced toward the West. They must feel
that they are at the edge of their world here. We buy two copies
of a volume of Barlach's pictures and Otl and I each write in
one of them the same text: "We are in Barlach's studio and are
looking at his works." Then all four of us sign our names in turn
and exchange the volumes in a mock-serious ceremony.

Everyone understands that Barlach was a thorn in the side
of the National Socialists. The fact that here in the fifties he
was included among the "formalists" and attacked is no longer
mentioned anywhere. Shame may be the reason to keep that
quiet now. While we are driving we tell the Aichers that Brecht
defended him and in so doing brought about his rehabilitation.
We talk about Franz Fühmann's story about Barlach, "The
Bad Year," in which he describes in a thinly veiled manner the
struggle of the artist for his truth and for honesty—with himself and against the intervention of the state and censorship.
We tell about the East German film cooperative's Barlach film
The Angel, for which Fühmann wrote the screenplay and
which could only be shown in an edited version. The Aichers
are not familiar with the name Franz Fühmann, have never
heard of him. I think, if anything at all announces that we have
moved apart, it is that the potential allies in East and West
Germany do not know each other.

We walk through the old Güstrow streets to the cathedral.
Everywhere there is a lot that needs to be done in order to stop
the impending decay; the Aichers refrain from making almost
any comments. In their minds they must see the clean little
towns in Allgäu, I think, in which not a single tile can fall from
a roof without being restored immediately.

Within me arises the word that may have been stimulated by
Barlach's figures and our conversation about Fühmann, as well
as by these deteriorating little houses along the street: futility.

We only glance at the houses on the cathedral square; in the cathedral we go past the acolytes' bench, past the burial niches of the Mecklenburg princes and their wives, also past the precious apostle figures of Claus Berg, which are reminiscent of the carvings of Veit Stoss.[2] The Aichers take note of the fact that they are in Protestant territory where, during the Luther period, Catholic cathedrals were first closed and then transformed into Protestant churches—inconceivable in the staunchly Catholic regions from which they come and in whose faith they were raised and have endured. We strive to reach the northern side chapel; we want to show the Aichers Barlach's angel—that is what we call the figure that is actually known as "The Hovering Man"; but for me, since "he" has the head of Käthe Kollwitz, the figure can never be a man, always a hovering woman, a memorial by Barlach for those who fell in the First World War, among whom was also Käthe Kollwitz's son Hans. It was removed from the cathedral by the Nazis and was later even melted down. Fortunately a bronze mold had been preserved, from which a second cast was made in Cologne after the war, which was turned over to the cathedral congregation in Güstrow in 1953. Because of that figure alone, we all felt that the visit to Güstrow was worth it.

It is midday. We are tired of sightseeing. Brief glances that we cast into some restaurants as we pass by reveal to us that any attempt to get a table here will be in vain. Since we had anticipated that this would be the case, we have a well-stocked picnic basket in the trunk, which we bring out and unpack at a rest stop in the woods along the Sternberg stretch of road. There are also cushions to sit on and boiled eggs, tomatoes, ham, cheese, coffee, and apple juice. Our mood gets better and better.

What are we going to do with the afternoon that has already

[2] Veit Stoss (late fifteenth-early sixteenth centuries), German sculptor of the late Gothic period. (Ed.)

begun? Well, aren't you tired? Not at all. Hesitantly: Well then, do you perhaps now want to see the excavation of a Slavic cult hall that was faithfully restored and rebuilt? Where? In Gross Raden. How far? Less than thirty minutes, just beyond Sternberg. Well, let's go. We can sleep in the car.

I catch myself being proud, when Otl Aicher, in the museum of the Slavic temple grounds in Gross Raden laconically says: Well done!, even though I do not know if he means the displayed wooden tools of the early Slavs or the manner in which the museum displays them. Most impressive is the open-air museum, which conveys a picture of the way of life of the Northwest Slavs a thousand years ago in this area, which they had once completely occupied, to which many place names still bear witness today. The cult hall, artfully framed entirely of wood, impresses us each time we come. Otl is most interested in the evidence pertaining to everyday culture—how the boards for the cult hall were shaped, how they were fitted together. We talk about the non-simultaneity of developments. When the Slavs, and also the Germanic tribes who later expelled them, were still working here with wooden tools and had no distinctive images of deity (at least they found none during these excavations), the Mediterranean region already had a thousand-year-old cultural and religious history behind it, the evidences of which still pertain to us and take our breath away. The influence boundary of these different cultures runs through Germany, approximately along the current border between the German Democratic Republic and the Federal Republic. The two parts of the nation, if we want to call them that, stand with their backs toward each other, the one group with their eyes turned westward, the other with their eyes turned eastward—and not just since 1945. Such differences, Otl thinks, should be better known and taken into account in the West. And now he can also understand why the people of Mecklenburg, although North Germans, are usually not tall, blond people, like the Frisians, for example, but, with the Slavic blood in their veins, are often round-headed and thickset.

We content ourselves with a long look at the open-air museum and dispense for today with walking across the plank path to the castle wall and to the restored cabin on the island, to which the former inhabitants probably retreated when they were attacked. The Aichers feel that it was important to come here; only this glance back into history gives a landscape vividness and depth.

Late afternoon. At home we are able to lie down for an hour. Gerd goes to the fishmonger's across the street and picks up the ordered fish and crayfish, brings sorrel from the garden at the same time, and gets up again soon to make the sorrel soup and to prepare the crayfish and the fish. When we are then sitting in the kitchen again after seven o'clock, the entire house smells like the fish. Sorrel soup, crayfish, and pike, all from our village. Cress and lettuce from the garden. Otl says: Inge, they cook here as well as they do at home. A happy moment for Gerd. Otl talks about his desire to write a cookbook without recipes someday, in which the basic foods would be assigned to meet the basic needs of human beings. Unfortunately he will probably never find the time to do that.

Following this glorious day, once more a spectacular sunset, in the colors that are only found in the North, but which are already autumnally toned down.

The news reports describe a situation that is becoming more and more critical. The stream of refugees from the German Democratic Republic via Hungary is swelling. The Aichers are worried about where that will lead. We brought along a hectographed program of the citizens' movement Democracy Now. The Aichers read it with deep sympathy, almost delighted: Yes, perhaps in the course of the transformation of the German Democratic Republic salvation for the Federal Republic could also be formulated. If we, the people of East

Germany, were to withstand the temptation to simply orient ourselves on the social and economic forms of the Federal Republic and to repeat the same mistakes that they had made: setting up profit and efficiency as the only criteria for the economy. He, on the other hand, says Otl, dreams of an alternative: to introduce work as the basis for existence again—without the state regulation that we have here—and thus to give the citizens who are committed to humanity out of inner conviction the possibility of a fulfilled life that does not have to detour into different substitute gratifications. In order to do that, one would have to transform the economy, which is now based on competitive enterprise and the megalomania that arises from it, from top to bottom—the German Democratic Republic, which will have to do it now anyway under penalty of its collapse, could perhaps become a model for that and take that opportunity to bring up a different Germany for debate—That would mean, we say, to continue to demand sacrifices from the people, for years to come—That's true—Where the thousands that are leaving are now signaling that they have had enough of doing without—Certainly. But documents like that from Democracy Now show that there are groups of thinking people in this country with a republican attitude. And the Monday demonstrations in Leipzig proved that those groups do not consist of dozens, but of thousands. Of course, we would have to be smart and not back the government into a corner too much, nor give it an excuse to intervene or even to shoot. Not bring the budding revolution into danger too soon. Make transitional offers, form a transitional government.

Now we begin with that immediately. Honecker, says Otl, will remain at the top for the time being, of course, but otherwise changes can cheerfully be made. Names are attached to functions, people who have no idea about their good fortune in misfortune. A list is created, one that now still seems utopian, but on the whole consciously makes compromises.

We should be patient, says Otl. Just because we have to accomplish a radical change in thinking, we need time, many steps and transitions, in order to move as many people as possible along that path, among them even some who are tied into the current system. If this approaching revolution were to result in a different state in the end—and it would have to do that in order to entrench itself—then at the end of this century it would at last have to be a polity that would not proceed from an abstract rational idea, nor from general principles, and simply lead back to a bureaucracy again, but a state that establishes a working relationship between the individuals on the basis of concepts and situations, one that does not subordinate itself to any overriding principle—be it called world reason or progress—but to the well-understood needs of the individual. I defend the autonomy of the subject, says Otl. To that extent I am an anarchist. And the Autonomous Republic of Rotis, the living and working place of the Aichers, which we became acquainted with, is, of course, a piece of realized utopia.

We are aware that the state that we have come to be, and which is now in its deepest crisis, drew its authentication from abstract goals, from a theory to which it wanted to adapt reality. Otl's practical approach to the problems also requires us to reorient our views. We see that he spreads out before us his vision, one that he could no longer believe would be fulfilled, and for which he now, here of all places, in this crisis situation in our country, suddenly sees a basis. We are skeptical and remain reserved; he notices it of course.

When we part, very late, he turns around in the doorway and says: If, however, two large population groups, from East and West, immature in their needs, encounter each other and are possibly supposed to or want to unite—what will then happen is something that I do not dare to imagine—Nor does he have to imagine that, we say.

During this night I lie awake for a long time.

THURSDAY, SEPTEMBER 27, 1990
Berlin, Amalienpark

Another "day of the year," for the thirtieth time. Without the hint on the calendar, I would not have thought about the duty that falls to me today. Am tempted to break off this project, more on the basis of a more deeply seated inhibition than on that of the usual disinclination. So I have been sitting inactive for half an hour in front of the sheet where I want to make notes. I have known, of course, for a long time what the cause is when I am "blocked": a resistance against insights that would be too close to me cannot yet be dissolved. Naturally, the rituals can always be described: getting up, eating breakfast, drinking tea, leafing through the newspaper, which, to my surprise, does not interest me at all, so that I already no longer remember what I have read. But in a time when everything else is "falling to pieces," those rituals seem far too trivial to me. The weather always takes place, so today cloudy, but not yet cold. The sun, I read on the calendar, rose at 5:54 A.M., and it will set at 5:48 P.M., while the moon will already rise at 2:50 P.M. and set again at 10:05 P.M. It is now 10:30 A.M, and I wonder, as I do every day, what phony activities I will invent for myself if I do not want to approach my desk.

Actually, it would be a shame to simply give up this series of reports now, which I have imposed upon myself on today's date since 1960, because—yes, why actually? Because the times have fundamentally changed? Because my position in this "new" era is too uncertain for me to be able to capture it in words? So uncertain that I could stop pursuing my professional responsibility? And that would be? Surely to continue to write my reports at least, to overcome my indolence.

Some of all these reflections I tell Tinka, who calls to ask if we are still "walking around somewhat whole on this earth." She is between two meetings, she is—who would have ever thought it?!—an associate in the state ministry for equality with the federal minister, who is, since the eighteenth of March, Lothar de Maizière,[1] is perplexed herself about the abilities that she is discovering within herself, is developing with her friend Marina, who is a state secretary, a campaign among East German women against the reintroduction of paragraph 218 (110,000 signatures!), is supporting the establishment of communal women's representatives, and is helping with a "women's report" in which the state of equal rights for women in the German Democratic Republic is documented. She recommends that I simply reflect upon the nice things that I have experienced during the last year. I say: I am thinking, and create a pause that is somewhat too long. She says: Well, for example the fact-finding committee![2]

All right, fine. If it is supposed to be something "nice" to investigate the infringements on the rights of demonstrators by the state security forces during the nights before the Fortieth Anniversary of the German Democratic Republic . . . Everything is relative, says Tinka, and she is right about that. In that fact-finding committee I actually experienced—and not only

[1] Lothar de Maizière (b. 1940), conservative politician who served as the first and only democratically elected president of the GDR immediately prior to reunification in 1990. (Ed.)

[2] Fact-finding committee: C.W. participated as a member of the independent investigating committee that examined the events of the seventh and eighth of October 1989 in Berlin and researched the encroachments of police and state authorities against demonstrators, right to the top of those institutions (for example, Minister of State Security Erich Mielke), in order to publicly indict them (see also the report of that investigating committee, *und diese verdammte Ohnmacht* [And This Damned Helplessness]," Berlin, 1991). (G.W.)

I—a paradox. As depressing and weighty as were the processes that were spread out before us and investigated by us, our collaboration was all the more encouraging and constructive. I leaf through my calendar: fifteen times, on every other Wednesday, it says there: Ten o'clock, fact-finding committee, Red City Hall. None of the many other appointments during this year appears that frequently. It became a habit for me to park the car in the parking lot behind the Red City Hall, to walk up stairs and through corridors that had meanwhile become familiar and enter the room where we meet, to take my seat, to greet with a handshake or a wave the others who also now have their customary seats, to spread out my notepad and materials, and to concentrate on the current proceedings. Even now, individual faces and figures pass before my inner eye as if in a film, prosecutor general, chief of police, lieutenant general, state security officers, police officers, the minister of the interior—I think back to when, less than a year ago, during the nights around the seventh of October, under orders from these people the demonstrators were loaded into trucks and taken to police stations and garages, where they were forced to stand all night with their hands against the wall and their legs spread, without food or drink, amid taunts and harassment, Annette among them; how the three of us looked for her on Sunday morning, in central Berlin, at the office of the prosecutor general, in the police headquarters; how only buzzing, unfriendly voices ever came from the loudspeaker; how the inner city of Berlin resembled a besieged city and I thought: Now power is showing its true face. I only have to remember that morning in order to stifle at the outset any sympathy for the representatives of that power, who, during the interrogations to which they are very unwillingly forced to submit, obviously evade, lie, do not remember, are not responsible for anything, and show no pensiveness, no remorse. For them it had been a matter of nipping a counterrevolution in the bud. Did they really believe that?

Now I am familiar, of course, with functionaries—a professional designation that is revealing in itself—and have experienced which people were able to last in which functions, who
was expelled, until we had to come to the conclusion that whoever rises to the top and stays there belongs to a negative elite.
But I had not previously been acquainted with the "function
holders" in the police, the army, and state security; they had,
whether they stood before us with or without a uniform, concrete in their veins and, I fear, in the convolutions of their
brains. Everything was clogged up; there was no path of entry
for thoughts and feelings that were foreign, i.e. suspicious to
them. After the meetings I often drove home feeling petrified
myself.

How different on the other hand were the mostly young
people who had demonstrated and came to us or were visited
by us as witnesses for the excesses of the ones who had
received orders from those others. We visited them in very simple, sometimes shabby, disorderly apartments; once I stumbled
in the dark through a colony of summerhouses, and I could
never doubt that what they stated, often awkwardly, was true;
never did one of them try to put on airs or perhaps to assume
a heroic pose after the fact. But we simply wanted to . . . , many
of them said, still bewildered by the severity with which the
state authorities had acted against them, from whom they really "only" wanted to wring a few self-evident concessions. And
to whom they had shouted, as their greatest provocation: We
are staying here!

I often thought: To share in this experience cannot be over-
estimated in its value. It was worth it to stay here just for that:
the unadulterated, pure, painful reality. Often, often I say to
myself: Do not forget that! Do not forget how from a larger,
heterogeneous number of people—none of them specialists,
not prepared for the tasks that would fall to them, most of
them strangers to each other, not without mistrust for individ-

uals among them, united "only" by a strong indignation with respect to what had taken place in their country, and the conviction that those who were responsible for it had to be found and punished—how from such an assemblage a group developed that was able to work, with a deliberate infrastructure, with a division of labor, discipline, and, the longer the more, with astonishing competence acquired by individuals in certain areas. And, the aspect that was perhaps most important for me: working in a spirit of friendship. We became acquainted with each other. Prejudices melted away. An atmosphere of mutual trust developed, which we urgently needed in order not to sink into depression when the facts and the relationships that we discovered threatened to depress us too much. The tension was often broken by a joke or a sarcastic remark that nobody misinterpreted. One could find understanding in almost anyone for the "conflict situation" into which each of us was entering . . .

I am writing this as a generalization, it occurs to me, and am avoiding identification of that "conflict situation." But I am supposed to remember "nice things" that I experienced, and I see that during these months for me nice things are tied to painful things. And vice versa? Painful things to nice things?

I interrupt these writings and go shopping. A mild, cloudy day. Strangers still greet me on the street. In the store that is open late on the corner of Kavalierstrasse I know where all the goods are located on the shelves; now I sometimes lose my orientation because of the new colorful articles that are put next to or that replace some of the old ones. By chance, shortly before noon, the store is empty when I reach the cashier's stand. Nonetheless, the cashier whispers as she tells me about the current state of her affairs. A West German supermarket chain is negotiating with the trade organization to take over this store. If not successful, the store will probably be closed. Then we will all be let go, the woman says, otherwise perhaps two of us can stay. But fighting and secret maneuvering is already beginning among the fellow workers; each of them is pushing her way to the front to be considered for the job that will perhaps remain. We have never known that sort of thing, she says. We really did not want that!—I know, of course, that is normal, but I do not have the heart to say that to the saleswoman.

We eat spaghetti, tomato sauce, and salad, silently. So what's going on? Gerd finally says—I am looking for the nice things that I have experienced this year—Who wants to know?—Tinka—And nothing occurs to you? Typical—Go ahead and start, I say, and he: Honorary doctorate in Hildesheim, honorary doctorate in Brussels, *Officier des arts et des lettres* in Paris, *Premio Mondello* in Palermo, and the corresponding trips through all of Europe . . . I say: Yes, yes. And think—and Gerd knows that I think that and does not say anything more—I mean something really nice.

Normandy! How could I forget that? Only two weeks ago, the trip with Renate[3] and Alain. The little town where we spent the night, Honfleur. Ebb and flow. The fishing boats that we saw from the window. The bright autumn light on the coast. Our almost reverential viewing of the Proust Hotel in Cabourg. The meal of fried fish, fresh bread sticks, and cold white wine right on the ocean, in the sun and the wind. And most important for me, the exhibition in Caen in the Musée des Beaux Arts: "*Les Vanités*": the trifles, vanities. Or, even more powerful: vanity—a word in which, through the linguistic similarity in French as well, another resounds for me: futility, *vainité*. I look for the picture postcard that I brought back with me: on a thick, bright wooden slab—old wood, notches, unevenness—in the middle a skull, bathed in reddish-brown

[3] Renate (b. 1948), Germanic studies scholar, and Alain Lance (b. 1939), poet and translator; friends of the Wolfs, translated C.W.'s books *No Place on Earth*, *Cassandra*, *Medea*, and *In the Flesh* into French. (G.W.)

light like the hourglass on the right, the half-faded red and yellow tulip in a spherical vase to the left of it. Only—or already?—about a fourth of the sand has run through the narrow neck of the hourglass. The picture is by Phillipe de Champaigne, who lived in Brussels and Paris from 1602-1674, and who was included in the "meditation about wealth, need, and salvation in the paintings of the seventeenth century" that this exhibition was trying to achieve. Difficult to describe the combined and contradictory feelings that arose within me as I walked alongside the pictures from skull to skull, from hourglass and stack of books to scythe and grave shovel and past the other testimonies of transitoriness that now awaken in me again as I look at the card. There is, of course, bewilderment that can also do you good. The recognition: yes, that is how it is, and others were able to experience and express it long before you did. Just what is "it"? Everything is horrible and futile at the same time. It passes away, at the latest when you pass away. And that will be soon. *Salvation*—a word that has always been foreign to me.

While I leaf further through my calendar, I realize: this year is not *a*, it is *the* year of change. As if an axis has been drawn into it around which the times "change." Now what is down was previously "up," thus visible, and what was—to us—previously invisible is lying on top. *Is* on top, I think, and have to laugh. Am able to stick with my self-ironic grin while my faithful, insolent calendar confronts me with all of the futile rescue operations in which I have worked my fingers to the bone during this year. An enumeration: I participated in the preservation of the Reclam Publishing Company, the Aufbau Publishing Company (establishment of an authors' council), in the Academy of Arts (which will probably now fuse together with the West Berlin Academy of Arts), and in the discussions in the PEN Club about its future. Participated in the establishment of the Basisdruck Publishing Company, in the newspaper *Die*

Andere, in a "cultural conveyor belt," in the futile attempt to establish a newspaper called *Berliner Tageblatt*, which progressed as far as the visit of a "founding group" to a notary, where I, however, recognized the futility of this endeavor and withdrew—*One* new establishment, however, seems to have been successful. In March Gerd and I were already at the notary's office to register Janus Press, Ltd.—the publishing house that Gerd was finally able to open and in which we are both now "partners." During the ritual at the notary's office we could hardly keep from laughing; at the tax advisor's office, however—also a new institution for us, a West Berliner whom friends in West Berlin had recommended to us ("The East Berliners really do not yet know how to deal with our crazy tax system!")—we broke out laughing at his helpless expression when Gerd, in response to his question of what kind of profits he wanted to make with his publishing house, responded unabashedly: None at all. He wanted to produce at last the books that had concerned him for a long time—Well then, said our tax advisor, then we must at least see to it that you do not incur too much loss . . . (You wanted to know what "nice things" I experienced, Tinka!)

The day needs a break. Lie down, rest, diversion with reading material that should be as far removed as possible from our problems. *Montauk* by Max Frisch, a book that gets better with each reading, or do I read this very personal book more intensively because I know that Max Frisch will die, not sometime, but very soon? When I visited him in June, he spoke openly about his illness: first, intestinal cancer, an operation that "succeeded," after that, tumors in his liver that are growing. He does not want chemotherapy, which would prolong his illness by perhaps only three months. He does not have any pain yet. He is putting his affairs in order. He is waiting. Emotionally hardly any losses, he says. But intellectually. The narcosis has damaged him, weakened his memory. The worst thing is the boredom. No more motivation to write at all. Hardly to read. He sits and ruminates, he says, but not really about "metaphysical questions," often about very banal things. Friends come and tell him goodbye. Recently his American lady friend from Montauk visited him; with her he took a ride on the Lake of Zurich, in a boat that had many children aboard. He did enjoy that. If the tumor continues to grow, it can press the bile duct closed. He is afraid of gradually becoming demented, of losing his identity.

Since I am drawing up the annual balance sheet: being together with Frisch, I think, the intimate, frank conversation belongs, as sad as it was, among the "good" memories. ("Well and good" does not have to be light and merry, does it, Tinka?) It is, by the way, ever more rarely that way. Could he think about other things at all, I asked him. Of course, he said. Sometimes the thought of his illness suddenly assaults him as if it were new again—I ask him about his past. Does he now see it differently than he did before?—Yes, he says. To the extent that he has to ask himself just why he tolerated or endured some situations for so long, when their fruitlessness was already clear to him. Wasted time—How I know that feeling! And this self-reproach: believed in the false gods for too long. (He, however, Frisch, probably means it in a private sense)—Where was the alternative? I ask. He does not know that either. We talk about what we had recognized as an alternative: honesty in writing. And that a person must even be distrustful of that—Peter Noll,[4] for example, says Frisch—whom he accompanied when he had cancer; who wrote about it— meanwhile it had become clear to him that he really did not draw very close to him; that the man began walking a kind of concealed path: just when he was writing.

[4] Peter Noll (1926-1982): His report "*Diktate über Sterben und Tod* (Dictations About Dying and Death)," Zurich, 1984, appeared with the "*Totenrede* (Death Speech)" by Max Frisch. (G.W.)

Concealed path! The term electrified me. Isn't that a cipher for our life as a whole? Wouldn't it be a title for a comprehensive written work?

Before I left, Frisch did say that he had retained his interest in politics ("to the point of intoxication!") and in friendships. The way it reads at the beginning of *King Lear*. The old man gives everything away; all he wants is love. He repeats that three times: Love. Love. Love.

I remember now that I thought: That is the key.

I remember now that I intentionally did not talk about my problems, which in comparison with his seemed trivial to me, until he himself began talking about them and proved to be well informed. Even he had not anticipated that kind of a collapse of the German Democratic Republic, he said. He now asked himself if he should have asked us sharper, more urgent questions back then. If we would have endured them. If we would then have rejected him. And he also asked himself what will happen to all of the people, for example, at the Volk und Welt Publishing Company, who really had attempted by all possible means "to support" him and other Western authors. Suddenly, in retrospect that must all seem superfluous to them and all their struggles must almost seem ridiculous.

Cult figures, he said, can only be worshipped or toppled. You yourself are now being toppled. You must all be careful that they do not take your lives out of your hands—(That penetrating feeling of expectation, even now.)

Write everything down, he continued. What you do not write down, you forget. You should not forget that—I said: Yes, yes, and thought: What for?

We forget. Perhaps we *want* to forget. If I now start awakening memories, I will not fall asleep at all. Gerd is asleep, with his book in his hand as usual. I try to empty my mind. At some point I must have fallen asleep after all. I awaken in the middle of a dream in which somebody whom I do not know gives me a bunch of flowers for Irmtraud Morgner's coffin.[5] Before my eyes the totally flower-covered coffin sinks into the ground—Irmtraud died on the seventh of May. She, too, knew that she would die and refused further treatment. We are already having to go to funerals rather often now, I think. But what do I mean here by "already"?—In my calendar I find that on the twelfth of May we stood at the graves of Brecht and Helene Weigel[6] in the Dorotheenstadt Cemetery and put flowers there. Their gravestones had been smeared with Nazi symbols and the insult "Jewish pig!" I did not want to admit to myself that even this would now belong to normality.

I get up and make tea, which I take with me to my desk. Duty calls, I say to Gerd, and he: If you would not view it as duty . . . I: As what else?—He: As fun, of course—variation of a standard dialogue between us.

So on with it! Let the "beautiful" show itself! Instead of that, the corridor of a building appears before me, almost dark, a niche into which someone beckons me to whisper something to me. It is the Cecilienhof in Potsdam, the man is someone who apparently pulls strings behind the scenes, even the strings of this "colloquium" of the Bertelsmann Company, one of the first East-West cultural events after the "*Wende* (turning point)," in which I unfortunately permitted myself to be misled to participate because many said to me: You cannot hide now! (They meant: in light of the frontal assault against my behavior and writing in the German Democratic Republic in the *Frankfurter Allgemeine Zeitung* a few days earlier.) But actually why not? It was a mistake to go, I think, and I already knew it at the time. The attacks continued, and they outspokenly demanded my confession of guilt as an entry ticket into

[5] Irmtraud Morgner (1933-1990) was an East German feminist writer. (Tr.)

[6] Helene Weigel (1900-1971), one of the outstanding German actors of her generation, Communist Party member from 1930 and artistic director of the Berliner Ensemble following her husband Bertolt Brecht's death in 1956. (Ed.)

the Western media landscape. (If, however, I had not gone, I would not have experienced with what presumption—no—arrogance, the Western business concern spread itself out in the building that had willingly been rented to it by what was still the German Democratic Republic, even in the holy of holies, the room in which Stalin, Truman, and Churchill/Atlee negotiated the Potsdam Accord, where their little flags still stand in front of their seats on the large round table, and where now—which was expressly and proudly proclaimed to us—now *we* sat, on elevated planks around that center. And outside on the terrace little tables and chairs beneath colorful Coca-Cola umbrellas invited people to relax.)

So what did that man want to tell me during the night in the dark niche of the corridor?

The following (I regretted very much not having a tape recorder with me, but I immediately wrote down his speech word for word in the hotel room): Naturally, it is a matter of a campaign against you. Of course it is not concerned at all with your past but with your activities in the present. That is disturbing. And of course anything concerning you that has even a faint odor of the left must be smashed. The German Democratic Republic must unconditionally be rendered illegitimate. Some other leftist guests that he had wanted to invite had been denied to him. And Lahnstein[7] had just said to him, when the subject came up of inviting me to a certain lecture series in Munich: We will leave that alone now. It has probably taken care of itself—You will no longer get a foot in the media's door here, said the man, but you do have your fans, and you can simply make yourself scarce and write.

I thought I was dreaming—that would probably be the currently appropriate cliché statement, and corresponding to that

[7] Manfred Lahnstein (b. 1937), German politician, member of the Social Democratic Party. (Tr.)

is also the fact that when I had finally found my way through the maze of half-darkened corridors to our hotel room, as sometimes happens in a fairy tale, a real object served as evidence for the reality of my experience. In my hand I had an undoubtedly expensive white rectangular box from the Prussian porcelain factory, on the lid of which Frederick the Second was engraved, whom we now again call the "Great." A gift of the organizer, "with compliments"—Oh, if only a person could always laugh properly at the right time!

Instead of that, I unfortunately fell into a depression, I remember, which I, when nothing at all seemed to help, intended to overcome with Arno Gruen's [8] help in Ascona, Switzerland; only Arno, the American, the psychoanalyst, had love problems himself and did not want to believe how serious my depression was, because he could see no reason for it—But just look at those who are inveighing against you! They are empty themselves and hate what is alive in you. Or they are offended with themselves for something and have to project their self-hatred at you!—I, again and again: Yes, yes, but there remains a shred that they are right about—He: *You* are not right. The guilt that you feel is a different one from the one that they want to make you believe. You must work that out for yourself; you must live with that. But you must learn to grasp the fact that they mean something totally different than you do.

Rather than devoting himself to my problems, he much preferred to sit with me on the hotel terrace. He told me about his childhood in central Berlin; his father, a Polish Jew, became well-to-do as a raincoat manufacturer. In America, where they immigrated, they were then poor again. He enjoyed even more telling Jewish jokes—In a bar in the USA a Jewish boy hits a

[8] Arno Gruen (b. 1923), Jewish psychoanalyst; emigrated from Berlin to the USA in 1936; lives in Switzerland, author of books appreciated by C.W. (*Der Wahnsinn der Normalität* [*The Insanity of Normality*], Munich, 1987, among others), with whom she participated in a friendly exchange of ideas. (G.W.)

Chinese man: Pearl Harbor—But that was the Japanese!—
Doesn't matter. They are all Orientals!—Then the Chinese
man hits the Jew: "Titanic!"—But that was an iceberg!—Iceberg, Rosenberg—all the same. We laugh. In the car Arno
shows me a passage in the book *A Man Died* by Soyinka.[9] The
prisoners get it straight in their own minds that their inter-
rogators cannot reach their souls. That is it!—Yes. Aside from
the inappropriate comparison, that is it, naturally, quite unam-
biguous. But in this instance it is a case that is not so unam-
biguous. It is a matter of that shred—Arno shook his head in
resignation and said: We'll talk about it!—In the hotel room, I
still remember, I noted down the joke and with it the first lines
of my "comforting aria" by Paul Fleming: And yet be undis-
mayed / And yet do not give up / Do whatever must be done /
Stand above jealousy . . . What must actually be done?

One day Arno was worried after all; it was the day on which
as if by agreement my "case" was discussed in all the media—
not just the newspapers—under headlines that, just how do I
put it: could "cause the blood to rise to a person's head," and I
had to ask myself: Am I perhaps really that monster? And I did
not know how I was supposed to get through the night. Then
he called from Munich, where he was on publishing business.
He had read everything; he apparently wanted to hear my voice;
he had read *What Remains* while traveling. He said I should be
very calm and wait and see. Everything was in there, of course.

Enough beautiful material, Tinka? There has not been any
mention of work at all yet, and neither can much be said about
it for this year. The publication of *What Remains*, which some
now read as an attempt to place myself among those who were
"persecuted" in the German Democratic Republic, others as
evidence for my "familial" amalgamation with the regime of
the Republic as a "state writer." Does one have to be malicious

[9] Akinwande Oluwole "Wole" Soyinka (b. 1934), Nigerian writer, poet and playwright;
received the Nobel Prize in Literature in 1986. (Ed.)

to subscribe to that interpretation? Or simply unaware? Can a person misunderstand a text that way? Should I have not published it now? I vacillate between different opinions, but actually I still do not know what is right—or what would have been right.[10] Strangely enough, the manner in which reunification is being carried out is now bringing people who were previously very critical of the German Democratic Republic to defend themselves against undifferentiated condemnation. (In the *Neue Zürcher Zeitung* I read that one can also now find Reagan's "evil empire" in the German Democratic Republic!) Recently my colleague Tr. said to me that he would now bite his tongue rather than make a public confession. As far as I can see, he has no reason for confessions of guilt.

What else? The work on the preamble for the new constitution![11] Since March an extensive working group has been laboring over it, commissioned by the Central Round Table, consisting of members of all parties represented in the national legislature and of experts from both German states. They assigned me to formulate the preamble. At first, when we still thought that the German Democratic Republic would exist somewhat longer, that this "third entity" would exist, which we irrationally wished for ourselves and whose contours briefly appeared, we worked on a "Plan for the German Democratic Republic." I participated in some meetings of working groups; I read constitutions of earlier German states, also those of other countries. The preamble, which I, of course, formulated following various drafts and discussions with the members of the working group, reads:

[10] C.W.'s book *What Remains*, Berlin, 1990, unleashed the so-called German Literature Controversy (see also: *Der Literaturstreit im vereinten Deutschland* [*The Literature Controversy in the United Germany*], Munich, 1991; *Der deutsch-deutsche Literaturstreit* [*The German-German Literature Controversy*], Hamburg and Zurich, 1991). (G.W.)

[11] "*Verfassungsentwurf für die DDR* (Constitutional plan for the GDR)," published by the work group "New Constitution of the German Democratic Republic" of the Round Table, Berlin, 1990. (G.W.)

Proceeding from the humanistic traditions to which the best women and men of all social strata of our nation have contributed,

mindful of the responsibility of all Germans for their history and its consequences,

determined to live as peaceful, equal partners in the community of nations, participating in the process of unifying Europe, in the course of which the German nation, too, will create its own national unity,

convinced that the possibility for self-determined, responsible action is the highest freedom,

building upon revolutionary renewal,

determined to develop a democratic and unified community that

> secures the dignity and freedom of the individual,
>
> guarantees equal rights for all,
>
> establishes the equality of the sexes,
>
> and protects our natural environment,

the male and female citizens of the German Democratic Republic give themselves

this constitution.

Meanwhile, following the election shock on the eighteenth of March and the resolution of the People's Chamber, we know the date on which the German Democratic Republic will join the Federal Republic. It is the third of October, a few days from now. A new constitution for the German Democratic Republic is now no longer necessary. The work group transformed itself unwearyingly into a "board of trustees for a democratically constituted union of German states" and is working on drafting a constitution for what I believe is a utopian structure. Even the preamble must be reformulated.

Probably never before in German history has so much energy been expended for impossible things as has been done this year. Wasted? I do not know. There may be a basic physical law according to which energy cannot be lost. Does that also apply to spiritual energy?

I ask Annette that; she must know. She says, here in this country a great deal of energy was stored up; it has now broken forth explosively. Much of it will go up in smoke, she believes. All of us did find ourselves in a state of mental emergency and we are now returning to normality—Normality? I say. You mean: entering a crisis—Mother, she says, you know yourself: that is now normality. And *must* be. It would be bad if we were to dismiss the crisis—Crisis as opportunity, I say. Smart daughter—When she is right, she is right, she says—And otherwise? I ask—She says: Tired. The clinic is doing me in. It can't go on much longer. I need a break.

I notice how tired I am myself, eat supper, am hardly able and hardly want to say anything more. G. leaves me alone, I go to bed, do not pick up another book, and fall asleep immediately.

At five in the morning I wake up and am determined to go back to sleep, but I already know that I will not succeed, as has so often been the case during these last weeks; that sleep flees all the further the more determined I am to catch it. So I adopt the other tactic. It does not matter to me at all if I sleep or lie awake; on the contrary, lying awake and giving free play to my thoughts is far preferable to wasting time with sleep, namely when I bring my thoughts to the point of floating freely, they wind up, I secretly hope, in the whirlpool of weariness and swirl into the dark abyss of sleep, but my thoughts are wide awake and do not fall for my trick. Individually they move wide-eyed and tauntingly past my inner eye. So fine, then I will observe how it grows light outside; there is an entire literature of such observations written by poor sleepers, and anyway, in the country one should consciously experience all times of the day, and it is actually a shame that I do not know when this darkness, which is still in front of the windows and which does not exist at all in front of our windows in Berlin, will be replaced by the first heralds of dawn.

Soon afterward, I do reach for the book that is lying on the old chair next to my bed. Actually I did not want to read Solzhenitsyn's *Cancer Ward* again. Actually I only wanted to find out if this book contributes anything to the basic thesis of the lecture "Cancer and Society" that I am working on,[1] too

---

[1] C.W., "*Krebs und Gesellschaft* (Cancer and Society)," lecture presented at the Con-

late, too slowly, too unfocused, and should it be a comfort when Gerd tells me on the telephone that I have always felt that way? I have forgotten it. I notice while leafing through the book how much I have also forgotten about that. How was it that I no longer remembered, I who pay so much attention to beginnings, that the book begins with the sentence: "On top of it all the cancer ward bore the number thirteen"? And that the unacknowledged superstition of the functionary Pavel Nikolayevich Rusanov is linked to his inability to bear the truth about the nature of his illness, which—first stage of the severe path to knowledge—robs him of all of his privileges with a single blow and, even before his biological end, throws him into social nothingness. Why did it not occur to me during my first reading that Kostoglotov, the main figure and counterpart to Rustanov, is first seen through the eyes of the latter—"semi-bandit"—and that we first learn the nickname that he gives to him and only then his real name? And why do I have to overcome an inner resistance each time I want to reach for the book? I read the initial chapters and note in my mind when I recognize something again and what it is. Yes, Kostoglotov forces his young fellow patient to read a book, and at the same time he impresses upon him: "But take note: education does not make the intellect larger"—"But what then?"—"Life."

Suddenly a child is busy around my feet; the child is wearing the striped T-shirt of Anton, his favorite piece of clothing, but it is not Anton, although in my dream I "know" that now, when his parents are "far away," I am responsible for him. It is another child with whom I walk through many corridors—colonnades—in a large house. It is a cute little girl; her name is Svetlana and she earnestly pleads with me to adopt her (a few days ago Anton said to us: As long as Mom and Dad are not

gress of the German Cancer Society in Bremen on October 24, 1991 (see: *Werke*, Vol. XII, pp. 326 ff.). (G.W.)

here I am your son). I awaken with the question: Isn't it the most evil thing to make a person angry?

It is seven-thirty. Now it is light outside, however; the window rectangle is clearly visible behind the curtain—What is the purpose of that sentence? Did it come from a different dream? And "Svetlana"? Why Svetlana? A Russian name—not surprising given my reading material. But doesn't it mean "the bright one, the radiant one"?

I pull back the curtain, the sky a gray cloth; from the elderberry bush beneath the window a few birds fly up. They will soon come back and continue to help themselves to the elderberries. I walk across the hall in my bathrobe to Anton's room; he is sitting on the floor next to his bed in his pajamas studying a Donald Duck comic book. I know that he is not responsive when he is reading, but I try again and again, ask him how he slept, express my concern about the coldness of the floor, do not even hesitate to express my wish for him to get dressed, receive in return a series of diverse grunts and a long accusing gaze to which I pretend to be insensitive (Man! This is just the most exciting part!). I use the old and contemptible device of blackmail. All right, fine, I say, then I'll simply eat a fried egg and ham alone. Gee whiz, he says, So really, you bug me, and sinks into his reading.

While I am in the bath, from the small radio comes the report that yesterday in the German parliament the viewpoints on the revision of abortion law clashed; that a total of six bills lie before the delegates, ranging from the bill that comes from Alliance 90/Greens to enact a woman's legal claim to the interruption of an unwanted pregnancy and to delete Paragraph 218 without replacing it, to the bill of a "right-to-life" group of the Christian Democratic Union that would permit abortion only if the health and life of the mother are endangered. The masculine hypocrisy that is complicated by the fact that it is often hidden from the hypocrite himself and that hides the ancient power play for dominion over wife and child behind the concern about "unborn life" makes me sick because that ossification cannot be broken down by any argument, by any sympathy for life that has already been born. It is too urgently needed for the preservation of the egos of its proponents. I miss part of the other news reports, while the images go through my mind of how I—when was that? End of the fifties, beginning of the sixties?—drove through the villages with R.W. in our bright yellow Trabant until we reached a village in Brandenburg, the name of which I have forgotten; how she there disappeared into a house that had a doctor's sign on the door; how I drove around the corner to wait, for a period of time that seemed endless to me; how she finally came out, white as a sheet, taking small, careful steps; how she sat down next to me without saying anything, but softly moaning; how I drove off without saying anything; how we hardly said a word during the entire, long trip back; how I took her home and put her to bed and during the next few days, when she began to have a fever and it grew very high, I was terribly afraid; but there was a female doctor who, although she would not have performed an abortion herself, was willing to prescribe the correct medications without asking any all too thorough questions . . .

So the UN Security Council has finally passed a general and complete weapons embargo against Yugoslavia, which is being expressly welcomed by the European Peace Conference that is convening in The Hague and intends to present results during the first week of October. I try to imagine the scenes that must lie behind the unbelievable report: violent battles south of Dubrovnik. The spontaneously arising statement: We really must be able to do something to stop it! is erased by a penetrating feeling of helplessness that dominates me more and more often.

I find Anton in the same position in which I left him almost half an hour earlier, sitting on the only open spot that remains for him on the floor, in the middle of hundreds of Lego blocks in the most diverse colors, which, as I know, are intended to be used in the completion of an extensive animal park facility, the beginnings of which are already visible beneath the table, together with the mass of native and exotic plastic animals that he knows by name, along with all of their habits, and for which he intends to build places to stay that are appropriate for them. I involve him in a conversation about the biotopes in tropical rainforests and hand him his clothes as I do so, which he actually puts on while lost in thought. He thinks about what material he might use to make a piece of tropical rainforest and while doing so watches over the production of his fried egg, about which he has precise ideal expectations that a real, earthly egg can almost never meet. It should be perfectly round, the white no longer "slippery," but the yolk sufficiently runny for him to be able to draw a network of rivers and brooks on his plate.

I cautiously turn the conversation to the subject of school. Whether he can imagine finding friends in his class. Sure, he says, Tobias is already as good as his friend. But it's funny, you know, usually the girls want to be my friends—And why is that?—Well logically because I protect them. There follows a long, detailed description of a chivalrous battle over a girl named Sophie, against the attacker Steffen, who had used the meanest tricks, but who simply had not succeeded against Anton's left hooks and sudden kicks and had in the end been given a warning that he would not forget very easily. Okay, I say, but tell me, have you never had the feeling that the others were envious because you could already read and they couldn't yet—No. Why would they be? It was only boring for me, not for them—And when your teacher had you read stories aloud—didn't anyone ever say to you that you are a show-off?—No, why would they? I really can read, and they noticed that—Oh, show-offs are people who brag about something that they can't do at all—Well sure, what else?

While I wash up, we again have to trace the travel route of his parents in the atlas and on the small globe; Anton wants to hear the verse again: In Europe everything is so big, so big / And in Japan everything is so small. The two of us know little about Nepal, aside from the fact that the people there are said to be very poor. Anyway, Anton says after a while, there would be no point in my sending them some of my clothes. The children there wear very different suits. I once saw that in a photograph—And would you send them your striped T-shirt otherwise?—Of course, says Anton.

He negotiates with me about whether we can already wash the last of the mustard out of a jar so that we will have one more jar from this mustard jar series that he thinks is "neat." He occupies himself with the question of whether the mustard producer can afford to give us a jar along with the mustard; that would really have to be expensive.

Carola[2] comes down the stairs, takes over Anton, and I get ready. It has begun to rain very softly; I cross the wet meadow to the car, exchange a few words with Carola about the amount of elderberries that there are this year; there are more every year, we still have juice in the cellar from last year, but should we let the berries go to waste? She will take a bucket and pick berries with Anton. With the key already in the car lock I straighten up once more and look around me. The old house with its red stone, the green door, and the white window frames, which, by the way, should be painted. The linden trees of different sizes to the right and left of the entrance, which are just beginning to change color. The sky above them, which meanwhile has become dark gray. For some time now I have consciously been laying in a supply of such images, something like provisions for the road for worse days. Now Carola claps her hands. An enormous flock of crows flies up from the larger linden tree.

[2] Carola Damrow: Ceramic artist, friend of the Wolfs. (G.W.)

So, first over the short stretch of cobblestone pavement. In keeping with the wishes of the mayor and most of the inhabitants, the street is supposed to be covered with a layer of tar as soon as possible. We are not enthusiastic about the prospect that our quiet village street will become a racetrack for rapidly moving cars, but other adjacent residents hope that this customer friendly street would then bring investors and buyers for the manor house on the lake, for example, which belonged to a nationalized factory in Berlin and which is now lying vacant; that vacation guests will move in there again and create some jobs for the unemployed women of the village.

Turn off onto the narrow macadam road that the cooperative constructed and which leads straight through their fields (but are they still "their" fields? I do not know), and as always at this spot try to look at the nest of the osprey that has been raising its young on top of a high-voltage transmission tower. Has it already left, gone south? I see nothing of the ospreys, but geese move in wedges across the sky. Every year the beginning and severity of the winter are predicted according to the time of the geese migrations.

While traveling on the road to Sternberg, which I know very well, it occurs to me why I have developed a resistance to the reading of Solzhenitsyn's *Cancer Ward*. I see myself sitting on the terrace of our house in Kleinmachnow, in a deck chair, with that book in my lap. It is warm, sunny, afternoon, and autumn; the poplars have cast their first yellow leaves onto the concrete of the terrace, a perfect idyll, and I am afraid. September '68. Gerd has driven to Potsdam with Annette; she has been summoned to a hearing before the state security police. Her boyfriend was stopped on his motorcycle because he was driving too fast, and he had the "Two Thousand Words" of the Czech writer Vaculík[3]

---

[3] Ludvík Vaculík (b. 1926), Czech writer and journalist. He wrote the "Two Thousand Words" manifesto in June, 1968, a treatise that would come to symbolize the will of the Czechoslovak people during the Prague Spring. (Ed.)

with him in a German translation. Annette had brought it with her from Prague. During the interrogation he said that he had heard the same opinions in our house. They searched his place. They would not find my diaries at our house; back then we hid them for the first time, and for the first time two gentlemen stood in front of our house. I brooded about what they could prove Annette guilty of, about what we should do if they kept her there. I tried to divert myself with the book and it did not work very well, but a slight feeling of fear or at least of uneasiness is still tied to the sight of that book. I know now where it comes from and will be able to ignore it.

In the physiotherapy department in the basement of the former outpatient clinic the same atmosphere as before still prevails, although, of course, the individual departments of the outpatient clinic were forced into private practice. Mrs. K. tells me about that while she gives me electric stimulation therapy and says that it is so absurd to break up a medical facility that functioned so well, whose individual domains were so well coordinated; it just could not be true that even that which had proved its worth in the East would have to disappear, and it was also economically insane that the expensive devices would now no longer be used jointly by all the doctors, to say nothing of the great disadvantages for the patients who would have had specialists for almost all illnesses in one single building. I ask if they were at least getting a financial benefit from it. Oh, she says, you know, of course, that we receive fifty to sixty percent of what the West German therapists receive. Recently they told us that if our training had really been that good, we would also have found a good job over there. So we are being punished because we did not leave our patients here in the lurch—Twenty minutes, all right?

I lie there and hear the conversations in the other cubicles; the main event is being discussed thoroughly. Last week somebody broke in here during the night; nowadays they start with the hospitals and outpatient clinics. Who knows what they were looking for. There are truly no treasures lying around here, but since then the night clerk has been afraid, and I can understand that. A person's life is no longer safe in general; when you consider how much the traffic has increased, you no longer dare to walk across the street. I lie there and enjoy the Mecklenburg dialect and the Mecklenburg fussiness. At the end I have to remind Mrs. K. that I have to acknowledge the treatment for her on my chart. Oh, she says, not so important. But it is your money! I say. Oh, she says and makes a gesture of refusal.

I wander through the furniture and housewares hall, with the intention of noting the changes that this past year has made in the range of goods that are offered; yes, even the housewares are on their way to the Western standard, the furniture as ugly as ever, whether Eastern or Western. I buy a bunch of wooden clothespins, guaranteed to be old East German products, and a similarly dusty trash can made of hard rubber, which stands hidden behind all of the new, sensational trash can models. In the supermarket next door as well, formerly the cooperative store, now Kaiser's, I have no desire to buy; a fryer, which is now no longer called a broiler, and basmati rice are almost my entire booty.

In the city, as if by a miracle, I find a parking place at the market, walk through a few streets, and muster the new businesses or those that have been dressed up with new advertising signs. On one corner there is a modern new textile shop— a pullover for Tinka for her birthday. For a long time I look for Conrad-Bächtle-Strasse, and it finally becomes clear to me that it must have been renamed Kütiner Strasse. Until now I had not given any thought to Conrad Bächtle; now I would like to know who he was. The Agency for Church Economy is situated in a beautiful, restored old half-timbered building; I have to speak to the Church economist. It is about a few square meters of land that they neglected to survey years ago when we bought our parcel of land. That was during "German Democratic Republic times," as they say now, not a problem. Land was hardly worth anything; above all it was not an object of speculation and the verbal assurance that we would take care of the survey sometime was sufficient for both of us; the piece of land next to us is used by neighbors who respect our customary law. Astonished, I listen to myself as I negotiate with the economist about the sale of that tiny bit of land; she does not show herself to be approachable. In principle, the Church no longer sells any land, and what I hear is that under the new circumstances it regrets that it ever did so. I suppress my displeasure, leave my letter to the Church council there, and admonish myself as I leave not to lose my sense of humor. Why shouldn't the "new circumstances," which, of course, means a new situation regarding to ownership, pose problems for me?

Treacherous, my urge to go into the discount store on the marketplace now after all, and to make purchases that suddenly seem immediately urgent to me, heavy bottles, heavy sacks. As I stand at the packing counter and pack up the goods, I hear a man behind me asking the cashier: Isn't that . . . my name follows. The woman answers in the affirmative. To which the man says: Honecker even gave her a luxurious house—It's working, I think to myself; I turn around and grin at the man and encounter the very familiar glassy stare. It is not a local man. Is that a comfort? When somebody tries to push through the door ahead of me as I leave, I push back as rudely as possible and force my way ahead. So, that was it then, I say to myself half aloud on the way to the car.

The day has become brighter; the sky is now a thick pane of frosted glass in front of a brightly lighted background. During the trip back the sun breaks through several times for a few seconds. I drive zestfully and sing: "*Jetzt fahrn wir übern See, übern See* (Now we go over the lake, over the lake)" and: "*Auf einem Baum ein Kuckuck saß* (On a tree a cuckoo sat)." A certain initial song is always followed by a certain series of songs; another one from this forest and meadow series is: "*Es blies ein Jäger wohl in sein Horn* (A hunter blew well on his horn)," with its large number of verses that almost fill up the time between Dabel and Borkow. This time I pay attention to how many of the linden trees that were freshly planted two years ago along the cooperative's road have grown in size; most of them have already developed a tiny crown. In my imagination they become full-grown linden trees in a moment of time, crossing straight through the beautifully rolling countryside; what an adornment, I will never walk in their shade, or how fast do linden trees grow? And its branches whispered, as if they were calling to me, I sang at the top of my lungs as I drove into the yard. Anton was there on the spot; they gathered three bucketfuls of bunches of elderberries. Carola is sitting on the rock and plucking them from their vine. On the ancient piece of granite—which we had brought from the lake, where it rested, to the front of the house, in a very risky maneuver, with the help of some men and heavy technology—Anton has built a bizarre landscape using stones and branches. Both of them are hungry for the potato pancakes that I promised them and that I finally produce, with a half-guilty conscience from the bag and not from freshly shredded potatoes. It tastes good, with sugar and cranberries. We try to picture what Tinka and Martin are probably eating in Nepal. It occurs to me that Anton, who at first, when they had driven away, avoided talking about his parents, now talks about them more and more frequently. Instead he avoids any conversation about school; at most he says: Yes, yes. I am going again now. But what frightened him so much on his first days at school, so much so that he could not sleep and could not eat and had to vomit in front of the school building, he cannot say. Isn't the teacher nice to you?

Yes, she is—Do the other children tease you? No, no—Should we practice writing a little more today? Yes, yes.

Lie down, the relief every day at noon, in the middle of the day a little vacation. Solzhenitsyn. I read myself into that well-known sadness again, which has accompanied me in my reading for a long time and which will not leave me anymore. I find the exact passage that I need for my lecture: Kostoglotov is talking to the adversary Rusanov about a book that he is reading at the time. It says in there that the relationship between the development of a tumor and the central nervous system has still not been investigated very much. That relationship, however, is remarkable! There is a spontaneous recovery, even if only in rare cases. "Do you understand what that means? Not healing, but recovery! Well?" How one of the mortally ill patients then says into the silence: "For that one must certainly . . . have a clear conscience," and how Rusanov indignantly maintains to the contrary: "That is really idealistic nonsense! Just what does the conscience have to do with it?"—Solzhenitsyn experienced such a spontaneous healing in his own body.

Anton wakes me up, he needs physical nearness, lies down next to me, cuddles up to me, lies quite still for a while; then he wants to read his beloved Jandl[4] poems, he knows where the book is, gets it, and insists that I read to him, although he knows the poems by heart and calls them out one after another in order to laugh himself sick in advance. "I / want to / play / do play / my child." Merry Christmas! he demands, and I read:

> open up the door
> open up the door
> then the little master can come in
> then the little master can come in

[4] Ernst Jandl (1925-2000, Vienna), Austrian writer, poet, and translator. (Ed.)

merry Christmas
merry Christmas
and I am only a dog
merry Christmas
merry Christmas
and I am only a dog

I make an effort to read the texts with exactly the same diction that Gerd is accustomed to using when reading them, but sense that it leaves something to be desired. Anton is generous and is satisfied. We are both in a good mood.

In the afternoon the sun really has broken through; I do not deny myself the pleasure of sitting down on the bench behind the house—my favorite place for reading and for making plans and notes—with my coffee and the newspaper. The headlines of the *Schweriner Zeitung*: Private investors have taken the bait. It is recognized, according to Fiduciary Director Breuel, who spoke to the press yesterday, that there are motivated and well-educated people in East Germany—Planned dismissals for thousands of East German dockworkers will only be valid with the simultaneous offer for absorption into an employment company. Twenty-four thousand men and women will lose their jobs in three waves of terminations by 1993—The situation in East German agriculture is coming to a head. The Minister of Agriculture calculates that four out of five people who are employed in agriculture will lose their jobs by 1994—Continuous arguments about the right of asylum—Revolt of the workers in Romania's capital city toppled the government—Following the closing of the post office in Jesendorf, the cooperative store is now also closed—No Soviet nuclear weapons in East Germany any longer—Eight thousand one hundred conscripts drafted from the new states—Mrs. Honecker received a German passport—By the end of July 2073 fatalities on East German streets.

I fold up the newspaper and interrupt the film that plays before my inner eye with every single news report. I look for the masthead. Publisher: Dr. Huberta Burda. Less than two years ago, in the same layout, this newspaper was the newspaper of the Socialist Unity Party. I wonder how many of the editors may have been kept in the transition.

It is after four. To the desk at last. The lecture, I am aware, is only an excuse for me to come to grips with the question that has interested me most for some time, and which, like other questions, was washed away during the past two years by the absolute primacy of the political domain. What is "the mind"? How does the mental principle relate to the brain? How are we to view the interpenetration of matter, even the human body, and the mind? And thus: how do "mind and soul" affect the body cell that suddenly "degenerates" into cancer? Too many quotation marks, I know, but how do I express linguistically that unity of mind, body, and soul? Very simply, actually, when I say: the human being. Only that we are trained always to include the division into three parts in our thinking about this concept.

I take up my notes about the conversation with Hans-Peter Dürr. He distinguishes between *real* and *true*. He sees no signs of a change in the one-sided thinking of the natural scientists. For them, *real* is what is measurable and they black out the entire remaining enormous (the right word!) realm of reality. So, according to Dürr, even the question "wave or particle" is basically wrong. Even the idea that an atom is a particle that constantly remains the same over time was quite wrong. Let's take an iodine atom, Dürr said. So fine, the statistical average of all iodine atoms decays in exactly the length of time ascertained by physics. The individual atom, however, is free to decay as early as during the next second or even substantially after the statistical average point of decay. In the microcosm an enormous confusion prevails, the mind as the source of everything creative makes an enormous abundance of creative offers; part of those alternatives solidify into substance that Dürr graphically and surprisingly calls "slag of the mind," which orients itself, like the substance of the macrocosm and that of the mesocosm in which we live, according to more or less mechanical laws. Such determinations suit us; they give us the assurance that we will find needed objects again as and where we left them. Not so in the microcosm; there everything is still open.

Dürr does not see the production of the cosmos from the mind as a kind of "big bang." Rather, that origin could be an original question that opened an alternative element: Yes–no. So–otherwise. Both–and. And this questioning entity immediately tied itself into a network of alternative questions at each of its poles, then again, again, and so on, increasing the number of possibilities at an enormous rate; this immense reservoir of possibilities could have—actually why not—created structures like "time" and "space" (which in this context probably deserve their quotation marks): a screen on which reality was to be projected.

I am now gripped by the same excitement that I felt that morning when we sat on our veranda and Dürr brought the concept "expectation horizon" into play. An expectation horizon forms, which brings about the event; in the place where the expectation is densest there is some probability that the event will transpire—but that is not at all certain.

A poetic principle, I said, and he: Why not? Someday science and poesy will perhaps come together again.

Spontaneously I apply his examples from natural science to history, to events that I have experienced. In the fall of '89 didn't we all feel the chokingly thick consistency of our common expectation horizon? Did not that density *have to* bring about "the event," catapult it out of itself? Physically we felt ourselves electrified by an unbelievable concentration of energy that had not been there a few weeks, even days before.

I quickly write a few sentences for the lecture: the meaning of the attitude of expectation, that is: of openness, of hope.

That one does not have to lie to the patient if one leaves the outcome open for him. That in processes that affect the individual, statistical probability loses much of its absolute validity. That it is always conceivable to reverse the process that disturbed the delicate balance of the cell and drove it to this frenzied acceleration. That we, perhaps, could again learn to respect the miracle of that balance . . .

For one or two hours, or even for longer, that already no longer conscious, continuous feeling of being "too late," with which I live, has left me; the clamp has opened and there is something like a free life, not under the yoke of false, destructive needs. Thus there must also be a life with each other, not just this blindly furious opposition; thus old Faust's grandiose self-deception is perhaps *not* the last word, I think to myself, and does it really have to be a *word* at all? Isn't a knowing glance, an unselfish deed now more effective that worn-out speech? Shouldn't . . . ?

My thoughts run hot. Anton appears in the doorway where the large poster with the portrait of Virginia Woolf hangs; he has just watched an animal film on television. Do I actually know how the survival of sea turtles near the South Sea Islands is related to the price of bananas? I do not know and now learn it. So: the sea turtles feed on jellyfish, don't they? And on the banana plantations poisonous fertilizers are used and herbicides are sprayed, aren't they?—Oh, and then the poison gets into the ocean and the jellyfish die . . .—Not really. Or yes, that's true, but that is not the main thing. You see, when the banana prices are very high, then the bananas are packed in plastic bags so that they are not damaged while being transported, because they are expensive, understood?—Understood—And many of those plastic bags, which are made of transparent sheets, are driven into the ocean, where the sea turtles think they are jellyfish and eat them; and then the animals die of starvation or choke to death—But that is terrible—It *is* terrible—But when

the prices are low and no plastic bags are used, then the workers on the plantations receive less pay—Sure. They can already
hardly live on what they make anyway—Thus: the turtles or the
people?—Anton remains silent and thinks. Then: I have an
idea. I would paint a large poster and hang it up here in the
field market. I would paint a sea turtle on it, very true to life,
and then I would have somebody write under it: Do you want
me to die?—Why *have somebody* write under it?—Well, I really don't know all of the letters yet. And then I would put slips
of paper next to the cash register, which people should sign,
saying that they will also pay a higher price for the bananas if
they are transported without plastic coverings. Good idea, I say,
and now we'll practice a few letters, all right?

We sit next to each other at the desk in the large room;
Anton negotiates: What? *Two* rows of "Mama," and then two
more rows of "Mimi"? And then the numbers after that?—
Come on, don't make a fuss—He writes without concentrating, does not like to exert himself, plays intermittently with the
sand-picture frame, and is happy about the landscapes that he
can produce with the sand that runs between the two sheets of
glass. I water the geraniums at the window and observe the
change in the sky and how early it gets dark now. By the way,
says Anton, do you know what would be even better? If the
people sign, saying that they will not buy any more bananas
that were packed in plastic bags—That would be even better.
But would they do that?

In her kitchen Carola has made beet rolls and spelt meatballs to go with them. The kitchen is filled with the sweet smell
of the elderberry juice that is running through the juicer. A bat-
tery of bottles is already standing on the windowsill. We talk
about the qualities of the elderberry, about the early departure
of the cormorants, and about the fact that the village cooperative store will soon be closed—it is not careful and its cigarette
and alcohol supplies are plundered every few weeks—and later

the post office, too. How are the old women in the village supposed to shop then? Where will they meet? Anton says: By the way, I know something else that would be better. You see, the people who own the plantations—they said that on television—they are rich. They should get less money and instead the workers should get more, even if the bananas become cheaper and are not packed in plastic bags. Otherwise the workers should not pick the bananas at all.

Carola puts Anton to bed and reads the evening fairy tale; I am called for the good-night song, which cannot be *"Der Mond ist aufgegangen* (The Moon has Risen)" under any circumstances; I finally find out why: because of the "sick neighbor" in the last verse, whom Anton then constantly thinks about. So we agree on *"Ein Sternlein stand am Himmel* (A Little Star Was in the Sky)" sung to an invented melody; we agree that he is still permitted to read, for half an hour? Okay; reassure ourselves that Anton's parents will be home again in three days, that we will pick them up at the airport, that they will undoubtedly be very suntanned.

Television crime drama. A rich man sets a trap for his wife's lover, but then shoots the wrong man. As I do almost every evening, I become irritated that I cannot extract myself from a crime drama, no matter how stupid or boring it is. Again I ask myself where all the television garbage of decades might actually be stored up within me, or what I could have done instead of sitting in front of the tube, my concession to the zeitgeist. Right after the end the telephone rings. Gerd knows that he cannot interrupt me until now. No, in Berlin there was no sunshine, but no rain either, dismal weather. Too much mail; you finally have to learn to throw some of it away—Rituals—Listen, I say: "In being find your happiness!"—does that mean anything to you?—Goethe—Well, of course. Which Goethe poem, if you please?—Well, for that I would have to know the first line—It is a late poem. Summarizes his worldview. Wait a minute: "Existence is eternal, nature's measures / Preserve for us . . . " It goes on something like that—Doesn't help me at all. I need the beginning.

During the "Political Barometer" program, of all times, the power goes off twice; in that way we are reminded that we do not live in the center of civilization. "The Crazy Show" then runs without interruption. Hard to believe, I say several times and then listen to and watch how the continuation of the permanent best-seller *Gone with the Wind* will be managed. So, the lady who will write this sequel is an employee of the community of heirs. Well, good luck, I say, comforted once more by the thought that I was not born later, when all authors will be employees of some interest group or other.

. . . "nature's measures / Preserve for us the living treasures / In which the universe did dress." So who says it? So that would be the end, with Goethe my memory always does yield something more. In the kitchen I prepare the chicken with mushrooms for tomorrow. Goethe has undoubtedly come to mind in connection with Dürr's trains of thought, so the first line must be related to that. Now I remember that it is a long poem, remarkable how Goethe's premonitions are becoming interesting for today's scientists again, even his actually "false" arguments against Newton about the nature of light. "To find himself in boundless sphere / The one will gladly disappear . . . " No, that isn't it. Although there are lines there . . . "In all the eternal makes its way: / For all to nothing must decay, / If it as something will endure." Those lines could also be in the poem I am looking for. Or not.

The pieces of chicken sizzle, a pleasant fragrance spreads through the kitchen, and I cut the mushrooms into thin slices. I feel that I am now quite close to the line that I am searching for; the rhythm works within me, tries out different words, new lines, and then it is there, very clear. My poem could not begin differently. Well, what time is it? Not yet midnight. I call

Berlin, hopefully you are not asleep yet, so listen, the poem begins: No being can to naught decay!

> In all the eternal makes its way,
> In being find your happiness!
> Existence is eternal: nature's measures
> Preserve for us the living treasures
> In which the universe did dress.

Just a moment, we'll have that right away. So, the poem is entitled "*Vermächtnis* (Legacy)," has seven stanzas and belongs to the very late group, between 1828 and 1832.

That's what I thought. But imagine: there must be an earlier poem in which he declares the opposite, specifically, that everything must fall into nothingness, and for that he very economically used the same line: In all the eternal makes its way— Very nice. Should be investigated sometime. But no more this evening, all right?

To my great irritation, the mushrooms have too much salt on them, and I won't be able to save the dish by cooking a raw potato along with them either. I take my edition of the Goethe poems to bed with me, not only because I must still find that poem but also because I want to indulge myself in the beneficial impact that Goethe poems always have on me. I turn pages, read, feel the desired effect, and also find what I am searching for, so it is called "One and All" and could be compared line for line with "Legacy," which was written barely ten years later and which ends, to my inner derisive delight, with lines that could not be more anachronistic:

> For seeking contact with noble souls
> is a most desirable profession.

SUNDAY, SEPTEMBER 27, 1992
Santa Monica, California

It is a quarter to ten in the morning. I am sitting in my office at the little computer. By means of an incorrect manipulation I just deleted the three single-spaced pages of the initial American impression that I had written the day before yesterday but had unfortunately not immediately printed. Fortunately there are the handwritten pages that I noted down on Thursday when I was waiting for the three suitcases that I had shipped as air freight. They arrived at around three o'clock in the afternoon, so that I was able to open the suitcase that contained the computer and call Erin in the Getty Center[1] and give her the voltage, after which she drove downtown and bought the converter that I needed because of the lower voltage here—and of course the salesman did not want to know the voltage, but the wattage!—now, praise and thanks be to God, the computer writes; it also deletes, however, things that it should not delete, but it does save me from having to adapt to using a Macintosh computer that is placed at the disposal of the "scholars" here.

This morning at a little after six, I was forced to wake up. My last dream image was of a blond, beautifully clothed girl who stood with her hand on a brightly painted railing and looked dreamily into the distance. I probably owe that dream to an episode of *Star Trek,* which I devotedly watch here in the evenings, which I, to be sure, do not understand word for

[1] From September of 1992 until June of 1993 C.W. was a scholar at the Getty Center for the History of Art and the Humanities in Santa Monica, California. (G.W.)

word, but thoroughly grasp the meaning, and in which just yesterday there was a planet on which the astonished *Star Trek*
crew members encountered their embodied dreams and fantasies, which they could live out there. Among those fantasies
there was also a blond, unfashionably dressed girl: Alice in
Wonderland. The girl in my dream, however, looked different,
and somewhat later, from another, earlier dream sequence the
sentence arose: I cannot know yet, of course, what depths are
being plowed here. The wheels are rolling and rolling and
rolling . . . Gradually, while I held my eyes closed and let that
casual, absentminded attention prevail, which can sometimes
fix the fleeting dream images in my memory, that dream did
arise again. A long emigration dream. We, Gerd and I, were
sitting in the car. It was clear, the "new money" would come,
and then we had to emigrate. A peculiar man with a broad, fur-
covered nose, whom we asked, confirmed to us calmly that we
had to go. Would many "go"? No, was the answer, most people, of course, wanted the "new money." In the dream I
became very much aware of our outsider role. The man, who,
according to our papers, was assigned to us for many years as
an informal colleague, played an important role in my dream
as a helper during our "move." In the end we sat tightly
packed together with him in the car. They said that we could
take even more things along; two women whom we knew very
well helped us to pack the car fuller and fuller; they did not
talk while doing so and had sad faces. I thought I should still
call our daughters and say goodbye, but they knew what was
happening and would remain here. Images appeared that I
have in my memory from my flight at the beginning of 1945;
everything took place in an atmosphere of disorder, disaster,
and homelessness that dominates all of my dreams.

(Yesterday morning, after the pictures of new outrages by
neo-Nazi young people in the former German Democratic
Republic—that is the only thing that people see and hear about

Germany here—I had seen interviews with school children. Good, normal faces. Smart opinions. None of the boys and girls was for the rightists, but neither did anyone know what should be done. And, what torments me: I do not know either, because I think this situation of young people dropping out of all social relationships—for which they are seeking a pseudo-social substitute—in serious cases, out of human civility, is structurally laid out in an industrial and competitive society.)

I must force myself to describe the first hours of the day— habits that are only beginning to become a pattern, which I will not remember if I do not note them down; I cannot rely on my memory even in small things and right now I am hungry for the details of everyday life—a hunger that makes me more and more unable to invent anything that has even a hint of the spectacular about it; although really, I say to myself, I cannot understand why I want to note down that earlier while still in bed I read in Dietmar Kamper's notes about his first stay in New York in 1982. Illuminating for me, his reflections about the "displacement of wishes" in that remarkable city, proceeding from the idea that the European emancipation movements were and are self-deceptions. Since the end of the Middle Ages we have known the ability to act in a way that is "only connected with confusion"; the "knowledge of doing" has always come "afterward," when it was too late.

So while I do my exercises—very cautiously; apparently the painful nerve is pressing very hard against my spinal column— a pain that very quickly becomes vicious and forces me, contrary to my intention, to take a pill even before breakfast, which appears to have been working for about an hour now— not only from the bed that is too soft (I banish the thought of what I should do here, where I am alone, if I were to have another prolapsed disk, for example, like I did last year). While I pull back the lamellar curtain on the bedroom window: outside the sun as it is every day, it will be hot, like yesterday, 90 degrees Fahrenheit, 32 degrees Celsius; while I shower, my thoughts revolve around Kamper's statement that the search for paradise led to the installation of hell on earth (and in New York, he believes, to a strange displacement of wishes: instead of paradise, the labyrinth). Manhattan means something like "island of the blessed," but we modern people do not have the slightest reason to mock the first immigrants' naïve perceptions of bliss, nor the exaggerated hopes of Christopher Columbus's crew, about whom they are having great celebrations here right now on the five-hundredth anniversary of his discovery. The hope for paradise mixed itself, of course, with sober economic thought in communism, to form a compound that could no longer be dissolved. The hope for paradise collapsed much earlier than the economy. I try to remember the stages in my own thinking and ask myself, not for the first time, what we were living for when after the collapse of hope only the shallow preservation of power had remained and the moral questions also presented themselves anew—as they again do now, because for many people in the former German Democratic Republic a new hope for paradise, which is hard for me to understand, is collapsing—"blooming landscapes," a paradisaical image—and so much depends on where the weight of that disappointment draws the majority of those people. And what would it mean for this precarious existing situation if what Kamper thinks were true: that emancipation and freedom are mutually exclusive?

And what does all that, I ask myself while I fix breakfast, have to do with the fact that here, in paradise, when I become aware of my situation, I am now subject again and again to attacks of a feeling of penetrating unreality? Flight? That would be too easy. Or do I want to have a look at how it is constituted inside, the paradise that now lies ahead all of us?

As chance would have it, while I eat my breakfast (Quaker's oatmeal, a toasted poppy-seed roll with the jams that I bought

on Thursday on Third Street, directly from the farmers), on
television there is a Sunday-morning worship service program
in an enormous hall, packed full of people who are listening
intently to the words of a preacher, who confronts this crowd
as a preacher of repentance, an actor, an animal trainer, and a
show master, and handles them according to the rules of mass
psychology; and all of them, or at least most of them, go along,
black and white. I can see their enraptured, fervently believing,
enthusiastically agreeing faces. Is one reason for this prevalent
chiliastic hope of salvation possibly the flip side of a life as
monads to which they are subject in their daily routines? "In
God We Trust" is written on their dollar bills—You can make
a difference! cries the preacher beseechingly, and at the end it
is announced that "changed women" are always ready to seek
out you and me and everybody.

On the way to the Getty Center I document all the details:
the Spanish façade of our hotel, the inner courtyard framed by
exotic plants, the sour orange tree in the middle, aware that the
light and colors that send me into euphoria cannot be captured
in any photograph. I walk—after five days!—an already accustomed route, taking pictures, how quickly we adapt, turn left
down Third Street to California Avenue, left again sixty or seventy meters, on the corner of Fourth Street push the button on
the traffic signal, wait until the warning red hand disappears
and a green pedestrian appears, quickly from that position take
a snapshot of the Getty Center that towers up on the right, a
fourteen-story modern office building, on the first floor of
which the First Federal Bank resides, to which I will probably
entrust my fortune.

It occurs to me that my dream sentence—The wheels are
rolling and rolling and rolling—could also be interpreted differently. Yesterday I rode with Martin R., the man from
Stuttgart who now leads a large and famous institute in Dresden, about three hundred miles across country: north along

the Coast Highway toward Santa Barbara, first past the expensive estates of Pacific Palisades (yes, I remembered how we saw them for the first time ten years ago . . .), then a large loop through the Santa Monica Mountains, which R. loves very much and which immediately fascinated me, too, ocher cliffs in all shades of color, uninhabited areas, now and then a ranch, horses, enormous cars in front of the rich houses, in which the male inhabitants, I heard, drive to L.A. to work. And the light, the slight intoxication comes from the light; I will not be able to describe that. For the first time again then that Coastal Highway, on the left the Pacific Ocean, a magical body of water, next to it the flat row of buildings with restaurants and cafés, to the right, towering up, the steep coastline. He envied me, R. said. For nine months I could see all of this as often as I wanted, it is his dream landscape, he had to depart tomorrow, i.e. today. As we wandered through the bizarre Spanish inner city in Santa Barbara, ate in front of a Mexican restaurant under a sunshade, tortillas filled with cheese and chicken, beans, before that we had enjoyed a margarita, for that had been the waitress's first question: Do you like a margarita? And to R.'s astonishment I cried enthusiastically: Yes, I do! And I recognized again the taste that I had never found in Europe, tequila and triple sec with lemon juice and crushed ice, at noon in that heat, but it did not matter to me. Then we drank an espresso on the next corner, talked about the thin American coffee, drove then to the "mission," to the Spanish mission, a monastery from which Spanish monks performed missionary work among the Indian population before 1600. Until 1848, of course, California belonged to Mexico, which, much to its detriment, had refused to sell New Mexico and California to the Americans; so they had to obtain those areas for themselves by war. We saw proof supposedly documenting the fact that the Indians were "content" with their conversion to Christianity; but the early photograph of a converted Indian shows him

as anything but "satisfied," on the contrary, grim. We read of
the draconian punishments that were inflicted by the Christians on the heathen: chopping off a hand for theft, chopping
off a leg for trying to flee. We saw the marvelously beautiful,
quiet monastery garden, filled with exotic trees and strange
flowers that blossomed in fabulous colors, a place of seclusion
and meditation where we heard nothing but the splashing of
the fountain and spontaneously had to say: Oh, isn't that beautiful?! (Just as on the first morning after my arrival, hardly
more than two hundred meters from my hotel, I had stood up
on the coastal bluff, looked at Santa Monica Bay, and said several times aloud to myself: Magnificent, magnificent, magnificent!) I sensed so much beauty as pure deception that is no
longer aware of itself, but only now, outside the influence of
that beauty, can I express it. They have counted that Columbus
in his ship's log mentioned the words *God* and *our Lord* one
hundred and fifty times, but the word *gold* one hundred and
thirty-nine times, and of what use are all the confessions of
guilt and professions of remorse of the Christian churches now
to the Indians whose tribes were exterminated and whose culture was destroyed? In saying that, I am aware that my anger,
my melancholy does not concern the Indians only.

We walked across the not really very large cemetery where,
over the generations, thousands of Indians and even white men
are said to have been buried. Today only a few large grave
monuments of Spanish-American families stand there. We
tried to imagine how contemporary and cultural history must
be layered over one another as human skeletons in this place.
As we walked, drove, and ate, our conversation continued to
focus on the legitimate structures of colonization, R. always
with a half-guilty conscience, probably asking himself if I num-
bered him, too, among the colonizers—which I did not do. He
is obsessed with his task and seems to be the right man in the
right place; for a West German, of course, can often save an

East German institution with which he identifies more easily than an East German can; but in the evening, in the dark, when we were already on the outskirts of L.A., a tiny particle of the many-eyed lindworm that was moving toward the city, which had already been shining in the sky for a long time as a bright red glow, he asked me if I considered the replacement of the elites to be among the legitimate developments of colonization; I said yes, and he asked if I suspected feelings of revenge on the part of the victors as being behind it; I said, an often unconscious need for revenge could play a role in it, they probably have to indemnify themselves for the fear of those who are now their subjects, which they had for a long time, without basis, as is now apparent; but the replacement of the elites does belong among the very oldest and indispensable control strategies of any new power; that the previous political elite will be removed is obvious, of course; there was not an economic upper class in the German Democratic Republic, of course, because nobody was able to accumulate a fortune in the capitalistic sense, so the owner class will also come from the West—especially since the right of former East German citizens to even the very modest ownership of houses, to the extent that they formerly had Western owners, is being contested; the fact that in the intellectual sphere the first attacks were directed at writers was also not a coincidence, of course, and with regard to the university professors—there the great liquidation is fully underway. I really did not think, I said, that they all could have or should have been able to keep their positions; only people who knew them and whose motives were not influenced by the initial East-West distribution struggles should have made the decisions . . .

We asked ourselves how this American West is different from the partially desolate industrial zones of the East. R. thinks that from the very beginning here in the West there was something like an idealistic vision that led to the fact that nature was not destroyed (except by settlement itself, through the big cities), that there are "creating areas" and industry that does not pollute the air. Actually, the mass transportation, in spite of the terrible pictures that are served to me every evening on television, does not make the same aggressive impression on me that it does in Germany, if only because of the speed limit, which is at least somewhat observed.

Where are you going, Madam? the watchman asked me down below. I had to sign my name in a book, for today is Sunday, of course, and the building is almost empty; in case of fire or other dangers they want to know where it might be necessary to save someone. When I got into the elevator on the wrong side, the watchman began singing a melodic scale with the little word *no*: No, no, no, no, no—until I understood that this elevator is not used on Sundays. So to the fourth floor, where everyone must go who wants to enter the Center, which as a whole, because of its treasures, is a high security section; I say "Hi!" to the second watchman who sits there (those are probably the only positions here that are occupied by blacks). From a little cabinet I take my personal security card with a photograph and two little keys, and because it is Sunday and the elevator is blocked, I go through a back door and climb a back stairway to the sixth floor, where there is not a soul today except at first the two girls and the young man—all of them black or brown—who are cleaning. Once a watchman walked past my door, which I leave open according to American custom, but otherwise I am alone. I get myself a cup of water from the kitchen, once a yogurt from the refrigerator, sometimes gaze across the parking lot for a long time, looking between tall apartment buildings at the ocean, which lies there flat and glitters in the sunlight bordered by palm trees. I look repeatedly at my watch and calculate the time difference between here and Berlin, but then do make a mistake when I finally call, because instead of figuring ahead I figured eight hours back.

Gerd's voice is quite near and I hear my own with a slight echo. When he is at the book fair in Frankfurt I will not reach him so easily anymore.

In one of the German newspapers that hang in the lounge, I find an interview with the American sociologist Amitai Etzioni, who belongs to the "Communitarians," a new political and philosophical movement that crosses party lines and strives for renunciation of crass individualism and consciousness of socially unifying values, to which belong: strengthening the family and emphasis of duty and responsibility for the society. He says that the American economy should take the Central European social market economy as a model and develop itself into a cooperative economy—up to now only the Pentagon has achieved that with its military economy. The absence of ties—even in the family—is one of the main causes for the American drug problem; there is no training of apprentices; the labor morale and the qualifications of American workers are startlingly low; the Americans can no longer afford their wasteful way of life; he fears that the enormous deficits in social policy could lead to the disintegration of the American society.

Now it is one o'clock; I am tired and hungry and will go over and make myself a pancake with mushrooms, then lie down and read. Now, however, having been warned by this morning's mishap, I will first print out the pages that I have just written.

Monday, the twenty-eighth of September: I did not succeed in doing that very thing last night, because during printing my color ribbon produced no color; I tried for half an hour, unwilling to believe what I saw, or unfortunately did not see. This morning Gretchen, the good spirit in our secretary's office, took great pains with it and just now a young man who looks Japanese arrived, an excellent computer specialist; he, too, capitulated ("Such a simple thing!") and now wants to try to find a branch office of the firm from which my little machine comes—they will probably have to call Germany. (But then that was not necessary after all; twice I drove deep into Los Angeles with Daisy, to a workshop that found the small part that was "broken" and repaired it for forty-five dollars; I am astonished at my dependency on mechanisms.) So yesterday I went home; the pancakes tasted somewhat peculiar with the slightly sweetened "Swedish pancake meal" and the over-salted margarine. I lay down and was happy with my quiet bedroom with the large, ivy-twined, screened window that is shaded at that time of day. I continue to read in Dietmar Kamper's notes from New York; fascinated for reasons that I am very much conscious of by his reflections on the causes of this increasing feeling of unreality, which he also seeks in the growing uneventfulness of modernity and in modern man's neediness, which is often hidden, even from himself ("Life here transpires to a certain extent with fatal certainty in established patterns. That is why insanity draws so close"). If you often let the radio and television set run, as I do, you get the impression that the Americans believe that there is a solution for everything, a remedy for every ill, relief for every pain, a cure for every illness, and they do not want to admit to themselves that from that very expectation of salvation, over time, a feeling of unreality, even weirdness arises. I, on the other hand, am aware: I am on vacation from reality. What happens to me here is not "real." Nothing does happen to me. The encounter with people—be they congenial or annoying—does not, of course, lead to obligation, tie, or responsibility. The relief that I experience makes it clear to me how intensively I experienced the pressure of reality "over there."

Kamper cites Steven Spielberg, the creator of E.T., that remarkable, actually monstrous and yet touching imagined being that drew the feelings of children and adults to itself for months: "The imagination is the only possibility of escape from the uneventfulness of modern times." It seems anachronistic to view the imagination as a means for expanding and condensing reality, a means that is in every way part of reality. In any case, Kamper believes that the "surplus of the fantastic" has penetrated to the heart of social life and "occupies the place that the gods once had." The unicorn on one of the "authentic" medieval tapestries is for him the symbol of imagination—"in reality," i.e. at the time of the matriarchy, it was, however, a calendar symbol composed of several female animals, and the horn of the unicorn itself was a phallic symbol; so on those tapestries that tell a story, it is perhaps not the imagination that is pursued and captured in the unicorn, but the "feminine principle"—and would that not amount to the same thing? And what does this mean for Medea toward whom all of my chains of thought are directed, when I let them run free?

Medea, the goddess, the healing woman who also heals through imagination—is she perhaps also slandered, persecuted, and ostracized by the male-dominated society in Corinth because of that surplus of imagination—since she did not kill her children after all, despite what Euripides ascribes to her? Apparently he needed a strong motif for the excess of hate that follows her through the centuries. So in order to explain that hate I would have to force the story open again. Medea, the sorceress who makes the men, even Jason, afraid. Who brought other values with her from Colchis to Corinth. Which, in the final analysis, is to be colonized.

I slept until four, fussily got dressed, and packed my bathing things; at five-thirty on the dot Kurt Forster called from the entry door. We drove the short distance to the Forsters' beautiful house on Montana Street. Françoise greeted me with the remark that she had already known me for a long time through my books. No strangeness arose; they showed me the bathroom of their daughters who no longer live at home, in which I was able to change clothes in order to swim in the beautiful oval swimming pool among exotic plants. In the house I found everything spacious, practical, and perfect—a word that occurs to me here so often. It is as if they find out the most practical way of doing anything and then orient themselves according to that insight.

We sat outside at a simple wooden table and ate radishes and nuts with a very good, dry, Italian white wine. Then began the long conversation about the Getty Center, of which Kurt F. has been the director for eight years, that is, he helped found it and assisted in determining its structure. My fascination was aroused by a materially well equipped apparatus that has devoted itself to the collection but also to the production of art. I foresee how often I will yet speak with varying partners about the problems that such a creation must necessarily produce, the tension between the laws of the bureaucracy and those of art production. I hear of the purchase of excellent collections that Kurt was able to convince the trust about, among them entire libraries and archives of emigrants and much German material; it is a matter of documenting the genesis of works of art; incomprehensible to me how such a mass of material could be brought together in eight years (I just received from Kathleen on the fourth floor an insight into the possibilities of the library and the acquisition of books, which, however, are overwhelming). Françoise did a great deal of work on Adolph Menzel [2] in East Berlin, is familiar with the history of the National Gallery, and remains close to some female associates with whom she was able to collaborate in a personal manner that one does not find in Western museums. She laments the fact that because they have combined with other galleries and museums effective work is now hardly possible.

We eat salmon and rice and mushrooms; the conversation remains lively. I learn that Françoise comes from a Hamburg

[2] Adolph Friedrich Erdmann von Menzel (1815-1905), German artist noted for drawings, engravings and paintings. (Ed.)

family that was not acceptable to the Nazis; some members of the family were involved in the twentieth of July and were saved because the leader of their subgroup committed suicide after his arrest in order not to betray anyone. Her fear of a possible repetition of the Weimar situation (this morning there was a report that neo-Nazis set fire to the Jewish barracks in the former Sachsenhausen concentration camp. A counterdemonstration by perhaps four hundred people). But you will go back? ask the Forsters. Yes, I say, what else?—We talk about how the old question, posed especially by intellectuals, of how much integration they can attempt without losing their integrity, is now—following the unification of the two German states (or rather: after the collapse of the one and the resulting possibility of the restoration of a German state within significantly expanded borders)—again posed differently than it was for us in the German Democratic Republic. The fact that there was a question there at all, and a problem whose solution could give one something to think about, is now no longer supposed to be true. The behavior that arose from a sum of conflicts, as well as mistakes, illusions, even wishful thinking and false opinions, and finally from insights that became more and more realistic, is now simply supposed to be gotten rid of as in a computer game under "true" or "false"—Again my impression that all of German history comes up and joins in here during almost any conversation that you might choose.

The American elections are being discussed everywhere. Françoise hopes that Clinton will perhaps squeak through; even if one must only hope that, she says, so that a different party will finally take the helm for a change and unravel the old tangled mess. The qualities of Clinton and his designated vice-president, Al Gore, of whom both have a high opinion, are weighed against the deficiencies of Bush and Quayle. Kurt fears that Bush will barely win; then in the houses of Congress the Democrats would have the majority and the government and the President would be immobilized.

At ten I am driven home and am very tired. Perhaps I still have not completely overcome the jet lag, or assimilating all of the new impressions very attentively is simply wearing me out. Lying in the dark, I suddenly hear the three notes—a triad— that always provoke a perfect quietude in me, even when "over there." Thus, as a consolation, they have accompanied me across the ocean. I quickly fall asleep.

I awaken at around a quarter to six; no dream fragment will let me catch hold of it. By now, it has been too long since I last dreamed. I am no longer tired. G. wants to talk with me about Alice Schwarzer's book about the deaths of Petra Kelly and Gert Bastian, which he is reading and which disturbs him because it allows for no other interpretations than that of the author. I remember how the report of that gruesome double death touched me last year in Santa Monica; something about it seemed typically German to me. I asked myself why I had to think again and again: That was a German couple, a weird German couple. This book by Alice Schwarzer does provide material for that feeling, but for my taste it presents too much prejudice and judgment, too little sympathy and sisterliness. At the same time, the relationship between those two people really would be worth an exact investigation and description, which would naturally not have to be uncritical— could not be at all. But with the standard of rigorous feminism a man—and a woman—cannot go ahead, it seems to me—the old question of how one does people more justice, with the dissection knife or with the understanding look that takes in one's own disputable points as well.

Newspaper reading at breakfast. In *Freitag* I read an article dealing with the question of just where the West could seek its friends in ex-Yugoslavia—in any case, not among the official politicians. As always, when I cannot avoid touching on that topic, I am offended at our inaction and my own feeling of powerlessness, which is not excusable just because most of the people around us share it. I have the impression that the number of problems that I do not see through, and for that reason also cannot comment about, is increasing, as is my uneasiness about the matter. For example, I read about the "revolt in Moscow," where Yeltsin dissolved the parliament last week and where there have been two presidents since then—he and Rutskoi. (Later, at breakfast, Gerd will read aloud to me what Falin writes about that: The German view of the most recent events in Russia is mistaken; what is taking place there is not a power struggle between "reformers" and "anti-reformers" but a struggle between two factions of representatives of the market economy. Yeltsin represents the "liberal," Rutskoi the "social" market economy. Only six percent of the population feels good under Yeltsin. Twenty-six percent of the people felt best under Brezhnev . . . No comment.) The "newspaper reader" of *Freitag*, Erich Kuby,[1] is concerned about the "Heitmann case." He mocks the fact that "Bonn's scandalmongers" now publicly rid themselves of the task of "making a federal president out of a Saxon pastor." I ask myself which would be worse: if the federal chancellor and those who defend his candidate really believed that he is being criticized because he comes from the East, or if they were to use that argument purely demagogically and wanted nothing but an indolent, clumsy federal president who presented a conservative image of the Federal Republic at home and abroad. Loss of reality by the rulers expresses itself in different systems through different objects and problems . . .

"The East Is Still No High Noon" is the title given to an article by a research group of the German Society of Applied Economics, which begins as follows: "Three years after the formal establishment of the unified economic system in East and West

---

[1] Erich Kuby (1910-2005), German author and journalist. (Ed.)

Germany it is becoming more and more obvious that the economic policy of the union, which focuses primarily on market forces, has failed. A self-sustaining economic boom is still not in sight even today." So it is a matter of a "reconstruction program" that would guarantee "reindustrialization and active labor market policies." That is probably right, I think to myself while I shower and get dressed, and yet there is also something that is not right about it, for all of the rescue suggestions focus on restoring the old monster, the industrial society in its old glory, thus also its priorities and values, thus also its alienation effect that led to the situation that people define and esteem themselves only in terms of work anymore and must feel that more free time is not only a social but also an existential threat. The industrial society needed generations to create that perfect, serviceable worker. How much time does it have to move work—*the* work—away from the center of life of most people to a peripheral place without the often cited "marginalization" bringing forth new dictatorships?

I am standing in the kitchen doorway; a light comes in that is new to me, a bright autumn light, less strongly filtered by the thinning foliage of the poplar tree in front of the window. Suddenly I see the new bright bench and the kitchen table as if for the first time; it is as if all the light from all of the kitchen tables of my life were gathering on this one; for the blink of an eye all of the family members and all of the guests that have ever sat at our kitchen table are sitting together around this one, I among them, in a changing, aging form. We looked at each other from many pairs of eyes across time. Some closed, irrevocably, others turned away, in shame, foreignness, hate, forever. New ones joined us, were welcome. The glow on the table remains, a laugh resounds, closeness comes into being. How we lived. How innocent we were. How cheerful, friendly, generous. How curious. Oh, as if not prepared for anything. Betrayal, at our kitchen table? We did not want to believe it.

Sought to stop the ones who were fleeing. Meanwhile a malicious hand snuffed one candle after another. Who directed it?
The others? I myself? A blink of an eye. I stand leaning against
the doorframe. The glow has faded. All day long I cannot forget that I saw it. That one moment saturated with reality
strengthens my perception of all other moments of this day.

Later, when we are eating breakfast, Gerd his beloved
smoked salmon, I my rye crisp with plum sauce, Gerd buried
in his newspaper—in the White House in Moscow the night
passed quietly—later I ask myself where the glow came from.
Outside it is a dreary, autumnal mood, the summer that was
too cool and too wet is ending too cool and too wet. I have to
get busy unpacking the enormous cardboard box from an eco-
logically minded office supply house, which has already been
standing in the corner for days. I ordered all kinds of boxes
and folders in order to perhaps get the paper chaos in my room
under control once and for all. I remember that I have been
trying to do that for decades, using new and varied tricks, with
little success; so I should probably grant myself the consolation
that it is not my fault, but that of the flood of paper that rolls
over me and really only partly originates with me. But next
week I will straighten things up from top to bottom for once;
and now I must first make a supplementary entry in my note-
book about how last week went. It is also one of my tricks, I
know, that I hope to use my time better if I note down how I
spent it and mostly did not use it. Günter Grass calls from
Hamburg. He wants to know how my mood is. I say, not all
that bad, I do meet reasonable people again and again. You
do? he says: Your words into God's ear, perhaps there still are
a few luminaries after all.

It is eleven o'clock; I sit down at my little machine to begin
these notes, for which this day is reserved, and I already
know—I have been at this exercise for long enough—I know
that at the very moment when I, at eleven in the morning,

begin to describe this day, the question will arise as to whether this text will swallow up the day, whether it determines its course, whether the day is lived for the sake of the text and the text is written for the sake of the day. In brief, whether self-observation leads to falsification, but what does not lead to falsification? I forbid myself to grope my way into that trap, which is always ready to snap shut at the bottom of my consciousness; I intend to stick to realities.

Telephone. It is the publishing company; it is about the texts that are supposed to be collected into a small volume next spring, and while I listen, express agreement and concerns, I remain superficial and carefree. It is still a long time until spring and I do not even know yet if I really want that little volume, if I want the foreign eyes on my writing at all, if I really want to endure it. Up to now everything has really been a game, a test balloon; everything is open; what do I care about the talk of dust jacket, number of pages, dust jacket texts. It is that way with me every time, Gerd says. Apparently I need that self-deception. He comes back from his morning walk earlier than I expected. The potatoes have not been put on yet. He now takes care of it, and I stir the cottage cheese. An editor from the radio calls; against my own rule I recently gave her an interview, which, as always, became longer than she had promised me, and which I, as always, did not break off when I noticed it, which she now has given, in part, to another station, for which she requests from me even more precise information that I do not want to give, which a newspaper would now like to print as well, after everything else—the usual media mill in which I always wind up when I break my rule, so that in the end I am always only angry with myself until I stop worrying about it. It is not worth it.

So we eat potatoes boiled in their skins, cottage cheese, and the kale from yesterday. We drink milk and talk about the event on Friday at which Gerd's Janus publishing house presented the book by Otl Aicher, tell each other anecdotes about the evening, which, strangely enough, never occur to us until days later. Again we discover how advantageous it is to share an experience with each other; it receives an additional dimension, more density, and even our often differing assessment of people, about which we once could bitterly argue, we now accept in order—we do not notice until a long time later—to gradually let them merge with our own views.

Before my afternoon nap I read the end of Alice Schwarzer's book, from which it becomes clear that she is also working off an old personal injury and old aggression in dealing with the case of the Kelly–Bastian couple. It would, I think, have done the book good if she had let that fact shine through earlier; but her many years of experience in how unmercifully they attack a woman who criticizes the patriarchy and reveals weaknesses herself probably compels her to suppress her own vulnerability or at least the expression of it. So now we are back to where they want us: one of the circles that now often dominate my thinking.

Martin comes. He just canceled his subscription to the daily newspaper *Taz* with an angry letter, which, in a review for the most part vilifying me, claims that Otl Aicher's concept of the culture of everyday life is "barbaric." That is unbelievable, we laugh, and yet it is a shame. That is one of the incivilities that consider themselves to be leftist and are based on ignorance, stupidity, and arrogance. One could ignore it if the signs were not multiplying that the—yes, indeed—left spectrum is again indulging in reciprocal accusations and demarcations, while the happily and unrestrictedly growing right is tying its diverse groupings and intellectual centers into a network.

Five o'clock, time to change my clothes, black pants, yellow silk blouse, black silk jacket; I put on my makeup and pack my bag. Gerd is already waiting impatiently in the hall when I do not yet know which shoes I should put on—a process that repeats itself again and again. Sometimes we can laugh about it; today we can't. It is after five-thirty when we leave. The hour of our arrival in Potsdam depends on the traffic. As always when we now go "into the city," we drive down Wollankstrasse; Schönhauser Strasse toward the city has been practically impassable for a long time because of construction projects. How much longer is that going to last? we ask again. I catch myself thinking that I will probably not live long enough to see Berlin as a traversable city again. Just beyond the railroad curve West Berlin begins; the jolting on the pavement ceases. Several times we stop at traffic lights; I open my eyes wide and try to fix the route that I have driven dozens of times in my mind. How foreign this West Berlin still is to me; how poorly I am still able to find my way around in many parts of the city; I am apparently unable to succeed in storing these new localities in my memory. I ask myself if an unconscious aversion plays a role there. We move forward briskly this evening. I stick to looking at the sky; it is dramatic, large, with dark patches of clouds that move rapidly toward the northeast; in between a sickly yellow, even a pale orange sometimes shines through. While we are turning onto the city highway behind the International Chamber of Commerce building, which I, by the way, have never entered, the news comes over the car radio. Schäuble[2] is giving support to Heitmann (How long will we still know that name?!); the Free Democratic Party now seems to be inclined toward Mrs. Hamm-Brücher after all; in and at the White House in Moscow things are quiet.

The trees along the edge of the street are beginning to change color; it now gets dark earlier following the change to standard time; the stream of lights from the cars that are coming toward us is very dense. In Dreilinden we now drive past the dilapidated border facilities of the German Democratic

[2] Wolfgang Schäuble (b. 1942), German politician and leader of the Christian Democratic Union; since 2005, Federal Minister of the Interior. (Tr.)

Republic; there was still a war then, we say. Those are legacies of the war. Is there peace now? (Shevardnadze had to leave the vicinity of Sukhumi, where he wanted to hold out until the Georgian population was evacuated, ahead of the attacking Abkhazian troops; so again a hundred thousand people take flight and Sukhumi, the "Pearl of the Black Sea," is destroyed. We say nothing about that and probably see the same images. Once we rode from Gagra to Sukhumi on the hydrofoil; the city, the white pearl, was set in turquoise blue and agate green; the sea and the hills with the orange groves, the harbor bay, dusty streets. For us it was the South. The photographs that I took back then could help my memory. I forbid my imagination to let the images of flight, misery, and destruction arise.)

And if the precision that I demand from myself on such a day were only good for making me aware of the chain of repetitions in which I have now already been enmeshed for a long time? The road to Potsdam that I traveled so often with my father— I remember everything again, his apartment in the newly constructed block that we pass, his gradual decline, which he countered with strong resistance, the few personal effects (what a term!) that he was able to collect during a life of more than ninety years . . . The former Hans Marchwitza House, which is naturally no longer called that, is closed up; from a side door we arrive in the Bacchus-Keller restaurant at the same time as Hermann Vinke,[3] with whom we have an appointment and who has come from Bremen. We sit down in a niche and begin going through the plan for this evening's proceedings once more. A young, cocky waiter comes to recommend a mushroom dish to us; in the Brandenburg woods, we hear, a person can mow chanterelles with a scythe, so we eat steaks with chanterelles, with them the unavoidable little potato balls, and drink wine

[3] Hermann Vinke (b. 1940), radio director of Radio Bremen, writer and publicist, edited the book *Akteneinsicht Christa Wolf. Zerrspiegel und Dialog* (*Inspection of Christa Wolf's Files. Distorting Mirror and Dialogue*), Hamburg, 1993. (G.W.)

with soda water. Then the two book dealers arrive, who are putting on the event this evening, W. & R.; they are even younger than I had imagined them to be. The one has a bald skull, wears round classes with nickel frames, and has a narrow black knit tie knotted around his neck; the other, his friend and companion, wears a mane of curls. Both of them cultivate the jeans and leather jacket style and are very willing to tell us their history as book dealers while they zestfully drink their beer. So: W. began to study at the university twice in the German Democratic Republic, was ex-matriculated or eased out twice, then got along with various jobs until an old Potsdam archivist, who recognized his obsession with books, hired him. That was his apprenticeship. R. had left the country and returned after the collapse of the German Democratic Republic. Both of them bought up books that could be had for pennies, or even for nothing at all, since they were supposed to wind up in the dump. On the day of the currency union they stood in the marketplace with a decorator's table full of books; even on that day they claim to have sold ten books, and the year 1990, of which other book dealers speak with open horror, became a dream year for them. When the August Bebel Bookstore was advertised for sale by the trust, they applied, and after a dishonest speculator was exposed and rejected they actually did receive the contract and a bank loan; then they were offered the opportunity to buy the building where the bookstore is located for an enormous sum. That put us against the wall, of course, says W. What did we know about money? But they received the bank loan, and after the renovation of the building they rented spaces to a wine shop and some attorneys, and now they are paying off the loans from the rents. But the store is operating. Where seven people previously worked there are now three and a half, including them; we would see for ourselves. Two lucky devils.

Before eight to the Stauden Gallery, which already existed

when we would come here to see my father, and which has now been taken over by younger people. A long, narrow room with paintings of Mecklenburg landscapes on the walls; two hundred and fifty people have come. I have doubts about whether a discussion will be possible here, which, of course, is what is important to me. Vinke and I must walk up onto a podium; I am naturally seized by doubts again as to whether I should have been willing to involve myself in this undertaking. What am I doing here? I think to myself. Isn't that simply pure presumption again? We must speak loudly into the microphone in order to be understood in the back. The topic is the volume *Inspection of Christa Wolf's Files* that Hermann Vinke edited. Alternately he and I familiarize the audience with the contents; I read from the letters that I wrote in Santa Monica and that are printed in the book. It has only been six or seven months; I still remember everything. It engraved itself upon my mind, and yet that is a completed phase; I sense that even now I can no longer convey my emotions of that time to the audience. Or is it the distance that I feel, a shield, unconsciously erected against a new deluge of uncontrollable feelings?

The discussion begins somewhat awkwardly. A man asks me if the sentence in *Cassandra*—that she is ashamed of having once thought: I just want the same thing that you do!—also applies to me. I can confirm that and I talk about how, in the campaign against *Divided Heaven*, I at first always said: But I just want the same thing that you do! and how I had to learn, rather difficultly, that that was not true.

Somebody asks me to describe my development since being permitted to inspect the records, especially my Interior Ministry records. I try to talk as openly as possible about the different stages, about the initial shock, the horror about myself, the despair about the impossibility of being able to expect a differentiation in public amid the general state security hysteria, about the danger of identifying myself with the characterization that I then experienced in public, about the therapy through writing and the gradual process of working my way out of the depression again until I reached my current state, where I believe that I can explain that episode—which will always remain a sore, even a dark point—on the basis of my development. While I am talking, I notice that I have taken too much upon myself after all, that I really am still too thin-skinned for that sort of forum, but now it can no longer be avoided.

An older woman spends a long time describing what she got from my books before the collapse of the German Democratic Republic; through them she became especially aware of the fact that we live in a male-dominated society; this whole matter of the records did not interest her at all; would I continue to write about women's themes. I say that I have retained my knowledge and insights, that there are structures that were basic to the East German system, just as they are also basic to that of the Federal Republic. Both were or are patriarchies; both were or are industrial societies—that will remain in the background of my writing, even when I do not treat feminist themes in the narrower sense.

One man refers to the appeal "For Our Country." [4] He has read one of my letters thoroughly. I explain there, he says, that in *Cassandra* I had described that Troy had to fall because it demanded human sacrifices; then, however, in the appeal *"Für unser Land"* I had apparently demanded the preservation of this country of the German Democratic Republic. Was that not a contradiction? I was rather glad to be able to clarify that. In

---

[4] *"Für unser Land* (For Our Country)"*: Proclamation campaign by initiators from the citizens' movement during the last year of the German Democratic Republic, last represented by Volker Braun, Bernd B. Löwe, Sebastian Pflugbeil, Andrée Türpe, Konrad Weiss and Christa Wolf, who put the text into the version that became known, which was introduced by Stefan Heym in a press conference on November 28, 1989 (see: *Für unser Land—Eine Aufrufaktion im letzten Jahr der DDR* [For Our Country—A Proclamation Campaign in the Last Year of the GDR], Frankfurt/M., 1994). (G.W.)

that appeal, after all, we had not been thinking about the old German Democratic Republic, about its preservation or even about its resurrection. For a very short historical moment we had thought about a completely different country that none of us will ever see. An illusion, and I already knew it was at that time. In spite of that, I participated in the appeal so that I would later not have to reproach myself for having missed an opportunity. For a moment I again feel the atmosphere of those months four years ago, into which I can otherwise hardly place myself anymore.

Suddenly the topic then changes to the state security police problem after all. Whether it is important to bring it up again and again and to grapple with it. There are differing opinions; I sense an aversion to the topic, and in that context I try to control myself sharply because I am not impartial. So I say, when the keyword *reconciliation* has been uttered, that there can be no reconciliation without knowing the facts, and even while I am saying it, I ask myself if I really think that or if I have only read it. This is one of a growing number of topics, by the way, about which I have no firm opinion. I would like to hear whether or not the people actually want a discussion of their past at all (but can one really "want" it if it is embarrassing and painful, or is it one of the typical German Protestant austerities to assume that after confession of guilt and remorse, forgiveness and catharsis will follow?—Until now it has always gone otherwise in history). Some say that they did want to think about the past, they just did not want the discussion to take place in *this* fashion: conducted by the West without sensitivity and differentiation; the practices of the Gauck Commission in my case are brought up as evidence for the fact that the state security police files are being used as instruments. I attempt to argue against it by saying that we actually have to get to the point of answering for our own lives, regardless of how difficult others make it for us, regardless of how much guiltier others are, but I know that those are unreasonable demands that have nothing to do with the lives of most people. As the discussion goes back and forth, I get the impression that they are again waiting for aphorisms from me about how things are supposed to go from here. I understand every sentiment and opposing sentiment from the audience; it is as if I had never been away, it is as if they had experienced during that time the same process that I did; and now I have to guard against an attitude of expectation to which I do not want to respond; I protest (what a beautiful word!) against any manifestation of nostalgia for the German Democratic Republic that permits one to beautify what one has said and done or, for the most part, not done during the recent decades, identify situations in which we (I say "we" and mean a small group of friends) really were quite alone, until the time when the manifestations of the state's disintegration became more and more apparent, the dangers were reduced, and more and more people came into conflict and finally into opposition. That was the normal course of events and nobody could reproach anyone for it, I least of all, but neither would I forget how despondent I sometimes was during the last years of the German Democratic Republic. Nor would they be any more likely to bring me to the point of sanctioning the manner and the haste with which everything that smelled like the German Democratic Republic and was therefore disreputable was dealt with. And while I say that, I see us with the eyes of those outside: inhabitants of a quarantined barrack, infected with the state security police virus. For the first time I believe I really understand what advantages that view brings, psychological advantages, for one must not become involved with these infected people. It is self-protection when you do not let them get close to you, and it is obvious that you can dispose of them at will. Then it dawns on me what harm this kind of "appraisal" causes, causes for both sides, and I hear myself saying, more forcefully than

I want to, but even for that, for humiliation and settling things, it takes two. Why did we not resist (but how? the opposing voice in me asks)? Why did the people from Bischofferode walk through the country and nobody go with them? (It is clear to me, and the next day I can read it. Those are the sentences that they quote in the newspapers everywhere.)

Somebody asks the beautiful question of whether or not the state security police records are the guilty conscience of the nation. I say: No, only in Germany could one arrive at the idea that records could take the place of conscience. After I read my records, I knew that those records do not contain "the truth," neither about the one for whose perusal they were assembled, nor about those who filled them with their reports. They contain what the state security people saw or were supposed to, had to, were permitted to see. They reflect a growing paranoia of the smallest intellects; the very language that they used was not adequate to record "truth," their very formulation reduces people to objects that they made use of. A few pieces of information can be drawn from them, frequently pieces of outdated information even about the informants, to whom the records grant no development and whom they now nail down on a point that they have perhaps overcome (which is why the decoding of the cover names of the many Interior Ministry informers who surrounded us in earlier periods did not interest us). I am quite happy that I can say that candidly, since, of course, I had my own Interior Ministry records published. I say: No, literature must probably present "the truth" about that time and about our lives.

They naturally pinned me down on that point: Just where is this literature? And why, a curly-haired young woman asks, haven't I spoken again publicly for a long time now? Somebody wanted to know what my removal to America stood for, if that was an escape. I insist upon my right to speak when I want to, and also to remain silent. I refuse to accept the advocate role that they again want to give me, appreciate the fact that they are partially right, but give examples of what I and others have said and written anyway, without anyone noticing, remind them, as I always do on such occasions, how many years after the Napoleonic Wars Tolstoy wrote *War and Peace*, and plead for the contemplation break that has to be granted even to writers. I do hear them say yes and sense that they silently stick to their demands; I notice physically how strong that claim has again become or perhaps always remained.

After that, book signings, individual questions. A young woman reminds me that she once visited me; I do not remember it. She wants to tell me how she is doing now after she saw her state security police files. She now knows who among her colleagues spied on her and is now so ashamed for those people that she cannot look at them anymore. They in turn know that she knows and also only creep around her. When she speaks to individuals they only give excuses and self-accusations that do not satisfy her. She simply does not know how she should deal with that problem. She is now doing theater with a women's group and wants to invite me to their next production.

A man in his mid-fifties with a jovially creased face speaks to me. He wants to apologize to me at last—For what?—For the fact that back then, when *The Quest for Christa T.* appeared, he followed the purported trend and called me a "stupid cow" and a "silly goose." He was a teacher. When *Patterns of Childhood* appeared, he had said: O.K., O.K. . . . But not until much later had he read *The Quest for Christa T.* again, and the scales fell from his eyes and he saw how unjust he had been toward me back then, and for that reason he wanted to apologize—I laugh and say, back then many thought and said that about me, but only he would say so.

It is almost dark when we drive along a wide curve through Potsdam in the car. While we travel I consider the fact that the problem of the young woman and that of the man—which are also my problems—complement each other and perhaps answer each other in part. How much time had to pass before that man could voice an apology for a comparatively harmless offense that nevertheless weighed on his mind; if that reflects some kind of law, in ten, fifteen, or twenty years the spies and informers of recent decades will (perhaps) utter their apologies . . . I don't know.

In the W. & R. Bookstore, which we knew well when it was still called the August Bebel Bookstore. Astonished by the successful renovation of the building and the rooms of the bookstore, which seems more spacious, more open, and more modern than before, especially because of the view into the romantic inner courtyard. The two book dealers explain their reasoned and skillful method of displaying the books; the customers should not stumble over the most trivial reading material immediately upon entering. In their store the demand for former East German authors continues unabated, and for that reason they could not do much with the Western best-seller lists. A press release just appeared, according to which significantly more reading still takes place in the new federal states than in the West. We go up the steep spiral staircase to the top floor. Cheese tidbits have been prepared, there is wine, there are six of us: a West German, a woman from West Berlin, a young man who left the German Democratic Republic and came back, three former East German citizens, all obsessed with literature and occupied with the writing, production, propagation, or distribution of books. We probably all feel that it is a good mixture; we talk, laugh, and tell jokes and anecdotes.

At around midnight on the deserted "pedestrian zone" in the center of Potsdam, eerily illuminated by lights on whip-shaped lampposts. For a few seconds I have an intensive déjà-vu experience. But here I have already . . . I stood here once before in the same light; I heard the same words of farewell; I already exchanged the same embraces once before . . . But that is impossible. I am simply tired, sleep during most of the trip back; Gerd is also tired but stays awake by driving. We do not say much; once I say that I could not do something like that again. Gerd says: You really don't have to. I brought along from the bookstore a book that is being discussed right now, have leafed through it, a thoroughly conceived story, I envy the woman who wrote it. When will I, or will I ever be able to write a book again about a distant invented figure; I myself am the protagonist, there is no other way, I am exposed, have exposed myself.

Before falling asleep, I read in an essay by Erwin Chargaff[5]: "Two Kinds of Mourning," which begins with the sentence: "A silent mourning has fallen upon the world." That is true, I think to myself, and then I find a diary quote by Kierkegaard from the year 1849: "A single person cannot help or save an era; he can only express that it comes to an end."

[5] Erwin Chargaff (1905-2002), Austrian biochemist; discovered two rules that helped lead to the discovery of the double helical structure of DNA. (Ed.)

Twelve o'clock noon. The day has "passed" to this point without even one hour of concentration for the *Medea* text. I ask myself how the hours have passed away again. (And yesterday, too, because I got up very early, only an hour and a half before breakfast, to continue working on the Akamas monologue.) I awoke for the first time at three-thirty, began reflecting about the event on the previous evening at the Academic Bookstore on Gendarmenmarkt, where the Links Publishing Company introduced its latest book, *In Matters of Biermann*, an annotated volume of documents in which six very young editors worked together with older historians, dug a substantial number of documents out of the Party archives and those of the Writers' Union, from which the beginning, the course, and part of the consequences of the Biermann affair can be reconstructed. I experienced—and I said so that evening in the bookstore—a peculiar feeling when I saw how young those editors actually are, younger than my children, and that they experienced those events back then as ten-, eleven-, and twelve-year-olds, that they thus particularize about abstract categories in the prefaces— were we a "group," and if so, based on what criteria?—that thus for me the whole thing probably reproduces the framework of the events correctly, but not the meat, the atmosphere, what we really experienced, and what is not documented. As it also came out in the memoirs of Hermlin, Klaus Schlesinger[1] and me, that

[1] Klaus Schlesinger (1937-2001), German writer and journalist. (Tr.)

we had forgotten many things and remembered some things differently, but that, of course, was not what I began to brood about in the night. Christoph Links had asked me that evening how I had dealt with the fact that Gerd was expelled from the Party and I was not. Very badly, I had answered, and then for the first time I frankly talked about how I had experienced those events back then: that I had insisted upon receiving the same measure of punishment as my husband; that Kant had tried to do me a service by presenting me under false premises in the meeting as being more willing to compromise; that I immediately protested, even twice, but that the assembly no longer had any desire to expel me as well and for that reason, against all objections on my part, voted for a strong reprimand. That at that moment I was taken by surprise, not quick-witted enough to do what I should have done: lay my Party membership document on the table; that I then later discussed with Gerd for days and nights what I should do. Walter Janka came to tell me: You do not leave the Party; you let yourself be expelled. That back then—rightly or wrongly—we had thought that if I had left the Party then, we would have had to leave the German Democratic Republic. And that for a long time I did not know whether I had done the right thing or not. I had told Erich Honecker, who had summoned me to an interview, that I had done the same thing as my husband and the others, that I would not recant anything, and that I wanted to be expelled from the Party and would not attend any Party function. I then did not go to a single meeting after that, and for that reason, because my comrades in the Writers' Union protested against it, I was "hidden" in the Party group of the employees of the Academy of Arts, where they left me alone. Now was that right? I asked. Viewed in retrospect, yes. But back then?

Early this morning I began to regret my openness. Naturally, there were representatives of the press sitting in the room, and of course they will use a confession like that against me again. Will I just never wise up, I asked myself (and also still ask myself), but of course that could not change anything anymore, and I remember the old saying that a word that has left the mouth can never be taken back. I recognized that I would not be able to fall asleep again very quickly and reached for the book in which I had been reading before midnight, Lutz Bertram, *Yoo Hoo, Dear Radio Audience*,[2] which was also published by Links, in which Bertram collected his interviews of recent years, among them one that he had with me in January of 1993, when I was in California and the waves rose in Germany because of the revelations by various media about my alleged Interior Ministry activities. The interviews throw spotlights on almost all of the explosive topics of the last two or three years, but also on funny side issues—a chief warden of the European Night Watchmen's Union, a congress of the Friends of the Ass. I read the interviews with Manfred Stolpe,[3] an impudent one—impudent on both sides—with Karl Eduard von Schnitzler, one with Walter Jens[4] about the unification of the two Berlin academies, one with Martin Weskott, the West German pastor in Katlenburg, who, with members of his congregation, retrieves piles of "disposed of" East German literature from garbage dumps, about readings with "garbage belletrists" that he organizes, and while I read, signals constantly flash on the second, third, and fourth levels of my consciousness, a storm of signals, called forth by certain names, fragments of memories that are linked to those names, or of reflections so numerous that it would probably take days even just to mention them all.

[2] Lutz Bertram (b. 1953), moderator for ORB (East German Radio Brandenburg), Potsdam station. (G.W.)

[3] Manfred Stolpe, from 1990 until 2002, Premier of the State of Brandenburg. Federal Minister of Transport, Building and Housing of the Federal Republic of Germany from 2002 until 2005. (Ed.)

[4] Walter Jens (b. 1923), German philologist, literary historian, critic, university professor and writer. (Ed.)

Gregor Gysi, Johannes Rau, Konrad Weiss[5]—entertaining reading because of the quick-wittedness, well-informed commentary, and chutzpah of the interviewer, who is, of course, blind, but about whose apparently excessive operating method, which even exhausts his coworkers, I would have liked to have learned more precise details than emerge from the final interview with him. Thinks very highly of himself, I say to Gerd. Then it was seven-thirty. I went to sleep again, am now awake, go take a shower, and hear the same Lutz Bertram on my little radio talking about the plague in India and the security measures of the airport authorities in Frankfurt. The doctor whom he interviews explains that in Europe and in Germany in particular, with its outstanding hygienic conditions, there is no expectation that the plague will spread, even if there may well be isolated cases, and they could be easily treated. I imagine the suppressed horror with which the listeners of many German radios receive such reports—for the plague is not simply an illness; it is a metaphor for uncontrollable terror per se. Other unpleasant news reports come from the radio while I calmly fix breakfast; of course, I will eat little myself because I want to reduce my weight before the hip operation—the World Bank, I hear, is meeting again, this time in Madrid, under police protection, of course, and naturally occupied primarily with the problems of the wealthy countries—the poor will have to see to it again that some crumbs are thrown their way, says the commentator.

Gerd eats breakfast with me again for the first time following his flu, which is lasting longer than he and I usually expect it to last for him; he eats his oatmeal porridge, I my rye crisp, and while doing so we leaf through the newspaper. Headlines: "Sloppiness and Chaos Swallow Billions from Taxes." "Police Follow Hot Trail After Attack on Man from Ghana"—that

[5] Gregor Gysi (b. 1948), German attorney and politician; Johannes Rau (1931-2006), eighth president of the FDR; Konrad Weiss, German author, publicist, director. (Tr.)

young man who opposed some skinheads on the commuter train, who were annoying women with blow darts, and who was beaten up and thrown out of the train for doing so, who was then run over—his leg had to be amputated—who lay on the tracks for ten hours. On the train there were about twelve people, nobody came to his aid, and what is completely incomprehensible, nobody even got off the train at the next station and reported the incident. Now the police implore those people in vain, even with the promise of immunity from prosecution, to at least come forward now as witnesses . . . "The Free Democratic Party does not concede defeat," "Clinton Justifies Invasion of Haiti," "Fidel intends to surrender himself if the USA, in possible negotiations, would respect Cuba's independence, the Revolution, and socialism." What a report, squeezed down small in a corner!—More and more people are having themselves buried in common graves for reasons of cost.

Under the headline "Fear and Uncertainty After Release from Confinement" there is a report about the state security police contacts of the "philosopher Wolfgang Harich." So: *Focus* had printed a state security police report that appeared from who knows where, in which there is a description of a meeting with Harich—there the latter had asked for advice as to how he should behave with respect to a letter from a West German Bahro solidarity committee,[6] which had been conspiringly sent to him. He had, to be sure, advocated Bahro's release, Harich says, but after his release from confinement he was simply afraid and had therefore inquired. Understandable, perhaps. We talk about the fact that with increasing age we find in the so-called media more and more names and review of events, which we either know or in which we participated.

[6] Rudolf Bahro (1935-1997), German politician (Socialist Unity Party) and journalist. He was charged with being a West German spy and in 1978 imprisoned for eight years. Released under an amnesty in October 1979 and deported to West Germany, he became a founding member of the German Green Party. In 1989 he returned to East Germany and spoke before congress. He was cleared of all wrongdoing in 1990. (Ed.)

Each time it then sets a chain of associations and images in motion.

Now, unfortunately, one of those telephone operas begins, which are about technical or financial matters and steal my mornings from me. So Mr. Buchwald calls—the new chief manuscript reader of the Luchterhand Literary Publishing Company—whose inglorious situation has cost me so much time and trouble during the last three quarters of a year. He wants to talk with me about the incorrect semi-annual publisher's statement, which I had questioned because the titles that were reprinted by Deutscher Taschenbuch Verlag are missing. Now supposedly the DTV statements did not arrive at Luchterhand at all, and besides that no money was remitted as would have been necessary. So I call DTV: The statements *have* gone out, of course, and according to contract the money is being credited against the advance that DTV gave Luchterhand. During these months I have almost become an expert in contract and statement matters.

I still have not sat at the computer. It is eleven o'clock; then the mail comes. A long letter from Rainer Jahnke[7] from his clinic in Rostock, where they have been doctoring around on the basis of the symptoms following his last session of chemotherapy, and where the actual examination by computer tomography still lies ahead of him. He writes about the autumn, about cranes, about the reading of the new book by Yevtushenko that lies ahead of him; they are already farewell letters, even for himself and to himself, I believe. He writes that on his nightstand stands the card with the Cézanne landscape. On the back I had written the Goethe lines that often dog me too: "I know that nothing belongs to me / But the thought that undisturbed / Wants to flow from my soul . . . "

[7] Rainer Jahnke (1939-1995), dramatic advisor at the Schwerin Theater; well acquainted with the Wolfs; died of cancer. (G.W.)

Somewhat helpless, as always in such instances, I tried to say with the words of someone else something that I do not want to say plainly to his face: that he probably has only a few more "favorable moments" to enjoy . . . Naturally, a brave letter like his also hides fear and a cry for help; I resolve not to fail to hear it.

Aside from two large letters with invitations that are illustrated and documented with programs, the letter of a West German who read *Parting with Phantoms* and refers to my answer to Jürgen Habermas,[8] especially to one sentence that he quotes for me:

> When I think of many of my West German writing colleagues—and it is really about them, about them and the other artists, not or hardly about the philosophers or the humanists on both sides—it is true that within the one German literature we (more strongly) related to different lines of tradition and also in different periods to differing literatures of other nations and areas of the world, depending on whether we lived in the German Democratic Republic or the Federal Republic.

On that question, my pen pal writes: "It is also true, and especially for the West German scholars, that with that sentence you exclude something," and then describes the great agreement in the book selection from the writers of '68, among whom he places: Adorno, Habermas, Luhmann, Marxist literature, psychoanalytical, socially critical literature, obviously fewer writers, both domestic and foreign. West German literature was for him, as for the West German left in general, without formative meaning. He explains that on the basis of a deep-seated distrust of our own language after Auschwitz. The fears that were expressed by Habermas are formed by sorrow-

[8] Jürgen Habermas (b. 1929), German philosopher and sociologist in the tradition of critical theory and American pragmatism, best known for his concept of the public sphere based in his theory and pragmatics of communicative action. (Ed.)

ful German history. There are good reasons to view even the history of the old Federal Republic of Germany and the German Democratic Republic as a warning. He concludes: "For me the principle of hope is tied to the West German counterculture that was addressed by Jürgen Habermas and to an East German genuineness, as it speaks from your books but was probably pushed all too quickly to the eastern periphery with the citizens' rights groups."

The genuineness, I think to myself, was not pushed to the periphery—it can hardly be driven out of a person, or can it? If one listens more closely to some complaints about losses, there may also be a complaint about the loss of genuineness, "depth" among them. The citizens' rights groups—yes; they became peripheral, which they of course were not, by the way, only for a very short time in the autumn/spring of 89/90. The East Germans who feel disadvantaged do not see their interests represented there (the others vote Christian Democratic Union anyway).

Besides that, in the opinion of many they wallowed too much in coping with the past, in a way that the stressed people could not bear. The whole thing cuts two ways. Each participates in his/her own way in pushing the past aside again, and I have begun to ask myself if it was ever different in history, if it can ever be different with larger masses of people. So that this work really would have to be accomplished to a large extent by the intellectuals, and specifically by the writers especially, who, of course—something that clearly emerges from this letter again—did have quite a formative impact on certain classes in the German Democratic Republic with their books, which was different from how literature affected the left in the Federal Republic. But now the intellectuals—that is one of my greatest worries—have been partially taken in by Kohl and the *Frankfurter Allgemeine Zeitung* and the rightist thinkers. Now, where there is no longer any communism, during elections the anti-communism that is directed against the Party of Democratic Socialism rages in absurd forms, from the red-stocking posters of the Christian Democratic Union ("Into the future, but not in red stockings") to the demand of the Social Democratic Party that the Christian Democrats, in those electoral districts in which the Party of Democratic Socialism has chances to win a direct mandate, urge its voters to vote for the Social Democrats to prevent the Democratic Socialists from entering the parliament. That very entry, however, would offer the Social Democratic Party perhaps its only opportunity, together with the Greens, to bring about the much implored "change," so that their slogan: "Every vote for the Party of Democratic Socialism is a vote for Kohl" is utter nonsense. Irrationalism is blossoming, and can be observed in intellectuals who let themselves be harnessed in front of the Christian Democrat cart and are not ashamed to sign an appeal in which it says that the liberal democratic fundamental order must not be permitted to be transformed into an antifascist democratic fundamental order: as if that were on the agenda—The bad thing about it: this entire republic is moving quite rapidly toward the right, and those intellectuals are firing at the left with all barrels. The Weimar Republic sends greetings, and sometimes I cannot sleep at night.

Now it is already Friday, the thirtieth, and because of constant interruptions I have not gotten any further in the description of my day; so I have to remember how I was finally able to begin writing the first lines on the computer after looking through the mail; how yellow autumn leaves from the poplar tree blew in through the open window, but the trees are still green and densely leafed; my longing for air and nature cannot be satisfied now, because I pay for any somewhat longer walk with such pain and blockages in my bad hip joint that I avoid escapades as much as possible. And the longing for the operation is increasing.

Before I start cooking the midday meal at shortly after twelve, a telephone conversation with Cornelia Geissler of the *Berliner Zeitung*, to whom I had agreed, even offered, to give an interview on the occasion of the appearance of the Biermann book, which I then, however, when she did not contact me for a week, had mentally canceled, and now she was horrified and insisted on it, and I, against Gerd's protest, gave in once more. (That interview has meanwhile been conducted and it left me very dissatisfied, confirmed my experience that I am not good at ad hoc formulation and should thus keep my distance from it; despite this, there were and are two additional interviews on the agenda this week.) Gerd says, What is the matter with you? Why are you suddenly so interested in publicity again? Why do you take on so much? I think I know why: because I promised some people from Alliance 90/Greens that I would speak out in favor of the change in Bonn—which is, of course, nonsense and only proves that I can only free myself with difficulty from the pattern of feeling that it is my duty to become involved.

In any case, I made my eggplant-tomato-ham soufflé with rice and it tasted good. Gerd wanted to give me suggestions while I was cooking, which I refused to tolerate, the usual kitchen aria, ending with Gerd's observation that we simply cannot cook together, which I deny.

At the table Christina says that she was supposed to reserve a table for a professor and some of his colleagues in an East Berlin scene restaurant, so she took the Jewish café right next to the synagogue; and now she reads in the newspaper that there are now, during the week of the Jewish Feast of Tabernacles, bomb threats against the Jewish establishments, that they are all closely guarded, there are armored combat vehicles on Oranienburger Strasse, and the customers of the Jewish restaurants are all being thoroughly searched. She was wondering if she shouldn't cancel that reservation for her acquaintances.

The bite of food sticks in our throats. Words like *terrible* come out of our mouths; we know, something is happening there which should never have been permitted to happen again. Jewish visitors to the restaurants say, Oh, coming from Israel they are used to those kinds of security measures, and during all those days the refrain goes through my mind: Just what will we still have to get used to, to what yet, and when will the point be reached again, where the democratic system—which I superstitiously do not want to put in quotation marks—can no longer "absorb" all this and rips apart? And what then?

Yes, I succeed in eating only a little, nevertheless the great weariness, as always, lie down, leaf through the newspaper; Gerd has read the autobiography of Philip Roth and is enthusiastic and amused. Sleep, each time in the afternoon that relief and the quiet hope that the break will last as long as possible; therefore postpone getting up . . .

In the afternoon the few steps through Amalienpark over to the building where my physiotherapist has her practice in the basement. She packs my hips in mud, and after that she begins to strike my legs over her shoulder and to pull the hip joint around in order to perhaps "open up" the interarticular spaces a little bit after all, and then she has never seen such a ruined hip before at all, she says every time. We talk about the amount of rent that she pays for her practice, 2200 marks. That is quite a bit, she says, and she would like to live here in Pankow, looked at one of the attic apartments that the West German foundation that has already bought up four of the buildings in Amalienpark is offering. They already cost more than 2000 marks now, and she would have to sign an agreement as part of the rental contract that she would be willing to agree if the apartment were turned into a condominium—price per square meter 4500 to 5000 German marks. At home we calculate that our apartment would cost at least 750,000 marks and that we, if we were to take out a loan for such a sum under the current conditions, would have to come up with more than 4000 marks a month just for the interest and paying off the loan. So should we insist on our ten-year rental protection? But move, when we are seventy-five? We pursue such deliberations with a halfway skeptical laugh and shake our heads . . . and then immediately have to occupy ourselves with money again. You see, Mrs. P. comes, a younger woman from Christina's circle of acquaintances, who expressed her willingness to help us with the decision about Christina's employment, remuneration, etc. "In the German Democratic Republic era," as we now say, she was a medical technical assistant. The toxicology institute in which she worked was very quickly liquidated. She was one of those who did not wait for a miracle but immediately entered a retraining program, for two years, as an insurance agent. Then with another East German colleague she opened a branch office of a West German insurance company in Weissensee. The two of them also founded a business association to help new independent business people deal with the authorities, and for us she has now set up wage tables from which we can learn how much salary expense we will incur if I employ Christina as my secretary, because I could deduct some of her pay from my taxes—if Christina were to earn as much net income as she needs to live on. If we create this job for four years, two or three years of it would be supported with a salary expense augmentation. So we talk about that, but hesitate because we still do not know how long Janus Press can exist, given the strain that the publishing house places on Gerd, and in view of the fact that he, with his uncompromising program, will hardly ever get into the black. I resolve not to state any reservations because of money, but only to put in a veto if I notice that in the long run the work exceeds Gerd's capacities. For what he does with and in this publishing company, is, of course, his life's work, which was unfortunately started too late; and that must not simply be broken off.

Mrs. G. from across the way brings a tray with magnificent mushrooms. She received more as a gift than she herself can eat; the woods are full of them. Gerd gets busy cleaning them; we realize that we will not be able to eat them all either and call Honza to ask if he can use some of them. Yes, gladly—this is something that both he and Benni can eat; they must live on a strict low-fat diet, so Benjamin comes rushing over to our place to pick up the mushrooms. Talks about the friendships that he is intensively cultivating, about the band in which he plays double bass and accordion and which will appear with other groups on Sunday on Alexanderplatz—under the peculiar name Xou are Point, which came into being in a difficult and accidental manner—he explains it to me. He is completely occupied, fulfilled, and sparkling with life; his hair has grown out again into a mop of curls, his voice breaks sometimes into the deeper range, the fuzz on his upper lip is becoming thicker.

Gerd withdraws to his bed; the afternoon has been too strenuous for him again; that infection has very long-lasting effects. The boletus mushrooms are a treat, "like little nuts," Gerd says. I behave as I should and restrain myself again, but drink a glass of red wine with them. I call Daniela Dahn,[9] who tells me that the broadcast that was supposed to run this evening on the Berlin-Brandenburg television station—a group discussion under the motto: "On the Day When the Unification Treaty Was Signed"—will be canceled. In addition to Gisela Oechelhäuser and Dani, who, through her book, *We Are Staying Here, or To Whom Does the East Belong*, has become a specialist for property questions in the unification, Schäuble, Krause, and Gysi were supposed to participate. On short notice Schäuble declined the invitation for himself and Krause. He would not sit down at a table with

[9] Daniela Dahn (b. 1949), German writer and journalist. (Tr.)

Gysi—Dani tells me why she could not come to our women's group on the previous evening. She had to participate in a suddenly necessary meeting of the renters' association over which she presides and which for several years, successfully until now, has warded off the danger that the buildings in which they live in Adlershof might be turned back over to the old owners. Now that security has come into question again through the senate, which suddenly no longer wants to recognize the ownership of buildings that were purchased after a certain set date. Dani also tells me about the abysmal lack of knowledge on the part of the Social Democratic Party in legal questions concerning East German property—We also talk about which party we intend to vote for; I want Alliance 90/The Greens to be in the parliament. Yes, so? says Christoph Hein somewhat later, whom I call to invite together with Christiane to Gerd's birthday and the election party: Do you really think that then something will change? Or that some publicly presented appeal from some writer will change anything? Of course not, I say. Hein talks about the company party of the Aufbau Publishing Company. He hardly knew anyone anymore; he is thinking about whether or not he can remain with them, but he still has time to make a decision since he still does not have any new prose.

I am interested in how the Berlin-Brandenburg television station will announce the cancellation of the Oechelhäuser broadcast. They are, of course, too cowardly to give the real reason. Because of appointment difficulties of some participants the discussion group cannot take place this evening. Oh, how I know all about that! But as a replacement there is now a documentary film, the announcement of which fortunately causes a memory to flash within me when I hear the name of the man that it is supposed to be about: Eberhard Tiede, and his fate: that he was from Riebnitz-Damgarten and killed himself. Didn't our friend K. tell us about the man a few weeks ago in Neubuckow? And that it was left up to him to speak the eulogy, and that while doing so he cited a few lines from my talk "Farewell to Phantoms"? So I stay with it, an East German fate from the time of the emergence. Immediately after the collapse of the German Democratic Republic, Tiede, department supervisor in the farm machine factory, seizes the opportunity to open a building construction and civil engineering firm, which is also thoroughly successful. Sufficient contracts, the banks give credit, and he travels to Hamburg to obtain it. Even while politically neutral, he becomes a close friend of Seite, the minister president of Mecklenburg-Western Pomerania, and of Rehberg, the chairman of the Christian Democratic Union group in the state parliament. Contributes only about 10,000 marks for the Party, becomes a model entrepreneur, living proof for the successful "East German boom." Begins to lose the ground from beneath his feet, his sense of reality grows cloudy. He builds up a hypermodern new enterprise; now loans become necessary, although contracts remain numerous and his expenses gradually exceed his income. He must raise half a million a year for interest alone, the leaf begins to turn, neither his assistants nor his wife, who is the personnel manager in his company, really notice it. The film begins with the playing of two audio tapes—Tiede said goodbye on his wife's answering machine; before that he had said to his bookkeeper that he was convinced that he would solve all of the problems, that he therefore intended to drive to Hamburg again, and then drove into a wooded area where he killed himself with the exhaust fumes of his car, not without having called his wife directly once more, who, however, did not understand what kind of a message he was giving her then. Nor would it have done any good, of course. A forestry worker found him. Rehberg did not even send condolences. Seite says in front of the camera that it is a tragic story, but nobody, of course, can absolve Tiede from the responsibility for this course of events. The friends turn away from Mrs. Tiede. She no longer has employment. Their little one-family house is placed as security in the bankruptcy estate. A bankruptcy liquidator is appointed who indicates that he will perhaps help good friends obtain certain fillet pieces at low prices. Mrs. Tiede also no longer has a home; she has found a place to stay somewhere. She understands neither her husband's behavior nor how it all could have happened. After all, he simply wanted to take advantage of an opportunity to make the most of his entrepreneurial abilities, an opportunity that finally presented itself to him. He was 51. The film is entitled: *Fatal Career.*

Bert Papenfuss then calls; he wants to talk to Gerd, but he is already asleep. After that, Tinka calls to ask what is happening with Father. A concerned conversation between mother and daughter. Thoughts about how he could avoid the pressure of traveling to the Frankfurt book fair next week.

Leaf through the *Wochenpost* newspaper. Under the headline: "Germany's Right Rolls" an article about a new publication: *The Self-Confident Nation: Swelling Goat Song and Additional Contributions to a German Debate*, edited by Heimo Schwilk and Ulrich Schacht, Ullstein Publishing Company. Twenty-eight authors, of whom I know only Hartmut Lange, Alfred Mechtersheimer, Ernst Nolte, Klaus Rainer Röhl, Ulrich Schacht, Brigitte Seebacher-Brandt, Botho Strauss, Hans Jürgen Syberberg, and Michael Wolffsohn as publicists. The author of the article, Bernd Ulrich, talks about the intellectual preparation of a drift toward the right in Germany. Apparently these authors actually feel that they have been pushed aside and disadvantaged, since even rightist and conservative papers no longer print their writings—to my amazement that is supposed to apply to Ernst Nolte. His car has already burned; in their mail the rightist thinkers sometimes find dead mice; they are being persecuted by the "antifascist struggle" of autonomous groups. They reveal an astounding hate for the "Habermice" and the descendants of the Frankfurt School, for everything that is leftist or that they consider to be so. Want to have success themselves by learning from the strategies of the leftists: first achieve an intellectual hegemony, then found a party like the Greens, and finally share in governing. Besides that, they proclaim a kind of catastrophism. Supposedly this right wing finds itself in a dilemma from which it will hardly escape, Ulrich believes, and he also says that the left offers no alternative to the national muck, but does not see any real danger in such rightist consolidations. I am not at all certain about that; too many symptoms of that sort have been piling up recently. So: however the election turns out—within the intellectual scene things are becoming very agitated.

Paper, paper on this day, and strangely enough everything that I read is tied together. Hebbel's diary notes[10] on his *Nibelungs*—of which I saw "Kriemhild's Revenge" last Saturday in the Deutsches Theater. "Nature owes man indemnification for the fact that it burdened him with the thought of death." . . . And in an article by Otfrid Ehrismann that was printed in the program, I find problems mentioned that are becoming more and more central in my exposition of the *Medea* material: "The fascination of the *Lay of the Nibelungs* in the reception history of the modern era was its manner of dealing with sufferings. The recipients felt themselves attracted by the images of death, but that is not an expression of longing for death, but fear of death."

Helene sends a fax: A dream story that Anton wrote in school. I read it several times, find it amazing, am moved by his imagination, his wit:

[10] Christian Friedrich Hebbel (1813-1863), German poet and dramatist. (Ed.)

First draft   Anton
The Bed School

In my dream it was about ten in the morning and I was going to
school. Strangely enough I—the "I" is Anton—kept my pajamas
on. In the school there were beds! I selected a four-poster bed with
a monitor for myself. On the monitor I could use numerous but-
tons to design the image and the voice of the teacher! I constructed for myself a little man from Mars with a bass voice. After a while
I fell asleep and received a strong commendation for it. I took the
four-poster bed home in my flying saucer and took my bed from
home to school. During my model pupil tribute I woke up.

(The teacher gave him an "A" in each discipline and wrote
below it: "You would really like that, wouldn't you?")

Perhaps the children will do things better, I think to myself.
I go to bed and to my delight, in a magazine I find a quote
by Woody Allen that simply wipes away much of the remaining deep talk: "Reality may be absurd and senseless, but it is
the only place where there is a good steak"—for which I
hunger, by the way, in these low-meat and low-fat days.
It is midnight on the dot when I turn off the light.

It is nine-thirty; as if I were not supposed to be successful in starting earlier, as often as I resolve to do. Too many mundane things have to be taken care of early on, today clean up the kitchen, go through the rooms—each time I am amazed at how much is still lying there from the day before, air things out, make the beds, today put a load of washing in the washing machine—30° C—and hang up the laundry, then turn on the dishwasher, because both machines at the same time overtax our electrical system. During the whole time occupied with my thoughts about this text. In the process something remarkable happens to me: I think Tinka's birthday is today, have Gerd call her to ask if we should come by this evening and take her the present—a beautiful necklace that we obtained in Lüneburg—then Martin corrects the error; says that he cannot proofread today because he is so confused as a result of the infusions that he is receiving from his physician this week. My doubts increase as to whether those infusions are appropriate—How is it that I mixed up the date of Tinka's birthday? What would Mr. Freud say about that?

The day began at midnight with the television news. The report that in New York the warring parties in Bosnia have agreed on a program for peace; immediately a commentary on it, how uncertain it still is and that nobody signed the paper, of course. That the Bosnians made it a condition that Karadzic be brought before the court in The Hague, but that this is very improbable, etc. Nevertheless, a ray of hope. I ask myself why

I do not feel a great relief. Probably my feelings simply became overstrained in this war, which is a nightmare. I imagine how the people there will live in misery for many years yet, how many things were irreparably destroyed; during the afternoon, in the text for the Luchterhand Publishing Company that describes the contents of the *Medea* manuscript, I wrote the sentence: "The female narrator lets it be seen that the behavioral patterns of the people who live in a society have not changed during recorded history." And that those behavioral patterns will not change, I could add. And ask myself if this apparently deeply ingrained conviction is jointly responsible for the fact that my drive to write has grown weaker (about which Lev Kopelev was very annoyed with me and which he vigorously denied when I recently suggested it to him in the hospital). Or where else does the "waning of the writing libido" observed by Trifonov come from? From the waning of intensity of feeling? From the frequently occurring reflection: But I have already experienced all of that? So that even the satisfaction of having completed a manuscript—like that of *Medea*, which was finally finished the day before yesterday and is now in the transcribing office—remains within limits. And yet there is something—perhaps only a habit, perhaps a discipline that has become trained into me over a long period of time—that causes me to write a piece of it every day anyway, and also to note down the events of my day.

There was an extensive report about relative successes in treating AIDS patients with a combination of two medicines. In a test period of two years about 38% fewer deaths occurred . . .

On another television channel a film was playing in which a highly intelligent boy puts a computer into his dead girlfriend in place of her brain, after which, however, she is no longer the same as before . . . I then went to bed, read another few pages in the book by the Italian Antonio Tabucchi: *Pereira Declares*, in which the narrator, who gives a remarkably distanced report, describes his first encounters with a young man whom he has employed as the obituary writer for the culture page of his small newspaper *Lisboa*. Time of the story: 1938, the Salazar era in Portugal, which is treated like the present— which it is, of course. And our feature writers trumpet out the challenge for us to write the novel of the collapse of the German Democratic Republic now at last. At twelve-thirty I turn off the light, reflect once more on the fact that I must utilize the enormous amount of material that I saved as a result of my participation in the investigative committee 89/90, and it becomes clearer and clearer to me that I should incorporate this very realistic material into an absurd, fantastic plot; or that an absurd, eccentric figure should encounter it. Resolve to think about that sometime in peace, when I have finished the assignments that I must still finish.

Before going to sleep I briefly think about what had upset us during the evening: It had turned out that a repair firm from Wedding had cheated us out of 900 marks in exchanging our old worn-out television set for a new, larger one; the man, a foreigner, was very self-confident and insolent on the telephone and cited the fact that the term of notice for canceling the contract expired on the same evening. His business was already closed and he would no longer accept faxes. Gerd tried anyway, but in vain. He then took a letter to the post office, but I am certain that we will not hear anything further from the firm. We were sorry about all that money, but above all we were angry that we were being so shamelessly cheated, and ashamed that we had not been more careful. That is the price we have to pay, we then said to ourselves, for being so trusting.

I woke up at seven; unfortunately the dream fled immediately, although it was vividly before my eyes during the first few seconds. It belonged to the new sort of very plastic, very strange, not really depressive, but often violent dreams that I have been dreaming since Mrs. L. has been massaging me in that intense and often painful manner, and since—both begin in more or less the same moment—Dr. J. has been treating me homeopathically (with phosphorus, by the way, the information of which is supposedly saved on the tiny lactose balls; after taking it two weeks ago there was an improvement in the condition of my leg, which now seems to have reached a certain stable level).

In passing I look in the mirror—not very pleasant. During this last year, since the operation, I have taken a large step toward old age (in other things, of course, I was forced to take very small steps . . .).

Gerd reads in newspapers that are lying around. I tell him what I saw on television last night when he had already gone to bed: Biolek [1] was hosting Reich-Ranicki. [2] How he presented himself. How he very unceremoniously stuck to all of his earlier effronteries; still boasted that through his scathing critique he increased the printing of the "bad book" by Grass; how Biolek agreed with everything he said; how he drew thunderous applause from the invited audience. Gerd says that of course the television people believe that they have to come to the assistance of one of their own.

I do exercises, experiencing pain. But I *do* want to exercise my muscles again. Instead of the hoped-for mobility, up until now the hip operation has brought only limitation of movement and pain, the deeper meaning of which I am not able to recognize.

And while I dress, again this slowing down of all tasks. Growing accustomed to it? Hopefully not yet.

Am in the practice of not eating much. So only two pieces of rye crisp with reduced-fat butter for breakfast, with it a few

[1] Alfred Biolek (b. 1934), German television personality, talk show host, producer and actor. (Ed.)

[2] Marcel Reich-Ranicki (b. 1920), German literary critic and member of the literary movement Gruppe 47. (Ed.)

North Sea shrimp, orange juice, tea (coffee is prohibited), and afterward some low-fat kefir. On the radio they are interviewing a minister of culture, education, and Church affairs from Lower Saxony. A female teacher who, as a member of the German Communist Party, had fallen under the edict on radicals and was fired, has been fighting the decision in court for fourteen years and has now obtained justice in the European Court. Of course nobody thinks of comparing that injustice with similar injustice in the German Democratic Republic, but I do think about how expensive it might become if that woman is also now awarded a verdict in her favor and compensation . . .

The newspaper. "Bonn remuneration coup on the brink"— no commentary on that lack of sensitivity on the part of the parliamentarians in increasing their own remuneration so richly. "Moving the government will be delayed"—into the next millennium—however, they are offering the poor officials unbelievable compensations. Andreotti "as if petrified in front of the judge,"[3] and some Italians already wish that they had the "*Pax Mafiosa*" back again. The judgment against O.J. Simpson is now due—that he is guilty seems perfectly clear to me, but the jurors will probably not vote unanimously. Now he is having his name patented. Then he would earn money on every T-shirt and every other article that markets his name. Free market economy.

It is now already six-thirty P.M. As usual, I am behind with these writings. This morning we searched together for the Schubert record *Winter Journey*, which Wolfgang Heise[4] once gave to me, about which I want to write a remembrance page for a book. I hoped to begin that today, but that hope has vanished because I had to wait almost two hours in Mrs. L.'s wait-

[3] Giulio Andreotti (b. 1919), Italian political figure, seven times Prime Minister. Accused of having Mafia contacts, he was eventually convicted in 2002, though he avoided formal conviction because of statutory limitations. (Ed.)

[4] Wolfgang Heise (1925-1987), German author and philosopher. (Ed.)

ing room, her "girls" had written down too many appointments for her and with my lengthy massage I am, of course,
always her last patient. So I just sat there, watched the female
patients come and go, among them some young, pregnant
women, since Mrs. L. shares her office with two gynecologists.
Otherwise we see hardly any pregnant women and few little
children on the streets. Gradually the young women are supposed to be recovering from the shock and slowly beginning to
have children again, I read. It is said that there has not been a
decline in births like that in the former German Democratic
Republic after the reunification anywhere, even during the
World Wars. I believe that nothing elucidates more clearly the
deep shock that this plunge into the market economy created
among the East Germans than this refusal to give birth. So in
the waiting room I very thoroughly read the *Berliner Zeitung*,
which I had fortunately taken with me; in it, with respect to the
debate that has been going on for months: "Nostalgia in the
East?" a contribution by Mrs. Bergmann-Pohl, whom I still
remember well as the president of the People's Chamber. She
concedes some difficulties for the East Germans during the
reunification, very reticently, of course, and under no circumstances the fact that the far-reaching alteration of the ownership situation was the actual characteristic feature of that
process, but claims that those difficulties were unavoidable.
That is the general line of the Christian Democratic Union and
partially that of the disastrously divided Social Democratic
Party: look ahead, join in planning, and do not look back.
Which they, however, for their part, do without embarrassment
whenever they are able to find fault with the German Democratic Republic or one of its representatives . . . Right now former East German prosecutors are facing prosecution because
in '89 they let the charges of voting fraud come to nothing. So
they are supposed to be condemned for what they did *not* do.
Now, God knows, I was fed up with those prosecuting attor-

neys, but whether they can get at them this way . . . I remembered the conversation with some younger people from the Church in the early summer of '89, in the garden of the St. Sophie Church with Pastor Passauer, after I had read in the Stephanus Foundation and we were discussing how one could deal with those obvious incidents of election fraud; I still remember, at that time I said: They cannot indulge in that again. And that was then also the death sentence for that kind of German Democratic Republic. They simply could not permit an authentic election—On one page there is a report about the case of the former president of the federal office for constitutional protection, Otto John, who is supposed to have been anesthetized and then kidnapped into the German Democratic Republic, and who sues again and again for rehabilitation; now there is a former KGB man who contests John's version and says that he was accessible to the KGB because of his high alcohol consumption, and that in addition at the beginning of '54 he had found the Soviet plan for the formation of a provisional all-German government plausible, which Adenauer, of course, strictly rejected in order to be able to tie West Germany to the West—Max Schmeling will be ninety and is still a legend for the young men. I remember how we listened to his fight with Joe Louis on the radio, how my father cried: "Pushing, pushing!" . . . I remember several social eras. The current one, which is so highly praised, is becoming as eerie to me as the two before it, but that is a broad subject . . .

Mrs. L. appeared with her hair cut short; she says that she suffers so much from losing her hair—I, by the way, am also experiencing that again just now. She listened to my report, which, of course, was quite favorable—four hundred, even five hundred steps once without a cane—just today again, however, I experienced pain in my muscle insertions, because I had exercised them. Mrs. Lau began to rub my neck, then to "adjust" me, then to work on my leg muscles, during which I had to move my knees. Some things were painful, but not as bad as during the first treatments. Then she "stretched my spine"; then she worked on my posture while still sitting. She told me about her impending move and that she then intends to concentrate more on Zen massage, about her allergy that she has almost eliminated through a fasting cure—Paula, who sits in the reception booth, is currently learning to be a non-medical practitioner and is already able to do color therapy. The nurse, Manuela, gives me the next-to-last injection of Calcinom and gives me a small lecture on permitted, desirable, and forbidden foods; so as much as possible I should not only give up the coffee—which I have done—but also drink herbal tea instead of the black tea. The women in the practice do that and eat rye crisp with it. Apparently the midday meal is omitted. I could not do that, I say, eat so little.

In the taxi, a driver with a moustache, whom I believe to be quite young; at first he is taciturn, then he complains about the fact that Berliner Strasse is closed again and again, that this subway construction never ends, that he always has to take the detour through Mühlenstrasse and then usually gets into the traffic jam at the traffic light on Breite Strasse. He talks in detail about the eating habits of his cat, which always has to stay in the apartment, and what a catastrophe it was when she once ran away; and then he began talking about his daughter, who is already twelve years old, describes how he recently came home, leafed through a "colorful periodical" that was lying there, *Girl* or something like that, how an eighteen-year-old candidly talks there about the fact that she has already been making pornographic films for two years, and another one, a younger one, asked about certain positions during sex. Well for God's sake, he asked his wife, who reads that kind of thing in our place? Well, your daughter, she said, she buys that for herself every week. Three marks forty, he said. Well she seems to have enough pocket money. They, his generation, had had the magazine *Das neue*

Leben; and there had sometimes been trouble when she had been a bit too impudent, politically, but something like that— no. They are just heating up the children to make a profit.

I get home before three o'clock; the other two have already eaten, of course; I take only five piroshki, but a large plate of salad that tastes very good, look at the mail, for once only three things, a report from the French committee to save Mumia Abu-Jamal, who is threatened with the death penalty in America and for whom I had also signed a petition; now a demonstration will be held on the Place de la République, to which I am invited if I should be in Paris. The second thing is the invitation to the Müggelsee Symposium on the seventh and eighth of October, which Horst Eberhard Richter and the Friedrich Ebert Foundation have organized, this time around the themes: Individualization of the society—hope or worry? and: German self-conception five years after reunification. I read the list of the convention participants. Mrs. Breuel is among them, whose practice as trusteeship director often disgusted me; but I know that I have no arguments against her efficiency, especially since the two of us have such different scales of values and she cannot imagine at all that what she views as a worthwhile social norm may perhaps not be the only possible normality for the coexistence of human beings.

The third piece of mail is a card from Pastor Weskott in Kathlenburg, whom we recently visited and who has saved to this point about four million books published by East German publishing companies, books that landed in garbage dumps or were supposed to be shredded, keeps them in a former chicken coop, and gives them out on Sundays in return for a contribution to "Bread for the World." He has learned that in the near future Grass will read in Northeim and is asking me to mediate in order that he might perhaps also come to Kathlenburg. I have already written to Grass and discussed the matter with Weskott on the telephone. (He had told me that he picked up additional pallets of books published by the Reclam Publishing Company from Riesa libraries, among them Volker Braun's *Hinze-Kunze Novel*, a book by Wolfgang Leonhard, and similar things. He has become an exquisite connoisseur of East German literature and the East German publishing companies.)

I lie down, read in *Pereira*, sleep until after four, prepare a tea-time meal in the kitchen, and gnaw on the end of a yeast pretzel. Christina says that they recently celebrated the twenty-eighth birthday of her oldest daughter. At that age she already had three children, and none of her three children has a permanent partner, let alone a child. Today it is that way with young people, they plan very carefully whether and when they intend to have a child . . .

I sit down at the computer again, write a letter to Manfred Krug,[4] who would like to publish the secret transcript that he made of our meeting in his house, in November of '76 after the Biermann expatriation—a meeting to which Werner Lamberz[5] had invited us in order to quiet us down, and whose shorthand notes show what kind of quandary we were in, how we tried not to let the conflict get out of hand, but in the process not to depart from our standpoint. I do not know how people who are not familiar with the heart of that conflict will read such a transcript.

Then continue to work on this text. Gerti Tetzner calls to ask about the best route to Rheinsberg, where our exhibition "Our Friends, the Painters" is still running; she wants to visit it with her friend Valeri. We talk about H., who now has strong anxieties about the future, of course; I tell her that I was able to obtain financial support for her through Maria Sommer.[6] Gerti

[4] Manfred Krug (b. 1937), actor; published *Abgehauen—Ein Mitschnitt und ein Tagebuch* (*Gone—A Recording and a Diary*), Düsseldorf, 1996. (G.W.)

[5] Werner Lamberz (1929-1978), member of the politburo of the Central Committee of the Socialist Unity Party. (G.W.)

[6] Maria Sommer (b. 1922), director of the Kiepenheuer Bühnenvertrieb (Stage Sales) Company, Berlin; member of the board of directors of the Wort Exploitation Corporation; close friends with the Wolfs, whose media rights she represents. (G.W.)

talks about a friend of her daughter, who has lived with a woman for eight years in the best of marriages, who has now broken out with AIDS contracted from earlier homosexual relationships. He is lying in the hospital; the process seems to go rather quickly; his wife is behaving in a wonderful manner, but his mother, who herself has ankylosing spondylitis, does not know anything about his illness yet, and her husband urgently warns them against telling her. She would collapse. Gerti has also known the mother for thirty years. She lives in Mecklenburg; Gerti wants to go to her place and sound out whether and how she perhaps might be told after all, so that she does not learn of it only when her son perhaps has only a few weeks left to live. She can deal with it, Gerti says. Through the death of her daughter she developed a different attitude toward death and also does not believe that with death everything ends.

I continue to write, now things that are already past, no longer at the same time as the events. Now, for example, it is already the next day, 12:45 P.M., and I have to think about what kind of a difference it makes when you can tell a story or even only describe a day from the perspective of its end, as opposed to when you simply take it down as it happens, without knowing what will come—then you cannot create any foci, place any emphases, and even the reflections become more meager.

I call Benni, want to know when he is going to Israel; Franci invited him to go, and he is looking forward to it very much. He is leaving on Sunday. I wanted to offer to Annette to pay the airfare for Benni, but she is not there, has a reading from her book, probably in the Xantippe. I get hungry, since I have eaten low-fat and little; Gerd fixes supper in the kitchen. He is expecting visitors. I eat a very small amount of fried potatoes and two thin whole-grain sandwiches with cottage cheese. Jana calls; we always want to get together and always find no time for it. Instead of that we have long telephone conversations. She just wrote a reportage about the Krishna sect in Berlin, quite long, she says, that would be an entire page. She offered it to the newspaper *Taz*, but does not know if they will accept it. It was difficult for her, also because the people were so nice to her as she conducted her research. But now she has treated them rather ironically and critically, and she asks herself if that is all right. In two years she will be finished with her course of study in journalism. Competition is becoming more and more severe in our business, she says. Who knows if there will still be any jobs at all then?—We talk for a long time about the purchase of the *Wochenpost* by Boetticher, and both of us doubt that even a good, new editor-in-chief and new people will get the newspaper on its feet again, above all, could make it into an all-German newspaper. For a long time the conversations with Jana have gone from one thing to another; she is interested in everything that happens in public. But to read a book in peace, she hardly gets around to that anymore, she says.

I watch the news. Mr. Rexrodt said that the economy in the new federal states is still a long way from being as far along as had been hoped; there can still be no talk of a self-sustaining boom, but otherwise the development can definitely be described as a success story—Tomorrow in New York Israel will sign the treaty about Arab autonomy in the Jordan territory.

I call Martin and ask if we should come by tomorrow evening, on Tinka's birthday. We do not want to bother them at all, I say, because I am not sure if they really want to see us. He declines. It goes through my mind that our relationships with Helene and Anton are slipping away from us. I am hindered by my leg from doing anything with them; their interests have changed; they do not need us anymore; at most I get on their nerves with my worries. I do not know if that is unavoidable and if then again another phase will come, as it did with Jana. It pains me, and I know that I am partially to blame. We work too much and are available too seldom.

I place the large, heavy manuscript packet on the table,

which a Mrs. P. sent me after we had talked on the telephone. It is the written estate of her son, who hanged himself three years ago at the age of twenty-two. I read what she writes about it and leaf through his writings; a sensitive young man who did not fit into either the German Democratic Republic era or this new era. I become grieved as I read; an oppressive feeling comes over me, which then becomes stronger and stronger as I watch the film *Sven's Secret*, in which a young woman teacher winds up in a school of a city neighborhood that is characterized by poverty, criminality, and prostitution, all of which is fully visible in the class where she is the teacher. The focal point is her relationship with this Sven, who is already an accomplished pickpocket and petty criminal and filled with longing for love that does not exist at home in his dysfunctional family. Gradually he clings to the teacher—I do not want to tell the story, but in its harshness and its hopelessness the milieu seemed to me to be authentic for most children; that Sven had a distant similarity to Anton, and suddenly it poured out of me, I started crying and could not stop. I was overcome by the misery about what is happening to the children everywhere in the world today. I saw very clearly how we all close our eyes to it and think only of ourselves and our little business deals, which are in part totally insignificant, and how this beautiful new era of the uncontrolled market economy must lead to a thoroughly criminal awareness, and what that in turn means for the children. I wept and started weeping again this morning when I told Gerd about it—Last night Gerd was on the veranda with a young student of German language and literature that wants to do an internship with him, and with Bert Pappenfuss.[7] When he came, he said that he gave Bert some money again, who whispered to him that he didn't have a penny again . . . I do not know why that comforted me somewhat.

[7] Bert Pappenfuss (b. 1956), German author. (Tr.)

Television, late: Roman Herzog met in Bellevue Castle with seven young people from East and West and chatted with them about their respective views and sensitivities, and about "growing together." The seven, of course, were hand-picked, had gotten dressed up, and were nervous. But apparently the need for such a conversation in front of television cameras had appeared urgent to the Federal President. He has heard everywhere that the Germans in East and West are still mentally very far apart.

I also saw a report about the last months of the German Democratic Republic, April, May, June, and July of 1990, up until the currency union. How much I have already forgotten again, how many details that seemed so important to me at the time have sunk into oblivion. De Maizière said in his inaugural address before the People's Chamber that not only the Party of Democratic Socialism had to answer for our past . . . Nice words. And today there are only accusations and hate.

It is after eleven when I go to bed, read *Pereira*, and turn off the light. I suddenly see the face of the small actor who portrayed Sven before me again, and I break out in tears once more, weep and sob for a long time, but so softly that Gerd does not hear it. So this day ends at midnight amid tears.

The last thing that I see on television at shortly before midnight the previous evening is the end of a Russian film: *Urban Matters*. I am touched by an atmosphere like that from the Soviet films of the "thaw" period, when we especially learned "the truth" from such films. It occurs to me that I have not seen a Russian film for a long time; therefore I stick with it. In his office, an older general shows the protagonist, who is likewise over sixty, a document (I cannot know what the document is); he takes note of it. The general says that he wanted to show him that document before anyone else. Then a reunion of old former Bolsheviks in a tavern; they devotedly sing a song in which the fascists are defeated, the protagonist is among them, also singing at the top of his lungs. Then a slender, thin, pale woman; she goes into an agency and is led into a room in which a document (the same one?) is lying on a table; she is permitted to look at it. It describes the fate of her father, who was shot in 1953. Among the signatures beneath the death sentence is also the signature of her current husband, the protagonist. Distraught, she goes home (a nice, large apartment of the kind that were allocated to the cadres). The man understands where she has been; she says that she wants to leave him. He puts on the jacket with all of his medals and goes to the city administration, where he is received very politely, and demands an apartment for his wife. The appropriate functionary asks him just how large his apartment is; that angers the protagonist. The functionary cannot give him an apartment for his wife. The woman tells him that he cannot understand her, his father was not shot in 1953, and she leaves. The protagonist calls after her: his father *had* been shot in 1953!—The final sequence: with his fur cap on his head, the protagonist climbs into his official car, which he apparently still has. He gives the driver an address, far out in one of the Moscow satellite cities, in an already dilapidated large-panel-construction building. Our man rings the doorbell of an apartment; the door is opened by a bare-chested young man who recognizes him. He disappears behind a door, pulls on a sweater, and says while doing so: "You should all be shot!" The woman has had a child by this young man. She is even thinner, careworn, quickly gathers children's clothing from the line in the kitchen. Our man says to her, she should come back to him, he cannot live without her. She shakes her head, then he says: She should not fool herself, without him she would not have obtained this apartment; then her face becomes stony, she hands him his cap and pushes him out. At the end his face in close-up, he says: You will all remain dependant on us forever—end of the film.

For that, while I was in the bath, another film played very quickly before my mental eye, in which a series of functionary types appeared, whom I had become acquainted with in the Soviet Union, and behind them faces of my friends, as well as scenes, dialogues, rooms and situations. I thought to myself, sometime I should actually write down my "Russian" memories, after which, of course, came immediately the question: What for? That prevents me right now from writing at all, least of all memoirs. I do know those times in which I cannot write, but it seems to me as though this state of not being able to write has taken on an additional dimension. Since the state structures and societies in whose spaces my memories "play" have collapsed, those memories have become strangely place-less, and I am also aware that they have no regenerating consignees; that is connected to the pressure that is exerted on our memories by the spirit of the times and that causes them to disappear; and what I want least of all is to submit indirectly to that pressure and to write justification texts. By the way: consignees will perhaps regenerate after all; we cannot predict where and with whom young people will perhaps seek remembrance and orientation in ten or twenty years, when the inability to reform and the destructiveness of the current system have become even clearer than they already are now, and that at a speed that we did not anticipate. So write down something after all, "just for me," I lie to myself.

It is exactly midnight when I go to bed. I am already looking forward to reading the latest Dick Francis crime novel, *Slayride*, which is meant for Tinka, for her birthday (she called my attention to that author), which I must therefore have read by then. Gerd is already asleep; usually, after ten-thirty he leaves me to my television excesses, which I do enjoy, however, even though I always experience a remorseful hangover afterward; only once does he turn over and ask with a murmur if I do not intend to turn off the light soon. I say "Yes" and continue to read; so the culprit is the agent of the Jockey Club in Norway himself. Best of all, as always, the little psychological insertions: that this Arne suffers from a persecution complex; that his wife has an orgasm while dancing with the Englishman David, and so forth. Dick Francis is a royalist; he would never insert a critical word about the crown into his successful crime novels; only now and again he expresses his aversion to communist dictatorships. In this book, however, a writer appears who drives the protagonist, is very likeable, and has radical leftist views.

Two o'clock when I finally turn off the light. Before I fall asleep, I experience the drama that I can sometimes call up before going to sleep: I "see" a story about which I have no previous idea. This time it is a woman; she is walking and I see her from behind, slender, wrapped in a dark overcoat; then I call her up for myself from the front, I see her face, tender and yet full of strength, sensitive, framed with blond, slightly wavy strands of hair—I see it before me even now. Unfortunately I have forgotten what the plot was that my sleepy, uncontrolled mind involved this woman in without my help; I did try to impress it upon my mind, but like so many things that I would like to impress upon my mind before falling asleep, in the morning it was lost.

I wake up at seven-thirty, no dream. Gerd is already lying awake reading; he always wakes up early, usually sleeps only six hours. I believe that it already occurred to me quite early that today is the "day of the year," but again I did not think what I always resolve to think in the morning: Today is the first day of the rest of my life!

Gerd complains about his reading material: Torsten Beck-er's *Beautiful Germany*, for which the Volk und Welt Publishing Company has such high expectations. They will probably not be fulfilled. The content: In the year 2010 the Wall will be built again, the German Democratic Republic introduced again, and Honecker will come back—it is not said why. And then instead of gripping satire, weak jokes and a bit about the Berlin Ensemble, in which the author, who is, of course, a West Berliner, once worked. Heiner Müller is described as "Fritz Meier," ridiculed by some, highly respected by others. Too bad for Volk und Welt, Gerd says, the publishing company urgently needs a best-seller.

When I get up, there is always the uneasy question of how things are with the pains in my leg. Today it is "all right," but my right hip does hurt. I take two Togal tablets with my usual pill cocktail. Before that into the bath. The news is especially depressing. The battles between the Israelis and the Arabs in the Gaza Strip have exploded; the opening of a tunnel for tourists by the Isrealis was viewed by the Arabs as a desecration of one of their holy places; that was the spark that flew into the powder keg. Netanyahu, who is responsible for all of that, broke off his visit to Germany early. One hope has been destroyed—In Afghanistan the radical Islamic fighters conquered the capital city of Kabul and as their first official act they dragged out the last communist president—who was staying in a building belonging to the UN, but was naturally left in the lurch by his guards—and hanged him on a lamppost in the city. Then they set out in search of other "undesirable" persons whom they could massacre. Many inhabitants tried to leave the city. The government troops had withdrawn to the North the day before. The Islamists proclaimed an Islamic theocracy in which barbarian laws are supposed to be valid. Another state in which the fundamentalists have been victorious—Konstantin Wecker[1] has been sentenced to two years and eight months in prison without probation for possession, purchase, and distribution of drugs.

While I am getting dressed I see that something like sunshine is trying to push its way through. Although the leaves show hardly any discoloration, an autumn mood clearly prevails in Amalienpark; it is probably because the leaves hang down silent and motionless, for example on the large beech tree across from our house.

Breakfast. Buttered bread with anchovies, tea. The *Berliner Zeitung*, which we now like to read first thing in the morning, during breakfast, thus delaying the beginning of the day—but aren't we retired? "Battles in Israel Out of Control." "At Mercedes 30,000 Protest Against Cuts." "Vietnamese Gang in Berlin Smashed." "Afghan Government Flees from Kabul." "Protests Against Less Sick Benefits." "Magdeburg SKET, Ltd. to Be Broken Up." "Banks See the Economy on a Growth Course." "Siemens Does Away with Around 1000 Jobs."

[1] Konstantin Alexander Wecker (b. 1947), one of the best-known German singer-songwriters, composer, author and actor. (Ed.)

"Bosnia Must Not Be Divided." "Is a Hot Autumn Threatening Now?" "Movement in the Conflict over Old Communal German Democratic Republic Debts"—To how many of these headlines will I still be able to assign content if I read them again a year from now?

There follows, as always, some housework: washing of the breakfast dishes, putting away the laundry that was washed yesterday, making the beds, airing things out everywhere. Now it is almost ten-thirty; I sit down at the desk to catch up on the last few days in my large calendar, in which I enter the events that have actually transpired (in contrast to the preliminary notes in the "little one"). A good opportunity to let them pass in review before my inner eye once more and by so doing to fix them in my mind as well: the opening of the exhibition of Martin's works in Rheinsberg, the Night-of-the-Mice event in Woserin, the dinner on Sunday with Hans Mayer[2] and the Pierwoss[3] couple in the Parkhotel in Bremen, in the evening the reading in the theater and the good discussion afterward, the fish supper in the Schnoor late at night, during which Mrs. Pierwoss told us very interesting things about her consulting work regarding sexual crimes at the Superior Court of Justice in Stendal (she as a West German psychologist in East German territory), Hamburg the next day—Monday—the magnificently luxurious Atlantic Hotel, the meal at the good Italian place with Armin and Annette Sandig,[4] in the afternoon the meeting with the Grassens in Sandig's studio, in the evening 1700 people in the Audi Max auditorium, and afterward at University

[2] Hans Mayer (1907-2001), literary scholar under whom C.W. studied Germanic literature in Leipzig 1951-1953; went to the Federal Republic in 1963; C.W. remained in close contact with the professor, whom she revered, until his death (see also: *"Ein Deutscher auf Widerruf—Rede für Hans Mayer* [A German Until Reevoked—Speech for Hans Mayer]," *Werke*, pp. 352ff.). (G.W.)

[3] Klaus Pierwoss: manager of the Bremen Theater, who continually invited C.W. to read from a new book. (G.W.)

[4] Armin Sandig (b. 1929), painter, president of the Free Academy of Arts in Hamburg, of which C.W. has been a member since 1986; a friend of C.W. (G.W.)

President Lüthje's house, where it came to a longer discussion, especially about literary criticism.

What good is this list? It could serve to help me maintain my impression that "in the West," among the people who read, campaigns leave no negative effect behind; that I still do not feel well when masses of people stream together to hear me read (and probably above all to see me). What do they expect of me? Why this demonstrative applause? I would not have accepted all of those engagements, of course, if I had known in advance that I would still be walking around with a crutch, which I do not always need during appearances, but often do, because I cannot know when my right hip will begin to hurt so much that I cannot appear. I still suppress the thought of the next operation that is due. But I no longer believe that I will once again be able to walk for longer distances without pain.

I also note down the evening with Richard von Weizsäcker[5] in our discussion group,[6] on which he lectured on "Unification Under the Sign of Globalization" and probably appeared to be too uncritical to many of the participants. He probably left with the impression of having gotten into a leftist nest.

It is eleven o'clock when I sit down at this text. I am looking forward to describing this day because it is a solid project that I can hold on to for two or three days, while otherwise my plans are still vague and even reading around in the manuscript City of the Angels does not help me at the moment.

Toward twelve I start off on my way to the market, after I have evaluated the pains in my legs and determined that it will probably be all right, with a "walking aid," of course. On the way I always take a series of steps without the cane, especially

[5] Dr. Richard Freiherr von Weizsäcker (b. 1920), German politician (CDU) and President of Germany from 1984 to 1994. (Ed.)

[6] Discussion group: Since 1989 C.W. has gathered a discussion group, to which she extends personal invitations, together on a monthly basis in order to discuss relevant political and cultural problems with prominent personalities as consultants, in a circle of intellectuals from East and West. (G.W.)

with the buckled pavement across the street. Several times women whom I do not know greet me with a friendly smile; I am not used to that in Pankow. It clears up even more at noon, so that I begin to perspire while walking. At the small department store—Pardon me! At the supermarket!—I see fewer Vietnamese than usual; some are even sitting idle, without cigarettes, on a bench. I ask myself if the supply of cigarettes has perhaps been cut off by the arrest of their gang leader. Then I plunge into Marktstrasse and listen to the Berlin jargon that surrounds me (Well, man, before, yeah, that was something else, but now everybody muddles around on his own!), hear the Turkish salesmen calling out their wares; if you even approach their stands they are immediately there and begin to lower the price. I buy a wallet for Gerd for five marks, so that he at least has one for the fair to which he is going next week, one that the money will not fall out of, buy myself a T-shirt, six eggs "from open air pens," fifty pfennigs each; at the stand the market woman calls out: "Three cucumbers for two marks!" A man with a shopping net walks past and says in dialect: "What? Three cucumbers for two marks? Then one costs sixty-six and a third pfennigs. That is too much for a cucumber. *Four* cucumbers for two marks—that would be right." Speechless, the woman follows him with her eyes. Then she asks her husband: "Did you hear that, Otto?" "A lunatic!" says the man.

After that I go to the Butter-Lindner store; they have neither veal nor beef sausage, only wieners made from pork, and they, of course, are prohibited for me; so I take turkey sausages, also take along a Harz cheese, and jellied fruits for Anton, then to the pharmacy, toothpaste and creams, have to give information as to why "my leg is still not getting better." I do not like to hear that, claim. But it *has* gotten better, the one that was operated on hardly bothers me at all anymore, it is now the other one. Oh well, says the pharmacist, an outsider cannot really discern that, of course—She is probably right about that. I shoulder my green rucksack and start out for home, and then, of course, my right leg hurts again.

I talk on the telephone with Angela Drescher[7] of the Aufbau Publishing Company; it is about the cheap sale or pulping of my book remainders that are still at Aufbau. We touch briefly on the book by Joachim Walter about literature and the state security police in the German Democratic Republic, whose appearance is immanent and which will once again create a high bow wave in the feature sections. I tell her that a few weeks ago in the *Süddeutsche Zeitung,* in an interview with Nadine Gordimer, a certain Mrs. Christiane Korff claimed that I denounced members of the opposition. Angela says that I should take legal action against it; I tell her that my editor, who is also a lawyer, got me an attorney from his firm, and according to her it is difficult to win such a case in court; then I heard nothing more from my attorneys. I wrote to the Korff lady and sent her *Akteneinsicht Christa Wolf* and urged her to at least take back the claim vis-à-vis Nadine Gordimer—but I do not hear anything from her either.

Gerd has cooked green beans and potatoes in their skins; with them there is white herring, one of our favorite dishes. Before that the mail, mostly advertisements, we should order Nuremberg gingerbread (we will probably even do that again for the families of our children); second-hand books are also offered. A member of the discussion group, formerly an East German historian, now retired, sends me a copy of a letter to Richard von Weizsäcker, in which he refers to the evening with him when he rejected my objection that one should be able to intervene and regulate the market economy (as he also reject-ed the observation by Mrs. Mann-Borghese that for the next century "a good shot of socialism" would be necessary to solve the problems). Now the professor writes that the market econ-

---

[7] Angela Drescher (b. 1952), publisher's reader for the Aufbau Publishing Company in Berlin; serves as reader there for C.W.'s books; friends with her. (G.W.)

omy has demonstrated its superiority and functionality, but the Basic Law, albeit vaguely, does imply a responsibility of property with respect to the general public. Thus it does not seem right to him to reject state intervention in the rampant growth of the market economy from the outset; one should consider what could be done and how it might be accomplished vis-à-vis the powerful interests of the industrial conglomerates and banks—which, of course, draw freely upon the help of the state when they have ridden their businesses into bankruptcy as a result of management mistakes . . . And so forth. Weizsäcker will be happy about that.

Wash up. Am very tired, look forward as always to my afternoon nap. Read for another quarter of an hour in the newspaper *Freitag*. Since the unification holiday, the third of October, is coming up soon, they have prepared a special supplement: "Six Years of Unity." First a lead article by Günter Gaus[8]: "Cold Buffet," one of those radically critical articles with which he consciously writes himself further into his outsider role. His theses: the German unification has failed as a formulated problem solution. The unification process has hardly ever gone beyond the intellectual horizon of an anti-communist crusade, in which plundering was among the freedoms. According to the prevailing West German perception, for forty years the people in the German Democratic Republic, to the extent that they were not criminals, were nothing but disguised West Germans . . . Is it possible to imagine anything more beautiful than the marketable model of a West German patented democrat?—The species of anti-communism of the German middle-class mentality is almost unique in the world . . . It is based on the demonizing of communism . . . Among East Germans there is a growing opinion that the replacement of the so-called dictatorship of the proletariat by the dictatorship

[8] Günter Gaus (1929-2004), German journalist, publicist, diplomat and politician. (Tr.)

of the market is not, in the long run, a sufficiently satisfactory social program . . . In the entire country the sheeplike patience is probably stronger than it was in the late German Democratic Republic . . . The Germans, so familiar with political fears, are now getting to know social fear again in the East and the West . . . But the end of social mercy really will, in the course of time, bring about a new, actually existing, national communality that does not yet exist for the time being.

In the supplement Michael Jäger investigates "the evaluation of the political potency" of the East Germans. With that, large photographs of Werner Schulz, Gregor Gysi, Rainer Eppelmann, Angela Merkel, Joachim Gauck, and Wolfgang Thierse[9]; the question is treated as to why there are so few politicians from the East in prominent positions, and why the few that are present cannot bring their respective parties to see the problems of the East more clearly. Under the title "The Man Who Came from the West" Regina General reports about Detlef Affeld,[10] who came as a helper to Brandenburg from North Rhine-Westphalia right after the collapse of the German Democratic Republic and tried to salvage some useable features of the East German health system in the Ministry of Health—and who now, with public reproaches and sent into temporary retirement, has to go. "Imperfections cannot be excused in him of all people." Under the title "The Demure Career Woman?" Claudia von Zglinicki writes about Rosemarie Will,[11] who at that time had not yet been elected judge of the Constitutional Court in Brandenburg—this, in the meantime, has happened. As a member of the Socialist Unity Party until 1990—she

[9] East German politicians who attempted, with some success, to make their way back into politics after the reunification. Angela Merkel has since become the chancellor of the Federal Republic. (Tr.)

[10] Detlef Affeld, former GDR health official who is involved with health politics in the Federal Republic. (Tr.)

[11] Rosemarie Will (b. 1952), jurist, since 1996 judge in the Brandenburg State Constitutional Court. (G.W.)

belonged, however, to its most reform-oriented wing—a wave of defamation and mud came at her in the press, but the Social Democratic Party in Brandenburg hopes to create a precedent with her election. How long Rosemarie Will can endure the heavy barrage remains to be seen—Egon Günther writes: "What is happening with art?" and begins to talk about film in particular, after he has unmistakably vented his fury about the unscrupulous profit orientation of capital and the help that the state gives to it in the process. "The old trouble is ending, now there is a new one." In the German Democratic Republic a person knew one censor or another. "Since you had a certain suspicion or often knew with certainty just who was doing something to you, in a tricky way you felt that you were in good hands . . . In what are called the differentiated, complex, and highly specialized industrialized nations of our day there exists a remarkably faceless, anonymous, but powerful current of tenuous, fleeting presences of an anti-enlightenment caliber. Exhortation of the third kind to enter the clandestine relationships where only sheer efficiency counts, and to create the event that can be measured in money, called film as far as I am concerned, but comparable to every other article of merchandise . . . " The fact that the trivial German film that is promoted has no chance of joining in the advancement of national identity, wants to be cool, only turns aside into shallow waters, and no longer wants to be a child of the enlightenment, as if that were possible, "causes unrest after six years."

And in my case, I think to myself, leads to the fact that this whole art business no longer has anything to do with me. But that it still touches a nerve in me when it concerns the "East"— that is something that I cannot hide from myself. So I note down what the relationships of today could call forth "later" . . .

Since I have a need to catch up from last night, I sleep until four o'clock in the afternoon. Dream while waking up: I am sitting on a seat outside of a streetcar, i.e. in the fresh air, and the

headwind blows the coat of somebody who is sitting or standing in front of me in my face, so that I have difficulty breathing and feelings of constriction. Tinka is suddenly next to me
and asks me something, but I do not remember her question.

While I make coffee in the kitchen, within the context of a
discussion of the last issue of *Sinn und Form* on the radio I hear
a review of the text by Volker Braun[12] in which he reports what
he subsequently learned about the female protagonist of his
Unfinished Story: that she was a representative of the Ministry
of the Interior and faithfully (what a word in that context!)
reported everything that she discussed with him—The wheel
of insanity can still be turned another revolution.

I sit down at the text again. Talk on the telephone with Jana,
who returned yesterday after nine weeks in Moscow, supposedly even thinner. Well, she says, she had little time to eat, is
almost finished with her article about the change in the teaching of history in Moscow schools, and she does not know yet
whether it will be printed in *Der Spiegel*. This time the farewell
to Moscow was hard for her; she became acquainted with
many people, and Moscow is developing into a cosmopolitan
city, unlike Berlin. We make an appointment for tomorrow at
Tinka's birthday celebration in the Café Kanapee. Tinka will
be forty . . .

Sometimes in the middle of the day I think very clearly to
myself: My time is running out.

Suddenly I have difficulties in saving this text on the computer when I have to stop: when I put in the password: TDJ96,
the message always appears: Codeword invalid or incomplete.
I finally let the word *TAG* (DAY) suffice, and then it works,
and the text has also not "crashed," as I determine with a precautionary check.

---

[12] Volker Braun (b. 1939), writer; close friend of the Wolfs; here an allusion to Braun's
contribution "*Das Ende der Unvollendeten Geschichte* (The End of the Unfinished
Story)," *Sinn und Form*, IV/1996. (G.W.)

As I am getting ready for the evening, Dr. B. calls from the Goethe Institute in Lisbon and wants to have the dates for our stay and the events that will take place confirmed once more: my reading and the scenic *Medea* reading, for which a troupe with Lothar Fiedler and Helge Leiberg will arrive.[13] How I would look forward to that trip and to Lisbon, if I did not have to fear that I will again only be able to walk with pain; I indicate something like that, so that they do not prepare a program for me that cannot be carried out. The lack of independence and the dependency on others to which I am condemned burdens me, but I try not to show it.

I eat two thin open-faced sandwiches and then the doorbell rings. C., an equal opportunities delegate in Marzahn, picks me up. "A friend" would drive us. The friend is sitting in the car, an ancient Volkswagen Golf. It is raining. I can hardly fasten my seatbelt because the belt does not work. All the windows are immediately fogged up; Brigitte, that is the friend's name, whom I can hardly see in the dark, has to roll the window halfway down in order to be able to see somewhat. She says she does not know the way to Marzahn very well but always takes the same stretch of road. We immediately get into a traffic jam caused by construction, which amazes the two women considerably: At seven in the evening! Then I learn that Brigitte really does not like to drive in the rain and that she especially cannot stand it when oncoming headlights blind her. In addition, where she is unsure of the way, as she proves several times at forks in the road: Oh dear, now I'm already on the wrong road again! Halfway there I am informed that she has had a driver's license for only two months and is still in the process of gaining confidence; I then become very quiet.

---

[13] The performance of *Medea*, with the painter Helge Leiberg and the musicians Lothar Fiedler and Tina Wrase together with an ensemble of actors, took place in Lisbon on October 15, 1996, in the Portuguese language. That performance was later followed by numerous performances at home and abroad, with C.W. as the narrator. (G.W.)

Before that I had learned from C. that she lived in Marzahn for a long time and did not find it at all bad until she moved to Pankow; now she no longer understands how she was able to endure it in Marzahn for so long. The population there is declining; more people are moving away than into the town, but the unemployment rate is not as high as it is elsewhere. The people are younger and all have a good education; even women's unemployment is not as high.

We actually make it; the Marie Women's Center is housed in a first-floor apartment of an "eleven-story" building. A few women who have no tickets are standing outside, but are still permitted to enter; some are already sitting in the café, a soberly and expediently furnished room with white plastic tables and black plastic chairs. The director, a dignified, good-looking blond woman, tall, who gives the impression of being kindly self-confident, once studied cultural affairs and has had this position for five years, a position that also completely fills her life. This women's center is primarily involved in advising unemployed women and in continuing education courses, which are probably also well attended.

Exactly thirty women fit into the reading room. I read the first two chapters of *Medea*, less than usual, because the most important thing for me is the discussion. The first woman, I estimate that she is in her early fifties, seems somewhat depressed and at the same time somewhat affected and read the entire book as a "book about us"—about our experiences in the last five or six years, and in Medea she also "saw me." Others do not go that far. One asks me about *City of the Angels*; years ago she heard my reading from it in the Pankow city hall. I try to explain why I have laid the manuscript aside and do not progress with it—it appears to be a mixture of the usual inhibition with respect to unscrupulously writing about myself and the feelings of futility and powerlessness that I have in the face of the societal conditions, which urgently stand in need of resistance, but I do not see the forces that could offer it. We talk about the crisis that I was experiencing in Santa Monica when I wrote *City of the Angels*, and that this crisis pressed the text from me. Now the necessity to write is apparently not as urgent—We talk about the scapegoat problem in *Medea*, for quite a long time about the exercise of male power through the millennia, and about what kind of men are capable of rising into the ruling class, and what kind of women; what happens to women when they also want to rise; how they deal with the "negative selection" that they encounter, highly neurotic individuals in neurosis-generating structures that almost force a loss of reality. C. would like to talk about *Medea* as a "feminist book," but the hint is not taken. We continue to talk about the problem of power that runs through my books, as one woman says; I cannot confirm that. It turns out that many of those who are present are familiar with most of my books, have not forgotten them, and emphasize again and again that in the German Democratic Republic they had "lived with them." But I sense German Democratic Republic nostalgia only in one woman, who, as it later turns out, was a theater scholar who lost her job. Now she works with children and finds, as she later tells us, that they no longer learn to read properly, as they did during the German Democratic Republic era, and that they also no longer read books. Others disagreed and also did not want to concede that in the German Democratic Republic *all* people read serious literature, otherwise the run on light fiction would not have been as strong after the fall of the Wall—Power *is* related to money, one woman says, and all of them talk about a possible alternative to the current system. One of them says that she has now arrived in the Federal Republic, but that she could not yet write down anything about this society. She works in a recycling business in which many women work. Most of the women there received a good education in the German Democratic Republic, are now doing something that is unrelated to their professions, but are not dissatisfied in doing so. C. was a computer scientist, the director of the women's center a theater scholar, her deputy a natural scientist—They ask how important the intellectual conscience is for a society and talk about the arbitrariness of moral values in science.

The discussion lasts for over an hour; afterward I sit down in the café with a glass of wine; we now talk more personally, six or seven women in the group, a casual, friendly atmosphere, familiar. In the West that would probably not be possible, even in a smaller group; that is because we all know about our experiences and we do not have to talk about them. Some of them say that they have wanted to write to me for a long time; unfortunately one or another of them will not do it. The conversation also turns to the autumn of '89; the years since then seem to become shorter.

During the drive back, C. says: That's just Marzahn, that is how the atmosphere is there. Once Brigitte takes a wrong turn. She, by the way, is a mathematician and has a job that does not interest her in an institute in West Berlin. She does not like to think about the fact that she is supposed to work for fifteen more years—The streets are now empty, making the driving less dangerous. I notice that I have forgotten my key. Our floor is dark, but then I see the flicker of the television set in the living room window. I ring the bell and Gerd opens the door in his pajamas. It is exactly midnight.

Wake up before six with the blissful feeling that I can still sleep for at least an hour. Try to do it, if at all possible without thinking of anything, and do not succeed. Reach for the book on the low nightstand, in which I began to read yesterday: *The Ordeal by Fire and Water* by Michael Maar. Read, with increasing enjoyment, about Rode's correspondence with Franz Overbeck[1] (about their mutual friend Friedrich Nietzsche, who had gone insane), that difficult, often tense relationship among the three of them, one that is not free of diplomacy and even betrayal, in which at the very end, after the deaths of two of them, the unfortunate Nietzsche sister also becomes involved. But then I became really interested in, that is: touched by the pieces about Virginia Woolf ("Two Oceans Under Two Moons"), about the interpretation of her diaries, actually of her as a person, whom many of her friends felt to be "cold," and about whom he shares the fact that as a twenty-four-year-old, following the loss of her mother, stepsister, and father, she also lost her favorite brother, Toby, and, with hopeful bulletins about the supposedly improving condition of the brother, who had in reality already been buried, concealed that loss from her seriously ill friend so that she would not collapse. Maar explains the inscrutable nature of those very plastic letters by saying that here for the first time the author saved herself in literature—something

---

[1] Franz Camille Overbeck (1837-1905), German Protestant theologian, perhaps best known in regard to his friendship with Friedrich Nietzsche.

that subsequently became her habit. Even in her diary, where there are sharp portraits of the people whom she encountered, so that one cannot be surprised that many of her friends call her "malicious," even "evil." Literature is demonic for the character, she herself writes in her diary, and I paused and thought for the umpteenth time about the nature of my occasional writing inhibitions. One can probably not be "good" and at the same time a good writer. While Virginia believed that one could not write good critiques if one were not a good person . . . That is remarkable. "The coldness," Maar writes, "the peculiar defect that cuts her off from osmosis and keeps her away from the nutrient bath in which the nice and normal people are interchangeable, does not change the truth of her moralism, which is not inferior to her feeling for style in any respect." And then he examines the origin of her excessive hunger for praise and finds that her delight in ridiculing others is the natural result of her early sufferings. "The poorly armored woman must keep the people away from her with a deluge of her wit's arrows."

The other essays in the volume are of a similar kind: profound pieces of knowledge, intense curiosity, the good nose of a detective, psychological perspicacity, but with it a definite respect for the often unhappy authors of the books that he takes up, authors who are encumbered with all kinds of physical and mental ailments: Arno Schmidt, for example, for whom he arrives at ugly characteristics, because of which I have never enjoyed reading his works and which I summed up, somewhat undifferentiated, under the concept *philistine*— even with him he remains decent and respectful. And how much more with Thomas Mann, whose late diaries he searches for the original reasons for the author's growing despair: the personal suspicion that he has "written himself dry." Maar talks about a "total chilling of his existence." "The kernel, you see, in which his entire despair is concentrated, is an icy one.

He cannot do anything about being that way, he suffers from it and can therefore no more turn off the coldness than the Devil in *Doctor Faustus*)" . . . Like Kay in Andersen's *Snow Queen*, which Mann loved: "Whoever gets the fragment of the Devil's mirror in his eye, loses his piety; he sees only the comical, the grotesque in everything anymore, can no longer love, and ends up in the ice palace. In the fairytale the fragment gets washed out. In life it remains stuck there, and that makes it into hell." And then the tension-breaking word of the late-born literary connoisseur: in the belief that he had written himself dry, Mann erred: "Art never left him."

Should write more about this book, of which I meanwhile—specifically on the afternoon of the next day—while we were awaiting guests, among them Tinka on her forty-first birthday, have already read much more. But yesterday, on the day that I must and want to describe, I then got up—after a few perfunctory leg exercises, which I have been grossly neglecting since we returned from Hiddensee, and for which I apparently cannot compensate through the weekly Feldenkrais exercises with Mrs. Sch., either—went into the bathroom, heard from the small radio the news reports about the earthquake in Umbria, about damage to the chapel of St. Francis of Assisi, where we once visited, which we now try to remember—In my mind's eye, I see little more than the facade, hardly anything of the interior of the chapel. Three fatalities were reported. Near Sumatra an airplane crashed with 234 passengers aboard, all dead. I ask myself if one cause of that accident could be the thick layer of smog that lies over all of Southeast Asia because of boundless deforestation and has claimed fatalities in its own right. And in Germany the politicians of the coalition and the Social Democratic Party are blaming each other for the failure of the tax reform. Somebody from the Taxpayers' Union calls it "shameful" what they are doing to the "position of Germany" and to the taxpayers for the sake of their power struggle . . .

All of this once again from the *Berliner Zeitung*, which is hastily perused as breakfast is being abbreviated today because of the planned shopping trip to Reichelt, but I do quickly take my pills, especially the pain pill, without which I cannot get around with my painful right hip. Draw out money at the bank and pick up the masses of prescribed pills at the pharmacy, an additional payment of almost eight marks, and then meet Mr. L. with his dog, who tells us about a disagreement that drove him out of his apartment. His wife, a physician, was suspended from her position as head physician in a clinic in East Berlin a few weeks ago, supposedly because of involvements with the state security police, which, however, did not exist, as she very believably asserted. Now she has attended a brief hearing at the labor court, and her employer will probably have to prove his accusations. Her suspicion: that he wanted to free up her job for somebody else.

On the way an advertising poster for Berlin Beer; Gerd begins to sing: We do not drink Rhine wine or champagne like the rest, we drink only Berlin Beer because it tastes the best. Was that actually a West German hit? Certainly, we say. So into the supermarket. Although it is still not quite nine o'clock, the parking lot is already one third full. I try in vain as always to restrain the shopping zeal that always overcomes Gerd when we prepare a meal for guests. So soup and hors d'oeuvres? Too much, I say. But I already have the oxtail! All right, fine! So I now go to the meat section. Fine. So I pick up shrimp, salmon, Serrano ham, and bologna. Too much, too much, I think to myself as I do it. So soup and hors d'oeuvres *after all*? It looks that way. Grand Marnier is needed for a margarita, which will be due again in the next few days. How much meat do you have? Eight slices, very nice loin, but they are very large slices. A loaf of French bread or two? Two, as a precaution. And dessert? Are we going to do the baked apples now? Who knows if anyone will still want that after the cheese? So only ice cream?

Ice cream and fruit with it. Cranberries. Fine. Milk, butter anyway. And grapes. I pay three hundred marks at the cash register.

I still need roses for Tinka's birthday. The flower shop on the corner does not have any especially beautiful ones, but I finally take twenty yellow roses. Mineral water still has to be obtained from the "little store," and then, after Gerd has had to go to the car twice in order to carry the purchases upstairs (I am almost completely unavailable for carrying), he goes to get freshly ground coffee because it "smells so good" in the kitchen.

The day is once again very beautiful, the most glorious, radiant autumn weather, deep blue sky for at least the last two weeks; every day I think longingly: Now I should be outside, but any "outside" that would require me to walk for a long time is denied to me, and Woserin is closed for us this year because the roof, floor, and stairway are being repaired and renovated.

I quickly write a few notes declining invitations that came in the mail. Today that does not seem to me to be a waste of time, as it usually does, because various ideas are whirling around in my head about how, after all, I can perhaps organize the material that I brought with me from America and at which I have been toiling in my thoughts and also a little bit on paper. Exploit the possibility that the most remarkable people can meet in that distant place—Santa Monica—people who still have to resolve something with each other from "back home," in both positive and negative ways. Then the ambient field, the city and the relationships there, would suddenly move into the background and align itself with the magnetic field. Much coincidence would play into it, coincidence of a kind that brings out the necessities that arise from the characters.

Suddenly something like courage to write is present again, even high spirits, which I have not felt for a long time. Sometimes you get the right book in your hands at the right time. And a calmly cheerful basic mood may add itself to that, a feeling of ease that even the blood pressure meter registered yesterday with values that were unusually low for me, so that I— in high spirits again, asked Professor F.[2] how much time I still had, in his opinion, to write something of greater magnitude, to which he replied: Oh, I believe, a lot. The prophecy, which I accept, has a lasting effect.

Gerd put on one of his beloved broths; so we eat noodle soup for lunch and lie down. I then leaf through the newspaper's weekend magazine, scan an article on the four hundred-and-fiftieth anniversary of the novel *Don Quixote*, which I have probably never read in its entirety, inform myself about Aleksandar Tisma's novel *Foreman,* which I will order for myself (*From the Hell of Guilt*), and find a column about Timothy Garton Ash's book *The File*, a report about the state security police dossier on him, from the time when he lived in East Berlin as a student. He visits the Interior Ministry people whom he finds in his dossier and "concedes that they had motives." Does not find them "evil," but weak, twisted. My mind is occupied with his observation that the Nazis did not have to employ anywhere near as many informers as the German Democratic Republic did—"because the Third Reich could depend far more upon spontaneous denunciations by enthusiastic Germans." He writes: "Probably no dictatorship in recent history had a secret police force that was as extensive and fanatically thorough as that of the German Democratic Republic. No democracy of recent times has undertaken more to expose the legacy of the bygone dictatorship than the new Germany." The budget of the Gauck Commission is higher than the defense budget of Lithuania, he knows. But he does not ask why. The fact that in the Third Reich there were more voluntary informers than in the German Democratic Republic also points to the fact that middle-class societies with unchanged property condi-

[2] Prof. Fritz Klein (b. 1924), historian; 1990-1991 director of the Institute for General History of the Academy of Sciences (German Democratic Republic). (G.W.)

tions were more natural to the Germans than communist societies that undertook nationalization. And the zeal of the Federal Republic to process and expose the National Socialist dictatorship was significantly more limited than it now is with the revelations about the East German dictatorship. (I consider to what extent it is valid or only a pointed witty remark that I made the day before yesterday, when that "Squirrel" Prize from Bordeaux was awarded to me in Potsdam.[3] I said to Günter Grass, who observed that nothing would remain of the German Democratic Republic: Yes there will. The Gauck documents! and then added: They promote forgetting while apparently fortifying memory. A German paradox—Manfred Stolpe, on the other hand, gave the opinion that literature will keep memory awake.)

Slept, set the coffee table on the veranda, the apple pie that Gerd brought; Pierre Dessus from Lyon, who wants to interview me for *Le Monde*, arrives quite punctually. He is a younger, very slender man with a noticeably long neck and a narrow skull; helps himself to the cake because he did not have any lunch. At first we talk a little bit in order to get to know each other. We find each other likeable. He liked *Medea*, he says; he sees it as a generally valid work, tested its effect on two French friends, neither of whom came to the idea that this was a book about German-German quarrels, quite in contrast to the German reviews that he had read. Then we were already in the middle of the interview, in part with the usual questions about the origin of the material, about its development stages, but also about "German" factors, to what extent the reunification has restorative characteristics, what is going on with German literature, which is no longer critical, etc. As always in such cases, I have forgotten most of it again and will have to

[3] With her translator Alain Lance C.W. received the Prix Écureuil de Littérature Étranger of the Bordeaux Book Fair for 1997 on September 29, 1997, awarded in Potsdam. (G.W.)

occupy myself with it when he faxes me the text, which I must and want to edit. He had brought only one tape cassette with him, and it was full after an hour and a half. We talked a little bit more "dry," and then the question arose as to what he could do this evening in Berlin; and he also did not have a hotel room yet. I called Volker Braun, who had Alain and Renate Lance spending the night, asked where they were going, and learned: to the Distel, a cabaret, and we were actually still able to get tickets at the door. We had to leave immediately; the performance began at six o'clock.

As always, Friedrichstrasse was again blocked by construction areas differently than it had been only weeks earlier. We crept in from behind. When we entered the anteroom of the Distel, a roar came from behind the door—five people had assembled themselves there to greet us; besides Volker, Annelie, Alain, and Renate, Giesela Oechelhaeuser[4] as well; she distributed the tickets, we were her guests and drank a glass of champagne upstairs before going into the performance hall. We had not been there for so long! Not since the collapse of the German Democratic Republic, and even before that not very often, but I remembered the meeting in which Walter Ulbricht had complained right here about the dreary, gray materials and the "formalistic" vases of the East German production and had been interrupted by Helene Weigel and others—it was later called the "vase discussion." And before that, Gerd was still with the radio station and we had only lived in Berlin for a short time, the trade organization had celebrated an anniversary in this room, for which Gerd had done the program for them and contributed a little verse that he had written himself: "Join with me in repeating Hans Sachs's words: We must never again divide Germany."

[4] Gisela Oechelhaeuser (b. 1944), cabaret director; 1990-1999 manager of the cabaret Die Distel; 1992-1997 moderator of the ORB program "*Am Tag als...*(On the Day When...)." (G.W.)

We sat in the third row; I enjoyed the program, which ran under the heading: "We Did Not Deserve That" and was dedicated primarily to unemployment and the shamelessness of capital. Gerd felt that the texts, especially in the first part, were often too didactic, and I also read that later in a review; people saw and heard there only what they already knew from the newspaper. That may be true, of course, but the actors were good, and it really is something different when you laugh about pointed formulations together with two hundred people. And the other spectators did that too. In front of us sat a whole group of West Germans; they enjoyed themselves immensely, especially when one of them was then turned on during a number by the performer and her husband identified her as "Elisabeth." At the end people called for an encore at the top of their lungs, but the performers remained firm. At eight o'clock they had to give the second performance.

We congratulated Oechelhaeuser, and she said that there was still some reticence in it. She had directed it and was able to judge. You need twenty to thirty performances before you move completely freely in the program and the actors also know where the points are. Only the audience teaches you that. While we are walking over to the Ganymed, where she had reserved a table for us, she talked about her constant fear of going into the red. In the summer they had three or four weak months, but now during the winter they were drawing crowds again. If this premiere went well, then the jobs would be secure for another fifteen months, but as early as the evening after a premiere they are already thinking with trepidation about the next one. They also have a second program with which they go on tour, and if a performer suddenly becomes ill, she jumps in with her solo program. They do not receive a single mark in subsidies, and when she recently turned to the senate to beg for 100,000 marks for an urgently needed air conditioning system, she encountered so many dif-

ficulties and would have had to lay her entire business operation open to scrutiny, with the result that she quickly desisted
from doing that and now asks the audience for contributions.

On the right, behind the door in the Ganymed, Thomas
Brasch sat at a tiny table drinking tea. He called to me; I turned
around and fortunately recognized him, although he had
changed a great deal. He has aged, a harder face, gray whisker
stubble. Wow, Thomas! Always that awkwardness when I meet
him, caused by a mixture of guilty conscience and the fear that
he could become aggressive again. How are you doing? Fine,
fine. How is the writing going? Fine, too. And at the same time
I knew that he has been working on a prose text for six or
seven years, has already written perhaps a thousand pages, but
it was supposed to be a novella and he does not finish it and
does not dare submit it for publication. And now I hear that he
is currently living above the Ganymed and has taken an apartment there that is much too large. He says he always wanted to
live that way someday, with a view on the water; his mother
had told him: When you become wealthy someday, move here.
Now he has not become wealthy, to be sure, but at least he has
moved here, even if he actually cannot afford the apartment.

Volker greets him, we talk a little more, and then I have to
go to the others at the table. As I am leaving, he says: Then I'll
come over sometime, and I, emphatically: Yes, please, do come
and visit us, Thomas! He will not come, of course. I see him
sitting at his little table for a while longer, then he is gone.

The Ganymed has only been open again for a short time, as
a bistro; we used to sit here often after the theater or with
guests. Under the tables there are supposed to have been listening devices. So what? We have a very amusing young
French waitress, striking and lively, and since we have three
French people at the table, it is very fitting. I drink beer and
eat roast beef. Volker, next to me, does not know what he
should order. A few days ago his doctor told him that he

should be careful about his blood sugar level. Now he hardly dares eat noodles anymore. We laugh. He complains about the many engagements, about readings that he, of course, cannot decline, if only for financial reasons, about the fact that these days he is no longer able to find cheap lodgings in which he could work for a month, which he had always done before in September. To my right, Renate says that they have now seriously begun to expand their cottage in the Champagne, that she has "been given rank as a civil servant" and has her steady job in the Aragon Archives, but that she has not yet recovered completely from the stress caused by her doctoral dissertation.

Later Gisela Oechelhaeuser sits down next to me; it occurs to me that she seems full of energy and talks a lot. She tells about her beautiful vacation in southern France, then in detail about the troubles of her male friend, who is unemployed, fifty-five years old, and does not get hired by anyone. She also describes how it falls like mildew over their get-togethers with West German acquaintances when P., in response to their question as to what he is doing, answers: Unemployed. The embarrassment that then arises.

We leave at around eleven; we still have to find a hotel for Pierre, of course. Neither on Albrechtstrasse nor on Friedrichstrasse is there a vacancy. It is Saturday, and on the next day there is a marathon in Berlin. We decide to take Pierre with us to our place, quickly clear off the not very comfortable cot in the small room, cover it with a blanket for him, and place a glass of water there for him; since he wanted to come back again the next morning anyway to get material about *Medea*, that is the most practical thing to do.

I am very tired, but satisfied with the day. Read a few lines about Nabokov's *Pnin* in the book by Maar, sense that all of these stimuli that are now flying at me are touching the place within me behind which the key to continued writing lies hidden. Quickly fall asleep.

M idnight finds me, as it so often does, in front of the television set. The final scenes of the Commissioner Beck series from Sweden are in progress. The murderer, who dismembered his wife and sank her in a lake because she found out about him and his buddy when they were breaking gold crowns out of corpses, has been caught, and the people from the national defense apparatus have been exposed; they wanted to use this case to deport a man from the Russian embassy who had nothing to do with it but has become a security risk through a love affair with a state secretary, and—in contrast to the unavoidable search successes—Beck sits there alone and dejected again, because he is not capable of keeping a woman whom he loves, in this case his colleague Lena.

In the current topics segment they show how the television teams from all over the world, which want to report from Bonn today on the results of the German parliamentary election, install their cables. Never before have so many reporters come, they say. After all, it is probably the last election with Helmut Kohl, the last election in Bonn, the last election of this millennium. A large collision on the highway in Bavaria is shown, which Theo Waigel, whom we see, just barely escaped. Every year the drivers simply race into the first fogbanks; even the rapidly moving emergency medical vehicle was passed by racers in the middle of the fog.

I turn it off, take my glass into the kitchen, drink a little more, feel the laundry in the bathroom to see if it will be dry by morning, move some pieces around, look around Amalienpark from Gerd's window, which I like to do late in the evening to see if there are still lighted windows, and do not find any this time. Go to bed. Gerd is asleep. I read for a while yet in the Langgässer biography *Sleep, My Rose* by Frederik Hetman, always searching for points of departure for the speech that I will have to make next February, when I have to accept the Langgässer Prize in Alzey. I will not conceal the difficulties that I have in approaching her; it seems to me that those difficulties will not decrease. I simply cannot imagine that woman; she comes from the same area as Anna Seghers, was born in the same year, and there are supposed to be two of Langgässer's books that are dedicated to Seghers in the Seghers Library. But she herself and everything that she writes is so saturated with Catholicism and mysticism that it is unspeakably foreign to me. Respect—yes, for the power of language, the wealth of images, but at the same time something like consternation. And yet also a great curiosity, more: a thirst for knowledge about her fate. So I read about her family home, her Jewish father, her courage and her strength to escape from the tight corner, to bring an illegitimate child into the world, who—disastrous for that child, Cordelia, during the Nazi era—was fathered by a Jew; in a marriage Langgässer has three additional children and has to experience how Cordelia is dragged off to Terezin. They are occurrences that I can hardly imagine for a mother—how she survives, "copes" with it, continues to write in spite of it (*The Indelible Seal*, complete in 1945). Today, of course, we can no longer imagine that most people back then did not know the extent and the manner of the extermination of the Jews. Langgässer receives an injunction forbidding her to publish, but "sinking into the role of the writer" is still possible for her—that is perhaps her salvation. That she does not emigrate in 1936—a professorship overseas is offered to her husband—in order not to leave her old and ill mother—how painfully well I understand that. Even more difficult—but that was just it: she did not *know*!—the fact that she declined the offer from Karl Thieme to send Cordelia to Switzerland. (Again and again we are in danger of seeking "guilt" in the persecuted people and the victims. Why didn't they save themselves in this or that way?! While all of the guilt lies exclusively with the persecutors!) So, then, secretly writes advertising slogans for a soap company . . .

Two miscarriages, then after that, by 1943, three births: because she, as a Catholic, did not want to prevent conception, to say nothing of having abortions? Or three desired children, in the middle of the war? And as if all of that would not be sufficient: multiple sclerosis.

Meanwhile the harassments and the persecution of Cordelia increase. Her mother keeps it secret from her until the last moment that she is "half Jewish" with three Jewish grandparents, is thus considered to be a Jew, and is subject to the racial laws. She has to wear the yellow star. Is no longer permitted to live at home. Only then does she gradually learn what her situation is. In an adventurous manner her mother obtains Spanish citizenship for her. And then the horrible situation in the Gestapo office where Cordelia signs a statement that she does not want to give up her German citizenship: because otherwise her mother would be prosecuted . . . Cordelia becomes a nurse's assistant in the Berlin Central Hospital, in the vicinity of which is also the home for the aged in which the Jews of Berlin are driven together. Cordelia is deported to Terezin; until 1946 Langgässer learns nothing about her daughter, who was transported on to Auschwitz and then very shortly before the end of the war taken to safety in Sweden. Later her relationship to her mother is disturbed. The daughter will write a book, with barely suppressed rage against her mother . . . That fate as a mother and those terrors veil for me the accomplishments of the writer, which hardly penetrate to me.—So how should I talk about that?

Gerd wakes up halfway, looks at the clock: It is almost one-thirty. Don't you intend to sleep?—I turn off the light, but cannot fall asleep; the fate of Langgässer and her daughter goes through my thoughts and through my initial dreams. I soon wake up again, toss and turn. I must have dreamt a lot during the night, bodies intertwined with each other, but otherwise I do not remember anything.

In the morning I wake up at around eight, Gerd is already reading, and I try to go back to sleep. I do not succeed; I reach for the other book that lies on my nightstand and which complements the Langgässer biography in an unbelievable way: Claus Leggewie's report: *From Schneider to Schwerte*—"the unusual life of a man who wanted to learn from history." "A representative of the Enlightenment without self-enlightenment" is what Leggewie calls Hans Ernst Schneider near the end of his book. Schneider was a "hereditary" officer in the SS Storm Troopers during the Nazi era, gave himself the new name of Hans Schwerte, and as such became a respected leftist-liberal colleague in the field of Germanic studies after 1945. After examination of the material and after conversations with Schneider/Schwerte, Leggewie has no doubt that his change of attitude was authentic, that in any case he did not deceive his colleagues and his students *about that*, and that to that extent he did not actually live a "double life." He has, according to everything he knows, no people on his conscience. Schneider, "like all Germans of his and later generations in the twentieth century, remained one and the same person, more precisely within the context of radically changed institutions and mentalities." L. finds fault with the manner in which the university came to terms with the "Schwerte case," when the deception—only two years ago!—was exposed, and he tries to make up for that discussion after the fact. He asks about the "genesis and effect of the members of the Nazi elite and their 'abolition' in West German society." He quotes Freud: "The biographical truth is not to be had, and if we had it, it could not be used," and closes his preface: "The usefulness of this biography should lie in the self-enlightenment of the Federal Republic of Germany and in the comparison of German intellectual types in the twentieth century."

While I continue to read, a comparison takes place within me between the biography of Schneider and my own. What if I had been born twenty years earlier? The external conditions would hardly have prevented me from drifting into National Socialism, even as an adult. And—a more relevant question— it is clear to me that my hesitant work on the new book is also connected with the problem of self-enlightenment: whether I pursue it deeply enough and where it will then lead me. And of course I try to visualize the treatment of National Socialist leaders and fellow travelers in the German Democratic Republic. With regard to more than ten million enrolled Party members in 1947, Eugen Kogon[1] is quoted as saying: "You can only kill them or win them over." In the German Democratic Republic, during the initial years there was a sharp, even often unjust quarrel with civil servants of the Nazi regime—of course most of them evaded the responsibility by escaping to the West, where the motto was clearly: win them over. That very thing was for us, of course, one of the main reasons for excluding the Federal Republic as an alternative for our lives.

In the "Schwerte case" Leggewie sees parallels to the "Hermlin case."[2] That seems to me to be an erroneous conclusion. Hermlin—in *Evening Light*—interlarded pieces of his biography with fiction. He did not deny his identity (not even

---

[1] Eugen Kogon (1903-1987), German publicist, sociologist and political scientist. (Ed.)

[2] Hermlin case: Allusion to the tendentious portrayal in Karl Corino's book *"Aussen Marmor, innen Gips"—Die Legenden des S.H.* (*"Outside Marble, Inside Plaster"—The legends of S.H.*), Düsseldorf, 1996. (G.W.)

by taking on a pen name), and above all he did not have any transgressions or crimes to cover up. This act of equating the two seems to me to point to a blind spot in Leggewie's view and argumentation with respect to leftists—By the way, while doing preliminary work for the yearbook for Hermlin's seventieth birthday, which just appeared, Gerd found an early letter from Hermlin in which he corrects him—Gerd. In an article about Hermlin he had adopted the claim (undoubtedly from biographical statements that were available to him) that Hermlin had been in a concentration camp. Hermlin wrote him that this was incorrect; he had never been in a concentration camp.

German personal records. Should I wish that I were not affected?

While Gerd leaves to buy croissants and a Sunday newspaper, I take a shower, and wash my hair, which, to my dismay, has been falling out in clumps since my last narcosis. Then we sit at breakfast and read the newspaper. *Der Tagesspiegel* brings the headline: "Recent Surveys See the Social Democratic Party Only a Very Short Distance Ahead of the Union By Now." That, of course, gets our discussion started again: For whom do we vote? The Party of Democratic Socialism should, even if it still carries around a lot of old ideas in the form of its older members, be in the parliament again, and the Greens should be strengthened so that the Social Democrats cannot avoid steering toward the Red-Green coalition . . . "Whoever does not vote remains silent," it says in the newspaper, and: "The Rushdie case remains controversial"—although the Iranian state president had declared that the Rushdie case was closed and that the government of Iran was no longer after his life. So now an Iranian newspaper writes that the appeal to kill Rushdie is "irrevocable"—"An additional 60,000 pages of the Starr report released"—the USA continues with the ghastly exposure of its president—who, however, has revealed himself to be an immature man. On the third page the racecar driver

Michael Schumacher is described as "shy, ambitious, rich—and fast." By the year 2002 he will supposedly receive two hundred and twenty million marks in salary . . .

"The interim results of the famine aid for the Sudan are depressing." An interview with Simon Wiesenthal, who will be 90: "The entire meaning of my work lies in a warning to the murderers of tomorrow." And, on page five: "Corporations in the maelstrom of a tightening defense economy." Under the pressure of the stolen gold affair "even German enterprises and corporations are showing a new mobility in the compensation of slave laborers and concentration camp prisoners." BMW, VW, Daimler, and Siemens are named, after that a whole series of the most well-known German enterprises; but it is primarily a matter of the four-year plan as the economic preparation for the Second World War. I have to think about how—it must have been in 1990—a man who had formerly been an industrial historian once said to me in Munich: If someday all the skeletons the great German corporations of the Nazi period have in their closets are uncovered, then a revolution really ought to break out here.

Gerd begins making the liver dumplings for the evening soup; I put the hand towels in the washing machine and take down the laundry from yesterday. I call Martin and remind him about the evening event at the Brecht House tomorrow, at which the yearbook for Gerd's birthday will be presented; I ask him just how he will vote now and we discuss the pros and cons—have all become tacticians.

We go to vote, to the school on Stiftsweg. It is a gray day, but warm; I immediately begin to perspire. Little groups of people are working their way toward the school; we are sent into different classrooms; the ballot is long, twenty-three parties. So I make my little crosses. Not an ideal election, I myself believe, but this time there was no "ideal" selection; we knew only what we did not want.

Outside Gerd announces whom he gave his second vote to. Well, well! I say, weren't we in agreement? No, he had always said whom he wanted to strengthen. Typical, I think. Also good. We meet our neighbors from the building, he has his little daughter on his shoulders, yes, they knew exactly how they would vote; they would always vote the same. We joke yet about anarchistic parties that we would like to vote for. Walking with my two crutches becomes difficult for me again; the stretches that I can walk to a certain extent with a minimum of complaint are becoming shorter and shorter; I have the impression that the joint in my left hip sometimes really pounds against the bone.

At home I begin writing this text, for the first time on the computer. Next to me lies a letter that arrived yesterday and which I intend to answer, from a Dr. Eva Glees, from Woodstock in England—a Jewish emigrant from Germany. She read *Patterns of Childhood* and writes:

"I could not stop—I was born in 1909, and the description of the life in which Nelly grew up awakened memories within me that I thought were buried. The many sayings and proverbs and the texts of songs were very familiar to me, as well as the way Charlotte talked." She writes that she also read *Medea* with great interest. Only after she went to the *Medea* exhibition in Bonn in 1996 did she also begin to read in German again . . .

Gerd calls; he has made rice pudding and applesauce, exactly the right food for today, I think. We lie down very wearily. Then I get my hands on the Sunday magazine section of the *Frankfurter Allgemeine Zeitung*, there is a text there—it is not actually a story—under the title "The Staff of Moses." The author tells how he lived in LA for a long time, bought a wooden club at a garage sale for twenty dollars, which the seller boldly called the staff of Moses (from a biblical film production), how he became acquainted with a young dancer with whom he wanted to make a film; with that intent he went to see her, taking the staff with him. She fascinated him with her bold dancing, and in the end the two of them talked about the staff, which he had laid across the back of a chair and a glass case. Then he stayed overnight and they forgot to put out the candle. He was awakened by a fire in the next room and could hardly get the girl to wake up. She was in shock and unable to act. He pulled her along with him and lost his orientation. Then suddenly the staff of Moses was above him; he again knew where he was, crept through beneath it, pulled the girl along with him, found the door, and they were saved.

The story was very believable to me, especially the girl's reaction, because three days ago—more accurately nights—I had experienced for myself how a sudden fright renders a person unable to act, when Gerd woke me up in the middle of the night (it was three o'clock) and asked for the number of the fire department; of course my subconscious reacted immediately with the memory of the fire in Meteln. I was so scared that I could hardly talk and asked what the matter was. He said only: Well, come and take a look! That upset me completely; I could not get up, my legs gave way, my heart raced, and I could no longer talk because my mouth was so dry. When I was finally in the vestibule I saw the reflection of flames in my room; I thought: It's fortunate that the diaries are in the safe! and asked myself what else I should quickly throw out the window. Then I was finally able to go to my window and saw that down below in the next yard a garbage pile was burning. The flames were shooting up quite high because they had already set fire to an elderberry bush; they crackled very loudly, and above all there were loud pops. Some kind of cans seemed to have burst. The fire department, which somebody else had already called, put out the whole thing in a few minutes. But I know now that I cannot rely on myself when I suddenly become severely frightened.

The story of the staff of Moses awakened the memory of the fire in Meteln once more, as well as that of the days afterward, of the help that we received from our friends, and of the alienation since then. Revelations, well all right. In spite of that I believe that the friendship was authentic. There is such a thing. "Double life"? I really don't know. I could actually write a novel sometime about a man who lives under another name after the collapse of the German Democratic Republic, perhaps in the first-person form. A protagonist whom I really could not condemn. And even I would write that book under another name, and that could even be the title: *Under Another Name* . . .

In the afternoon we listen to the news, the election turnout this Sunday was probably higher than during the last election. Then it is reported that in 1964 the world was faced with a third world war. The USA had planned an action against China to destroy the atomic weapons there, but was kept from doing it at the last minute by military advisors who had calculated the possible course of events. Remarkable how cold such reports leave me. Apparently I have meanwhile become prepared for anything.

At the computer again. Gerd is preparing the table for the evening. He walks back and forth; dishes rattle. At five-thirty I become restless and sit down in front of the television set. There are pre-election programs, among other things one that makes fun of a parliament session, which I find funny. Gerd carries platters of ham and pickled mushrooms past me, lets me taste, I think they are "too old" and he exchanges them for newer ones. In the election studios they show who is there, who will do what, who will later commentate the results (in the Work Group for German Public Radio most of the commentators wish that they might be spared the change; they are bank people, entrepreneurs). The tension increases; the leaders of the election tally groups say that they already know how it will turn out, but that they are not permitted to say anything yet; instead it is shown how those predictions materialize. It is finally six o'clock and the first prediction comes immediately: The Social Democratic Party is ahead, the Party of Democratic Socialism has 5%. I cannot yet believe that we will someday experience an election that must not depress us. Christa Vogel[3] arrives; we drink champagne, the computer projections stabilize, and cheering Social Democrat and Democratic Socialist parties blend together. The bozo from the Christian Democratic Union makes a speech in which he praises the services of the Christian Democrats and Kohl. I wanted to see him lose, but when he then appears, I feel hardly any satisfaction. He carries himself well, is a good loser, all right, the Kohl era is past, we say goodbye, may things go well for him. The Brauns come and we say: Well, have you toppled another regime? Volker, when asked how he voted, does not give direct information; one should always vote for the opposition, he says. Meanwhile Schröder and Lafontaine step in front of the cameras together[4]; I hope that Lafontaine will continue to have influence on Schröder. Maria Sommer comes and announces to whom she gave her second vote. Frank calls and gives congratulations regarding the election. Annette arrives. She was at Lake Constance for a convention; the most beautiful part was the landscape, she says. We still watch the television screen; the Party of Democratic Socialism fluctuates, but always remains above 5%. Nobody would have thought that, not even Gysi, who is happy and says that if he were to need them to be elected Federal Chancellor, Schröder would receive the votes of the Democratic Socialists in the parliament, if not, then he wouldn't,

[3] Christa Vogel (1943-2005), dramatic advisor for television; friends with the Wolfs. (G.W.)

[4] Gerhard Schröder (b. 1944), German politician, member of the Social Democratic Party, Federal Chancellor 1998-2005; Oskar Lafontaine, Social Democratic Party leader. (Tr.)

because actually Schröder is too "central" for him. During the course of the evening it becomes clear that Red-Green has a majority, at first only of three, then of seven votes. Today, a day later, we know that it is twenty-one and that the Social Democratic Party is beginning coalition negotiations with the Greens—must begin them, for on the evening of the election we still had the feeling that it would rather create a Grand Coalition, Germany needed a "stable" government, but the representatives of the Union and the Free Democratic Party said that they were not available for any coalition; the majority was sufficient for Red-Green, so now let them govern. Gradually it became clear that they hope that Red-Green will soon fail, and then they could sweep up the fragments. Kohl also stepped down as party chairman. Schäuble, who would probably have led his party to victory, said: The Kohl era is over. And many said that. And what almost pleased me the most: neither in Mecklenburg nor in the cities of Brandenburg that are administrative districts in their own right did the rightists get into the parliaments—I had hardly dared hope for that.

Back to the evening. We were all there and ate the excellent liver dumpling soup, but then Tinka and Martin also came, and finally Ruth and Hans Misselwitz[5] as well, and it became crowded in our room. Hans came from the Willy Brandt House; there the young voters had begun to shout slogans: "Red-Green! Red-Green!" In our group more or less everyone made their voting decisions known. Volker was probably the most skeptical with regard to the future government (with which he is undoubtedly right, but it might be that the unexpectedly strong election victory will also bring a shift in mood and force Schröder and Lafontaine to make reforms or make reforms possible for them). Ruth Misselwitz, who attended the

---

[5] Ruth Misselwitz (b. 1952), pastor of the Pankow Protestant Church congregation; together with Hans Misselwitz founder of the Pankow Peace Circle in the network of peace, environmental and human rights groups; friend of the Wolfs. (G.W.)

different election parties of the political parties in the Pankow
city hall, had not found the Christian Democrats, instead she
came from the Democratic Socialists, where she was received
with cheers and plied with wine. Strangely enough, everyone in
the group was in favor of the Party of Democratic Socialism
being in the parliament and watched the computer projections
eagerly, until it was established that with 5.1% they had made
it this time. At around ten o'clock the results were established:
Social Democrats 41.8%, Christian Democrats 34.6%, Greens
6.6%, Party of Democratic Socialism 5.1%, Republicans and
the German People's Union remain insignificant at under
2%—that was one of the greatest joys of the election evening.

Our visitors left and Gerd started dealing with the dishes—
I could hardly help since I cannot walk without a crutch and
thus can hardly carry anything. I channel surfed around a little
more in the groups of Sabine Christiansen and Erich Böhme;
of course they did not give any new knowledge, but Späth and
Egon Bahr, for example, dealt with each other in an amazingly
objective manner, just as previously the Social Democratic
Party had taken pains not to humiliate the losers with their
feeling of triumph. For the first time a ruling Chancellor was
defeated for reelection in the Federal Republic, and the East
German states shared in that tendency completely (in Saxony
a 27% loss of votes for the Christian Democratic Union!). It
may be that this joint announcement of the will of the people
will lead to more inner unity—anyway, everywhere in the new
federal states—quite in contrast to the old ones—the Party of
Democratic Socialism received at or above 20% of the votes.
That is the decisive difference.

At midnight I lay in bed.

MONDAY, SEPTEMBER 27, 1999
Dresden—Berlin, Pankow

At midnight, when this twenty-seventh of September begins, I am still lying awake, in Dresden, in the double bed of Horst's guestroom, a way station on the road from Kreisau/Kryzova to Berlin. I sense that I will not fall asleep for a long time; in the classical manner the images of the day pass in front of me, the morning departure from Kreisau, the German-Polish meeting place for European youth on the grounds and in the buildings of the former estate of the von Moltkes, where I had read from *Patterns of Childhood* the evening before, and Veronika Jochum von Moltke had played the piano; the short drive around the village, which, like all Polish villages, exhibits the decaying face of the twenties and the thirties, up to the Mountain House, in which the Moltkes actually lived and in which the men and women of the Kreisau administrative district met, far away from all the centers, thus favorable for their conspiring purposes, probably less favorable today for this meeting place. The house, like the entire estate, restored and renovated in the most wonderful way as a possible memorial and research facility for this segment of the resistance against Hitler. I see the three children before me, who come toward us on the threshold and apparently live there with their family; a girl has a white dog in her arms and tells us its Polish name when we ask. I see the empty rooms furnished with shelves, the still modest library, beer bottles and food fragments from the previous evening on one of the tables, music from another room; we do not want to disturb and quickly leave again. We stand on the "mountain" and look out over the wonderful hilly landscape all around us; here they had an unencumbered view. Gerd gathers up a few apples under a large old apple tree; I photograph the castle grounds that we can see from up here. I lie here and call all of it to mind in order to fix it in my memory, the new road to Legnica that we drove this time, how I look at the town name Gross Rosen again and again. There was a concentration camp there, I say, Franci was there, and Gerd says, wasn't Fred there, too? We no longer remember that exactly; at some point on the right a modest sign that points to the State Museum of Gross Rosen, a few kilometers later a signpost pointing left, black writing on a white background. Do we want to drive there? Yes. Through a little village, past a rusty, dilapidated production facility, which seems threatening in these surroundings; it is an overcast day, rainy, I remember that we did not know what awaited us, then to the right the parking lot; we turned in and saw the gate, a physical blow. I know, it is that gate that does not let me sleep, "Work liberates," I forced myself to photograph it as we approached, for Honza, I thought to myself, also for Franci. I wake up more and more, remember how we went into the museum, which exhibits documents about German fascism in Poland and of course also about the division of Poland between Hitler and Stalin, and at the sight of the maps I remembered how, during the previous evening, when we were sitting together in the large dining hall of Kreisau after the reading, Eva Urban, the Polish director of the Kreisau Foundation, who had come over from Wroclaw, suddenly felt compelled to talk about her seven years in Siberia, about the fact that the Russians took one and a half to two million Poles away to Siberia, intellectuals, judges, military people in any case, and refugees from the western areas . . . Remember the dark eyes of Eva Urban, her restraint as she said, the Nazis had only had twelve years, but the Soviets seventy . . . But now we want to change the topic, she said, as I remember; she is seventy-three and walks awkwardly, supported by a cane. She had read *Patterns of Childhood* twenty years ago "with burning ears"—But I see behind all, *in front of* all other images the gate. In the museum a relief of the camp, the multitude of barracks, of which today only the stone bases remain standing. The camp, of course, stood on a kind of high plain. The map with the mass of side camps, many more than we knew about. The Polish visitors, often couples, the youth, apparently boy scouts, a group accompanied by a priest. The young woman in the museum keeps a list of visitors. We see how she writes "*Niemci*" by our names and makes two lines behind it.

At some point I fell asleep. I wake up in the night because I have to go to the toilet, dreamed that I was supposed to give Freya von Moltke something and that I did not succeed in formulating it, although I knew it was quite simple. (After the reading Veronika Jochum had called Freya in Vermont, and I spoke with her as well. We remembered our meeting at her place more than six years ago, when we were in Hanover, New Hampshire.) The stairway to the bathroom is narrow, creaks, but I am happy that I can manage it, even though my left leg is still weaker than the right one and not always free of pain. After a while I go to sleep again, am awakened by the call that the bathroom is free. Admire, while I am getting ready, how cheerful and thought-out everything is here, while at our place, especially in my room, I sometimes have the feeling that chaos will break over us in the near future.

Breakfast in the winter garden, in radiant sunshine; it is cool outside, however. The *Dresdner Zeitung* offers precautionary derogatory comments by top people in the Social Democratic Party on the approaching publication of the "exposé book" by Oskar Lafontaine. He is reproached for cleverly marketing himself, for letting the publication run in the very media that formerly attacked him the most. A short report about a radio discussion between Grass and Walser the previous evening; only comments on the reunification are quoted. Grass: "There is still no blessing on it." And "something took place that can no longer be erased: the act of taking possession. The West made a grab for it." Walser: It was difficult "to take over such a broken-down thing." "No society would have gotten along there without losses of justice." There is a report: "East Germans read less than West Germans." At the time of the survey just 56% of the West Germans read a book, but only 43% of the East Germans. It may well be that they (can) hardly buy books for themselves anymore; it is also the fact that part of the motivation to "read" in the German Democratic Republic— the public information deficit—is gone.

We talk about Horst's and Helga's daily routines, about their physical workouts twice a week in a fitness center, about the students that Helga still tutors, about Horst's devotion to the wind tunnel, about his teacher, Professor A., who turned eighty-five the day before and receives a relatively small pension—as a West German professor he would have received four or five times as much, about the good performance of Horst's pacemaker. He repeats that he can hardly grasp how much we are still on the go, how many events I still participate in, and when I hear him talk that way, I cannot comprehend it myself and resolve to decline several more invitations for the coming year.

At 8:45 A.M. we depart, the route through Dresden that is already familiar now, through the long construction zone on the highway, then over the rough stretch that is also still rather long. Gerd says: But with Poland—no comparison! The sun hangs rather low to our right, flits past the tree trunks, and the flashes disturb me.

I turn off the radio, and we travel almost silently. Whenever possible, Gerd drives very fast; apparently he wants to set a record. I begin to think about what I could do in February at the poetics lectures at the university in Göttingen. Perhaps I should talk about the diary as a literary genre and as raw material for literature, ask myself the question of how a "fate," "a life," evolves from the experience of the everyday routine, day by day, when and how the mundane routine is transformed into something deeper, into temporal fellowship; the concept of time in general, inviolable in its simple expanse minute for minute, in which usually nothing at all "happens." I imagine the endless minutes of the concentration camp prisoners, the monotony that undoubtedly makes that time shapeless in their memory, and our hunger for experience, for "events," which for its part also kills time. (Jana says, to her sorrow she has hardly any memories of the time when the German Democratic Republic collapsed; she is irritated that she did not write down anything.) My desire to retain everything as far as possible, to eat up the time through these writings, which I would need for the "actual" writing, and later, when I read the diary manuscripts again, to discover that I would have forgotten almost everything if I had not written it down. Where does what we experience go? And to what extent does it form us anyway? Which literature claims, of course, when it falsifies by taking certain proceedings, certain thoughts and manifestations of feeling from the stream of everyday events and giving them meaning. It is not a coincidence that *Patterns of Childhood* is based on a travel diary, not a coincidence that the structure of *Stadt der Engel* is also based on a diary; *What Remains* is the description of a day, likewise *Accident*. Apparently I believe that I can only be "authentic" in that way and escape the adulterations that literature also means . . . So should I talk about "the authentic" in Göttingen? How the pure course of time brings forth phenomena like "conscience," even "love"—or are those hollow questions?" What does *carpe diem* mean?

In the car I always almost automatically begin to sing, and now it is to that point again, usually the same songs, "*Ich hatt einen Kameraden* (I Had a Comrade)," "*Es leben die Soldaten*

(Long Live the Soldiers)," "*Hohe Tannen weisen die Sterne* (Tall Pines Point out the Stars)"; suddenly I hear: "*In den Ostwind hebt die Fahnen* (Into the East Wind Raise the Flags)"—a song that I have not thought of for many years; Gerd knows it and he is as startled as I am at the lines: And a land gives us the answer / And it wears a German face / There has been much blood shed for it / Now the ground won't hold its peace—Where does this song from an earlier historical era come from now? Did it wash up within me as a result of our visit to Poland? Again I become aware of what layers of history are stacked together within me. I quickly seek other songs, "*Wer recht in Freuden wandern will* (Whoever Wants to Hike with Joy)," "*Dona nobis pacem, Die Glocke läutet vom Bernwardsturm* (The Bell Rings from the Bernward Tower)," "*Entgegen dem kühlenden Morgen* (Toward the Cooling Morning)," "*Die Gedanken sind frei* (The Thoughts Are Free)" . . . Quite soon we are at the Schönefeld crossing, we have decided not to drive through the city, but along the eastern ring, as an experiment; the stretch is longer, also partially restricted by construction areas, but no traffic lights, and therefore much faster on the whole. We drive past the new housing developments along the stretch, neat cottages that all look like toy housing developments. When we drive up in front of our door, I look at my watch and proclaim: Two and a half hours. Truly a record.

Gerd must carry most of the baggage upstairs; climbing stairs is still difficult for me. My left leg is weaker and hurts; even the physiotherapist and the orthopedist do not know if that is really still from the "bursitis" or if it can simply be traced back to the failure of the largest muscle ("the one that we eat as a filet from an animal"). The mailbox, which has not been emptied twice, is totally stuffed, on the answering machine thirteen phone calls. Throw open the windows, clean out the bags; Gerd immediately begins to clean the mushrooms that we bought along the road in Poland, magnificent rough-stemmed boletus mushrooms and chanterelles; we discuss whether or not we should fry them all, whether that will not be too much, and then Gerd saves out some chanterelles and dries them on the windowsill. I begin opening the mail. Most of it fortunately into the wastepaper basket as always, advertisements or announcements of events that I will not attend. A card from Helene in the USA, from her tour through California ("I am now familiar with everything in Disneyland"); in the year 2000 I am supposed to give a lecture at a convention for the continuing education of teachers; a written interview is requested by the local newspaper of Vöringen, where I will read at the end of October; *Arte* "needs" me for a television interview about my feelings ten years after the fall of the Wall; on the same topic I am supposed to write an article each for two Italian newspapers; Stralsund women who protested against the war in Kosovo want me to come there as a "peace researcher"; nothing that I will really accept, but everything has to be declined and costs time.

While the potatoes are cooking and the mushrooms are frying, I unpack the suitcases and the washing machine gets filled up. I feel quite strange, not really dizzy, but something is wrong with my head; I must lean against the door frame, perhaps a lack of circulation, a pressure in the area of my stomach. Gerd says, you have overexerted yourself; we are no longer able to simply put such a tour behind us. He is also tired.

On the answering machine, besides news for Gerd's publishing company and some messages that people will call again, there is also a call from Günther Gaus. His voice is hoarse; he has his third chemotherapy treatment behind him; he is doing "quite well"; he asks if we can see each other at our place on the tenth of October, the election Sunday. I think of him very often; it is so important to me for him to "defeat" the illness—but isn't that again a word from a completely false category, for the course of events for which I hope so much for him?

Jana calls and wants to know how it was in Poland. Old

Grandpa did want us to get together some evening this week, she says. We agree that we will meet on Wednesday evening, either at our home or in a restaurant.

The mushrooms taste delicious, but I continue to feel "light-headed." After washing the dishes, I take my blood pressure: 146/86, completely normal, but a pulse of only 45. Is that what is making me so drowsy? I remember this feeling, but do not know when and where I have already experienced it. I am happy and relieved to lie down; then I read in today's *Berliner Zeitung* about a German-French colloquium that took place in Genshagen, topic: "How historical memory is transformed into political identity." A French sociologist and the former French ambassador in Germany explained that for France it is only now slowly becoming possible "to accept politically" the events at the time of the Vichy regime and the bloody colonial war in Algeria that ended in 1963, as "historical events." Such a transition period is apparently a "necessary phase of silence." Another man gave the opinion that the temporary suppression of a painful part of history is a prerequisite for finding a social and political consensus. I think about the brute force with which East German citizens were supposed to be compelled to remember everything quickly and self-critically after 1989, while at this convention it was also confirmed that the "German populace has only been ready for a few years to approach" National Socialism "in a truly honest manner." The history of the Third Reich is more present in Germany now than it was ten or twenty years ago. Claude Lanzmann said: "Only when history no longer clings to your own body are you ready to accept it."[1] The writer Bernard-Henri Levy reports that Joseph Fischer[2] said to him while looking at photographs

---

[1] Claude Lanzmann (b. 1925), French filmmaker and professor of documentary film. (Ed.)

[2] Joseph Martin Fischer (b. 1948), German foreign minister and vice-chancellor in the government of Gerhard Schröder. (Tr.)

of the Bosnian massacre that his patriotism feeds on his memories of Auschwitz. For Levy that was "a soothing and important moment that reconciled me with Germany."

I remember my excitement about Walser's[3] speech in St. Paul's Church last November/December, when I was in the hospital and often followed the reports about him and the reactions to it on television until late into the night; how I at first could not believe that the accusations against Walser were justified, but that he then increasingly confirmed it himself, especially in the closing discussion with Bubis.[4] And how the whole thing now, after Bubis's death, seems initially to have been shoved into a drawer. But it will occupy our minds again and again. And I also ask myself if the NATO bombardment of Belgrade can really be justified on the basis of Auschwitz—in spite of the crimes of Serbs against Kosovo Albanians. I know, the tension of yesterday—the visit to the place of German resistance fighters in Kreisau, the confrontation with a location of the greatest horror that Germans brought about, in Gross Rosen—continues to affect me.

Even after sleeping I still feel a slight absence of blood in my head, but my pulse has normalized, and we decide to go shopping. A letter that I had written for little Helene's birthday has come back—the stamp fell off. It has to go back into the mailbox quickly. The book dealer has me sign a few books in passing, for a customer to whom she will send them abroad. On the way I have to stop and catch my breath again and again, yes, yes, I will have it examined when we get our precautionary flu shots next week before we go to the book fair. At the watchmaker's shop we pick up the watch that belonged to Gerd's father and which he gave his grandson for Anton's coming-of-age party. It was repaired for 126 marks. At the market the pur-

[3] Martin Walser (b. 1927), German playwright and novelist. (Ed.)
[4] Ignatz Bubis (1927-1999), German businessman, politician (Free Democratic Party). (Tr.)

chase of vegetables, grapes, potatoes—Gerd is always ahead of me; for certain goods he goes to certain stands where they already know him. We walk down Ossietzky-Strasse, because I want to buy thinner stationery; the building that houses the store is surrounded by scaffolding and we have to go up a stairway to a back door; the paper that I finally take is only one point thinner than the other and unfortunately also not quite white. Further along Wolfshagener Strasse, I am happy to be able to walk so far without any support, almost painlessly; I can live with that, I think to myself. Past Annette's place, up in the window there is nobody visible; Gerd buys milk and butter in the organic grocery store. Heavily laden he goes up the stairs ahead of me; I come slowly behind him sweating and wheezing: unpack at home, we then fix tea, I call Honza. Tell him about Gross Rosen. Yes, he says, that was the central camp where Franci arrived with her sister and her mother. They had actually been interned in the side camp at Christianstadt, from where they had to walk to a distant munitions factory in the forest to work, often in ice and snow. He had always wanted to go there, even with Franci, but then it was suddenly too late when she died—I want to know what is happening in his battle with the medical society and the health insurance agency, who are denying him continued treatment, blood detoxification for his metabolic disease, on the basis of an expert opinion. Since this disease is extremely rare, there is no long-term study about the fact that it could be the sole cause of a heart attack (at the age of forty he had already had two heart attacks), thus the treatment can only be regarded as "preventative" and is therefore not covered by the health insurance. Honza is in the process of writing to everybody under the sun, filing petitions; I implore him not to let it get to the point where he could get into a critical phase again, ask him to work it out with his treatment center that he can temporarily be treated at our expense. He says, that will be difficult and that it is also very expensive; I say: You, otherwise I'll go there! Finally he agrees to find out if it is possible to pay privately for the blood detoxification that he needs weekly. Tinka calls. She is also upset because of Honza; she says that we have to go to the newspaper, otherwise nothing will happen. We make an appointment to go to a Spanish restaurant tomorrow, on her birthday, with her family. After her return from the Ukraine, where she had an exciting, good seminar with "great" women, she was very tired, but things are going better now again. Was she there at the right time to wish their little son a happy birthday? I ask. She says: Our little son was not there! He was at a party, then went out with his friends, and came home at one. Entry into the young-man phase, I say. She says: It's about time! Then Anton comes to the telephone briefly and I belatedly sing "Happy birthday to you" to him.

I go to the window and look at Franci's tree, the red beech. I tell it that we were in Gross Rosen and that we will take care of Honza.

There is a call from the Luchterhand Publishing Company. Did I receive the leaflets for the edition of my collected works? Yes, and I also like them, but a mistake has been made with the Bettina title: It has to read: "But the *Next* Life Begins Today." They are taken aback; hopefully the mistake is not in the books as well—the first four have been sent to me—then: No, in the book and in the press annotation the title is given correctly. An advertising mistake.

I call Günter Gaus and he answers immediately. Even after the third chemotherapy treatment his condition is "not bad." Occasionally, when the white blood cell count declines completely, he feels very lethargic, but he is determined to be in Berlin on the tenth of October, Berlin's "Election Sunday." We arrange for them to come to our place at five-thirty to watch the election results, and that we will then eat something together. Now and then, he says, he lies down, visualizes things on the basis of the book that I sent him, and lets "the Indian River flow through him," which is supposed to wash away the bad cells. I praise him for that. I believe in the effectiveness of visualization.

Now I simply sit down in front of the television set and watch an ancient episode of *Derrick*; after a while Gerd joins me. We eat bread, cheese, and grapes. On the screen we are informed that a year ago today the new government was triumphantly elected, and what has become of it? Ten years ago the demonstrations in Leipzig, the "cradle of the quiet revolution." And how far has democracy progressed since then? A woman civil rights advocate says that oblivion is spreading and that the injustice of the German Democratic Republic is still far from being completely specified—The extradition proceedings against Pinochet are being negotiated, with documented incidents of torture—All a part of our past, I think to myself, but how does "the past" come into being? The US government expects that the current year will bring a 1.15 billion dollar budget surplus, more than ever before—And with that to the stock market . . .

Sonja Hilsinger wants to know what I have to say about her afterword, etc. for the next volumes of the collected edition, but I just now found the material here and have not yet been able to look at it—A long television evening, while after a while Gerd strikes his sails and goes wearily to bed. I have become alert again. There is a rerun of the film *King of St. Pauli*; I watch parts of it, the scenery is shaky, the whole thing is a sentimental fairy tale, but the actors in part quite good. On another channel under the title "Love, Desire, and Passion" there is a documentary about the chemical prerequisites for those feelings; the hormone oxytocin, which accompanies all sexual processes, emerges as significant. The "crafty chemistry of love life" is described, the physiological explanation of extramarital affairs . . .

Eberhard Görner calls[5]; he had had to leave Kreisau very early in the morning because he is making a film in his native village. He wants to say once again how important it was that we were in Kreisau, how glad and happy above all even Veronika Jochum was (her father was the famous music director Jochum; she studied in the USA under the greatest piano virtuoso and became acquainted there with her husband, Wilhelm von Moltke, the brother of Freya), she would like to appear with me again by all means, etc.

In passing I read in the feature section an article by the American Andrew Gimson, "Chancellor of the Political Class," a sharp attack upon Gerhard Schröder, his "dangerous lack of authentication and reliability after only one year in office," who, for example, is now propagating the Euro against his better judgment, but does not say that the compulsory savings are in part being forced upon him by this "sickly premature birth," and who is supposedly increasing Germany's "democratic deficit."

In the current topics segment, the Russian minister president says that in Chechnya "the last bandit will be destroyed"—Supposedly there is "progress" in the negotiations about the compensation of the Nazi forced laborers by German industry, which held them as slaves (if I remember correctly, Franci, her sister, and her mother each received 3000 marks for their slave labor!). Father Kurt Gumpel is pursuing the canonization of Pope Pius XII—the "pope who remained silent." There are supposed to be two letters in which he describes the Jews with loathing. The father: "A miracle will happen to make a saint of Pius XII."

The weeping mother of the baby that was kidnapped from the Friedrichshain hospital appears on the screen. Please, please, help me find my baby . . .

[5] Eberhard Görner, German theater director, screenplay author, film director. (Tr.)

On into the new day there is a rerun of the Sunday broadcast by Sabine Christiansen, in which that West German sociologist appears, the one who discovered that the East Germans are simply lazy. Poor Hans Modrow tries to argue against him with some pipe workers or other in Riesa, but he, of course, does not grasp anything: If you could not get this and that there, why didn't you then go somewhere else? That is how we did it . . . As is always the case now, Thierse must try to treat both sides fairly; I ask myself what the media are trying to accomplish by planting such a divisive factor now in the already very difficult process of "unity," shake my head, and go to bed; read a few more pages of Fred Varga's crime novel *The Disconsolate Widower of Mount Parnassus*; since it is not very exciting I soon fall asleep.

T he day begins at midnight with the final passages of a Japanese film on television: *Dance on the Edge of the Abyss*. I saw nothing more of the dance; what I see is a dying Japanese film director who persuades his doctor to let him out of the hospital in spite of a much advanced case of cancer, because he still wants to shoot the great final sequence of his film; the younger doctor, who initially views medical ethics differently, then agrees with the decision of this patient to die working, and earlier as a result; amid the applause of the nurses the old director leaves the clinic in a wheelchair, pushed by his wife, who is completely devoted to him. The doctor remains at his side as he directs the final sequence of his film, a musical piece, in a large theater with many people in the audience, collapses in the process, then lies on his death bed, even makes the amazingly large audience laugh as he dies, and finally dies "peacefully."

As a film, weak, sentimental, but since we were at the funeral for Tina Wrase[1] only a day earlier (how often we are at cemeteries now, when friends are buried who were younger than we are!), that theme of death touched me—just as I live each day in general, of course, with the thought of death, and often, during everyday activities, ask myself: How often will I still do that yet? How often will I still see, experience, and think that yet?

---

[1] Tina Wrase (1960-2000), musician, played saxophone and alto clarinet in the team of the *Medea* production (see above). (G.W.)

Until now that thought has come without fear; only when I must have a doubtful clinical finding checked, I notice: it does matter to me. I like living. Often I had thought that like my mother I would die at the age of sixty-eight years; since that did not happen, I no longer set a limit for myself.

At twelve-thirty to bed; as usual my thoughts wander around the family circle before I fall asleep. The day before, I had spoken with all of them on the telephone. Jana[2] is back from Crete; here the aftereffects of the suicide of her friend Felix in prison are overtaking her again; the attorneys now finally intend to pursue something with a higher authority that had filed an objection to Felix's temporary release and his later work release. Jana says that each time she sees exactly how senseless and how unnecessary his death was, she wants to vomit. Honza almost poisoned himself with poisonous mushrooms in Kamern; above all, however, he has slipped into sleeplessness again, because he learned that the general health insurance office is postponing the examination of his individual case, which the medical commission finally proposed for his case of metabolic disruption, and intends to leave everything up to the court, and who knows when that will deliberate. We are really worried about Honza. All the others bring us joy: Anton, who has just turned sixteen, who shot up to be taller than Tinka in one year, with his new deep voice and his refusal to talk about himself, except with Helene, who is splendid all around and went to a tavern in the evening with her brother and his friends the day before yesterday to buy them their first official beer, which can be drawn for them, of course, when they are sixteen—a kind of initiation rite. Anton was promptly asked for his identification. They could all use some more money, since they have occupations or perform jobs that are not appreciated in this society. Benni was on the answering machine. He lost his wallet and his account is also empty. Later in the evening: the wallet has been found, his situation has become less critical . . . I laugh softly to myself, think about how my "situation" was when I was twenty.

I read a few more pages in the Benjamin novel by Jay Parini: *Benjamin's Crossing*, in the fourth chapter, where it talks about Walter Benjamin's work on his crossing book, in exile in Paris, in the reading room of the Bibliothèque Nationale, at a table at which more and more seats remain empty because more and more users of the library leave Paris in flight from the advancing Germans. He is quoted as saying that he wanted to "make the areas arable on which until now only insanity has thrived. Forge ahead with the sharpened axe of reason and without looking right or left, in order not to fall victim to the horror that entices from the depths of the primeval forest." The world, it says there, which Benjamin knew, was dominated by self-deception and mythos. "He was depressed by the spirit of consumption and the hunger to buy that was visible everywhere, an insanity that was expressed in an unsurpassable manner in the shopping passageways . . . Through the passageways the actually rational city structure was transformed into an irrational labyrinth, into a nightmare of interconnecting tunnels, to an inwardly directed spiral that culminated in a kind of mental implosion." Benjamin: "What the mythical dimension of all labyrinthine forms creates is the downward whirlpool; once the spectator has entered, he is seized and drawn into a complex world without visible or predictable existence." The longer I read in that chapter, the more fascinated I became—for two reasons: first it seemed to me that in this image of the downward spiral I had apparently found the basic structure for my text "Descent into Hades," and secondly the figure of Benjamin reminded me more and more of my friend I., who has been working on Walter Benjamin for decades without ever finishing the book that he wants to write, and who seems to have a rela-tionship with women that is similar to the one that Benjamin probably had: passionately hesitant—Benjamin: "In ancient Greece the places where one descended into the underworld were indicated. Even our waking existence is a land in which there are hidden places leading down into the underworld; it is full of inconspicuous places into which our dreams flow." The topic of discussion is the "minotaur that must be slain, who lies half asleep on the floor of the labyrinth." The modern era as the age of hell—that is, as I clearly sense, my topic. Alienation in its contemporary form. In the form in which I have experienced and still experience it: "socialistic," capitalistic alienation.

Do the Chinese crane exercise and fall asleep at around a quarter to one.

Woke up at around six. It promises to be another magnifi-cent day. Gerd is already reading in the Thomas Mann biogra-phy by Hermann Kurzke; he creates breaches in the biography on the basis of certain points of view, he says, but he is learn-ing quite a bit. He must have known the Mann family well.

In the Benjamin novel I read the chapter "Lisa Fittko in Gurs." Remember our trip to southern France years ago, to Marseilles, to Les Milles—we were following the tracks of those who had gone before, in this case Anna Seghers and her husband. And we? Do we leave tracks of our own?

I sleep again until nine, a rare occurrence, and then quickly get up. Through the bathroom window I see: a magnificent day. The trees are still green.

Gerd is already sitting at the typewriter. On the little table in the vestibule lies a fax from the "Wildgarten Citizens' Initia-tive," an open letter to the "ladies and gentlemen of the Pankow district council," in which they once more urgently plead that the building permit for the parcel of ground behind our building be rescinded. It is supposed to be developed with several buildings, but in the process the wild garden will be lost and of course the bird habitat will be destroyed and our quality of life would be significantly decreased. I do not see how that can be stopped.

On the radio: Off the island of Paros a Greek ferry sank with 400 people aboard. Forty bodies have already been recovered, forty-four people are still missing. Supposedly the captain was down below watching a soccer match on television instead of navigating his ship from the bridge—Memory: how we were on Paros to negotiate with a peculiar team about a filming of *Cassandra*—Does every key word trigger a chain of memories?

Still on the radio: Mr. Merz of the Christian Democratic Union says, if need be, the Christian Democratic Union will enter the election campaign with the pension reform. When the trucks blocked Berlin yesterday ("a truck rally"), to demonstrate against the increase in fuel prices and against the pollution tax, Christian Democratic Union functionaries mixed in with the people and agreed with what they said. On the front page of the *Berliner Zeitung* the headline: "Truck Demonstration Fails to Reach Goal: Government Insists Upon Pollution Tax": "In their insistence on the pollution tax the federal government is now receiving the backing of prominent artists. The writers Günter Grass and Christa Wolf are supporting an action of the graphic artist Klaus Staeck and the Social Democratic Party politician Erhard Eppler, who are supporting the retention of the controversial tax," and so forth. Typical that none of the other signers are named. It is naturally a declaration of will against the current, but it disgusts me how every interest group thinks only of itself and how totally indifferent they are to what kind of world their grandchildren will live in or simply not be able to live in anymore.

I drink tea, eat muesli with shredded apples, toast.

In the feature section an installment of the novel *The News* by Alexander Osang is printed; I read in the timely continuation, in which a woman journalist talks with the special commissioner for state security police documents, in order to set him on the trail of a colleague about whom she has heard the rumor that he was an Interior Ministry informant: the only East German journalist who has become a newscaster for the national radio system. The special commissioner calls Lander's supervisor, disturbs him very much with a harmless inquiry in which, of course, no suspicion is voiced; Lander is immediately withdrawn and not permitted to report the evening news— A dossier about him was not found, only an index card.

While I am reading, the name "Joachim Gauck" resounds from the radio, and then his voice. He is resigning as of 3 October, of course, and is thus being asked to give an accounting. Did he not, in order to render the German Democratic Republic illegitimate, sometimes go too far in publishing documents?—No, he acted strictly according to the law. Sometimes he also expressed his opinion simply as a citizen, for example in the case of Christa Wolf, who, as a very young person, had become entangled with the state security police, but had then severed her ties with them, as one could clearly see from the many files kept on her and so forth. The interviewer then also expresses his opinion in the sense that of course the "campaign" against C.W. was "excessive."

Headlines: Opposition Wins Victory over Milosevic—Kohl Ignites Argument About German Unity—IMF Chief Köhler Calls for a War on German Poverty (the fox is minding the sheep!)—Pension Discussion is Taken up Again—Anger in the Precincts (in the federal parliament). A trucker: "The French drivers would have done it completely differently and simply shut down everything with their trucks and buses"—Protests on the Opening of the Monetary Fund and World Bank Convention in Prague—Dozens of Demonstrators and Police Injured—Ban on Attack Dogs Soon EU-wide?

The most necessary housework. Already 10:30. To my desk at last! Quickly a few letters. To the director of the production class at the film and television college in Babelsburg (what a stream of memories the mention of the name of that town now awakens within me again!), where one of his students wants to use quotes from *Divided Heaven* in his examination film, an annoying situation since the quotes have nothing to do with the film and I already refused to approve them once; but in order not to prevent the screening of the film at festivals, I reluctantly give my permission.

A German literary scholar would like me to describe my meetings with Uwe Johnson for his Johnson anthology—but I want to reserve to myself the right to talk about Uwe Johnson in whatever form and at whatever time I want (another stream of memories).

A woman who is a German literary scholar receives permission to look at the reviews of *Cassandra* that are in the archives.

For a long time I have been aware that I must spend larger and larger portions of my working time on information about earlier works and experiences. Apparently I have slipped out of the status of being a contemporary woman and into that of being a witness of the times.

I finally turn to the Seghers materials that are lying on my desk, for the speech that I have to give in the Academy on the occasion of her one-hundredth birthday.[3]

The last issue of the *Argonaut Ship*, galley proofs of her story "Jans Must Die," which was just recently found at her son Pierre's place in Paris, the pocket book that was just published by Aufbau with her letters from the first year after her return from exile (*Here in the Nation of the Cold Hearts*), and the galleys of the first volume of the Seghers biography by Christina Zehl Romero. Although I am only supposed to speak for twenty minutes, I want to do it thoroughly and perhaps even fundamentally.

[3] C.W.'s speech on the occasion of the one-hundredth birthday of Anna Seghers (*Werke*, Vol. XII, pp. 747ff.). (G.W.)

The problem of failure, which is almost unavoidable for people like Seghers—given the way German history has unfolded. Her idealistic origins in the chiliastic ideas of Laszlo Radvanyi. Her especially intimate tie to that man and the ideology that he and she represented. The partial failure as a writer is probably tied to her decision—which was made in exactly that year of 1947—to use her art to educate that morally destroyed German nation. *The Decision* is then evidence of the—once again partial—failure caused by its concession to the illustrative elements. Did she see it that way herself, have any idea of it? I did not want to see it that way back then— Later then, in the German Democratic Republic, she experienced what we all experienced: standing with her back to the wind, between false alternatives. Just that she had no choice at all to go perhaps to a different country.

There are few intellects in present-day Germany who are ready and able to view such a biography as an expression of German history and far less as evidence of personal failure and personal guilt. If one asks only who was right, everything simply runs in the direction of today's utopia-free situation, in which the individual interest groups are held together by their tenacious fight for an edge, for penny and mark, and terms like "public spirit" and "solidarity" only sound hollow by now and are reserved for noncommittal Sunday speeches.

I am invited by the Südwestfunk network to a broadcast occasioned by Anna Seghers's birthday, which I decline because I already have other things to do for it; the organizer says, but I must know, after all, that I am the only one who can still say something authentic about Anna Seghers—I now hear that sentence very often, for varying reasons. Sometimes it is correct, but I always dispute it.

I go out, do some shopping, it is very hot, twenty-five degrees Celsius, and I sweat.

Before eating I quickly call Uta Birnbaum,[4] who had yesterday left an unexpected message on the answering machine, after we had not had any contact with each other for ten years. Then she says that she saw me on television, and then it weighed heavily on her mind again that they had not called us anymore although we had actually done so much for them back then—What we "did": when she and Stefan Schütz went to the West in 1988, like many of our departing colleagues, before leaving they sat in our kitchen on Friedrichstrasse, and Stefan asked us to keep a thick bag for him in which there was his manuscript, which he did not want to take across the border with him, although they did have permission for it. We were supposed to hand the bag over to the person who came and spoke the key word "father." We stowed the bag in a dark cabinet corner in which a few similar pieces were stored; one day Günter de Bruyn stood at the door and said in a sepulchral voice: "Father." We laughed a lot. Now I learn from Uta Birnbaum that the bag was taken to the West as journalist baggage by Sibylle Wirsing.[5] She herself has meanwhile retired, they live in a small cottage in Oldenburg; Stefan Schütz no longer has a publisher and writes manuscripts for the drawer. They are still grateful to us—I really see no reason for that now.

The mail. A bunch of catalogues that seem to multiply in all directions, more and more companies offer things for sale, from whom I have never ordered anything, in addition requests for contributions, bank vouchers, ludicrous offers: I should adopt one of the slabs of the information box on Potsdamer Platz, which are now being dismantled and auctioned off!

Adolf Dresen[6] sends me his article "The German Dilemma,"

[4] Uta Birnbaum, theater director; went to the Federal Republic in 1980 with the writer Stefan Schütz (b. 1944). (G.W.)

[5] Sibylle Wirsing, German newspaper journalist. (Tr.)

[6] Adolf Dresen (1953-2001), theater director; following productions at the Deutsches Theater in Berlin, went to the Federal Republic with an East German passport; 1981-

which had already appeared in the *Berliner Zeitung* under the title "The National Dilemma," but, as he explains in an introductory note, abbreviated, with his consent; he himself had previously eliminated some paragraphs—passages that did not conform to political correctness; he had also changed the title, thus exercised self-censorship. His cuts in the manuscript had been "cuts of cowardice," and now he was sending the entire article to a few friends. The article begins: "Something is wrong." The world is growing together, at the same time states are dissolving into small and extremely small units. The passages that he did not publish in the newspaper concern themselves with the fact that people also have reasons for finding a neighborhood with foreigners difficult and that for hypocritical reasons we do not take their reservations and fears seriously—I think that too, however.

Before going to sleep I read the chapter in the Benjamin book in which Benjamin is described in the Parisian café and then together with his sister Dora—it becomes more and more clear that the author is actually not a novelist; his style is dull and short-winded. I sleep. Dream for the first time in a very long time—perhaps for the first time at all—a dream of my former family. The four of us are in a large room that very distantly resembles our bedroom on Fritsche-Strasse in Leipzig; it also has windows in a rounded-off wall, below the windows is a cot upon which first my mother lies; my father lies in one of the double beds, my brother Horst as a child—eight to ten years old—in a kind of child's bed at the foot of the double beds. He pouts and whines to himself that he has to go to school again in the afternoon. My mother and I comfort him, but make fun of him a little bit without talking to him—in real

1985 theater manager at the theater in Frankfurt/M.; beginning in 1985 independent opera director in Vienna, Paris and London; friends with the Wolfs after 1989; discussed with C.W.'s discussion group his book *Wieviel Freiheit braucht die Kunst* (*How Much Freedom Does Art Need*), Berlin, 2000. (G.W.)

life perhaps I never joined forces with my mother confidentially and humorously against another member of the family; my mother looks like she did in the photograph from the year 1929, when she is holding me in her arms as a baby. She has short cut hair, a "bobbed hairdo." I then lie down on the empty bed next to my father and fall asleep, dream that I am lying there and sleeping in the middle of my family, and I feel unbelievably well as I do it; I feel completely safe and secure and do not want to wake up at all. It is a long time before I make it clear to myself where I am in reality, in which bed I am lying, and that Father and Mother have been dead for a long time. A regret that even amazes me.

On the answering machine there are a lot of calls, fortunately most of them for Gerd. I drink tea. I sit down again at the desk, write a page of the speech for Anna Seghers, begin with two anecdotes, of which the one is her reaction to the Walter Ulbricht speech in the State Council Building. In response to his claim that we needed a socialist *Egmont* and a socialist *Faust*, she, thoughtfully: Yes, Comrade Ulbricht, with the *Egmont*, it may just be all right. But what are we going to do with Mephisto for the *Faust?*—To which he says: Well, Comrade Anna, we will solve the question of Mephisto yet!— I ask myself how she herself saw "the question of Mephisto" back then and begin to read in her essays on Dostoyevsky. "Everything is permitted"—she worries about that claim.

At six we have to leave, drive to the Francavilla Restaurant on Exerzierstrasse, where Dietrich Simon is waiting for us. At first his deputy in the Federation of Publishers and Book Dealers is still there; he gave me a copy of the federation's periodical, after all, I had been on the board of trustees since 1990 and my name was on the letterhead. I had no idea about that. Probably forgotten.

We order calf liver and rice, prepared with wine vinegar, therefore somewhat sour. I drink beer, Gerd white wine with soda water, Simon water. He does not want to endanger his driver's license again. We talk about our health, about experiences that Simon had with Hochhuth, who is not only his author but also his friend. I am interested in the small character traits of my colleagues.

We then talked about the publishing companies, of course. I told Simon that the Luchterhand Publishing Company is negotiating with me about the pocket book rights that are expiring with Deutscher Taschenbuch Verlag, which it would like to use for the "Luchterhand Collection" that will be starting up again next year. Simon doubts, as I do too, by the way, that the titles in that pocket book series can have sales comparable to those of Deutscher Taschenbuch Verlag. As a publishing company, Volk und Welt is finished for all practical purposes. Simon now sits there in his office in the empty building on Oranienplatz with only one assistant and an intern—We talk about *Hadesfahrt*, Simon encourages me to finish the text and then show it to the publisher. It has meanwhile become clear to me that it must become the story of a failure.

I indicate what I intend to do with the Seghers speech and tell some Seghers anecdotes that he does not know yet. He also thinks that I should tell them now. He asks about *Stadt der Engel.* An unending knitted stocking, I say, and I do not know at all if I would still like to see that published. He thinks that I should still experience that, what the people say about it, how they will praise and cast aspersions at it—I think to myself, I have more than enough of both.

In the middle of this I get miserable cramps in both thighs, brought on by the chair edges that cut into the flesh. I have to walk around for a while outside to get rid of the cramps. Gerd goes to get the car. We drive Simon to Brunnenstrasse, where his car is parked in the yard of the senator for culture. He had left word with the doorkeeper that he would come back yet and pick it up, but the doorkeeper's booth is empty, the barri-

618 - CHRISTA WOLF

er to the yard closed, and there is an iron gate in front of it as well. We must wait quite a while before the woman comes, lets us in, and lets Simon out with his car.

Silently we drive home, up the Brunnenstrasse and then the Wollank, as we have already done so often; we listen to jazz, I am not too tired, it is only ten o'clock. A nice, warm evening. At home then in front of the television set, the usual ritual. Evening news. Kohl's speech in the "tear palace," attack against the Social Democrats; he is taken back into the lap of his party with loud applause—Survivors of the ferry accident off Paros tell their story, once again the faces of people who have escaped death.

We then watch an episode of "Windshield Wiper," one of the better ones; Kohl is taken to task of course, one of the participants delivers a good number as a Turk, which ends with the idea that the Turks would help the Germans win the Third World War with German tanks—A good parody of Reich-Ranicki.

G. goes to bed. As so often, I remain sitting there (which he, as he does so often, criticizes). An old rerun of *The Old Man*, with Angelica Domröse, she gives me the excuse to remain with it until the end; of course it was then also she who cleverly drove her husband, who is afraid of going blind, to commit suicide.

Now it is a quarter to one. Tired. A few lines yet in the Benjamin novel.

Light out.

Otto Ihlenfeld (1897-1989), father of C.W.

Hertha Ihlenfeld, née Jaekel (1899-1968), mother of C.W.

Horst Ihlenfeld, b. 1932, brother of C.W.; his wife Helga.
Frank Ihlenfeld, b. 1964, their son, nephew of C.W.; his wife
Sabine; his son Bastl.

Dieter Wolf, b. 1933, brother of G.W.

Annette Wolf, b. 1952, daughter of C. and G.W.; in her first marriage
married to the film director Rainer Simon, b. 1941; in her second
marriage married to Jan ("Honza") Faktor, b. 1951, Czech writer.
Jana Simon, b. 1972, daughter from first marriage,
Benjamin ("Benni") Faktor, b. 1979, son from second marriage.

Franci Faktorová (1926-1997), mother of Jan Faktor, German Jewish
woman from Ostrau, deported from Prague to Terezin and
Auschwitz, liberated 1945, until 1968 editor of *Literárni Novyni*,
close friends with the Wolfs from 1959 on. Together with Jaroslav
Putik (b. 1923) she translated several books by C.W. into Czech,
after 1968, because of a prohibition to practice her profession,
under another name.

Katrin ("Tinka") Wolf, b. 1956, daughter of C. and G.W.; Martin
Hoffmann, b. 1948, painter and graphic designer, her lifelong com-
panion; beginning in 1990 book designer for G.W.'s Janus Press Pub-
lishing Company, Ltd.,
Helene Wolf, b. 1982, their daughter,
Anton Wolf, b. 1984, their son.

Der geteilte Himmel, Halle (1963); *Divided Heaven*, translated by Joan Becker, introduction and bibliography by Jack Zipes, Adler's Foreign Books, 1965.

Nachdenken über Christa T., Halle/S. (1968); *The Quest for Christa T.*, translated by Christopher Middleton, Farrar, Straus & Giroux, 1971.

Lesen und Schreiben, Halle (1971); *The Reader and the Writer: Essays, Sketches, Memories,* translated by Joan Becker, Signet, 1977.

Kindheitsmuster, Aufbau-Verlag (1976); *A Model Childhood*, translated by Ursule Molinaro and Hedwig Rappolt, Farrar, Straus & Giroux, 1980.

Kein Ort. Nirgends, Berlin (1979); *No Place on Earth*, translated by Jan van Heurck, Farrar, Straus & Giroux, 1982.

Kassandra, Luchterhand (1983); *Cassandra: A Novel and Four Essays,* translated by Jan van Heurck, Farrar, Straus & Giroux, 1984.

Patterns of Childhood (formerly *A Model Childhood*), translated by Ursule Molinaro and Hedwig Rappolt, Farrar, Straus & Giroux, 1984, 1980.

Störfall: Nachrichten eines Tages, Luchterhand (1987); *Accident: A Day's News*, translated by Heike Schwarzbauer and Rick Takvorian, Farrar, Straus & Giroux, 1989.

Die Dimension des Autors: Essays und Aufsätze, Reden und Gespräche, 1959-1985, Luchterhand (1987); *The Author's Dimension:*

Selected Essays, introduction by Grace Paley, edited by Alexander Stephan, translated by Jan van Heurck, Farrar, Straus & Giroux, 1993.

What Remains and Other Stories, translated by Heike Schwarzbauer and Rick Takvorian, Farrar, Straus & Giroux, 1993.

Parting from Phantoms: Selected Writings, 1990-1994, translated and annotated by Jan van Heurck, University of Chicago Press, 1997.

Medea: Stimmen, Luchterhand (1996); *Medea: A Modern Retelling*, translated by John Cullen, Nan A. Talese, 1998.

Leibhaftig: Erzählung, Luchterhand (2002); *In the Flesh*, translated by John S. Barrett, David R. Godine, 2005.

Ein Tag im Jahr: 1960-2000, Luchterhand (2003); *One Day a Year: 1960-2000*, translated by Lowell A. Bangerter, Europa Editions, 2007.

About Europa Editions

"To insist that if work is good, no matter what, people will read it? Crazy! But perhaps that's why I like Europa . . . They believe in what they are doing above everything. Viva Europa Editions!"
—ALICE SEBOLD, author of *The Lovely Bones*

"A new and, on first evidence, excellent source for European fiction for English-speaking readers."—JANET MASLIN, *The New York Times*

"Europa Editions has its first indie bestseller, Elena Ferrante's *The Days of Abandonment*."—*Publishers Weekly*

"We certainly like what we've seen so far."—*The Complete Review*

"A distinctly different brand of literary pleasure, thoughtfulness and, yes, even entertainment."—*The Ruminator*

"You could consider Europa Editions, the sprightly new publishing venture [...] based in New York, as a kind of book club for Americans who thirst after exciting foreign fiction."—*LA Weekly*

"Europa Editions invites English-speaking readers to 'experience all the color, the exuberance, the violence, the sounds and smells of the Mediterranean,' with an intriguing selection of the crème de la crème of continental noir."—*Murder by the Bye*

"Readers with a taste—even a need—for an occasional inky cup of bitter honesty should lap up *The Goodbye Kiss* . . . the first book of Carlotto's to be published in the United States by the increasingly impressive new Europa Editions."—*Chicago Tribune*

www.europaeditions.com

www.europaeditions.com

The Days of Abandonment
Elena Ferrante
Fiction - 192 pp - $14.95 - isbn 1-933372-00-1

"Stunning . . . The raging, torrential voice of the author is something rare."—*The New York Times*

"I could not put this novel down. Elena Ferrante will blow you away."
—ALICE SEBOLD, author of *The Lovely Bones*

Rarely have the foundations upon which our ideas of motherhood and womanhood rest been so candidly questioned. This compelling novel tells the story of one woman's headlong descent into what she calls an "absence of sense" after being abandoned by her husband. Olga's "days of abandonment" become a desperate, dangerous freefall into the darkest places of the soul as she roams the empty streets of a city that she has never learned to love. When she finds herself trapped inside the four walls of her apartment in the middle of a summer heat wave, Olga is forced to confront her ghosts, the potential loss of her own identity, and the possibility that life may never return to normal again.

Troubling Love
Elena Ferrante
Fiction - 144 pp - $14.95 - isbn 1-933372-16-8

"It's the first time a novel ever made me get physical, and it was the first good mood I'd been in for weeks."—*The New York Times*

"Like Joyce's *Ulysses*, this journey draws vigorously on its cityscape. Naples is one of those sun-drenched spooky cities, thrumming with life and populated by ghosts, spastic with impermeable local culture."—*Time Out New York*

Following her mother's untimely and mysterious death, Delia embarks on a voyage of discovery through the streets of her native Naples searching for the truth about her family. Reality is buried somewhere in the fertile soil of memory, and Delia is determined to find it. This stylish fiction from the author of *The Days of Abandonment* is set in a beguiling but often hostile Naples, whose chaotic, suffocating streets become one of the book's central motifs. A story about mothers and daughters, and the complicated knot of lies and emotions that binds them.

Cooking with Fernet Branca
James Hamilton-Paterson
Fiction - 288 pp - $14.95 - isbn 1-933372-01-X

"A work of comic genius."—*The Independent*

"Provokes the sort of indecorous involuntary laughter that has
more in common with sneezing than chuckling. Imagine a British
John Waters crossed with David Sedaris."—*The New York Times*

Gerald Samper, an effete English snob, has his own private
hilltop in Tuscany where he wiles away his time working as a ghost-
writer for celebrities and inventing wholly original culinary concoc-
tions—including ice-cream made with garlic and the bitter, herb-
based liqueur of the book's title. Gerald's idyll is shattered by the
arrival of Marta, on the run from a crime-riddled former soviet
republic. A series of hilarious misunderstands brings this odd couple into ever closer and more disastrous proximity.

www.europaeditions.com

Minotaur
Benjamin Tammuz
Fiction/Noir - 192 pp - $14.95 - isbn 1-933372-02-8

"A novel about the expectations and compromises that humans create for themselves . . . Very much in the manner of William Faulkner and Lawrence Durrell."—*The New York Times*

An Israeli secret agent falls hopelessly in love with a young English girl. Using his network of contacts and his professional expertise, he takes control of her life without ever revealing his identity. *Minotaur* is a complex and utterly original story about a solitary man driven from one side of Europe to the other by his obsession.

Total Chaos
Jean-Claude Izzo
Fiction/Noir - 256 pp - $14.95 - isbn 1-933372-04-4

"Rich, ambitious and passionate . . . his sad, loving portrait of his native city is amazing."—*The Washington Post*

"Full of fascinating characters, tersely brought to life in a prose style that is (thanks to Howard Curtis' shrewd translation) traditionally dark and completely original."—*The Chicago Tribune*

This first installment in the legendary *Marseilles Trilogy* sees Fabio Montale turning his back on a police force marred by corruption and racism and taking the fight against the mafia into his own hands.

Chourmo
Jean-Claude Izzo
Fiction/Noir - 256 pp - $14.95 - isbn 1-933372-17-6

"This hard-hitting series captures all the world-weariness of the contemporary European crime novel, but Izzo mixes it with a hero who is as virile as he is burned out."—*Booklist*

"Chourmo . . . the rowers in a galley. In Marseilles, you weren't just from one neighborhood, one project. You were chourmo. In the same galley, rowing! Trying to get out. Together." In this second installment of Izzo's legendary Marseilles Trilogy (*Total Chaos, Chourmo, Solea*) Fabio Montale has left a police force riddled with corruption, racism and greed to follow the ancient rhythms of his native town: the sea, fishing, the local bar, hotly-contested games of belote. But his cousin's son has gone missing and Montale is dragged back onto the mean streets of a violent, crime-infested Marseilles.

www.europaeditions.com

The Goodbye Kiss
Massimo Carlotto
Fiction/Noir - 192 pp - $14.95 - isbn 1-933372-05-2

"The best living Italian crime writer."—*Il Manifesto*

"A nasty, explosive little tome warmly recommended to fans of James M. Cain for its casual amorality and truly astonishing speed."—*Kirkus Reviews*

An unscrupulous womanizer, as devoid of morals now as he once was full of idealistic fervor, returns to Italy where he is wanted for a series of crimes. To avoid prison he sells out his old friends, turns his back on his former ideals, and cuts deals with crooked cops. To earn himself the guise of respectability he is willing to go even further, maybe even as far as murder.

Death's Dark Abyss
Massimo Carlotto
Fiction/Noir - 192 pp - $14.95 - isbn 1-933372-18-4

"Beneath the conventions of Continental noir is a remarkable study of corruption and redemption in a world where revenge is best served ice-cold."—*Kirkus* (starred review)

"Dark and, in part, extremely brutal stuff, but an interesting game of taking action and responsibility, of being able to—and not being able to—forgive and make sacrifices."—*The Complete Review*

A riveting drama of guilt, revenge, and justice, Massimo Carlotto's *Death's Dark Abyss* tells the story of two men and the savage crime that binds them. During a robbery, Raffaello Beggiato takes a young woman and her child hostage and later murders them. Beggiato is arrested, tried, and sentenced to life. The victims' father and husband, Silvano, plunges into an ever-deepening abyss until the day, years later, when the murderer seeks his pardon and Silvano turns predator as he ruthlessly plots his revenge.

www.europaeditions.com

Hangover Square
Patrick Hamilton
Fiction/Noir - 280 pp - $14.95 - isbn 1-933372-06-0

"Hamilton is a sort of urban Thomas Hardy: always a pleasure to read, and as social historian he is unparalleled."—NICK HORNBY

Adrift in the grimy pubs of London at the outbreak of World War II, George Harvey Bone is hopelessly infatuated with Netta, a cold, contemptuous, small-time actress. George also suffers from occasional blackouts. During these moments one thing is horribly clear: he must murder Netta.

www.europaeditions.com

I Loved You for Your Voice
Sélim Nassib
Fiction - 256 pp - $14.95 - isbn 1-933372-07-9

"Om Kalthoum is great. She really is."—BOB DYLAN

"In rapt, lyrical prose, Paris-based writer and journalist Nassib
spins a rhapsodic narrative out of the indissoluble connection
between two creative souls inextricably bound by their art."
—*Kirkus Reviews* (starred review)

Love, desire, and song set against the colorful backdrop of modern
Egypt. The story of the Arab world's greatest and most popular
singer, Om Kalthoum, told through the eyes of the poet Ahmad
Rami, who wrote her lyrics and loved her in vain all his life. Span-
ning over five decades in the history of modern Egypt, this passionate tale of love and longing provides a key to understanding the
soul, the aspirations and the disappointments of the Arab world.

Love Burns
Edna Mazya
Fiction/Noir - 192 pp - $14.95 - isbn 1-933372-08-7

"This book, which has Woody Allen overtones, should be of great interest to readers of black humor and psychological thrillers."
—*Library Journal* (starred)

"Starts out as a psychological drama and becomes a strange, funny, unexpected hybrid: a farce thriller. A great book."—*Ma'ariv*

Ilan, a middle-aged professor of astrophysics, discovers that his young wife is having an affair. Terrified of losing her, he decides to confront her lover instead. Their meeting ends in the latter's murder—the unlikely murder weapon being Ilan's pipe—and in desperation, Ilan disposes of the body in the fresh grave of his kindergarten teacher. But when the body is discovered . . .

Departure Lounge
Chad Taylor
Fiction/Noir - 176 pp - $14.95 - isbn 1-933372-09-5

"Smart, original, surprising and just about as cool as a novel can get
. . . Taylor can flat out write."—*The Washington Post*

"Entropy noir . . . The hypnotic pull lies in the zigzag dance of its
forlorn characters, casting a murky, uneasy sense of doom."
—*The Guardian*

A young woman mysteriously disappears. The lives of those she has
left behind—family, acquaintances, and strangers intrigued by her
disappearance—intersect to form a captivating latticework of coincidences and surprising twists of fate. Urban noir at its stylish and
intelligent best.

www.europaeditions.com

The Jasmine Isle
Ioanna Karystiani
Fiction - 176 pp - $14.95 - isbn 1-933372-10-9

"Grim yet gorgeous, here's a modern Greek tragedy about love foredoomed, family life as battlefield, the wisdom and wantonness of the human heart and the implacable finality of the hand of fate."—*Kirkus Reviews*

A modern love story with the force of an ancient Greek tragedy. Set on the spectacular Cycladic island of Andros, *The Jasmine Isle*, one of the finest literary achievements in contemporary Greek literature, recounts the story of the old sea wolf, Spyros Maltambès, and the beautiful Orsa Saltaferos, sentenced to marry a man she doesn't love and to watch while the man she does love is wed to another.

Boot Tracks
Matthew F. Jones
Fiction/Noir - 208 pp - $14.95 - isbn 1-933372-11-7

"Mr. Jones has created a powerful blend of love and violence, of the grotesque and the tender."
—*The New York Times*

"More than just a very good crime thriller, this dark but illuminating novel shows us the psychopathology of the criminal mind . . . A nightmare thriller with the power to haunt."
—*Kirkus Reviews* (starred)

Charlie Rankin has recently been released from prison, but prison has not released its grip on him. He owes his life to "The Buddha," who has given him a job to do on the outside: he must kill a man, a man who has done him no harm, a man he has never met. Along the road to this brutal encounter, Rankin meets Florence, who may be an angel in disguise or simply a lonely ex porn star seeking salvation. Together they careen towards their fate, taking the reader along for the ride. A commanding, stylishly written novel that tells the harrowing story of an assassination gone terribly wrong and the man and woman who are taking their last chance to find a safe place in a hostile world.

www.europaeditions.com

Dog Day
Alicia Giménez-Bartlett
Fiction/Noir - 208 pp - $14.95 - isbn 1-933372-14-1

"In Nicholas Caistor's smooth translation from the Spanish, Gimé-nez-Bartlett evokes pity, horror and laughter with equal adeptness. No wonder she won the Femenino Lumen prize in 1997 as the best female writer in Spain."—*The Washington Post*

In this hardboiled fiction for dog lovers and lovers of dog mysteries, detective Petra Delicado and her maladroit sidekick, Garzón, investigate the murder of a tramp whose only friend is a mongrel dog named Freaky. One murder leads to another and Delicado finds herself involved in the sordid, dangerous world of fight dogs. *Dog Day* is first-rate entertainment.

Carte Blanche
Carlo Lucarelli
Fiction/Noir - 120 pp - $14.95 - isbn 1-933372-15-X

"This is Alan Furst country, to be sure."—*Booklist*

April 1945, Italy. Commissario De Luca is heading up a dangerous investigation into the private lives of the rich and powerful during the frantic final days of the fascist republic. The hierarchy has guaranteed De Luca their full cooperation, so long as he arrests the "right" suspect. The house of cards built by Mussolini in the last months of WWII is collapsing and De Luca faces a world mired in sadistic sex, dirty money, drugs and murder.

www.europaeditions.com

Old Filth
Jane Gardam
Fiction - 256 pp - $14.95 - isbn 1-933372-13-3

"Jane Gardam's beautiful, vivid and defiantly funny novel is a must."—*The Times*

"This remarkable novel . . . will bring immense pleasure to readers who treasure fiction that is intelligent, witty, sophisticated and—a quality encountered all too rarely in contemporary culture—adult."
—*The Washington Post*

Sir Edward Feathers has progressed from struggling young barrister to wealthy expatriate lawyer to distinguished retired judge, living out his last days in comfortable seclusion in Dorset. The engrossing and moving account of his life, from birth in colonial Malaya, to Wales, where he is sent as a "Raj orphan," to Oxford, his career and marriage, parallels much of the 20th century's dramatic history.

The Big Question
Wolf Erlbruch
Children's Illustrated Fiction - 52 pp - $14.95 - isbn 1-933372-03-6

Named Best Book at the 2004 Children's Book Fair in Bologna.

"[*The Big Question*] offers more open-ended answers than the likes of Shel Silverstein's *Giving Tree* (1964) and is certain to leave even younger readers in a reflective mood."—*Kirkus Reviews*

A stunningly beautiful and poetic illustrated book for children that poses the biggest of all big questions: why am I here? A chorus of voices—including the cat's, the baker's, the pilot's and the soldier's—offers us some answers. But nothing is certain, except that as we grow each one of us will pose the question differently and be privy to different answers.

The Butterfly Workshop
Wolf Erlbruch and Gioconda Belli
Children's Illustrated Fiction - 40 pp - $14.95 - isbn 1-933372-12-5

Illustrated by the winner of the 2006 Hans Christian Andersen Award.

For children and adults alike . . . Odair, one of the Designers of All Things and grandson of the esteemed inventor of the rainbow, has been banished to the insect laboratory as punishment for his overactive imagination. But he still dreams of one day creating a cross between a bird and a flower. Then, after a helpful chat with a dog . . .